DARK DIAMOND

By Neal Asher

Agent Cormac series
Gridlinked • The Line of Polity
Brass Man • Polity Agent • Line War

Spatterjay trilogy
The Skinner
The Voyage of the Sable Keech
Orbus

Standalone Polity novels
Prador Moon • Hilldiggers
Shadow of the Scorpion • The Technician
Jack Four • Weaponized • War Bodies

The Owner series
The Departure • Zero Point • Jupiter War
World Walkers

Transformation trilogy
Dark Intelligence • War Factory
Infinity Engine

Rise of the Jain trilogy
The Soldier • The Warship
The Human

Cowl

Time's Shadow trilogy
Dark Diamond

Novellas
The Parasite • Mindgames: Fool's Mate

Short-story collections
Runcible Tales • The Engineer
The Gabble

NEAL
ASHER
DARK DIAMOND

TOR

First published 2025 by Tor
an imprint of Pan Macmillan
The Smithson, 6 Briset Street, London EC1M 5NR
EU representative: Macmillan Publishers Ireland Ltd, 1st Floor,
The Liffey Trust Centre, 117–126 Sheriff Street Upper,
Dublin 1, D01 YC43
Associated companies throughout the world
www.panmacmillan.com

ISBN 978-1-0350-3793-3 HB
ISBN 978-1-0350-3794-0 TPB

Pan Macmillan does not have any control over, or any responsibility for,
any author or third-party websites referred to in or on this book.

1 3 5 7 9 8 6 4 2

A CIP catalogue record for this book is available from the British Library.

Typeset in Plantin by Palimpsest Book Production Ltd, Falkirk, Stirlingshire
Printed and bound by CPI Group (UK) Ltd, Croydon, CR0 4YY

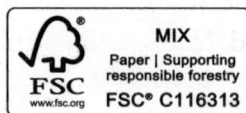

MIX
Paper | Supporting
responsible forestry
FSC
www.fsc.org **FSC® C116313**

Visit **www.panmacmillan.com** to read more about all our books
and to buy them. You will also find features, author interviews and
news of any author events, and you can sign up for e-newsletters
so that you're always first to hear about our new releases.

Five years ago, I watched the two Falcon Heavy side boosters come into land at Cape Canaveral Space Force Base. Honestly, it was like something in a game animation and seemingly too perfect to be believable. Others, I've seen landing on drone ships with names taken from Iain M. Banks' Culture books. Just recently, I saw a huge booster for the *Starship* come down to be caught between two metal arms – y'know, they caught something the size of a skyscraper like a dropping stick – and that was an astounding feat of engineering. But these are not in isolation, since SpaceX, as of last month, has launched over a hundred rockets in 2024.

Meanwhile, the guy who brought this about, the guy who is aiming to make humanity multi-planetary by putting us on Mars, has a few other projects on the go, like building electric cars, burrowing tunnels under cities, putting up a satellite internet system and, perhaps the most important of them all, preventing the totalitarians of our world from killing free speech.

So thank you, Elon Musk, for bringing to reality, right before my eyes, those things I read and dreamed about as a teenager.

Acknowledgements

Thanks to the staff at Pan Macmillan, and elsewhere, who have helped bring this novel to your e-reader, smartphone, computer screen and that old-fashioned mass of wood pulp called a book. These include Bella Pagan (publisher), Michael Beale (editor), Melissa Bond (editorial manager), Neil Lang (jacket designer) and the Pan Mac marketing team; also freelancers Jessica Cuthbert-Smith (copy-editor), Robert Clark (proofreader), Steve Stone (jacket illustrator) and others whose names I simply don't know.

Glossary

Atheter (The): A highly advanced space-faring race who, during their time, encountered the civilization-destroying Jain technology. Eventually, to escape this technology, they committed a form of racial suicide by sacrificing their civilization and intelligence. Their animal descendants still exist on the planet Masada. They are gabbleducks – creatures that speak nonsense and whose behaviour is always strange.

Augmented: To be 'augmented' is to have taken advantage of one or more of the many available cybernetic devices, mechanical additions and, distinctly, cerebral augmentations. In the last case we have, of course, the ubiquitous 'aug' and such back-formations as 'auged', 'auging-in' and the execrable 'all auged up'. But it does not stop there: the word 'aug' has now become confused with auger and augur – which is understandable considering the way an aug connects and the information that then becomes available. So now you can 'auger' information from the AI net, and a prediction made by an aug prognostic subprogram can be called an augury. – *From 'Quince Guide' compiled by humans*

First- and second-children: Male prador, chemically maintained in adolescence and enslaved by pheromones emitted by their fathers, and acting as crew on their ships or as soldiers.

Prador adults also use their surgically removed ganglions (brains) as navigational computers in their ships and to control war machines.

Golem: Androids produced by a company Cybercorp, a ceramal chassis usually enclosed in a syntheflesh and syntheskin outer layer. These humanoid robots are very tough, fast and, since they possess AI, very smart.

Haiman: An amalgam of human and AI.

Hardfield: A flat force field capable of stopping missiles and energy beams. The impact or heat energy is transformed and dissipated by its projector. Overload of that projector usually results in its catastrophic breakdown, at which point it is ejected from the vessel containing it. Hardfields of any other format were supposed to be impossible; however, it has been revealed that they can be made spherical and almost impenetrable . . .

Jain technology: A technology spanning all scientific disciplines, created by one of the dead races – the Jain. Its apparent sum purpose is to spread through civilizations and annihilate them.

King of the Prador: The king who ruled the prador when they attacked the Polity was usurped by another prador who had been infected with the Spatterjay virus. The new king, and his family, have been highly mutated by this, resulting in extreme body changes and increased intelligence.

Nanosuite: A suite of nanomachines most human beings have inside them. These self-propagating machines act as a secondary immune system, repairing and adjusting the body. Each suite can be altered to suit the individual and his or her circumstances.

Ophidapts: People taking on some of the appearance of snakes, including the fangs, scales and eyes, either through cosmetic or genetic alteration.

Polity: A human/AI dominion extending across many star systems, occupying a spherical space spanning the thickness of the galaxy and centred on Earth. It is ruled over by the AIs who took control of human affairs in what has been called, because of its very low casualty rate, the Quiet War. The top AI is called Earth Central (EC) and resides in a building on the shore of Lake Geneva, while planetary AIs, lower down in the hierarchy, rule over other worlds. The Polity is a highly technical civilization but its weakness was its reliance on travel by 'runcible' – instantaneous matter transmission gates.

Prador: A highly xenophobic race of giant crablike aliens ruled by a king and his family. Hostility is implicit in their biology and, upon encountering the Polity, they immediately attacked it. They originally had an advantage in the prador/human war in that they did not use runcibles (such devices needed the intelligence of AIs to control them and the prador are also hostile to any form of artificial intelligence), and as a result had developed their spaceship technology, and the metallurgy involved, beyond that of the Polity. They attacked with near-indestructible ships, but in the end the humans and AIs adapted, their war factories out-manufactured the prador, and they began to win. They did not complete the victory, however, because the old king was usurped and the new king made an uneasy peace with the Polity.

Quantum crystals: Can be used to store masses of data in a distributed fashion throughout any system, including the human body. This form of storage is being experimented with by the Polity and can take the place of a memplant – a device used to record a human mind.

Runcible: Instantaneous matter transmission gates, allowing transportation through underspace.

Sparkind: Units of four Earth Central Security special forces soldiers, usually consisting of two humans and two Golem.

USER: Underspace Interference Emitter. This device disrupts U-space by oscillating a singularity through a runcible gate. It is used to push ships out of U-space into the real, or realspace.

U-space: Underspace is the continuum spaceships enter (or U-jump into), rather like submarines submerging, to travel faster than light. It is also the continuum that can be crossed by using runcible gates, making travel between worlds linked by such gates all but instantaneous.

Cast of Characters

Arach, the Spider Drone
Manufactured in Factory Station Room 101, Arach is a highly weaponized spider format war drone. He became a long-time companion of Agent Ian Cormac and the brass Golem Mr Crane.

Captain Blite
A trader whose business edges into illegality. During a deal that turned sour he encountered Penny Royal, who killed his crew. His second encounter with the AI was when it used him and his ship as an escape from the world of Masada. With his ship under the control of the black AI, Blite witnessed its obscure business in the Graveyard and elsewhere, and came to realize that it may be correcting past wrongs. After recognizing this, he and his crew were abandoned again on Masada, but the advanced technology left aboard their ship (not to mention their first-hand knowledge of Penny Royal) meant they became of great interest to the Polity AIs. Blite escaped the Polity and continued to pursue Penny Royal, once again finding himself dragged into its obscure manipulations, until Penny Royal dropped itself into a black hole and 'went beyond time'. The AI left him a piece of itself: a dark diamond. Since then, many years have passed and he is now the owner of a trading and haulage company called Penny Transport.

Ian Cormac, the Agent

An agent of Earth Central Security integral in the defeat of the scientist Skellor who acquired lethal alien Jain technology, and a rebellion by disenfranchised war drones and AIs infected with the same technology. During these actions he acquired the ability to jump himself through U-space. He also learned that the chief AI of the Polity, Earth Central, had been facilitating these enemies in an effort to drive the evolution of humanity. He destroyed that iteration of Earth Central, which was soon replaced, and with his new abilities made it his remit to keep the Polity AIs in line.

Mr Crane, the Brass Man

A high-series Golem android who was broken by murder tapes and reprogrammed to become a killer for the gangster Arian Pelter. He was torn apart during the same action in which Cormac killed Pelter, but was later resurrected by Skellor using Jain technology. Finally defeating his reprogramming, Crane changed sides and became Cormac's ally.

Penny Royal, the Black AI

An artificial intelligence constructed in Factory Station Room 101 during the Polity war against the prador. Its crystal mind was faulty, burdened with emotions it could not encompass when it was hurled into the heat of battle. Running the destroyer that it named *Puling Child*, it fought and survived, then annihilated eight thousand troops on its own side before going AWOL. It changed into something dark then – a swarm robot whose integrated form was like a giant sea urchin. Blacklisted by the Polity for ensuing atrocities, it based itself in the Graveyard – a borderland created between the Polity and the Prador Kingdom after the war. There it continued its evil games, offering transformations for the right price, but ones that were never good for the recipients. It was nearly destroyed in a deal that went wrong. Later restored to function by the scorpion war drone Amistad, it apparently became a good AI. It righted many of the wrongs it had done, before dropping itself into a black hole and moving 'beyond time'. It is regarded by the Polity as a paradigm-changing threat.

Prologue

Captain Blite

Fate had conspired to leave him with one working and clear eye, and just enough muscle in his neck with which to raise his head and look at what remained of his body. There wasn't a lot of it. Not that he believed in fate, of course – well, not in any vague religious, supernatural sense. He rather felt that Fate in his particular case had a name still spoken of with awe – and of course the retrospective, spectator-titillation of those who weren't there when a particular black AI started fucking with causality, or didn't have any skin in the game.

Smoking rubble lay all around him: chunks of composite, shards of ceramal, foamstone that had apparently heated up enough to melt, and drifts of ash still glowing red inside. Thick, heavy smoke boiled through the air and each heaving breath he took failed to draw enough oxygen into his lungs. Even so, he could see that his legs and arms were gone, while his torso looked like a pork roast, nicely prepared and shaped into a neat cylinder, but having been shoved into an oven that was far too hot. It surprised him that he could feel no pain, until he did. Then he transitioned into the nightmare of not having enough air to breathe *and* not enough with which to scream.

Again.

1

1

Blite – Present

Captain Blite had met some interesting people over the years, and some had, surprisingly, been younger than him. But there was something about this guy. He didn't look particularly enhanced – he wasn't obviously boosted and hadn't grown his body taller, as seemed the fashion nowadays. He looked much like your standard Polity human of Blite's early years: a melting pot human. He did have that sinewy tough appearance of people Blite had known in the past, which in those days had hinted at someone who could move fast and violently. He had silvery hair cropped short, a face conventionally handsome but with lines that told of strain and thought. All of it could be a look straight out of a catalogue, though, and mean nothing at all.

But still . . .

The guy wore a long, light coat of some fine, slightly metallic fabric over a black T-shirt, black leg-hugging combats and enviroboots. This old-fashioned style was one that came around again and again, as Blite well knew. Watching the man come down the wide aisle on the viewing deck, he became immediately wary. He knew there must be a contract out on him because a year ago, when he'd gone off from his company Penny Transport to tick off a few more things on his bucket list, there had been two attempts on his life. And, frankly, this guy looked like a killer.

The man gazed at Blite directly. In his left hand he held a drink, and his jacket hung loosely enough to conceal a weapon. Surely he wouldn't try anything here? The AI of this passenger ship was eternally vigilant, while the crew consisted of an interesting bunch of very capable humans, high-series Golem and a couple of war drones. Blite knew there was suppression tech around him, undoubtedly including lethal weapons concealed in the walls, while the disc-shaped bumps in the ceiling were almost certainly pendant security drones. He'd chosen to go on this cruise precisely because of all this – so he could relax for a while and not have to keep looking out for the next threat. Damn it, he was a legitimate businessman now and owner of Penny Transport. He thought he'd left that sort of nonsense behind him.

The guy sat down in the seat just one along from him and put his drink down on a side table. They both sat there gazing through the chain-glass wall opposite, beyond which sat a gas giant, striated with cloud like Jupiter, but in shades of green and gold, a large asteroid the shape of a caraway seed in silhouette, and the Fortense space station just sliding into view. This was a thick slab twenty kilometres long, with spaceships docked along one edge like contacts on an old computer chip.

'It's quite a view,' said the man. Calm voice, but there was something in it.

'Yup, it is that,' Blite replied.

'You'll be going through the runcible there to travel to Callanasta, then by ship to your company base on the Lustra moon Perihelion,' he said.

The man turned towards him and studied him evenly. Blite had never believed all that rubbish about seeing something in a person's eyes. They were just balls of jelly, after all. You didn't see stuff there, just the focus of their expression. But in this case he was, briefly, prepared to believe there was more there. He saw intensity in this man's gaze, as well as strength, and something else that seemed utterly beyond the norm. He swallowed dryly, realizing that, for the first time in perhaps a century, he was looking at someone who scared him. This made him angry, of course.

'Who the fuck are you to know my travel plans?' he said.

The man smiled; the expression didn't have any warmth in it. He held out his hand.

'My name is Ian, formerly ECS.'

Fuck, fuck and fuck! Blite didn't want to shake that hand. This Ian might be lying and nanotoxins could be concealed in a handshake, but he found himself reaching out anyway. A brief clasp, nothing special – just a hand. He now understood his initial reaction to this interloper. He didn't believe the 'formerly', since Polity agents never retired.

'And why is ECS interested in me?'

The man turned back to the view and Blite felt relieved to have those eyes off him. 'I told you, I'm retired from ECS. Though I have to admit that certain connections remain and that's how I learned of their interest.'

'In what way?' Blite just hoped the answer would be simple, prosaic and nothing to do with rather complex events he'd been involved in long ago. He'd already been interrogated about those and there was nothing more to say.

'You were really lucky with that assassin on Earth, weren't you? Almost as if you were prepared for him. Managed to disable his weapon and then pump shots in through a vulnerable part of his armour.' Ian turned back again and studied him coldly. 'How many attempts did it take for you to get it right?'

Blite now felt really worried. Nobody should know how he'd done that and, as far as he understood the process, nobody *could* know.

'That's a strange thing to say,' he commented.

No doubt about it now. He needed to get back to his company at Perihelion and keep his head down there. He needed, rather than leaving it in the hands of others, to get a grip on the ongoing investigation into who the hell was trying to kill him. He really, really did not want to be a person of interest to ECS, not again. Not after everything that had happened before. He'd thought the AIs would never leave him alone, never stop investigating every aspect of his life. He'd thought the questions would never end.

'It happened in New York, didn't it?' Ian continued, gaze sliding back to the view. 'And strange power outages occurred at the same time, running equatorially around Earth. Along the Atlantic coast a cold ocean current swept round, and the sea farms had some problems with die-offs. They put them down to the sudden drop in temperature, but that didn't really account for it. Nor was the cold current accounted for.'

Blite forced a smile. 'I expect it can be made to fit some conspiracy theory, but I'm failing to see what it has to do with me.'

The man turned back to study him again. 'There was a rash of sunspots that year too, and they were outside of projections.'

'I still don't see—'

Ian snapped up one hand. 'Just listen. Investigations were made into the individual attempts on your life. They led nowhere because cash payments and instructions had been delivered to the assassins beforehand. With the killers all dead and you still alive, the investigations were shelved. But now AIs have made a connection between the attempts on your life and other curious phenomena and, considering your history, that becomes very interesting.'

'Yes, I see how that might be the case.' Blite wanted to get the hell away from here. He didn't like where this seemed to be going at all.

Ian continued, 'Earth Central Security is aware now, as is Earth Central, our beloved AI ruler of the Polity. You need either to disappear for a good long time or to find a way to stop these attempts on your life. If you don't, and they continue, and those other phenomena continue . . .' He shrugged. 'I don't need to go on, do I?'

'No, you don't.'

Ian, the erstwhile Polity agent, abruptly stood up. He took up his drink. 'Let us hope that we don't meet again.' He walked away.

Crackling groans were issuing from his mouth by the time the mask went on. As soon as it started feeding him oxygen he had the air to scream, but this faded out as something went into the side of his neck and awareness of his body slid away. He could still see, however, as a scorpion-like autodoc climbed onto his chest, dug in sharp limbs to hold itself in place and extruded a mass of self-guiding pipes and wires from its mouth.

'How the fuck is he still alive?' someone wondered.

He couldn't move his neck now, but the vision in his one eye continued to work. He saw two people in hazmat suits move into view. One of them stooped down beside him, putting a couple of cylinders on his stomach behind the doc, then connecting fluid tubes to the machine.

'Tough bastard, whoever he is,' said this one – a woman, by the voice.

'I think he's still with us,' said the other. 'Put him out.'

He didn't feel the injection or the alteration to the nerve shunt on his neck. The world just went away and then, seemingly without transition, it had changed when he next came to. He was hanging semi-weightless in clear fluid, in a tangle of pipes and wires. It seemed they must have found one of his arms and reattached it. He moved the skinless limb and noted it only possessed a forefinger and thumb. His mind seemed to be ticking along just fine, but the fact he wasn't suffering the horrors had to be due to drugs, targeted neural suppression, and some tinkering with his nanosuite.

'Stop waving that about,' said a voice apparently in his ear. 'You'll pull out some of those feed tubes.'

He was in a regrowth tank and through the fluid, and the glass containing it, he could see someone standing there. Obviously they'd attached hardware to his skull so he could hear. Could he talk? He tried – just subvocalizing and forming the words without actually moving anything, because there was no air in his lungs and he wasn't breathing.

'Where am I?' he asked.

'Tideville on Callanasta,' the woman outside replied.

He recognized her voice as that of one of his rescuers, but that wasn't the main thing which now occupied his mind. He remembered arriving on the Fortense space station and, after his talk with that ex-agent, he'd had no wish to hang around, so he'd bought a runcible slot to head here as soon as possible. What he couldn't remember was actually going through the runcible to Callanasta.

'What happened?'

'Runcible failure,' she said incredulously. 'Can you fucking believe it?'

He could, and now the horrors began. Runcibles didn't fail any more, and he couldn't help feeling that this failure had been deliberate, connected to the attempts on his life – this *had* been an attempt on his life. If that was the case, then this whole thing had just gone nuclear, literally, and investigative AIs would be buzzing around this place quite soon, if they weren't already. He needed to get out fast, before connections were made.

He raised his mutilated arm in front of him. 'Yes, I can believe it.'

'It's crazy. Hasn't happened in a hundred years – not as bad as this,' she said. Then, 'Anyway, I need information from you. The AI is down and we're having problems identifying survivors. Costs for your medical treatment are obviously covered, but we need some details on who you are, and if there's anything we should be aware of regarding regeneration of limbs and other repairs.'

He considered this briefly. The AI might be down, as she said, but others would soon take up the load. Almost certainly his DNA was in the system and they would quickly enough discover his identity. He then reconsidered. No, that was rubbish. Even if an AI was down, others would be functional and connected and he would have been identified by now. She wanted to ask him something else.

'My name is Blite, but you already know that,' he replied. 'What do you really want to know?'

'Okay,' she admitted, coming closer to the glass. 'We've scanned you and everything is much as other scans, and we can of course fix you. However, there's something impenetrable to scanning – a crystal set in the bone of your skull – and we have no idea what the hell it is.' After a pause she added, as an excuse, 'We don't know if it'll interfere with any of our procedures.'

'It won't interfere with anything you do,' he replied, not entirely sure it was true. 'It's just something valuable to me that some people tried to take away from me once. I had it put there so they couldn't.'

'Oh, I see . . . but it's impenetrable . . .'

'It is indeed.' He didn't elaborate and instead said, 'Now, I need to make a U-com call to someone. I want you to give me a vocal netlink, and I need it quickly, as well as some privacy. If you give me that, perhaps I'll elaborate on what exactly I have in my skull.'

After a long pause she turned and walked away, saying, 'You're in – just speak.'

'Carlstone 87876523BIT,' he said. He didn't mind that he was probably being overheard because the code was a one-time thing. The 'BIT' amused him – it stood for 'Blite in trouble'. After a delay of a minute or so, a sound like that of an antique phone connection being made burred in his ears, then a moment later someone spoke.

'What's happened now?' said his second-in-command of Penny Transport.

'I'm in a regrowth tank on Callanasta, in the town of Tideville,' Blite said. 'Burned, and have lost all but one of my limbs. I need you to put a medical transport team together and get me the hell out of here fast.'

'We heard about the runcible,' said Carlstone. 'Hell, you were in that?'

'I was indeed. Get me back there, quick as you can. Also, I want our security up to max, and I mean *max*.'

'Potential for attack?'

'Just do what I say. I don't have much privacy here.'

'We're on our way.'

The connection broke with a click.

Blite hung in the fluid, waiting until, inevitably, the woman came back.

'You still want to know what's in my head?' he asked.

'Sorry, but I've never seen anything our scanners can't get through.'

'It's a piece of Penny Royal,' he told her.

As she walked away laughing, he tried to smile, but nothing in his face worked. Then he remembered the one who'd once tried to take this piece from him, forcing him to have it implanted. The thief – the terrified thief.

Blite – Past

The art gallery had been laid out on three levels, and Mr Pace's sculptures sat on pedestals in cylindrical chain-glass cases. Mr Pace, whom Penny Royal gave immortality, and who was thankful to lose it again. Using the touch consoles at the base of each display, one could black out the background behind the sculpture and revolve the pedestal, also turning on lights of various hues. Another touch could bring up a menu in the chain-glass itself, which allowed magnification down to the microscopic on any portion of each sculpture.

Blite stood gazing in at the sculpture of a prador – one of the implacable alien enemy of the Polity, still out there, beyond a border space called the Graveyard. All the tools provided here for potential buyers' close inspection of these artworks were irrelevant in the case of this collection. Before his death, Mr Pace had lined up the sale to a planetary AI; on subsequent investigation Blite had discovered that the buyer concerned, here on Abalon, had just been obeying orders. The ultimate owner of it would be Earth Central itself, and the collection would go on display in the Terpsichorean Museum of Art in London.

This sculpture was beautiful, yet ugly too, and menacing. It had been formed of translucent yellow and green glass, even with glass internal organs. Its limbs were distorted and there were whorls in its deformed shell. He was sure now that, impossibly,

11

it depicted one of Sverl's children, even though Mr Pace could simply not have encountered those rebel prador when he made it. The AI Penny Royal again – fucking about with time and causality.

The prador here was special to Blite. Like all of Pace's sculptures, it activated under the warmth of a hand, but unlike others, this one had once activated, then stayed active, even after he took his hand away. It had been just a few months ago, when he'd gone to find it after receiving a message, especially for him, from Penny Royal. The sculpture had something for him, he'd been told, which turned out to be three ruby memcrystals containing the minds of his dead crewmen. And, of course, all of that had been impossible, if one thought in Blite's terms and not like something with godlike powers. These crystals, along with this collection, he and his old crewmate Greer had been asked to take to Earth, where they would be 'interviewed' by AIs about events leading up to Penny Royal inserting itself into a black hole and, apparently, moving beyond time. One other item had been with the crystals too. Unconsciously, Blite now raised his hand and closed it around the black gem he'd had fitted into a pendant hung around his neck.

A piece of Penny Royal. Why the AI had given it to him he had no idea. He'd just known the moment he first touched it that it was his. He didn't know if it was in any way active – it was a touchstone and a connection to those events that somehow acknowledged his part in them. And, if he was honest, he felt special owning it.

He would have to hide it when they went to Earth. He'd leave it aboard Pace's ship during those interviews and, if at all possible, he wouldn't mention it. If they found out, the AIs would take it away from him for examination. No. He realized the ship wouldn't be safe enough. The AIs, or AI, that would interview him would almost certainly take Pace's ship apart. It would have to go in a shielded container and then into a secure box with Galaxy Bank here. Since he was a very rich man now, and his account was with them, they'd run around to provide him with whatever he needed. This would have to be his next task.

'Okay,' he said, and turned away from the case.

He'd seen everything now. Pace had been a supreme artist. He'd also been one of Penny Royal's projects when that AI hadn't been quite so nice. It had effectively given Pace corporeal immortality by dint of a nigh-indestructible body. And if he did destroy it anywhere, he was perpetually backed up, so mechanisms in his home world could rebuild him. By the time Blite had encountered him, the man had wanted to die, and finally he had.

On the lower floor, Greer was looking through the collection. Blite raised a hand to the heavyworlder woman and by gesture indicated that he'd meet her later for a drink, then headed out of the gallery. Things were up in the air for her and for him. They were both very independently wealthy, but those interviews with the AIs were still to come, and what then? He'd always been attracted to the idea of retiring on a resort world, drinking cips in some sunny beach bar and generally being indolent. But, even now, with nothing to strive for any more, no scrabbling after money to pay for some upgrade or new component for his ship, or acquiring a cargo for transport and involving himself in some barely legal deals, he could feel boredom growing.

He moved outside. Here the buildings were oddly curved structures that loomed over the crowded street. Apparently they were the product of some architectural artist the ruling AI here had transported in. People paid a premium to live in the upper apartments, and business concerns similarly paid out to rent shop space on the lower floors. Blite didn't like them much –

they reminded him too much of the rib bones of some giant beast, and as if the street were its spine. There were aspects of this world he did like, though. The Abalon AI wasn't one of those heavy-handed planetary AIs that controlled everything. It allowed business that slid into that grey area Blite preferred. It could be dangerous here, it could be chaotic, but on the whole it wasn't too boring. His attitude soon changed when a girl ran into him in the crowds and knocked the wind out of him.

Blite staggered back and glared at her. She looked at him in shock. She appeared young, clad in a scrappy environment suit and heavy jacket, thin elfin face with artfully messed yellow and blue hair. As ever, that could have been a look from a catalogue.

'I'm so really sorry,' she said.

Blite waved a dismissive hand at her. She nodded in gratitude, smiled and ran on, dodging through the crowds. He watched her go, while making a grumbling sound in the back of his throat. Such a prosaic encounter, after all he'd been through. If only she knew. He continued on towards his rented apartment. It was only when he was climbing the stairs to it that his hand strayed to his breast again, underneath his suit, and he realized the pendant was gone.

Blite – Present

His regrowth in the tank continued apace. The hardware they'd attached to his skull was in fact an induction aug, and he found it had many more functions than enabling him to speak to, and hear, those who came to visit him. He could link into the AI net and search out information he wanted. He could enter virtualities and play games, or live a life of his choosing while his body healed. Instead he chose to contact Carlstone again, to keep

harrying him, then drifted into ten-hour periods of unconsciousness while he waited.

After the first ten hours, he could see skin forming on his arm.
It was doubtless developing on what remained of his body too,
but he couldn't see that. The woman was there again when he
woke.

'We've been overloaded,' she told him. 'Our procedure with
you was to be stabilization first, then we'd bring you out under
the printerbot and autosurgeon, but apparently you're being
transported out of here?'

'Yes, that is the case.'

'I never realized you were *that* Blite.'

'That Blite?'

'The extremely wealthy owner of the Perihelion moon and
Penny Transport.' She paused. 'And you weren't lying about what
you have in your skull.'

'I always tell the truth, me,' Blite lied.

'Anyway,' she continued. 'We would have been taking you out
of the tank by now for surgery and printing but it seems your
people will be arriving soon. If we start work on the next procedures, we won't be able to interrupt them.'

'Just leave me here,' Blite informed her.

'And what about—?'

Blite didn't hear the rest because he'd already instructed the
induction aug to put him under for another ten hours.

When he next woke a ceiling was passing overhead, punctuated
with alternating light squares and the bumps of security drones.
Curved glass now lay close to his face. He couldn't make out
much about the figures moving with him, beyond the fact that
they wore combat armour and carried weapons. One of them
was almost certainly Carlstone, come to get him out of here as
instructed.

'Everything good?' he asked via his aug.

'No problems,' Carlstone replied. 'Taking into consideration what we discussed after initial contact, we're taking you out by ship. Two of our trade ships are here and we're going in one of them.'

'How long till we're aboard?' Blite asked.

'An hour until we're aboard the shuttle and launched, then three hours till we're on the ship.'

'Flight time?'

'Eight days.'

'Why so long?'

'More secure route.'

'The ship has been swept?'

'It has, and its unit is . . . prador.'

That meant the controlling mind of the ship was the flash-frozen ganglion of a prador and not an AI. Good choice, Blite felt, because right now he didn't trust any AI. He queued up the aug to knock him out for another four hours but then hesitated. He felt a bit mean about his responses to the woman who'd been one of his rescuers and had obviously been curious about him. He should have overcome his inclination to reticence and engaged her in conversation. But about what? She would probably have wanted to know more about those past events surrounding Penny Royal, and he'd grown tired of telling that story – mostly because of telling it to the interviewing forensic AI Carnusine years before, while it hinted that it would really like to examine him more closely, and did he mind? He hadn't allowed it – or rather, they'd allowed him not to allow it. Perhaps she wanted to know more about the crystal in his skull, and how and why it had got there. There was no danger in that. He'd never been secretive about it. In fact the crystal – the dark diamond – was the one which kept secrets. Maybe another time he'd hunt her down and be kinder, but right now he had problems to deal with, and someone else to hunt down who might help him get to the bottom of all this.

Blite – Past

Blite was devastated. When he reported the theft of the pendant he described it as holding a black jewel but dared not elaborate on that. He also described the girl who'd stolen it, using an induction aug to access his memories for a more precise depiction of her. Turned out her name was Meander Draft 64XB and she was on record, location presently unknown. He threw some money around and employed the types he was used to employing to hunt her down. But eventually his schedule began to catch up with him.

AIs were getting tetchy about him not turning up on Earth for those interviews; Earth Central itself had sent him a message. He became aware that his delay on this world, just to look for a missing pendant, would bring that pendant to the notice of those AIs. They'd start to wonder why he considered it so important; they'd speculate on it having some connection to the events they wanted to interview him about. In the end, he paid out more money, left instructions for the search to continue, and funds for a large – but not too large – reward.

Done, thought Blite bitterly.

His belongings were packed in two grav-cases and now his time in this Abalon apartment was up. A small shuttle awaited at the space port and Mr Pace's, or rather the ship Pace had given him, awaited in orbit. The collection of glass sculptures had been packed away safely, transported back up there, and was now in the hold.

Time to go.

He strolled along the street, his two cases drifting after him. He regretted leaving this place and was anxious about what was to come when he arrived on Earth, as well as still pissed off about the theft of his pendant. At the end of the street, he took an aircab to the space port and was soon strolling through the wide entrance to the shopping complex that backed onto the designated landing pad. There wasn't much security here. Cargos coming in were scanned in a limited manner for dangerous weapons, but since your average fusion node could be converted into a heavy weapon, and a lethal biological could be concealed in a pinhead, it was just a hat-tip towards security. The gates to the landing pad had scanning too, but you were only stopped if you couldn't be identified. He walked straight through.

Wide steps led up to the pad. Once he reached the top, he looked around. The shuttles were set out in rows and of various designs. Stacks of cargo crates were everywhere, autohandlers and older driven versions loading the crates onto trains of wheeled pallets, people standing talking or wandering about too. Small cargo ships and shuttles were here. The larger stuff lay beyond, where bigger ships loomed and cranes shifted over stacks of huge cargo containers. He walked along a row of shuttles, finally spying his own far ahead, half concealed behind stacks of plasmel crates. As he drew closer, he turned to his luggage and waved a hand ahead.

'Go aboard,' he said tightly, and the two cases overtook him.

He slowed his pace, knowing he was dawdling because he didn't want this next stage of his life to begin. He felt irritated and low, as if he had a hangover he'd failed to medicate. He needed to move on – get his mind on other things. Looking at all these cargos and all this *business*, he pondered on how, with the wealth now at his disposal, he could do things so much better than he had before. Did he really want to sit on a beach with that cips? How long would it be before he started thinking about importing his favoured version of that drink? How long before he looked at price lists, import tariffs, tax structures and how to get around them? He grunted to himself and stepped past a large stack of plasmel crates, finally ready to board the shuttle.

'Please,' said a shaky voice.

He halted, hand sliding down to where he usually wore a gas-system pulse gun at his hip, then straying away again.

'I'm sorry,' said the voice.

He couldn't see anyone at first, but stepping forward further, he noticed her sitting in the gap between two stacks of crates, with her back against one of them. She looked up at him. Her face still appeared young but had rings under bloodshot eyes. It was thinner, with the bone structure sharply highlighted by shades of grey. There were deep scratches on her neck, as if she'd raked herself with her fingernails. Her hair was messy, not stylishly so, just messy, and had streaks of something drying in it – probably vomit. Certainly, her torn and battered envirosuit had vomit down the front, and he could smell a horrible mix of body odours. She reminded him of the kind of people found in back alleys on less salubrious worlds, lost in addiction and lying in their own shit and urine.

'You,' he said.

'I thought it would be enough . . . enough for you to follow the trail,' she said, and then her gaze wandered away from him as she groped into a pocket of her suit. She took out the pendant and, with a shaking dirty hand, nails broken and bloody, held it up for him. 'Please take it.'

Without a second thought, Blite snatched the pendant from her. He inspected it, immediately suspicious it was a copy, but the moment his finger touched the black crystal he knew it was his own. He slipped the chain over his head, then tucked the thing inside his shirt so it rested against the bare skin of his chest. Something unwound inside him and the world seemed suddenly brighter. He peered back down at the girl, wondering what to do about her.

She was already rising now, and the transformation was startling. Her face suddenly seemed prettier, like life had returned to it. She stood straight and strong and peered down at her soiled clothing in disgust, before sighing out a breath and her gaze straying to where the pendant lay against his chest. He realized she now looked less of a girl and more of a woman.

'I don't know what to do now,' she said. 'It just wouldn't let me keep it . . . it showed me things.'

Blite now had questions. He reached out to grab the shoulder of her suit, prepared to drag her inside the shuttle. Her hand came up with a blade in it – glinting chain-glass – and he knocked it aside, grabbing for her with his other hand. He caught part of her sleeve but the knife sliced down, thankfully cutting the fabric rather than his fingers, and she slid lithely past him to run away. He watched her go, knowing he carried far too much bulk to go in pursuit, and anyway, what was the need? He turned and headed for the shuttle, wondering whether to cancel the search for her, but then decided against it. He could tell this hadn't been just an opportunistic theft; he wanted to know why she'd stolen a pendant that, on the face of it, looked like tourist tat, and what it had done to her.

Blite – Present

'Those are mine?' Blite enquired aboard the ship.

Carlstone had always been the height of efficiency and Blite admired the way he tended to every detail, but he'd outdone himself this time. Blite had awoken on a surgical table in a sealed surgery, a gleaming autosurgeon backing away from him, an organic printer folded down at the foot of the slab, and other equipment all around. He was presently pointing with his partially restored arm at a row of cylinders along one wall.

'We brought your stock of cellular printing substrate.' Carlstone, who looked more like the ECS soldier he'd once been than the administrator of Perihelion he now was, stood behind the glass of the clean surgery. 'It's all there: bone, muscle and skin – the lot. But I thought it might be an idea to wake you first, bearing in mind what we discussed.'

'That someone has been trying to kill me,' Blite said. 'And that the runcible failure on Callanasta might have been no accident.'

Carlstone nodded. 'You said you wanted to augment.'

Blite nodded – he could do that now. Yeah, he wanted to boost himself up, make sure he was a lot less vulnerable to injury, which seemed a rational choice. He shuddered, a hint of the horrors rising, but still thankfully suppressed. Of course, Carlstone couldn't know – in fact no one could or should know – that it was the injuries which most concerned him, not the possibility of dying. Yet it seemed that somehow a particularly spooky 'retired' Polity agent called Ian might know. He put that aside for the moment. One thing at a time.

'Yes, I want everything we have,' he said. 'What do we have?'

Carlstone shrugged. 'Depends how concerned you are about your appearance.'

'I want it to be more or less the same.'

Blite had never really gone in for much in the way of body modification. He still looked mostly the same as he had as a youth, when in fantasy virtualities he'd always been given the role of the blacksmith, or in others the heavy, the enforcer – the

21

guy who broke people's bones for fun. Heavily muscled, just through genetics – though maybe now looking on the point of turning to fat – he liked his body as it was, because it was Blite.

'Very well,' said Carlstone. 'And how quickly?'

'Yesterday.'

'Then we can toughen up your bones and weave cable muscle into your present musculature, including some in your heart, and we can put in subdermal armour. However, all those will need support by altering your lung capacity, the carrying capacity of your blood, organ processing etc., and that'll be via reprogramming your nanosuite, so it will take a little while to catch up.'

'Anything else?'

'We could give you fire-resistant skin, but it never looks quite right.'

Blite peered at him. It seemed Carlstone was having one of his all too rare moments of humour.

Carlstone continued, 'I would also suggest nerve enhancement and the incorporation of an aug to run all the integration processes.'

Blite grumbled.

Carlstone added, 'It can be an induction aug you can remove at any time.'

'You neglected to mention something else,' said Blite.

'I was waiting for you to mention it.'

'You brought it?'

'Yes, I did, but I strongly suggest it's something you avoid.' Carlstone grimaced. 'Too many imponderables there. First off, we don't know how it will interact with your other enhancements. Secondly, it was developed, or it evolved, in the Kingdom, aboard the King's Ship. Let's face it: even the AIs don't know enough about the Spatterjay virus, and what they do know is fucking scary. This one . . .' He shrugged. 'It's fast-acting, I'll give it that.'

'We'll leave it for now,' said Blite. 'But I want a batch of it prepared to go in my thigh bone, with an externally activated pump.'

'You're the boss,' said Carlstone tightly.

'Now get all that other stuff done.'

Blite reclined, thinking about this virus. On the world of Spatterjay, it turned its hosts into a reusable food resource for the leeches which spread it. Those hosts then became something really *really* tough, and the virus worked with all species, including the humans of Spatterjay, called hoopers. It had made some of them very strong indeed, the toughest being the Old Captains, whose strength and durability hadn't really been properly measured, but lay beyond most Polity enhancements. It sounded ideal if you didn't want to end up dead, but it had its drawbacks.

If you were sufficiently injured, the virus used an eclectic collection of genomes from its previous hosts to increase your survivability. And this could turn you into a monster, so it had to be controlled. The things it did were also based on a malfunction of something else it contained, which few knew about: the genomes of a squad of Jain soldiers. The Jain had been an alien race whose vicious technology had been hanging around and destroying civilizations since the Jain themselves had disappeared long ago. Add to this the version of the virus they'd obtained from the Prador Kingdom, which was a mutated or modified strain that worked much faster than the centuries it usually took to create an Old Captain, and Carlstone's reservations were warranted. However, as Blite drifted into unconsciousness, he had the strong feeling it might be something he would need, and soon.

2

Matheson

Matheson stepped out of his tent, dumped his pack by his feet and peered down at the marks in the dirt. Some were still visible, though the hailstorm in the night had obliterated the rest. Sleer tracks. They'd come visiting to grind whatever version of eating apparatus they had – that being dependent on what stage of sleer they were – against the open-cell monofabric of his tent. They weren't much of a threat to him, having little chance of penetrating the material, but they'd interrupted his sleep, and he liked his sleep. He decided he'd have some target practice on the pests today as he continued with his associates towards the 'farm'. He looked around.

Jurgen, their guide, was out of his tent and shrugging on his pack. The other three tents of the Brice brothers and sister were still closed. Ricardo, the Golem, had yet to return from his nightly perambulations. And Nightshade, the spider drone, was squatting on the roof of their ATV, gazing off towards the horizon. Matheson turned back to his own tent, opened the flap to check he had left nothing inside, then stepped back, tapping the control on the flimsy console by the flap. With a hissing sound, the dome-shaped tent released air from its open-cell foam and steadily collapsed. As it did so, microfibre memory mesh began to fold it, and fold again, until finally it became a small block that could fit into the palm of his hand, flimsy screen on top. He slid it into a pocket in his pack, picked up the pack and walked over to Jurgen, who was already collapsing his own tent.

'So today we should reach the boundary of the farm,' said Matheson.

'Weather permitting,' Jurgen replied, looking up at the sky.

'No such thing as bad weather, just bad clothing.'

'That's all right for you to say,' said Jurgen, eying the high-tech power armour Matheson wore. 'If the hail comes again, I can always just give you directions to the pass.' Jurgen shrugged.

'And I pay you the rest of your fee?'

'Of course.'

'No, you get us to the pass and I pay you there, as agreed.'

Matheson turned away. The Brices were up now, all efficiency and readiness as they collapsed their tents and ran weapons checks. Sheen Brice, the sister, didn't look very different from her brothers. All three were heavily boosted, extremely tough, and the best bounty hunters in the sector. Matheson auged in, running his own weapons check as he slung on his pack. His multigun was strapped onto the back of it at the moment, and he saw no need to unlimber it until they were closer – his gas-system pulse gun and flak pistol would be enough to deal with any sleers or droons that might come after them. Gazing into the distance, he wished he could have used a grav-car to take them beyond the pass, but their target at the farm apparently had detection gear, a couple of particle cannons and a missile launcher. Airspace over the farm was a no-fly zone, as agreed by the authorities of this world they were on, Cull.

'I still don't get why they're so complacent about us being here,' said Ulnar Brice, stepping up beside him. 'The machine has citizenship – you'd think the authorities would protect it.'

'That's because it can protect itself better than the police of Cull,' said Ricardo, casting his voice from a distance as he walked towards the encampment. 'You've seen how they are here: low-tech projectile weapons.'

'But as a matter of policy?' said Ulnar.

'It told them it needs no protection.' Ricardo had broken into a run, his cast voice dopplering oddly. Finally he arrived by them. 'As I understand it, the thing rather likes all the attempts to collect on the Polity bounty that's been placed on its head. It is, after all, a killer.'

Matheson grimaced. There'd been numerous attempts to bring the machine in, either whole or in bits – the bounty specified that either way would garner payment, though the more intact the thing was, the more money would be forthcoming. And the bounty had recently gone up . . . Whatever. The machine, the fucking machine, would be returned to the Polity in bits because this was personal. Because this was *the* machine. Matheson remembered the day when his mother had told him his father was dead, having tried to collect on a bounty for a separatist terrorist called Arian Pelter. Growing up, he'd trained himself for the same profession, but by the time he was ready, Arian Pelter was long dead. He'd found out about the machine, though – how it had killed fifteen bounty hunters, including his father. It had torn off his head.

Matheson learned his profession properly and gained deep experience over more than a century. He forgot about the machine until, in his hundred and seventieth year, ennui hit. He survived it, barely, but only because he remembered his past and decided to make the machine an end goal to give him purpose. Coming out of ennui, he discovered that bounty hunters with higher resources than him had tried and failed to get to it, and he realized he wasn't ready. But now a series of profitable successes had provided the equipment they wore and carried, and wealth enough to employ a war drone and the Brices. What had once been a distant purpose enabling him to survive had become present reality.

Matheson now eyed Ricardo, clamping down on his growing dislike. They'd worked together for many years and he had trusted the Golem more than he did most other such machines, which wasn't a high bar. This was because Ricardo was a human mind loaded to a Golem chassis. But over the last year, during two previous hunts, the man-Golem, who'd always been precise about necessary precautions, had begun to make them burdensome. Almost certainly this was because the high-value target prior to those two hunts had nearly done for Ricardo, with a particle cannon demounted from a warship. Matheson speculated on Ricardo in comparison to the machine they were going after now. He knew that with their new equipment he and the Brices could bring Ricardo down, and his chassis was a modern series. However, the machine at the farm had been altered and adapted. It'd been loaded with a murder tape to break its Polity programming, armoured in some fashion, and it was rumoured to have integrated some form of alien technology, though the last seemed highly unlikely.

'We all ready, then?' he asked, looking around.

Jurgen gestured across the gritty ground and they set out. They'd used the ATV previously where it had been a flat plain, but ahead stretched a rockscape with buttes of multicoloured outcrops jutting up here and there. This area lay athwart the jagged peaks where the supposed pass ran through, though they'd never been able to obtain satellite imagery or even a map. At the end of this, just behind those peaks, was a small plateau upon which lay the farm. It was inaccessible by any way other than on foot – apparently the machine had blocked off other routes.

Matheson had considered climbing gear but didn't fancy getting caught on a steep face by his supposed prey. Grav-harnesses weren't an option, since the machine had ways of detecting grav disturbances. The thing had laid out its game and he would play by its rules only so far.

'Hey, Nightshade! You going to sit there all day?'

The spider drone turned and observed him with glittery red eyes. Matheson felt a brief primal shudder at the sight of this three-metre spider, seemingly fashioned of grey iron, scrambling down off the ATV and coming after them. But Nightshade seemed okay. His contract had been open, and many other bounty hunters had used him and recommended him. That spider body was loaded with good weaponry. Matheson nodded to himself. They had the edge, with a man-Golem, a spider war drone, state-of-the-art power armour and weapons, and the EM disruptor shells for their multi-guns, which should bring down any damned rogue machine. And they had an ace in the hole too, which Matheson had strictly ordered the others never to discuss within Jurgen's hearing.

They trudged throughout the morning between rocks, along rough stream beds and past hills and buttes. A sleer came out of a hole at the base of one of the buttes and started to head towards them. The nightmare thing vaguely resembled a scorpion, was as big as the spider drone and had an excess of manipulators to the fore. Before Matheson could even reach down to his flak pistol, Sheen had nailed it with her laser carbine. In a cloud of smoke and fire the sleer retreated, body segments revolving independently. It never reached its burrow, just falling apart with those segments rolling away like burning tyres.

'Save your ammo,' said Will Brice.

He had a point. All of them apart from Jurgen, Ricardo and Nightshade wore power armour; one good solid kick would be enough to deter the creatures.

Jurgen next led them to a stream that wound down from the mountains. They ascended alongside this, below layered sandstone cliffs that grew steadily taller. The path here seemed quite worn and, where it went up over fallen slabs, steps had been carved in the stone. Matheson caught hold of Jurgen's shoulder and gestured to steps lying ahead.

'This looks well used,' he said, suspicions arising about where they might be being led. 'I thought the machine kept itself isolated.'

'He does, generally, but he's running a farm. He grows biotech stuff up there and sells it. Traders from the city or the plains come up here.'

'And they have no problems?' Matheson didn't like how Jurgen referred to the thing as 'he'.

'They're not coming to collect on the bounty.'

'Ah, so it's a peaceable machine usually, just defending its agrarian idyll?'

'He likes his sport,' Jurgen replied, heading for the steps.

The path wound steadily higher and the declivity the stream had cut steadily narrowed. Ahead, stretching across between the two cliff faces, he saw a tree trunk lodged in place. There were ropes hanging from this, most of them flapping loose but one still holding a body up there by the neck.

'This is as far as I go,' said Jurgen. 'The edge of the plateau is a further four hundred metres up.'

On the sandstone slabs below the tree trunk lay remains that had obviously, at one time, been suspended above. There were headless skeletons clad in body armour, and skulls scattered around, lodged in crevices. Sheen climbed up onto a rock to inspect some of them.

'Polity commando kit,' she called down. 'Maybe twenty or more years old.' She held up a skull with a helmet still in place.

'Army surplus,' said Will. 'You can buy it anywhere.'

'So, will you transfer my payment?' said Jurgen.

Now, Matheson felt, it was time to start playing the game his way. He had no doubt that Jurgen had some kind of deal with the machine up above. He led the hunters here, doubtless assessing their capabilities, then sent some kind of report. It was time to remove him from the equation. He reached down and drew his weapon, but Nightshade had moved close and now reared up. A hissing crackle raised dust from Jurgen's clothing and he shuddered, going down on his knees with a baffled expression. The spider drone caught him and laid him down on his side. It had effectively saved his life by hitting him with a load of stun beads.

'You're too kind,' said Matheson.

'The police here may turn a blind eye to bounty hunters going after the machine, but maybe not to the murder of one of their citizens. Let's keep this clean.'

Matheson holstered his pulse gun. Nightshade was right, but Matheson still didn't like the spider drone's inclination towards morality. That had been in the reports from others who hired him. Apparently, he only killed those who directly attacked him or were, not to put too fine a point on it, bad people. It bothered Matheson that he might well fall into the latter category.

'This does not look good,' said Ricardo from up on the rock where he'd joined Sheen. 'If these guys were wearing army surplus, it seems they obtained a standardized batch for them all to wear. They were all boosted, auged and had other cybernetic enhancements too.' He held up the bones of an arm held together with gristle and ligaments, and a joint motor at the elbow. 'And look at this.'

He dropped the arm and picked up something else, then tossed it down to them. Will stepped in to catch the item and swung round, brandishing it. It was a heavy carbine of some kind.

'ECS high-power laser carbine with side slug launchers and EMP viral warfare facility,' he said. 'We ain't in Kansas any more, Toto.'

It was an expression Will had used a couple of times before: when he'd learned what their mission would be here, and when he'd seen the ship Matheson had bought following their last big bounty. Matheson reminded himself now, as he had on those previous occasions, to look up the phrase, since he had no idea what the man was talking about. Another object spiralled down from the rock and thumped in sandy dust. Matheson stepped forwards, stooped, and picked it up. A small flat gun – a pulse gun of a familiar design. This was the kind of weapon legendarily carried by Polity agents. He discarded it. You could buy them anywhere.

'I suggest a reassessment,' said Ricardo, jumping down from the rock and landing lightly. 'We need more information.'

Matheson stared at him, his growing dislike abruptly grounding in reality and finding justification. In a Golem chassis, Ricardo had super strength, speed and durability, but inside that chassis he was still a man. In retrospect Matheson realized that the precautionary approach which had made Ricardo so useful arose out of cowardice. He saw in an instant how Ricardo had always tried to put his fears across logically, in terms of the mission, but really he was craven. Oh, he would happily rip off the head of a victim, but any hint of danger to himself and that 'reassessment' would come out. Matheson grimaced at his twenty-twenty hindsight, as he saw the logic of this fear which had led the man to install himself in a Golem chassis in the first place.

'We need no more information,' said Matheson. 'There's a killing machine up there with a huge bounty on its head and we're going to collect.' He looked around at the others. 'Close up visors and initiate the 'ware.'

He watched as the Brices closed their visors and worked their wrist controls. Shimmering lines appeared at the tops of their heads and traversed down their bodies, seemingly erasing them from existence. He turned to Ricardo, who shrugged, then disappeared in the same manner. Ricardo didn't wear armour but had the same chameleonware installed in his body. This was their big edge – on top of their superb armour and weapons. He looked around for Nightshade – but the spider drone had already disappeared – then closed down his own visor. As soon as it snicked home all the others reappeared to him. Their 'ware was linked so they could see each other, since being invisible to each other would almost certainly result in some friendly-fire incidents.

'Where's Nightshade?' asked Will over com.

'Scouting ahead,' the spider drone replied. 'More casualties up here – you need to come and have a look. Ricardo might not be far off the mark.'

Matheson felt a stab of anger, but suppressed it. None of them knew about his father and how he'd died, and he didn't want to start showing any behaviour they might consider irrational. No matter what did lie ahead, they were going to the farm. He waved an arm at the others and led the way up.

Here and there along the path lay wreckage. Two grav-platforms rested against the cliff face like huge discarded coins, weaponry still mounted on them. On one a corpse was draped over what looked like a particle cannon. Another pile of wreckage at the foot of a cliff, after a long scar through the sandstone, looked to be the remains of an armoured grav-car. Then ahead he saw Nightshade, standing in front of something crumpled below steps which led upwards beside a waterfall.

'I think I knew him,' said the spider drone. 'His name was Plunder – veteran of the war like me.'

This wreck of a war drone was the usual nightmare rendition of something nasty and insect-like. It had a short flat body at the back, from which protruded a barbed sting. From its thorax six legs had protruded, some of which it had lost, the rest bent and broken. Its head had been birdlike, from what he could see remaining of it. As he drew closer, he noticed a large hole – big enough to drop a man through – had been burned right through its body.

Nightshade turned and looked at them. 'So, we've had what looked like a unit of Polity commandos here, a Polity agent, grav-mounted weapons and now a war drone. Perhaps this machine we are hunting is even more dangerous than we supposed.'

The Brices were looking at Matheson and waiting for his response. Ricardo was gazing at the ruined drone with an odd lost expression.

'This is staged,' Matheson said finally. 'No way did the machine take all of these out at once. As I understand it from Jurgen, the machine allows people up here to the farm to collect its crops. It probably doesn't react unless attacked.' He gestured at the drone and back down the pass. 'I'd bet these didn't come here all together but separately, over many years. Then, after they were killed, the machine put them here.' He pointed to the war drone. 'That probably made the mistake of flying in. Jurgen tried to imply the machine likes killing bounty hunters, but putting these here indicates otherwise – it's trying to turn us back.'

'This is not a good idea,' said Ricardo.

'Shut the fuck up, you coward,' said Matheson.

'Oh, a coward, am I?' Ricardo enquired.

'Yes, and it's become more obvious ever since you were beamed.'

'A coward,' Ricardo repeated. He gazed at Matheson for a long moment, then abruptly swung around and began walking back the way they'd come. Matheson stared at him, not quite believing what he was seeing.

'Where the hell are you going?'

Ricardo just kept walking.

Matheson felt the rage surge up; he drew his flak pistol and began firing. Ricardo stumbled as shells slammed into his back, but they couldn't do much damage to his Golem chassis. Abruptly he jerked into fast motion and went dodging and weaving down the pass. Matheson lowered his weapon. Pointless exercise.

He turned to the others. 'Anyone else want to run?'

'We're good,' said Will. 'If it all turns to shit, doesn't necessarily mean we'll end up dead – we'll just have to get out, fast.'

'Nightshade?' Matheson asked.

No expression to read there – just those glittery red eyes. 'War drones don't make the mistake of flying straight into heavy weapons.'

'How many disenfranchised war drones have you known that chose a way out?' asked Matheson.

'He has a point,' said Sheen. 'Probably decided to go down in flames.'

'Okay,' said Nightshade. 'But I am not suicidal. If this does turn to shit, I'm gone.'

'So, we continue,' said Matheson, heading for the steps up the side of the waterfall.

The last stretch before the upper plateau consisted mostly of these steps. Matheson felt himself boiling inside, but his certainty had drained away. Yes, it seemed likely the dead had been positioned there as a deterrent, but, fuck – a war drone brought down? Anyway, Will was right. They had their chameleonware and they had their weapons. If things got too hot up above, they could lay down a lot of fire and flee. At least then he'd have more of an idea what he faced and be able to return better prepared.

After two longish climbs they came to a short length of steps up to clear sky. Matheson unhooked his multigun from his pack, extended the support arm from his suit and fitted it into place, plugging in the power lead and ammo feeds from the pack. Targeting and weapons selection came up in his head-up display. The Brices did the same and they auged together, running a final weapons check. Nightshade opened two hatches in his back end and protruded a pair of miniguns, while other hatches slid open on the war drone's body too. They were ready for the final climb. Matheson waved a hand and led the way up.

From the last few steps the vista opened out ahead of them. The plateau wasn't huge – just five kilometres across. The scene was bucolic, with neat fields laid out between fences, around a farmhouse that seemed transplanted from some ancient age on Earth. He took in the scene, looking for the machine, then his gaze fell upon a nearby flat rock, raised like a dais directly in the path. Lying on this, like some exhibit in a sculpture museum, was an object. It consisted of a thick mass of glassy and metallic fibres, some seemingly frayed, ribbons of a variety of materials, grey and black nodes like seeds, and thin ribbed wires of some black substance. It had been tied into a knot nearly a metre across, with the two ends of the mass protruding for over a metre on either side.

'Oh, I see,' said Nightshade.

Matheson heard a sound and turned to see that Nightshade had retracted his cannons and was now closing up his other lethal hatches.

'What do you see?' said Matheson.

'That Ricardo made the right call, and this is where we turn around and go home.'

'Talk some fucking sense, drone.'

With one forelimb Nightshade indicated the knotted mass. 'That is a Mobius AI, and it's not looking too good, is it?'

'You're fucking with us,' said Will.

'Bye bye,' said Nightshade and turned around to head back down the steps.

Matheson wanted to fire on the thing, just like he had on Ricardo, but you didn't open fire on a war drone – their reactions could be instantly lethal. He watched him disappear out of sight.

'What now?' asked Sheen. 'We had some serious edge when we came up here and it's now looking increasingly blunt.'

'Look,' said Will, pointing.

A figure had stood up, out in the fields. It was humanoid and obviously quite tall, wearing a long khaki coat and a wide-brimmed hat. Even at this distance, Matheson could see the brassy metal of its face and hands.

'The machine – Mr Crane,' he said, aiming his multigun and lining the figure up in the crosshairs.

Five of his EM disruptor shells hit this big Golem one after another. One caught him straight in his face, with a resounding clang and flash that turned his head and sent his hat arcing away. Three hit him in the chest and one in the stomach, their explosive output of EMR blasting his long coat away in tatters to expose the brassy metal of his torso. Matheson broke into a run towards him. It hadn't been in their plan to attack like this, but Matheson knew that if he didn't do something immediately, he might lose the Brices too.

After a few seconds of shock, the three Brices opened fire as well. Since he'd hit the Golem with EM disruptors, they used rail beads, cracking through the air as they broke the sound barrier and went far beyond it. Mr Crane jerked in a familiar dance of someone being shot multiple times. A beam lanced through smoke – Sheen firing a high-intensity laser. Crane stumbled out of the crops, which seemed to be the upper red and green leaves of biotech podules, with the remaining tatters of his coat flaring away. He was now clad only in ragged smoking trousers and big toe-capped lace-up boots. Ridiculously, he was still clutching the hoe he'd been using. But then he raised it like a spear and threw.

The Golem blurred, his arm disappearing momentarily. Matheson heard a ripping crack over to his left and received injury alerts through the aug connection. Sheen. He saw her tumble backwards several metres, as if at the front of a blast wave. She landed on her side then came upright to her knees, groping at a shaft sticking out her chest. The other length of the shaft protruded from out of her back, the metal business end of the hoe glowing white hot. Matheson just gaped. Their armour was the highest rated and little but rail-beaded, densely compressed ammo could penetrate it, yet . . . this? Sheen keeled over, flatlining over the aug – at least she was backed up in a memplant in her skull. There might even be a chance to get her body functional again, since death nowadays had little to do with the heart stopping. The suit and her internal nanosuite would be busy trying to save what it could by vitrifying her.

Matheson opened fire again, using a rotating selection of the firing options on his multigun, his suit kicking into assist to take the recoil of the rail beader. Crane staggered back through a growing ball of fire as, after a shocked pause, the Brice brothers opened fire too. Then the fire went out and the Golem was gone.

'Where the fuck is it?' said Will.

They began to pull closer together.

'Behind you!' shouted Ulnar.

Mr Crane appeared behind Will Brice, reached out with those big brassy hands and closed them on either side of his helmet, then turned it. Will flatlined immediately and dropped, his head on backwards. Matheson fired again, another mass of EM disruptors, but Crane had disappeared once more.

'Chameleonware, it's got chameleonware!' shouted Ulnar.

No shit, thought Matheson. It also seemed their 'ware didn't hide them from him, while in that glimpse he'd caught of the Golem, there'd been something else too. Their firing had caused damage, with one plate of the armour over his torso hanging off to one side. And, exposed within, organic yet metallic ropes twisted and writhed.

Ulnar began firing around himself randomly and Matheson ducked down, having to roll towards a nearby boulder as some of those shots came dangerously close. He watched the man, sick inevitability in his guts. Saw his multigun ripped away and arcing over into the fields, then Mr Crane appeared before him, chopped with one hand, and stepped away. Ulnar's headless corpse dropped, his head bouncing through the smoking foliage to one side. In an instant, Crane was standing before Matheson.

Matheson opened fire with everything he had. Crane disappeared behind this fire and the shattered debris of shells, then his arm reached out of it, his hand closed around the barrel of Matheson's multigun and crushed it. The gun exploded, slamming Matheson back into the boulder. His visor was charred and, after a moment, the chain-glass decohered, falling to powder in front of his face. He had no idea what could have caused that. He was bruised, battered and scorched where fire had got through the armoured joints, but otherwise intact. He looked up as the Golem stepped forwards to loom over him.

Crane still wore his ragged monofilament trousers and large boots, while his damaged chest plate was open, and other rings and plates of armour rucked up. Those metallic snakes continued to writhe underneath, but now an inky-black meniscus, like a flood of oil, began to cover them; this seemed somehow worse. Crane reached in and pushed the chest plate back into place, with the stuff bubbling around the edges. It seeped and shifted elsewhere too, in closing fractures, and perhaps it was pushing from the inside as dents popped out and his armour smoothed. Was it his version of blood? He peered down at Matheson with eyes of the same blackness, as deep as Hell.

'You killed my father,' Matheson said, feeling ridiculously like some character in a badly written virtuality.

Crane shrugged and began to reach for him. Then, right at that moment, something huge appeared and slammed into Crane from the side, ploughing his feet through the earth and carrying him on as if on the nose of a monorail train. In a glimpse, it looked like someone had flown a grav-car into the Golem.

Matheson flinched back, splintered debris stinging his face. What the hell was this? He heaved himself upright for a better look. Crane lay sprawled in earth mounded up by the impact and seemed a little dazed. Beyond him, having cut long grooves through the soil and skidding to a halt, stood a prador. Where the hell had that come from? Matheson gaped at the thing as it turned, and he saw odd irregularities – he now wasn't so sure this was a prador. The shape was all wrong, with the body being flatter and wider, and a carapace rim protruding out above its legs. It didn't have a head turret either, just hooked-out mandibles either side of a mouth, with eyes above in a straight, almost machinelike line. Its legs were long and bladelike, and its claws long. It resembled something else, he realized, and the aberrant memory arose of prill – crustaceans on the world of Spatterjay.

Crane heaved upright as the creature stalked towards him. Side-on to him, Matheson saw that the impact had damaged the interloper too, bulging up the front of its armour, with splits open there. He also noticed it wasn't alone. Two more of them were skimming across the podules field, and he couldn't tell whether they were running or grav-planing. The nearer one halted, as if assessing its options, then opened fire – a high-speed Gatling cannon flashing from a hollow at the centre of one claw. The shots sent Crane tumbling again, while the creature skidded back on the recoil. Finally coming to a stop, Crane shot up straight to his feet as if angry. He eyed the nearer creature, glanced at the other two approaching as he brushed clods of earth from his body, then stepped to one side and disappeared.

The creature didn't move, just stood facing where Crane had been. Matheson now thought these things had to be war drones – they came in all shapes and sizes and very often aped crust-aceans. Whatever. He'd come here to take down the Brass Man and failed, and now shit was happening well above his pay grade. Time to go. Slowly, he pulled himself round to one side of the boulder. Looking back, he could see a straight run over to where that Mobius AI lay. Past that and he'd be out of here. However, his leaden legs and the ache of his body indicated he wouldn't be getting there fast. He found himself turning back to watch the creatures, his urge to run undermined by a combination of physical incapacity and curiosity.

'I wouldn't hang around here,' said Nightshade. 'Unhealthy for you now, and it will be later. Mr Crane is not as forgiving as me.'

The drone wasn't visible, but the voice had issued from above. He gazed up at the top of the boulder and could see nothing, but he'd lost his visor, so wouldn't see Nightshade with his chameleonware running.

'You know him,' said Matheson, realization dawning.

'Of course I know him.'

'Fuck you, Nightshade.'

'So, you haven't figured it out yet. My name isn't Nightshade.'

It was just like his epiphany about Ricardo's cowardice. Of course, he had researched the history of Mr Crane, and of course he knew the content of the fictional virtualities about him. The problem had been separating out fact from fiction, but now it seemed he had found one of them. The Brass Man's war drone companion was, indeed, a fact.

'You're Arach,' he said.

'Yeah, that's me.'

Splinters flew down from the top of the boulder and Matheson realized the spider drone had jumped. The other two prador creatures had arrived now, and it seemed all three were grid searching the field. Arach's landing point became evident when, with a shuddering impact, one of the creatures over there dipped. The spider drone shimmered into visibility, miniguns pointed downwards, and opened fire. He held in place for a second, with fire and shattered slugs spraying out all around, then the recoil lifted him, as if launching on rocket engines. The prador creature staggered to one side, its back smoking and holes punched right through to where messy-looking organics hung out of its underside. It looked about done, but the others reacted. Their cannons flared, smashing the drone through the air, with hot broken slugs showering from his body. Arach was taking a pounding, but Matheson noted the drone must have superior armour and ammo. He landed in a crouch, somewhat dented, and then disappeared. Meanwhile the first creature he'd attacked slumped. Yes, the stuff hanging out of its underside indicated something living within that armour. But now it seemed Arach's chameleonware wasn't effective, as one of the remaining two opened up with what appeared to be a near white-shifted particle cannon from its other claw, hitting the drone twenty metres from its previous

41

position. Arach replied with a series of missiles, blasts taking off two of that creature's legs and flipping it over onto its back.

Then, over to one side, Crane reappeared. Ridiculously, he'd retrieved his hat, which sat on his head, smouldering, but he'd also brought heavy armament, though Matheson had no idea what the black tube might be. Crane snapped into motion, hurtling towards the remaining creature as it tracked Arach through the fields with its cannon, smoke and fire trailing the drone. Crane skidded to a halt just ten metres away as the thing swung towards him. Holding the tube in two hands, stretching it back under his arm, he opened fire.

'Fuck,' said Matheson, flinching from the glare.

A bright white beam stabbed out from the tube and struck the creature straight in the face. As his vision began to clear, Matheson managed another glance back and saw that the tube was being eaten away by this fire. Must be something like an iron-burner, he supposed – a device converting all its substance into a dense particle beam. It was an old-fashioned weapon, but no less effective for all that.

The creature staggered back and went down on its rump, a glowing hole where its eyes and mouth had been, its mandibles fractured into splinters by the heat. Crane shut his weapon off and strolled over to the one Arach had flipped over, even as it flipped back onto its feet. The iron-burner flared again, now burned down to less than half its length. The creature dodged and weaved as it closed in, its armour flaring. Crane finally discarded the nub of the device, which was still sputtering fire, and launched himself forwards, crashing into the thing. He grabbed a claw and, bracing a leg against the creature, tore the claw away. He then moved in close, punching and tearing. The noise was appalling – like a grav-car going into a scrap shredder. Matheson saw Crane levering up a lump of armour and stabbing a hand inside. He began ripping stuff out that could have been either mechanical or organic. And the creature finally collapsed.

Definitely time to go.

Matheson heaved himself to his feet and set out at a staggering run, until he reached the defunct Mobius AI. Glancing back from there, with smoke mostly blocking his view, he did get a glimpse of a wide-brimmed hat on a brassy head. He stumbled down the steps, trying to reason out 'what next?' but could only think of survival. Later he would ponder all he'd seen, but his aim here no longer seemed achievable. Seriously, how the hell could he take down a Golem like that? He'd been self-indulgent. After clambering down the stairs, he started to feel dizzy and had to stop, leaning against a rock with his thoughts whirling. When a backpack thumped down in the earth beside him, he jerked and came close to shitting himself.

'Maybe, after this, you can spread the word about Mr Crane,' said Arach.

The spider drone appeared on the top of the slab, then moved forwards to lean over and peer down at him. Gazing back up at the drone, Matheson felt some of his hate return.

'You and Crane . . .' he began, but trailed off because he didn't know what to say.

'A drone has to keep himself occupied,' said Arach. 'Crane became tired of the bounty hunters wrecking his property and damaging his crops long ago. I became bored with farming, so I went off to try out bounty hunting, and here we are.'

'So you protect a killer,' Matheson sneered.

'When Crane killed your father he was a different creature. In fact, he was more like the creature you are now.' Arach raised one leg and indicated the backpack. 'Take them and consider yourself lucky those things attacked.'

'Were they drones?' Matheson asked.

'No, not drones.' Arach scuttled to one side, tilted back, and looked up towards the sky. 'Something has changed. Someone is coming.' Abruptly the spider drone leaped off the rock and onto the path, then scuttled back towards the steps.

Matheson watched him go, then stooped down to the backpack. He pulled it open and saw Sheen gazing up at him. The heads of the other two were in there too. All had memplants, so they could be resurrected. He hoisted up the pack and set out. They would owe him for this, which was always useful. He thought too about the corpses, the wrecked war drone and the wrecked Mobius AI. Maybe, sometime, if ever he became confident of success, he'd be back. But he couldn't really envisage that happening.

Matheson didn't know why he was carrying the heads. A little bit of work with his cat's claw commando knife and he could have extracted the Brices' memplants in a moment, and they'd then have sat neatly in his pocket. He just couldn't do it, though. He guessed there was some squeamishness, but not about blood and bone, more about the fact it exposed the reality that a human life could be recorded on a lump of ruby the length of the last joint of his little finger.

He moved on down the valley, only pausing to think of his inventory of defences, when he saw a second-stage sleer clinging like a scorpion shadow to a sandstone cliff. His multigun was broken trash somewhere above, and at some point he'd lost his flak gun too. He still had a gas-system pulse gun at his hip and the knife in his boot. Meanwhile, self-repair was eliminating the suit's error reports, and suit assist was becoming available. Chameleonware could only hide everything below his neck, since his visor was gone, and the helmet sections were jammed down into his neck ring. With both functions being power hungry, he couldn't use them for long, but long enough should any of the pests attack him. He carried on, legs rubbery, torso aching and now burns through his joints making themselves known. It seemed a penance to trudge down the valley on minimal assist, with the weight of the Brices' heads in the bag on his back.

At least he was alive.

He steadily worked his way down and looked towards where they'd left Jurgen lying. The man wasn't there, but that was unsurprising. Arach had probably either given him a briefly paralysing shot, or come back and revived him. He went on past all the grisly warnings Crane had left here, and finally reached where they'd camped for the night. As expected, the ATV that'd been parked over by the rock was gone. He swore under his breath at Ricardo and continued. The man-Golem might have taken the ATV, but he wouldn't be getting back aboard Matheson's ship. Or even if he did, he wouldn't be able to fly it.

'So, you're alive,' said a voice.

He spun around, hand dropping to his gun, then just watched as Ricardo came out from behind a rock. The Golem halted, reached up to scrub at his hair and looked shamefaced.

'No thanks to you,' Matheson replied.

'But I was right, wasn't I?' said Ricardo.

Matheson pointed at where the ATV had been parked.

'Where?'

'Jurgen.' Ricardo pointed up. 'I saw him take it while I was on my way down.'

Matheson said nothing more and just turned away, heading towards the space port. After a few paces, Ricardo caught up with him and walked at his side. This annoyed him intensely. Had Ricardo been a man he would have been dead by now, but there was nothing Matheson could do with the armament he possessed, beyond burning up the man-Golem's syntheflesh outer covering. He glanced over to him, chewing on ideas. If he drove Ricardo away, he'd have no chance for payback. If he kept him close, he'd be able to put the man in the way of some sort of Golem killer. The only drawback, of course, was that he wouldn't be able to make Ricardo suffer.

'The Brices?' Ricardo asked.

Matheson halted and turned to him. 'I think you sometimes forget you've got Golem senses.' He hauled the pack off his shoulder and tossed it to Ricardo. The man caught it easily in one hand and held it up.

'Oh,' he said.

'Come on,' said Matheson. 'With luck we'll make it back to the ship by dark.'

'Okay.' Ricardo slung the pack over his shoulder, giving a tentative and painful smile. The man probably thought he was working his way back to being accepted into the fold – that his cowardice would be brushed aside because of how useful he could be. Not this time.

Matheson just kept walking, giving monosyllabic replies whenever Ricardo tried to start up a conversation. But then occasionally, he'd lean into some exchange to keep the man reassured; to keep him thinking he'd be forgiven.

Matheson peered through a dim evening fog at the diffuse lights of the city, and then over to the side at the red and green lights around the space port. He thought about heading into the city to see if he could track down Jurgen, but then, what did it matter? The ATV had been a rental, and it was possible Jurgen would bring him trouble with the local authorities. He had, after all, been about to kill the man, and still owed him half of his guide fee.

'Down there,' said Ricardo.

Matheson nodded and turned onto the path winding down to

a road lit up by orange street lights. That was a recent addition here, as were groundcars. Cull had reached a general technological level of twenty-first-century Earth, barring aberrations like the space port and items brought in for trade.

'I've called a cab,' Ricardo added.

When he'd seen the road in the distance, Matheson had considered doing the same, but that meant turning his aug back on, and he'd had it off while on the way down from the plateau. He hadn't wanted the distraction, needing time to think on what to do next. Yes, he still wanted to take down Crane, but what had happened up there, and what he'd seen . . . well, a new approach would be required.

They reached the edge of the road and gazed out at scattered chunks of carapace and other remains of first-stage sleers ground into the surface, as a triple formation of lights picked them out. The car, a low lump the shape of a beetle with windows all round it, slowed past them, then turned and came back.

'Ricardo?' a voice called from the window.

'Yup, that's me.'

The driver was something of an anachronism, Matheson felt. He wore handwoven cloth, and leather liberally studded with metal. His long hair was tied back, while a helmet, sword and some big heavy slug thrower lay on the front seat beside him. He eyed them as they climbed in, particularly focused on Matheson's heavy suit, before switching to the bloody bag at Ricardo's feet.

'Careful with the upholstery,' he said.

'It's good,' Matheson replied, suppressing the urge to pull his pulse gun and grind it into the back of the man's neck.

'More like you have been arriving,' the driver commented as they sped back towards the city.

'Really?'

'Since the bounty on Mr Crane went up. We've got two more ships down and notification of more on the way. Where do you want to go?'

'The space port.'

The drive was swiftly over, as they pulled into a parking area by the port. Ricardo produced a handful of octagonal coins and handed them over.

'Have a good one,' the driver told them.

Cranes and gantries were strewn across a port slab like many on other worlds, and apparently delivered here as a gift from the Polity. The whole area was fenced but not exactly overrun with guards. The government didn't seem too concerned about who arrived, but *what* arrived, imposing import taxes on Polity goods. Apparently some parts of the fence were left untended, though, with the collusion of a few guards, and deliveries came in by way of being thrown over to a growing number of gangs. It was always the same.

At the gate Matheson held out the ID ticket he'd been given upon leaving this place, and a guard clad in a beige uniform with occasional archaic accoutrements studied it, then checked a list.

'There were three others with you.'

'They're with us now,' said Matheson, gesturing to Ricardo, who swung round to show the bloody pack.

'Crane?' said the guard.

Matheson just nodded.

'There'll be more like that soon enough,' said the guard and just waved them through.

Matheson eyed some small, converted, in-system barges, and one or two attack ships, of the kind still knocking around after the war. He noted a large rectangular vessel that had probably been a passenger transport, and guessed it belonged to one of the new arrivals. His ship lay beyond it: a spherical thing five hundred metres across, with its surface seemingly assembled out of blocks. Passing the other vessel, he peered at people he recognized running a grav-sled loaded with equipment down the ramp. Finally arriving at his ship, he reached up with reluctance to turn his aug back on. Immediately numerous messages from other bounty hunters arriving here came up for his inspection. He sidelined those and linked to ship controls. Even as he drew close, the ship recognized him and began lowering a ladder to an airlock seven metres up. He belayed that and sent another order. With a thump, a ramp door opened instead, and lowered. He really didn't feel like climbing the ladder on minimal assist and, as he'd been pondering on, he would need the armour's remaining power elsewhere.

He and Ricardo walked up into the lower hemisphere hold space – this was divided off into sections, with hardly anything in them at all. He took it easy, because he needed to deliver instructions to the ship's computer, carefully working through his plan while checking what power remained in his suit. He paused and looked to Ricardo. Then, as if accepting that perhaps he'd come to some major decisions about his life, he gestured at their surroundings and said, 'You know, this ship has a lot of space down here. It doesn't always have to be bounties. We could move some cargos.'

Ricardo nodded, maturely accepting this concession to reality and deliberately not gloating. Matheson felt further contempt for this man in a machine, as he led the way into another of the holds.

'Put them there for now. They can go in the freezer later.' He gestured to racks holding spare equipment.

Ricardo walked over to the racks, taking the pack off and slinging it onto one of the shelves – the Brices sat amid the spare guns and boxes of ammo. As an afterthought, he pulled across

49

a strap and secured them. 'We should take out the memplants and dispose of the rest.'

Matheson had turned to look at another piece of equipment in here – a clamp. To go after Crane, he'd made many preparations, including this one, but had decided it was redundant the moment they arrived and he'd confirmed what the situation was. Though the major part of the bounty was payable for Crane in pieces, a series of bonuses could be claimed, the largest of which was for him to be intact. There had always been the chance that, with the EMR shells, they could have immobilized him without destroying him. However, with him intact, there would also have been the chance he could reactivate, so Matheson had needed some way to immobilize him aboard. It had been a good idea, albeit negated by the dangers of transporting him from the plateau, since this clamp had been too bulky to transport up there.

Matheson now studied the device. It consisted of two thick slabs of ceramal running on columns at the corners and driven together by hydraulic rams. The aim had been to put Crane between the two slabs and simply compress him there. Thinking on what he'd witnessed up on the plateau, he doubted the thing would have worked had Crane become active in it. However, it was rated highly enough to work on any other Golem.

'We should dump this thing,' he said.

Ricardo shrugged. 'It still has value, and we could sell it to someone.'

Matheson stepped over to the rack and rested a hand on the bag containing the Brices' heads, as if communing with them. He then abruptly turned, apparently angry, and gestured at the clamp.

'Fuck it. Get the thing disconnected. We'll leave it on the pad when we get the hell out of here.'

'If you say so,' said Ricardo, turning towards the clamp.

Matheson turned back to the rack, auging to his suit and ramping up assist. Once in contact with the ship, he checked that it had followed his instructions. Yes, nearby computing was shielded, and the power supply to the clamp was a direct line and couldn't be interrupted without unplugging it. He stepped along the rack a little from the Brices, while also ensuring that his suit shielding was up to maximum. No other preparations to make. The ammunition cases sat next to a couple of spare multi-guns. He reached over to a long box, flipped the catch and opened the lid. The EMR disruptor shells were in magazines of ten, held together in a flimsy fibre frame. He drew one towards him, his body interposed so Ricardo couldn't see what he was doing, pulled out all the shells from one magazine and auged into them, giving them a one-second delay. Nine went into his left hand, while in his right he popped off the safety cap of the other, pressed the activator down with his thumb, and held it there as he turned.

'It seems a waste,' said Ricardo.

Damn, the man-Golem had already unplugged the power cable and was standing there holding it in one hand.

'You're right,' said Matheson. 'I've just thought of a use for it.'

He threw the first shell hard, his thumb coming off to initiate it. The thing hit Ricardo in the chest and exploded, blowing open his shirt and blackening syntheskin. Electrical discharges spread out from that point, running down his arm into the cable, and down his legs into the floor. Matheson advanced, throwing another shell. This one ripped deeper, peeling up syntheflesh and exposing grey metallic ribs. Ricardo made an odd huffing sound and staggered back. Another shell at his feet brought him down on one knee, and a fourth set his artificial blond hair smoking. Dropping the cable, he started to come up again, but then just swung down, forehead thumping against the floor.

Matheson watched for a second, then to be sure tossed another shell under the arch of Ricardo's body, and leaned close to jam yet another into the back of his trousers. As the last one blew, he kicked the man-Golem over towards the clamp, before grabbing up the cable. He quickly inserted the plug. His movements were jerky, his suit delivering error reports because, despite its shielding, the thing was suffering from the EMR pulses too. Ignoring the detachable remote, he used the simple button to test the clamp, watching its display come on and the hydraulics whine and shift. Ricardo moved again, one arm snapping out and a hand groping for Matheson's foot. He stepped back and, one after the other, used the remainder of the shells. Then, with his suit thumping and crunching, he grabbed Ricardo and heaved. The man-Golem was as heavy as expected but crashed down on the lower platen of the clamp. Matheson hit the button, but at the last Ricardo tried to throw himself out of the thing.

The upper platen came down hard on full power, like a drop forge. It caught Ricardo half out of the thing, its edge diagonal across his back from one shoulder to hip bone. Ricardo's right hand was just a finger's length away from the controls. Hydraulics whined, crushing down his torso until, with a crackling sound, it collapsed to half its thickness, while his legs kicked out on the other side. Hand still reaching, Ricardo looked up, then his arm and his head dropped down. Matheson let out a shaky breath, next, considering the proximity of that hand, went over to get some tools. As he returned, his suit finally gave up and he had to spend some minutes removing it before setting to work. He unbolted the clamp's controls and moved them well out of reach. He'd considered cutting off Ricardo's arm, but knew that, even with an atomic shear, it would take some time, and he didn't want to get close to it. That done, he headed for the door.

'Why are you doing this?'

Matheson turned. Ricardo had raised his head again. His mouth wasn't working but his voice wasn't generated that way. Matheson noted that however generated, the voice had an irritating whine in it.

'You know why.'

'This is stupid. I was right about Crane.'

'You're a coward and you betrayed me.'

'What are you going to do?'

Matheson eyed him. He hadn't really thought much beyond this point, but now he did. 'I can't cause you pain, so maybe I'll drop you into a slow descent into a sun so you can have a few months to contemplate that.' He closed the door on his way out.

Blite – Present

Perihelion looked like Earth's moon, but with a large chunk taken out of it. There'd been much speculation about how that had occurred. A meteorite impact couldn't have done it, because an impact hard or large enough to excavate so deep would have smashed the moon apart, or resulted in it becoming molten and eventually reforming into a sphere. Methods of dating the formerly molten material inside the crater had put its occurrence at just over two million years ago. AIs had come here and, it was rumoured, the giant research vessel *Jerusalem*. The nearest they'd got to an explanation was that the crater had been carved out by a weapon similar to a contra-terrene imploder. Blite never thought it a sufficient one. Imploders crushed down matter, fusing some of it, and a resultant secondary explosion would have broken up or melted the moon anyway. The crater was simply too neat – a perfect hemisphere cut out.

Blite was currently on a bed with an orthopaedic frame on.

The thing consisted of splints and motors, and special materials that could grow stiff or soft where required. Apparently it was necessary, to stop him snapping his own bones and doing other damage. The surgeon had woven in cable muscle, as well as put in some bone strengthening, but now his adjusted nanosuite needed to catch up with the rest of his body – high carrier haemo-globin, an expansion in lung capacity and efficiency, boosted compact glycogen storage and dense fast-conversion fats. If he used the muscle too much, he was told, areas of it could run out of oxygen and die. There were also other things that needed to be controlled and monitored, such as the acceleration of his nerve impulses, which could inadvertently have him breaking not just his own bones but those of others, and the expansion in efficiency and capacity of, well, all his other organs. All of this was being monitored, controlled and integrated by the induction aug on the side of his head, in conjunction with the suite. He could use the aug for all the other general functions too, like connecting to the ship and looking through its cams at Perihelion. Though he preferred to use his screen-painted wall and gesture control.

His company base sat in the base of that crater, a large mass of buildings now with over a thousand employees – a growing complex he visualized as one day filling the crater to its rim. At present it sat like a squashed metallic spider right at the bottom. Landing pads were positioned outside it, between its 'legs', but they were only for shuttles. The main ships of Penny Transport here – slab-like cargo haulers or heavy tugs that could shift large masses such as tanks of material, or even the odd useful asteroid – were docked around a ring station just out from the moon. That structure was mostly robotic and run by one of the few artificial intelligences he trusted: an old war drone called Absinthe. It bore the shape of a huge lizard, rendered in chrome and gold, and possessed more than enough mental watts to run cargo transfers and refuelling there. Absinthe was one of the disenfranchised drones, who'd spent most of its time since the prador/human war knocking about in the Graveyard. At present, Blite's ship was heading towards the ring to dock. Now it was time for him to move.

With movement limited by the frame, Blite heaved his legs over and sat on the side of the bed. He stood and walked to the door, feeling mildly irritated by the constraint, since the aches and pains of major surgery and rebuilding were fading now. In the corridor he smiled and, acknowledging crew and the team Carlstone had brought, he headed for the bridge. As he entered, he inspected the set-up. The captain sat in the usual throne in the middle, a panoramic screen wrapped round the fore, and two or three crew were at stations around the wall. Integrated drive control, he noticed. The ship, the *Bracken*, was a huge and powerful thing; its cargo was larger still. It controlled subsidiary drives scattered about the surface of that cargo, which consisted of half a million tons of tree trunks. Carlstone had suggested they park the cargo somewhere and just use the ship alone, to get here quicker. Blite had scotched that idea because, well, it'd mean loss of profit, but he also didn't want others to get the impression he was running.

'Captain,' said Captain May. She sat there just looking kind of bored, then, as if something had kicked into motion inside her, she abruptly stood up and gestured to her chair.

'No need for that,' said Blite. He'd retained his title 'Captain' because that's who he was, though he should really have been addressed as 'Owner' or 'Director' or some such – titles he wasn't fond of. May slumped back into her chair, her expression bland. He had a sense of something odd about her since the last time he'd seen her, something off, but he had no time to investigate that now.

He walked out past her to gaze at the ring station ahead. The cargo vessels currently making transfers, being refuelled or awaiting assignment, were all docked around the rim. One other vessel was docked inside it. It looked like a spearhead attached to a short length of shaft. To the rear of that shaft were clustered the usual collection of fusion drive throats. Halfway along it, U-space nacelles jutted out. Other objects of a less salubrious nature protruded all down its length. The thing was a kilometre long and had space for small cargos, because Blite never wanted to miss out on opportunities, but the main purpose of its design was to be fast and very capable of protecting itself. He gazed approvingly at his ship, the *Coin*.

'Get me Absinthe, if you would,' he said, turning to May.

'He's waiting – he wanted to talk to you earlier.'

'And why wasn't I told?'

'Carlstone suggested the longer you stayed still in your cabin, the better.'

'I see.' He gestured towards the chain-glass screen.

A frame activated in the meta-material sandwich of the screen and opened to show the gold and chrome head of a monitor lizard. It blinked at him and flicked out a forked tongue.

'Good to see you, Blite,' it said.

'And you, Absinthe. How are the preparations for the ship?'

'Fuelled and ready to go,' Absinthe replied. 'All the other items are perfectly functional too.'

'The mind?'

'Not a very talkative item, but efficient.'

'My preference. You checked the provenance?'

'Yes. It's the flash-frozen ganglion of a prador female originally from a wartime destroyer crashed on Samver in the Graveyard. Used by a coring operation, which was taken down by, well, the usual, and all their remaining assets were sold off. It was given the choice of extinction by the forensic AI that examined it, but refused that.'

'Okay,' said Blite, tightly. The coring trade still existed in Graveyard borderland between the Polity and the Prador Kingdom. There, some villains infected people with the Spatterjay virus to make them durable, then supplanted their brain and a portion of their spinal column with prador thrall technology. The resultant organic robots were sold to the prador, mostly. The 'usual' taking them down meant Polity agents, and Blite was in agreement with the agents' often brutal methods.

He glanced back up at the main view screen then to May. 'Take us in.'

She nodded an acknowledgement, and he felt the steady clumping like heavy footsteps proceeding from far back in the *Bracken* and drawing closer. The thing was detaching from its cargo, since both together were just too large for manoeuvring near the space station.

Carlstone led the way through the space station and four soldiers, from his personal force, joined them. Clad in vacuum combat suits and heavily armed, they had the same look as him: ex-ECS. Blite wondered about the necessity for this here, in his own territory, but guessed you couldn't be too careful.

'You have the specialists you asked for aboard,' Carlstone said, 'mostly recruited from Penny Transport.'

'Good,' said Blite, while raising his hand to look at the brace wrapped around it to stop him snapping his own fingers.

'Your security professional will be me,' said Carlstone bluntly.

'I would rather you stayed and were here running things.'

'Penny Transport just about runs itself now – you recruited operators with a degree of independence. And I'm not going to let the reason it exists out of my sight when someone has gone as far as sabotaging a runcible to try to kill him.'

'It doesn't really run itself,' said Blite.

Carlstone nodded. 'I've trained a good team here and Reltor was to be my replacement when I retired.'

'Retired?'

'Yes, in two solstan years.'

'Still not sure it's a good idea, you coming.' Blite was thinking the man might be . . . restrictive.

'I'm coming,' said Carlstone stubbornly.

Blite scowled at that, but knew by Carlstone's expression that there'd be no further arguing with him.

'Who else?' he asked.

'You'll see shortly.'

The ring corridor was wide – walkways either side of a maglev track that ran cargo containers. This was for small cargo exchange, since the station wasn't really a delivery point. Blite noticed the lack of personnel here and reckoned it had to be Carlstone's doing. He wanted clear shooting, should there be any assassination attempt. The outer ring wall was punctuated by large cargo ports, interspersed with personnel airlocks. Blite paused at one to glimpse the *Bracken* heading back out to attach up to its cargo. He frowned at the thought about May's odd behaviour, then moved on. Ahead, coming into sight around the curve, Blite now saw some personnel and handler drays taking items through a large port on the inner ring to his vessel, the *Coin*. It was a silly name, but after naming other ships bought in for Penny Transport he'd just about run out of connections to Penny Royal. Drawing closer, he saw one handler dray carrying a rack of missiles inside; it was always good to be prepared.

Carlstone's four men edged in close as they approached – there were people here, so the danger greater. Before reaching the main port they turned to a smaller port, went in through an armoured door, then in zero gravity passed through a transparent tube to the airlock for the *Coin*. It had room for two men at a time, so two of the guards went first, followed by Blite and Carlstone, then the other two.

Once inside, they were on ship's grav and, well familiar with this ship and getting a little peeved at Carlstone's protectiveness, Blite led the way up a curving corridor to the bridge. The moment he stepped inside he felt at home. Four people were at consoles. The screen-painted upper wall gave the appearance that everything above the consoles was open to vacuum. And his captain's chair sat there, right in the middle, ready for him. He then noted that something else seemed oddly familiar – a bulky female figure bent over a console, peering at something on a screen.

'Greer,' he said, surprising himself with the name.

She stood upright and turned towards him. The heavyworlder woman who had crewed with him in the past had changed very little. Her long blonde hair was in a plait coiled at the back of her head. She was showing more than a little of her large boobs, pressed up now by her tightly folded arms. And she still looked as if she could tear someone's head off.

'What the hell have you got yourself into now, Blite?' she said, tapping one foot.

He shrugged. 'Seems someone keeps trying to kill me.'

'But a runcible, damn it?'

'Looks that way.'

He felt suddenly uncomfortable. She grimaced at him and he felt further discomfort. She knew he wasn't telling her everything – even after such a long absence she could see through him. He turned and headed towards the captain's chair and sat down in it. Greer followed him.

'What has Carlstone put you on?' he asked, glancing across to where the man had gone to seat himself at one of the consoles.

'Weapons,' she replied with a tight smile. 'This ship certainly has its fair share of those.'

'That's everything aboard,' Carlstone announced. 'Hatches closing and umbilicals detaching.' He paused to spin his chair around and face towards Blite. 'But I suspect we didn't get moving fast enough.' He waved a hand, but really used an aug instruction to bring up the view.

A frame appeared in the screen paint to the fore, where they had a view of the inside of the station ring. This frame showed starlit space with a glare off to one side, which soon revealed itself to be the gas giant as the view swung over. There, coming round the great orb, were objects like glittering shards of shattered metal. The frame focused in, revealing four Polity attack ships, with polished metal squid bodies and various combinations of U-space nacelles to their rears. Behind them came a dreadnought. The thing was a standard lozenge with protruding nacelles, and weapons much like those of the *Coin*, but orders of magnitude more powerful.

'I think some explanations are going to be in order sometime soon,' said Greer, rapidly heading to her console and sitting down.

The frame remained on the approaching ships, but beyond it the station had begun to drop away. Another frame flicked up, showing Absinthe looking dyspeptic.

'I've just been told that no ship is to leave,' said the drone. 'Apparently Polity marines are coming to search the station.'

'We've just been told to hold position too,' Carlstone added. 'Else we'll be fired upon.'

'Weapons all online,' said Greer doubtfully.

Blite stared at the approaching ships, running through options and discarding them. The Polity didn't yet know which ship he was aboard, so any firing they did would only be to disable. Still, he could see no way out. The Polity would confine every ship here and search this place until they found him.

Then the questions would begin, and the examinations – probably once again on some highly secure moon allotted for the purpose.

'Somebody wants to talk to you,' said Carlstone. 'I told them you're not here at Penny Transport, but I just got a package detailing all the arrangements I made to move you here.'

'Put whoever it is through to me, but route it through the station and scrub my background,' Blite replied. 'An AI would be able to work out which ship I'm on from that.'

'Okay, doing it.'

Another frame opened up in the screen paint, black at first. As the image there surged forwards to occupy the frame, he noticed numerous other icons opening for further com. Carlstone seemed to be handling that for the moment and, at a glance, he could see the coms were from the numerous cargo ships docked or in transit about the station.

'One further thing,' said Blite, 'record and relay this conversation. Let everyone listen in. And transmit it, with imagery of those ships, to the Polity net too – general distribution.' He now looked directly at the image in the frame and felt a moment of dread. The spherical crinoid form, with its numerous feathery limbs spread out from a central point, was all too familiar. He'd never actually had any dealings with a Mobius AI but knew them by reputation. The difference between the AI Carnusine, who'd interrogated him previously, and an AI like this echoed that between a bureaucrat and a Polity agent.

'Who am I addressing?' he asked.

'Mobius Straeger,' the thing replied.

'So, Mobius Straeger, I am fascinated to know why you've turned up here at Penny Transport and effectively shut down a legitimate business with threats of violence.'

'Very clever, Blite,' Straeger replied. 'But I am here on a

legitimate ECS mandate to arrest and interview the chief suspect in the terrorist destruction of the Callanasta runcible, whose death toll has now passed ten thousand.'

'And that suspect is?'

'Why, you, of course.'

'I barely survived it – my entire body had to be rebuilt.'

Carlstone turned, frowning. He nodded to a screen, where text appeared: *We just lost access to the Polity net – viral blockade on anything from here.*

Blite kept his expression bland.

'You *impossibly* survived that incident,' said Straeger. 'You were the individual who passed through when the buffers failed. At the time of that failure, and ever since, entropic effects have been observed all around Callanasta. The sun has developed an extreme rash of sunspots and temporal anomalies have been detected. Considering your past involvement with the AI Penny Royal . . . you have some questions to answer.'

Blite noted Greer, Carlstone and others looking at him speculatively. Yes, she'd been right: some explanations would be in order should they get out of this and on their way. He paused contemplatively, then replied, 'I too have some questions I need answers to, and I won't find them locked in some Polity black site being taken apart by a forensic AI. I'm also fairly certain that if you start examining me in the way you probably now have a mandate for, you're just going to create bigger problems.'

'So you think you know better?' Straeger enquired. It gave a kind of shrug, with a wave of movement passing out from its inner core. 'Irrelevant, since I now have a near-hundred per cent certainty on your position.' The frame closed.

Blite turned to Carlstone. 'What are the others saying?'

'That they can cover us while we escape.' He nodded, and one of the icons expanded into a frame showing Captain May.

'We have four high-volume cargos,' she said. 'They won't use heavy weapons since, we presume, they want to capture you alive. We'll burn out between you and those ships – should give you the run you need.'

'This is an idea, but it's not something I'm betting your lives on,' Blite replied.

'We choose where, and on what, we bet our lives.' She seemed to be excited by the prospect.

'Okay, let me think on that.'

The frame collapsed back to an icon.

'Feasible?' he asked Carlstone, his glance sliding around the bridge to include the others.

'Station grav interferes with U-space jumps, which is why we need to be clear of it before jumping,' said Paidon – a black-haired beauty who knew more about drive technology than anyone he'd ever met. 'They may give us the time we need.'

'Good idea,' said Greer, 'but that dreadnought could yet use heavy weapons. I guess it'll take them a few minutes to cut through the millions of tons of timber May is hauling, but . . . they'll probably deploy a USER.'

Underspace interference emitter. As soon as one of those devices was deployed, no one would be going anywhere. He suspected the Polity force hadn't deployed one yet because their effect lasted some time, and they wanted to grab him and get out of here fast.

'What the fuck?' said Carlstone.

In the frame showing the approaching ships, one of the attack ships was now tumbling, fire sketching a line across space from its shattered drive nacelle. Even as Blite took that in, another one exploded completely. Blite gaped, then watched as the two remaining ships flashed out of existence, obviously jumping away somewhere and not intentionally.

63

'Explosions detected inside the dreadnought,' said Carlstone flatly. 'I have no fucking idea what's going on . . . . Com coming through.'

A frame opened again and he saw it was the one from Mobius Straeger, but the AI appeared there only briefly before fragmenting and another image coming through. It was a side view of a man clad in black fatigues, black T-shirt and a long jacket of metallic fabric, walking along a corridor. He held a short laser carbine in his right hand, pointing it upwards at the ceiling for a moment, then aimed it forwards at something and fired. Explosions flashed ahead of him, smoke billowing and debris bouncing past. In his left hand, down at his side, he held a thin gun. He had silvery hair cropped close to his head.

The agent.

'Mobius Straeger is having difficulties, so you have your window, Blite,' he said. 'I told them not to interfere with you leaving.' He turned towards the frame and his background cleared to show a munitions store. 'I suggest you run now.'

'*You*,' said Blite.

'Run,' said the agent. 'Now.' The frame blinked out.

Blite didn't overthink it. 'Tell May and the others to do as she suggested. And we go now!'

Icons blinked out along the bottom of the screen-painted wall. Other views came up while the bridge crew pulled across and clicked home safety harnesses. As the *Coin* surged under fusion, he saw other ships breaking away from the station and accelerating. A great shadow pulled across as May's ship, under powerful acceleration from its onboard engines, and its subsidiaries spread all over the great mass of timber, drew between the *Coin* and the dreadnought. Other views showed the dreadnought opening fire – royal blue particle beams striking that great mass and tracking through to take out the subsidiaries.

A giant tanker flanked it, taking fire on a collection of giant cylindrical tanks. Explosive emissions of its cargo of hexafluoride erupted in glittering fountains. Then suddenly a blast peeled up part of the dreadnought's hull and all the particle beams went out.

'I don't know who that fucker you just spoke to is, but he's effective,' said Greer.

The four cargo ships hauling their high-volume loads had shifted into an overlapping line by the time the particle beams came back on. Blite felt sick enough about them standing in the path of those weapons, and even more so when he saw that just about every single cargo ship and transport was now out from the station, and moving into the path of beams too.

'How long?' he demanded.

'Getting clear of the disruption now,' said Paidon.

Blite flipped up a screen from his chair arm and checked her calculations. Too cautious.

'Hit it now,' he said. 'They're risking their lives and so should we.'

Paidon hesitated for just a second, then punched it. Reality lurched to one side and Blite experienced all the effects of an unshielded jump, because they weren't far enough from station grav. Objects around him multiplied in curving lines to infinity, and everything twisted in a direction he couldn't point to. He felt abruptly nauseated and bit down on the urge to throw up, until gradually, by and by, the effects faded.

'We're clear,' said Paidon woodenly.

Yes, they'd risked their lives just like those in the cargo ships . . . only a niggling internal voice was telling Blite that he hadn't really risked his. He knew that if the jump had been unsuccessful, he would have gone through it again, and again, until they were clear. The screen view now filled with a grey representative roil of U-space, and he noticed that everyone was looking at him expectantly. He sighed.

'Well, I guess you deserve to know as much as I do,' he said. 'I didn't really figure it out until New York . . .'

Blite – Past

New York's second sun was setting on the false horizon. Blite gazed across at it, taking in a city in silhouette that hadn't changed in three centuries, excepting of course the transit tubes to the upper level, and the giant pillars that supported it, disappearing into the false sky. The pillars, Blite recollected, were of carbon-fibre composite, once developed for the 'Skylift Project' – an orbital elevator made defunct by the development of anti-gravity. Many other cities had grown and changed over the years, preserving what they could of old structures under diamond films, in atmosphere-controlled bubbles and under hugely complicated preservation orders. In New York, they'd gone another route by building a giant platform thirty kilometres across above it. There the second city had risen, with its skyscrapers, sky bridges, platform parks and other paraphernalia of the modern metropolis.

Well, he'd seen the preserved lower city now. He'd drunk Manhattans, eaten doughnuts and a variety of traditional foods, been inside the Empire State Building and seen many other relics. Another tick on his bucket list. Now it was time to see the upper city, then get the hell off Earth. After his lengthy interrogations with AI Carnusine at a black site, about the events surrounding Penny Royal, he hadn't really wanted to come here, even after so long, to the capital world of AI dominance – just in case Carnusine had further points to raise. But, damn it, he'd decided not to let that get in the way of him seeing the things he had, supposedly, wanted to see.

He headed across the roof port to a row of dropshaft openings, selected 'ground', and stepped inside. The irised gravity field took hold of him with a lurch, then wafted him downwards. After passing numerous openings, he finally slowed to a stop before one and stepped out, walking along a corridor to what looked like a lobby. Only when the glass doors slid aside to reveal an indoor arboretum did he realize the dropshaft hadn't taken him to the ground floor. He was sure he'd pressed the right icon on the touch screen, yet he was also sure that the hotel arboretum was on the fourth floor. Some fault with the shaft? That lurch when he'd first stepped in hadn't been usual. Instinct kicked in.

Someone had already tried to kill him once. On Mars, in Marina City, a sniper had aimed for him on one of the streets. Luckily he'd still been wearing his envirosuit with its safety helmet, after venturing to one of the Martian parks where the old environment had been preserved. The whole incident had been rather confused, because the shot had given him a concussion. He had memories of blood and brains, of falling many times, of somebody screaming and of dying. But next he was being dragged into an ambulance, dazedly watching ECS grav-cars settling in the area. No results, as yet, had been forthcoming from the investigation into that.

Blite dropped a hand to the gas-system pulse gun at his belt. Another reason he'd persuaded himself to come here had been the lack of restrictions on personal protection. He scanned around, inside the arboretum, tempted to turn and head back to the dropshafts. However, he didn't like that it had delivered him to the wrong floor – it might do something else, like deliver him to the basement at terminal velocity. He'd use the stairs which, if he remembered correctly, were on the other side of this arboretum.

He took a step forwards and then halted. Of course, if someone was after him here they might well have predicted he'd head for the stairs, which seemed a perfect spot for an ambush. He backed out of the doors and took a left, pausing to touch a map screen on the wall to get his location. Circumventing the arboretum, he walked a complicated route round to a different set of short stairs down to the next floor, then took another complicated route to the main stairs and down. Finally reaching the lobby, he skirted around the edge, keeping close to the wall and eyeing all the people either relaxing on sofas or heading off somewhere. At the doors he was even more cautious, going out fast when a luggage robot came through, and putting it between himself and most of the lobby. He stepped outside, breathing a sigh of relief and thinking maybe he was being a bit too paranoid.

The killer was waiting half a block down the street.

An old trash truck with rubber tyres and a diesel engine was tipping the contents of a large metal wheelie bin into its back. He gazed at it with a raised eyebrow, realizing it was some history-in-action. The machine probably parked in a museum after its day's work. He sauntered along the pavement towards it, and a figure stepped into view from near its front end. The man, big and obviously boosted, wore combat armour and had his helmet up with the chain-glass visor closed. This wasn't standard dress in any city on Earth. The man stepped forwards, raising a stubby laser carbine, and simply fired, even as Blite's hand dropped to his pulse gun.

Blite felt the explosive evaporation of skin, muscle, lung tissue and heart send him staggering backwards. He saw the gout of steam and smoke, and smelled cooking flesh as he went down on his rump. Death wasn't immediate. He had time to look down at the fist-sized smoking hole through his chest, time to put down a hand as he slumped and to feel grit against his palm, then to see the smoking slurry from the exit hole across the pavement behind him. His vision finally darkened, pain messages began to arrive, but too quickly grew dull as the world receded down a long tunnel.

There was no confusion in the next instant – not like on Mars, which now came clearer to his mind. He remembered how there, some particular awareness had made him step aside, so he took the first shot in his shoulder, then a second killing shot through the head . . . when he died the second time. He remembered the terrible panic when the scenario began to play out again, and he threw himself down – the third act being the shot which smacked off his helmet, and his memory fractured by concussion.

As before, he went into a replay. He found himself once again approaching the dumpster, but this time with the knowledge seeping into his mind of danger and the imminence of death. He stepped aside, grabbing for his pulse gun. The first carbine shot seared along his forearm and punched into his lower torso. He staggered back and went down on one knee, managing a snap shot that flared off the armoured thigh of his attacker. He fired again, hitting the killer in the chest, but pulse gun shots were just not good enough to penetrate that kind of shielding. Another carbine shot to his head flipped him over into blackness a moment later.

Again the dumpster, and the urgency he felt was greater now; the memories clearer. He immediately dropped to one knee and opened fire, even as the figure stepped into view. Five pulse gun shots sent the killer staggering backwards, but he regained his balance and fired back, sending Blite into dark yet again. Patterns turned in the dark, crystalline kaleidoscope wheels. Blite felt something jerk him about as if in irritation, and the hint of some immense dark intelligence.

He was further from the dumpster the next time. Perhaps he

should just turn and run? He did run, but towards the vehicle, dodging behind it as it was lifting the bin. He crouched, steadied his aim, and fired directly at the carbine. His shooting wasn't as good as it should have been, and he died behind the dumpster with a shot through the neck. Only on the following occasion did the carbine explode, after which he flung himself into a dropkick at the armoured figure. The man fell, and Blite came down on top of him. The weak point, he knew, was under the arm. He jammed his weapon into the man's armpit as a blow like a beam end hit his chest. He pulled the trigger and kept it down, emptying the weapon into the suit, and finally, when the composite armour gave way, into the chest underneath.

When he finally stood up he *knew*, on a level beyond feeling the dark diamond hot against his chest. Through that thing Penny Royal was looping time to keep him alive. Why? He shuddered at the thought that Penny Royal saw him as a friend to meet up with at the end of time, then put that aside. More likely the AI had some presently obscure purpose for him, and the diamond. He needed to keep it somewhere safer on his body, because his life depended on it, and sure as shit someone wanted him dead.

3

Cormac – Present

As he made his way through the dreadnought he thought on AI cold calculations. Sometimes, if a certain person died in a certain place at a certain time, thousands of other lives would be saved in the future, in that place or elsewhere. This had its utility, like shooting the man who had his finger on the detonation button, but how far did you take it? Too far was often the answer with AIs. The old iteration of Earth Central had facilitated many threats from alien technology, rogue AIs and internal revolutionaries in order to lever slow, bumbling humans into post-humanity. This was obviously a better state for the human race, despite the casualties. And that was why he – or rather in the final moment his companion at the time, Mr Crane – had destroyed that iteration of Earth Central. The AIs needed to know they weren't all-powerful and didn't have free rein over humanity. They had to be aware that someone out there could stop them.

Him. Ian Cormac, ex-ECS agent.

'Why are you interfering?' asked the Mobius AI Straeger.

'Morality,' Cormac replied.

Around him fires burned hot, fed by the oxygen line he'd routed here. The storage cylinder that ran a feed to one of the ship's railguns was like a furnace that no human could possibly survive, but then Cormac wasn't actually in the cylinder. Using his unique abilities, his body was just a dimensional slice away, into U-space. He looked around one last time. The fire wasn't so hot that it would damage the cases of racked USERs and breach their singularity containment, but hot enough to render them disfunctional for some time. Not that they were really a problem now Blite had escaped.

'Your presence here indicates you are aware of what is happening around him,' Straeger complained. 'Something is interfering with causality. Thousands have died because of him.'

Cormac focused, his gridlink feeling hot in his skull, and shifted through the ship, checking the extent of his sabotage. He linked into ship's computing to check there too. The dreadnought AI was oddly somnolent; it seemed Straeger had plugged into the control circuit. He searched where he could in the data realm and found no sign that Blite's U-signature had been recorded, but then pulled out quickly as Straeger reached for him with ensnaring tendrils of coding. Even though Cormac had acquired the ability to jump through U-space, and manipulate it after a fashion, he was by no means a god and should never underestimate the abilities of the likes of this AI.

'And you know you're simplifying the situation,' he replied. 'Thousands have died because apparently someone has been trying to kill him.'

'Your use of "apparently" indicates doubt,' Straeger noted.

'You have a mind, so you think about that. You're behaving like some antediluvian doctor trying to cure symptoms rather than the disease.'

He U-jumped again, this time putting himself in a corridor leading to Straeger's location. Even as he semi-materialized there, pulse gun fire nailed him at the chest. But he wasn't quite back in the world of those energy weapons and only felt it as a hot flush in his body, with the shots passing through him and scoring the wall behind. He wasn't completely invulnerable like this, though. A very high-intensity laser with compacted photon density could burn him. And being in that attack ship as it blew up hadn't felt comfortable at all, during the fractions of a second it took him to escape it. Weapons that manipulated U-space or generated high-point gravity could get to him. He knew, for example, that ECS was developing a weapon just for him called a singun, whose shots generated point singularities. He should feel honoured. However, semi-materialized like this, he also couldn't affect the world around him beyond the reactions to his apparent presence.

He strode forwards. The Polity marines Straeger had positioned all around its location weren't really there to try to kill him, but to prevent him fully materializing here and maybe seeking to kill Straeger. The AIs knew he tended to avoid getting into fights that resulted in innocent human casualties. Two marines stood at the end of the corridor. They still kept him in their sights but stopped firing. Touching data surfaces, he could hear them communicating with their colleagues to cover other locations around Straeger. He kept walking and stepped forwards to go between them. One of them instinctively moved to block him, but he just walked straight through the woman. She shuddered and he felt the essence of her organism as he passed through.

Going around two more turnings, he saw other marines moving into the area as he came to the circular armoured door. It was closed and Cormac moved to step through it but then, detecting the subtle wash of *something*, he halted to inspect his surroundings. First he concentrated his U-space vision on the door to map out its internal technology, integrating and understanding it in the amalgam of his gridlink and mind. The thing was loaded with sensors, and there was USER technology in there. He turned away, now scanning the local area and inspecting the devices in the walls, as well as others focused on him throughout the ship. Understanding hit him – a weapon would activate on that ship in the shuttle bay and the trap lay in the door.

Cormac pushed at the dimensional barriers, the ship inverting around him and matter turning to its inverse, so material objects appeared to be holes spearing into infinity. He shifted and, as ever, it felt more like moving the material world to a new position around him when he semi-materialized inside Mobius Straeger's abode.

'So this wasn't about Blite,' he said.

'I'm not sure what you mean,' said Straeger.

Cormac clamped down on irritation. 'That Polity attack ship blowing up had nothing to do with my sabotage. Seems you're prepared to sacrifice your own to take me out.'

The AI sighed then said, 'I wondered how long it would take you.'

Cormac felt suspicious of the chagrin in the thing's tone. The crinoid-form AI hung in mid-air in the middle of a spherical chamber. It was perfectly spherical itself, and over two metres across. Within this its feathery manipulators shifted around like static discharges inside a plastic globe, but from Cormac's perspective, the AI looked uncomfortably like a large eye.

'How did you manage to find out about my connection to him?'

'It would be very foolish of me to tell you how, but, yes, as you've no doubt divined, we recorded your encounter with Blite.'

Cormac nodded. It seemed highly likely the AIs had detected the causality anomalies around the assassination attempts on the man earlier than he'd supposed. They had clearly been monitoring Blite with some sophisticated technology which, since he himself was a bit of a flaw in causality, had almost certainly detected Cormac too.

'Your whole intent was to push me into intervening here so you could snuff me out?' He continued scanning his surroundings, looking for traps beyond the U-space tech in the door he'd circumvented.

'Miscalculations have been made. The attack ship AI chose its own course in response to you. The cargo captains running a barrier like that was a surprise,' said Straeger blandly. 'But since you are here and talking, perhaps we can . . . discuss some matters.'

'Those being?' Cormac kept his focus on his surroundings. This all stank. Sure, an attack ship AI might choose suicidal destruction to take out an opponent, but as far as that barrier was concerned . . . AIs like Straeger were rarely surprised.

'I do have a mind, as you suggested, and I and some others, including the present iteration of Earth Central, have been thinking very deeply about what's been happening around Blite. There have in all been seven attempts to kill Blite, not the few he supposes.'

'Attempts he didn't notice?'

'The first ones simply placed things in his path. On Charadon, where he stayed for a while trying out retirement and lying on a beach drinking cips, he formed some habits. One such habit was to take a morning swim out around a particular islet. A nearby research facility was studying spearpigs and due to a strange accident, some of them escaped and ended up precisely where he usually swam. That day he decided to go out on a fishing boat. When subtly questioned about this by one of your erstwhile profession, he showed some confusion about his routine, which he put down to the amount of cips he'd been imbibing.'

'Disruption, presumably?' Cormac noted the chattiness – the AI was trying to lure him into a false sense of security.

'It was particularly hot the rest of the summer there, due to the sunspots.'

'Entropy,' said Cormac.

'Yes, precisely the kind of effects we saw when Penny Royal started playing around with time. But now we would like to know what you know about it all, and how.'

'And I should tell you this, why?'

'Because there is a gradation to the attempts on his life. Obviously they have been increasingly overt up to the sabotage on the runcible he was travelling through. One might suppose growing desperation to kill him. However, the attempts run perfectly up a stepped scale in the entropy they generate. It seems to us that these aren't really attempts to kill him, but to find out if there are limits to whatever keeps pulling his nuts out of the fire.'

'Whatever?'

'Very well: limits to how far Penny Royal will disrupt things to save Blite's life. And that is something we don't understand as yet. The black AI went beyond time and, we feel sure, to the Omega Point – the end of time.'

Cormac allowed himself a superior smile. 'Not entirely.'

'What?' Straeger contracted to a metre across, manipulators frozen in place.

'As with you, I'd be foolish to tell you how I know certain things. Suffice to say, I found out something odd was occurring around Blite. Instead of watching him very closely, I did some digging into his history, running through from when Penny Royal entered Layden's Sink black hole. You didn't see what I saw – I suspect that due to the nature of the object itself. I saw it on simple cam imagery. Blite acquired a pendant, which held a black gem.'

Straeger unwound a little, limbs turning like multiple second hands of an infinity of ancient clocks. 'I see it now,' the AI said, obviously having done a massive search through recorded data.

Cormac continued, 'That pendant was stolen from him on Abalon, but when he left there he somehow had it back again. I focused my searches on it. Despite Carnusine's long interrogation of him, Blite managed to keep it concealed, even though he was quite open about it being "a piece of Penny Royal".'

'How did we not see this?' Straeger protested.

Cormac paused there. Though it seemed Straeger was being straight with him – well, as straight as such AIs could possibly be – he now had doubts. He'd dealt with many AIs since acquiring his ability, and their many attempts to capture or neutralize him had given him a sense of them. Rapidly reviewing the conversation in his gridlink dispelled his doubts. Straeger was lying, but about what he didn't yet know.

'A gem that has the power to shift time to preserve someone's life should have little trouble in concealing itself. Especially if it is, as I think, an anchor into realtime directly from Penny Royal,' said Cormac.

Straeger now expanded to its full extent again and said nothing for some time. When it finally spoke, a greater element of seriousness had entered its tone, and yet this seemed false too. 'Revise and review: the precision of the steps in entropic disruption that the attempts on his life have caused are beyond present AI ability to calculate. Something out-Polity is doing this. There is a highly intelligent alien element at work here, with deeper knowledge of Penny Royal than we have. I should have captured Blite. I need to look at that crystal.'

'But you're not going to, because of breadcrumbs.'

'Eh?'

'Whoever's been doing this has been measuring the capabilities

77

of that crystal. The attempt to steal the object was particularly inept, which might suggest it was a half-hearted one. But whoever it is doesn't operate with such imprecision.'

'I see.'

Cormac nodded and reached into his pocket, taking out an object he clutched in his fist. 'Blite, finally having been driven to track down who is, supposedly, trying to kill him, will take his only available option, since other trails of breadcrumbs don't exist. He'll go after who tried to steal the gem and work from there. Somebody, or something, is reeling him in. It has purpose, and Blite is integral to that.'

'Still . . .' Straeger hedged.

'You will not go after Blite. This is my warning.'

Cormac materialized fully, for a few microseconds, then disappeared. It was just a couple of microseconds shorter than the response time of the photon-dense beam that cut through the space where he'd been standing. The beam, its power levels immense, sliced through the wall and through the interior of the ship, luckily missing the marines, and even punched out of the hull.

'Fuck,' said Straeger.

Hanging even more divorced from realspace than before, and beginning to drift, Cormac used his U-sense to trace the course of the beam back to the ship docked in the dreadnought's shuttle bay. So that was all of it? Straeger had been lying about its intent here, which had really been to set up that shot, simply to kill him? Had the situation involved something less than temporal anomalies and Penny Royal, Cormac would have accepted that explanation, but he didn't now. He flung himself away through U-space, out of the ship, to a new destination. The anomalies were promulgating and the game, whatever it was, had shifted into a higher gear.

Straeger

The AI hovered in hot metal-laced smoke and turned his attention to an object that had bounced on the floor, settling upright. The little rubber dog gazed up at him with a cartoon expression. Straeger backed away abruptly and contracted, making a sound like chips sizzling in a fryer. Without tracking anything this time, he again fired up the weapon sited aboard his ship in the dreadnought's shuttle bay. The photon-dense beam flared bright, evaporating the small toy, and passed through surrounding infrastructure at a slightly different angle. Abruptly realizing the danger, Straeger shut off the thing, but on tracking it through internal cams and sensors, he realized he'd been too late. The beam punched through the structure of the ship, exploding hot clouds of gas wherever it had room to expand. It sliced sideways, ever so slightly, melting beams and cutting into a tall wall packed with hexagons. Oily fire exploded out of the slice as the beam incinerated fourteen marines in stasis, and one who was awake and had gone in there to pull out more of them.

This had been harder than he'd expected, but not because of the damage and loss of life. Holding off on taking that shot, while lying convincingly to try to glean what the agent knew, had been a major strain. Now he'd missed the shot, the intensity of emotion rising up out of entanglement rolled through him in waves. He fought to hold himself back from wreaking further destruction. Like, for example, annihilating Penny Transport and every ship in the area. He held on and rationality slowly returned. He'd failed to kill the agent, but still remained on course for other objectives. Now his usurpation of this Polity operation was at an end.

Trovek, the marine commander, had already been asking some highly pertinent questions. He'd communicated with the ship AI, which, since Straeger had absorbed the thing, meant the communication had come directly to him. The man now had his doubts about the mission. Surely the lighter touch first proposed would have been better? Surely the planned covert penetration of Penny Transport, followed by a fast snatch, would have put Blite in their hands? He'd questioned the change of plans shortly after Straeger came aboard, for it seemed to him such confrontation would drive Blite to flee. Straeger's aim here had been precisely that, but also to draw in the agent and nail the fucker. The probability of that had been low, but non-zero was still non-zero. It had been contrary to Earth Central's orders concerning Cormac, though, since kill on sight had been rescinded.

Straeger sent a signal to open the door and rolled out into the corridor. However, he took the precaution of keeping his beam weapon targeted close to his location. If Cormac returned, it would be another chance to fry the man, although he doubted the agent would come back. The AI continued along, calling in his subminds – he'd distributed smaller versions of himself, just a little larger than a human head, throughout the dreadnought. Meanwhile, urgent com was coming through from Trovek. What the hell just happened? Why did that attack ship explode? What the hell was that weapon? Even as he began to disconnect from the dreadnought, Straeger saw the marines on the move. Trovek's questions were simply an expected response, but he and others were positioning themselves around Straeger. The AI paused, considering the situation. He was still digesting the dreadnought AI, adding its knowledge and experience to his own. He couldn't put it back, and its absence would be noticed upon his departure. Now it was time for him to do the next logical thing: accept a full and complete break from the Polity AIs he pretended to be aligned with.

'Straeger,' said Trovek, this time not over com but from directly ahead.

Straeger gazed at the man. He and his marines had suited up in heavy power armour and armed themselves with multi-guns, which were also loaded with disruptor shells – that acquisition hadn't been noted in the system. Straeger paused again, moving and reacting as slowly as a human. Not that he couldn't think at a rate orders of magnitude faster, but the thousands of threads of causality generated from every moment needed to be assessed to inform his next action. He tracked through enough of these possibilities to see them collapsing into the same future, and he understood his limited options here. Next, reaching out through the system, he found the dreadnought's store of contra-terrene devices. Cormac's sabotage had rendered the CTDs impossible to fire – not that Straeger would have allowed that – but they still held their lethal loads of antimatter. They'd sufficiently remove anything other AIs might want to investigate. It amused the AI that, considering the telemetry he'd allowed to be broadcast back to the Polity, containing edited reports from Trovek and other marines aboard, the assumption would be that Cormac had destroyed this vessel.

'Do you have a problem, marine?' he asked.

'Too fucking right, I have a problem,' the man replied.

Straeger subtly altered the aim of the beam weapon to the marines.

'Then perhaps you should tell me about it,' he said, as he tweaked the aim and set a firing routine. He began backing up, away from the marines, trying to draw them towards him. Annoyingly, the travel path of the beam did intersect with that

CTD store, and the idea was for him not to be aboard when they exploded.

Trovek and the marines halted. There must have been some aug communication between them Straeger hadn't been privy to. He had never bothered penetrating their military com because in essence they were ephemeral. But now it seemed certain they had properly traced the source of the photon-dense beam, ascertained it could be used against them, and placed themselves precisely where its use was impossible. The AI realized he would have to get his metaphorical hands dirty.

'Why did you drive a confrontational attack against Blite? Where is the dreadnought AI? And why the fuck did a weapon firing from your ship just kill fifteen of my people?' Trovek demanded.

Something didn't quite make sense. Trovek was being uncharacteristically confrontational, which meant he was deliberately aiming to unbalance or distract. Straeger scanned out and around, finally detecting the marines two decks below and three above. Their suits were running chameleonware, so they were difficult to detect, but their 'ware and enwrapping chameleoncloth couldn't quite conceal the two weapons they were positioning. Judging by the dimensions, these were heavy particle beamers quite capable of cutting through the ship infrastructure. Though he appeared to have questions, Trovek had already come to a decision about Straeger.

'Seems to me you don't want answers,' Straeger said and surged towards them.

They were expert, effective human fighters. The AI measured their response time as fractions of a second, but fractions of a second too slow. The deck behind Straeger erupted in molten metal and burning composite as the purple blaze of an in-ship-fired particle beam punched through. The marines snapped shut their helmets and visors, opening fire – all ten of them perfectly aligned to shoot past each other, like one functional machine of destruction. For Straeger the microseconds rolled past like long drawn-out moments of introspection. He opened holes in his structure to allow the disruptor shells to pass through, then hardened around those holes as the first shots blew on a proximity detonator. Lasers scored across him, sizzling up threads and burning through meta-material ribbons. Pulse shots zeroed on his core, but he tubed them away into the floor. He shrieked as he advanced, because pain was a necessary warning mechanism, useful both biologically and in AIs. He fed the upshot of this pain into an energy circuit akin to excitement and anger, or perhaps an emotion that wasn't human.

Glassy tubes bent into knots, routing pulse gun shots back out, spanging off heavy armour and burning trails through the walls. He knotted threads and lased from them, stabbing out with an accurate shot in the blue range. This went straight in through the barrel of one multigun and blew its disruptor magazine in cascade. The marines' formation itself became disrupted, one man sprawling back, his visor gone and half his face burned away, his shooting going wild. Then Straeger was in among them. His fibres, braiding themselves into ropes, bound up limbs, scored across visors issuing chain-glass decoders, and hurled two men so hard against the wall they left dents, while slamming another up into the ceiling. He issued molecular sharp spikes, punching for joints and connections. His S-con interfaces touched on suits and issued informational warfare, and shear-fields running on cat's claw edges shaved through armour. Four marines died in the first second, two more in the third, and by then all were beyond fighting. He found himself holding them all, corpses too, up in his structure, and he gazed into Trovek's raging expression.

'You fucking murderer,' the man said, the words taking longer than the fight had.

Trovek sent a signal at that moment. Obviously he'd given orders previously that the AI must be destroyed, or otherwise removed from the ship, and that sacrifices might need to be made, including his own. Both particle beams hit at once. Floor and ceiling disappeared in fire. Marines burned up and melted. He saw Trovek fall away screaming, though his yells had a belligerent fuck-you edge. Straeger felt his body ablating away, almost down to fifty per cent, before he threw himself out of it. No more slow leisurely rolling through the ship now. Folding in his remaining fronds and ribbons, he balled up and accelerated on grav, hurtling around bends and finally bouncing down a drop-shaft. The particle beams fired four more times but only singed him once, since there were now no spotters nearby. He finally hit a surface etched with quadrate spirals. It opened under him and he fell inside.

Immediately he sent the order to open the bay doors. Since the dreadnought AI was a dissolving part of him, he had full control of at least this mechanism. He felt much irritation about those he couldn't control via that route: the humans. The fallacies of inclusion and respect for them as singular entities had always been annoying to him. They were a negotiation and a concession that AIs hadn't needed to make, and they had made these before anything like Ian Cormac had turned up to punish infractions. He felt some sympathy with the iteration of Earth Central that had been crushed to powder in the hands of Mr Crane, but also a degree of disinterest. Humans should be pushed into the future, by those who cared whether they existed or not. Straeger did not.

As he rolled through the tubes of his ship, he began opening up again, absorbing subminds as they quickly boarded and came to him. His vessel, an asymmetric claw of technology over two hundred metres long – inevitably named the *Claw* – was packed with weapons and machines that *were* perfectly under his control, and sans any humans. He withdrew the struts which braced it against the walls of the bay, and detached umbilicals. Then, nudging with steering thrusters, he eased out into vacuum, while at the same time initiating his ship's chameleonware. Still with some connection to the dreadnought, he noted the marines and other personnel out of hibernation were working hard to get U-space communication up and running. Given time, they'd succeed. But they didn't have time.

Swinging his ship around to interpose the dreadnought between himself and the ships around Penny Transport, he targeted carefully and then opened fire with the photon-dense beam. It splashed at first on the dreadnought's armour; had this not been a static target, he couldn't have succeeded – the ship would have evaded, deployed shields and fired back. It wasn't capable of doing so, however. After long minutes the beam punched through the hard shell, vaporized softer internal structures, paused for a microsecond on further armour around the CTD store, then burned in. An eye of intensely bright fire opened within the dreadnought, then the thing spread and shattered like a balloon on the blast. Straeger started his fusion drives and rode out with the blast front, his ship taking damage from burning debris, but nothing consequential. Then, once sufficiently far away, he dropped into U-space.

Cormac may have survived, but events remained on course from Penny Transport, and other opportunities would arise as they approached the inception point Straeger had calculated for. Unfortunately, the closer they got to that inception point, the higher its probability became. Straeger would prefer to have Cormac dead long before then, so it was now time to head for the next kill opportunity. Straeger didn't know what the temporal anomaly would be to draw Cormac there, and he put data-gathering in place to ensure he'd be ready for whatever was necessary.

4

May

Captain May gazed at screen images of space all around the docking station. Her own cargo of cerulean oak, from which she'd detached her hauler, had eventually been stabilized by the remaining subsidiary drives attached to it. Now hundreds of EVA units had come out from the station to snare up the stray tree trunks and other debris. She focused on one of them – an ellipsoid body with swivel-mounted ion thrusters top and bottom, two robot arms protruding with large three-fingered grabs. It took hold of a drifting tree trunk and began towing it back to the main mass. About a quarter of the trunk had been burned away, and this reflected in microcosm the total loss: about a quarter of the load had been burned up by that particle beam from the dreadnought. She shook her head and turned her attention to the icon flashing on one screen, and via her aug initiated it immediately.

'About damned time!' she said.

'I have been busy, as you can imagine,' Absinthe replied.

'What . . . what are the losses?'

'I am assessing them,' the lizard drone replied, 'ongoing and transmitted to our agent on Earth. We are already filing a massive damages claim to ECS.'

'And they'll pay?' It was distraction really.

'Oh yes. ECS has a fund precisely for that purpose.'

'Anyway, I don't mean *those* losses.'

'Understood. Numerous injuries ranging from a barked elbow to one broken spine, but no deaths.' Absinthe paused for a second then added, 'In Penny Transport.'

May took in the spread of wreckage and shook her head.

'Still, that dreadnought out there . . .' Just saying the words sent fingers creeping down her spine – a sensation she'd not felt in a long time. The damned thing had exploded. Surely they'd had nothing to do with that?

'The dreadnought is not really our concern. None of us fired on it.'

'So what the hell *did* happen here?'

'You know what: the Mobius AI Straeger came to arrest Blite, you and the rest blocked those Polity ships and he escaped.'

'Now you're being deliberately obtuse. Even with what we did, Blite's chances of escaping were minimal, what with four attack ships and a dreadnought out there. One of those attack ships blew up too, and others just U-jumped out of here. I don't think they went willingly either. And, fuck, Absinthe, again: an ECS dreadnought blew up on our doorstep!'

'Somebody intervened,' said Absinthe. 'Though apparently is not responsible for the major detonations you saw out there.'

'Who? Who the hell can so royally screw up a Polity operation like that?'

'You wouldn't believe me if I told you.'

'Try me.'

'Ian Cormac,' Absinthe replied.

'Fuck off.'

'Told you so.'

'I'm supposed to believe that a character out of virtuality fiction came to our rescue? Is this some kind of war drone joke?'

Absinthe looked off to one side. 'Anyway, I have things to deal with. I can't keep chatting to you here. Oranth will be taking your load on. Your ship is about the fastest here with its subsidiaries in place, and you have another mission.'

'Eh? Another mission?'

'You'll find out about it shortly.' Then the frame showing Absinthe winked out.

May looked around at her bridge crew – just Davidson and Akanthor – and the two ophidapts gazed back at her. As ever, their snake/human faces were difficult to read.

'Another mission. My, my,' said Davidson.

'Subsidiaries?' Akanthor enquired, giving an odd smile that revealed her fangs.

'Pull them in and have them attached to the frame. I'm going to take a shower.' May stood up and departed the bridge, her thoughts washing around in her skull like muddy water. She was loyal to Blite and Penny Transport because he'd given her the break she so badly needed – granting her the loan which had enabled her to go from in-system hauling to interstellar cargo. Blite had effectively paid for her ship, the *Bracken*, and the repayment terms were the best. It was fine that she'd been summoned to transport Blite away from that mess on Callanasta, but now it seemed he might have had some connection to the runcible failure there, and she'd come to understand why Mobius Straeger and ECS were after him. She'd put forward the idea of the blockade to the other captains before finding out about all this, and they'd agreed to help Blite escape. Subsequent events here now had her questioning her choices, though only mildly, and with an odd indifference.

May tramped down the corridor from the bridge and halted before her cabin door. There she paused. Maybe Blite was involved in something illegal? She knew he had been at one time, but since starting Penny Transport he'd always been a straight operator. Then, of course, there was his past involvement with the AI Penny Royal. He had been co-opted by the AI to transport it around as it righted some of its own wrongs, and prior to it dropping itself into the Layden's Sink black hole. And that was . . . difficult.

She palmed the lock and the door clicked open. Walking in, she closed the door and began stripping off her jumpsuit as she headed for the shower. She was down to a T-shirt and knickers when she felt a weird wash of cold and some disturbance in the air.

'Sorry to catch you like this,' said a voice behind her. 'I don't usually invade people's privacy, but there's some urgency.'

She froze, replaying what she'd seen when she walked in. There hadn't been anyone in her cabin. Without turning, she thought about where her pulse gun sat holstered, hanging in her wardrobe. She hadn't fired the thing in years and had no idea if it was charged. She turned towards her two armchairs. A man was sitting in one of them.

'The fuck?' she said.

He sat relaxed, with his legs crossed. Black fatigues and black shirt, long coat of some silvery metallic material. His hair was closely cropped and silvery grey. His face was mediocre handsome and his expression mild. His eyes fixed on her, and she felt more naked now than she had been about to be. Abruptly she stepped to the shower cubicle and grabbed a big towel from the rail, then wrapped it about herself. It offered some comfort.

'I listened in on your conversation with Absinthe,' he said. 'I can confirm that the destruction of the dreadnought was not my doing. Apparently Straeger is not what he first appeared to be and is covering his tracks.'

He reached into his coat and pulled out a gun, but made no

threat, simply putting it down on the coffee table before him. She stared at the thing, horribly fascinated. It was a thin gun.

'What do I look like to you?' he said.

'With that –' she gestured at the weapon – 'a Polity agent. It's a look many like to adopt, and thin guns sell very well.'

'I was once an agent, but now I'm more of an independent operator.' He rested back in the armchair. 'Oscar Wilde said that life imitates art more than art imitates life.'

'Who?'

He waved a hand dismissively. 'A writer from way before the Quiet War. Anyway, the AIs understand the essence of this. If you turn reality into fiction, it saps the potency from that reality. The wargame virtualities where people fight prador are an example of this, as are the ones where one can hunt down and neutralize black AIs.'

'What the hell are you talking about?' Even as she posed the question, May had a damned good idea of where this was going.

'They took the, well, there's only one way to say it: they took the reality of a Polity agent who acquired certain powers and turned against the Polity, and they made this into fiction. It was one of their many attempts to ameliorate the threat I posed to them.'

'I don't believe any of this,' said May.

He nodded calmly and pulled back his sleeve. Around his left wrist was a wide metallic band with a holster facing towards his palm. With his right hand, he pulled a shifting star of black metal out of the holster and tossed it into the air. The thing whirred viciously and came to hover in mid-air a metre above her head. There it spun faster and protruded chain-glass blades, the sound it made becoming even more murderous – if that were possible.

May backed up against the wall.

'Shuriken,' she whispered.

'What do I look like to you now?' he asked.

Her mouth was dry, but she felt a thrill she enjoyed. Like a lot of Polity citizens, she'd spent her time in virtualities and the legendary agent of Earth Central had been in many of them. The man in the seat even looked like him. And now this: the impossible Algin Tenkian weapon – a thing made by a nigh-mythical weapons-maker and possessed by one person.

'Ian Cormac,' she said.

He stood up. The Tenkian throwing star tucked in its chain-glass blades and somehow folded up its main body too, as it shot back to his wrist like a hawk returning to its handler. The savage sound stopped as it snicked home. He pulled his sleeve over to cover it, picked up the thin gun and returned it to a holster under his jacket.

'How much of it is true?' she asked.

'Rather a lot of it,' he replied, heading for the door. 'And we're going to visit one of those truths, because things are getting complicated. I and some friends of mine are more involved than we expected to be.'

'What?'

'This is your new mission,' he added, and departed. May still had room for doubts until that moment. But the guy walking through the door, without the benefit of it actually being open, dispelled a great many of them.

Blite – Past

Blite gazed out of his cabin window at the view. A few hundred yards of red regolith lay between him and some containment spheres. The spheres were set in the ground just out from the edge of another structure, where ships were docked and weapons turrets protruded. The sky above had an odd greenish cast with stars sparsely scattered. After the journey here in the hold of a Polity dreadnought, he'd had no idea of the location of this ECS black site. He'd seen the huge icy planet it orbited, but that was no help. All he did know was that he really didn't want to be here any longer, at the same time wondering if he would ever be able to leave.

He couldn't leave. He had no access to a spacesuit, or even an envirosuit; getting anywhere that might make escape possible wasn't an option. He was under constant scrutiny, and privacy simply didn't exist. He'd learned from the AI Carnusine that even his shits went off for intensive analysis, and he was probably watched while doing them. Anyway, he wouldn't have put it past the AI to have implanted trackers during one of his 'examinations', and who knew what else? There had been many endless questions and, via an induction aug, the AI had delved into his mind. Some periods during those examinations were vague to him now, and he suspected they'd gone beyond mere questions. He felt sure he'd been examined physically, maybe even taken apart and put back together again, with the memory of that erased. He thought he'd been here for months, quite possibly years, but his grasp on time had failed and he had no way of checking. Which, in all, begged the question: how the hell had the AI missed it – the piece of Penny Royal?

Blite walked over to his screen, at present set to mirror, and studied his haunted expression. He touched the screen to activate it and called up satellite views of his ship. Well, it didn't look like a ship now – more like some cetacean blown apart by ingested dynamite. Rib bones, organic hull, implanted systems, and the whole paraphernalia of the thing was spread over a volume of space that was kilometres across. Amid this, termite-things and similar components of Carnusine were at work. It looked like an infestation eating a corpse. Apparently they were now reassembling the thing, having gleaned every scrap of data they could from it, and preparing to bring it back down to the surface. Maybe, at last, this was all coming to an end, and he'd finally be able to sit on that beach and drink himself into a coma with cips.

'Is there anything you would like to tell me,' had been one of Carnusine's initial questions.

He'd had nothing at all he wanted to tell the AI, but he'd also been aware there was nothing he could conceal. Rather than be taciturn, as was his inclination, he'd decided to get one thing out of the way immediately. The Polity escort ship had arrived even as he launched Pace's biotech ship from Abalon, so he'd had no real chance of hiding the pendant anywhere. He'd considered ejecting the thing on a course through vacuum and picking it up later, but the idea had caused him almost physical pain. Anyway, Greer had informed him the escort was scanning them perpetually. Realizing that Pace's ship would be taken apart, just as he was now seeing, he'd known he couldn't conceal the pendant aboard. It was going to be found and there was nothing he could do about that. So he'd been upfront about it.

'I have a piece of Penny Royal,' he'd replied, and lifted the pendant out of his shirt to show it.

Carnusine, in its complete form, consisted of what looked like metal termites held in a strap-work metal cage. The AI had shifted in place in front of him, its voice taking on an odd edge: distant, distracted. 'That is a black diamond. Interesting crystal structure of very high density. Likely formed on a brown dwarf.'

'A piece of Penny Royal, which I'm sure you want to examine.'

'I am sure that you think it is a piece of . . .'

Blite had waited for the Mobius AI to continue, but nothing came. Puzzled, he'd slipped the pendant back into his shirt. The

AI froze, all its components immobile as he'd never seen them before. The world seemed to stutter around him, and then the AI was in motion again.

'Is there anything you would like to tell me?' Carnusine had asked again.

Blite had thought about what it'd just said. He'd known, in the heart of his being, that the crystal in the pendant was more than just a black diamond. He'd felt utterly sure that, to this AI, it should be more important than Pace's ship, himself, Greer and those crewmen the AI had resurrected in virtuality to question. Was Carnusine playing some game?

Blite had shrugged. 'I have no particular wish to tell you anything. Just get to your questions and I'll answer them as best I can. I have nothing to hide.'

The pendant, meanwhile, had felt hot against his chest.

Blite – Present

'Your timing is excellent,' said Broden, 'and I for one am glad to be able to give you something worthy of the considerable sums you've paid me for my services.'

Blite eyed the man sitting before him, then flicked his gaze to Greer, sitting on his left, and Carlstone on his right. Both were keeping their expressions blank, but he could still see the anger in Greer, and Carlstone's puzzlement. Greer he could perfectly understand. Anger was often a comforting set point for her. This had been triggered when he told her about the black diamond, because he'd been keeping it from her all this time. That anger grew when he revealed details of all the attempts on his life, and it took on a new dimension due to the fact he'd not been in contact with her about the matter either. She would settle down eventually to a low boil – likely to be expressed should anyone get in their way during this search for the girl. Carlstone was more worrying. His puzzlement was probably to be about the way Blite had survived the attempts on his life. He rather suspected the man didn't believe the explanation he'd given.

'Please explain my excellent timing,' said Blite.

Broden was an outlinker: bones like glass, little musculature, painfully thin but perfectly designed for his zero-gravity environment. Outlinkers could also survive in vacuum for a short while, by expanding on internal pressure, all orifices sealed, nictitating membranes for their eyes and pores closing. Right now, down on the surface of Abalon, he wore a motorized support suit so as to move about easily, his thin bald skull cupped by a padded support that also closed around his fragile neck. Precisely why he chose to live on this world was a conundrum, but Carlstone's investigations had isolated him as the best private detective here. And Blite now wanted the thief found at all costs.

'I've been chasing rumours for decades. Some leads took me off-world, as you know, and all turned into dead ends. Seemed she was tied up with the Mortons here before she stole the item from you, then disappeared.'

'Local syndicate,' Carlstone interjected.

Blite nodded. He'd read all the reports so knew about them.

'The Mortons employed her to steal . . . the item.'

'Seems that way,' said Broden vaguely, then continued, 'I have people in with them who reported on their hunt for her after she left them. She hid very well for some years, but when she attempted to have her face changed, they grabbed her.' Broden shrugged. 'I tried to find out what happened to her following that, but I just kept hitting a block. Most of the funds I've spent recently have been to run a deeper penetration of the Mortons, to try to find out. Then recently she reappeared out at Clander.

I was just putting together another report for you about that to see what you wanted to do.'

'How did you pick up on her?'

'I employed a nefarious AI to inject a constant search through all cams, readers and so on around the world. In fact, the search program is practically an AI itself. It found her by facial recognition, then confirmed this with a DNA reading taken by micro-laser spectrograph. She probably thought it was an insect sting.' He paused for a second, then added, 'Odd DNA she's got.'

'And you have eyes on her now?'

'The search program is keeping track, but I've also moved my people into the area to cover all points of egress. She's still there, in the Mortons' –' he raised his gauntleted hands to make quote marks – 'country residence.'

Blite looked over at Carlstone. 'You have all this?'

Carlstone tapped his aug and nodded, then gestured to the wall behind Broden. A satellite image appeared, showing a sprawling residence in a forest of blue pines. Blite noted where the trees had been cleared back from a security fence, with gun towers along the fence and other installations on the roofs of the scattered buildings.

'Tell me more about the Mortons,' he said.

Broden shrugged. 'Pretend separatists who're into every form of crime going. The Abalon AI's light touch has allowed them to expand their reach. It's rumoured that the AI is losing interest . . .'

'Explain.'

'It's concentrating on the terraforming here and has left everything else, where it doesn't interfere with its plans, to human governance. And we know where that leads.'

'But not completely internalized, like one of those AIs getting into U-space math?' Blite asked.

Broden glanced back at him. 'No, not completely.'

Blite stood up. Good to be reminded there was a controlling AI here which, at any time, might receive a message from Straeger, or send data about him out into the Polity net. 'Then we need to move fast. Carlstone?'

Carlstone stood up, Greer too. The man replied, 'The guys are ready – swift penetration, snatch and grab.' He shrugged. 'But surely, if she was employed by the Mortons, it's them we should be after?'

'I want to talk to her first, to glean some idea of which Mortons we need to question,' Blite replied. Carlstone was right, really, but he thought that only going after the woman was the right thing to do. Oddly he felt guilty about what had happened to her – felt he owed her something. He looked back at Broden. 'I take it she's guarded?'

'They'll be around, yes.'

'And what's the criminal status of those guarding her, and elsewhere in that residence?' Greer suddenly asked.

'Scum,' Broden replied and, knowing precisely what Greer was really asking, added, 'The Mortons have been involved in the coring trade – mostly off-planet but plenty of people have disappeared from here, too.'

'And this internalizing AI has allowed that trade?' asked Greer disbelievingly, though she'd received the answer she wanted: she had a pass to kill Mortons and those working for them.

Broden shrugged. 'Let the primitive humans do their thing until so sickened by it they start stepping away from their primitivism. It's a pattern repeated throughout the Polity, where AIs prefer the stick to the carrot.' He gestured at the screen. 'It's a fact that the Mortons keep their activities closely under wraps, which makes it difficult for the police to bring them down. I know for sure there's a push in the local police service for more gridlinking and other upgrades to break their cover.'

Blite snorted an acknowledgement. It was well known that AIs often gave humans free rein to fuck up, sometimes on a planetary scale, with the ultimate aim of forever pounding in the same lesson: you can be better.

'Let's go,' he said.

Cormac

Cormac relaxed in his cabin on the *Bracken*. He'd considered sitting on the bed in a meditative pose while he continued to explore, as he'd been doing for so long, his ability to manipulate U-space. But in a fit of rebellion, he sprawled back on the bed. Seriously, he didn't want to be seen as some strange unhuman aberration, and in his mind such poses were related to that. Sitting in a meditative trance was the kind of thing Horace Blegg would have done.

Instead of exploring his talent, he reviewed the time that'd passed since Mr Crane crushed the previous iteration of Earth Central. Following that, Cormac had interfered on many occasions when he found AIs driving humans towards AI upgrades, regardless of the cost in human lives. He'd seen worlds apparently allowed to secede from the Polity, but then become nightmare totalitarian states, and he'd tried to prevent that. However, he'd discovered that very often this occurred because of the boredom and inattention of the AIs in charge, not by design. The kind of AI interference in human destiny he had fought mostly didn't happen any more. For the last few decades, he'd been travelling and watching, but it seemed the drive to make humans 'catch up' had waned. He suspected this was because AIs, which had often been referred to as post-humans, were evolving and becoming less human themselves. Their perception of time was different, while their need to bring humans along with them had faded, become vague.

As an outsider, he'd seen the events concerning Blite and Penny Royal, just as he'd seen the Jain threat arrive in a particular accretion disc, and then be quashed. He'd considered getting involved, but felt both of these were beyond his remit. He couldn't keep watch on the AIs *and* counter all the external threats the Polity faced. So why had he become involved now with everything that was happening to Blite? This wasn't about the AIs playing their games; as far as he could assess, it concerned some outside alien influence. Sure, he could rationalize it all, and connect it to the murky doings of the likes of Mobius Straeger, but he was too honest with himself for that. He'd travelled and kept the AIs in check, but now he was bored. He wondered if this might be a form of late-onset ennui, since he'd not experienced it at the usual age, now a century behind him. Whatever. He was entangling himself in something that had much more of a human element, and that pleased him.

The ship shimmered around him, and now he glimpsed a world as an infinite tube through the continuum of U-space. He found himself drifting, up off the bed and beginning to slide into the wall behind. He got a grip on himself as the U-space engines of the vessel – tangled manifolds of energy, matter and pseudo-matter to his perception – pulled out the cusps holding them, and the ship, in U-space. As the ship surfaced into the real, he thumped down on the bed, solid and human again. He lay there until the expected message arrived.

'Okay,' said May through Cormac's cabin intercom. 'We're here, at Cull. Akanthor is talking to the authorities, and I don't see any problems about getting permission to land, though I do about *where* to land – lot of ships down there.'

Cormac smiled tightly. While surfacing from four jumps to

confuse any pursuers, though he suspected Mobius Straeger might have guessed where he was going, he'd accessed the AI net for data on this world.

'Bounty hunters,' he replied.

'What?'

'A long time ago, Polity AIs offered a huge bounty for one of those we're here to collect, intact or in pieces. After numerous failed attempts, the hunters gave up and looked elsewhere. Now it appears some unknown party has substantially increased the reward, bringing them back again.'

'Why does anyone want this . . . person so badly?'

'Because he has Jain technology inside him.'

'Oh.'

Cormac got up off the bed and walked to his cabin door. This time he didn't neglect to open the door before going through it. He'd resolved to be a lot more human around his own kind. As he walked along the corridor to the bridge, he considered his explanation. It was plausible and probably to a certain extent true that the Polity wanted Crane because of the Jain tech, but he was sure of the involvement of another element: a degree of 'fuck you' from the AIs. Because of Cormac's own abilities, they couldn't nail him, though of course they continued to try, and like vengeful humans were going after viable members of his 'family'. Whatever Crane was, he didn't have the ability to manipulate U-space, so they knew it was possible to grab hold of him, with enough force. Another element in play here was that by putting Crane in constant danger, they might lure Cormac in. But they always underestimated Crane, as had been the case when a Mobius AI led a special mission to seize him. The debris of this still mouldered down there on Cull. But the other party now involved, and the expanded reward? He felt sure that, just as with the attempts on Blite's life, there'd be no trail to the source of that money.

Cormac entered the bridge and gazed at the image of Cull up in the screen paint. Memory intruded of his fight with the Jain-infected biophysicist Skellor down there, and numerous other events that had occurred. He shook his head, dismissing them, and focused on the moment. The two ophidapts were glancing at him surreptitiously. They didn't quite believe what Captain May had told them about him. It didn't matter.

'We've been given permission to go down,' said Akanthor. 'I get the impression it's a bit chaotic.'

Cormac nodded. 'I rather think no attempt has been made to refuse permission. Those that have landed there, and the others doubtless heading this way, will be heavily armed with high-tech weaponry. The local police only carry projectile weapons, usually for dealing with sleers coming into the city, or driving off the odd droon.'

'Ah,' said Davidson abruptly. 'It's *that* world!'

May, Cormac and Akanthor looked at him questioningly.

'I know about droons and sleers but just didn't make the connection till now.' The ophidapt man looked at Cormac challengingly. 'The world where you fought a Jain-infected separatist, and from where you finally dumped him on a brown dwarf.'

'Exactly,' said Cormac mildly. How old were the three here on this bridge – into their second century, perhaps? Certainly May was, if he read the indications from her correctly. Nevertheless, all three seemed like infants to him. He turned to May. 'If you would, captain.' He gestured to the world, then walked over to sit in a spare chair.

'We can't land in that space port,' she said, gesturing vaguely about herself, as the fusion engines kicked in and Cull began to draw closer.

She was right, of course. The *Bracken* was a huge ship, whose length would stretch right across the landing slab, were it not already crowded. He'd checked the vessel for a shuttle and found only a couple of vacuum transfer vehicles – nothing suitable for landing. It seemed May and her crew used local services when they wanted to go down to a planet they couldn't land on.

'We're not landing there,' said Cormac. He gridlinked to the ship's system and brought up coordinates in a lower area in the screen paint.

After a moment Akanthor said, 'We're not forbidden to land there, but advised it might be unhealthy. Apparently there's a missile installation up in the mountains, and a particle beam weapon at that location. Somebody there doesn't want visitors.'

'We won't be fired on by those weapons.' Cormac glanced around at them. 'The plateau in the mountains is our destination. However, if we try to land there directly, you can be damned sure we'll be fired on by others who are heading there. They'll not want anyone to rescue their target.'

Still linked in, he accessed ship cams. They weren't over the space port, but high-resolution imagery had been recorded as they came over the world. He viewed this imagery in his gridlink and then, as an acknowledgement of humanity, brought it up to the left in the screen paint. Numerous vessels of all kinds were down there, and the port was loaded with stacks of supplies and many disagreeable types in combat armour, lugging a variety of heavy weapons. Out of one large vessel he could see treaded ATVs coming down a ramp. Beyond the space port, a group of such vehicles was heading out fast, leaving an arrow of dust behind them. Further out still, he could see ATVs gathered in the foothills of the mountains and figures moving up through the pass. He might have arrived just in time to prevent appalling damage and loss of life – he would see.

'Not looking too rosy down there,' May commented. 'This ship is just a cargo hauler.'

'Which is why we're not landing on the plateau,' Cormac replied. 'Now, if you'll excuse me.' He sat back, closed his eyes – not because it was necessary but as a firm signal that he didn't want to be interrupted.

'Arach,' he said in his mind.

'Weren't in a big hurry to get here, were you?' the drone asked acerbically.

'It seemed a good idea to confuse my trail.'

'Mobius AI after you?' said Arach.

'Good guess.'

'I'm a good guesser now. Been around Crane too long and something is wafting over to me from that tech inside him. I've noted some alterations inside me. Seem benign . . .'

'Let's hope so.' Cormac replied. 'So tell me – your message was rather terse. Some kind of attack and a temporal anomaly has occurred . . .?'

'Yeah, I knew the words "temporal anomaly" would get your attention.'

'They did, but how does it relate to this Matheson character you mentioned?'

'Matheson is a side issue. When Arian Pelter controlled Crane, he killed this Matheson guy's father, who was a bounty hunter too. He came here with some moderately serious weaponry, and chameleonware, to avenge his father and collect on the Polity bounty.'

'A rather long time after the fact.'

'Call it late-onset vengeance.'

'Okay, but I'm not sure why you mentioned him in your initial message.'

'Just when Crane was about to cream Matheson, there was an intervention. Three armoured creatures arrived and attacked Crane.'

'Arrived how?'

'Still not clear on that. This is the anomaly that's suspiciously temporal. Where it arrived, part of Crane's podule crop is dying, because the chemical energy has been sucked dry. Looks like an entropy spike.'

'Interesting,' said Cormac. 'And the creatures?'

'I've done a cursory analysis. Never seen the like before. They're prador, highly mutated by the Spatterjay virus but not along the lines of the King's Guard. Most of the changes come from the genome of a Spatterjay crustacean called a prill. And that's not all. The things are cyborgs – loaded with some seriously advanced tech.'

'Recognizable tech?'

'Polity and prador methods of construction blended together . . .'

'And?'

'As though prador have been doing what they had been doing ever since the war, in stealing Polity tech, adapting it and extrapolating from it.'

'I see,' said Cormac. 'Explainable for today, except for that entropy spike. Again, someone is fucking with causality.'

'Looks that way.'

'Okay. We'll arrive soon but sadly probably not in time to pull you both out of there before an attack. Can you persuade him to move?'

'He's working in his fields – trying to save those podules.'

Cormac grimaced, closed the link, then tried another he hadn't used in some time. Meanwhile, May's ship descended fast through atmosphere. He could feel the grav changes and the lurch as steering thrusters powered up, but this was to be expected, since the vessel was no passenger transport.

The link just blanked for a while, then it opened with a rush of data that had his security screaming and attempting to close things down. For a microsecond he considered slamming it shut. The reality of Crane was that he'd been repaired with Jain technology and it was now apparently subdued within him. However, further understanding of this tech, arising from events out at the Jain-tech occupied accretion disc, had highlighted further dangers. This point was emphasized by the fact that Crane had become increasingly strange and dysfunctional over the last few years. Yet Cormac just shut off the security, wondering again if he was hitting delayed ennui and taking foolish risks.

A virtuality fell into place. Cormac found himself standing on the plateau, up to his thighs in wilted podule leaves, with Mr Crane to one side. The Golem wore a long coat, baggy trousers, heavy lace-up boots and his hat. Cormac knew they weren't necessarily the same items as before, since Crane kept a supply of them. The Golem had a fluid tank strapped on his back, running a tube to some kind of injector he'd stabbed down into the ground and into one of the podules. After a moment he pulled the injector out and stood upright, looking across to where Cormac was apparently standing. Crane waved a hand at the extent of the wilting. He was annoyed and this came across well. He blinked brassy lids over eyes like midnight, and waited.

Crane only spoke occasionally, and then with such brevity the meaning might be hard to nail down. He tended to integrate data at a higher and more complex level. Cormac wanted to tell him to get out of his fields, since his crops weren't important – that bounty hunters were on their way up and, in the ensuing attempts to take Crane, everything here would probably be destroyed anyway. Instead, he collated and sent a mass of data concerning events surrounding Blite, and those 'temporal anomalies'. Crane blinked; it felt to Cormac as if he'd dropped the data down a well. Crane held up a hand and hanging from it appeared to be a black diamond in a pendant, along with a general query. Cormac put together further data on the events surrounding the AI Penny Royal's apparent apotheosis, and sent this too. Crane nodded, then went over and injected the next podule.

'You can't stay here,' said Cormac. 'I know you have some attachment to the people on this world. But how long now, with the increased reward, before your presence becomes a danger to them all?'

Crane sighed, pulled out the injector and stood upright again. He turned and strode out of the fields. In the virtuality, Cormac followed him, noting the completeness of the illusion – he could feel the soil underfoot and the brush of the podule leaves against his legs. He sent coordinates for the area of the plain, beyond the mountains, where May's ship was even now beginning to settle. Crane acknowledged these with a nod as he reached his farmhouse, pushed open the wooden door and stepped inside. Still following, Cormac looked around. The house was a neat and functional farmhouse from an era long past. A scrubbed wooden table stood in the centre of the room, surrounded by chairs. There was a wood-burning stove with its stovepipe running up the wall and across, finally exiting through the ceiling. A sink and cupboards ran along one wall, and through one door Cormac could even see a bed. All the accoutrements of human life were here, none of which Crane needed at all.

The Golem went into a back room filled with agricultural equipment, much of it antique but some advanced Polity tech. He stripped the tank off his back, uncapped it and emptied its contents into a floor drain. He then turned on a hose and began washing it out.

'Come on,' said Cormac, irritated.

Ignoring him, Crane racked the cleaned tank and injector, and stepped out of the equipment room. Cormac watched impatiently as he took up a backpack and put inside a spare set of boots, a folded coat, trousers and, of course, a spare hat. He then headed outside again. As Cormac followed him around the house, he considered this behaviour and came to the same conclusion he had when noting it before. Crane acted like someone meticulously imposing order on his immediate environment because of the chaos inside himself. This didn't bode well, considering what the Golem had inside him. Around the corner, Crane stopped and pointed.

Arach was here, standing beside the remains of one of the creatures that had attacked Crane. Cormac glanced across the nearby field to see the other two resting side by side there. They'd dragged this one in for examination. He walked over and peered inside a piece of carapace that Arach had cut and levered up, seeing an intricate tangle of organics and tech. This looked close to dense-tech levels. And though this was something that a present-day war drone might have advanced to, he had a sense of utter wrongness pouring over from Crane. He then received coordinates from him, off to the edge of the mountains. Without words, Crane conveyed his intentions.

'Okay, you're right,' said Cormac, as Crane went over, stabbed down a hand to grab it, and began towing the thing over the ground.

'More than I've got out of him in fifty years,' said Arach, miffed, and showing he'd been included in the virtuality.

'I'll see you at that location,' said Cormac, closing the link and dropping out.

Blite

'It's too early for that,' said Carlstone, looking Blite up and down disapprovingly.

'I'll be the judge of that,' Blite replied. He tapped the induction aug on his skull. 'I'm monitoring.'

Having removed the frame supporting his healing joints, he still received alerts when he moved too quickly. Shortly afterwards muscle aches and stabs of pain arrived from microfractures, along with a tight feeling in various organs as they laboured to deal with the damage, but his nanosuite seemed to be on top of it. He looked around at those in the room. Carlstone was clad in combat armour, much the same as that of the four in his security detail. They carried pulse rifles, sidearms and a selection of other armaments on bandoliers. Carlstone wore a pack with feeds and a support arm running to a multigun, presently folded back against his torso. Greer, whom Blite couldn't stop coming with them, wore an old-fashioned combat suit without assist or other additions – it just stopped most shots. She had a heavy gas-system pulse gun at her hip and, poking up from its sheath on her back, a double-headed axe. Blite eyed her for a second. He hadn't seen that thing out of storage since before the Penny Royal farrago, in the days when those they traded with were less than salubrious.

'Are we all ready?' he enquired.

'I would have preferred a larger force,' said Carlstone.

Blite shook his head. 'You know why not: the more noise we make here, the more likely we are to draw AI attention. I want to go in and out as fast as possible, with minimum casualties.'

Carlstone looked across at Greer and raised an eyebrow.

Blite turned to her and repeated, 'Minimum casualties.'

'Sure.' She reached up and touched the head of the axe. 'I'll be gentle.'

It wasn't a particularly reassuring answer. Blite gestured to the door.

Broden had provided them with rooms in one of the rib towers in the central town. This also had a private grav-car port – a small platform jutting out from the side. An armoured and armed grav-car Blite had brought out from the *Coin* awaited them. He hoped those weapons and armour wouldn't be necessary – that they'd be in and out before anyone realized what was happening – but he wouldn't put it past the Mortons to try to bring them down as they escaped. They clambered inside the vehicle, two of the security detail taking the pilot and weapons control seats, the rest settling down in the back. The car lifted hard and fast, and was soon hurtling through the sky away from the city.

'What if she doesn't want to come with us?' asked Greer conversationally.

Blite gestured to a pepper-pot stun gun at his waist.

'Ah.'

There seemed little more to add, so he focused through his induction aug to link to the systems of the grav-car. As he'd suspected, screen paint had been used all around the interior. He activated a section and noticed Greer jerk in surprise, then look at him in annoyance. It made it seem as if the floor had disappeared, with their chairs and other equipment now sitting out on open air. Neat square fields, divided by wide hedges and drainage channels, sped along below. The population of Abalon was low – just over two billion – so there were few agricultural areas like this. These, as he understood it, supplied fresh produce locally to the city, as did other such areas to other cities, while major food production lay further south. It didn't take long for them to pass over these, and to the Clander Forest. One would have supposed, like on Earth, that the fields had been carved out of the forest, but it came afterwards. The whole world had been terraformed from a lifeless orb, the crashing comets that had supplied its water also shoving it into a prime position in the Goldilocks zone of the sun. Its transformation into a living world had thereafter ensued. It wasn't over yet and, under its controlling AI's influence, it still retained the cachet of a frontier world.

They sat watching the view. The endless forest wasn't exactly interesting, but it was mesmerizing. Time passed – it does that.

'Three minutes to the landing zone,' said Carlstone from up front. 'We've got low-grade chameleonware running, and the detectors haven't picked up any scans. Maybe closer?'

'Maybe straight into their back yard?' suggested Greer.

'We land where planned.' He looked across at Greer. 'In their back yard would be provocative, don't you think?'

The car began to slow, then turn into a descent spiral. Lower down, networks of drainage channels and one circular clearing revealed themselves. The clear area had been the site of a terraforming machine, since removed, which had something to do with airborne bacteria altering the atmosphere. With it being a perfect landing spot close to the Mortons' residence, Blite had nixed the idea of putting down there, since it was almost certainly watched. Instead, Carlstone brought the car down in one of the nearby drainage channels, settling into half a metre's depth of water and a layer of mud. Greer got up and worked the door control, setting it to open down as a ramp. Blite was a step behind, noting a slight ache in his back because he'd stood up too quickly. Carlstone and the others were up and ready as Greer stepped out. They all scrambled up the mossy bank and quickly into the trees, squatting down, ready to dive for cover – all except Blite, who, checking a map in his aug, just set off at a steady walk towards the residence. A moment later Greer fell in beside him, checking her surroundings suspiciously. The security squad spaced themselves out in the trees, doubtless assuming the best positions tactically. Carlstone came up on his other side.

'They're unlikely to hit us here.' Blite paused, waiting for gunfire to break out, then continued, 'We use stun initially, if we have to, and only resort to other weapons if they start trying to kill us.' He eyed the axe on Greer's back.

'You seriously expect a reserved response?'

He grimaced.

Within twenty minutes they came to the fence – buildings lay beyond it amid a sparse scattering of trees. Carlstone waved one of his men forwards and turned to Blite. 'No detectors in the trees we could find, but our equipment isn't state-of-the-art.'

The man who'd moved to the fence ran a hand scanner over it, checked the results, then took items out of a pack on his belt. He ran a wire in a circle against the fence and initiated it. With a fizzing sound, the section of fence inside the circle parted company from the rest – he pulled it out, tossing it aside before moving through. The others quickly followed. Blite checked the map of the buildings in his aug, locating the one Broden's people had last seen Meander Draft 64XB being taken into. They headed straight towards it. Still no response, maybe they were going to –

They came around some bushes to his right, running silently. With his vision already enhanced, Blite took in their form. The two Rottweilers had gleaming ceramal teeth, additional lumps on their skulls and excessive heavy musculature. As they ran, they started growling, and through this came slurred words, 'Grrret you aaasfucker . . .' Enhanced guard dogs uplifted to near-human intelligence, doubtless loaded with natural and artificial aggression.

'Awww,' said Greer.

Blite looked askance at her as he drew his stun beader. He fired, hitting the nearest in the face. It staggered but kept going, until pulse stun fire from one of the security detail brought it down. The other one abruptly skidded to a halt, then started barking and dodging from side to side, making it a difficult target. That was one alarm, but Blite had no doubt another operated straight out of their enhancements as the lights came on. He squatted, surveying his surroundings, and saw figures appearing, just as Greer leaped through the air and came down on the barking dog. It collapsed with an oomph, and then they were rolling in the dirt, the dog trying to bite through her arm. Blite shook his head, fired at a half-seen figure and ran on. Pulse fire laced through the air and he saw two go down, webbed with the electric discharges of stun. The reply was the stab of a laser carbine, raising fire from one of Carlstone's men, who staggered and then dived, rolling for cover. No stun shot that: the gloves were off.

'Greer?' Carlstone asked over aug as they ran from cover to cover.

'Leave her,' Blite replied. He had no idea why she'd decided to wrestle a dog, but had every confidence she could look after herself. With his stun gun holstered, he pulled the short stubby laser carbine off the stick patch on the front of his suit. Someone stepped out ahead of him, raising a heavy gas-system pulse gun. He dodged to one side, firing and flaming a leg. The woman dropped, shrieking. He stepped in close and slapped the weapon from her hand as she tried to target him again, then brought his hand back in and punched her in the face. His fist went in with a crunch and she slumped. Pain in his hand. He'd broken her face but probably also his fingers. A shiver of shame ran through him – he'd misjudged the blow with his new strength and might have killed her. He couldn't quite accept gloves off.

Carlstone's security detail was firing in short bursts. One of them limped heavily, his armour still smoking. Carlstone himself now opened up with the appalling firepower of the multigun, shredding trees and turning sections of wall to gravel. Blite let them cover him as he finally came up to a steel door inset in a stone wall. The thing had a coded lock. A glance up at a nearby window showed it barred, confirming that Meander must be a prisoner. Thankfully the door wasn't ceramal. He shot out the lock, burning right through with his carbine. One kick against it drove his other foot into the ground. It bent the door in, exposing locking bars all around. He began burning through these, but impacts in his back slammed him forwards into it. Another shot hit him as he turned and a huge figure came towards him, holding a flak gun. The man was smiling as he now aimed at Blite's face. A whickering sound in the air was followed by a crunchy thud. The man's expression turned puzzled as he staggered a step forwards. He then fell flat on his face with Greer's axe embedded in his spine. She ran over and heaved it out, her expression crazy delighted.

'What are you pissing about at?' she asked. 'Go get her.' She ran off.

Blite saw that Carlstone and his men had formed a loose ring out there, taking cover and firing at others who'd also taken cover. Well, any chance of subterfuge had gone out of the window with that barking dog. Heaving himself up, he burned out more locking bars, meanwhile auging through to the grav-car and summoning it. He kicked the door again and this time it crashed inside. One room lay beyond, utterly bare but for a single chair bolted to the floor. Out of a room beyond, in which he could see a low pallet bed, stepped Meander. Her hair was a blonde mop. She looked thin and worn. He noted bruises, missing teeth, burns and drug shunts on her arms. She could barely walk. Why? Was this all done to glean information from her? Knowing people like the Mortons from many past associations, he guessed she might have turned from a prisoner, to be interrogated, into a plaything. He felt less guilt now about the woman he'd punched.

'*You*,' she said, and he could see her tiredness swept away by dread. She turned back towards the room and halted. She had nowhere to flee.

'I just want some answers,' he said. 'And I won't use the methods they have here.' He kicked the chair and surprised himself when it broke from its fixings and crashed into the wall.

She turned back with fear still written on her face and he wondered just what the hell holding on to the black diamond had done to her, but she nodded, briefly. He turned, heading to the door which led out of the building. 'Carlstone! All of you! On me.'

He stepped out of the door, only a little way – he didn't want to give Meander room to flee past him – which, he felt, seemed likely. Carlstone and the other four began laying down heavy fire as they retreated towards him. The grav-car loomed in the sky and he auged into its controls, opening its ramp door and bringing it down. It descended fast, landing with a crash before him, the ramp door open on the other side. He turned to find Meander directly behind him, reached out carefully to take hold of one thin arm, and towed her along with him.

'I won't run,' she said.

He ignored this and kept hold of her anyway. Round the other side of the car, the others were piling in. Blite pushed Meander in front of him and, turning his back, kept himself between her and the shooting from the surrounding Mortons. A series of hits caught him at the top of the ramp, throwing him inside with her, his back flaming. He stood quickly, pushing her to one side as shots spanged inside and a laser seared across the wall opposite the door. The security detail were all in the car now. Two men were down on the floor, one with his suit smoking and face blank with the drugs the suit had injected. The other had the front of his suit open, pushing something into a seeping hole in his chest.

'Get us the fuck out of here,' said Blite, looking to Carlstone and the other man in the seats ahead. 'Wait! Where the hell is Greer?'

'She's coming,' said Carlstone dryly.

Blite peered around the edge of the door and saw Greer dodging towards the ramp, something heavy over one shoulder. Pulse shots and lasers zipped through the air, but she seemed to evade them with ease. She hit the ramp just as it, and the car, began to rise, and then fell inside, rolling, dumping her load on the floor and coming upright.

'Now that was exciting,' she exclaimed. 'I've really missed this since you went legit.'

The ramp door closed and the car jerked under the impact of a missile. Burner acceleration kicked in, taking both Blite and Greer off their feet, sending them tangled together to the back of the car. A second hit occurred a few seconds later, but that was the last of it. As he extricated himself from Greer, she said, 'We're a little bit battered.'

He noted the long list of damage coming up in his aug from his suit, and the larger list from his nanosuite. 'Yeah, we are that.' Now he pointed. 'But perhaps you can explain this.'

'Always wanted one,' said Greer.

The Rottweiler lay on its side, long red tongue hanging over ceramal teeth.

Blite transferred his attention to Meander. She looked as okay as she could be, with arms wrapped tightly around her legs and chin on her knee, her eyes wide and terrified.

5

May

'Those coordinates are fifteen kilometres away,' said May, standing at the head of the ramp. 'And a lot of it is rough terrain.'

The agent nodded. 'Any closer and we'll be noticed, then probably targeted by a variety of missile launchers and other ground weapons. As you said, this ship is no war craft. But this is close enough. There's a calculation concerning load and distance, with my abilities.'

May glanced back at her ship. It looked like some sleeker vessel in the process of construction. Behind the heart-shaped front end, containing the bridge, and crew and passenger quarters, extended the long frame with all the subsidiaries attached to it, like scattered iron-coloured seeds on a half-eaten cob of sweetcorn. Running through this, the cylindrical section contained Engineering and a small cargo section, mostly packed with spares and repair materials. At the terminus of that sat the rear engine section, with fusion drive at the back and U-space nacelles protruding to the sides. Down here, on the surface of a planet, its actual size impinged. At a kilometre long, and less than half a kilometre wide, it was small in comparison to many behemoths out there, but it was still a lot larger than many cargo ships, and certainly bigger than the one she'd had before. Even now she had yet to explore its interior fully.

'Your abilities . . .' May said blandly. The guy had been quite chatty and sociable over the last few days of the journey. He'd told them much about his time with ECS and the threats he'd faced, filling in detail and dismissing whatever was fiction, but she noted how he smoothly moved conversation away from anything concerning his 'abilities'. And still, despite his obvious attempts to be more human, she found him spooky, yet rather enjoyed that reaction.

'What about them?' he said.

'They're limited, then?' she asked

He gave a tight smile. 'I can transport myself through U-space a considerable realspace distance – the limitations are usually due to the vagaries of that continuum. However, when it comes to transporting anything more than the personal items around my body, things become more difficult. I once transported a load from orbit to Earth, then back again. Didn't like the blood running out of my ears afterwards.'

'So this is how . . .'

He looked at her and stepped away. She felt a similar sensation to that of when a ship dropped into U-space, and briefly saw where he was stepping before snapping her attention away.

'Damn,' said a voice behind her.

May opened her tightly closed eyes. Where Agent Cormac had been standing, dust swirled. Looking back, she now saw Akanthor and Davidson had come down from the ship's bridge. Both of them had made it a game of trying to find faults in the stuff Cormac had been saying. She realized they didn't experience the visceral feeling she had about him, and didn't really believe he was who he claimed to be. She guessed this doubt had now been dismissed, however. The two moved forwards to stand at the head of the ramp with her.

'You know,' said Akanthor, 'I was okay with it – I get my money to ferry around some delusional friend of Blite's. No problem.' She looked at May. 'But what the fuck have we got ourselves into here?'

'Serious shit,' said May. 'But we're paid to help out Blite, who I feel I owe more than just a good employee attitude. You two can opt out any time you like.'

Davidson moved up on the other side. 'No need for that. We're of the same opinion.' There seemed an extra firmness to his words, as if he was trying to persuade himself of that.

Just beyond the ramp, dust swirled up again and the air above it shimmered with what appeared to be heat haze. With a crackle like gunfire, Cormac reappeared there, his hand down on a large spider drone. May recognized the shape of something like a black widow but with thicker legs. Its coloration was that of heat-treated polished metal, spread with iridescent patterns, its eyes bloody red. Cormac stood upright, taking his hand from its back. It scuttled away from him, then turned to face him. The patterns shifted on its carapace and May guessed at some form of chameleonware there. Cormac looked up the ramp at them before disappearing again.

'There was a spider drone in some of those stories,' said Davidson.

'Perhaps we'll soon learn which of them were true,' Akanthor added.

'It was a bit part,' the spider drone said, as it swivelled around to face them and head up the ramp. May felt an immediate atavistic fear, but stood her ground. She noted the ramp sink as it stepped onto it, the metal bowing a little. *Dense tech*, she thought. The drone came right up to them.

119

'I'm Arach, as you probably guessed. Pleased to meet you.' It held out a forelimb to her. She studied the complex high-tech foot, with its hooks, gecko strips and the concentric convolutions of some other gripping surface, and took hold to shake it gingerly. The drone did the same with the other two, who shook silently but politely. Lowering the limb, Arach added, 'I didn't catch your names?'

'Sorry.' May shook herself. 'I'm May.' She pointed to the other two and introduced them. Arach dipped his head in a nod, then scuttled around to face back down the ramp.

'Now,' the drone continued, 'if you enjoyed those stories you're in for a treat, or maybe, depending on your nature, a bowel-loosening moment.'

Perfectly on cue, the dust swirled again and Cormac appeared with that crackling sound. Next to him a figure stood a head, shoulders and much of a chest above him. May saw the brass face and hands, and the black eyes below the wide-brimmed hat. Her gaze traversed down the buttoned-up coat, down the baggy trousers, to the heavy hobnail boots. She understood now that the virtualities had toned things down a little. The Mr Crane of those had been smaller, lighter-looking, and didn't seem to invade reality quite so heavily. She swallowed dryly.

'Fucking legends,' Akanthor muttered.

Cormac

After delivering Crane to the ship, Cormac jumped back to the pick-up location for the third round trip. There was one last thing to collect. As he stepped back into the real, he raised a finger to probe at his ear and inspected the fingertip. Fortunately it didn't come away bloody. He grimaced. Mass was a factor in this and

Crane did weigh about the same as Arach, but something else had made it unusually difficult to transport the big Golem. Cormac had felt it to a lesser degree on other occasions long ago – Crane had considerable drag in U-space, almost certainly due to the Jain tech inside him. That the drag had increased over the years signified something; he didn't like to think what that might be. He walked over to the one of the three creatures that Crane and Arach had killed and brought here. What was it? A prador or a biomech drone? The distinction was hazy. He studied it, using his U-senses actually to peer inside and see the amalgamation of organics and hard technology.

Crane had been right to bring it along. Even examining it like this and running a series of analytical programs in his gridlink, Cormac could divine little beyond what Arach had learned. They needed to get it into a laboratory somewhere, take the thing apart, and do some serious data crunching. Crane could assist in that respect, but he tended to be a bit too unpredictable. He might withhold information, or simply decide to destroy the thing, or grow bored partway through and wander off. Better to take it to an AI who specialized in this sort of work, and Cormac already had a candidate in mind. He smiled. It would perhaps surprise the new iteration of Earth Central just how many AIs, drones, Golem and haimen didn't agree with the thesis that humanity should be pushed to uplift itself.

He stepped back and checked his surroundings. Crane had dragged the thing down a narrow valley from the plateau, into a small copse of nettle elms and tea oaks. A stream trickled past, and nearby sat a boulder with a seat roughly carved into its upper surface. It was, he knew, a place of contemplation for Crane, and the fact it was a peaceful, beautiful spot somehow reassured him about the Golem. He went over and sat on the boulder, in no hurry to make the next U-jump and frankly, after Crane, feeling the need for a brief rest. A breeze tickled his face. He watched something vaguely like a turtle nose out of the stream, see him, then splash back into it.

So what the hell was going on? Something had been attempting to kill Blite, but the increasing severity of the attempts might be to measure how much that black diamond, now embedded in his skull, could twist causality. All he knew was that whoever, or whatever, was screwing with Blite was tracking the man quite closely. There seemed to be intricate plotting involved, but was what happened here, with these creatures, relevant? The only connection was the temporal one. Maybe that other unknown party wanted to quash potential allies of Blite? Whatever it was, he would have to be careful – something had to be analysing threads through time and acting on them, he felt sure . . .

A whoomph up above threw debris and smoke into the air. Cormac peered at this, then brought his attention lower, gazing through the U-continuum. He saw the gravity plane of the world, with all matter reversed into a convoluted abyss, but all running through his gridlink to give him a real-world interpretation. Crane would not be pleased by what Cormac saw: it seemed one of the bounty hunters had just put a missile into his farmhouse and turned it into a burning ruin. Many of them were up there now, and spreading out. One group was even heading towards this same valley. As ever, events would not wait on his contemplations.

He stood up and headed over to the creature, reached down and placed a hand on its carapace. The thing felt slightly warm, and he sensed in it the wrongness Crane had indicated – a weird kind of *weight*. Now noting the profile and severity of the damage, he realized its armour wasn't as durable as normal prador armour and probably served some other purpose. Like all the puzzles this thing represented, that would have to wait for analysis. First, he needed to get it back to May's ship. He took a breath, concentrated on doing the thing which defied conventional description, extended the U-field which normally generated just out from his skin to encapsulate it, then jumped.

As soon as he entered the U-continuum he felt a similar drag to the one he'd had from Crane, and he knew something was very wrong. The coordinates, right down to the foot of the ramp up into May's ship, began to slide away, and the abyss folded around him, extending into a tube. It was as if he'd transported far too close to a runcible gate – something he'd done before and never intended to do again. His mind kicked into high gear, integrating with his gridlink. He was being drawn somewhere else and it seemed likely to be a trap. He pulled together all the data he could glean, formulated a loose plan and instructions, opened a link actually within U-space and shot it over to the only mind capable of receiving it in the microseconds he had. He followed it up with a brief addition concerning Captain May. Receiving an acknowledgement that had something in it of 'I told you so', he fell away, deep into the abyss, new coordinates coming up like a claw to grab at him.

May

'Mr Crane,' said Davidson nervously, holding out his hand as Crane walked up the ramp. May noted the ramp sink under the Golem's weight as it had done for the spider drone. Something seriously odd about that, since the Golem shouldn't mass so much.

Crane loomed over them. He peered down at Davidson's hand then held up his own. Though it looked to be made of brass, May guessed it must be some other extremely hard and tough material. He flexed it a couple of times. By now Davidson's nervousness had segued into an instinct for self-preservation. He abruptly lowered his hand and stepped to one side. May didn't blame him. That brassy thing looked capable of crushing rocks to powder. Crane stepped on past them, ducking his head to go through the entrance. He disappeared inside the ship, heading straight up towards the bridge, May noted.

'Doesn't say much, does he?' she commented.

'Not the greatest conversationalist,' Arach replied. 'Right now he's crunching data from Cormac, who'll not be rejoining us.'

'What?' May peered at the drone.

'Seems the creature was a trap, or maybe something about the tech in it is throwing Cormac off course. We don't know enough.'

'What?'

'Are you hard of hearing?'

'What creature?'

Arach gestured inside the ship. 'Maybe explanations can wait for later? The bounty hunters have satellites pointed down here, and now a lot of them are heading in this direction. We need to move out of here fast.'

May whirled around and headed inside. Akanthor and Davidson quickly fell in behind her, Davidson hitting the ramp control. Arach clattered after them as the ramp began to close up. Maybe legends had arrived, and they were getting involved in something . . . legendary, and she felt a frisson at the thought of this, but she needed to stay focused on reality. Obviously, those hunters were after either, or both, of the two who'd just boarded her ship. There were a lot of them, and just a glimpse at the ships down at the space port told her they had way more armament than hers. She hurried up to the bridge, calculating. Her advantage here was the sheer power of her hauler and, therefore, its speed.

On the way to the bridge, she noted with annoyance the

footprints in the composite floor. Hobnail boots with that weight above them hadn't done it much good. She'd have to have words with that Golem. She nearly giggled at the thought, and as she entered the bridge she glanced at Crane standing against the back wall. She had the weird sense of something shifting inside him, yet he was perfectly stationary. As if in response to her inspection, he closed his brassy eyelids. She stepped away and threw herself into her chair.

'Davidson,' she snapped. 'Configure the subsidiaries.'

'On it,' Davidson replied.

A clattering sound drew her attention; she looked round to see Arach, with legs folded up, squeezing through the door. The drone only made it so far and couldn't seem to squeeze its abdomen through, so it just settled there. May dismissed him from her thoughts, hit a control on her chair arm to bring up a joystick, and gripped it firmly.

'Akanthor, watch for weapons fire.'

'Already am,' Akanthor replied.

May engaged the grav-engines, running them up to full power, then as an afterthought initiated the forward screen. The ground was already dropping away yet there'd been no sensation of that. Sensations would ensue shortly, and some of them might be quite painful.

'Incoming,' said Akanthor.

Fuck, that was quick. May hit her other chair arm and a touch console folded out. She operated it fast, bringing up a series of displays. One showed her ship as a glowing dot, with five further dots speeding towards it from the space port. Two more views showed her ship's hull as two bead-feed miniguns rose out and tracked. One fired, its front end glaring, and two of those missile dots disappeared. Another two dots then appeared, rising from the plateau in the mountains.

'Secure for acceleration. Those subsidiaries online?' Another view on the screen displayed the subsidiaries on their back frame folding round to all point in one direction. She pushed the touch console and joystick down, keying in preparations, and leaned back. Padded clamps rose to take her arms, another cupped her head, while the seat folded around her torso and legs. A glance to one side showed Akanthor and Davidson similarly protected.

'Arach, you know what happens next?' she asked.

'I know. Don't worry about us,' Arach replied.

'I'm not worried about you, but get out of that fucking doorway.' She swivelled her chair around to be sure. Crane had now squatted and driven his hands through the floor to grip strengthening beams there. She really needed to have a word with him about the damage he was causing her ship. Yet, with his eyes closed, it seemed his pose had less to do with the acceleration she was about to apply, and more to do with him controlling himself. Arach shifted, then with a whining, clattering sound, his abdomen compressed. He came through the door and settled down, probably bonding to the floor. The door rolled out from its space in the wall, sucking into place on its seal. May turned her chair to face the front screen.

'Hitting it,' she said, and did so.

The hauler's fusion engines ignited. She shifted the subviews down to the bottom, and the main screen view to the sky above. For a minute into the fusion burn internal grav compensated, but then she felt the acceleration trying to tear her out of her chair to the left. Now the bridge pod shifted, which was why she'd needed Arach out of that doorway, orienting them so acceleration drove them down into their seats. May kept her finger on the joystick control, pushing it until the bones in her hand were creaking, feeling that if she let go it would end up jellied in the chair arm. She watched the missile tracks.

'Dropping . . . back . . .' Davidson managed.

May felt like nodding agreement, but of course couldn't move her head. Reluctantly she switched over to her aug. The joystick and the touch console slid from her grip and her hands dropped down onto pads. As ever, she grimaced at her disinclination to use her aug, knowing it arose from her admiration of Blite and his same reluctance.

'Dropping back,' Davidson repeated through the connection. 'We're outrunning the missiles but we've got ships in orbit on the move.'

All the screens and more opened to her internal perception. The view was much clearer now through ship's sensors; she could see two vessels under acceleration – one the long slab of an old-style attack ship, and another just a great pear-shaped blob of armour and weapons. The views blinked for a second and then came back. Her body felt tight, her pulse thundering. She'd just passed the point where a normal human, if such a thing still existed, would have blacked out. The aug, allied with her nano-suite, was compensating: increasing her heart rate, opening blood vessels to her brain and closing them elsewhere, tensioning up her muscles to their maximum, shutting down nerve impulses. This would hurt later.

More missile tracks showed, this time from the armoured ship. Their own guns fired again – a minute-long burst. The missile tracks disappeared, but at the last so did one of the guns, just fragmenting and vanishing. They really weren't supposed to be used under such heavy acceleration, being designed to deal with space debris while doing realspace hauling. She'd need some upgrades to the ship if her involvement in events like this continued. The thought caused an odd feeling: a surge of excitement quickly sliding into emptiness.

The sky began to darken, stars coming out. The view of those approaching ships became clearer too. She checked data, but knew they weren't ready to jump just yet. It then occurred to her she had no set of coordinates to jump to. She turned her internal attention to the ship's mind which, like many in Penny Transport, was a flash-frozen ganglion of a prador female. Blite had little trust in AIs; therefore neither did she. She considered where best to go, but it didn't really matter, just so long as it was *away*. A new link winked up and, without her giving permission, it opened. U-space coordinates appeared. May activated her chair again and swung it around, its motors rumbling with the strain. Arach was unreadable, of course, but Crane's eyes were open and he was looking at her. She took the coordinates offered and shunted them over to the ship's mind, along with the instruction to jump the moment it became possible. Crane tilted his head in acknowledgement. She looked into his black eyes and it seemed there were flecks of light in there now. She turned the chair again, not wanting to see him.

'Clear of atmosphere,' Davidson intoned over the link.

'Let's hope we wake up from this,' said May.

She fired up thrusters, turning the ship until the subsidiaries pointed back along their direction of travel, or as near as possible, since the standard fusion engine was still fired up. She paused for just a second, seeing something lancing out from that armoured ship again. Fuck. Particle beam. She fired up the subsidiaries.

It took a second. The bridge rumbled as it reoriented. She knew she would not be conscious when they jumped to U-space, just before a black hand slammed down on her and took her away.

Cormac

With U-space folding around him, Cormac found his options to U-jump anywhere but to the new coordinates imposed swiftly diminishing. However, U-space being a continuum lying beneath the conventional dimensions of time and distance, he could still effectively slow his transition. He did so, freezing the folding all around, peering hard with his U-senses into his situation.

He was being pulled to a particular location. If this was a trap, he had no doubt that something nasty awaited him there. Quite likely it would be oblivion. The dead creature was pulling him on this course, so he needed to let go of it. Mentally, he began to pull on the field encompassing it. The action had all the difficulties of trying to change course while falling down a cliff, but he did have some traction on what stood for air in that analogy. The U-field began to draw back into him, then snapped out again. He pulled again, but felt the ugly sensation of the creature beginning to shift into him. The result of this would be him appearing at the coordinates melded to it in a screaming mess. Fuck that. There was only one other way: he had to pinch off that section of the U-field. It would screw him, leaving his abilities disrupted for some hours, just when it seemed likely he'd need them. It was the only option.

He tightened the field at the point lying between him and his burden, steadily piling on pressure. U-space began to fold again, taking him closer, if such a term could be used, to his arrival point. The strain started to tell. His gridlink felt as if it wanted to take flight from his skull, and he knew that blood coming out of his ears would be the least of his problems. It finally snapped, and he glimpsed realspace perception of something shattering like glass, with the creature falling away. This perception was the start of his U-senses disrupting, but he at least had the satisfaction of knowing the creature would arrive at those coordinates without him. He'd still emerge close by, of course, and hoped that his instinctive manipulation of U-space, despite the disruption, would prevent him materializing inside a rock.

U-space inverted, turning out reality, solidity and the dimensions of time and space. Cormac fell, arms windmilling, then his heel hit something and he was tumbling down a slope. Old training kicked in and he turned the fall into something balletic, shedding energy and slowing, skidding down through smoothly rounded spheres, as well as commas of gravel and white salty-looking dust. He came to a halt on the slope, standing upright, and saw he was on the side of a mountain, with others rising above. Turning to look below, he saw a deep green ocean hurling waves against tall knife-like boulders. He felt elated to have survived, until he took his first breath.

Coughing, he dropped to his knees. He suppressed the overpowering urge to gasp for oxygen in air that didn't contain it and was almost certainly laced with toxic gases. Something snapped into being in the air beside him, then fell to the slope. The glassy mass seemed alive, but he had enough cognition to recognize help when offered. Scrambling over to the thing, he picked it up. The jellied cup of matter, run through with pipes, half-seen mechanisms and cilia woven along two outside edges, was shaped on the inside to fit a human face. He slammed it in place without a second thought.

The thing deformed around his features, sinking close to his skin. He felt objects entering his nostrils, forming around his mouth and probing at his eyes. Since the alternative was suffocation, he sat back and let it happen. He huffed out the last of his breath as cool jelly filled his eyes and, unable to fight it any longer, took in a breath through those things in his nose. Air came in clean and, he recognized, highly oxygenated. As he gradually recovered, using rigid self-control to quell his panic, his vision returned as clear as it had been before. Finally, he stood up again.

'So who are you?' he asked.

He felt tendrils spreading back from the mask along his cheek-bones then entering his ears, and guessed he'd soon be getting an answer.

'What you call me is immaterial,' replied a flat voice.

'Well, thank you . . .' Cormac considered for a second, then finished with, '. . . Mask. Where the fuck am I?'

'Soon to be in . . . deep shit if you don't move your ass.'

The first words had been as flat as before and androgynous, but those that came after the pause had taken on character and the tone of a woman's voice. He wondered if he was talking to an AI which had just adapted to talk to him on a more human level.

'Move my ass where?'

'It doesn't matter, just so long as it's away from your present location. They have the creature now and will soon figure out someone, or something, came through with it. Your U-signature was pretty loud and messy, as was the translocation I used to send you that mask.'

Cormac looked around, studying the terrain. He now recognized the oddly shaped lumps of gravel as splash from a particle beam strike. It was likely this had hit above, then all this stuff had rolled down. Walking on it, he'd leave no trail, but it would be hard going. Down the slope lay a lot of white powder where he'd make tracks, and over to the right, running upwards, he could see clear stone. He quickly headed off across the gravel, slipping and sliding until he reached the stone, then began climbing up.

'Good choice,' said the one he'd dubbed Mask. 'The p-prador snap-back point, when they are U-jumped a second time, is up there – same location for tachyon evaporation.'

Cormac couldn't quite make sense of that so repeated, 'Good choice?'

'Knowing someone came through and broke away, they'll expect you to head in the opposite direction.'

'Tell me what else I should do,' said Cormac. It occurred to him that if this was an artificial intelligence speaking to him, he might well have been correct in naming it Mask – it might actually be *in* the mask he was wearing.

'Head a bit to your right as you go up,' said Mask. 'A lot of holes in the mountain up there were made during a war they've all but forgotten, and you need to hide and evade.'

'And then what?'

'You recover your abilities and get the hell out of there.'

Only as Mask said this did Cormac's physical condition hit him, perhaps because the surge of adrenalin was fading. He felt battered. His head ached, with the pain seeming to ooze out of his eyes, ears and nose. When he tried his U-senses, he just got a view of grey and silver swirl that immediately elicited panic and a further painful twisting in his mind. At least he was seeing the continuum, though in the same way as a normal human being would. When he made an effort towards jumping, he found the ability dead inside him. He'd suffered this before, the time he'd jumped too close to a runcible, but it hadn't been this extreme. He kept moving up the slope, pushing hard to his limits.

'This raises the question of where exactly this place is,' he said dryly.

'Your location physically, with of course some compensation for orbital dynamics, planetary shift and your instinct not to end up inside a rock, is close to what it was before.'

Though he now guessed what had probably happened, he said, 'Doesn't look much the same.'

'The plateau is still up there, and that's where they've put their machine. Bombardment centuries back was what rearranged the landscape otherwise. The ocean was a surprise to everyone – a local crustal collapse into a giant underwater reservoir.'

'Centuries,' Cormac repeated.

'Along this particular timeline on the probability slope,' Mask replied blithely. 'Of course, it's a future that might not exist for you.'

'How long in the future?' Cormac asked.

'Just over a thousand years,' Mask replied.

'Okay,' he said, trying not to be appalled.

Straeger

Like a dandelion clock weighted with dew, Straeger dropped through atmosphere. He was trying not to be angry at all his threads of prediction being in disarray. The anomaly he'd detected here on Cull involving Mr Crane had been a lure for Cormac, and another potential kill zone in which to catch the agent. According to Straeger's prediction, the man should have been turning up here sometime hence, aboard a simple cargo hauler that was vulnerable to attack. But something had dislocated the timeline, and he'd turned up a lot earlier. And though he'd arrived in that ship, the data indicated he hadn't been aboard it when it left, yet thus far there was no sign of him on the surface.

Below, amid rolling hills, Straeger could see the lit sprawl of the city. The humans of this world were primitive and had regarded their *guest* here, Crane, with awe and reverence. Their attitude was somehow akin to ancient cargo cults and had been a hindrance to any Polity actions against Crane, as well as anything Straeger cared to do. He came in to hover over the city as dregs of anger and offence rose out of entanglement and he contemplated punishing the humans below him. He quickly moved on, sliding over the lights and into the wilder lands beyond. Punishing such people was beneath the rationality of a being like him, surely? The larger – in fact immense and potentially infinite – picture was the one that must concern him.

As he drifted to the farm, he continued to absorb the local com, mostly of the bounty hunters who hadn't given chase after the *Bracken*, and from the sensors he'd positioned here long ago. He learned of the most recent attempt on Crane, and that the hunter concerned, one Matheson, had survived. Having obtained initial data on the man, who currently occupied his ship in the space port, Straeger did some further checking. He'd come here accompanied by a spider-format war drone, which explained a lot. If the drone was Arach, as seemed likely, this must be why Cormac had received notification of the event so quickly, and come here before predicted. However, it still didn't explain why he hadn't left aboard that ship, or why there was no sign of him on the surface now.

With the sunrise, Straeger settled down towards the plateau, while concentrating on the data gathered by his sensors scattered there. Some bounty hunters were still in the area, though most were trekking down to rented ATVs parked below. A few were in and about the ruins of Crane's house, picking through the remains in the hope of finding something profitable. A perhaps more thoughtful one of their kind was running a biosensor over the podule crop, likely seeing this as a chance for a profit. Straeger ignored all of them as he touched the ground and rolled, hissing, through the leaves. Instead he focused on the group gathered around the remains of two wrecked, armoured organisms which seemed to have been the source of the anomaly here. He listened in, hearing that they'd sent for grav-motors from their ATVs to move the things out. They felt sure there'd be a market for them somewhere. They would be disappointed.

Straeger finally came to a halt directly over one of his sensor arrays and punched a few tendrils to plug into the thing directly where it lay, two metres down, and thence into the quantum storage crystals in order to download the clearest picture obtainable. After finding out Cormac wasn't where predicted, double-checking the recorded data here had been his secondary aim, since temporal anomalies tended to screw this kind of sensor-gathering. By direct download, he quickly assembled the full picture of events here. It amused him to watch Matheson and his bounty hunters striding in, see the man-Golem Ricardo abandoning the quest, then Arach's inevitable betrayal. He watched the fighting and felt himself wincing with sympathy for the things that had attacked Crane. His entanglement-engendered hatred for the Brass Man, which was ephemeral to the larger picture, became somewhat tempered by respect. It could not be denied that he was a formidable machine. Matheson escaped and then, after a bucolic hiatus, Crane began dragging one of the attackers away, while other bounty hunters closed in. And then Cormac arrived.

Straeger watched intently as the man U-jumped Crane and Arach down from the plateau to the cargo hauler on the plain beyond. Even now, after so many years of data-gathering, he studied everything in fine detail. But still he could get no intimation of how a soft human could bare-brain his way through U-space without being ripped apart. Sure, his gridlink enabled him to make the calculations required, and to interpret U-space for his linear-evolved brain, but where were the watts that threw him into, and then out of, that continuum? Where was the shielding of a 3D being required to survive a multidimensional environment? And then, after moving Crane and Arach to the shuttle, Cormac returned.

The man stood surveying his surroundings. It seemed in overlay that he focused directly on Straeger for a moment. He then shrugged and stooped down to the machine-organism to place a hand on its damaged carapace. Straeger fined down the data as far as possible, complementing it with what he could glean from the data of other sensors, and broke it down almost to nanobytes. A U-field generated around the man and extended to encompass the creature. He and it then blinked out of existence, but didn't reappear by the cargo ship. Further data indicated no U-signatures or anomalous twists in U-space, either about the planet or up in orbit. What the hell had happened? Straeger ran through it again and again. It was only when he focused entirely on the U-space map that he saw it. Temporal tension on the entire machine-organism had been released by Cormac trying to U-jump it. The thing had dragged him off *somewhen* else.

Straeger detached from his sensor array with a strange mix of emotions roiling inside. His aim to kill Cormac here had failed, but other options were opening out in a probability cascade. He looked over to the bounty hunters around the remaining machine-organisms. They'd spotted him. Four who were close to the thing were watching cautiously, while three others had flicked their suits into full assist and were now heading as fast as they could to the pass down below. Evidently the fleeing three were wanted for crimes in the Polity and didn't want to stick around. The four who stayed were either without guilt, brave or stupid. They were no concern.

Straeger began rolling towards those remaining, hesitated, then abruptly altered his course after those fleeing. Coming here, he'd been aware of the other presence and knew that at some point he had to acknowledge it; he had to touch upon the source of the entanglement that drove him. The three disappeared into the pass, shooting frightened glances over their shoulders. Finally reaching the edge leading to the carved steps, Straeger watched them scrambling down, one of them actually losing his footing and tumbling down the last of the steps. In its way it amused him that they considered themselves important enough to be chased, then he swivelled his attention to his real reason for this diversion.

The Mobius AI, tied into a knot, still sat on the flat slab of rock where Crane had placed it. The operation it had been part of had apparently been straight out of ECS; though, apart from the agent involved, the soldiers had been mercenaries just equipped with Polity military gear. In the end, it had been illegal in terms of Polity law – a black-book operation instigated by a rogue AI – and Earth Central had hammered those involved who'd survived. Yes, Crane was dangerous, a killer, with Jain tech inside him, but he was outside Polity jurisdiction, and the more conventional AIs had calculated that going after him directly, if unsuccessful, would result in him becoming *more* dangerous to the Polity. Part of that calculation concerned Cormac too, because he might take exception to an attack upon one of his allies, and no AI, including the current Earth Central, wanted him turning up inside their defences.

The rogue AI that had conducted the operation now sat before Straeger, while the soldiers and agents continued their slow decay into dust down in the pass. He probed the knot to find what he had before: that Crane had knotted the AI not only physically, but mentally too. Its entire consciousness was locked into a loop, feeding back into itself perpetually, for it had in effect been locked into a time crystal. The thing only existed now to replay endlessly the last twenty minutes of its existence. It was nominally alive in this state, but undoing the loop would only bring about its dissolution, for it would turn to dust. It almost seemed as if Straeger was seeing, in this entity, a microcosm of the larger problem he faced. He hissed at the thing, moving off, and now noting a boy trudging up the steps towing a conglomeration of grav-engines like a misshapen balloon.

Straeger rolled aside and watched. The boy halted upon seeing him, spoke over com to the others here, then continued past. Straeger returned to his thoughts about more recent events here, thinking hard. Some other influence was involved, and Cormac had been dragged, perhaps inadvertently, elsewhere. Maybe there'd been intent behind what happened to Cormac, perhaps to kill him, as Straeger wanted to do, but he had no guarantee of that and needed to prepare other options now etching themselves out of his predictions. Abruptly, because it had been rumbling in his mind at a low level, he set out towards the hunters.

'What do you want?' asked one of the five hunters, stepping ahead of the rest while the others were busy attaching grav-motors to the machine-organisms.

Straeger halted and gazed at the scene. What *did* he want? Clarity, and a firm course into the future. Right now, though, he wanted to introduce elements that were alien to his predictions, to counter the anomalies developing from here. What he wanted was a weapon. He properly focused his senses on the creatures at their feet and quickly gleaned a general picture of what they were. In some sense they weren't dead. Though Crane and Arach had ensured the destruction of their major ganglia, their viral transformation maintained a facsimile of life while it searched for survival heuristics. They were mutated prador and cyborgs. Also, he saw that their U-space protective armour, and other tech inside them, remained intact enough to be useful. Combine that with a method of U-jumping, which wasn't in them, along with a guiding intelligence, and he'd have a perfect counter-weapon to someone who could jump at will through that continuum. Straeger didn't want to be that guiding intelligence – he needed to remain in oversight, to track the temporal threads. Anyway, getting involved in U-space combat seemed a good way to end up dead. So who could he use? Seeing the neatness of knots and closed loops, he focused towards the space port where Matheson was aboard his ship, along with the decapitated Brices and the man-Golem Ricardo. He'd defied predictions by surviving and seemed like a loose thread. The neatness of the narrative didn't escape Straeger.

'I want those,' said Straeger, extruding one glassy tube to indicate the highly mutated cyborg prador.

'They're ours – we've claimed them,' the man objected.

The last of the grav-motors was being attached and Straeger felt the impatient push of entanglement. Within himself, he eased weapons into a state of readiness, only marginally higher than before. Then he checked himself. Was he allowing his frustrations and irritations to influence him like some human? What would result from him killing and thieving here? What causal threads might that open out? Better to acquire what he wanted quietly, for he'd made quite enough noise destroying a Polity dreadnought and didn't want other AIs making connections.

'Name your price,' he said, linking into and rapidly penetrating their com. There were two groups of bounty hunters here, and two Galaxy Bank accounts he found. He made connections to them and then to a series of black ECS accounts he was sure Cormac used, and which he'd been using too.

'A million New Carth shillings each,' said the man.

The others moved away from the two cyborgs and up behind the man. They all had hands near, or on, weapons, but that was just a customary response. They had to be smart enough to realize they had no power here.

'You are being excessive,' said Straeger.

'I don't think so. If a Mobius AI wants these, then their value has to be very high.'

'I will pay you half that.'

'Make it nine hundred thousand . . .'

The negotiation went the expected and customary route to start zeroing in on eight hundred thousand. At the correct juncture, Straeger said, 'I have no time for this. I will pay you eight hundred and fifty thousand each, but you must make yourselves available to the ECS inquiry concerning events here.'

'Okay . . .' said the man, looking warily to one of the others, who tipped her head slightly in agreement.

'Done,' said Straeger. 'Check your accounts.'

The man checked a wrist screen while the woman obviously auged into her account. Judging by their expressions, they were happy with the arrangement.

'The extra is for those grav-motors, which I will need too.' With a thought, he swept the motors from the woman's control and initiated them. The defunct cyborgs abruptly rose a metre from the ground and Straeger began to roll forwards. The hunters quickly got out of his way as he moved in between the two things, snaring up some items that had fallen off – such as a couple of legs – and wedging them into holes in their carapaces.

'Remember, you must keep yourselves available for ECS interrogation,' he said, deliberately choosing 'interrogation' because of its negative connotations. 'I suggest you go to the nearest Line station and make your presence known.' He rose into the air, the cyborgs on either side. The hunters watched him until he was a few kilometres up, and then turned away to head down from the plateau. He knew for certain that 'ECS interrogation' would keep them closed-mouthed about events here, and out of the Polity for a long time to come. And now he had some other bounty hunters to collect, and a weapon to create.

6

Blite

Blite watched the autosurgeon fold away its various implements, cleaning them as it did so, like a cat licking its paws. At the last, it disconnected the nerve shunt from his neck, and feeling returned. This time, unlike many other occasions when he'd been under a surgeon, pain returned too. His body felt battered from head to foot, complemented by an ache that seemed to issue from deep in his bones.

'I have pain,' he complained.

Iris Masarkian Drope grimaced at him from behind the glass of the cleanroom control booth. She'd been one of the first on his list of recruits for this venture, since she was the best human surgeon-doctor he knew. She peered at her screen for a moment and then, in irritation, raised a complex hologram. In this she manipulated things for a short time, before banishing it. She stood, stepped over to the door, then entered the surgery area.

She was a tall, bony woman with a big nose, an intense gaze and black hair tied back. She hadn't bothered with the usual cosmetic enhancements and retained the body she'd been born with, or rather the one she came out of the tank with. For all that, she was still attractive. She wore a loose silky blouse of a silvery green material and tight red jeans. These concealed a lot of her technological augmentations, though he could see the metallic veins down the backs of her hands and running up the sides of her neck to her large twinned crystalline augs, as well as webbed across her skull under her hair. In her eyes he perceived a metallic shifting, like the internal mechanism of an ancient clock. She stepped over to him, with a metallic tongue rising up behind her head. This then opened out into twenty of the same and curved inwards, forming her sensory cowl. Obviously, this haiman woman, part human, part AI, had decided the sensors of the surgery weren't sufficient for her requirements. She stood gazing at him, then nodded. The tongues of her cowl straightened and collapsed back together, retreating into the carapace on her back.

'It's quite simple really,' she said. 'You became excessively physically active before your enhancements had established them-selves. You fucked yourself up, and though I've repaired most of the damage, the ongoing adjustments are struggling to get back on track.'

'But the pain?' said Blite.

'Take a pill.' She shrugged dismissively. 'Or you could try activating that package in your thigh bone,' she added disapprov-ingly, and turned away.

Now he could see her carapace, for the back of her shirt was open. The thing was metallic and its form followed the muscu-lature of her back, though at the sides he could see its engaging legs entering ports that ran down the sides of her body. Ports of various other designs scattered its surface too. He knew the thing had a great deal of processing power, and he'd once asked why it was so damned bulky. She'd told him that the carapace supported the synergy between her mind and the AI crystal in her twinned augs. It provided physical support for her body and the soft matter of her brain, mainly to prevent that organ simply winking out like a blown fuse. A standard haiman answer, but Iris was an anomaly.

Haimen were usually reclusive, or consorted only with their own kind. Because of their abilities, those who didn't were much sought after and usually ended up in charge of major projects for large corporations, or Earth Central itself. Yet here she was, working for a haulage company – his Penny Transport. It had taken Blite aback when she'd agreed to do so, and surprised him further when she agreed to come on this trip. He kept in mind that she'd be a damned sight more useful than just being in charge of Medical.

Grunting annoyance, Blite heaved himself out of the surgical chair. He padded naked over to a nearby fabricator and input an instruction. A second later he was taking out a pair of loose shorts and pulling them on. His combat suit was presently being repaired, while the clothing he'd worn under it had gone into recycling. He'd dress properly later in the room he had here, in this building they'd rented on Abalon from Broden, but right now he wanted to see how the others were doing. Iris stood by the exit door, waiting for him and, as he walked over, opened it and stepped out with him.

A short stretch of corridor, decorated with strange blue pot plants that looked decidedly carnivorous, led them to another door. This opened and a bulky boosted man, dressed in shorts just like Blite's, stepped out.

'Captain,' he said with a nod.

Blite recognized Armand – the man in Carlstone's security detail who'd received fifty per cent first-degree burns, and a couple of fragmentation slugs in his bowel. He looked fine now. Everyone aboard had their supply of printerbot substrate, and Iris had worked on him and the others first, probably with the intent of leaving Blite to contemplate his stupidity.

'All good?' Blite asked.

'I've had worse,' said Armand. He grinned. 'And I haven't had so much fun in a while.' He walked off.

Blite watched him go, understanding that ex-ECS military had a definition of fun slightly divergent from his own. He stepped through the door after Iris. The room had three beds. The other soldier lay on one of them, with all sorts of feed tubes plugged in, while Carlstone sat on the edge of his bed. The soldier, Kostis Raseer, nodded cheerfully.

'I thought him the least injured,' Blite said to Iris.

'Bullet in the spine,' she replied. 'Little bit of slow nerve regrowth and he'll be up and about soon enough.'

Carlstone stood and headed over to them. 'In all, not too bad,' he said.

Blite raised an eyebrow.

'Nobody dead,' Carlstone explained.

'None of ours,' said Blite with a frown.

He now took in the rest of the room. Meander was in another bed, asleep, a scanning array poised above her. Her mouth hung open, and he could see that Iris had fixed her teeth, and her arms now looked smooth and undamaged. Before he could say anything about her, his eyes fell on another occupant. A low pad had been extruded from the wall and on it lay the Rottweiler Greer had brought from the Mortons' place. It had been dying from the pulse gun burns through its chest, though that hadn't stopped the thing attempting to bite off Greer's face when they returned to this temporary base. He could see none of the damage it had received now. The dog also had a thick optic plugged into that expansion of its skull.

'You fixed the fucking dog before me?' he exclaimed.

'Those in the greatest need come first,' Iris told him blandly. 'Also the most deserving.'

'Well, thanks.'

'You weren't about to die, and that creature was only following an enforced program.' She pointed at the dog. 'I'm currently reprogramming it for Greer.'

'So it will be loyal to her?'

'Nope. As per Greer's instructions, I'm taking out all the enforced stuff. It will have a free mind.'

'And a muzzle, one hopes,' said Blite huffily.

He turned away and walked over to Meander's bed. He grimaced down at her, not quite sure why he felt so strongly, nor precisely what he was feeling. Fatherly concern? Or something rather more carnal?

'Why is she still out of it?' he asked.

'This one is a puzzle,' said Carlstone. 'Perhaps a larger part of the puzzle entire than we supposed.'

'What do you mean?'

'Better for Iris to explain,' he said.

Blite turned to her, noting that her sensory cowl was back up and open as she peered down at the woman on the bed.

Iris nodded. 'Fixing her up wasn't too much of a problem. I just had to run in high-spec nutrients and fluids once she dropped into hibernation. I suspect the Mortons discovered this about her, since the lines of old scar tissue, which are fading, run deep.' She stepped over to pull back Meander's lips to further expose her teeth. 'These aren't printed replacements. They grew back within an hour, once she'd had what she needed. Just as her body repaired all the other damage itself.'

'Hibernation?' Blite asked.

'Speeds the process of repair,' said Iris, releasing Meander's lips and turning back to face him.

There was something excited and acquisitive in her expression; Blite didn't like it. He shrugged it off – haiman, go figure. 'I'm not sure what you mean by all this,' he said, feeling a bit stupid, since at his age he really should.

'She's biotech. You only see it this extreme in the Polity, on one or two worlds. I've run pattern matching on the tech and it doesn't match any of them, so she must have come from an out-Polity biotech world.'

Blite accepted this with a nod. That was something he would follow up on later; right now he had more pressing concerns. He asked, 'So why's she still in hibernation? I want to speak to her. I need to know which Mortons instructed her to grab my piece of Penny Royal.'

'Repairs still to make,' Iris replied with a frown.

'That scar tissue?'

'In a sense,' Iris hedged.

Blite looked around at Carlstone. 'Some clarity would be good here.'

Carlstone shrugged. 'She's biotech and capable of massive self-repair. I've been checking with Broden and, from what he says, the Mortons out there are notable sadists. They've had her for years . . .'

'I see.' Blite reviewed his recent orders and actions. He now felt he'd been far too restrained. They should have gone in full force and not bothered with stun shots.

'The repairs,' Iris said as he swung back to her, 'are continuing in her brain. This brings to light another problem when it comes to your questioning her. She's capable of, and actually doing, some self-editing. It might well be that when she wakes up, she'll have no answers for you.'

'Can you wake her up now?'

'I could, but I'm not going to.'

'Why?'

'She's suffered enough, Blite.'

Though he hadn't known Iris long, Blite understood this was the end of the conversation. He wasn't happy about it and felt sure she was holding something else back, but he didn't want the girl to suffer unduly either. He turned to Carlstone. 'Get onto Broden. Find out the best candidates among the Mortons to provide some answers.'

'And then what?' asked Carlstone, his expression turning slightly cruel.

'Then we ask some pertinent questions.'

Cormac

The rock slope became steeper and Cormac transitioned from walking to climbing. When he spotted shapes up in the sky, he dropped down into an old lava channel, concealing himself as best he could. He groped for his thin gun and felt it there, still firmly in its holster. But he withdrew his hand and considered lining up attack programs in his gridlink for Shuriken, wishing he had a heavy particle beam weapon too.

'There they are,' he said, as the shapes descended out of view.

'Heading for your last known location, though they don't have exact coordinates. You need to keep moving and stay hidden,' said Mask.

Cormac peered over the edge. Four of them, just like the corpse he'd tried to transport, had appeared. They flew with their legs folded underneath and their carapaces glinting a metallic sheen – as he'd noted while examining the corpse, they didn't wear separate armour but had incorporated it. He began crawling up the channel. In reality, he stood little chance against them without his abilities. Shuriken might be able to carve off a few legs, and he'd probably be able to take out an eye or two with his thin gun, but getting through that main carapace wouldn't be feasible . . . though there'd be options once his abilities returned. Mask was right: he had to keep hidden until that time came.

He kept going, glad of the tough fabric of his clothing. As he reached the top of the channel, he paused to look down. The four had landed low on the slope and were meandering around down there. He rolled onto his back and checked the compacted supplies around his belt and in various pockets. He had food concentrate and a small medical kit, spare clips for his thin gun and power supply for Shuriken. Also one or two other items to which, he decided, he must add a breather mask. But right now, the most useful items were his clothing. He exposed the small control panel just under the right lapel of his silvery jacket – he really didn't feel up to gridlinking to it – and input instructions. The meta-material engaged its chameleon effect and the coat turned the colour and texture of the surrounding rock. A second later, he saw it establish a link to his trousers and boots, and they likewise camouflaged themselves. He stood and scrambled upwards.

It wasn't perfect concealment, since it only defeated a limited amount of the EMR spectrum, but it seemed this would be enough. After he'd climbed a few hundred metres, he looked back down again and saw the creatures had moved even lower, perhaps thinking he'd tumbled right down. He kept going.

'So what the hell are they?' he asked.

'What the hell are what?' Mask asked distractedly.

'Those creatures down there.'

'Spatterjay-virus mutated prill-prador cyborgs. Since your time, a prador family have risen to dominance with these modifications.'

'And what the hell is the situation here? Is the Polity at war with the prador again?'

'The Polity, as you know it, no longer exists, just as the Prador Kingdom as you knew it is gone. Suffice to say that an enclave of humans is at war with an enclave of prador. And that will have to do, until I calculate just how much I can tell you.'

'Why?'

'Because causal threads have already been overstrained. Time travel is still as dangerous as it ever was, Ian Cormac.'

Cormac let it drop for now, since he was running out of breath to talk. Soon he reached a slope he could stand up on, and he managed to run up it. All around, he could see further signs of warfare: glassy spills from beam strikes, and a moment later he entered a similarly glassy crater which looked as if something had taken a chunk out of the mountain with a giant ice-cream scoop. He paused there to get his breath, since he was now completely out of sight of those things below. He checked his condition. A lot of his aches and pains had receded, his nanosuite having repaired and cleared damage in his brain and body. He tried his gridlink and it fired up. All its usual disconnected functions were available, including his ability to crunch U-space data. The normal outside connections weren't there, obviously, but, searching for outside signals, he did get a series of complex icons that made his head ache again. They were four, and maybe five dimensional; looking at them felt like gazing into the holes and twists of U-space.

'I have possible gridlink connections,' he stated, moving carefully up the slippery side of the crater.

'Connect to this one, none of the others,' Mask replied.

One of the icons shivered, jumped and flashed bright green, shot through with rainbows. It was a thing like an organic sensory manifold, stretched into a line in one part of his perception, this being time, and curved into a spiral in another. He mentally reached for it and the thing opened in his skull. The impact of the data felt physical, and he found himself falling, then sliding, back down into the crater. Some data came clear – stuff that gave him a local 3D map – but even that strayed into other dimensions. It was all too much to parse and he felt himself retreating from it, shoving in security and simple blocks. After a few seconds, bandwidths tightened, limiting his access. He briefly glimpsed a schematic and function data on the mask he wore. But then the one either in it, or communicating through it, took that away too. From the remaining connection he could demand nothing, only receive what Mask chose to send.

'Sorry about that,' said Mask. 'I forgot your limitations.'

Cormac stood and climbed up the side of the crater again.

'Bullshit. If you're as advanced as you'd like me to believe, you wouldn't have forgotten. And being sufficiently advanced, you wouldn't have had the urge to show off.'

'You got me,' said Mask, which immediately made Cormac think that he hadn't. 'This is where you need to go – lots of hiding places there.'

He received a section of the 3D map with his location indicated on it, as well as the positions of the four prill-prador. Out of the crater he took the shortest route and, just twenty minutes later, reached a point where the mountain had been burned through with beam strikes, bearing the appearance of worm-eaten wood. He entered one of these arrow-straight caves, out of the bottom of which water trickled.

'The beam strikes punched through to cave systems. I suggest you go deep and find places where access for our friends outside will be difficult.'

Cormac squatted by the stream. It looked completely clear but, still, he took a toximeter from a belt pouch and tested it. The stuff was potable, so he drank, scooping it up into his mouth. After the first drink, he abruptly realized he'd been breathing

151

through his mouth and it lay open to the air. Feeling the edges of the mask, there he found swiftly vibrating cilia. Somehow it was cleaning the air and adding oxygen. When he stooped to put his mouth straight into the water, he could feel the cilia beating faster, and the mask grew cool against his skin. It had decided to take a drink too.

'I don't know what—' he began, standing up.

Fast movement. Danger. His thin gun was in his hand in an eyeblink, identification made, and he fired three shots. The first-stage sleer – a thing vaguely resembling a fifty-kilogram scorpion – nosedived halfway through its run at him, three smoking holes in its head, and smoke rising behind where the shots had penetrated right into its body.

'The fuck,' he said.

'Perhaps I should also have mentioned the caves are occupied,' Mask allowed.

Matheson

Matheson observed the plethora of ships gathered around Cull. The essentials of U-space travel were bolt-ons: the U-space drive and its controlling intelligence, which, as many now well knew, did not require some high-functioning Polity AI. This meant that, with enough wealth, a person could haul anything sufficiently atmosphere-sealed between star systems. That accounted for the presence here of what Matheson recognized as an old touring submarine out of Carth. Other ships were interesting to him too, like one that appeared to be half of an old ECS dreadnought, and another consisting of two cargo barges linked to form something like a catamaran. Then there was another vessel that seemed to have no antecedents. The thing bore the appearance of an asymmetric crab claw holding something bright and complex within its grip and showed no sign of exterior U-space nacelles. It looked far too expensive and shiny to belong to bounty hunters like the rest. Perhaps it was a pleasure yacht, belonging to some rich tourist out of the Polity come for the show. Matheson scowled at the idea as he put his ship into a steady orbit about Cull.

He had some things to think about and deal with. Now installed at last in his chair in the bridge, he eyed the cam feed from the hold space and wondered if he was being stupid capturing Ricardo like this, just for some payback. His encounter with Crane had raised second thoughts about his aims here, just as it had given him a healthy respect for how tough Golem could be. Shortly after their ship launched from Cull, Ricardo had managed to move a short distance under the clamp, so Matheson had gone down there again. While Ricardo tried to persuade him to release him, and promised he wouldn't do anything, Matheson had moved all the weapons out of the hold. He'd then brought in a deposition welder, stripped syntheflesh off Ricardo's legs and welded them to the lower platen. An attempt to do the same on the other side had nearly put him in the reach of the man-Golem's arm, whose joints had a range of motion beyond human. Ricardo had apologized profusely for trying to grab him, and Matheson had left, welding the hold door shut behind him.

Keeping Ricardo aboard was a severe danger. The man in the machine was a coward but, as Matheson had discovered over his years of bounty hunting, that often made someone more dangerous. Now, sitting in orbit off Cull, he checked ship's systems and discovered that, yes, in the event of contamination, a hold space could be ejected from the ship. Ensuring all of that was in operation, and then setting an aug subprogram to keep watch for any further activity from Ricardo, he finally felt some of the tension seeping out of him. Now it was time to deal with the next thing.

Numerous messages awaited his attention. All the bounty alerts he shuffled over into storage without having much interest in them. Some links might be worthwhile investigating, as they came from other bounty hunters who were still here. Recognizing one, he opened up contact and a frame appeared in the screen ahead of him.

'Hey, Andre,' he said.

A holding delay ensued, followed by a routing protocol. Investigating that, he saw that Jessikon Andrew's ship was down in the space port, while he himself was out in the wilds. A picture of the brute of the man filled in over a background displaying the plateau and Crane's burning house.

'Matheson,' said Andre as his image updated to real time. 'You're alive.'

'Fortunately,' Matheson replied.

'What the hell happened?'

Matheson considered keeping the information to himself but could see no advantage in doing so. Speaking tersely, he detailed his hunt for Crane and how disastrously it went wrong. Andre nodded along with the commentary and, since the imagery showed him head to foot, Matheson could see the man pulling pieces of podule leaves and inserting them into a hand-held test unit.

'Pretty much what I thought,' said Andre, 'which is why I only ran supply here, and why I cut my ties when the others went after that ship.'

'Too many hunters have failed,' Matheson agreed flatly.

'More importantly, even ECS backed off here. I've seen what's in that pass, and up at the top there. Anything that can take out a Mobius AI, and has allies like Arach and Ian Cormac, is not

to be trifled with. Add in those weird prador-things and . . .'
Andre shrugged.

'What's this about a ship?'

'You've been out of the loop. Imagery from up there shows
Crane and Arach boarding a cargo ship which landed on the
plain – big-fuck hauler. It took off and an alliance of hunters
went after it. Lot of confusion about how they actually got to
the ship too.'

'And those things that attacked Crane – what happened to
them?' Matheson asked.

'Two crews allied down here and grabbed the remains to maybe
sell them off. There's some odd technology in them that might
have value. Then things got a bit strange when a Mobius AI
rolled up and paid megabucks for them.'

'Fuck,' said Matheson.

'What're you going to do now?'

'Some things to resolve. I'm not really sure.' As the conversation meandered to a close, Matheson realized that his long-time
aim to collect the bounty on Crane seemed to have transformed.
It had lost emotional weight and dropped to the level of spectator
curiosity. Annoyingly, he was beginning to have some empathy
with Ricardo; that just wouldn't do. Leaving Andre to check that
podule crop, he turned his attention to another comlink request
– despite him shutting it down earlier, it kept coming back up.
In irritation he snapped the thing open, ready to shout down
this impertinent interloper.

'Virtual,' said a voice at once.

'Who the fuck are you and do you think I'm stupid?' Matheson
replied.

'It wasn't a request,' the voice informed him.

Matheson felt a surge of panic and went to shut down the
link but wasn't fast enough. The bandwidth snapped open from

voice-only to virtuality and beyond. He saw a whole host of out-parameter and overload warnings as he fell into a grey base-format virtuality. It wasn't full immersion: he retained his perception of his real surroundings and the one current auglink showing him the cam feed on Ricardo. Within the grey depthless space, Matheson appeared as a stock representation, slightly younger, in much-repaired combat gear and with a face that never reflected what he was actually thinking. Ahead of him appeared something inchoate – almost like a planetoid swirling with cloud. Virtualities were supposedly intended to give a greater breadth of communication that could cover all the senses. People used them so they could seemingly see and be with whoever they were talking to. But he now understood that wasn't the purpose of this one, as he attempted to raise a hand, in his captain's chair, to shut down his aug manually, but found he was paralysed.

'Who the hell are you?' he asked again, speaking in the virtu-ality but unable to do so in reality. It was a place-holder question, because he had a damned good idea what he was dealing with.

'You are not unintelligent, for a human, and have the required data from your conversation with Jessikon Andrew,' the interloper replied.

'What do you want to know?' Matheson asked, hoping that information was the only requirement here.

'There are many things I want to know, but very few I need to know,' the interloper replied. 'You failed to collect the bounty on Mr Crane.'

'Failure presupposes a time constraint.'

'Tell me, in detail, what happened down there.'

'If you listened in on me and Andre, you already know.'

'Very well,' said the thing before him. 'So, presuming you are still intent on hunting down and capturing Crane, who killed your father, what will be your approach now?'

'It just needs some rethinking,' Matheson hedged, while pushing at his invisible bonds. He found himself able to tilt his head slightly to see his hand on the arm of his chair, and there slightly raise one forefinger.

'And have you done any of that?'

He hadn't really, but he spoke off the cuff, in the hope that it would keep his captor distracted. 'Crane seems immune to disruptor shells. He's got chameleonware too, and is probably faster and tougher than late-series Golem. Maybe the rumours are true about some alien tech inside him. I need an edge.'

'You had edges, apparently.'

Matheson pushed with his mind and body. The paralysis had to be due to a feedback overload into cranial nerves, since it was slowly dying away. Anyway, that was as much as he knew about the way it could be done through an aug. The lock on his ability to control anything else via the aug was a programming thing – some kind of comlife inserted like a virus. He just needed to be able to move so he could manually shut the damned thing down. He finally replied, 'My Golem betrayed me, while spider drones are common – how the hell was I supposed to know Nightshade was *that* spider drone?'

'You mean Arach, companion of the Brass Man, Mr Crane, and the Polity agent Ian Cormac?'

'Those were just fucking stories!' He could move two fingers now and slightly raise his hand.

'Stories are useful. When real events become "just a fucking story" they lose their power. People who consider themselves intelligent laugh wisely at them, because of course they know how things *really* work.'

Momentarily distracted from his efforts, Matheson just stared at the thing hovering before him. He'd known about the virtuality fictions from when they first appeared in his youth. He'd only ever experienced one of them before, abandoning it in distaste upon finding he couldn't convincingly alter the narrative so that he managed to destroy Crane. He'd felt sure the things had arisen from some creator who, having heard about Crane, just incorporated him in some common super-agent fiction. But now things began to click home in his mind, and he understood that if he'd accepted those fictions to be true, he would never have come here expecting to bring down the Brass Man with conventional weapons, even advanced as they had been. That was all irrelevant now, and not as important as discovering he could slightly raise his forearm and had just regained some aug control.

'Okay,' he said. 'Then I need other edges.'

Putting together the instruction was painfully slow; before, it had always been autonomous. The main screen shuffled through numerous frames, then discarded all but one, showing the only ship altering its orbital trajectory out there – the one like a metallic crab claw. Interpreting the data from what was falling into his aug was slow too, but soon enough he saw this ship was heading his way.

Matheson continued, 'I'll be heading to a place I know, to have the Brices fleshed up again, and where I can maybe get hold of something . . . effective.'

'Like what?' the interloper enquired.

'Disruptor shells don't have the power or the duration, but if I could nail Crane with a vortex laser . . . lock him with an informational warfare beam.' Plenty of bullshit ideas were available, all beyond his scope or his inclination now, but it was nice to fantasize and throw that fantasy at the thing before him. 'We could then hit him with an imploder . . . it would have to be a tactical version . . . semi-imploder, since without any remains we won't be able to claim the reward.'

'This is very interesting, and something we will discuss face-to-face,' the interloper informed him.

There it was. The whole conversation was a place-holder.

'I don't think we need to discuss things face-to-face,' he said, still watching the other ship approach. It seemed that the confirmation of physical confrontation fed energy into his fight. He lifted his forearm higher, hand quivering as if he was trying to raise it under heavy-gee acceleration.

'I think it is a very good idea,' said the interloper. 'You see, it occurs to me that you are having second thoughts about going after Crane, and suffering the illusion of choice.'

Raising his elbow was the hardest battle, and he could hardly believe it when he finally got his fingers to his aug. Resting his forefinger on the small button, he suffered a surge of anxiety, feeling sure that so simple an intervention couldn't work. He pressed the button.

The virtuality winked out of existence and local reality crashed back into him. The fact he suddenly felt no restriction on his movement showed him that he'd been wrong about the paralysing overload. Something more sophisticated had been used, which was unsurprising, since he was now sure what had deployed it. Now, sans aug control, he flipped open a console on the arm of his control throne. He worked touch and texture controls to bring up the weapons manifest, as if to assure himself he still had access to his ship's selection of missiles and beam weapons. They were just a desperate option. Right now he needed to get the hell out of the Cull system.

'And it occurs to me,' said the voice from that virtuality, now hissing close to his left ear, 'that you may not willingly accept the edges I have come to give you.'

Matheson froze, something frigid scuttling up his spine.

'Fuck,' he said.

Matheson closed his eyes and sighed out a breath. Something was fizzing behind him like static over com and a feeling, like one got standing too close to a hardfield, was raising the hairs on the back of his neck. He wished he hadn't abandoned his armour. He wished he had weapons to hand. But he also wondered whether any of them would have been in anyway effective. Despite all his security, someone had managed to get aboard his ship and creep up behind him. Opening his eyes, he stood up and stretched, fixed a nonchalant smile on his face, and turned. Any attempt at a casual, dismissive attitude died with confirmation of what he'd suspected since the thing had pushed into his aug.

No, not *someone*.

The thing had been described as resembling a terran sea creature called a crinoid, but also like the head of a dandelion. Both descriptions meant little to Matheson – to him it was precisely what it was: the mobile body of a Mobius AI. The spherical machine, or organism, or whatever, stretched over two metres across. Its fronds, tentacles and tendrils spread out from a central point to create the sphere. These consisted of glassy tubes, flat ribbons, threads and fronds of various colours. Scattered throughout were nodules, inflating into being and deflating out of existence. The thing was in constant motion and seemed to be swimming in electrostatic energy and field interfaces. The sound of static, he realized, did echo that of the sea, so perhaps this accounted for the first description – like waves hissing on a shingle beach.

'Well, this is a surprise,' he said.

He reviewed his history and winced at all the bad things he'd done, and thought got away with. There wasn't a crime on the books he hadn't committed. Most had been outside Polity jurisdiction, but enough had been within it for him to have a healthy tendency to avoid going anywhere within the grasp of ECS. He eyed all those tendrils and extrusions, horribly aware of the capabilities of the thing before him. Just like earlier forensic AIs, it could take him apart and inspect him physically down to the nanoscopic level, and mentally to extract every detail of his life. And, as he had heard, there might not be any anaesthetic involved. He felt like a murderer brought before a hanging judge.

'Come with me,' said the AI.

Matheson frantically riffled through his options. Maybe if he ran he could make it to a spacesuit and eject out into vacuum, then persuade one of the other bounty hunters to pick him up? No, he couldn't outrun this thing – it was as inevitable as fate. Or maybe, if he got to a weapon, he could . . . the thought died there as he realized the only sensible option in that scenario would be to put the weapon in his mouth, direct it towards where his memplant lay in his cortex and hold the trigger firmly down. Just then the ship shuddered and he knew that the approaching vessel had docked.

The AI rolled towards the doorway to the rear of the bridge – it had opened without Matheson hearing. With a sizzling, the thing crammed into the narrow corridor beyond, filling it from wall to wall and ceiling to floor. No way past. He took a hesitant step after it, then halted. He suddenly became angry. Yes, the situation was a shitty one, but he was damned if he was going to track around after the AI like an obedient dog.

'What the hell do you want?' he asked.

'I want the inception-point nodal event to occur, and I want to be able to track the threads with more precision. I probably want it in an infinite number of timelines. But more important to you is what do you want, Matheson?'

161

He had no idea what that first bit meant and just dismissed it, since he couldn't hope to understand the workings of an intelligence like this. He focused on the second.

'I want to survive,' he replied.

'Of course you do, and the way for that to happen is for you to do what I tell you to. Come with me.'

'What's your name?'

'Straeger,' the AI replied.

Matheson walked after the thing, pondering on that name and feeling a sinking sensation in his guts. Straeger was one of the older ones, with a nasty reputation. He didn't know much more than that about it. Then, because it no longer mattered, he reached up to turn on his aug. A moment later he accessed data on this Straeger. The thing had worked for ECS but, like a lot of its kind, seemed to have gone its own way. The data showed him it had been involved in bringing down various criminal operations, but beyond that all he got was stories and unconfirmed rumours. What did surprise him was that ECS had recently posted a reward for any information concerning this AI. It seemed it might not be the paragon of lethal virtue he'd supposed. He didn't know whether that was better or worse for him.

The AI slid into the spiral stairs and went down. Matheson kept a good few paces back – any closer than two or three metres and his skin started crawling. Down in the volume of the hold, it expanded out and took the wider tunnel towards one section of the space, finally rolling to a stop before the door Matheson had welded shut just a few hours ago. The thing extruded one of those glassy tubes and tracked around the door over the deposition weld, a shimmering light glowing at the point of contact, and the weld disappearing. The door thumped up on its seal and swung open, Straeger deforming and sliding around it into the hold. Matheson suddenly realized something: the thing was now in a hold he'd made preparations to eject!

He stood at the doorway and auged to the ship's system, checking. Yes, he could send the order right now and blow this hold out into space, but thereafter things would become problematic. He was standing right next to it and would end up out in vacuum too. Even if there was some way to prevent that, he would have achieved little. Creatures like the thing ahead of him were as at home in vacuum as anywhere, and it would just come rolling back to him, while his chances of a rapid departure had already been shut down by the ship that had docked. He hated it – feeling this powerless and the necessity of being this realistic. He did nothing and stepped into the hold.

By the time he'd entered, the AI had already opened the clamp and was in the process of debonding Ricardo's legs from the lower platen. The thing also had tendrils running into the man-Golem's chest which, even as he sat upright, expanded with a crackling sound back to its customary thickness. Ricardo turned his head, further than any human could turn it, and gazed at Matheson. With the AI withdrawing, he stood up and walked around the clamp. Matheson held his position. Fucked if he knew what was supposed to happen here, but he knew what he'd do if he were the Golem. Ricardo came towards him, but just reached out a hand and pushed him aside, before heading off into the rest of the ship.

'I hadn't decided what to do with him yet,' said Matheson.

Straeger just rolled over and through the clamp, crossing the hold. Matheson quickly moved out of the way.

'Come with me,' it said.

Matheson watched it heading for the central stairs, knowing that the longer he didn't do something, the deeper in he would be. But again, what the hell could he do? Standard Polity AIs were dangerous enough, but these things were as inescapable as fate. They had all the tools of a forensic AI, the tools too of a war drone, and they were mobile in any environment. He realized, in retrospect, that it had probably known about his ability to eject the hold and correctly predicted that he wouldn't. He was now the plaything of a god . . . or a demon.

He trudged after the thing, up the stairs, into the workshop and medical area of the ship, and through to the equatorial airlock where the other ship had docked. As they reached the open airlock, he heard a sound behind and looked back to see Ricardo. The man-Golem had retrieved a pack which was shedding cold vapour because it had come from a freezer. It seemed the Brices would be accompanying them aboard.

The airlock on the other side was a standard enough affair, with an adjusted portal to bring it down to the human-sized one of his own ship, but beyond it things became non-standard quickly. The tunnel was just a little bit wider than the breadth of Straeger, highly polished, and had no flat floor. The moment he stepped into it he was in zero gravity. He propelled himself after the AI, with hands and feet thankfully finding the walls weren't slick. Occasionally he caught hold of the edge to a circular or oval gap, and through these saw something of the ship's interior. Its machines were there, bound in webs of organic-looking girders, optics and s-con power threads. It looked somehow incomplete, and Matheson didn't understand why until he saw the back end of a railgun feed. It had no casings, and all of its working mechanisms were exposed. This made sense. Human ships restricted access to their workings for safety, atmosphere integrity and to prevent easy interference with delicate or dangerous technology. This was the ship for an AI that was the core of the machine and could tinker at will, knowing precisely what it was doing, and needing no protection. Quite likely he was able to breathe now because Straeger had contained air in this tube, which usually wouldn't have been the case.

They finally came out into an open area in the ship's structure. Through gaps all around, he could see other tubes worming between those webs and machines, but mostly his view was blocked by an accumulation of technology here. He recognized the tools of a high-tech laboratory and manufactory linked into some seemingly chaotic system. He could identify nanoscopes and nanofactories, a series of chain-glass cylinders that looked like regrowth tanks, with all their surrounding paraphernalia. Then his gaze fell on objects hanging in polymer bands, like insects caught in a spider's web. At once he saw they were two of the things that had attacked Mr Crane, along with what looked to be various pieces of the same.

'Why am I here?' he asked, catching hold of one of the web girders, which looked like a metallic bone.

Straeger extruded one of its glassy tubes and, though there was nothing human about the thing, he had the sense the AI was pointing. He turned to look at what it wanted him to see, and there watched Ricardo. The man-Golem was over at a wall of folded manipulators, clinging to a stanchion with one foot now operating like a hand, and taking one frozen head out of the pack. He held it up – it looked like Ulnar Brice – and a ten-fingered hand folded out, plucking it from his grasp. The head tracked through machinery, skin and flesh peeling away, and a trepanning tool going in to remove a chunk of skull. Matheson just glimpsed the memplant being extracted as the head moved on and Ricardo fed in the rest.

'I have a general-purpose cell substrate,' said Straeger. 'Their own DNA will prime it, essentially inoculating it so it converts to their pattern. Their brain matter can be mostly repaired and memories reinstalled from their memplants, and with the further adjustments all of that is negotiable.'

'Their memplants?' Matheson asked.

'I'll keep them here on my ship and connected as backups. They'll be a useful resource if I have to remake them again.'

Matheson saw three grey tubes retract out of sight to leave their contents behind: three headless skeletons nested in tubes and wires. Peering closer, he saw that the bones had a nacreous glitter and recognized a biotech fix. The bones were made of a substance similar to oyster shell and very tough. He watched as skinless skulls were popped into place, saw them disappear under thimble-like protuberances and heard the burring of a bone welder. But obviously there was more involved, because when the thimbles retracted, the skulls became lost in nests of fibres that looked like some part of the Mobius AI itself. Some tension sighed out of him. He understood, though it seemed as non-standard as the contents of this ship: the AI was resurrecting his comrades. Next, coming down from the head end on each skeleton were doughnut matter printers, humming into life. Matheson turned from that and faced the AI.

'I heard you acquired those from the planet,' he said, pointing to the prador-things hanging in their web. Even as he did this, he saw activity there too. Things that looked like mechanical lampreys were hoovering over their surfaces, with intense, painfully bright light at their contact points. He turned away, but could see grooves of their paths as they etched away the metal.

'I retrieved two of them and they have provided much data,' Straeger replied. 'It seems their armour enables the creatures to jump through time in U-space, without having a major fusion-reactor power source, energy shielding or drive-created U-fields.'

'Right . . .'

Straeger continued. 'The advanced version of the Spatterjay

virus within them toughened up their organics, probably to the limit of what is possible, but it is the reactive alloy that does most of the shielding. Organic creatures, even if they have a way to make the calculations and initiate a U-field, should simply be torn apart in that continuum, which begs the question of how he manages to do it. This is a source of considerable puzzlement and irritation to many AIs, including me.'

'Who?'

'Ian Cormac.'

'What?'

'Since it was Mr Crane, the Brass Man, who killed your father, you presumably know who I am referring to.'

'So that's real?'

'Mostly.'

As he absorbed this, Matheson just felt like laughing. To his cost, he'd discovered that Crane was as depicted in the fictions, and that the war drone Arach existed too. So why not the super-agent who could jump through U-space and punish AIs that strayed from the path of virtue? Why not anything, really, since it seemed he'd stepped into one of those fictional virtualities, and all the rules of reality were rapidly departing through the airlock? He turned and looked over to Ricardo and the Brices. The man-Golem was just hanging in place, still holding the pack he'd brought the heads in. Matheson suspected Straeger had done something to him – had control over him – because the Ricardo he knew would have been asking questions and trying to negotiate his way out of this. Meanwhile, the Brices had undergone their first bio-printing pass, and now the skeletons were glistening. He could see precursor organ structures in there, membranes and veins, and some musculature. Something about all of it didn't look right, yet he didn't see it until the printer doughnuts were halfway back up them and more had been deposited. There seemed to be a great deal of fibrous stuff in there, mobile by itself, writhing and growing.

'Fascinating,' said Straeger.

'What the fuck is that?' Matheson asked.

'It's the Spatterjay virus, but a more advanced form than you will find anywhere in our time, though I understand the prador have been tinkering with it for a while. Depending on the suppressants they use, the native version takes decades to establish itself in a human being. That is to say, it takes decades to establish itself if the human is to remain a human being. This version is highly programmable, and its growth rate is phenomenal – it's growing faster than my printers can lay down tissue.'

'You're turning them into hoopers!'

'As I said, some toughening of the organics is required to enable the U-jumps.'

The relief he'd felt waned, but it didn't go away completely, because at least it wasn't him there under those printers. He wasn't stupid. He wondered if somehow, in its twisted morality, the AI felt it could do what it was doing because the Brices were themselves on a wanted list. Or did it simply consider humans as disposable biological mechanisms to use at its will? But of course, in these thoughts, he was anthropomorphizing. He, the human, had more akin to the crinoid this Straeger resembled than the AI had to him.

'How will they jump in U-space?' he asked.

'I can't copy what he does, because I'm not even sure what it is and how he does it. But I can create a reasonable facsimile. The jump-field technology is too large to fit in just one human body, so must be distributed across you all and controlled by one mind.'

'Controlled by one mind,' Matheson repeated, turning again to look at the AI as if he could somehow read it just like a person. He noted that a structure had appeared within it – a small dome of intricate crystal valence electronics, bound together in an s-con grid.

'Indeed.'

'I've never seen a U–space engine smaller than a car,' he said, desperately now because he had some visceral hint of what was coming.

'You would be utterly surprised about what ECS research has been coming up with for decades, and failing to contain.' Straeger paused contemplatively. 'The drive is mostly in the armouring, which will have to be at the biological integration level, while certain other adjustments will need to be made too.'

Matheson got it then. He pushed himself roughly away from his hold, heading for the exit from this place. Rationally he knew escape was impossible, but he couldn't deny his instinct. He bounced off one of the chain-glass cylinders, hit a stanchion and hurled himself onwards. In a glance, he saw Straeger still in place, but something else was on the move. That something hit him hard, adamantine hands closing on one leg and one arm. The face of Ricardo looked up at him and showed eyes that were blank and metallic.

Struggle was futile, but struggle he did as he fell into the light and fibrous body of the AI. A burning sensation ensued as threads began to penetrate his skin. He saw his clothing and Ricardo flung away, like so much detritus not useful in the coming task. The pain increased to unbelievable agony, but he couldn't scream, and some larger perception fell on him, as though he was gazing through the AI's senses. He saw himself peeled open, down to muscle and bone in an instant. His skull broke into segments, spreading out to orbit his bare brain, while his eyes hung out, tethered by optic nerves. The object Straeger held went down onto the soft matter and sank there. Rational thought began to flee, yet, in those last moments, he understood he was being weaponized like the Brices. And though it seemed events on Cull had been all about Crane, the target for which they were being remade was Ian Cormac. He also perfectly understood that, though advanced and beyond him as far as any AI could be, Straeger was also cruel.

7

May's first thought of *I feel like shit* was swiftly capped with *I'm alive*. Without moving, because she knew that would hurt, she checked out the situation through her aug, first linking to damage reports. The particle beam had missed its first shot as the subsidiaries kicked in. The second shot had touched just as the *Bracken* U-jumped away from Cull. A channel a metre wide traversed the ship from front to back, penetrating deep enough to have opened the forward section to vacuum. The brief explosive decompression before they dropped into U-space had elicited a response from the safety systems. It now appeared that hard bulkhead doors had slammed into place, and some areas had filled with breach foam. Her cabin, Akanthor's cabin, and an unoccupied one were no longer available. She grimaced, but then dismissed the matter. Personal items she wanted to retain would still be in there, buried in the foam, and there were other cabins she could use. Of much more concern was one of the U-space nacelles.

This item, protruding from the ship just ahead of the frame which held the subsidiaries, had also been briefly touched by the particle beam. It was giving an unfamiliar readout, and frankly she had no idea what that meant. When they finally surfaced

171

back into the real, would the ship arrive there turned inside out? Or it might mean nothing at all.

Now she checked things through internal cams. On the bridge, Akanthor was up and on the move, walking towards the exit like someone with the worst hangover. Davidson still sat in his chair, fingers up against his aug and no doubt looking at the same damage she'd seen. She then did a double take: Akanthor was heading towards the door across an area of floor previously occupied by a large spider drone; Mr Crane had gone missing too. She scanned through the ship. They weren't in any of the remaining twelve living compartments, or anywhere in that area. She scanned further back to the engineering and factory section. Here, with a variety of machines, they could turn out various components for ship repair, and much besides. She found Crane standing next to a printerbot making something, while Arach was further back, towing a sled-load of equipment towards one of the larger airlocks. The load included one mobile hull-repair printerbot and a stack of composite plates.

May gaped. The idea of going outside while the ship was passing through U-space elicited a thrill of horror, but then she reconsidered. Out there, the spider drone would still be encompassed by the ship's U-field, since it extended at least three metres from the hull, and wouldn't suffer the effects a human would have. Obviously, these two had been unaffected by the massive acceleration of the subsidiaries, and the ensuing drop into U-space, and had got straight to work. The time had come for her to get to work too.

May opened her eyes, meanwhile sending the instruction for the chair to unfold from its protective grip. The moment it released her, she felt her bones and muscles creaking and aching, and stabs of pain throughout. Linked to her nanosuite, her aug delivered its diagnosis. She'd received her lumps, but they would pass soon enough. Right now she wanted to see exactly what Crane was up to. She didn't need to check on Arach, since it seemed obvious the drone was heading out to repair the damage from the particle beam.

'Always a delight,' she said out loud, pushing herself out of her chair and standing.

'Ain't it just,' Davidson replied. 'You've seen what Arach is busy with?'

'Yes, but now I want to see what the other one is doing.'

'Tried a penetration of the printerbot,' Davidson replied, 'but I'm locked out of programming I don't recognize. It's not just the bot either. Fabricators and gross materials machining is going on down there.'

'You want to come with me to see?'

Davidson shook his head and pointed down at his leg. 'Not right now. I think next time we do a refit my chair is going to need some work. Broke my damned shin bone.'

'You get injury fees for that,' said May, forcing cheerfulness.

'I think we'll all be collecting on that by the time this is over,' Davidson said dryly. 'Presupposing we're able to collect.'

May smiled, shrugged and headed to the door.

'Oh, captain,' said Davidson. 'Why did you choose those coordinates?'

'I didn't,' she replied. 'I don't even know where they are.'

'Realspace position is not in any known system. It's interstellar – nothing there.'

May shrugged again and headed out of the bridge. Were they on course to catch up with Blite or somehow to intercept Cormac? She had no idea and, oddly, the tension of not knowing seemed fine.

When she finally arrived in the manufacturing section of Engineering, she found Crane away from the printerbot and sitting on the floor, surrounded by numerous components. He looked up at her briefly then continued his chore: assembling something, the parts of which she knew she'd never have been able to pick up even in standard gravity.

'What are you making?' she asked, although she expected no answer.

Crane continued constructing the thing, pushing together printed or machined components with solid clicks, occasionally picking up a deposition welder to fix something. She noted some of their supply of superconductor going into a long tube with the iridescent shine of meta-material inside. She noticed feed tubes running to a chamber at the rear, and for a moment she thought the Golem must be making some form of thruster. The thing lay three metres long, and bulked out a metre thick as a final section began to go into place. Now she had an intimation of what it really was, and walked over to one of the nanofactories busily producing something that was going into a series of large storage cylinders. Checking its screen, she saw code in a language she simply didn't recognize. She turned back to Crane, pointing to one of the cylinders.

'Particulate?' she asked.

He acknowledged this with a dip of his head.

May turned away and headed off to one of the available cabins. She wanted a shower and a change of clothes, while she pondered on just what sort of particle cannon Crane was making, and what its necessity might mean for her ship in the near future.

Blite

Blite felt better, a lot, lot better, but he had still put the body frame back on. Iris had been adamant about that, and he really didn't want her getting tetchy when he might need her. As he and Broden strolled along the pavement of Abalon's capital, apparently dressed casually, he gazed up at the tower block. It stood forty floors tall, with a dropshaft running up the centre. Broden and Carlstone had negated the idea of using that, since the Mortons, once they became aware their territory was being invaded, might turn it off while Blite, Carlstone, Greer and the twenty mercenaries Broden had recruited were in transit. They'd take the stairs.

'Tell me again about the people in here,' he said.

'Mortons and their employees,' said Broden tightly.

The outlinker's suit, now concealed under a long coat, was a heavier version than before and he carried a stubby, mean-looking multigun strapped to his side. The twenty mercenaries, randomly converging on the area, bore similar armament, as did Blite. The weapons had multiple options, including a variety of stun settings. Though he'd revised his opinions about the Mortons, Blite still couldn't rid himself of the idea that just killing anyone who got in their way was wrong. Broden wasn't so reserved.

'And any employee of the Mortons knows exactly what they're all about,' Broden added. 'Anything they are doing here facilitates their criminal operations, even if it involves legitimate businesses. These people have been a thorn in the side of this world for too long.' He patted the weapon under his coat. 'As I suggested: just stomp them.'

Blite shook his head. 'We stun until they reply with lethal armament.'

'Good way to get some of our people killed,' said Broden disapprovingly.

'We're better than them,' said Blite, but now he questioned his decision. He knew he wouldn't die in there. Even if a nuclear warhead took this place out while he was inside, he'd end up back at the point before he even entered, time and time again.

'You in position?' he asked over com.

'We are,' replied Kostis, now fully recovered from the bullet in his spine.

Blite glanced at Broden, then down the street to where Carlstone loitered. The others were appearing from different streets, casually sauntering in this direction. It was time.

'Okay,' he said, 'let's do this.'

Broden stepped off the pavement onto the groundcar road and Blite came after him. On the opposite side of the road, they moved along towards the entry portico. This had the appearance of a series of stone arches supporting a solar-tile roof.

'Concentrating your security in one place tends to leave weaknesses elsewhere,' Broden had said earlier.

The entry portico contained a sub-AI security drone, and other weaponry in the arches leading up to the double doors. Those doors looked like heavy old wood but were actually ceramal, while the glass panes in them were chain-glass. Through them Blite glimpsed the lobby – there were some people sitting or moving about behind a counter, and a scattering of security guards. He and Broden walked straight past, with others now heading towards them, all converging on a point where the tall windows, inset in thick apparently stone walls, overlooked the street.

'And their security is designed with local threats in mind, which has left one big gaping hole there: chain-glass,' had been another of Broden's earlier observations.

It appeared that Broden, while gathering information for Blite and learning how the Mortons operated, had acquired a huge antipathy towards them. It was only as they'd been planning this operation that Blite had realized the man must have been formulating ways to take the Mortons down for a while. A piece of technology that would help them towards that end now sat in Blite's pocket. Five other such items also sat in the pockets of those who were, even now, drawing opposite the tall windows, and loitering. One of them was Greer, her axe turned the other way up to conceal it under her heavy coat, her new pet pacing along beside her. Blite grimaced. He hadn't been too happy about that idea, but Greer had assured him that she and Groff had had a long talk and the Rottweiler would be a useful addition.

Coming opposite his designated window, Blite took the round flat object, much like an ancient makeup compact, out of his pocket. He leaned towards the window and, directly through it, saw a boosted man in armoured uniform peering out at him. Too late to wait now: having seen him lean in, the others were doing the same. He smiled at the man and slapped the decoder against the glass. The thing stuck as he took his hand away, and then thumped. The chain-glass turned white as the decoder implanted the key to unravel its chain molecules, collapsing it all to dust. Blite stepped back, drawing his gas-system pulse gun, but with a crackling sound, shots snapped past him, taking the guard in the chest before he could. The man staggered back, pieces of his armour splintering up and fraying into threads, but he still reached for his weapon. Broden's next shot was the vicious hiss of a laser, straight into the guy's face. He fell, screaming.

Blite went through, glancing down at the man writhing and yelling on the floor, his face boiled under a chain-glass visor that he was groping at. He moved on and opened fire with stun shots towards the reception desk, but his weren't the only ones. He saw men and women clad in businesswear, unarmed, collapsing. Over to his right, two more guards ran into a spray of slugs, bloody mist exploding from them as they went down. Behind, he heard a sharp crackle that ended the shrieks of the guard there. Glancing back, he saw a look of vicious satisfaction on Broden's face and realized he'd accepted much about the man because of the impression he gave of outlinker weakness, but he was a killer. Broden ran off, heading for his designated stairwell.

The mercenaries all piled in, bringing down almost immediately anyone who came into the lobby. Shots rang out from the stairwell, and Blite saw two of Broden's men go down. A shape streaked across to the stairs and leaped in. He heard snarling and a shriek, and the firing stopped. The idea of only stunning people was gone now.

Blite reached the stairwell and saw a man there, his back against the wall, shivering and trying to stem the blood jetting from his neck. He felt ashamed, but when the man reached for the weapon on the floor beside him, Blite fired once, blowing the side out of his skull. He didn't know when he'd switched over to lethal rounds and, even though he'd just killed someone, the shame died too.

Been getting soft in your old age, he told himself.

From above there came further snarling and another scream. 'Told you,' said Greer, coming up beside him.

Four mercenaries joined them and they began to climb. Four stairwells and four parties led by Blite, Carlstone, Broden and one of the mercenaries. They ran up, targeting in their visors, hitting anyone who appeared. A woman tumbled down, scattering papers, a shot bored straight through her forehead. Blite stepped over her and kept going. As they passed each floor, the mercenaries sowed stun grenades. Occasionally they passed someone with his or her throat ripped out and Blite wondered just what the discussion between Greer and the dog had been.

Ten floors up, they ran into heavy fire. A mercenary went down. Greer fell back against the wall, cursing, armour splintered around her leg and blood leaking out. Blite switched to a new setting on his gun, as did the other mercenaries. They squatted, taking braced positions, plugged subsidiary power leads into the battery packs they carried and a feed from another pack, putting suits on maximum assist. The rail beader setting could work for a maximum of a hundred shots. The beads themselves, being hyperdense and very heavy, couldn't be carried in the weapons, so fed in from the packs. They began firing, the shots passing through walls, maybe some stopped by armouring, but most not. After a fusillade that rained wall fragments and filled the stairwell with dust, they advanced again. The heavy fire had ceased.

Limping after them, Greer said, 'I hope no one hit my dog.'

The dog wasn't there, but the corpses were. Blite paused, guilt rising up in him again.

'Okay, seems they're on the move,' said Kostis over com. 'Five of them with some heavies.'

'Need backup?' Blite asked.

'Are you kidding?'

He waited. The objective thus far had been achieved and there was no reason to keep climbing . . . to keep killing. After a little while Kostis came back on, sounding a little out of breath.

'Okay, we got them – heading out now to collect them.'

Kostis and the three other soldiers had settled their grav-car on the roof, concealed by a water tank and solar array up there, and with its limited chameleonware engaged. The craft itself had a heavy stunner. They'd just needed to wait until the Mortons in the penthouse decided to run to their grav-cars.

'Good job.' Blite turned to the others and pointed down the stairwell. 'Okay, we're out of here.' He noted Greer's moue of disappointment, guessing this stemmed from her not even getting her axe out. But she shrugged and turned away, raising a device to her lips and blowing in it. He heard nothing but knew it wasn't for his ears. The three remaining mercenaries made no move to go, however.

'We get out of here,' he repeated, looking at them.

One of the mercenaries, a calm-looking grey-haired man, shook his head. 'That ain't what we've been paid for.'

Broden . . .

'What have you been paid for?'

'Going to the top,' he replied with a shrug.

Blite nodded, not inclined to argue the point. He simply turned and followed Greer down. Her dog Groff joined them in the lobby, muzzle bloody and tail wagging for Greer.

'Sfun, sfun,' said the dog, 'sdinner now?'

Cormac

Cormac ventured further into the mountain's cave network, moving steadily along the burn hole of the particle beam strike to where its initial energy had begun to dissipate. He enhanced his vision via his gridlink, then, as an afterthought, did the same with his hearing. Here the cave walls were no longer smooth, while melted rock had poured out to leave deep channels, crevices and side caves. With there now being so many hiding places around him, he drew his thin gun again and held it loosely in his hand, lining up a new series of attack programs in his gridlink for Shuriken.

Rustling movement sounded to one side. He turned and fired as the sleer came out of the crevice, nailing it with just a single shot through the head. He didn't know how many of these things there were, or how long it would be before he ran out of ammo. The creature kept coming, though, and he backed up, keeping it targeted. He wasn't sure what stage of sleer this was and didn't really care – it was bigger than the last and its body form at variance. It finally hit the floor, smoke rising from its head, and turned to face him. He held off, waiting to see if it would charge again. Instead it writhed in a manner that displayed its alien body format. Its segments turned like tyres independently of each other, and in different directions, legs rising up to the back or disappearing underneath, some segments upside down in relation to others. It almost looked as if it was unscrewing itself, then confirmed this by separating into two halves. The front end collapsed, while the back end aligned its legs with the floor again, turned, and ran off.

'Passing strange, those fuckers,' he said.

'Second-stage,' Mask commented. 'You killed the front end but not the rear. It's incapable of feeding but still capable of mating. Life continues.'

Cormac nodded to himself. The entity speaking to him could definitely see what he was seeing.

When Cormac didn't reply, Mask continued, 'Fortunately for you, there are only first- and second-stagers down here, and their nymphs.'

'Oh, yes, I feel so lucky. Any droons down here too?'

'Droons don't exist here any more. Since this is a world occupied by p-prador, and droon acid can burn through even their high-tech carapaces, they wiped them out.'

'I don't know whether to feel sad about that or not.'

'No need to feel sad – I'm sure their code is backed up somewhere, and I'm pretty certain I have one or two in environmental encystments.'

Cormac moved on, edging around the front end of the second-stage sleer. 'Environmental encystments? Do you mean a zoo?'

'Yeah, pretty much.'

Cormac smiled. He needed to keep talking. He didn't know what it was, but Mask had mentioned something it, or she, shouldn't have – something concerning their technology and the way they lived in this time. He kept moving, the fissures and side caves growing larger around him. With enhanced hearing, he began to pick up more movement and, concentrating on that, came near to stepping over an edge. Peering down, he saw a drop of five metres into a natural-looking cave that intersected diagonally. This must be where the final energy of the particle beam had dissipated, with fissures starred off all around. He looked for a way down but then, with a degree of irritation, turned to face up the way he'd come.

First- and second-stage sleers were pouring out of the walls like termites from a disturbed nest. He target-framed and counted at least twenty of them. Raising his gun, he fired at the leading three, his shots perfectly on target as they always were, hitting two scuttling along the floor and one on the ceiling. The one above fell, the two on the floor curled up – one a second-stager shedding its back end, which, once free, ran straight towards him. He stepped aside and watched the thing tumble over the edge, hit the bottom, do its curious rearrangement of its body segments, then shake itself and run off. Returning his attention to the others, he shrugged at the inevitability of them still charging towards him. He'd hoped that killing a few in the lead might deter the others, but it was a vain hope – he knew all about their hostility. It seemed a universal rule that anything with an exoskeleton and more than four legs was going to try to eat you no matter your response.

'Fuckers,' he said, initiating Shuriken with a thought.

He flung out his left hand and Shuriken departed its holster – a spinning black star with crystal at its centre. Its spin ramped up, and it expanded as it folded out its main body, then its chain-glass blades. He noted that the blades gleamed anew, and there was the glint of something else along their edges. They shimmered there with a blue light. He frowned. This was an iteration he hadn't seen before, though he knew that the Tenkian programming was a deep and ever-growing thing, stored in its crystal and along the chain molecules of its blades. Shuriken perpetually upgraded itself based on environmental factors and information gleaned from data links. He knew it connected into the AI net in the Polity for this purpose, and now wondered if it had made connections here and learned some new tricks.

Shuriken cycled up, the sound it emitted transitioning from that of an ancient helicopter drone to a high-pitched whine. This was new too, and probably something to do with that shimmer he could see. The star dipped and shot forwards. It turned vertically to hit a second-stager in the face and, with a sound like a circular saw going through wood, traversed it to the tail. It turned horizontally to hit the next, even as its previous victim fell into two neatly divided halves. This second one collapsed on its side, spilling the top half of its body to reveal an internal cross-section like an anatomical picture. Zipping up, Shuriken beheaded two more on the ceiling, then went straight through a rocky protrusion to hit another. Cormac watched rock fall as it was sliced through, mirror smooth. Shuriken continued, now perhaps not showing off so much as it steadily turned all the sleers into the kind of neat cuts one might find in an alien meat market. Finally it came back, shrugging away ichor and fragments of flesh and carapace, to spin before him. He eyed it, pretty damned sure it was waiting for his approval. He held up his left hand, sleeve pulled back.

'Nice job,' he said.

Seemingly satisfied with this, Shuriken folded in its blades and body, shot down and revolved small before his hand, then slowed and inserted itself in its holster with a neat snick. Cormac lowered his arm, put away his thin gun and looked for a way down into the cave below. He decided not to mention to Mask that his Tenkian throwing star had now acquired a highly advanced shearfield he'd never seen before. Shuriken was obviously keyed into the local version of the Polity net, and he didn't want Mask to block that.

'That thing is a bit of a puzzle, even in our time,' Mask commented as Cormac began to climb down.

'It's here now?' Cormac enquired. 'Isn't it theorized that an object cannot occupy another time continuum where it still exists?'

'So it was theorized in your time, and generally only in entertainment virtualities, not in the minds of AIs looking at the math,' Mask replied. 'You are here in this time too, albeit now as scattered components of stellar dust.'

'Well, thank you for sharing that with me,' said Cormac snappily.

'But our aim at the present is to prevent the you right here falling into the same state. You need to hide. The p-prador detected your noisy weapons and are on their way.'

Blite

Blite had declined Broden's offer to become further involved in 'taking down the Mortons'. He'd made a final payment to him from the account of Penny Transport because he felt the need to cut ties with the man. Broden's mercenaries had left the tower building a burning mortuary, escaping from the roof as local law enforcement arrived in the street. The man planned to move on and destroy the rest of the Mortons' operation too. Blite wondered if this would truly be for the good of anyone, because it seemed likely Broden would just end up occupying the power vacuum created. Anyway, he had what he wanted right here. Gashiir Morton was the boss. The other four, whom Carlstone and his soldiers were questioning in other rooms, were high up in the Morton organization too.

'You've wasted a lot of time and effort,' said Gashiir.

The man wore rumpled and expensive businesswear. They'd searched him and removed all his neatly concealed weapons, while a spider block sat over his aug preventing communication with anyone outside this room. The man was bulky with boosting, conventionally handsome, had a spade-shaped black beard below a shaven head, and skin with a bluish tint. Blite had thought he might have the Spatterjay virus in him, so had had Iris check. It turned out he was part adapt, with one of his parents being a human adapted to a high-gravity low-radiance world. Apparently his skin contained photosynthesizing cells to provide extra nutrients, hence the bluish cast.

'Tell me about my wasted time and effort,' said Blite. 'I want to get this all completely straight and don't want to have to start asking *harder* questions.'

Gashiir was sweating. Though trying to come across as cool, centred and in control, he clearly feared where this might be going. Doubtless, in his own experience, anyone captured and then strapped into a chair like this did not have a rosy future. Blite, meanwhile, wondered if he would've been prepared to torture information out of this man, though of course Iris had made that cease to be a necessity.

'Meander Draft 64XB is an interesting lady,' said Gashiir. Blite noted the use of her full name – Gashiir was trying to insert as many words as he could to expand the gap between now and what he expected to come. The man continued, 'She was pretty much below our radar when she first came here, which was about a year before you came previously too.'

'How did she get here?' Blite interjected.

Gashiir shifted, perhaps trying to raise his hands from where they were strapped to the chair arms. 'That was a bit of a puzzle for a while – she was very resistant to interrogation.'

Nice to be reminded, thought Blite, of what they'd done to her.

'My brother Colson finally nailed it down from a few things she said. She in fact came in on a trade ship that was working with us – she crewed it as a biotech specialist, which was useful. She'd signed on in the Graveyard.'

Blite nodded, keeping his expression bland. Quite likely that trade in the Graveyard had involved cored and thralled human beings. He didn't like the trade, nor did he like that Meander had been involved as a biotech specialist, since that meant she'd probably been tending to the human blanks – those walking corpses which resulted from coring and thralling people.

'And then she continued in your organization, whereupon you gave her a new task?' Blite tried.

'Nope. As soon as she got here, she just quit and headed off.'

'So you went after her?' Blite prodded.

Gashiir shook his head. 'She wasn't important enough to be bothered with, beyond arranging an accident for her if she ever turned up again. She'd probably seen things aboard that ship . . .'

'So, she turned up?'

'No, but then that shit Broden brought her to our attention again. You work with that guy? Do you think yourself a moral man?'

Blite ignored the barb. 'He brought her to your attention again how?'

'We found out Broden was running a penetration of our organization. We knew him of old as something of an irritant we intended to deal with when the time was right. What we couldn't understand was how he'd risen from being an irritant to a real threat. He just hadn't had the funding to be such a problem before.'

'I see.' Blite stepped away from where he'd been leaning against the wall with his arms folded, walked over and pulled over another chair to sit astride it, with his hands along the back. 'So what did you find out?'

'We found out about steady payments he'd been using to expand his organization. We managed to get some time on a forensic AI submind that showed us the payments were coming from Penny Transport. You.'

Blite nodded, kind of annoyed that he thought the man was telling the truth. It should be more difficult than this. 'So you found out the source of Broden's funding . . . what next?'

'At first we thought you wanted a foothold on this world. That your aim was to take us down, supplant us. Penny Transport is big and wealthy, so this was a concern.'

Blite's annoyance increased. He knew he had a bit of a reputation for some dodgy dealing, but that arose mainly from his past. He'd liked the barely legal and illegal deals, the risk, and the thrill of fighting to keep his operation running. He'd also enjoyed putting one over on the likes of the man sitting before him, and coming out of it with a profit. But in no way would he have countenanced supplanting a criminal organization such as that of Gashiir Morton. With people like this man, and the things he did, Blite's response was usually pretty much along the same lines as Broden's. He frowned: *Getting soft.* Anyway, now he was legit . . .

'Continue,' he said tightly.

'It came as a big surprise to us that you had Broden hunting down just one individual – that woman – while he used the funds you supplied to penetrate our organization. Did you know that? Did you realize that while he was searching for Meander, his main objective was us? Did any of that come across in whatever he communicated to you?'

Blite didn't react. Gashiir, seriously worried about his immediate future, was still taking the time to try to undermine an enemy. He finally replied, 'Of course I knew. Broden had surmised that Meander, a thief, had likely been employed by you, or that she would be someone you were aware of at some level. That he also wanted to bring you down was just a side benefit.'

Gashiir frowned. Just for a second, Blite wasn't sure why he'd defended Broden like this, since the man certainly hadn't made his antipathy towards the Mortons clear, then he realized why. In many ways Broden was like a younger version of himself. He now remembered many occasions when, supposedly in search of the best way to make a profit, he'd gone out of his way to right some wrongs.

'And anyway, you're getting away from the point,' he added.

'Okay.' Gashiir nodded, some sweat dripping from his brow. 'The fact you had so much interest in Meander made her of interest to us. So we started looking for her properly. We deployed facial recognition, put out a reward and used sub-AI micro-drones in the cities. She finally revealed herself to us when she went to one of our surgeons to have her face altered – probably because she'd found out either Broden or we were looking for her. We would have missed her had not the surgeon noticed something strange and informed the street boss in that town.'

'Strange?' Blite echoed.

'To change her face, she needed structural splints and other implants. Seems her biology is such that any simple surgery to rearrange her features would only work for a short time. She always heals back to her original appearance.'

Blite suppressed the urge to agree or confirm anything about Meander's odd biology. He just nodded for Gashiir to continue.

'The street boss immediately recognized her and delivered instructions to the surgeon. He nerve-blocked her and waited for us to come and grab her.'

'What did you learn from her?'

Gashiir grimaced. 'She was surprisingly resistant, and Colson discovered that each time she healed from interrogation, she'd lost memories. But he found out enough to know we'd been wasting our fucking time. You're a surprise to us, Blite.' Gashiir eyed him with perplexity. 'All that wealth and power, and you expend a small fortune on tracking down a petty thief who stole a fucking ornament from you. Yeah, maybe it had some sentimental value, but we learned that she even returned the thing to you!'

Gashiir had slipped into anger. Blite just sat silently and waited. After a short time, the flush left the man's cheeks and he looked pale and ill. The ire had briefly displaced his awareness of his situation, but now it was back again.

'Having learned all this,' said Blite, 'why did you keep her for so long?'

'Colson.' Gashiir shrugged. 'He found her biology and her ability to heal herself swiftly very interesting. He has interests like that.'

Blite abruptly stood up and headed for the door.

'Wait!' Gashiir almost shouted. Blite turned back to him and he continued, 'That's all of it. That's the truth. You're not going to get any different version of these events out of me. It was your interest here that led us to grabbing . . .' Blite walked out of the room, closing the door behind him.

Out in the corridor Iris was waiting with a small trolley neatly arrayed with medical equipment. He ignored her for a second and took a breath to cool his anger. The Mortons hadn't sent Meander to steal the gem, and it seemed likely Broden had been a little parsimonious with the truth. The man had used Blite's funds to his own, perhaps understandable, ends. He ground his teeth and turned his attention to Iris's trolley.

On the top level, lying in a kidney bowl, sat a dark bean-shaped augmentation. Iris sat on a couch along one wall, arms folded, eyes metallic and shifting while she was lost in her mental realm. Blite picked up the aug.

'This is it?' he asked. He glanced along the corridor, now seeing Carlstone and Armand approaching.

Iris focused on him. 'Yes, that's it.'

'Does it hurt?'

'Not really,' she replied, but her expression seemed just a little cruel to him.

'How come you're in possession of such a thing?'

'Misspent youth.'

Blite put the interrogation aug back into the bowl. Once Iris attached it to Gashiir's head, the man could be made incapable of lying, while she could closely examine his thoughts. Initially, Blite had been prepared to stay here and listen to what might be revealed. But now, utterly sure that Gashiir had been telling the truth, he had some thinking of his own to do.

'This may take some time,' Iris added, standing up.

Blite shrugged at that. Having rented this building through Broden, he'd decided to question Gashiir here on Iris's advice. He would have preferred to do it aboard his ship, since they had more resources there, but the space port received a great deal more AI attention than elsewhere. He wanted to stay under the radar, though he wasn't sure he was making a good job of that here.

Receiving no reply, Iris opened the door and pushed her trolley into the room. Blite heard Gashiir's 'Fuck,' as she entered. He thought his torturer had just entered. It occurred to Blite that perhaps she had.

'Done with the others?' Blite asked Carlstone as the man came up.

Carlstone shrugged. 'They back up his story, and with sufficient mismatch of detail to make it likely the truth. But we have to be aware we're dealing with professional liars.' Carlstone had been watching Gashiir's interrogation via aug.

Blite nodded. 'Ream him good. Confirm the story, or otherwise, but also strip a copy of all this guy's other activities. Coring trade, everything.'

'And then what?' Carlstone asked.

'Then hand the copy, him and the others over to Broden,' said Blite. Broden annoyed him and would be receiving no more funding, but his cause was just . . . perhaps.

Carlstone nodded, looking satisfied.

'Then we're out of here. Get all the—'

Blite instantly recognized the rumbling crash as the non-accidental variety. It shook the building. The other sounds came as confirmation: the sawing of a particle beam, the vicious whirr of a fast projectile weapon, and distant explosions.

May

Through an outside cam, which blocked the U-continuum so it seemed there was simply a grey wall some metres out from the ship, May watched Arach lay in a final piece of hull composite on top of the others he'd put in place below. He then stepped back. Like a smaller deformed cousin of the spider drone, the printerbot scuttled in and began deposition welding. In her aug,

May watched sensors reporting in that the hull was again completed to a whole in that area.

'We need more robots aboard,' said Akanthor. 'Maybe Arach fancies a job here?'

'I think Arach would take exception to you calling him a robot,' May replied.

She turned her attention to the cam view into the engineering section. Crane had been busy. He'd made two of those big fuck-off cannons and was now working on something else. She rather suspected, by the format, that it was a shield generator.

'What the hell is it doing now?' asked Davidson, who'd limped back into the bridge only ten minutes ago, complaining about the efficiency of their autosurgeon. His nanites had splinted his shin bone internally, but the surgeon had done the final repair.

May returned her attention to Arach. Towing the sled, the spider drone had left the printerbot behind and headed up along the hull. She could see no reason it would be doing this – perhaps taking in the view – until it arrived at the stub of wreckage that had been one of their bead guns. Arach set to work, cutting stuff away and removing the remains of the gun, careful not to let the debris fall into the U-continuum. Nobody was entirely sure whether such a thing might be a collision risk, but it was best to be cautious.

'Ah,' said Davidson. 'Now we know where those cannons are going.'

May searched for aug connections besides those she usually used in the ship with Akanthor, Davidson, the ship mind and subsidiary computing. Two icons stood out. One was just plain weird, being a tangled wormy mass but with a definite brassy tint. The other was, inevitably, a spider. She sent a connection request and it immediately opened to her. She included her crewmembers too.

'You got questions?' Arach asked.

'Crane has made a couple of particle cannons and now seems to be making a hardfield generator,' she said. 'You're going to put one of the weapons there, and the other on the other side. I'm guessing the place for the generator is just forwards of the subsidiaries. No technical questions.'

'Moral questions?'

'Nope. You seem to be preparing my ship for a fight. I'd like to know who we might end up fighting.'

'You just escaped bounty hunters. Use your brain.'

'I am very capable of using my brain,' May replied dryly. 'Perhaps you can be capable of remembering that you're a guest and passenger aboard my ship, and that you put me and my crew in danger!'

'Sorry,' said Arach. 'Spent too long with that brass bastard and lost some conversational politeness. We haven't escaped completely – they are bounty hunters so have their methods for tracking down and following people . . .'

'Oh, hell,' said May, abruptly feeling stupid.

'Our U-signature,' Davidson interjected.

The ship wasn't some state-of-the-art Polity warship, so it had no way of concealing its U-signature, nor had had any necessity to do so. Those ships in orbit around Cull, and quite possibly many down on the planet, would have recorded their U-signature and now be following them. When they reached their destination, bounty hunter ships would undoubtedly arrive shortly afterwards too.

'Two particle cannons and shield generator are not enough,' said Akanthor. 'We need to keep bouncing until we can put ourselves near some Polity military installation.'

'That is where you are incorrect,' said Arach. 'They are precisely calculated to be enough, by the brass bastard. They will get us to our destination and to cover, and thereafter, some other weapons will become available.'

'Our surface point to the real is in interstellar space.'

'True,' said Arach. 'But there is something there.'

'What's there?' asked Davidson.

'A weapons cache Crane knows how to access. It will just take some fancy flying to make cover within it – it's a planetoid filled with caves,' Arach replied.

'A planetoid filled with caves,' May repeated.

'If you're as good a pilot as supposed, you should be able to guide the ship into cover in less than ten minutes.'

'They'd need to be big caves,' Davidson noted.

'They are,' Arach continued. 'We have the coordinates within the planetoid. We also calculate that the bounty hunter ships will appear eight minutes after our arrival there. It may be that the weapons and the hardfield will not be required.'

May felt the drone was getting rather chatty, almost as if he didn't want her asking questions about something he'd said previously. She thought about that for a little while, considering further questions, but before she could ask whose weapons cache it was, Arach had more to say.

'But the weapons and shield may be required so, perhaps, rather than sitting on your hands up there, you would like to help? We've got some infrastructure below these old guns that needs removing or altering, we've got power feeds to run, and you are quite right about where the hardfield generator needs to be positioned.'

May sat there feeling foolish again.

'And we have just under an hour and a half to get it all done,' Arach added.

She stood up abruptly. 'Okay, send me details. Send us all details.'

Instantly, schematics of three areas of her ship snapped into her mind. Components and structure were highlighted, indicating what had to be removed, while attached was a list of other required components, and links to further schematics showing where they needed to go. Davidson grunted in surprise.

'Well, fuck me,' said Akanthor.

AI fast, of course. It seemed that Arach, if it was he who'd laid this out, had been very thorough. May began to look for errors – she was contrary like that. She matched the component list to the ship's manifest of components, but found the drone, or Crane, had got there before her. Some things needed to be manufactured. Further links starring those off led to printers and nanofactories in Engineering already at work on them. May stopped herself delving any further, since she was wasting time looking for problems. She decided to be as efficient as her acquired passengers.

'Akanthor. You take the stuff inside the port gun, and you the other, Davidson. I'll set to work on where they want the shield generator.' The port gun was the undamaged one, so removing what needed to go and preparing the area for the new weapon would be easier – hence she'd chosen to send Akanthor there, because the ophidapt woman had less technical expertise than Davidson. The damaged gun would have things that'd need doing beyond the schematic and work order.

May headed out quickly. She didn't need to issue any other instructions about equipment required – her crew were her crew for a reason. They'd do a good job. She could hear them coming after her as she quickly went down to Engineering. There she observed Crane at work, his hat hanging on a nearby machine and brassy head gleaming as if he was sweating, which was of course unlikely. He ignored her as she headed into a storage area and picked up cutting equipment, also linking to a mobile tool chest and printerbot. Akanthor and Davidson were in there with her a moment later, doing the same. No words now, just getting on with work.

She walked to the task she'd assigned herself, schematic and order of work at the forefront of her mind. Without even pausing for consideration, she fired up the cutter on a laser setting and began slicing out through the inner hull, sending a suppression order for the breach system there. After taking out bracing struts and inner layers, she stacked them on the floor. Further stuff she removed with a debonder, or took out fixings. Once the bulk was extracted, with a remaining skin of hull left above a circular opening, she instructed the printerbot to take the debris back down to Engineering, and to collect an iris hatch from there. This would sit in the hole when she removed the outer hull. She'd need to close off bulkhead doors and evacuate this area as she did it. She debated with herself whether to program the bot to put the hatch in place, or suit up and do the task herself. She realized she felt calm and happy for the first time in a while.

Maybe Arach could have come in here and finished this task in a tenth of the time she was taking. But it wasn't all about the efficient deployment of resources. Drones, Golem – and in fact any AI – were good with mechanisms, and that included the soft mechanism called the human brain, and knowing what it needed.

Matheson

Matheson opened his eyes, and then his mouth to scream at the agony. Only now it was a memory of pain, immediately swamped by far too much other input. His conventional senses were pretty much as they had been before, but something else had been added. He could see much of what lay around him beyond his current position. His view encompassed Straeger's ship and his own, and a number of views out into vacuum too.

'I don't feel right,' said Sheen Brice.

He looked at her there, hanging in lianas of tech, all plugged in, pumped up and transformed. Like her brothers, she'd been boosted, heavily muscled and almost mannish. It seemed that in rebuilding her, Straeger had returned her to some wasp-waisted basic female form, but beyond that, she didn't look right either.

Her skin was a drowned-man blue, with its discoloration emphasized by metallic veins running all over her body. Matheson recognized these as haiman tech, just as he recognized the circular objects all over her as data interfaces, rising up out of the largest conglomerations and intersections of those veins. But recognition didn't stop her looking as if she was suffering from some hideous pox. She was bald, he noticed, with fewer interfaces up there, which seemed odd, while her eyes, when she shifted to look towards him, were still the same startled blue.

Glimpsing a limb beyond her, Matheson focused with his new sense and saw this was lost among the same entangling tech – Ulnar and Will had been similarly changed. Upon seeing them, and understanding that this sense had nothing to do with collecting up photons, he looked at himself. The tech tangle around him was nowhere near as dense, and he was floating in fluid in one of the regrowth tanks he'd seen earlier. Straeger had used a different approach with him, since he'd been complete when coming here. The disassembly still cycled in his mind, while pain memories tried to elicit screams. His alterations were also at variance to those of the Brices. His skin was blue, yes, and the veins and interfaces were there on his body as well. However, he had much more of them on his bare skull, almost like rashes of glassy freckles running back from his forehead. He supposed that they connected to the gridlink Straeger had installed there, and which, he now understood, was the reason for his wider sense. He'd previously used his aug to peer through the cams scattered throughout his ship. This was the same ability, but increased by an order of magnitude, incorporating data from other sources converted to visual information.

'What the hell is this?' asked Ulnar Brice.

'You answered your own question,' Will replied.

Matheson swept his attention away from them, searching his surroundings. Now, with his senses encompassing so much more, he confirmed his speculations about Straeger's ship and its open machines, but he couldn't find the AI within it. Next, looking to his ship, he still couldn't find the AI in total, but instead saw hundreds of smaller versions of it busily at work there. He then realized he *was* seeing the AI; it had broken up into swarm form. He focused in, trying to glean some sense of what it was doing, and that's when the gridlink kicked in fully.

It was much like an aug, but with bandwidth taken beyond the limits of such exterior devices. He understood the theory: being distributed around the inside of the skull allowed it to have a broader range of access to the brain, up to and including changing, and in some cases making, neurochem. In the past it had been the case that a gridlink could feed information into the brain, so one could simply know it, while an aug could not. In more recent years, though, that division of process had become increasingly blurred.

Data loaded and he knew at once what Straeger had done, and was doing, on his ship. The armour, weapons and drive had all been improved, but within time constraints of which only another hour remained. Understanding those alterations and integrating them perfectly, he tried to focus on those that'd been made to him and the Brices. Further data dropped, but this was more difficult to elucidate than simply extra thermocouples installed in ship armour. The fibres of the Spatterjay virus had turned them into woody, tough creatures. Metallic processing tech had been interlaced throughout too, surfacing in those veins and interfaces, yet it seemed to be an open-ended thing requiring other components.

Then the next components arrived.

'What the fuck?' said Sheen.

He saw her looking at her legs, as some hazy grid began to blister out a few millimetres from her skin. This grew, spreading up her legs to her body, down her arms and up over her head. Transparent pipes routed in all around her, then darkened and began flooding in some liquid metal with the appearance of mercury. It spread out, binding to the grid and enclosing sections in shiny metal. This then seemed to frost over, as if abruptly acquiring an oxide layer. Over her calves, thighs, forearms and biceps, it appeared solid, while in the joints between, accordion segmentation rippled into existence. It was all obviously armour of some kind, bonding to her skin and, as he watched, it plugged into her interfaces too.

'Damn,' she said as this growth closed in on her neck and travelled upwards. She tilted her head back, looking like someone drowning, trying to snatch their last breath. She made a horrible gasping sound as it finally enclosed her head completely.

Matheson stared at her transformation in horror, as all the pipes began to detach and snake away. Via their connection, the Brices were shouting questions and demanding answers, but Sheen fell away from language as rising out of her pain came the reality of suffocation. Beyond her, Matheson could now see the same happening to the brothers, and then looked down as he felt a burning sensation in his own legs. The grid sped up quickly to encompass him, his whole body burning, and he still had no facility to scream at the pain.

'What the fuck are you doing, Straeger?' he shouted, terror rising.

The sense of connection through his gridlink expanded, and he now recognized it had been there all along. He flashed his attention over to his ship and there saw the small versions of the AI coagulating as it headed back towards the airlock tube. Straeger gave no answer, but Matheson did get a sense of its close observation of him as the metal began to feed into the pipes around him. Realizing something, and desperately seeking some way out, he again checked his surroundings, yet found no sign of those prador-things aboard Straeger's ship. He put together some of what Straeger had said and began to understand where this strange metal had come from. He saw Sheen, now completely disconnected and floating, writhing in place as she suffocated. He watched her fingers extending into claws, and sharp slicing edges appearing along her forearms.

'Initially weapons cannot be carried,' said Straeger. 'It is therefore necessary to form part of the armour to that purpose.'

Matheson had so many questions, but he couldn't voice them as his surroundings twisted and changed. He recognized this because, like many captaining their own ships, he'd tried once or twice to look on raw U-space. The experience had nearly killed him, and right now it seemed to be tearing into his mind. Groping for some solution, he found his gridlink responding. Spacial coordinates retracted infinities into something bearable. He felt a definite sense of connection to the Brices as they screamed silently in their armour. This connection elucidated as his armour grew to his neck, and then up to enclose his head. His scream remained down deep, but seemed to be boiling his mind in waves of giggling madness as his world shut down into blackness.

He tried to breathe, not believing that something so horrible could be happening to him. He managed to hang on at least long enough for his gridlink to interpret his surrounding view of U-space and convert it into something that wouldn't drive him instantly mad. Through his connection to the Brices, he sent this perception to them, but their suffering continued. Then, as he struggled for air and yet remained lucid – a contradiction which threatened his sanity – he found the gridlink connections to autonomous functions of his body. Shutting down his lungs was easy. Removing the signal to his brain that told him he was suffocating was harder, but he found it eventually and fell into a strange quiet. He relayed this to the Brices, understanding in that instant that they were subsidiaries of him, utterly under his control. Their suffering immediately diminished too, and then babbling protests and questions rolled through him. Too much of it made little sense and edged into the gabble of minds on the edge of breaking, so he shunted them aside.

'Straeger,' he said.

'It's not as effective as I would like,' the AI replied. 'To maintain its utility as a transport vessel in U-space, the armour is not so tough in the real sense – little more than simple steel. But it will serve for my purposes.'

'And what are your purposes?' Matheson asked tightly.

'You need only think of your own,' said the AI. 'It's time for you to take yourselves back aboard your ship.'

More than the words came through as his gridlink increased its processing, until seemingly vibrating in his skull. He recognized the connection to the Brices as more than an informational one and expanded it to outline and encompass them in three dimensions. As he did this, he saw Straeger rolling back through the airlock, the lock closing behind it as the two ships detached. This brought home that his method of going aboard would be different.

'Go now,' said Straeger.

Matheson reached for the bridge of his ship, coordinates

shifting and calculations running in a way that went beyond his understanding. He pushed. U-space drove aside his gridlink interpretation of it, in all its raw insanity, and he shrieked. Then, with a thump like a mine going off, he and the Brices were in the bridge of his ship and dropping to the floor. He landed in a crouch and looked over to the three of them, all down and ready as he was, with burning lines running over their armour as if fuse paper had been ignited there. He stood upright, feeling as if a hundred blades had sliced through his body, but also that his flesh was shifting and melding. He felt like he wanted to puke, but where would it go?

'I have input coordinates to your ship,' said Straeger in his skull. 'Go there. Kill Mr Crane. Pursue him if necessary. And kill Cormac.'

He saw that his ship had become something more formidable than it had been before. He could jump himself and the Brices through U-space, and who knew what other abilities and strength might arise out of that, considering the fact that the Spatterjay virus packed their bodies? But how the hell were they supposed to bring down the brass Golem with what, in the end, were little more than edged weapons? Straeger's orders were also debatable and didn't necessarily align. However, as Matheson reached out to the mind of his ship, one thing was certain: he simply couldn't disobey.

8

Cormac

There was simply no way to go quietly and stay hidden. As he moved through the cave system, the ever-aggressive sleers kept appearing and trying to do what they did. He found a long side cave that looked narrow enough to block access for the prill-prador and turned into it. Halfway along, a large second-stage sleer sat in his path. It just hissed at him rather than charging, until he drew close, and then it did charge.

He shot it three times through the head, because here he had no way of keeping away from it until it died from just the one shot. It nosedived, legs rattling against the walls and body segments turning. As its front end died, it tried to separate, but instead pulled out a long plug of organs, crawled part way up one wall, and just clung there as this plug fell out, as well as other organs, in long drools of ichor. It was bleeding out.

Cormac edged past, gun pointed at it all the time, but neither the front nor the back end responded to him. Further on, the side cave opened out into a small chamber with no other exit. Another creature lay against one wall. It looked vaguely reptilian, had six legs and a big cow-like head with stalked eyes. Its body, under its scaled hide, didn't look right: many scales were rucked up over swellings he guessed weren't part of its natural form – swellings that were moving. He could hear a constant grating, crunching sound and thought for a moment it came from those mobile swellings. However, when the stalked eyes turned really slowly to observe him, he realized the creature was grinding its ruminant teeth together in agony.

Since his first encounter with the sleers here, and after Mask's explanation of part of their lifecycle, he'd accessed information on them in his gridlink. The second-stagers grabbed prey after mating, paralysed it and injected their eggs. The sleer nymphs fed upon the prey while it was still alive and fresh, finally killing it. It seemed that in the latter stages the paralytic tended to wear off, hence the movement of those stalked eyes and teeth. He observed as black hooks protruded from one of those lumps and sliced back and forth. The small head of a young first-stage sleer protruded. He pointed his gun at it, expecting the usual immediate hostility, but the thing ignored him, eating away at its surroundings and dropping scales on the floor. Cormac watched the thing, then swung his gun aside to put a shot through the ruminant victim's head, presuming its brain was there. It slumped, the teeth-gnashing stopped, and its stalked eyes coiled up.

'That was illogical of you,' stated Mask. 'The p-prador can detect your weapons.'

'I don't always function with logic,' Cormac replied. 'Do you?'

'I have my weaknesses, as you noted before,' Mask replied, voice fully female now, as if she or it had forgotten to stay in character. 'I'm just surprised is all – you are somewhat at variance to your legend.'

'Nice to know I'm still remembered.' Cormac turned back to the way he'd come in. 'This isn't going to work. If those . . . p-prador are intent on putting me down, they just need to send some missiles this way.' He moved quickly back into the cave, as fast as he could. When he passed the sleer he'd killed earlier, he wondered if it had been the mother guarding its brood. Probably. Nature was so kind.

'You are remembered, but if you don't find somewhere to hide soon, you'll end up being remembered in an entirely different way, on a different timeline, by other iterations of the people here.'

'Finding caves too narrow for the p-prador isn't an option,' said Cormac. He paused, reached down and touched the hilt of the commando knife in his boot, but then dismissed the idea. 'The sleers come to me if I stay in one place and I doubt I can kill them quietly, or otherwise deter them. The p-prador will thus locate me and then it's still just a matter of sending a missile. I need other options.' Perhaps Shuriken, with those new shearfields, could take the p-prador? No, he couldn't rely on that – he had to get back into his game.

'Then you need to find that other option,' said Mask blandly.

Cormac kept moving, putting together various instances in their conversation that indicated foreknowledge on Mask's part. Time travel was involved here, and that opened up a whole gamut of possibilities. He felt sure Mask knew how he would succeed. This raised another stray datum. He hadn't been entirely sure what had happened with Blite – he just knew that manipulation of time had enabled the man to survive via a series of highly unlikely circumstances. He had some hint now of that mechanism and wondered if it applied to him, here and now.

'Where are they now in relation to me?' he asked. Even as he posed the question, he set to work mentally. He began pushing his U-senses. His head throbbed warningly, but he damned it and kept pushing. He could see the U-continuum around him, shapeless and indifferent, straining from his perception. The pain increased, but he lined up a program in his gridlink and shunted it straight into his nanosuite. A hot flush ran through his body and rose up into his skull, as the nanosuite went into a specific-ally designed emergency mode. It would help him as it scavenged resources and made faster repairs, but it was very energy-hungry. The thing would also adapt, evolving under his push. He took out one of his protein bars, began munching it, and just kept pushing.

'They're two kilometres back,' Mask replied. 'You lucked out: taking a direct route to your last weapons fire, they ceased following your course and are heading to a point too narrow for them to get through. Maybe that was a mistake, or maybe they are simply being methodical. I estimate you have about fifty minutes before they are on you, if you stay in the main cavern.'

Breakthrough . . .

U-space finally opened up around him. He received the usual view lying beyond normal human perception. Objects became holes curving off to infinity, folded up in the sheet of gravity. He gazed at the immensity of his hand, larger than universes, and noted the world around him receding to an infinitesimal point. He was indifferent to a perception that sometimes sent other people crazy – those people who, contrarily, had something closer to the senses he possessed. Those who gazed upon a mere grey and silver swirl wondered what all the fuss was about. He perceived and understood it, but still needed assistance for further interpretation. The gridlink programs he now ran were somewhat like those found in the minds of math introvert AIs – straying into multiple dimensions, describing a plenum that linearly evolved minds struggled to encompass – and somewhat his own design and gut-level understanding of it all.

The gridlink translated and now he could see, in human terms, everything around him, in ways not limited by distance or by anything, like rock, that would have blocked EMR. He reached the main cave again and began searching for what he needed.

Just then, the floor shifted slightly and a rumble reached his ears – hearing was a meagre and almost irrelevant portion of his perception now.

'Earthquake?' he wondered out loud.

'No. You were right about the missiles,' Mask replied.

Cormac's perception may not have been limited by distance now, but it was by how much data he could encompass. So in essence he could only look at a few cubic kilometres at a time. He shifted his viewpoint back to look for the p-prador. He traced the course they'd taken and found them at a point where the cave they'd traversed had narrowed. He saw one of them fire again, spitting out a couple of missiles from a launcher that was folded up from the creature's back. The missiles streaked off into the narrow cave. He tracked their course, checked the map of the cave system all around, and saw them impact against a wall of rock that lay only tens of metres away from the enclosed cavern he'd just left. Another p-prador fired something else, and he saw gleaming objects like metallic soap bubbles speeding after the missiles. Some kind of search drone, he had no doubt. These creatures wouldn't stop until they found him, or his remains.

After sending out the search drones, the four creatures turned back along their course. Still pushing his U-senses, Cormac returned to searching his immediate surroundings. He ran another program for this, to sort the data quickly, and immediately saw some areas highlighted. One was a section of cave blocked at both ends, but it was half full of water and he simply didn't fancy that if alternatives were available. He spotted another option – a section of shaft similarly blocked – but it lay at the edge of the present reach of his perception. Though U-space supposedly negated the concept of distance, that hadn't entirely been his experience of it. The further he went from the centre point of what he could perceive, the more effort it took, and right now

207

he didn't think he was up to making a big effort for a jump. Then he found a perfectly spherical cave, separated from all other spaces around it by hundreds of metres of rock. It was perfect.

He fixed the location in his mind, ready to flick back to it in a moment, then wandered over to the edge of the cave here and sat down. Discarding the wrapper of the protein bar, he took out another and began eating. He felt really hot now, and his skin hung strangely loose. This had occurred on other occasions when he'd required this nanosuite emergency mode. Already his body was eating its way through his meagre supply of fat. He'd upgraded long ago in this respect and had the highest-density fats feasible, along with triple carrier haemoglobin and many other enhancements, but he'd limited himself to enhancements which didn't actually alter his appearance. Vanity? No, he just wanted to maintain the visual cue that had some AIs shitting computer chips.

'I note that you are not running and hiding,' Mask observed.

'That's because it's a rather pointless exercise,' he replied, while again observing the p-prador. 'You can see what those hard-edged bastards are doing?'

'Ah, yes.'

The creatures were now deploying more of those micro-drones, a few speeding off down the main cavern, while others went to explore the side caves. It didn't matter where he went in the present system: he'd be found. He couldn't, after all, go through a cave large enough for him and too small for those drones.

'I wonder why they didn't deploy those first,' he said.

'Overconfidence,' Mask replied. 'They figured out someone had been dragged through time with their fellow and probably thought it would be a simple matter of extermination. That you managed to evade the arrival point didn't matter, because you could be hunted down at their leisure. But now they are starting to realize you might be a bit more of a handful than they supposed.'

Cormac nodded, in no doubt that the mask transmitted his acknowledgement. He concentrated internally, pushing repairs to all those fractured blood vessels, clearing dead and malfunctioning cells, and tweaking the nanosuite program to optimum results. He watched it adapt and sometimes dredge up alternatives via a connection to the data stores in his gridlink. After finishing the second protein bar, which was also veined with fat and packed with other nutrients, he started immediately on the last one. When he did this jump, he wanted to be at the best he could achieve, and not end up shifting back into the real inside solid rock – that would screw anyone's day.

He kept his perception on the p-prador, watching them drawing steadily closer, then stood up and moved along the cave, tracking a channel until he found a pool of water. Again he tested it before drinking his fill. The water was highly alkaline but not poisonously so. As he finished drinking, he looked up with conventionally human vision and observed one of the silver bubbles floating towards him.

'Could these search drones be weaponized?' he asked.

'Yes, they could be.'

He pulled his U-space vision in, focusing down and down until his entire perception was of the drone only. It did contain complicated tech, but also some of surprisingly antiquated design. Fashioned of bubble and nanoscaffolded metals, the incredibly light object flew using simple internal propellers. He relaxed, sure its airy lightness negated any possibility of explosives, or anything with the energy density to drive a weapon, but he still ran its schematic through his gridlink. Interesting results arose concerning the technology – it was highly integrated with full spectrum EMR detection, running in the layered meta-materials of its skin. But the analysis told him it had a very low likelihood of being dangerous. Expanding his perception again, he saw the p-prador picking up their pace, obviously now aware of the location of their prey. He stood up, limbs aching, and began to walk away from them, keeping an eye on the drone as another joined it. The things might not be explosive, or sport any conventional energy or projectile weapons, but they could still carry nanotech or poisons; he didn't want them close.

'We haven't discussed where I go next, should I escape these hunters,' he observed.

'No, we have not. Your escape, as such, will be utterly dependent on your capabilities. There is some vague data on that in my present, but not sufficient.'

My present. Mask wasn't from this time and place? Cormac filed that away for later inspection. He now noted the drones getting closer; he drew his thin gun, and snapshot twice. They disappeared with dusty whumphs and a brief flare of green light. He placed his hand over his mouth and ran. It was just a precaution, but he hadn't liked the look of that spread of dust. After a few hundred yards, he found his limbs turning leaden and stumbled back to a walk. His Shuriken holster automatically tightened on his wrist, as he'd been feeling his belt automatically tightening too, and his clothes hung on him as he burned resources. Briefly drawing his U-space perception back to himself revealed that the mask had darkened. No doubt it was struggling with the output of his breath – the increased carbon dioxide and other gases, and the organic waste. He realized that merely shifting away from the p-prador wouldn't be sufficient, and so he listened for nearby movement.

The p-prador drew close enough to be sure of a kill if they sent missiles. He winced a smile at the fact that they hadn't. They might have chimerical biology and cyborg bodies, but they were still prador at heart – now seeing their prey, they wanted to be in at the kill. He cursed: even though the sleers had been constantly attacking, now that he actually needed one to attack, there were none. Then, rounding a melted-looking boulder, a first-stager lunged at him. He casually shot it three times through the head, while wondering about the intelligence of these creatures. Since he'd killed so many, were they trying to ambush him now?

He kicked the thing a couple of times to ensure it was dead, then reached down and dragged it out into the middle of the tunnel. Even the effort of this left him panting. From behind in the cave, he could hear the clatter of hard feet on stone, while other drones began to come into sight, but hung back. He squatted by the sleer, his hand on warm carapace, pulled his U-senses in around him, while linking again to that spherical cavern. He began generating his U-field and extended it out around the sleer, the effort seeming to wrench muscles throughout his body. He looked up at the p-prador which came clattering and crashing into sight, then jumped.

U-space tore at him and he could feel the sleer trying to break free in the same way he'd wanted to separate from the p-prador corpse before. He maintained his grip through an agony that lasted no time at all, and eternity. Then with a thump they arrived, dropping a few centimetres onto the hard painful angles of a surface. His U-senses collapsed, and even with light-enhanced vision he found himself in darkness. He remained still and just breathed, ensuring he at least had that. He felt terrible, and for the moment dismissed all the alerts coming up via his nanosuite-gridlink connection. He reached down to a belt pouch and by feel took out a small bead, then tossed it upwards. It stuck against a surface up there and turned on, flooding his surroundings with light as bright as day. Hurriedly he brought visual enhancement down to human normal, whatever that was. And he looked around.

Bright amethyst, tourmaline and clear crystals jutted in all around him. It seemed a fairy cavern, bright and magical, and he realized he'd transported himself to inside a geode within the mountains. Even in the most extreme circumstances, fighting to survive, beauty could come along and leave him gaping. In this he took comfort because, in being able to appreciate such things, he hadn't become bored and indifferent to existence. Reaching down to his boot, he drew out his commando knife and turned to the sleer. Now, sadly, he was going to make a mess in this place.

Blite

Blite just stood there blinking for a moment. It seemed highly likely that the Mortons had just attacked. Carlstone turned away, fingers up against his aug, then turned back, looking puzzled.

'The explosion was in Creston Street, a kilometre away. Someone is killing civilians . . .'

Blite looked back to the door of the interrogation room as Iris stepped out of it. Did they really need to remain here any longer? He had no doubt that if Morton operatives had found the location of their boss, they'd be coming in heavily armed. Was there any point in risking people's lives further?

To Iris he said, 'Leave it – no need to confirm what seems blatantly obvious. Go get Meander on a grav-gurney and take her up to our car.' He swung back to Carlstone as Iris returned to her trolley to pick up a few items, then slipped them into her pockets. They didn't have to pack much up here, since most of the equipment had been rented from Broden.

'Tell everyone to grab their stuff,' he told Carlstone. 'We're heading back to the *Coin* now.'

Carlstone nodded, and he and Armand left. Blite walked fast towards his room, but on hearing that particle beam sawing again, he broke into a run. There was something wrong about this being the Mortons. Seriously, would they be firing up heavy weapons in a populated area? They existed in the grey area of the planetary AI's light-touch policy of letting the humans fuck up. That usually lasted only as long as the troublesome humans stayed under the radar, and were sufficiently entrenched as to be an irritant too difficult for the AI to remove. Why the hell would they start an attack a kilometre away? It made no sense.

Blite crashed into his room, shrugging an apology to no one in particular for breaking the door. On the floor a couple of bots, similar to autodocs, were working on his suit. His support frame lay folded up to one side. He scowled at the frame, ignored it and went over to the suit. As he began pulling it on, the two bots fell away, waving manipulators at him in protest. When he powered it up, meta-material armour inflated, and unneeded assist became available. Next, reaching up, he initiated his induction aug and got a readout from the suit. The bots had fixed the major damage and had been finishing some cosmetic stuff when he came in. He picked up his pulse gun from the bed and holstered it, then grabbed up the carbine. One last look around the room – he didn't have much here – and his gaze fell on that frame again. Fuck it – he'd leave it here. He headed out.

Nobody was out in the corridor, so he headed for the stairs, up to their armoured grav-car. The sounds, as of battle, were closer now. He auged again for information, receiving Carlstone's order of departure. There weren't that many from the ship here. Greer had gone downstairs with some of them to take a groundcar from the basement garage, and was already heading away.

213

Carlstone waited up at the grav-car, Kostis was with Iris, on the way up, while Armand was looking for him. Blite tried to key into the local net to see if he could gather any information on the attack. Nothing – the local net was disrupted. Armand appeared up at the top of the stairs as he began to climb.

'Any idea what's going on?' Blite asked.

Armand looked a tad overexcited.

'Fucking hell, you have to see this.'

At the next landing Armand kicked open a door, led the way down a short corridor, then turned into a cafeteria. He carried on, up to a window stretching across one side of the building, and pointed. It didn't take long for Blite to figure out what the man was pointing at. Fires down there, flashing police lights, and a blast picking up a police street cruiser and flinging it, tumbling. He could see armed cops in the area. Reluctantly he enhanced his vision using the aug and brought more into focus. He could see a Golem – this being obvious because half her police uniform and syntheflesh had been stripped away. And damned if there wasn't a war drone down there! The thing bore the shape of a giant stag beetle. As it backed up over wreckage it was firing at something in the smoke and dust. Just beyond this, a four-storey building abruptly collapsed, flinging out more dust and smoke.

'You're seeing this?' Carlstone asked him via aug.

'I'm seeing something,' Blite replied.

'Five of them appeared half the world away. Apparently there was some sort of weird anomaly I don't have much detail on. The planetary AI demanded they land and stay in one place to be . . . assessed. They ignored it. Warning shots were fired, and then a particle beam strike. Surprisingly resistant. Took an orbital railgun to take out two of them.'

Smoke and dust cleared, with three shapes surging out of the haze. Blite immediately thought they were prador, but then began to reassess. They just didn't look right. He could see no head turrets, and they were wider and flatter, almost like inverted saucers with legs. The stag beetle drone continued firing at them, railgun shots sending them staggering. The explosions left mere dents in their armour, the particle beam stabbing in and only etching over the surface like acid. The three abruptly separated to make themselves more difficult targets, then fired weapons from their claws. The beams that lanced out were first the familiar royal blue of particle beams, but then brightened into an intense white. They intersected on the drone's head, splashed, then penetrated. An explosion in the drone's body raised its wing cases and spewed out molten components. It began to lift into the air, perhaps deciding it had had enough, but now, from launchers that snapped up on the back of the three, a series of missiles looped in. They struck the drone, exploding, and it dropped, smoking, out of the fireball as a large mangled sphere of scrap.

'Fuck me,' said Armand in awe.

Blite tilted his head in agreement. War drones that bore that shape had been made during the war, out of factory stations like Room 101. Those that'd survived the war and were still around had all upgraded and evolved. They were usually packed with dense tech and very dangerous indeed. That these creatures had just destroyed one demonstrated how dangerous *they* were. He also considered what Carlstone had said about *some kind of anomaly* and just knew these fuckers were here after him. But why?

'We get out of here, fast,' he said, turning away and breaking into a steady lope. As Blite hit the stairs, Armand came up directly behind him. Blite accelerated. He'd been lucky those things had arrived half a world away, with the result that the AI had been able to respond and put things like that war drone in their path. Or had he been lucky? He really didn't want to end up dying in the wreckage of this building and have to go through all this again and again. As he ran he auged to the ship, selecting the aug icon for Paidon and requesting contact. Her face appeared in inner vision, seeming to peer at him curiously.

'Prep the ship for immediate launch once we arrive,' he said. 'No permissions and as fast as possible. Prepare the Laumer drive.'

'In atmosphere?'

'Damned right.'

'That's going to piss off the AI.'

'Just do it.'

She shrugged. 'You're the captain.'

They were a floor below the one with the grav-car platform when the building shuddered. Just above he could see Iris guiding the grav-gurney through a door Kostis had opened.

'Move faster!' he bellowed, soon reaching the door behind them.

Beyond lay an area scattered with equipment and packing crates. Glass doors stood open onto the platform – the grav-car was there with its ramp down. Kostis and Iris had broken into a run, the grav-gurney speeding ahead and up the ramp, Meander's arm flopping off the side. A massive blast issued from below and the building lurched again, then he felt a sickening sensation he usually associated with too much cips or an earthquake. His balance felt strange, and he realized the whole building was going over. Kostis and Iris went up the ramp even as it started to close up. Bright white light flared and one of those beams punched up through the building, blasting molten debris up into the air.

Everything suddenly seemed to lurch into slow motion, except the beam tracking across, carving a channel through foamstone and composite, the roof sagging on either side. He saw Armand slipping on molten material, holding up a hand as if to cut the glare, then disappearing in fire turned orange by his brief presence. The world slewed again under Blite, and he found himself putting out both hands as if he could somehow stop himself. Those hands disappeared in two orange streamers – the beam ate up his arms, and then the rest of him. He just had time to feel a sense of *here I go again*.

Was it better this time to remember clearly the possible futures? At least in this scenario the first of his multiple deaths were without pain, though the ones where the beam burned off his legs, and tracked on to cut the grav-car in half, had not been so good. He'd spent far too many times lying in rubble before the prador-thing tracked him down and incinerated him there. This only changed when, immediately after the first beam strike had dropped him on the rooftop, he tried something radical: he drew his pulse gun and blew his own brains out. After that he fell conscious into blackness, with the crystal throbbing in his skull. A sense of omniscient inspection breezed over him, leaving a wake of amusement. The revision next time put him further back, so he assumed Penny Royal, or some fragment of the same, had intervened in the usual process.

'Do you know what's happening?' Carlstone had asked.

'Yes, I fucking do! Move fast and move now, or we're all dead!'

This time there'd been no interlude with Armand to look out of the window at the approaching prador-things. Blite's urgency propelled the man ahead and they arrived on the roof earlier. And yet, it was almost as if reality was trying to correct for these revisions. He saw Kostis and Iris ahead, just behind the grav-gurney carrying Meander. They got aboard as the ramp began to close, as before, and Blite ran with the horrible expectation of burning up yet again. He and Armand hit the ramp next and dived inside. Rolling, Blite looked back into that familiar flare of bright white as the beam punched up through the roof and tracked across.

'Get us the hell out of here!' he shouted.

The floor hit him hard in the back as combined grav and thrusters went straight to full power. They hurtled into the sky, the rib-shaped building still upright this time. A side wall exploded outwards, and the creature shot out. It accelerated towards them on blue-green thruster flames, and Blite knew that yet again they'd not moved away fast enough. But then it dipped, its underside exploding downwards, and the straight-line vapour trail of a railgun strike appeared a second later. The AI had got itself a clear target. Blite breathed relief as the ramp door finally closed up, but immediately started to get the horrors. It had taken him an age the others simply couldn't know about to get here. The moment still existed, though, and they weren't out of danger yet. He closed his eyes and delivered instructions to his nanosuite, whittling down the adrenalin, shifting neurochem so he wouldn't fall on the floor and coil up, hoping the world would go away. At last, with some grip on himself, he auged to the grav-car and switched on the screen paint. Now he could see the creature falling, still amazingly intact after a strike that would have vaporized most things. His relief was short-lived, as it still managed to fire missiles directly towards them.

'Evasive!' he managed to shout, just a second before they impacted.

The car shuddered on the blasts, crabbing sideways through the air. Fire blasted in through the back end, flinging Kostis past him, while Iris made a strange keening sound and fell back, slumping to the floor with her left arm missing. Acceleration died, and then came weightlessness. Blite didn't need Carlstone's, 'We're going down,' as confirmation. He considered how differently he'd play this when, inevitably, he had to go through it all again. Then, out of chemically induced calm, he told himself, *Hey, you're not dead yet.*

May

They were done. May scanned over the shield generator and its heavy array of thermocouples, as well as other energy convertors. Her satisfaction with a job well done had its subtext. Still wearing her spacesuit, she turned away and headed for the bridge, meanwhile auging through to Arach, who was coming up from Engineering.

'It doesn't have an ejection port,' she said.

Shield generators took on the weapons load against the shields they generated and rapidly converted the energy into other forms. They could in fact be used to recharge a ship's laminar storage remotely via a high-intensity laser or particle beam, but there was a delay during conversion. If a shield was hit with more energy than it could handle, the generator would begin to melt down, or even explode. Should this happen aboard warships, the delay and the reading of energy levels gave enough time for the generator to be ejected through a port, to finish its destruction safely out in vacuum, and before it caused damage inside the ship.

'That will not be necessary,' the spider drone replied.

'How can you be so sure?'

'Because of centuries of experience with tactics and logistics,' Arach replied.

'You're not being very clear,' May replied, slowing as she saw the huge figure of Mr Crane walking ahead of her towards the bridge.

219

'Okay,' said Arach. 'Clarity. If we're hit with anything sufficient to destroy the generator, ejection makes no difference. You don't have a second hardfield generator to take up the load, and you don't have the ablation and defensive armour of a warship. The moment that generator fucks up, you'll have a particle beam carving the ship in half. The damage an overloaded generator might cause is simply irrelevant.'

May turned, seeing Arach now coming up behind her.

'Thank you for the explanation,' she said out loud, and tightly.

'Think nothing of it,' Arach replied.

She turned away, wanting to rail at the drone, but having no real direction for her abrupt and uncharacteristic anger. She followed Crane as he ducked through into the bridge. The big Golem went back to stand against the wall, as he had before, but this time planted his feet wide apart and folded his arms. What this particular pose implied she didn't want to think about. She dumped herself in her chair and looked across at Akanthor and Davidson, who were watching her intently. Anger slewed into incongruent excitement.

'Okay, prep for heavy manoeuvring.' She sat back and auged to the chair controls. It folded around her, and down on the arms she had access to the joystick and touch screen. Davidson and Akanthor did the same. Davidson was on damage control and repairs now, as well as the subsidiaries. They'd distributed the *Bracken*'s population of robots throughout – printerbots and others with deposition welders – and scattered patches were ready to be applied to the hull. She felt this was simply make-work as they'd either be safe or dead within a matter of minutes. Akanthor was on scanning and energy distribution, chiefly because that concerned the shield generator. Behind her, May heard Arach compressing himself to squeeze in through the door.

'You ready there, spider drone?' she asked, swinging her chair around to face him.

'I was born ready,' the drone replied.

'Born?' Davidson interjected nervously. 'First time I've heard it described as that.'

'Stamped out, printed and assembled, then,' said Arach. 'My memories of Room 101 are vague, starting with when I fell straight into a prador assault.'

You fucking what? thought May, and then, *But of course.* It made sense that the drone had been made in the war factory with the worst rep going.

'I'm still concerned about the EMR,' she said.

She hadn't noticed what the drone had been doing until he flipped up a section of the floor and delved down inside with one foot.

'I have multiple data links to the weapons, which are unlikely to fail, and now . . .' something clicked and crunched in the floor, and the spider drone's leg went down deeper, '. . . and now I have a hard link to them, and to all the ship's systems.'

May sank into deeper aug connection with the ship and could feel the drone there – an alien interloper. It wouldn't surprise her, should things get seriously traumatic, if the drone took over completely. At present, raising a schematic, she could see his connection to the weapons and, of course, the sensors for targeting. She swung her attention to the ship mind, felt the busy roil of calculations and its dumb pleasure in that. She ignored that and went to the human count, seeing just a couple of minutes of ship time remaining before they surfaced into the real.

'It will take ten minutes to make it to cover in this planetoid, but the bounty hunters should arrive in eight minutes,' she said, now sounding as nervous as Davidson.

'That about covers it. You've inspected the coordinates?'

May blinked and pulled up the data, while also translating it into a visible image. The line schematic of the object turned before her, transparent, to show an internal tunnel system around one shaft that delved down about eight kilometres. This was her target – one of the few large enough to accommodate the *Bracken*. She had to guide her ship down about six kilometres, then take a convoluted route through side tunnels to reach a small internal chamber. It occurred to her, as when she'd looked at this before, that she wasn't seeing all of it. Maybe the entire thing was filled with such tunnels. Something nagged at her about it. She knew about Polity installations of a similar nature but, as far as she understood it, ECS would be unlikely to leave an active one unattended. And if they were to abandon such a place, they'd have stripped everything out, including the weapons. But she was sure she'd heard of something else, and the words *dark wanderer planetoid* just kept playing in her mind.

'A Polity installation?' she asked abruptly.

'There is a very vague connection,' Arach replied. 'Thirty seconds remaining.'

May gripped the joystick and raised a link to it in her aug.

'Vector switch,' she said to Davidson. 'A6 through to C12 on standby.'

'Yeah,' Davidson replied bluntly. They'd already gone over this ad nauseum.

'Ten, nine, eight . . .' Arach counted them down, and then they were there. May felt the weird wrench go through her and caught sight of the infinite, for she was one of those who could do no more than glimpse the reality of U-space. They thumped out into the real, leaving a trail of spontaneously generated photons up out of the quantum foam. May dropped the imagery of the planetoid in overlay onto the real object in the distance, even as she slammed the joystick forwards. The image turned to fit, and she pinpointed the location of the shaft they needed. Now other things began impinging, even as one of the particle cannons fired up and incinerated an object hurtling towards them – it passed in a cloud of glowing gas. Space around here was scattered with debris.

May ramped up acceleration, her chair tightening around her and her nanosuite kicking in to keep her conscious. The bounty hunters would appear at, or near, their own arrival point, so it made sense to run hard for the planetoid, then decelerate around and behind it. She should be able to keep it mostly between them and their pursuers, as she took her ship down into that shaft. However, after taking a few seconds to assess their surroundings, she pulled the acceleration down. There was simply too much debris for a maximum acceleration run to be safe.

'What the hell happened here?' she wondered, through her aug.

'The war,' Davidson replied.

She began running an identification program – frames fell over various debris, closing in around them, then coming up with brief analyses. There, the front end of a slab-like early Polity attack ship. There, the U-space nacelle from a late wartime destroyer. Over there, the burned-out hull of a prador assault craft, and beyond it the ripped-open hulk of a prador destroyer. Still something nagged at her.

'A lot of war,' said Davidson, puzzled.

The minutes counted down as she guided her ship between the larger masses, while Arach kept on firing up the weapons to incinerate smaller chunks in their path, or shift them aside through explosive ablation. Maybe this had been the real purpose for these weapons. She checked timings. Five minutes had passed.

'Wait a second,' said Davidson. 'That's not wartime.'

He highlighted a hulk, and then the decals on its hull.

'That's SGZ out of Stratogaster,' said Akanthor. 'Graveyard coring and thralling bastards. Well deserved, whatever happened to them.'

'And definitely after the war,' Davidson added. 'Getting a bad feeling now.'

They passed the planetoid and May used the reserved subsidiaries to flip the ship over, now decelerating around it in a curve.

'Here they come,' said Arach. 'I'm dropping some watchers.'

May checked and saw the fist-sized sensors zipping out from their port. They hadn't been discussed, but she guessed it made sense to do this. Via the ship mind, she received data surges and translated them into a perceivable map. Eight distinct U-signatures had appeared in an arc behind them. Imagery then clarified of the vessels now emerging, taken from the multiple inputs of all the sensors Arach had launched. A second later a particle beam lanced out from the ship that had fired on them before around Cull, seemingly drawing a slow line across vacuum. May tracked vectors, fired their upside thrusters and watched the beam slice past them, to carve a glowing line in the face of the planetoid.

'Shit,' said Arach.

What was his problem? It'd been a miss, hadn't it? But then other sensor data began coming in. She saw weird U-signatures appearing and registered energy surges, all *inside* the planetoid.

'Bringing us down to one in ten subsidiaries,' said Davidson.

'Check,' she replied.

She fired up the main fusion drive for remaining deceleration. The planetoid grew huge ahead, with the shaft mouth clear. Another alert showed up and she saw missiles heading towards them. They wouldn't arrive until the ship actually entered the shaft, which might make things a bit hectic. Had Crane and Arach factored that little gem in? Too late for any change of plans now, however.

The particle beam fired again, the ships behind accelerating towards them. The beam seemed to waver and spiral in its course, and she recognized that the aggressor had shifted targeting to cover a particular area. They knew where she was heading, and now that beam hitting home had moved from possibility to certainty. A second later the iris over their shield generator opened and the thing fired up. In the imagery she was getting, extending across EMR along with a U-space overlay, she saw the perfectly circular disc appear behind. The particle beam tracked across and splashed on it, the thing turning from light amber to black.

'Fucking powerful,' Akanthor commented.

The mouth of the planetoid's shaft rose up towards them as she heard explosions inside her ship, and the waft of burning reached her nostrils. That was worrying, since the bridge door was shut in order that the bridge could reorient to deceleration. And then the shaft swallowed them.

May concentrated totally on flying, while also bringing on collision programs. She felt the shift in grav as the gravity of the planetoid impinged. Shaft wall sped past. It was just rock, but with odd striations in it from whatever method had been used to bore it out. The shield blackened further on a huge explosion, and then it went out. Their particle cannons fired up next, filling the shaft behind with explosions as Arach took out the other arriving missiles. May damped their speed but then, after a glimpse at what lay behind, ramped it up again. No more missiles were coming their way, but chunks of stone were zipping down fast, followed by the ponderous fall of boulders nearly the size of the ship. It was going to be tight.

Hard deceleration next, and she kicked in further subsidiaries for that, overriding Davidson. The ship lurched down to a slow roll, with the side shaft coming into sight. She kicked with the subsidiaries again, throwing the ship into the side shaft, and winced at the crash as she clipped a part of it on the lip of the entrance. Debris tumbled past behind, shortly followed by those leviathan boulders. A slew of damage reports arose and she dismissed them in irritation. She pushed hard on the controls, using the joystick but also complementing that with aug control, mapping grids flashing red before her. After another crash against the wall, followed by breach alerts, she killed velocity, dismissing the alerts too. No need to go so fast now. She doubted any missiles would be following them in here, and Davidson confirmed this a moment later.

'Sealing up some holes,' Davidson said tightly, then added, 'I don't think we'll be going back out that way.'

'There are many other exit points,' said Arach.

Yes, because this whole planetoid is riddled with tunnels, May thought.

Seven turns through the tunnel, and then easing through the last because the clearance was mere metres. She finally flew the ship out into the chamber they were aiming for, grav countering the light gravity of the planetoid, then feathered down until the ship crunched onto the stone floor. May looked around. Smaller tunnels speared away from this place. Across the floor lay what appeared to be technological junk, but laced together with what looked like metallic fungal growths. There was workable technology here, but any order to it was perhaps only perceivable by a complex, fragmented and insane mind.

'I calculate,' said Arach, 'that you have by now figured out where we are.'

May felt a shiver run down her spine, but it was Davidson who replied out loud, his voice flat and precise, as if he was trying to control his fear.

'This is Penny Royal's planetoid,' he said.

9

Matheson

The hunger and thirst quickly reached the edge of tolerance just a few minutes into the U-jump to the coordinates Straeger had provided. Meanwhile Matheson fought a perception of that continuum which threatened to tear his brain out of his skull. He sat in his captain's chair as he struggled, feeling logic and his grip on reality sliding in and out. The Brices were just sitting on the floor behind, arms wrapped about their shins, and in some manner communing. Their arrival point lay a few hours into the future, and he knew he needed to snap out of this cycle if he was to survive, if they were all to survive. The door to the rear of the bridge opened and Ricardo stepped inside.

'Matheson,' he said.

Matheson was out of his chair in an instant, clamping down on his sudden urge, and gridlink calculation, to U-jump across the bridge. He strode towards the man-Golem, while raising a hand to look at the sharp points of his claws.

'You fucker,' he said, but the words were only in his mind and his face was a frozen thing, embedded in metal. He came to a halt before Ricardo, aware that the Brices were up and oriented like predators on *his* prey. How much damage could he do to Ricardo with weapons that were, as Straeger had said, little more than sharp steel? And anyway, the fact he couldn't swear at, or threaten, the man-Golem sucked away his impetus. He just stood there, clenching and unclenching his hands.

'I have the data on what Straeger has done to you,' said Ricardo, and now Matheson could see the man-Golem wasn't right either. He looked thin and drawn, which for someone in a Golem chassis made no sense. What could be seen of his skin outside the bland grey overall he wore had also taken on a metallic hue, while his eyes had turned topaz yellow. As he stood there, he reached up to his now-ragged blond hair, plucked out a lump, and let it drop to the floor.

Ricardo continued, 'The Spatterjay viral form needs sustenance and suppression, otherwise you'll turn into something that ceases to be of utility to Straeger. You must eat.'

The dead, leaden words further stalled Matheson's inclination to attack. Straeger had obviously done something to Ricardo. Though he had no solid evidence for it – aside from the pain throughout his own body, and his mind teetering on the edge of madness – he reckoned it was probably worse than any punishment he could have thought of for Ricardo. He forced himself into the nearest thing he could accomplish to relaxation, noting the Brices simultaneously straightening up, then raised a hand and pointed at his enclosed face.

'I can't fucking eat,' he said, but only in his mind.

Ricardo just stared at him, obviously not having heard, then jerked as if prodded. He raised a hand and pointed at Matheson's enclosed face. 'You have been provided with the tools but must acquire the skills.'

Abruptly it became too much. He didn't think about methods of attack, or how dangerous a Golem could be, as he stepped in and swept his fist from left to right as hard as he could. He hit the side of Ricardo's skull, knocking the head right over to the shoulder. Ricardo's feet left the ground and he spun, legs over head, to crash into a console to the left of the Brices. Matheson staggered in the other direction and, when he caught his balance, saw why he too hadn't gone over. Two long dents in the floor showed at the edges of his feet. He raised his hand. The blow had deformed it, with the back of his hand bent around and fingers sticking out at the wrong angles. Part of the armouring had also split to reveal an open wound, a sliver of exposed bone and slowly shifting fibres. It hurt, but not as badly as it should have done. Not even thinking about what pain it might cause, he clenched it back into a fist. Bones crunched as it tried to obey him, and steadily it regained its correct shape, shedding a spill of seemingly half-coagulated blood as the split closed. It wasn't quite there yet, he could feel it, but it was rapidly healing. He lowered it and looked over at Ricardo.

The man-Golem lay sprawled below the console with his head still over at an unnatural angle. The Brices had turned to orient on him, like a pack of dogs Matheson could unleash at any moment. Straeger wasn't sending them off with inadequate weapons, to die at the hands of Mr Crane. The Spatterjay virus packed into their bodies had made them ridiculously strong – perhaps as strong as, or stronger than, a Golem. But if they didn't eat and take viral suppressors, just as Ricardo had said, that same virus would turn them into something monstrous and utterly beyond Straeger's control. So there had to be a way.

Ricardo's head straightened up with a crackling sound, and he carefully climbed to his feet. He looked at the damaged console, then down at the dents in the floor, then, as if prodded, advanced a few paces and halted. He raised a hand and pointed at Matheson's head again, as if making some point.

Matheson reached up and explored the covering over his head, but just found a slick surface that he could hardly feel through the armouring also over his hands. He focused in with that other new facility of his which interpreted U-space, and he hauled up cam and other data to allow him and the Brices to see. His face lay there, under the metal, and now he could see lines of division in the armour. One ran from just below his chin to the crown of his head. At both end points it bifurcated. From his chin, lines ran along his jaw bones to end against the accordion structure around his neck. From the crown, they ran down the back of his skull to the same at the back. There had to be a way to open up this covering and yet, searching his gridlink connections to this armour, he couldn't find it. Rage flushed through him and he reached up to his face, digging for the line of division, bending the metal in with unnaturally strong fingers, and at last finding a grip. He pulled, hard, tearing open the covering at the front line. Finally, long suppressed since the armour engulfed him, his scream came out.

The pain was horrifying – so much worse than from his broken hand – and yet it also seemed to have a dull edge, as if somehow dislocated from him. He went down on his hands and knees. Through his wider sense, he saw the Brices in a weird pose, with their hands up at either side of their faces and held there, as if frozen in some act of worship. Also through that sense, he could see himself, and now realized that the armour covering had been melded to his human skin. He saw his face, like an anatomical model stripped down to the muscle, leaking blood as thick as jam, while twists of blue and white fibres writhed over its surface. Despite the pain, there came an immense relief too, as he was able to gasp in his first breath since being enclosed in this suit. He screamed that breath out, more in rage than pain, and then ended it, pushing himself back upright onto his knees. The pain began to fade, with the spread of hard scales expanding on his face like crystals on the surface of a fluid. He recognized this wasn't skin growing back, but perhaps something from the virus's eclectic collection of alien genomes. He wondered too if, with such hunger and thirst in him, he'd grown a leech tongue.

'Straeger likes us to suffer,' he said, thankful his mouth did actually feel right.

He stood up and focused on the Brices. They were still in that weird pose. The talk between them continued, but had turned into something he no longer recognized as human speech. He brought it into focus in his gridlink, and further opened his link to them. It seemed that their locked screams and suffocation had robbed them of human speech. He spoke to them anyway, through this connection and out loud on the bridge too.

'Open your face coverings,' he said.

Human speech returned to them in waves. He heard Will saying, 'No no no,' even as his fingertips dug in at his forehead and chin. What had seemed nonsensical jabber now clarified from Sheen as an ancient rhyme, repeated again and again. 'Beware the Jabberwock,' she was telling her brothers and him. What Ulnar might have been saying he had no time to interpret, as the man quickly wrenched open the covering and dropped, bellowing, onto his back. The other two shortly followed him down. Will was the first back up and swinging towards Matheson, skinned face twisted with rage and pain, as iridescent scales grew and his eyes seemed to glow red.

'You should let us die!' he spat, taking a step towards Matheson, but then seemingly unable to take another one.

With breathing, it seemed some modicum of sanity had returned to Matheson and, despite something dangerous and giggling sitting inside him, down deep, he could think more clearly now. Straeger had provided the tools but not the skills, Ricardo had said, and in his gridlink he could see the schematic of his new armour and its intrusions into his body. Then three

231

more schematics were overlaid on this – slaves on the master copy.

'That's a problem,' he said to Will, making an alteration to the schematic and holding up his right hand. 'We're loaded with some advanced form of the Spatterjay virus. If I left you in your armour, unfed, you wouldn't die.'

Will closed his eyes and shrugged himself under control, as the others got to their feet too. Matheson remained focused on his finger. The change came with heat and a burning sensation at its tip. The spike of his claw there lost its frosting and turned mirror bright, before sinking back down and returning the armoured covering there to the semblance of a normal human finger. He considered a redesign of his face covering, which he could do easily enough in the gridlink, but then understood the horrifying truth: the armour *was* his skin. Did this mean to eat, drink, breathe and see in a normal fashion he'd have to tear it open every time? There had to be another way . . .

'I have provided nutrients,' said Ricardo, now stepping forward, turning and opening the bridge door. He headed off without looking back and, hearing him talk in such an unnatural manner again, Matheson wondered if any of the original man remained.

'Come on,' he said to the others, and went after him.

The ship, despite being a damned good vessel for a bounty hunter to have acquired, didn't extend to cabin fabricators, so Matheson headed straight for what he and Ricardo had come to call the kitchen. Even before reaching the door into that place, he smelled food – his body responded by writhing and twisting where there should have been no movement at all. It seemed the Spatterjay virus inside him was hungry too, and making its wants known.

The sliding door remained open and Ricardo was inside, with his back to the preparation counter and EMR cooker. Like some servant out of ancient times, he stood with a tea towel draped over one arm, clutching a serving dish in the other. The table, bolted to the floor in the centre of the room, had been neatly laid out as never before, with glasses, plates and cutlery that hadn't been part of this ship's manifest previously. Also, beside each setting, were air-blast injectors. Matheson pulled out a chair and sat, watching the Brices hesitate as they hungrily scanned their surroundings. Then humanity reasserted and they took their seats.

'What's this?' asked Will, picking up one of the injectors.

'Viral inhibitor,' Ricardo replied tonelessly.

Will raised it and injected himself in his face, then discarded the thing. They all followed suit, now knowing what was living within them. When Matheson injected, he really felt things slowing down inside him, and some return of human feeling. He looked up when Ricardo went around scooping out meat and vegetables, depositing them on every plate, and had a flash of insight. Ricardo was the coward, and if Straeger had examined him on as deep a level as such an AI could, it must know this about him. It seemed to have turned him into a servitor, to look after the actual fighting men, but this was only the visible humiliation – he wondered what other tortures might not be on display.

The food was heavy with garlic and herbs he didn't recognize, though he knew the first of these acted as a viral suppressor, and probably the herbs did too. He cleared his plate as Ricardo came around filling up their glasses with wine from an actual bottle. The grotesque facsimile of civilization that Straeger had imposed fled from his mind as Ricardo came to fill his plate again. Finishing the second helping, he realized that no matter how much the Spatterjay virus had changed his body, it would still have waste he needed to eject. He pushed his chair back to look down at his groin, and could see the shape of his genitalia there. But inevitably, there was no opening.

'I'm feeling more human now,' said Ulnar Brice, his words hissing.

Matheson looked at the man's red eyes, and a hollow between them seemed like another eye ready to open. The man's tongue poked out a little way, showing an opening at the end, with what seemed like small teeth wheels revolving inside.

''Twas brillig,' Sheen agreed.

Will turned and studied them for a moment. When he returned his attention to his plate, Matheson could see the despair in his expression as he scooped up more food. Matheson stood up abruptly. After they were first enclosed in their armour, he'd cut them off because he couldn't bear their suffering, and now he couldn't bear what that suffering had done to them. He needed time alone to think this through, and sitting here exchanging nonsensical statements wouldn't help. He drained his glass of wine, grabbed a bottle of water from a cupboard and headed out, raising the armour's schematic in his mind as he did so. He needed to alter his armour, and by extension theirs too – if they were closed up in it again as they had been before, he doubted that what would be revealed next time it opened would be human at all.

Cormac

Raw sleer wouldn't have been his first choice, but Cormac was used to making do with whatever he could get his hands on. His commando knife, with its ceramal blade honed sharp as chainglass, still required some force to get through the carapace. He butchered the thing, separating the segments, removing the legs and opening them, exposing various organs and taking some out. Meanwhile, he checked the biological data on the creatures in his gridlink. With storage in his skull being enough for a series of vast libraries, that data was complete and up to date from the last time he'd linked into the AI net.

Ascertaining that the musculature was edible, though lacking in some nutrients, he began carving off pieces and inserting them into his mouth. The taste was somewhat fruity and the texture unpleasant, so he shut down his taste buds for the chore. He soon turned them back on again, because the texture was even worse with taste off. His nanosuite was still in emergency mode, and the nanites in his stomach and intestines, so the process of digestion was faster than normal. Meanwhile, he ran feedback through his gridlink to ascertain requirements, running search-and-match programs with sleer biology.

Many of the organs contained toxins, but also nutrients he required. After filling himself with the muscle meat, he began making adjustments so his suite could convert and break down any toxins and access those nutrients. He picked up an organ that looked like green liver, chopped off a piece, and ate it. Without his nanosuite working, this would have killed him within an hour. Instead it just felt hot in his guts, like a shot of whisky. The organ meat itself tasted quite good, surprisingly – almost like a curry. He grimaced and continued eating, working his way through different parts, including its eyes too. It was good he'd tried so many varieties of strange foods over his long lifetime; it ensured he felt no squeamishness at all.

As he monitored himself within, and just sensed things on a normal level, he felt the food dissolving into his body. At some point, remaining detritus would reach his large intestine, but it hadn't got there yet. His belt loosened to accommodate his expanding torso. Meanwhile, steady reports of physical damage began disappearing. He started to feel a lot better too, as the pain in his skull receded.

'That wouldn't be my favoured cuisine,' said Mask.

'Ah, so you can still access me through hundreds of metres of rock. That's interesting.'

'You could also do that sort of thing in your time, with terahertz-scanning beams,' Mask replied.

Cormac smiled. Mask had effectively told him that their communication method didn't involve such terahertz radiation now. He therefore pushed to bring his U-senses back online and felt good when they came up easily. He focused in close, as he had on one of the prador search drones, and studied the mask over his face. The technology was a combination of organic and mechanistic, just like those p-prador, but now he saw something more. Distortions in it, like flaws in a diamond, actually extended into the U-space continuum. U-com, in the mask – very advanced organic tech.

'What do you usually eat?' he asked.

'Whatever I need to,' Mask replied. 'Don't get me wrong, I would eat as required, and as you now are, but my preference is for roast glister.'

Cormac blinked. Glisters were crustaceans from the world of Spatterjay – the source of the virus that had enabled the p-prador to make their partial transformation towards prill, which were also crustaceans of that world. Some connection? And was Mask maybe an Old Captain? Could she be one of the long-lived and nigh-indestructible inhabitants of that world? Perhaps there was a link between the humans here, if human she was, and the . . . Cormac halted this train of thought. The great mass of open-ended speculation from that simple glister comment made him realize he'd been played by an expert. Mask had deliberately derailed him.

His strength continued to grow, and his clothing tightened. Musculature had expanded and just the dregs of repairs remained.

His body, in conjunction with his nanosuite, was now laying down reserves. Triple-density fats were growing, their cells filling and packing with lipids, but also with other nutrients and minerals. Now, with waste beginning to enter his large intestine, and his bladder filling, he paused to gaze down at the remains of the sleer. He'd eaten nearly half of the thing – maybe twenty kilograms of watery meat.

He slowed the steady eating, monitoring his body more closely and being more selective about what he consumed. Certain nutrients were a requirement, but he didn't want the fats to expand any further and become a hindrance to movement. He began to bring his nanosuite down out of emergency mode, whereupon it informed him of numerous mutations in its function, some useful, some not. That was the thing about nanosuites: they were more complex than the bodies they occupied, subject to similar biological laws, but over a shorter time span. Now, concentrating less on suite data, his conventional physical response told him he'd eaten too much. He put down the latest chunk of something gristly and leaned back, feeling slightly nauseated. Bowel and bladder now distended, he did what was required, a bit embarrassed knowing Mask could see this, then telling himself not to be such a fool. He slid the remains of the sleer over the mess, then stepped away to another part of the geode where the surfaces weren't so sticky.

Weariness now impinged – a pure human reaction. He could choose to sleep while his body finished various tasks, and he knew he'd feel better afterwards. Instead, he dismissed the fatigue and focused his attention on his abilities. Extending his perception out from the geode, he found the p-prador in a nearby cave. All three were motionless and facing in towards his position. Certainly, they had detector gear, otherwise how would they have come so quickly to his arrival point on this world, in this future?

And what would their strategy be now? Their weapons couldn't reach him here . . .

Cormac abruptly stood up. The creatures had demonstrated a grasp of the function of U-space perhaps equivalent to his own ability, if not more advanced. He shouldn't make assumptions. It might well be that they could send something to his present location, and the fact they hadn't could be due to another prador trait of pride. Or they might not be able to send something themselves, but the technology for doing so lay where the p-prador corpse had been dragging him, and even now they could be making the request. Instinctively, Cormac wanted to jump away immediately, but he suppressed this, needing to check whether his abilities were fully up to spec – he hoped they would be repaired enough to do something that would divert attention.

He focused down on the sleer remains and opened himself to U-space. He encompassed the remains, but then pushed further with finesse, running a program to incorporate spatters and other debris in the U-field. In fact, everything he'd brought here. Maintaining his position in the real, though fading somewhat, he reached out to a cave beyond the four p-prador and flung the remains there. They faded before him, leaving clean crystal, and he perceived them reappearing in that cave in mid-air, then slopping to the floor. The p-prador turned at once and set out to that location. Cormac smiled and, sending a signal, held out his hand. He glanced once around the inside of the geode, pleased he would be leaving it in the condition he'd found it. The light dropped from the ceiling into his hand, and he put it out. Time to stop running and get proactive. Time to really let the creatures pursuing him know who he was, if only briefly.

Blite

The grav-car they were in dropped through the air. But, even though its grav-engine had been knocked out, some of the thrusters were still working. Blite just hung on to internal hull struts as Carlstone fought to bring the car down in one piece. Armand was up with his back against one wall, clinging on also. His suit was charred, but the face behind the visor seemed fine. Kostis had moved up front with Carlstone. Iris had stopped keening and, clinging on with her remaining arm, she peered down at the severed stump of the other. The bleeding stopped abruptly, then grey liquid bubbled out, spread over the stump to harden, and sealed it. She looked up.

'That was a shock,' she said without moving her lips.

'Understandable,' Blite replied out loud, but also via his aug.

'The human rises at unexpected times,' she observed, her voice coldly clinical now, but her expression kept twisting, as if she didn't know whether to be angry or somehow smug. It was very odd.

A building loomed up as Carlstone fought the controls. The grav-car clipped it, rucking out chain-glass windows like scales off a fish. Blite wanted to say something, but then realized the man had deliberately hit the building to change their course, as the car fell into a long street with rib-bone buildings looming over it on either side. People were there, running for cover. Blite felt a bit sick about that and just hoped they'd all get out of the way in time. He turned his attention to the grav-gurney.

Meander was still in place, though a little in disarray, twisted in the straps. The gurney had locked down to the floor. He inspected her body, looking for damage. She abruptly straightened out into a position flat on her back, her arms coming in and hands gripping one of the straps. Unconscious? Was she aware on some level of the danger, and putting her body in the best position for the circumstances? She opened her eyes and looked straight at him. He loosened one hand and gave her a thumbs-up and a wink, which was about the only reassurance he could offer. Fear displaced her initially puzzled expression. He guessed this wasn't because of any real awareness of the circumstances she'd found herself in. She was scared of him.

'Get braced!' Carlstone called.

They were now skimming along over running figures. Surely Carlstone had better choices than this? Again he wanted to say something, but again suppressed it. He'd always had confidence in the man's expertise, so if Carlstone aimed to bring the car down in this street, that was because any alternative would cause greater damage and loss of life. At the last the car tilted and the grav-engine fired up, sending compression waves through the car that Blite felt twisting his bones. The engine dropped out with a hissing bang, a hot glow shining up through cracks in the floor, and then the smoke of burning composite belching out. It had been enough. The car turned, clipping a long fence of metal palings, then hammering through the upper foliage of a tree. A second later it smashed into the trunk of another tree, exploding it to splinters. Blite managed to hang on, fingers digging into metalwork. Iris and Armand slammed into the bulkhead behind the cabin. A chaos of broken trees, mounding earth, fire and smoke ensued. With a final shuddering crash, the car came to a halt.

Blite released his hold, seeing Iris and Armand still mobile. He went into the cabin. The chain-glass screen was down, with its top edge jammed into the back wall, the cabin truncated. Carlstone was already ducking out from underneath the screen, but Kostis would be going nowhere. The screen edge had gone straight through his neck, leaving a long smear of blood along its underside. Where was his head? There . . .

Carlstone moved into the back area, holding Kostis's head in one hand by the hair. He brought it quickly down to the floor, while pulling out a shearfield blade. He scribed a circle in the occipital, levered out a chunk of skull and delved inside. A second later he had what he wanted: a finger-length cylinder of ruby trailing a skein of hairlike fibres. He stripped the fibres away and inserted the memplant – everything Kostis was – into one pocket.

'You good, Armand?' he asked the now-standing soldier.

'My suit and my nanosuite are on top of it,' Armand replied.

'Becoming a habit,' said Carlstone. 'Maybe you need an armoured hotsuit?'

'Funny man,' Armand replied.

'I'm missing something,' said Blite.

'Fifty per cent burns,' Armand told him. 'Again.'

Blite nodded, then to Carlstone, 'The ship.'

'We move,' Carlstone said. He swung his gaze over Iris.

'I'm good,' she said, a bitter snap in her voice.

Blite returned his attention to that head, now an organic lump leaking fluids. He'd had a memplant himself when interrogated by Carnusine, and the AI had removed it for study. When they released him, the AI had offered to return it to his skull but he told Carnusine to keep it as a souvenir. Over the ensuing years of ticking things off his bucket list, and building Penny Transport, reluctance had grown in him. Had he subconsciously understood what the black diamond was doing, even before it became blatant? Could it be that he'd always had some sense that he had no need for a memplant, already possessing something that wouldn't allow him to die? Now new thoughts occurred. If he had a memplant like Kostis, would the diamond still intervene? Did it distinguish between him and a recording of him?

'Is there something we need to know?' asked Carlstone acerbically, interrupting his thoughts. Blite grunted a response and turned away.

They collected scattered weapons. Carlstone abandoned his wrecked multigun pack and found a laser carbine. Even Iris took up a pulse weapon in her remaining hand. Blite, having not been thrown about so much and retaining his weapons, stepped forwards and stooped over Meander. Her eyes were closed again, but whether out of fear or unconsciousness he had no idea. He had to assume the latter, so he undid the straps, hoisted her up and draped her over one shoulder. Carlstone nodded, then turned to the ramp door which, with a blast, separated from the car and tumbled over a pile of smoking foliage.

They set out, moving slowly at first through the wreckage created by the crash, then speeding up once in the spaces under the trees of this arboretum. Blite allowed Carlstone to lead, to dictate their course. He'd once again proved his worth in the way he'd avoided dropping their car on a crowded street. Blite knew there would have to have been some very fast logistical and tactical calculations to do that. They ran.

'So, Captain Blite.'

The communication hadn't come via a request, but sliced through his aug security as if it wasn't there. In internal vision, he glimpsed a metallic face icon, but then this slewed away. Perhaps the planetary AI understood he was busy, so didn't want to give him too many distractions.

Blite kept it subvocal; he didn't want his distraction to spill over onto the others.

'Yup,' he said simply.

'I was told to keep a lookout for you, but the reasons for that have been somewhat obscure. This is not unusual when Mobius AIs are involved. So, these prador biomechs are here after you, are they?'

'That has become apparent,' Blite replied.

'Three thousand two hundred and four, including one of your men, have died, Blite.'

Just for a second Blite felt a surge of shame, then he became angry at the manipulation.

'And I didn't kill anyone,' he snapped. 'I came here to rescue someone from the Mortons – a criminal family you've allowed to stay in business because of your "advancement of humanity" bullshit.'

The AI just seemed to accept this and asked, 'Where are these creatures from?'

'I have no fucking idea. I just took off when it seemed evident they were coming in my direction.'

They ran out from under trees and across open ground thick with grass and weeds, some of them unnervingly mobile. No problems, however, and they came to another paling fence. Carlstone began slicing through it with his carbine.

'No, some other datum is missing. Your behaviour, from what I can gather of it, was of a man who knew too quickly that these creatures were after him.'

'If you say so.'

'You are hiding something, Blite. Why did you grab this petty thief from the Mortons? Why go to such expense and trouble?'

'Are you actually an AI?' Blite asked as they went through the fence.

'Just probing . . .'

'I don't have time for this,' Blite spat back.

'She stole something from you, but precisely what that was is unclear. Oddly unclear. The highest likelihood is that it is something to do with Penny Royal . . . ah, and now the Mobius AI has deigned to provide new data. Attempts on your life. Temporal anomalies.'

'Straeger,' said Blite.

'Who will be arriving shortly,' said the AI.

'Then best direct your questions there.'

'I will do so, but, meanwhile, you must surrender yourself to me. I will provide detail on how you can get out from under this.'

'Go fuck yourself,' Blite replied.

The link simply blinked out.

They ran out along a slab path, Carlstone leading the way. The city had many paths like this and very few groundcar roads. Blite glanced up as a series of military-looking transports sped overhead towards a distant pall of smoke and dust. Even as he looked over in that direction, he saw the arrow-straight vapour trails of orbital railgun strikes appearing. He hoped the AI had nailed a few more of those bastard things.

'We need a car,' he opined.

'Most of the cars here are under AI oversight,' said Carlstone, looking thoughtful.

'Just been talking to the AI,' said Blite.

'Me too,' Carlstone replied.

It was well to remember that AIs were quite capable of conducting thousands of conversations all at once.

Carlstone continued, 'It wasn't so subtly referencing my service in ECS and what my duties should be. Apparently I'm not a good citizen.'

'Heh,' said Armand. 'You got that spiel too.'

Blite glanced at Iris. She shrugged. 'Completely different approach with me, concerning human development in conjunction with AI. But the essence is the same: the AI wants us under its control.'

'It'll try to lock down the ship,' said Carlstone.

Blite looked at him. 'We need options.'

'I'm on it,' Carlstone replied, his expression introspective as he began some heavy aug work. They kept moving down the path, and a minute later he gestured to a side alley and led the way in. Blite noticed that this led away from the ship, but he went anyway. Stupid to start questioning the man's decisions now.

They wound their way through narrow alleys, scattered with pots of geraniums and overhung with rainbow bougainvillea. Iron railings ran around small yards and stone steps leading to tea oak doors. Blite became aware that explosions and the sounds of destruction and conflict were drawing closer, while they were still heading away from the space port.

'This a good idea?' he finally asked.

'The best in the circumstances,' Carlstone replied.

A shape appeared in the alley ahead of them, legs spread, shiny composite teeth exposed and tongue lolling. Greer's dog didn't look threatening; it was almost as if Groff was grinning.

'This way,' said the dog, turning and bounding off down the alley a short distance, then going up some stone steps to a door. 'Break door,' he added. Blite noted the dog's speech had become a lot clearer than before. No doubt Iris's work on his mental enhancement and artificial voice box.

Armand, just behind the dog, didn't hesitate. He drew a pulse gun and shot out the lock, kicking the door open. The dog led the way in, and they followed into someone's home.

'What the hell?' said a man standing in a hologram of the city, obviously following the events nearby.

'Sorry about this,' said Blite. 'Short cut.'

Before the man could react any further, they ran on after the dog to another door. No requirement for 'break door' as

Carlstone, now ahead of Armand, opened it and stepped through. They came down into another alley, followed that, and took a turning that led out onto a groundcar road. Even as they reached this, a car running on adaptive wheels slammed to a halt, throwing up flakes of stone from the road, and its doors popped open.

'Get in!' Greer yelled.

Groff was up beside her in an instant. Armand and Carlstone piled in too, and Blite lowered Meander to Iris, who pulled her inside. He paused then to look back down the road. Smoke was belching from a building down there, and dimly through it he could see pulse shots flashing. Up in the sky a drone slid over – not a wartime machine, but one of the utile things AIs tended to fashion nowadays. Pale yellow beams stabbed down from it and tracked around. Blite noted the spiral pattern running down them and recognized vortex lasers – informational warfare beams. One of them nailed something just this side of the smoke. Invisible at first, it then appeared in a mass of shifting pixels. Until now, Blite hadn't understood why the AI hadn't nailed all of these creatures with satellite railgun strikes. The accuracy of such shots could be down to mere centimetres. Now he understood. They had some form of chameleonware, and obviously of a sophisticated kind, so the AI required close spotting from a drone. A missile spat up out of the smoke behind, looped around, and smashed into the drone, blowing it to shreds. As the vortex lasers winked out, the creature it had detected disappeared. A railgun strike came down a moment later, spearing into the road. The road erupted, but there was no sign of the creature.

'Fuck.' Blite piled into the car and Greer stamped on the accelerator, spraying stone as the adaptive wheels dug in. The acceleration was almost that of a launch, and it took Blite a short struggle to get properly seated in the back, crammed up against Iris. Glancing to the front, he saw now why the car was capable of road-wrecking acceleration. Part of the console had been torn open and Greer had inserted optics from a device lying down by Groff's rump. The vehicle was out of AI control.

'At least two of them,' said Carlstone, from where he occupied the front passenger seat with Groff. 'I think the third might have been hit, but that's not confirmed.'

'It's strange they didn't use chameleonware all the way,' Armand said tightly.

Blite looked past Iris to Meander, who still seemed out of it, then to Armand. The soldier's face looked pale and sickly, while burn plasma and blood were leaking out of splits in his burned suit.

'Energy,' said Iris flatly. 'Chameleonware is energy-hungry. A greater puzzle is what the hell they are. From what I've seen, their technology is advanced. Their weapons are like something out of recent ECS development, and I've never seen 'ware recover so quickly after being brought down by a warfare beam.'

The conversation paused as Greer took them around a tight corner so hard Blite thought he'd go through the door and end up on the street. He saw they were still heading away from the space port, and then thought: *Of course.* Behind them, back at the corner, the side of a building exploded, showering foamstone across the street. Those things, whatever they were, were still in pursuit.

'Prador,' said Carlstone.

'I agree they have something of that appearance. But the body form is too shallow, and they don't possess a head turret,' said Iris.

Blite glanced at her again. She was peering at her arm stump. It was nice to know she'd retained enough humanity to be embarrassed by her whining scream when she lost her arm and was now trying to appear all coldly analytical.

'I don't need to look at their body form, just their behaviour,' said Carlstone. 'Yes, chameleonware is energy-hungry, and they've obviously limited its use somewhat because of that, but otherwise their strategy is all prador.'

'Yes, there was no need for so much death and destruction for them to achieve their objective.' Iris turned to look at Blite, her gaze unreadable. 'Whatever that objective might be.'

Out of the city centre, Greer took the car up to high speed through a residential sprawl. The hyox engine began making a buzzing and grinding sound, obviously having been taken to its limit and beyond. Turning to look back, Blite now saw orbital railgun strikes following them out, while more drones had appeared and were tracking around with vortex lasers. A shadow fell across them and he flinched. It then came clear ahead and began to settle, its front end in a park and back end ruining someone's Japanese garden – he'd never been so glad to see his ship. The *Coin*'s ramp was already down, and it settled on the road.

Blite auged through to Paidon, 'Fast off, once we're in,' he said.

'Carlstone has already made me aware of the urgency,' she replied. 'And oddly, that wasn't entirely necessary.'

Sarcastic woman, thought Blite, as the car decelerated with a lurch, blowing out of its engine compartment something red hot and shaped like a slice of orange, which rolled clattering to the foot of the ramp.

'Out!' Greer shouted.

They piled out of the car and headed for the ramp. Halfway up it, Blite paused and looked back. A pall of thick black smoke had risen, with railgun strikes etching lines through it. Over that way he saw yet another building going down and felt another stab of guilt about that. Continuing inside, he headed for the door at the back of the hold space, and it was as if, in that moment, the universe was again trying to correct some balance.

He turned to look back again as Greer and Groff were coming up the ramp. Bright light flared behind them, throwing them into silhouette, and then their silhouettes melted away. Blite instinctively threw himself sideways, feeling the wash of intense heat across his face and hands. The beam, half a metre wide, punched through the door he'd been heading for, and burned on into the ship. An emergency protocol kicked in and slammed the ramp closed to cut off the beam, then the ship lurched into flight.

Blite lay there, looking at his charred right hand and feeling the burn on his face. He looked over at Meander, sprawled and singed but still breathing, then to the door. Iris, Armand and Carlstone were gone. Well, all but for someone's leg lying on the deck. Over by the ramp door, all that remained of Greer and her dog was soot settling through the air. The utter injustice of it clenched up his insides and brought him to sitting upright. Meander had now turned her head and was watching him with eyes that seemed strangely luminescent. Hardly thinking the matter through, he drew his pulse gun and put it up against the side of his head. He wasn't killing himself, merely resetting the universe to a just course.

Fifteen, maybe twenty shots and reruns? The whole began to blur in his mind with variations on who survived, and how those who didn't survive, died.

'Don't enter the ship!' he shouted, on the final iteration. 'Get under the ramp!'

It would have worked to save them all too, but Groff was injured and limping, and Greer turned back to snatch him up. And then, perhaps not hearing his warning, she ran up the ramp.

'Get down!' Blite shouted.

The beam lanced straight towards the hold, for it seemed the direction of the shot never changed. The top parts of Greer and Groff evaporated. Pushing himself back to his feet, Blite stared at the remains smoking on the ramp, then wearily drew his pulse gun and raised it to his head.

'What the hell!'

Death didn't come as expected, as his shots flashed upwards to zing off the *Coin*'s hull, after Armand clung to his arm. Blite swung his other arm around in a slap that sent the man sprawling. He shook his head at this foolishness, then reached up to touch the bump in his skull – the gem felt hot and seemed to be throbbing again. He then checked his weapon and knew he was procrastinating. He raised it to his skull once more, just as the stun rounds slammed into his back and sent him staggering. As a wave of blackness of a different kind crashed down on him, he hated himself for feeling grateful it was unconsciousness and not death.

May

There was atmosphere inside the planetoid, but Arach had advised against any attempt at breathing it.

'I'm still registering enough oxygen,' said Davidson over augcom from the bridge. 'And no toxins – it seems really close to Earth normal, except for an excess of argon.'

'The gas mix is not the concern,' Arach replied as he scuttled along after Crane across the stone floor. 'Stray nanites – which might decide to turn you into a mobile autogun – are.'

'Was it such a good idea to open the ship, then?' said May, gesturing back to the ramp.

'I'm too big for your airlocks,' Arach replied. 'And there are levels of risk. I did tell you to stay in your vessel.'

'I want to see this place,' said May, still puzzled why Davidson and Akanthor hadn't been so in love with the idea. She'd read their attitude and had ordered them to stay in the ship to keep on the sensors and make repairs. Their fear surprised her. It was something she would have to investigate in the future.

As she followed the spider drone and the Golem, she studied her surroundings. The stuff here did look like the detritus in a junkyard, but now she could see patterns. It seemed Penny Royal had laced together the parts here it had wanted to use simply without discarding the rest. She saw connected laminar power storage, links between processing units, strange metallic fungal growths binding together optical storage substrates. This all offended her sense of neatness, but of course she couldn't doubt the power of the insane, fragmented mind that had created it.

Crane strode through all this to a tunnel that speared off into darkness. It was just three metres across and oval. He took off his hat when it brushed against the ceiling. Arach just about filled the tunnel ahead of her. As May followed them in, she ramped up image enhancement in her visor, and noted things getting a bit tidier. Silvery inlays ran along the walls, quadrate and regular. Doubtless this was neatness out of necessity, but for what purpose she had no idea.

'Looks like a pre-Quiet War integrated circuit,' Davidson commented. The two of them, back at the ship, had the visual feed from her suit.

'It's nanotech,' said Arach. 'Touch nothing.' The drone chortled at some private joke. May, who'd just been reaching out, snatched her hand back.

The tunnel ran straight for a while, then began to curve to the left and upwards.

'Signal is getting dodgy,' Davidson commented.

May wondered at that. A mere curve in the tunnel shouldn't have been enough to stop the signal bouncing out back to the ship. The tech in the walls was clearly having an effect.

'Running a relay through me,' said Arach. 'Better?'

'Yes,' said Davidson, 'and now we're seeing what you're seeing too.'

The further along they went, the thicker the inlay grew, until it was bulging from the walls – thick silvery cords. May noted that other stuff had come in from elsewhere too, through holes and ducts. It all seemed to have coagulated into a feed towards something lying ahead.

'How does Crane know about this place?' she asked. 'And how come he thinks he can use its weapons?'

'Long story,' said Arach.

'I'm not doing anything other than walking at the moment.'

'Mr Crane has some technology inside him,' Arach stated. 'It's a technology he managed to turn to his own purpose. However, it's dangerous and tends to fight his control of it, attempting to return to its original purpose.'

'Destroying civilizations,' said Akanthor flatly over the link.

May felt a shiver run down her spine. She'd played in that virtuality and, at the time, thought that Crane having Jain technology inside him had just been an authorial fix to explain how difficult he was to destroy. But it was true, as Cormac had told her before too. That fucking Golem had technology inside him which scared even the AIs. No wonder there was such a huge bounty out for his retrieval, whether in pieces or otherwise.

'Yup, that's the one,' said Arach.

'What's this got to do with Penny Royal?' May asked.

'Well, Crane decided he needed some help in dealing with that problematic technology. Obviously he couldn't have gone to ECS – he would have ended up locked down in one of their black facilities.'

'They have those?' Davidson asked.

'Indeed,' said Arach. 'It's not just legendary agents and

homicidal Golem the AIs have turned into fictions that can be denied. Neat technique that: anyone asks about a black facility and the reply can always be, "You spend too much time in virtualities. This is the real world."'

'Anything else like that?' Davidson asked.

Before Arach could reply, May said, 'I would have thought Crane bright enough to realize that going to Penny Royal for help wasn't such a great idea either.'

Crane glanced around at her and her throat felt abruptly dry. Perhaps she was getting a hint of Davidson and Akanthor's attitude now.

'It was later on, when Penny Royal was becoming a good AI,' said Arach, dripping sarcasm.

'So just prior to the thing taking a nosedive into a black hole,' said Davidson. 'I've always been a bit unclear about events surrounding that AI. Something happened at the planet Masada involving it, then it disappeared for a while . . .'

Arach waved a leg dismissively. 'Atheter technology kicking off. It was resolved.'

A couple of simple statements that opened up a huge number of questions, and probably deliberately so. May decided to stay on point.

'And after those events, Penny Royal came back here and was a good AI, and Crane came to visit?'

'Yeah. We paid for transport with diamond slate on a trader's ship, while I tried to persuade the brass bastard he was being stupid. As you can imagine, I got nowhere. I stayed aboard the trade ship, well clear. Crane took a shuttle over here.'

'So you've no idea what happened then?'

'Some idea. Crane doesn't talk much, but I got the gist through other connections. Penny Royal was a fragmented mind combining, if you like, good and evil. The good had prevailed to create

253

something highly moral, but kinda disconnected from the prosaic affairs of lesser beings. It seemed the AI was lost in introspection but, when Crane arrived and made his request, the response was powerful – we even felt it out on the ship.'

'What response?' Akanthor interjected.

'Hilarity,' said Arach tightly.

Around the curve of the tunnel its terminus came into sight. There was a glassy bubble ten metres across, and silvery branches from the tunnel had veined it inside. Other objects were in there too, like the metallic fruiting bodies of those branches. Crane walked inside, stepping over branches to reach a growth like a flat mushroom, and climbed up onto it. No room on there for Arach and May, so they stood off to one side. Crane put his hat back on, then took something out of his pocket and began fiddling with it in one hand. May saw he held a small rubber dog. This just seemed ridiculous; crazy in these surroundings.

'So Crane got what he wanted from Penny Royal, without the usual drawbacks?' she asked, peering through the glass bubble and seeing that it appeared to be attached to the wall of another shaft.

'He got something, but what it was I cannot say.'

'That still doesn't explain how he understands this place, and has access to its weapons.'

Arach reached up with one limb and placed it on the edge of the mushroom. 'It was shortly after his visit that Penny Royal departed. We saw the launch of the original destroyer the AI controlled, though it hardly looked like a ship any more. In fact, let me show you – I can access the system here and run a hologram.'

An area within the bubble turned black, scattered with stars. Out of left field the planetoid came into view, the focus coming down on a silvery dart rising from the surface. This resolved into a Polity destroyer, but one that seemed to have something seriously wrong with it. It reminded May of an insect that had been the victim of a parasitic fungus. Splits had opened down its length, with vine-like growths tangled all through, and fruiting bodies protruding on fat stalks which also looked like U-space nacelles. The ship headed out into space and then started to shed chunks of itself as fusion drives kicked in from various orifices all over its hull. The thing began to distort, with areas folding in as if under the impact of faulty U-drive. Metal and composite disappeared, and black crystalline substance welled out in their place. As the fusion drives started to go out, she could see U-effect all around it, and it began to leave a photonic trail. At the last, all that remained was a long dart of matter consisting, seemingly, of long black crystalline blades: Penny Royal. Then in a flash the AI disappeared.

May staggered, as if the effect she'd seen in the recording had impinged here and now. She looked around to see the tunnel mouth dropping down, to be displaced by long metallic and slimy-looking rails. A glance outside showed the shaft walls passing as the bubble they were in rose up it.

'The fuck?' she said.

'Entirely unnecessary, I think,' said Arach. 'Maybe Crane is putting on a show for you.'

'You still haven't told me how he knows how to operate things here,' she said.

Arach sighed and continued, 'Seems Penny Royal was off about its business, and left the keys to its home to Crane. Apparently this place would come in useful. Crane stayed down here for a solstan month, and I had to become a bit threatening to stop the trade ship leaving. But they were happy with the load of diamond slate Crane brought back when he eventually returned.'

'Come in useful,' Akanthor repeated. 'Almost like the black AI could see the future.'

May shivered yet again. As with so many major events that'd occurred in the Polity, she'd taken an interest in the story of Penny Royal, but soon grown bored with the dearth of facts and the endless speculation. It occurred to her that this might have been as deliberate as turning main actors into fictions – as though the AIs wanted to keep things nicely vague. As if they really didn't want humanity to know what course they were upon. She'd come across a lot about the black hole the AI had dropped itself into, and other related reports about Penny Royal now sitting beyond time, but she had no real idea what that actually meant.

The bubble rose to the mouth of the shaft and kept going, the landscape of the planetoid opening out around them. She stepped aside to stand on a clear area of the glassy substance and peered down, seeing they were rising on a silver stalk. Slowly the motion drew to a halt, and she estimated they now stood about a kilometre above the surface.

'Okay,' said Arach. 'Time, since you are here, for you to make yourself useful and tell them to go away.'

'What?'

'It'll be warning shots at first . . . I think.'

The black area of the bubble flickered; now, scattered across it, she could see the pursuing ships out there in vacuum. Around this, frames began to pop into existence. In each of these were types she recognized from throughout her career: hard-looking men and women, comfortable in space armour, and a variety of designs of vacuum combat suit. All of them seemed to be peering at her closely. She felt a brief stage fright, but then remembered the damage to her ship and how close it had come to being destroyed.

'I'm presuming you all know where you now are,' she said.

Signifiers appeared below many of the frames, and she could see the occupants talking, some waving their arms, some asking questions of her, and almost certainly talking to each other. No voices came through to her, however.

'Your detectors will surely have picked up the activity within this planetoid. We initiated that as we arrived – powering up an interesting variety of weapons.' A little bullshit was required here, though from Arach's reaction when they'd detected that start-up, she guessed he'd feared the planetoid was about to fire on them. The place had history. Looters had come here. Some had gone away with hauls which were usually bought up by Polity AIs, or locked down, or destroyed by Polity agents. Some formed the mass of debris out there. She smiled when, during her pause, two of the frames simply winked out. Checking the view, she saw two ships accelerating away, and a moment later dropping into U-space.

'I suggest the rest of you turn your ships around, just like two of your fellows have done, and leave. This is the only verbal warning you'll receive.'

She looked over to Arach, who dipped his head in acknowledgement, then switched her attention to Crane. He put away the rubber dog, reached up and pulled his hat down tighter on his head. Around them everything seemed to slide slightly out of reality, as if seen through thick glass. A white beam of energy lanced out, then ran a sinusoidal path along the line of ships, touching not one of them. At once the ships began firing up drives and pulling away. May watched them disappearing and the frames winking out. She'd recently checked to see what the reward was on Crane, and it had been huge enough to tempt even her. Despite that, she reckoned the power readings on that beam had been sufficient to loosen a few bowels.

After a long quiet period, she said, 'As simple as that?'

'No, not that simple,' said Davidson. 'I've been running diagnostics. Remember that damaged U-space nacelle?'

257

'It's fucked, I take it,' said May, feeling a surge of guilt as she remembered dismissing all the damage reports as they flew in.

'Damned if I know. All I do know is that it's no longer attached to our ship.'

10

Cormac

Cormac materialized in a cave some distance from the p-prador. He began walking while gridlinking programs into Shuriken, then drew his thin gun to snap shoot a lurking sleer from the ceiling, stepping over its corpse indifferently. Retaining his U-sense vision, he saw the p-prador abruptly turn to his location, and smiled.

'What is your strategy now?' Mask enquired.

Cormac ignored this and focused on two search drones that had appeared ahead. He reached out to encompass them, dismissed them through U-space to materialize in solid rock off to one side, and kept going. The creatures had been moving fast towards him until he did that; now they slowed and began unfolding missile launchers, as well as opening the throats of weapons in their claws. After a second, one of them surged ahead, while the other three held back. Sacrificial – he recognized that at once. He waited.

A couple of minutes later, the creature skidded into sight around the corner ahead. It fired on him immediately with its particle weapon, the beam lancing straight through Cormac's chest. But he'd made a partial shift into U-space and felt it only as a warm spot – rather like the effect of eating sleer organ meat. As the beam snapped out, he came fully back into the real and leaped aside, launching Shuriken with a flick of his wrist, and firing pulse shots straight into what looked like the creature's eyes. Shuriken whined up to speed and sped along the roof. The creature ignored it and fired its Gatling cannon, filling the cave with slugs and lethal ricochets. Cormac crouched down in a side cavern as Shuriken looped back, the new glimmer to its blades visible. The weapon hammered into the creature, taking off a couple of its legs. The creature tilted back, orienting on this new danger, and tried to hit the throwing star as the thing wove a fast pattern around it. The weapons fire brought down a load of stone, and the distraction allowed Shuriken to zip in again, hitting the creature's carapace. The shriek was ear-numbing – not from the creature but the struggle to cut it. Cormac received feedback on this as the star shot away again in a shower of sparks. Energy levels were down by a third. Minimal penetration. So, he'd learned what he needed to: Shuriken could whip off a few legs but, despite the new shearfield, couldn't penetrate that carapace armour. Time to end this.

Via U-sense, Cormac looked inside the creature, then extended his field to encompass Shuriken. The star seemed to shrug an acknowledgement. He felt a light tug, as if the star had gained the same kind of inertia as that p-prador corpse, or perhaps because of technology at the location where he'd translocated it. Then the star shifted out of the real – still visible to him as an infinitely black star-shaped hole – and back into the real, *inside* the p-prador's carapace. There it spun and shifted, slicing through internal organs and some hard lumps of dense tech. The creature shrieked for real this time, but when Shuriken passed back and forth through its ring-shaped major ganglion, the shriek turned to the hiss of deflation, and it collapsed. Now Cormac tried to grasp the throwing star and pull it back out, via U-space again, but it was difficult. Shuriken swayed with the tug from U-space, remained inside, and cut forwards. No time to deal with that right now. Cormac grimaced, and stepped partially out of the real as the other p-prador launched a series of missiles up the tunnel towards him.

The missiles struck, blasting out white fire filled with spinning wheels of hyper-diamond wire shrapnel. He felt the heat of the blasts wash through him, rock melting and tons of it dropping from the ceiling. He advanced, walking through falling rubble and gobbets of lava. Ahead, the p-prador were retreating. He briefly focused on Shuriken, still inside the creature it had killed, and cutting to the fore where its mouth lay. A backwash of what stood for thought in the weapon revealed that it was working with the schematic of the creature to find a way out. No time to wait for it, though. He shifted forwards, out of the fire and falling stone, then materialized, extended his U-field and waited. On cue, the creatures launched further missiles. With processing ramped up beyond human, Cormac snatched all the missiles and shifted them away. Two of them were on target, materializing inside two of the creatures. Disappointingly, they didn't detonate, but their velocity and the heat of their motors was enough to destroy much of what lay inside those carapaces. The two skidded forwards under the impact and just slumped, wraiths of fire flickering out of leg sockets.

The other missiles exploded all around the remaining prador. The creature moved with surprising speed. Hurled up on the blasts, it turned on thruster flames, hit the melting ceiling and ran along it, bouncing off falling boulders, and was soon out of the fire. Cormac acknowledged this with a nod – good to remember just how they could move. He stepped through U-space after it, appearing in the cave just ten metres behind, and once again extended the trap of his U-field. Instinct outweighed sense, and the prill-prador turned to open up with its Gatling cannon. He netted the shots of its brief fusillade and, as it turned away to run again, he transferred the cloud of slugs to its location. Many of these appeared outside it, warranting him again stepping partially into U-space, since they were on the previous trajectory. Many also appeared inside the creature and tore its internals apart. It flipped over and landed on its back, legs kicking briefly, then folding in. Cormac stepped back into the real.

'Well, it seems you have the powers required,' said Mask.

Cormac didn't answer; he simply turned and looked back down the cave. Shuriken zipped into sight through boiling fire, shedding molten rock. The star came up before him, spinning and smoking, and remained where it was even when he held out his arm. A check on its programming showed it needed to cool down from the temperature of glowing iron.

'It seems I have the power required for what?' Cormac asked.

'For you to go home,' Mask replied.

Cormac absorbed this as he continued to check Shuriken. The star had cut various actuators inside the corpse to open the armoured covering over its victim's mouth, and had come out that way. He also noted a deal of strange programming working in the weapon. Not only had it acquired those shearfields, but it also seemed to be acquiring other facilities from the local version of the net. Finally, it folded away its chain-glass blades and inserted itself in its holster. The holster began recharging the star, and he knew he'd have to insert the other power supply he carried soon after that.

'Go home how?' he asked.

'Pretty much the same way you came,' Mask replied.

Blite

Blite jerked awake, groped for his pulse gun and came up empty. It seemed he'd been divested of his armour too, and wore only a pair of shorts. Vision was blurred at first, but then the *Coin*'s medical area resolved around him as a backdrop to Iris and Carlstone. Even though this area had its grav-plates, Blite could still sense the ship had taken flight and they were out in vacuum. There was something missing, he knew; something was going to hurt him, yet he hadn't figured out what it was.

'Where's my gun?' he asked, abruptly sitting upright, the vision of Greer and her damned dog dying on that ramp now sliding into his consciousness.

'You don't need it here,' Carlstone replied, watching him carefully.

Armand had stopped Blite's arm before, but the stun shots that'd knocked him out had come from Carlstone.

'You never truly believed it, did you?' Blite asked.

'It's a difficult thing to grasp,' Carlstone replied, 'I saw down there that you knew when things were going to happen, and how to avoid them. But I couldn't help my reflex to stop you killing yourself. Only retrospectively did I understand it. And unfortunately, I can't reverse time.'

The man spoke succinctly and analytically, and Blite wanted to rail at him for his idiocy and demand his gun back. He stopped himself. Carlstone might not be showing it, but he was certainly punishing himself more than Blite could have. And in all honesty, Blite felt much of the guilt lay with him, in procrastinating at the end there and allowing others to act. Now, if he was given his gun back, what would he achieve by blowing his brains out again? Sure, he'd leveraged the diamond to save the lives of others before, but the thing's prime purpose was to save his life. Shooting himself in the head now wouldn't shunt him back to before Greer's death; it would just take him back far enough for altered circumstances to prevent him taking that shot in this moment. He could see how the further into the past her death fell, the greater were the odds against him somehow being able to prevent it. How many times would he have to shoot himself in the head? A thousand? A million? He swung his legs off the side of the bed and stood up.

'What's the situation?' he asked, voice catching. The horrors arrived then and he closed his eyes, concentrating on the feed from his nanosuite as it adjusted neurochem and other reactions throughout his body to what lay in his mind. How many times could he die and remain sane?

'We're going nowhere,' Carlstone replied.

Blite opened his eyes and gestured to the door. Carlstone moved ahead of him. He glanced at Iris – still lacking an arm. Though she was looking at him, it felt as if she wasn't seeing him. It was unusual for her not to have something to say, but then they'd all been through a lot. He followed Carlstone.

'We half expected some action from the planetary AI,' Carlstone told him as they reached the bridge, 'but it let us leave the surface. No action on its part was required.'

'Not required?' Blite asked, looking over to Greer's empty seat beside the weapons console and wincing.

'It's a USER effect,' said Paidon. 'No one is going anywhere.'

'Where's the USER?' asked Blite.

'Nowhere,' she replied. 'That vessel out there sowed some U-space mines. We're trapped here for a good few hours, unless of course it drops some more. Apparently, Mobius Straeger is aboard it.'

Blite eyed the weird-looking ship. The claw-shaped thing wasn't any design he recognized, but if it belonged to a Mobius it'd be lethal. Especially that Mobius. He felt almost grateful to it, and the AI, for the problems they presented. He didn't dwell on the reason. Carlstone went over to his position and straight into deep com, plugging his aug into a console with an optic. Judice, a human woman uplifted to Golem, and Breil, a lightworlder, were analysing data Carlstone began throwing their way. He sighed, walked over to the captain's chair, and slumped into it.

'Straeger have anything to say?' he asked.

'No direct communication from the AI,' Judice replied. 'Though I am getting sub-AI requests for data.'

'Give him what he wants, just so long as it doesn't negate any advantages we might have.' He couldn't think what those advantages might be, but thought it best to throw that in there. 'Weapons?'

They all looked over to the weapons console, then away again with varying expressions of chagrin, grief and guilt. Judice abruptly stood up and walked over there to fill the empty chair. She began checking things as an almost embarrassed silence settled.

'It's not a Polity dreadnought,' Judice said, finally breaking the silence. 'But we've been getting some weird readings from the thing. No idea what weapons a Mobius AI might have.'

Blite turned to their pilot and U-space expert. 'Paidon. You didn't use the Laumer . . .'

'Straeger dropped the mines as we left the surface. I thought it best to keep that card close to our chest,' she replied.

Blite glanced at Breil, who simply nodded an acknowledgement. That would be one datum to hold back, though he doubted an AI like Straeger didn't know already. He sat there rattling his fingers against the arm of his chair, then thought, *Screw it*, and started to get up.

265

'Something happening with the ship,' said Judice.

Imagery came up on the screen. The claw-shaped vessel, which really wasn't much bigger than the *Coin*, had fired up fusion drives and was on the move.

'Trajectory?' he asked leadenly. Carlstone had more soldiers like Armand aboard, but Blite really didn't want a fight here if Straeger aimed to dock. They might win, but he doubted much would be left of the *Coin* afterwards. He was also reluctant about going up against the nominal good guy or guys, though in reality he was thinking about the likelihood of there being ECS marines aboard that ship, not the Mobius AI.

'Not towards us,' said Judice.

'Something going on down there,' said Carlstone.

'Breil?' Blite asked, sitting back into his chair, relieved by further distraction.

Breil replied with calm assurance. 'That last satellite railgun strike took out another of the creatures, leaving just one, which went to ground. It blew a hole through Teleman Street and dropped into the underground vactrans.' He gestured and a frame came up showing the city from above, scattered with fires and partially shrouded in smoke. Lines of collapse webbed across the city, bringing down buildings and dropping roads into the ground. The fires abruptly went out and most of the smoke disappeared.

'What was that?' Blite asked.

'From twenty-three minutes ago. The creature bust open the vactrans vacuum system and it sucked everything down. Incidentally, it crashed a train with four hundred people aboard – no survivors.'

'Fucking thing,' Carlstone muttered.

Breil continued, 'Planetary forces have dispersed to cover ground access. The AI also shut the vacuum doors beyond the city. The creature is, apparently, trapped down there.'

Blite returned his attention to Straeger's vessel. The thing had hit orbit now and begun descending fast. He realized that, though Straeger had prevented them from leaving, they weren't its main focus at this moment.

'How long would it be on the Laumer drive to move us beyond the U-space disruption?' he asked Paidon.

'Half an hour, maybe.'

'Get everyone locked down for that, but take us out on fusion, nice and easy for now,' he told her, then to the others, 'And give me as much imagery from down there as you can.'

A further series of frames opened up, giving good views of the city from above, even as he felt the slight kick of the fusion drive firing up. More frames opened, showing something he couldn't identify for a moment, until he saw the surviving creature moving along the glassy curve of a vactrans tunnel. It seemed they had imagery from below the city too. Yet another frame stayed on the AI's descending ship. He auged into all this data, then did a double take on that ship's speed of descent and abrupt vector changes. If the thing had marines aboard, even with internal grav, they would have needed to be in gel stasis. He suspected it had only one passenger, quite capable of surviving a lot more than soft humans could. The frame flickered to a new view showing the ship falling onto the city. It tipped claw down, and blasted out a bright fusion flame from some arrangement within the grip of that claw. Below it, trees caught fire in a park that Blite felt sure was the one they'd run through. At the last it flipped, grav effects throwing burning wood and smoking earth out in a spiral wave below, then it came down on its side. This confirmed the pilot for Blite – they tended to a have a low regard for the damage they caused during pursuit.

The ship sat there immobile in its landing damage for just a minute, then a split opened in its side. The vessel dwarfed the whirling sphere of threads that came out, glowing with internal light. However, checking the data feed in his aug, Blite saw that the Mobius AI had taken on mass, increasing in size from a couple of metres to fully ten metres across. It shot along, over the burning park, and hit the railings without pausing, leaving a melted-out hole behind. It then rolled along, following a couple of streets, and Blite felt relieved that it didn't feel the need to go through someone's house as they had. Its destination lay ahead – he could see the local police rapidly moving away from the entrance stairs down into the vactrans. A war drone like a short golden centipede backed up, and spotter drones scattered from the sky above.

'Mobius AIs,' said Carlstone tightly.

'Indeed,' said Blite, then to Paidon, 'Full power on fusion.'

How long ago had these AIs started appearing? Less than a century or so, to his knowledge, though they might have been around for a lot longer. They seemed to be a law unto themselves, rather like some rogue security organization in a pre-Quiet War human government. But in reality they couldn't do the things they did without permission from Earth Central or ECS. They had a reputation for causing destruction and death to achieve their goals. Some compared them to Polity agents in their focus and inclination to kill, but Blite felt that unwarranted. Polity agents did kill, but in a surgically precise way, and with cold efficiency. As he watched cameras pick up the Mobius AI in the vactrans system, he tried to remember stories he'd heard in which such AIs were involved. Oddly, he found he couldn't remember one.

'Should be reaching it any time now,' said Breil.

Blite dismissed his puzzlement and focused on the screen. The Mobius AI filled the tunnel – bright around its edges, as if it had needed to fold in some of its substance. On another frame the creature turned, launched three missiles, then jettisoned the launcher from its back. It seemed likely they were the last of its stock, since the thing, with its fellows, had been causing destruction along their course around half of the world.

The missiles slammed into the AI and filled it with bright fire. The blast carried debris both ways along the tunnel and, as the fire died, the remains of the AI were left as a ring around the inside of the tunnel, a hole right through its centre. Blite couldn't quite believe what he was seeing. Had the creature managed to destroy a Mobius? No. The ring collapsed into a sphere – a smaller form of the AI, now maybe six or seven metres across. It rolled forwards. The creature opened up with its Gatling cannon this time. The slugs hit and penetrated the AI, but just hung in its substance as bright spots, slowly fading.

'They must use internal manufacture,' said Carlstone. 'Probably driven by fusion nodes like a war drone.'

Blite nodded agreement. The missiles had surprised him, as had the sheer quantity of slugs the creature slung out. If this thing had been a normal prador, it would have been out of ammo by now. The fusillade continued and the AI just kept rolling into it. Blite used his aug to bring up a close and enhanced view in his skull and saw the shifting threads of the AI. He watched one of the slugs within it, hot and bright at first, then, as it cooled, stretching out and blending in. The AI was incorporating the slugs into its substance and replacing what it had lost.

It seemed the creature began to divine this, or ran out of ammo. Its cannon shut down and it now fired its particle beam. Blue at first, the strike just fed into the AI and spread out through its threads. Blite had no doubt that, after garnering material from the slugs, it was now drawing materials and energy from the particle beam. The power of the beam then ramped up, going to blue-white, then bright white. It flashed through the substance of the Mobius AI, blowing smoking black debris out of the back end, then began to cut across. The AI ceased rolling and surged ahead. As it did so, it opened a hole in its body that tracked with the beam so it simply passed through the AI, hitting nothing, and then the AI engulfed the creature.

The beam stabbed out a few more times, then shut down. Blite replayed this with enhancement and saw the creature's mandibles cut away by tightening bright threads and dragged into the substance of the Mobius. The creature continued to fight, slicing with sharp legs and something starting to spin around the edge of its carapace, flickering blue – some kind of cutter. The Mobius AI grew bright, then brighter still, then a blast finally took out their view down in the tunnel.

'Look,' said Breil, pointing.

On the city view an explosion opened a street, and out of that rose a fountain of fire. Using enhancement yet again, Blite could see within this the blackly silhouetted creature, and around it a widely spread mass of wispy threads. He stared and made a decision.

'Hit the Laumer now,' he told Paidon.

Straeger

Mobius Straeger acknowledged a dangerous opponent. The initial shots with conventional weapons had been almost a hat-tip towards the usual form of combat. The creature had used up its remaining missiles, knowing they would at least cause some damage. It had fired off half of its internally manufactured cannon slugs on the same basis, then stopped firing them after seeing little result. Scanning the thing heavily, Straeger had watched the slugs going back into the creature's dense-tech manufactories, to be turned into particulate that would top up the supply to its particle weapon. The energy density of that beam had been surprising, and Straeger damned his own arrogance for not fully assessing the data the planetary AI had sent him. It happened – Straeger was after all a post-human, and as inclined to error as his forebears.

A slow advance, while assessing, then became contraindicated, so Straeger hit the thing fast. He grabbed it, wound Q-carbon threads around the limbs wielding its weapons, and cut them off. *Tough little fucker*, he thought as he did so. He soon found out that he hadn't completely neutered it. The shearfields were another surprise. Having in the last few seconds fully incorporated the data from the planetary AI, Straeger comforted himself that at least these hadn't been used until now. The fields cut the threads of the AI's being, but they also incorporated viral warfare, spreading disruption where they cut. It was, he decided, time to end this. Any advantage to be gained in examining the creature fully intact was now receding.

Straeger began driving in Q-carbon nanodrills, finding weak and damaged spots all over its armour, shuttling the drills in down the severance points of the mandibles, worming in through joints and data ports. By slow degrees, in AI time, which was a matter of seconds, he started shutting down the creature's shear-fields. As these went down, he could detect some other system coming online in consonance with them. He detected a power cycle in a superconductor grid, linked to power sources throughout the creature's body, and to meta-material layers in its armour. A mere few microseconds later, he understood what was happening and began shifting his body format to compensate, dryly aware that he might not be able to do this fast enough. The power surge ablated those layers, turning them to an intense electrostatic blast.

This blast took Straeger and the creature – now depleted of power but amazingly still alive – up through the roof of the tunnel in a column of electrostatic fire. As Straeger held on, he noted data coming from a portion of himself he'd left onboard his ship. Blite had fired up the *Coin*'s Laumer engine and was running. Perfect timing, really. Blite had once again demonstrated his precisely tuned instincts.

Straeger fed off the energy of the blast, grabbed what materials he could, and again started to tighten around the creature. Out in space, the *Coin*'s Laumer engine was generating an ion trail from the disrupted quantum foam. Blite was the perpetual bait to draw Cormac in, but the agent hadn't intervened here, and certainly wouldn't be turning up now. And yet, with just a slight disruption, Straeger's probability map of the future – which had highlighted the temporal event here – had only shifted a small amount. This meant the agent must still be a part of it, even though at present he was missing. Matheson and the Brices were one counter he could use against the agent, but still the course of events wasn't clear.

He needed more information. He needed to examine this creature, and the remains of the others the planetary AI had taken down. He needed to know why they were so much tougher than the three that had attacked Crane. And why were they trying to kill Blite, as well as Crane? His probability map of the future had intersected on the event here, but detail had been lacking. The temporal flashes that gave him glimpses of the future landscape, and promised almost unlimited power over time itself, were tantalizing, but frustratingly few.

May

Striding ahead impatiently, May reached her ship well before Crane and Arach, who didn't appear to think there was any urgency. She gazed at it, and here and there picked out signs of damage, but it was only when she walked around the other side that she saw where the nacelle had gone missing. Looking back along their path in, she could see no sign of the thing.

'Davidson, take a look back down the tunnel. See if you can find it,' she said.

'Okay, but I have my doubts it'll be intact.'

As she walked back around the ship, one of the subsidiary engines on the central framework detached and rose up on compressed air thrusters. It turned, and then briefly sputtered a chemical flame to send it shooting off down the tunnel. They did have a collection of survey drones aboard, but she could see how this would be the quickest solution.

'The important stuff might be intact,' she said as she ran up the ramp, moved to the back of the hold and opened up the airlock set in an inner bulkhead door. 'That kind of tech is well protected.'

'If you say so,' said Davidson. 'Anyway, be good to get a proper look out there.'

She wanted to cycle straight through the airlock but, remembering what they'd discussed before heading out, she programmed the decontamination routine for nanites.

It took a short while to kick in, and did so with some ominous crunching sounds. It was probably like Davidson's seat – long overdue for maintenance. Ultraviolet darkened her visor and as this faded, the airlock seemed to fill with straight threads. Small flashes surrounded her, a mini fireworks display, as micro-lasers zapped anything floating in the air. They then raised smoke from the surface of her suit as they burned away any dust there. Next a hot flush ran from the top of her head down to her feet. It felt like a powerful active scan but was in fact a nanite EMR disruption routine. A shower of highly acidic boiling water ensued, to be sucked away through drains in the floor. Later, when they closed up the hold again, they would have to decontaminate in there, presumably with Arach and Crane still inside . . .

She finally stepped into the main ship with her suit steaming. Even as she did so she paused, wondering about Arach's claim that he was too big to fit through the external airlock. She now realized that didn't make sense. The drone happily moved through internal corridors built on a human scale, while the external airlocks were made to take three people all at once. She'd ask him, but right now she needed to know where that damned U-space nacelle had gone. Sure, she'd seen Crane and Arach fabricating some complicated tech, but she doubted they could build one of those things.

She picked up her pace to the bridge. As she entered, Akanthor and Davidson looked her up and down, Akanthor frowning as she turned away. Both of them looked seriously worried. She was supposed to have put her suit in a sealed container for further decontamination and felt their disapproval. She also understood that the recent events had added to whatever load they were carrying. Screw it. She headed over to her seat and dropped into it.

'What have we got?' she asked.

'Imagery coming in,' said Davidson, gesturing to the main screen.

This gave the view from the subsidiary as it took the route out they'd taken in. When it reached the shaft, she saw the tunnel entrance mostly blocked by boulders, but there was room for the engine to go through. It drifted out into the shaft, and now other frames opened to show the views up and down. The nacelle wasn't in the tunnel, so it seemed likely they'd lost it in the shaft. Davidson sent the engine out over the jam before she thought to instruct him, and there ran deep scanning. Still no sign of the thing, though the scan couldn't penetrate all the way down through the debris.

'Try up top,' said May, suppressing a hollow panic growing inside.

The engine sped up the shaft, igniting its chemical thruster again to speed the process, and soon shot out of the planetoid's surface. Another series of frames opened, showing surrounding space – if they couldn't find the thing on the surface, the next place to look would be out in vacuum where they were first attacked. It had to be somewhere between their U-space exit point and the ship, otherwise they either wouldn't have exited U-space at all, or would have exited turned inside out.

'Got it,' said Davison.

One of the frames expanded to show the surface. A hundred metres out from the mouth of the shaft lay the nacelle. It rested completely intact at the end of a trail scored through the dust, and even had its stanchion still attached. May felt a surge of relief, realizing how it must have simply been swiped off as she took the ship down into the shaft.

'Damn it,' said Davidson. 'We've got another one coming in.'

A new frame expanded to blot out the first, showing a large ugly-looking spherical ship hammering towards the planetoid.

'Arach,' said May, after opening the spider drone's com icon. 'We've got another visitor.' She riffled through aug connections to find the one through Arach's eyes. The view made her head ache – it was 360 degrees and straying beyond the human visual spectrum. Finally she got it. The spider drone occupied a small chamber, the walls lined with metallic tiles like polished aluminium. He was working on some object in the middle of the chamber. The thing looked like a neuron, formed of a mixture of dull ceramal and the same polished metal as the tiles. She saw him severing connections that speared from it to the walls like neural dendrites or axons.

'Yeah, looks like Matheson came to join the party. I wonder if he got round to resurrecting the Brices,' Arach replied.

'What exactly does that mean?' she asked, abruptly angry.

'Matheson is a bounty hunter, like the rest out there. He came after the brass bastard just prior to those creatures attacking him. The Brices, two brothers and their sister, were part of his . . . hunting party. They were just heads in a rucksack last time I saw them.'

Akanthor and Davidson looked around at her, watching her reaction. It was another sign in their behaviour which led to a conclusion from which she'd been leaning away. Although they'd been onboard at the start of this, they were now having serious second thoughts. She was losing them.

'Whatever,' she snapped. 'Crane needs to go back on that weapons system and send them away.'

'He's on it.'

Another view came up. It slid off the edges of human perception and again made May's head ache. She saw Crane standing on the mushroom platform in that bubble as it rose out of the surface of the planetoid. The view twisted around and out into open space. She saw the debris there, and the approaching ship. The white laser whipped up from the planetoid's weapon and this time it wasn't a warning shot. It splashed on a hardfield, however, and the ship carried on relentlessly, shedding a hardfield projector like a burning star as it did so. May winced and managed to shut down this view. AIs might be able to handle multiple inputs like this, but she had her limitations.

'That ship has been upgraded,' Arach commented.

Due to the strain of handling it mentally, May routed the imagery to the main screen, shutting down the visual feed from Arach too. Matheson's ship sped in, dumped another projector, then took a hit on its armour. She expected this to be it, but the thing rolled out of that too and stabbed out with a particle beam. It then launched a swarm of missiles. She hadn't realized how close it was until now, as the frame expanded to show the horizon of the planetoid and a huge explosion blowing fire out of a shaft mouth. A further shift showed Crane's bubble up on its stalk, with missiles zeroed in on it, then they began exploding on impossibly curved hardfields, drowning out the view in fire.

'Now that was . . . interesting . . .'

Noting the edge to Arach's voice, May brought his visual feed back up. Arach abruptly stepped forwards and grasped the object in his forelimbs, then backed up, tearing away remaining connections. Perhaps he'd finally decided there was now some urgency.

On the screen, the ship veered into a hard gee turn that she knew should have pasted the crew all over the walls, then it dropped down into the burning mouth of the shaft it had just fired into. The white beam tracked across the surface there, scoring a burning trench, and then winked out.

'We need to move to the surface and do something about that nacelle,' said Arach.

'Getting out of here might be a problem.' May reviewed the drone's flat tone, wondering if this was less about getting to the nacelle, and more about escaping the planetoid now this ship had entered it. Something wasn't right. She didn't think mere bounty hunters could survive a Penny Royal weapons system.

'We'll take a different route,' Arach replied. A second later a new map of their surroundings arrived, dropping into the system and her aug to show a course through a series of tunnels and another shaft to the surface.

Davidson flicked up a display from external cams showing Arach coming into view, still clutching the item he'd cut free. Moving fast, he shot across towards the ship, up the ramp and inside. May felt his arrival through the bottom of her seat.

'Close the ramp,' he said. 'We're out of here.'

'What about Crane?'

'He'll be joining us later – he has some business to attend to below.'

'Okay.' May sent the instruction to close the ramp. 'We move.' She set her chair to wrap round her, grabbing the joystick and focusing mentally through her aug. Thrusters and grav-planing fired up as Akanthor and Davidson similarly sat back in their chairs and made themselves safe . . . Or as safe as they could be in circumstances obviously not to their liking. May turned the ship and aimed it towards the relevant tunnel mouth. She took things slowly, careful not to bash it against the walls this time.

May dismissed most aug views, since they were screwing with her perception. She glanced to the frames open on the screen. Fire had cleared out there, and she saw Crane's bubble descending into the planetoid. It didn't take much thought to know where he'd be heading but, whatever happened below, she should concentrate on the one task ahead. She flew the tunnels, finally entering a shaft like the previous one, and moving up it. Coming out to the surface, she rolled the ship towards the original shaft, located the nacelle there, and settled the ship down beside it in a dusty explosion.

'Well, we need to suit up and get to work,' she said as her seat unfolded from her.

The ramp was already going down, and one of the frames showed Arach heading out, shortly followed by a pair of print-erbots and a quadruped grappler.

'Bring a scaffold,' said Arach. 'And other items.' The list arrived in her aug with methods, material and work orders linking away from each item. The same list had gone to the other two, whose expressions glazed over upon receiving it. She stood up. On screen, Arach had already lifted the nacelle stanchion to crawl under it, and as she watched he began dragging the thing back to the ship.

'I take it there's some urgency,' she finally commented.

'As yet to be determined,' Arach replied dryly.

Matheson

Matheson was pleased with how he and the ship had performed. The power of the beam from that planetoid had been ridiculous and, gridlinked into the system to run the calculus, he'd understood they couldn't withstand it for long. The glancing shot on the hull had been at the limit, but perfectly calculated to save on burning out further hardfield projectors. His ship's particle beam strike had then scoured that shaft of a portion of the weapons system down there, and the missile strike had been a suitable distraction, giving them the time they needed to go down that shaft. Now his ship sat at the bottom, amid rubble that had fallen from above, and he had to decide on the target.

With his U-space sense at full extent, he could just about see the other ship on the surface; making calculations for a jump there became a movable feast, blurring in and out of feasibility. The distance was certainly a problem, and it seemed that something in the ship's hold was interfering too. Tactically the ship should be the first target, confining Crane and the rest here to be dealt with at leisure, but he scotched that idea for now, since it would take the other crew some time to fix up that nacelle, if they could even get the thing working again. Anyway, the other target – Mr Crane – was now down in the tunnels and heading towards them.

'The Brass Man first,' said Will, for Matheson was again sharing his vision with them.

'Uh-uh, uh-uh,' said Ulnar

'Brillig,' said Sheen.

Matheson studied them on more than just the visual plane. They'd all changed drastically. Ulnar was the worst of them, as he'd lost his facility for language. Sheen wasn't much better, since it seemed she could only use the words from that ancient rhyme. Only Will had retained the majority of what he'd once been, laced through with a burning red-eyed anger. Matheson could see the man had enough mental function to understand perfectly the horror of what Straeger had done to them.

'Close up your armour,' he instructed.

Without questioning, they all reached up to the shells of armour either side of their heads and closed them across their faces. On the suit schematic level, Matheson watched the armour bonding and closing the gaps, with threads spearing out to reconnect and pull everything down tight. They didn't panic or fight this time, as they could still see clearly through his U-sense, while the ability to shut down their breathing and not suffer the effects of suffocation had been installed in them all. He reached up to his own face armour and hesitated.

He'd changed things during the time they'd had available, and some of that was visible in the Brices before him. Whereas before the only line of division had run down the centre of their faces, they now had lines marking out their eyes and mouths. When he allowed it, they could open metallic eyelids and lips. This enabled them to see and breathe without having to tear down to the raw muscle of their faces. Other changes appeared lower down, with tubes opening to their anuses and their urethras. This was messy, but it worked without being painful.

Matheson sighed and finally reached up to close his face covering across. In himself he inspected the process more closely, seeing the linkages of fibres and meta-material meshes – all the odd and disparate layers of the armour. It reminded him of a

Polity warship's armour, with all the complexity of human skin. But it was their own skin. With it closed up and his breathing shut down, he concentrated outwardly.

Crane was some kilometres away, marching down a tunnel towards them. Did the Golem think he was coming to fuck over some merely human bounty hunters trespassing on his property? Matheson saw no reason Crane would think otherwise. He considered his last attempt on the Golem and remembered that plate of dislodged armour showing the snakish organic technology underneath, as well as the black oily stuff. Crane could be damaged. Crane could be killed. However, Matheson also remembered how the Golem had fucked them over, and knew that in no way should he be underestimated.

'We hit him hard and fast,' he said over com to the other three. 'Create weaknesses, then work on those, pulling them open. Tear him apart.'

'Gyre and gimble,' Sheen agreed.

'Uh-uh,' said Ulnar.

'What about weapons in the area?' asked Will.

'Good thought,' Matheson replied.

He concentrated on the tunnel Crane was striding along, though it wasn't entirely clear at this distance. Technology of an unknown nature was laced through the walls of it, but there didn't seem to be much they could use against him. Anyway, he didn't want to risk a jump to somewhere he couldn't see clearly, and where the calculations strayed into chaos. However, scanning along Crane's route, he saw the perfect location. Nearly a kilometre ahead of his present position was a cubic chamber, with the ceiling up high. Part of the ceiling had collapsed, dropping many large and useful rocks. That collapse had damaged various machines in there too, scattering lengths of pipe and other items that could be used as weapons.

'There,' he said, highlighting the area for the Brices.

'We go now?' asked Will.

'No – Crane has Golem senses, and who knows what output we're giving off. Likely he'll know we're waiting for him and be ready. We jump in as he reaches that place, then hit him.' He paused to contemplate something he now understood to be a possibility. 'Be ready for fast relocations. I can, I think, jump us all individually.' Once they were all there, he knew they'd attack – he'd seen in the way they'd turned on Ricardo when they first boarded the ship that this compulsion was already deeply and firmly embedded in them.

'He's getting close,' he said.

Indeed, Crane was moving a lot faster than had at first been apparent. Matheson calculated for the cube chamber, with U-space swirling into his consciousness and seemingly fogging out the translated view. He felt the U-field generating from his armour and extending out to encompass the others, like bubble membranes joining. Crane continued marching on, then slowed in the chamber to look around at the wrecked machines. Perfect.

Now.

It was no less traumatic this time than it had been the first. Matheson couldn't stop his internal scream, and the other three echoed him during an eternity and an instant. But even with forces he couldn't name twisting and shearing his body inside, he managed the calculation to fling them into a ring. Unfortunately, some part of his calculation must have been out, as they appeared three metres above the floor. They dropped. Matheson hit the stone and went down into a crouch, but he felt so ripped up inside that he was sure, if there'd been any gaps in his armour, he would have flooded out of it in a slurry. A pause of a second or two ensued as his U-sense cleared. He'd come down directly ahead of Crane, who had come to a halt. Ulnar was to the right,

Will to the left, and Sheen behind the Golem. The diorama broke with a high-pitched shriek.

The length of pipe was a blur through the air, and it landed with a resounding clang on the side of Crane's head. Sheen had been the first to attack. Another weird pause ensued as Crane's hat tumbled through the air and fell slowly in the low gravity. Then Ulnar and Will closed in, driving high and low kicks that landed with the same dull clangs. Sheen, it seemed, then forgot all about tactics and reverted to some earlier female state. She threw aside the bent lump of pipe, jumping on Crane's back and groping for his eyes with those long clawed fingers. Matheson took the opportunity to run forwards and launch into a hard dropkick at the Golem's chest. Crane staggered back, bowed over. Unbelievably, Will had also managed to break up a rib of Crane's armour on one side and was pulling at it with all his might. Then Crane appeared to have had enough.

Matheson understood the delay. The Golem had been abruptly confronted with something that, even with his enhanced senses, it took him a moment to puzzle out, but now he recognized he was in real danger. He reached up and grabbed Sheen. Matheson managed to roll to one side as Crane slammed her down into the floor. And she was *in* the floor, with the thing having dented down beneath her and some form of foamstone exploding to flinders all around. Matheson rolled in past her, seeing the gory splits in her armour. Yet she held up something in one hand, shaking it at the air in victory, and he recognized one of Crane's black eyes. He grabbed the Golem's leg, and got his shoulder against it, bracing against the floor to try to bring him over.

Crane swivelled, raising the other leg and stamped. The hobnail boot slammed down on Matheson's side and, as his grip slipped from the first leg, he saw his lower body had now become as wide as it had been thick. It hurt badly, and yet the edge of this felt dulled as before. Something bulged out of a split in the front of his armour, and he nauseously recognized intestines. He rolled away, seeing Will slam into a wall. Crane then turned to grab Ulnar, spin him over, and pile-drive his head into the floor. Matheson dragged himself further away and tried to get back to his feet, only then realizing his legs weren't working. Sheen tried to rise too, but Crane's boot came down hard on her chest, slamming her even deeper down, with pieces of organic matter shooting out of those splits in her armour. He plucked the eye out of her hand, inserted it back in place, and turned to Will as he peeled out of the wall and dropped to his knees. A kick slammed the man back into the same place and he dropped again.

So this was it? With all that Straeger had done to them, and Matheson's power to jump them through U-space, Crane had dispensed with them in a fight that took less than a minute. Now, he had no doubt, the Golem would finish them off. Seeking escape, Matheson reached out with his ability, but he found U-space a fractured mosaic around him and his calculations made no sense. He understood: Straeger had inserted the technology in their armour which enabled him to jump the others and himself, protecting them from the effects of it. The armour was now broken and, even if he could jump them, he doubted they'd survive the process. He watched and waited for the end, in some sense feeling relief and yet dreading how it would come about.

Crane stooped and picked up his hat, carefully dusting it off, putting it back on and adjusting it. It seemed ridiculous that this was his first concern. He then unbuttoned his ragged coat and began transferring items out of its pockets into those of his trousers. Next, discarding the coat, he peered down at the damage he'd sustained. Numerous dents were visible on his torso, and an ab muscle rib of armour had been ripped up and bent to one side. In the gap Matheson noticed a tangled intestinal mass, slowly writhing, then something black and oily sliding across it, as he'd seen before. Crane simply bent the rib back into position and held it there for a moment. When he took his hand away, it remained in place. A second later, with a crackling sound, one of the dents evened out, though Matheson could see cracks around the impact point. The big Golem then stepped forwards and peered down at him.

Matheson dragged himself back and pushed up into a sitting position, expecting the end to come swiftly now. Instead, Crane squatted down before him, watching, nothing recognizable in that Apollonian brass face. The inspection went on for a while, until something distracted the Golem. He looked over to one side and reached down to toy with an object on the floor with one finger. Matheson saw this was a knife-like sliver of armour from one of them. Crane picked it up and inspected it closely, then abruptly he stood, dropping the thing into his trouser pocket, turned and walked away.

Cormac

Cormac walked out of the cave into a bright but cloudy day. He hurriedly returned to the cave as hail the size of eyeballs started bouncing and shattering off the rockscape outside.

'The weather is still pretty much what it used to be here, even if the air is unbreathable,' he stated. 'What happened to the human population?'

'They moved on,' Mask replied morosely, in such a way that Cormac knew this discussion would go no further.

'So my way out lies up, over there?' he gestured towards the mountain's peaks.

'Indeed,' Mask replied.

After delivering the explanation for what needed to be done, this entity – whether a female from the far future communicating through his mask, or something else – had ceased to be so chatty. Now it seemed that his stay here had a limit, Cormac wanted to learn more. Logically Mask's reluctance to tell him anything was about causality; with time travel involved, knowledge could be a very dangerous thing indeed. However, instinct told him his invisible companion's reluctance was due to something else akin to sadness, fear, or maybe even regret.

'What's waiting for me up there?' he asked.

'About a thousand p-prador in various stages of development, led by something like a father – a senior p-prador,' Mask replied. She sighed, and then continued, 'You will have to design your response to what you see. You'll know what to do. The device is your only route back.'

Cormac gazed at the hail, wondering why the hell he was waiting for it to stop, and why, in the end, he'd asked that previous question. He extended his U-senses, encompassing the mountainside that ran upwards. The full extent of this brought him to the peaks, but not to the plateau lying beyond. Next he tried to shift the centre point of the U-sense sphere over to the plateau, but encountered resistance. This was similar to what he felt around a runcible, so whatever lay up there must be comparable technology. Noting that the hail was local and not above, he U-jumped, taking himself to the mountain peaks.

A frigid wind blasted him, his coat flapping. He gazed down onto the plateau once occupied by Mr Crane's farm – it looked very different now. Around the edges were dome-shaped dwellings similar to those the prador built along shores and down into seas, linked by pipe tunnels. A horde of p-prador swarmed around these, and hundreds of them were rising into the air even now, around a nominally spherical vessel. He didn't need much in the way of analysis to realize the protrusions, all but swamping the spherical shape, were heavy weapons. He gazed at it a moment longer, noting its similarity to old-style prador war drones, but writ huge. What would be their aim with it now? If they wanted him dead, no doubt they were going to—

He shifted swiftly over to another peak as the place he'd occupied exploded under railgun strikes. He felt as if he was skidding over a slippery surface, sliding around, and he put this down to the object at the centre of the plateau. The plateau itself had been levelled perfectly and coated with a substance like milky glass. At the centre stood four horn-shaped monoliths, with their tips pointing inwards. They looked like the horns of an old-style runcible, but those were usually twinned and held the U-space cusp between them. The added dimensionality, with time travel being involved, made sense. Around these horns stood what he assumed were weapons installations. This must be a trap for anything that snapped the temporal tension on the p-prador which had been sent back to attack. He couldn't help but think it was just for him, because anything else U-jumping the p-prador would be a ship, and only a very small ship would be able to pass through that thing. He would've arrived right at the centre of it had he not severed his connection to the p-prador corpse, which he could see still lay at the centre down there.

The spherical vessel rose higher, the p-prador accompanying it abruptly dropping away from the point that lay between him and it. He shifted again, probing, with the resistance to him going down as he did so. Again, another railgun strike hit behind him, shredding stone and tumbling down part of the mountainside.

'It's not a case of simply U-jumping in there,' he said.

'I know,' Mask replied gloomily.

Arriving further down an inner slope, he scanned around at suitable rocks, reached out with his U-field to grasp them, then flung them off to various locations. He found resistance to flinging one of them down towards the plateau. The ship or drone – the *weapon* – which had fired on those locations this time whipped out a white-shifted particle beam. The rock he'd flung inwards didn't arrive where he'd intended. The disparity shot a warning stab of pain through his skull. He wouldn't be able to shift himself down there, not all in one jump. He began walking, partially shifting into U-space, the ground feeling mushy and insubstantial under his feet. The weapon reoriented on him and began firing. White fire lanced through his insubstantial body and initial warmth grew steadily more intense. He could see rock melting and soon found himself walking through a furnace. He broke into a run to escape it, reaching a cliff edge, then went over the edge and fell, perpetually fighting to adjust his vague connection to the reality around him. His fall slowed, the beam tracking into the cliff behind and exploding a shattered course, with globules of molten rock filling the air. It was almost as if he'd fallen past the action of some giant arc welder.

He continued to assess and plan as he went. He knew what his tactics should be now, but he needed to be closer, in a real sense. Scanning around, he located the 'senior' p-prador Mask had mentioned, or whatever it was, by its size. It was now over to the right of the plateau, beyond the device, surrounded by the main horde of smaller p-prador. Cormac's feet touched the roof of one of the domed buildings and he ran down it as if over a quaking bog. Leaping to the ground, adjusting, running, his ghostly form having a sliding grip on the real. The weapon descended, the p-prador falling in behind it.

Now.

Cormac came fully back into the real, reached out with his

U-field to grab one of the p-prador and shifted it directly inside the substance of the weapon. A microsecond later he faded as a railgun strike nailed his position. He ran towards the senior p-prador, with the ground erupting behind him, his head aching and a trickle of blood leaking from one ear. His perception was distorted now, so close to the device, yet he still saw the effect of his previous action. The weapon shuddered in the air and started spinning, all its armaments firing, but at least not at him any more. Domed houses exploded, p-prador fell burning from the air, explosions in the surrounding slopes generated landslides boiling like pyroclastic flows. As he ran on, the p-prador pulled in protectively around the senior, just as he'd hoped they would. Above, the weapon abruptly shot to one side and crashed into the mountainside. This caused yet another landslide, but the thing stuck there like a cooling ember, red heat glowing from inside.

White particle beams intersected on Cormac. He turned as if to evade them, heading towards the runcible device.

'The senior, of course, has ultimate control,' he said.

'You are correct,' Mask replied, her voice distorted and tinny.

Around him Cormac could feel the hum of power; he could also sense it in ways beyond human. According to Mask, his mere act of U-jumping at this point would put him straight into that tunnel to the past, unless the p-prador here stopped him. He passed into the centre of the device, heading for the corpse, and finally came to a standstill over it, still immaterial. How much time would he have? Seconds, if that. He flung out an arm. Shuriken shot away, straight towards the senior, as immaterial as Cormac and linked into his U-field. It passed right through the creature's carapace, to inside. Cormac materialized, also bringing Shuriken back into the real, and the star began cutting. He simply wasn't quick enough, though. Sun-bright fire filled his world and

289

he closed his eyes, wincing at the imminence of destruction he probably wouldn't feel.

'I didn't allow myself to know,' said Mask. 'I cannot hold.'

Cormac opened his eyes. Brightness still surrounded him and he turned it down to a manageable level. He was standing inside a sphere, with something inset in its surface. Power continued to thrum all around him too. His movements felt hindered and, glancing down, he saw a transparent film covering him from head to foot. The mask had expanded to cover him entirely. He re-focused on the object.

'Mask,' he said.

'Quickly now,' Mask replied.

Mask bore the shape of a human woman, but a large one fashioned of glass, filled with a melange of organs and mechanisms. Her arms were extended, fingers long and blending into the surrounding sphere. The head was bald and the eyes black. Threads of blue fire ran convoluted paths through the body.

'Shuriken,' Cormac said, stepping over and crouching by the p-prador corpse.

'Gone.' Mask replied.

In that instant, Cormac felt an information packet arrive in his gridlink. He expanded his U-field and it snapped out to the limits of the sphere, then he jumped into U-space. The destination he chose was simply the same spot. He had time to realize that he was once again transporting the corpse as the shift changed and something seemed to grab him, as it had before, dragging him into a long tunnel. A scream pursued him down it – a human scream. He felt the implosion behind, the pain growing in his skull, as if his gridlink was trying to tear free. Brightness died and, with a thump, he materialized over the crushed leaves of a podule crop, dropping down into a crouch, the corpse crashing down beside him. He then stood.

'What the fuck?' said a figure standing nearby.

Cormac pulled off the mask, which had now retracted back to his face, then focused on what was in front of him. The combat suit, the belligerent face of a heavyworlder man, and the stubby laser carbine swinging towards him. Everything still swirled in his head, laced through with a feeling of terrible loss, but instinct remained. He stepped in, spinning, and launched his foot hard, straight into that face. The man flew back and crashed down on his back. Cormac went over and picked up the carbine, pointing it at him, but the man didn't seem inclined to get up again. Cormac felt some satisfaction with that, but then looked down to the empty holster on his wrist, and winced.

11

Blite

They were away, into a U-space jump, and Blite couldn't quite believe it had been so easy to escape a Mobius AI. In his aug, he suspiciously began rechecking the data they'd received from the planet, at the same time starting a diagnostic search through the system and following it up by running a scan on the ship's hull to ensure nothing untoward had been inserted or attached to it either. He then realized he was procrastinating again.

'Program a series of further jumps to shake him,' he ordered.

Paidon nodded gravely. 'It will have to be a minimum of five to be sure. Mobius AIs are tenacious. Any particular direction?'

Blite considered this for a moment. 'Just keep us well away from Polity worlds – make them all deep-space locations.'

'Six or seven jumps, then,' Paidon replied.

'What?'

'We need more. Clearer U-signatures left in open vacuum,' she explained.

Blite grunted and stood up, heading for the exit. It then seemed to take too little time for him to reach the door to the cabin he'd been aiming for. Using captain's prerogative, he pressed a hand against a palm-lock coded for one person and the door unlocked. He pushed it open and walked inside, halted and looked around.

Greer's cabin looked little different from his own, except for the basket on the floor with its bunched-up blanket and a chew toy shaped, perhaps ominously, like a prador. He stepped over to her console and pressed a hand against the screen. The thing recognized him and a series of options came up. He had to scroll through a number of them until he found 'In the event of my death'.

With a sigh and something nagging in his chest, he pulled out the chair, sat down and stared at the numerous subheadings. There was a lot to read through, and he reckoned on it taking him a while to nail down what he wanted. Reluctantly, almost feeling as if he wasn't giving her the attention she deserved, he sat back and auged into the console, running searches his aug generated from his needs and wants.

Greer was rich, as were all his erstwhile crew, and had laid things out pretty neatly initially. But then over the years she'd added a lot, the latest concerning Groff, which of course no longer applied. She'd provided for the animal, with funds in his name and an application for Polity citizenship filed and awaiting Groff's examination by AI. But that stuff wasn't what Blite was after. He soon discovered she'd been memplanted and had provided for her installation in a body regrown on Earth, where her DNA was kept on file. It surprised him to also learn this wasn't her first death, for she'd been loaded to a new body only ten years before. He avoided following that thread to find out what'd happened then and concentrated on the now. The beam that struck her had certainly destroyed her memplant too, which meant that kind of resurrection was impossible, but maybe there'd be something else.

He found it. When she last died, she'd backed up her memplant to Soulbank. This meant Greer could be brought back to life, but with the last ten years missing from that life. For this, he and others could provide data, out of which an AI could create a memory construct of her last ten years, should that stored version of her want it. Knowing Greer, she wouldn't, but would rather enjoy finding out for herself. So Greer could live again. But as he stood up and wandered over to sit on the bed, it didn't feel like that to Blite.

He wiped at his eyes, brushing away a tear or two, and felt them dry, the nag in his chest receding. He realized something had changed in him. This no longer felt like an adventure pursuing a mystery to be solved; it had become something he must doggedly see to the end – for Greer's sake, if not his own. He stood up and headed for the door, receiving com from Iris as he stepped through it.

'She's awake,' said the haiman woman, directly through his aug. He kept open links to her and Carlstone because he knew they wouldn't contact him unless for something important. This time, having gone so deep into what he'd been doing, he had a moment of confusion, thinking Iris was talking about Greer. He then understood the woman was referring to Meander.

'She seems confused,' Iris continued. 'Understandably so, considering the—'

He cut her off, turning off the induction aug and removing it from his skull. They were useful devices but he didn't like them much.

Iris was standing outside the door to Medical with her hands on her hips, looking pissed off. He studied her left arm, which, the last time he'd seen her, had been missing. The thing was translucent with hints of veins, bones and less organic mechanisms visible inside. It didn't have those metallic veins running over its surface like her natural arm before. He couldn't tell whether it was biological or mechanical, and he wondered whether she had taken a step towards, or away, from some haiman ideal. Seeing the direction of his attention, she raised her hand and inspected it, then abruptly lowered it in irritation.

'You cut me off,' she complained.

He ignored that and asked, 'You were telling me it's understandable that Meander is confused, what with the self-editing she's been doing. How much mind does she have left?'

'Plenty enough to increase our confusion, I would warrant.' Iris turned and pushed open the door.

They entered a short corridor through Medical and turned into a small recovery room. Here Meander sat upright in bed with a tray of food before her. A lot of food. She took no notice of them as she quickly and methodically fed herself, doubtless taking in the requirements of her curious biology. Finally, after draining a glass of some milky fluid, she looked up. Her face immediately turned as white as the contents of the glass had been, her shock evident. Blite held up his hands.

'I'm not here to hurt you,' he said.

She continued to stare at him wide-eyed for a short time, then closed her eyes and dipped her head. When she opened them and looked up again, colour had returned to her cheeks, and somewhat of a glitter to her eyes. She looked at each of them, finally focusing on Iris. Blite looked round. Something odd and fleeting passed from the haiman woman's expression, and it settled into hard and emotionless.

'Okay,' said Blite. 'I'll take it from here. I've got things to talk about with this . . . girl.'

Iris gazed at him steadily for a moment, assessing, then turned back to the door. 'Go easy,' she said, yet it seemed a throwaway injunction.

Blite walked over, snagged up a chair, reversed it and sat astride it by the bed. He considered his own appearance and knew that many found it threatening. Not much he could do about that.

'I don't know why I'm frightened of you,' said Meander. 'I don't know who you are.' She returned her attention to the tray and began eating again, automatically. Watching him and waiting.

'I'm Captain Blite,' he said and held out a hand.

She paused to shake his hand, and the strength of her grip surprised him.

'Meander Draft 64XB,' she replied. 'Pleased to meet you.' She wasn't – he knew that. She continued eating.

'What does the 64XB stand for?'

'Sixty-fourth generation extremophile Brandt line,' she replied.

Good, that meant not all her memories had been edited away.

'I don't know what I'm doing here,' she added.

'You arrived on Abalon via a Morton trade ship out of the Graveyard,' Blite explained. 'There you stole something precious to me. It has elements of AI that had some kind of effect on you, and this is why you fear me. You returned this object to me.'

'A black crystal – a diamond,' she said, no longer eating. Abruptly she put the tray on a side table and returned her focus to him. 'I remember that . . . thing.'

'Why did you travel to Abalon?'

He saw the confusion. 'I don't know.'

'Okay . . . maybe that'll come to you. On Abalon, before you returned the diamond to me, I employed some people to search for you. Even after you returned it, I had them continue searching, because I wanted to know why you stole it. Do you know why?'

She shook her head quickly. He grimaced. She might be lying, and he shouldn't allow her appearance to mislead him. Though she looked like a young woman, for all he knew she might be older than him. She looked weak, but the strength of her hand-shake told him otherwise.

'Anyway, certain circumstances concerning that diamond led me back to Abalon. I learned that my search for you had come to the attention of a criminal organization there – the Mortons. They captured and tortured you, at first for information and then for entertainment. They tortured you over many years, and I rescued you from them.'

'I am aware of many survival revisions,' she said. 'The details have been removed as psychologically damaging.'

He nodded, feeling a sinking sensation. Iris had been correct. The Mortons had tortured her for information, and her ability to edit her own mind for survival had probably erased information this Colson Morton had thought interesting, which was probably the stuff he wanted too. And now another sneaking suspicion had arrived. Maybe there was simply nothing to learn. He stood up, noted her flinch, and so stepped slowly back.

'Maybe you'll remember more at a later date,' he said. 'But understand that you're safe here – no one will harm you.' He turned towards the door, wondering what the hell he needed to do now.

'I know something,' she said suddenly. He turned back and she continued, 'It's important. It sits in my mind like some kind of centre point, yet . . . my fear of it should be gone. The diamond . . . that place.'

'What place?'

She stared at him, haunted. 'An infinite dark plain. The sky above is fire, and I am trapped there . . . trapped there for ever.'

He had no idea what that could mean, though it seemed to indicate a connection between her and the thing. He thought about those creatures who'd tried to kill him on Abalon, about time travel, about all the other attempts on his life. He couldn't see the theft of the black crystal, the dark diamond, as something disconnected from those.

'What's your home world called?' he asked as his thoughts whirled.

297

'Yospen,' she said, looking oddly anxious. 'Will you take me home?'

He shrugged. 'I need to talk to you some more, but, when we're done, I should be able to put you on a ship heading there. Where in the Graveyard is it?'

'I don't know. I don't remember the coordinates.'

'Anything you can remember about it?'

'It orbits a class-six supergiant. Heavily populated . . . biotech.' Her confusion showed again, but then she looked up brightly. 'It wasn't always called Yospen. It used to be called Yossander's Penny.'

Blite was out of the door in a second, reattaching his aug even as he felt the *Coin* drop out of U-space ready for another jump. He caught Iris's look of satisfaction on the way out and forgot it a moment later. They had a destination now, if they could find it.

May

They were following Blite now. Arach had apparently used a U-space connection to the Polity net to hunt him down, and found where the *Coin* had gone. Why, she wasn't sure. Whether she should be involved or not, she was sure, even though this had gone way beyond her contract to transport the agent to Cull. She liked it. She liked that her involvement in all this made her feel . . .

The moment the ship materialized into the real, May breathed out a sigh of relief, which then transitioned into an odd feeling of disappointment about nothing having gone wrong. Reattaching the U-space nacelle had been simply a case of some heavy engineering, expedited by Crane's return. She'd asked about the bounty hunters and when Arach replied, 'They won't be bothering us,' had decided not to pursue that any further. Actually connecting up the nacelle, and balancing it with the other one, had been another matter. All the readouts had been in parameters, but she was no AI and didn't know what she didn't know. Arach had told her it would be fine. She hadn't argued, wanting to be away from that benighted place.

Shortly after they surfaced into the real, a sense of leaden inevitability drowned her remaining relief and even disappointment when Akanthor turned to her to say, 'We need to talk.' May dipped her head in acknowledgement; she'd seen this coming.

'Just file your resignations,' she replied in a bored voice. 'You'll be given everything owing to you, including danger money and any bonuses Blite decides on, if we ever see him again.' She glanced to Crane, standing in his usual position at the back of the bridge, now wearing a new coat, and then to Arach occupying the floor space behind her. They weren't the kind of crewmembers she would usually employ, but they were efficient.

'You don't understand,' said Akanthor.

'I understand your agreement to help out Blite dissolved under pressure,' she said, trying to be annoyed and failing.

'It's a very human thing,' said Arach. 'You should perhaps be thankful they went along with you for as long as they did. I would guess you're three months in, Akanthor?'

Akanthor nodded. 'Yes, but you weren't guessing, were you?'

'Not really,' the spider drone conceded.

'What are you all talking about?' May demanded, still searching for annoyance and failing. Then, finally understanding what 'three months in' probably meant, she felt stupid and just said, 'Oh.'

'Life continues,' said Arach.

'You're having a baby?' May finally asked.

299

'Well –' Akanthor shrugged – 'two, actually . . . and they'll first arrive as eggs.'

'What?'

Akanthor reached out and touched Davidson on the shoulder. 'Our ophidaption is genetic and we've been quite committed to this.' Davidson hardly noticed. His expression was intent, focused on something via his aug.

May's mind was finally gearing into motion. Ophidapts were usually those who made cosmetic and structural alterations to their bodies. They often had snake fangs, like her two crewmen, but they were usually just implants. It seemed Akanthor and Davidson had made alterations at the genetic level, or had inherited this. Most likely it was the latter, because those who were born into it often considered themselves a partially separate species and were committed to maintaining said species.

'Wait a minute,' said Davidson. 'Maybe we need to deal with this later.' He turned his chair and waved up at the screen fabric. 'The shit has been hitting the fan here.'

One of the frames that appeared on the screen showed highways of damage through Abalon's capital city, whose space port they were aiming for. Other frames showed what had led to that damage, and further scenes from just a few days ago. Though she'd been holding off on the input, upon seeing footage of a Mobius AI rolling out of a weird ship down in that wreckage, May auged into the local network for data. She felt her guts tightening on discovering this AI was Straeger, then a relaxation after seeing the AI had departed two days ago. Running through other imagery, she consolidated the story.

'Same things that attacked you,' she said, looking to Arach and Crane. 'It seems Straeger grabbed them before leaving.'

No reply was immediately forthcoming. She glanced at the two ophidapts and saw, by their rigid poses, they were lost in the same data she'd delved into. Perhaps Arach and Crane were similarly occupied?

'Indeed,' Arach finally replied. 'And other data are interesting. Where was Straeger when last you encountered him?'

'At Penny Transport,' May replied, not sure what point Arach was making.

'Other data are that Straeger was here when Blite was here. The AI dropped a U-space mine to prevent him leaving, then instead of going after Blite, pursued one of those creatures on the planet. I can guarantee a Mobius AI's personal ship would have been quite capable of disabling the *Coin*, and yet Straeger allowed Blite to escape on Laumer drive.'

May thought furiously. 'Obviously ECS considered those creatures of greater importance than this entropy stuff involving Blite.'

'I don't think ECS was in the decision-making process,' Arach replied. 'ECS has recently put out a reward for information on Straeger's activities. An attempt by the planetary AI here to detain it didn't work out too well either.'

'Straeger has its own agenda,' said Akanthor.

'And it seems,' said Davidson, 'ECS wants to ask it about how it happened to survive an exploding dreadnought.'

May nodded, then focused via her aug through ship's sensors. The whole situation was steadily becoming more complicated, but she doubted they'd resolve it sitting up in orbit discussing it. And anyway, she felt it was time to be on the move to the next thing. She hated herself for feeling this way, but she didn't want to have to take into account the reluctance of her crewmen any more. The next thing would come once they were on their way, and she was no longer responsible for them. The next thing would keep her occupied . . .

She zoned out of the continuing conversation in the bridge. There wasn't much traffic around this world, since, according to data she accessed, it was pretty much self-sufficient. The movement of people here was mainly via the planetary runcibles. She did, however, note a number of disreputable-looking ships in orbit – the kind of patch-up jobs often found in the Graveyard. After a brief squirt with the fusion engines, she was in atmosphere, with streamers of cloud ribboning past. Bright day faded to night, broken by thruster steering, then the ship filled with the sliding roar of atmosphere as they headed towards the space port. This was big enough for the *Bracken*, so there was no need for a shuttle ride. She saw dark forest sliding underneath, then city lights and what looked like one or two fires still burning there. With a blink, she enhanced and all became as bright as day. Slowing further, and then pausing over the city as a ship launched from the space port, she gazed down at the mess. Once her slot was ready, she took her ship in over the space port and brought it down nice and neat, where required.

May came out of it feeling oddly disappointed, seeing as she'd been doing what she always loved doing, and looked around. Crane, Akanthor and Davidson had gone from the bridge. She pinged the latter two and found them in their joint cabin. Crane, meanwhile, had gone down to Engineering and was working a machine there. She didn't bother to ask what he was doing, instead swinging her chair around to face Arach.

'So how do we find out where Blite went next?'

'We go and talk to Broden first.' Arach turned to the door from the bridge and squeezed through, compressing his abdomen to do so.

'And he will know?'

'He doesn't,' said Arach as he ambled away, 'but he may have other useful information.'

May leaped out of her chair and followed. She thought about her weapon, still in a cabin filled with crash foam, but really, she didn't need weapons with a companion like Arach. She just followed him down to the personnel airlock, which he squashed into first, demonstrating it hadn't been necessary to open the hold on Penny Royal's planetoid, and confirming for her that the purpose had really been to bring in the object now sitting in there. The inner and outer doors of the lock then remained open, since the atmosphere outside was breathable. It brought in a waft of burning and the aroma of pine. While she waited for Arach to clear, Akanthor and Davidson arrived, two trunk dogs hovering along the floor behind them. They must have packed up their stuff during the journey – this all seemed to be happening too quickly.

'We're sorry about this, but hope you understand,' said Akanthor.

May still felt shreds of resentment, but they dispersed when she studied the woman more closely and noted the slight swelling of her torso. Any other time she would have thought Akanthor had been allowing a build-up of fat via her nanosuite, for whatever purpose. Now she knew the real reason: Akanthor wouldn't countenance risking lives that had no choice in the matter.

'I understand. I'll shoot updates to your net accounts whenever I get a chance. I hope we'll meet up back at Penny Transport sometime.'

'We still like the job,' said Davidson. 'Just, in the circumstances, not this particular iteration of it.' He turned and looked back as Crane loomed in the corridor behind and began trudging towards them. 'Stay on point, May, and –' he hesitated for a long moment – 'take care of yourself.'

As he and Akanthor stepped into the airlock, his last comment puzzled her. Of course she'd take care of herself – she always did, didn't she? Their luggage paused behind them, then slid out with an increased hum of old grav to drop down the length of the ladder. She turned to Crane. 'What've you been making?'

Coming to a halt, Crane shook his head slowly. He wasn't going to tell her, but she could see he was clutching something in his right fist. She went through the lock, Crane coming in quickly behind her, and soon stood on the composite of the space port slab. She surveyed some familiar infrastructure: the fuel tanks for older ships, rows of handler drays, a couple of cranes and a meagre scattering of vessels. A memory arose and she remembered coming here before, to pick up a mixed cargo of multicoloured marble mined here, as well as various woods and a load of tea. There'd been no extensive customs checks from the light-touch planetary AI, though she wasn't sure what its reaction would be to her companions. She focused on Akanthor and Davidson and saw they were lingering. Time to say goodbye properly. She walked over to them.

'So this is it,' she said. 'Let's not draw it out.'

Akanthor grabbed her in a hug, then stepped away. It surprised her to see moisture in the ophidapt woman's eyes. Davidson hesitated a moment then did the same.

'It's been good,' he said, then frowned past her shoulder.

She turned to see Crane had come up behind her. Davidson backed up abruptly beside his partner, and Crane stepped up to them. He held out his huge hand and opened it. May saw that perched on his palm were two rubber dogs, like the one she'd seen him toying with in Penny Royal's planetoid. Davidson and Akanthor just stared at them, then looked to May for guidance.

'They're gifts for your children – just take them,' called Arach from where he stood, gazing towards the city lying adjacent to the space port.

Davidson swallowed nervously, stepped forwards and carefully took them from Crane's hand.

'Why . . . thank you,' he said, but Crane was already turning away.

May felt sure the things would be dropped in a bin at the earliest opportunity. But then Arach spoke out again. 'Keep them safe and pass them on to your children. When an AI receives one of those it's a warning that has them shitting computer chips. In this case, it's a promise. There's a code written inside them. If your children are ever in serious trouble, they just need to send it . . . but it has to be *very* serious trouble, mind.'

Davidson pocketed the things, nodded to May and, without a further word, he and Akanthor turned and headed off. As May watched them go, she wondered if the two toys would still end up in a bin. Having Crane come to your rescue didn't sound like an ideal solution to any problem.

'A shame they went, since you needed them,' said Arach. 'But understandable from their point of view.'

'Too dangerous,' said May, feeling a slight frisson as she wondered what they'd be getting into when they went after this Broden.

Arach scuttled around and faced her. 'Yes, you are.'

As they moved off, she couldn't understand why she didn't question that.

Cormac

He was back. Recovery was quicker this time, as if having done this once his facility with U-space had adapted. However, Cormac did run his nanosuite in emergency mode again, and had to tighten his belt. When he opened out his U-senses just a minute or two after his arrival here, it functioned cleanly, and the warning ache in his head quickly faded. He ran analysis of his condition via his gridlink, which was also perfectly online, and came to some conclusions: the trip to the future had been a causal anomaly, a push into a probable reality, while coming back here had been a reversal of that. The fact he suffered ill effects related to that portion of the future he'd brought back within him: materials ingested, knowledge in his skull, and of course the p-prador. Perhaps his reasoning strayed into the specious, but it felt right. He grimaced and focused through his gridlink on the data of the now.

Net permissions on the world of Cull were limited. The AIs were feeding through data to provide a rose-tinted view of the Polity, and to be helpful, but with just enough held back for those living here to want more. The AIs were patient – eventually rulers here would be pushed by their population into joining the Polity. Accessing the net, he ran his usual security protocols to conceal his identity and began gathering data, steadily worming his way through the blocks. Keying into satellite imagery, he saw the remaining bounty hunter ships down at the small space port and started to walk in that direction, not being inclined to shift over there until he was up to date. He then halted and turned to look back at the corpse of the p-prador. Did he need it any longer? Yes – the thing was loaded with advanced technology and might provide further useful information, even though he now knew what the thing was. But how to transport it? Might it snap him back into the future again?

'Ah, fuck,' said the bounty hunter.

Carbine resting over one shoulder, Cormac stepped back towards him.

The man sat upright, reached up, and straightened his nose with a liquid crunching. It didn't seem to bother him overly much. He turned and looked at Cormac. 'Was that really necessary?'

Cormac shrugged. 'You had a weapon and you were turning it towards me. In your line of work, you should know how hesitation can get you dead.'

The man nodded, then looked at the p-prador. 'What the fuck?' He put down a hand and heaved himself to his feet, then looked around. In the distance, far over the other side of the fields, more hunters were heading for the pass down from the plain, doubtless towards the parked ATVs below.

'Why are you still here?' Cormac asked. 'Crane is out-system with some ships in pursuit. No bounty here now.'

The man looked back at him. 'Trying to find some way to rescue a profit out of this shit-show.' He gestured to the crop they stood in. 'I thought these podules would make a good cargo now I can get a grav-loader up here.' He grimaced. 'Seems the local government has claimed them, though, and told us all to leave at once.'

'But you haven't left . . .'

'I was about to when someone kicked me in the face.'

'No inclination to force the issue and just take the podules?'

'I know they're not well armed here, but I was just running supply for another outfit. The final payment on the retainer disappeared along with those guys.'

As the man spoke, Cormac checked what he could via the net, though the hunters who'd come here kept tight security and didn't use it as much as legitimate Polity citizens, for obvious reasons. Facial recognition of the man gave him a wide selection of possibilities, which he quickly fined down with other information.

'What's your name?' he asked, already knowing it.

'Jessikon Andrew,' the man replied.

Andre, as everyone who knew him called him, was of a similar type to Blite, as he had been long ago. He worked on the edge of legality and sometimes strayed over it. No, wrong assessment. Blite had his own particular morality that Cormac admired, while this guy wasn't quite so admirable. Some of the illegality he strayed into involved the coring trade and, should he venture back into the Polity, someone of Cormac's previous profession would come down on him very quickly, followed no doubt by some pertinent questioning from an unsympathetic forensic AI.

'And your name?' Andre asked.

'Ian Cormac.'

Andre laughed, but then the laughter stuttered to a halt and the man turned to look towards the smoking ruins of Crane's farmhouse. He'd just made the connection.

'You're shitting me.'

Cormac unshouldered the carbine and gestured to the p-prador corpse. 'Go over there and sit on that thing.'

Andre eyed the carbine as it centred on his face for a moment and casually traversed down his body to his right leg. He waved an arm angrily, then walked to the corpse and sat on it. Cormac went over to stand close, U-senses opening out. Via the net, he'd already located Andre's ATV down below, but he did feel some reluctance about what he intended to do now. Mask had told him about the 'tachyon drag' of things sent into the past, as if flung back in time on a piece of elastic. In trying to transport this corpse, he'd activated all of that at once, and it had dragged him into the future. Mask had told him that he too had created an elastic link to his own time and would be dragged back once he was within the time runcible – as indeed had happened.

He stepped closer and put a hand down on the carapace, pushing his U-sense harder. He even went so far as to push just a little way into U-space until he, Andre and the corpse began to fade from their surroundings. He could sense some drag there, but it no longer had the *weight* it had when moving it the first time. He just *knew* it wouldn't drag him as before. He snapped his hand away, thinking. Something had happened. Mask had intervened in some way, beyond stopping him being fried. And the meta-human, or whatever Mask was, had also screamed at the point he left, quite possibly dying. He could see no reason his U-field had expanded in the way it had; he felt sure this had been deliberate. Just as with the memory package sitting in his gridlink, Mask had wanted him to take the thing with him. He made his judgement.

'Fuck it,' he said, and extended his U-field, shifting the three of them to that ATV.

No tunnel opened to drag him away, and he fell quickly to the coordinates he'd chosen, though he did feel a perceptible tug, like a side current. There was something else different about the transition this time, however. He felt a threat, as if something just at the edge of his perception was chewing towards him, making a machinelike grinding squeal as it did so. He didn't pause. He didn't alter his time sense to more assess this properly, and just fell through. They landed with a dusty thump. Cormac staggered, then stepped back, carbine centred on Andre. But the man wasn't about to attack him. He was still sitting on the p-prador, gripping the edge of its carapace and gaping at his surroundings.

'Oh, hell,' he said, then focusing on Cormac, 'For real?'

'Indeed,' Cormac replied.

The ATV, a big cigar-shaped machine with adaptive wheels and a loading crane folded on its back, stood out in the open with space clear all around. Beside it rested a variety of plasmel crates, likely unloaded by that crane. With the kind of people who'd come here, Andre wouldn't have left either his vehicle or those supplies unprotected. Cormac eyed the antipersonnel laser on the roof towards the back of the cab, then turned back to the man.

'So your venture here hasn't been as profitable as you hoped?'

Andre shrugged.

'What kind of ship do you have?'

'In-system cargo barge converted for U-space.'

'The mind?'

'Plugged-in submind,' Andre replied, though it amused Cormac how the man didn't mention he had a modern submind that had been slaved.

He gestured to the p-prador. 'I need to transport this somewhere for examination and I can pay. A thousand New Carth shillings a day, or equivalent amount in any currency you desire. Hard or Net Bank.'

'Okay, but I'll need something up front, and I'll need to know where we're going.'

Cormac nodded, attention focused through his gridlink to where he'd already found the man's Galaxy Bank account. He selected one of the numerous ECS black ops accounts to which he'd gained access and routed over ten thousand shillings. He always enjoyed drawing on ECS funds when needed, since it almost made him an operative paid by the AIs to audit their behaviour.

'We're going to Hune. It should take you about five days in your vessel, plus some waiting-around time, then on to a destination to be decided. Check your Galaxy Bank account.'

Andre stared at him, blinking, then raised an arm to operate a touch screen on the sleeve of his combat armour. After a moment, he made a clicking sound with his mouth and flicked to something else.

'Okay, let's get this loaded,' he said.

Having watched him in the virtual realm, Cormac was glad to note that he'd shut down the instruction to the ATV's anti-personnel laser, which had been to nail anyone who wasn't Andre walking within a perimeter around it.

Blite

The latest jump brought them to a risky destination. Blite clumped up from his cabin and entered the bridge. The whole crew was in place, with Judice on weapons, Carlstone running tactics and probably tracking local com, Paidon on the drive system and piloting, while Breil was quickly sorting data. Now they were within a Polity solar system, they could key into the AI net. This was something Blite could see no way around, since they needed information.

It had seemed counterintuitive to head here, a world deep within the Polity, but Carlstone explained the rationale. It was a certainty that wherever they connected to the net, they'd be detected, identified and AIs would know about it at once. Here, however, they'd chosen a long-established high-population world. The latter had resulted in five runcibles on the surface and a lack of ships in orbit. The former meant its defences were huge orbital stations that weren't capable of chasing after Blite. The position of the world also meant a lack of ECS warships in the area, since they mostly concentrated out towards the borders around the Line worlds.

Blite stood just in from the door and eyed the captain's chair, then shrugged, walked over and sat down carefully. He'd found himself doing a lot of things carefully now, ever since inadvertently shattering his favourite teapot.

'Do you have anything for me?' he asked, looking over to Breil.

Breil looked around. 'It was a quick and accurate search. The AIs have at least two-thirds of the Graveyard nailed down in detail. No world there called Yospen, and no world called Yossander's Penny either, but there is one called Yossander's Hold.'

'That's interesting.' Blite eyed the images in various frames, now up on the main screen, of the world they presently orbited, more interested right now in what the reaction might be to them here.

It was Earth-like, but half again the diameter. Even from orbit it was possible to see vast cities rising from the continents, like technological boils, to penetrate the stratosphere. From their perspective, half the world was luxuriating in the light of a red giant, while the night side looked like a forest of lit-up Christmas trees. Four moons orbited – so encrusted with tech and structures that it was difficult to tell that they were moons. The two defence stations were even bigger than them, and these rectilinear monsters bristled with weapons. This wasn't a world likely to fall to alien attack without the battle lighting up the galaxy like a nova.

'The stations?' he asked.

It was Carlstone's turn to answer. 'Nothing but the usual queries and warnings. They're not really taking much notice of us being this far out.'

Blite pondered on the lack of reaction to them. Perhaps Straeger hadn't put out an apprehend alert, and maybe had larger concerns with those prador-things. Or maybe the Mobius AI was just letting them run out on a leash. He wasn't sure which might be worse.

'We're fully updated?' he asked.

'On all key matters,' said Breil.

The ship's data storage updated from net traffic on anything concerning Penny Transport, and anything else Blite or the others had defined as of interest. It couldn't get everything, of course, because that would take crystal storage larger than the ship. Something else would have happened too: the moment they connected to the net, notification of Greer's death and the destruction of her memplant would have gone to Earth. Probably, in the next few days, printerbots would be making the first passes on constructing her skeleton, depending on demand, of course, and whether this was the method of rebirth she'd chosen.

'Okay, Paidon,' Blite said. 'Get us moving, and let's take a look at this Yossander's Hold. Breil, run data on it to screen.'

'Will do,' he replied. 'I've also got a message here from Absinthe.'

'Run that first.'

A frame opened in the screen paint to show the tongue-flicking monitor lizard head of the war drone. For a moment, he was looking at something off to one side, then he turned to face towards Blite.

'Bastards have locked us down,' said Absinthe. 'The place is crawling with agents and ECS commandos, including Sparkind and a plague of small Mobius AIs that I think might be subminds. They're recording everything, interrogating minds and people, but then I don't suppose you'll be surprised about that. Since we're suing ECS for damages, I have managed to negotiate some concessions, so not everything has stopped. Carlstone's replacement is, as to be expected, doing a good job, and most of the workforce is taking it in good part – seeing it as an interesting interlude. All detail is attached to this message. Good luck with whatever shit you've got yourself into out there, Blite. With any luck, everything will be back up to scratch by the time you return.'

The image blinked out. Blite got an 'I told you so' look from Carlstone, before the man turned back to his console. The ship, meanwhile, was in motion again, with the defence stations drawing away to their left. Next up, the frame expanded and broke into numerous windows. Blite gazed at the text, the imagery, the streams of code and virtuality links, and he knew he really ought to stick the induction aug back on his head to dive into it. Instead he glanced across at Breil. 'Give me a précis.'

'Hold on,' said Carlstone, holding up a hand. 'Just looking at the stuff Absinthe sent. That Polity dreadnought blew up after we left.'

'What the hell? The agent did it?' Blite said.

'Maybe,' said Carlstone, 'but there's other data. Straeger was aboard that ship and now ECS has a reward for information on the AI's activities.'

Blite didn't know what to do with that, so instead said, 'Breil – that world?'

Breil turned from his console and reached up to touch the aug permanently fixed behind his ear. It was one of those glassy slugs that took auging as far as it could go in most humans, before they had to go Iris's route and start putting support systems into their bodies.

'Yossander's Hold is a diaspora world that was discovered just a decade before the war. A biotech faction headed out from Earth for the same reason the Cyberat went – to avoid the supposed inevitable AI extermination of humanity. They were a gloomy lot back in the day. When it was rediscovered, the colony population of twenty thousand had grown to over a hundred thousand through cloning, artificial wombs and major DNA rewrites on those clones. The world itself was at the proto-life stage when they first arrived, but they worked quickly, seeding the oceans and the land masses – one main continent and a large collection of what are called drift islands. Modified corals stabilized the islands, and an atmosphere was establishing. During the war, they were hit by a prador bioweapon but weren't occupied. The data we have now is that they survived, have a stable atmosphere, a population of over three billion and are stage three biotech. They trade within the Graveyard and beyond. In fact, they have more dealings with the prador than with the Polity.'

'Politics?' Blite asked.

'Biotech line families are in charge of various areas. Low conflict between them, but it is there. There's also a factional problem that's been growing ever since they discovered the AIs didn't slaughter humanity, and since they climbed back up out of the pit the prador bioweapon created. Many of the families have a messianic focus on biotech – no technology allowed at all that's not grown. Others have accepted the melding of hard and soft tech, and the fading of their distinctions.'

'And of those families . . . what do we have on the Brandt line?'

Breil winced. 'That's where things start to get a little confusing. Our passenger says she's Meander Draft 64XB – sixty-fourth generation of the extremophile Brandt line. There are four Brandt lines. Definitions of extremophile seem to be used on some basis I cannot parse, but they're all only to the thirtieth generation, where a generational number is even used.'

'I see,' said Blite, catching looks from Carlstone and Paidon. He'd told the bridge crew about the constant rewinds of his deaths, the entropic effects, and the fact that causality was being fucked with by the gem now embedded in his skull. As did he, they doubtless saw the time travel implications in Meander's name – how could she be from a generation that didn't exist yet? 'How long before we get there, Paidon?'

'Depends whether you want to go straight there or not.'

'Yes, take us straight there. I don't see any Polity warships following us into the Graveyard, do you?'

'A few weeks, then. The world is nearer to the prador border than here, and edging into rift space. The prador probably never occupied it because it was well off to the side of the main front.'

Blite put his hands down on his chair arms and pushed himself up. 'Keep me apprised,' he said, and began to stand.

'Hang on,' said Breil, looking over to Carlstone, 'Are you getting this?'

'U-com, routed from fuck knows where,' Carlstone replied. He looked around at Blite. 'Could be Straeger getting in touch. Should we allow it?'

Blite sat back down and stared at the image of the station. If the AI had tracked them down and was about to tell them to stay put, they were in as bad a position as they had been over Abalon. They could Laumer their way out, but still might be fired upon.

'Allow it,' he said.

Carlstone worked his controls and a frame opened. It showed nothing at first, then an image began to fade into view. Cormac sat there on some large object strapped down in a small cargo hold. Blite did a double take when he realized the thing was one of those odd prador. He focused on the man himself. Cormac looked drawn, with his clothing hanging loose, but his expression gave away nothing at all.

'Blite,' he said. 'I understand you've encountered some of these fellows.' He slapped a hand down on the surface he sat on.

'Maybe,' said Blite.

'Run me an update on all that's occurred with you.'

Blite hesitated. Cormac had warned him of dangers and got him out of a sticky situation, but he still didn't trust the machinations of Polity agents – no matter that he claimed no longer to be one.

'I'm particularly interested in this Meander female, too, and your current destination,' Cormac added.

How the hell did he know that, and how much more did he know? Blite was inclined to be parsimonious with information but, again, guilt about his apparent invulnerability kicked in. In all this, he wasn't putting himself at risk of dying, but that didn't apply to everyone around him, as he was all too aware. For things to run at optimum, he needed all the information, and allies, he could get.

'I sense your reluctance,' said Cormac, a hint of irritation crossing his features. 'I suggest a packet exchange.' He slapped a hand on the carapace again. 'I can tell you all about how I acquired this prill-prador, or p-prador, and where it led me. I'll also have more to tell once it's been examined.'

Blite looked over at Carlstone and Breil. 'Put together something for him and send it once he's sent his.'

'Everything?' Breil asked carefully.

Blite sighed. 'Yes, everything.' He turned back to the screen. 'Did you blow up that Polity dreadnought?'

Cormac winced. 'No – I suspect Straeger has something to do with that.'

Blite nodded. 'Straeger came after us to Abalon. It grabbed one of the p-prador on there, so anything you learn he probably already knows. He also allowed us to run.'

Cormac tilted his head and fiddled with the holster at his wrist. He looked up. 'Then he has some idea of where you're running to, or he knows that he'll find out.' Cormac stood up, waved a hand. 'I've sent my packet.'

Blite looked around at Breil and gave him a nod. A second later the screen frame flickered out. Standing up, Blite absorbed the agent's subtle warning. Either some form of tracking was on his ship, or someone aboard had a different paymaster. He glanced over at Carlstone, who was frowning, obviously having caught it too. Blite tilted his head at the man, who acknowledged this by tapping a finger against his aug. Carlstone would look into it. Without a further word Blite turned and headed back out of the bridge, not liking that he must now distrust his crew, and that Carlstone wasn't excluded from that.

He stomped back down through the ship towards Medical, but halfway there stopped, thought about things for a while, and instead went to his cabin. There he took his time making himself a pot of tea to calm himself. He had no idea what the fuck was going on, and it would have been stupid to go to Meander to start reaming her for information she probably didn't possess. He had to remember that, however Penny Royal's gift to him had fucked her over, it had left her frightened of it and of him. It would be counterproductive.

Having made the pot of tea and poured one cup, Blite sighed and grudgingly reached into a pocket and took out the induction aug. The expansion of contact and available information filled up part of his skull at once, which was why the things were so damned seductive. He harrumphed, sipped his tea, then sought out an icon and made contact. A surprising delay ensued; he had a sense of data being shifted about and slotted away, then Iris was there, glaring at him. Was it her real face, or a representation brought up automatically, or one chosen by her? He had no idea about that, and no idea whether it mattered.

'Obviously caught you at a busy moment,' he said.

'I'm always busy,' she replied. 'I don't have room for the so-human ability to be indolent.'

'Well, that's nice for you.' Blite sensed something odd about that reply, but continued with his concerns, 'How's the patient?'

'A great deal better, and I suspect that keeping her here in Medical has become contraindicated. Meander is another who doesn't seem inclined to indolence.'

'She's bored, you mean?'

'Certainly.'

'Okay, I'm coming to get her.'

Iris just dipped her head and cut the connection. Blite was about to take off the aug when, because it was both seductive and convenient, he used it to assess ship's status. Only a third of available cabins were occupied, and he selected one just a short distance up this corridor from his, amid other occupied cabins – he wanted her close and not off on the periphery. He sent orders and the cabin robots got to work, raising a Spartan accommodation into something more comfortable: inflating open-cell lumps into mattress, cushions and pillows, unpacking compressed blankets, towels and other such items, connecting up the cabin fabricator and plumbing. He then finished his tea before setting out.

Iris stood waiting in the corridor outside Medical, head dipped and arms folded. She looked up as he approached. 'So we're heading to her world?'

'It seems likely it may be, but there are anomalies.'

'Yes, I'm aware of them and their implications, as you must be.' She sighed, looked away for a moment, then back. 'Meander is sixty-fourth generation, while they're only into thirtieth generations there. Time scales on generations can be highly variable, but I would note that even I don't understand all the biotech in Meander, and she has a lifespan as potentially limitless as that of you and me. The missing thirty generations.' Iris shrugged.

'A thousand years, perhaps,' said Blite. He'd briefly dipped into the information the agent had sent – the fact the man had been dragged a thousand years into the future, where it seemed these p-prador came from, then returned. He knew Iris would have integrated all of it. Rather than elucidate anything, it had just added more confusion.

'Could be,' said Iris, 'but then if you're using advanced biotech and churning people out of artificial wombs, it could be a lot less.'

Just another thing they didn't know, thought Blite, as he turned to the door and pushed it open. He gazed at the row of beds, and the cleanroom surgery lying beyond at the end. Meander was standing there, gazing in through the window, with her hands behind her back. It struck Blite as a somewhat military pose.

She turned abruptly and gazed at them. Something flickered in her expression at the sight of him, then went away. She was dressed now in a skin-tight envirosuit and looked a lot less like the waif he'd first seen. He headed over. She spoke before he could make the prosaic enquiries about her health.

'You're Blite,' she said. 'You save the world.'

12

May

The town was a wreck of collapsed buildings, with streets dropped down into what May learned over aug had been a vactrans system, and piles of smouldering rubble. Air ambulances were strobing through the sky, with rescue workers on the ground, including skeletal Golem taken out of the AI cache, and a variety of robots. Crane abruptly halted and looked down one long street that didn't appear quite so damaged. May tracked his gaze to a Mobius AI rolling along towards them like a dandelion head. It abruptly halted as though it'd hit a glass wall, then zipped off to one side to fold up and drop through a hole in the rubble. Crane checked the security of his hat, made a snorting sound, and walked on. That was when a nearby pile of rubble shifted massively, and a great mass of scrap dragged itself out.

The thing lay two grav-cars long, walked on a few remaining legs and was a burned and melted mess. Studying it more closely, May saw the remains of a wing case and one protruding stag beetle antler, and recognized it from footage she'd been viewing intermittently since leaving the ship. She'd thought the stag beetle drone completely trashed. It was, pretty much, but the packed remains were crawling, with silver worms dipping in here and there, or out, in anemone-like sprays. As it moved, shrivelled and burned items were dropping away, and other objects were shifting around the remains of memory-metal frameworks, straightening up. It dragged itself in front of them and halted, folding out a mangled minigun of a similar design to the ones Arach could deploy.

'Got a little bit too exciting for you?' Arach enquired, moving forwards and slightly raising the hatches on his sides.

A humming clicking issued from the wrecked drone. The weapon shifted slightly, evidently targeting Crane. May had no confidence the weapon could fire.

'Ancillary voice . . . Norbert . . . Glyph presentation corvine,' the stag beetle stated, then added, 'Fuck it. Assistance.'

Arach rattled round to look at May and Crane, and gave an eloquent shrug. 'Norbert here has been through the wars. He lost half his mind in the attack, is rebuilding, and will download the missing half from the local AI. He needs some help, which he has requested from me, since he doesn't trust the Mobius AIs lurking around here offering to put him back together.'

'Why doesn't he trust them?' May asked.

'We're a private kind, us from 101, and Mobius AIs are impertinent. You'll have to talk to Broden alone.'

'I don't even know what to ask him!'

'Get any information he has on what Blite did here, and where he might have gone. I'll catch up with you later.'

'And if he doesn't want to talk?'

Arach raised one limb and pointed at Crane, then turned and scuttled forwards to the stag beetle drone. May watched as he reared up to the side of the wreck and began to delve inside with his forelimbs. Crane just gave a shrug and set off again. As May followed, she saw hatches opening in Arach's thorax, to issue jointed tentacles bristling with manipulators at their ends. The weapon continued to track Crane until they were past. It didn't surprise her how little trust people of any kind had for the big brass Golem. If just ten per cent of the virtualities were true, then she was walking with what might be a nigh-indestructible psychopath. A laugh rose at the thought, and then died.

Crane trudged on, hobnail boots crushing rubble to powder. He seemed to know where he was going, so May kept her mouth shut and just stayed with him. They took a convoluted route through the streets and into an area of the town where there wasn't so much damage. One building was down in a great smouldering pile, and as they came opposite this Crane halted, hesitating. He walked over to stand next to the pile. Small seeker robots, like silver harvestman spiders, were crawling all over the rubble. As she watched, May shuddered at the sight of a military autodoc, like a scorpion with too many legs, scuttling up a beam and dropping into a hole to disappear out of sight. Crane watched too, then abruptly moved forwards to a large square door of ceramal lying in this pile.

'What are you doing?' May asked, not really expecting an answer. She then looked up as a shadow drew across and an air ambulance dropped into the street.

'Under,' said Crane, surprising her.

Standing in the rubble, he reached down and, with one hand, caught hold of the edge of the door. Perhaps this had been a bank or something, and the door had been to the vault. The thing looked heavy and solid. Crane heaved, his boots sinking down into the rubble. May quickly backed up as, in one dusty rush, he heaved the thing over, then darted forwards, sideswiping a falling beam and sending it clanging away. As the door crashed down, he disappeared in dust for a moment, then came out carrying a young woman, clothing bloody and ragged, and the autodoc clinging to her chest with pipes running into her mouth and torso. He trudged out, taking her to two skeletal Golem who were unloading a grav-gurney from the ambulance. The two halted and abruptly backed up. Ignoring them, Crane laid the woman on the gurney, then began heading up the street again. May hurried after him.

'Careful, you're undermining your reputation,' she said as she caught up.

He halted, turned to look at her with those black eyes, then gestured her ahead of him and pointed to a nearby building. A woman sat on a low wall between pillars in the portico at the front, smoking a cigarette.

'Broden,' said Crane, and just halted in the street.

This was the most she'd heard from him in all the time she'd known him; she didn't think he was going to become any more loquacious. Moving ahead, she walked up to the portico. The woman just flicked a glance at Crane, then stared at May while puffing on her cigarette. It was an antediluvian habit many took up just for optics. She wore old-style camouflage fatigues, and had obviously gone for a historical African mercenary appearance that was probably a rent-a-thug look from a catalogue. Down beside her rested a pulse rifle and she had a heavy-looking handgun holstered at her hip. May didn't know what exchanges had been made, only that Arach had spoken to this Broden and they were due to see him.

'We're here to see Broden,' she said.

'Really?' said the woman, casually flicking away her cigarette. 'He's rather busy at the moment.'

'We're after information about Captain Blite.' She pointed over her shoulder. 'Mr Crane here is anxious to find him.'

The woman smiled tightly. 'Mr Crane,' she said. 'Look, Broden is recruiting, but he's not overburdened with a sense of humour and needs serious people. If you really want in, then I suggest you head over to Chanville and apply there.'

May didn't know how best to move forward now – should she insist? She turned to Crane and shrugged. He just stood out there in the road looking back towards the air ambulance as it took off. Would he do something? She had no idea, and she wasn't sure she wanted him to. His rescuing that woman seemed likely to be an aberration. She turned back.

'Our companion, the war drone Arach, has been in contact with Broden – I think he knows we're coming. I work for Blite, as did Broden.'

'Arach,' said the woman, her tight smile fixed. 'Go away. As I said, Broden wants serious people not cosplayers.'

'We really must insist,' said May.

The smile diminished and the woman dropped her hand to the butt of her sidearm. Crane abruptly walked in from the street to come up beside May. She supposed that standing out there, he'd only had the appearance of a big man. Now, looming up beside her, his sheer scale had become clear, as had a face seemingly made of brass. The woman's expression changed. She abruptly came off the wall, snatching up her pulse rifle.

'Biggle, get down here,' she said, then looked up into the roof of the portico.

A security drone, much resembling a miniature version of one of those strange prador, dropped down on a column. It possessed a multipurpose limb on each side, and from underneath it extended a series of barrels. One of them was squared off and silver inside – a particle cannon. It swung from side to side, targeting each of them, while red lights ran frantically around its rim.

'I see,' said the drone.

'Leave now,' said the woman, putting her pulse rifle across her shoulder and now utterly confident.

Meanwhile, above her, the drone had set his arms to work.

Reaching above, he began unplugging cables and feeds. Once most of these were free, he reached down; the sound of a socket driver alerted the woman – she looked up again.

'What the hell are you doing, Biggle?'

'I was contracted for building security in the expectation of an attack from the Mortons.' He waved a limb at May and Crane, then with a shrug dropped the cannon to hang by its power and particulate feed. 'This is way above my pay grade.' With a crunching sound, the drone turned and detached from its column, dropping down to hang hovering in the air. Backwash from its grav-engine raised the woman's dreadlocks. She swung her rifle down to bear on Crane, but kept looking to the drone as it hung there. In an abrupt motion, it flew out of the side of the portico. She watched in disbelief as the thing went bobbing up the street, then reached back and touched a small aug behind her left ear.

'Biggle just fucked off,' she said.

Before she received a reply, the door swung open and a thin outlinker stepped out in a bulky armoured suit. He surveyed the scene, nodded to May and focused on Mr Crane. After a second, he reached out and put a hand on the barrel of the woman's pulse rifle and pushed it down.

'I'm Broden,' he said. 'I didn't really believe it, and I'm not sure I do even now. There are Golem who copy the look of a certain fictional character.'

'Seems your security drone was a believer,' May replied.

Broden tilted his head to one side – the pose of someone frantically running through data in his aug. 'Yes he does, but he was being overly dramatic and has a tendency to wind up his comrades. He's gone off to check the surrounding area.' He shot a glance at the woman, then continued, 'Until now I never realized those fictions were based on historical fact, nor did I know that Crane was recently driven from his hideaway on the out-Polity world of

Cull.' He blinked, still glassy eyed. 'You are May Esteem, one of Blite's employees and you went to Cull, so that ties up.'

'We're only here for information on Blite,' said May.

Broden shrugged. 'I already sent an update on all that to this . . . Arach. We snatched a woman from the Mortons – she'd stolen something from Blite – and now he's gone off with her, likely to the Graveyard.' He hesitated. 'Though . . . more information is coming to light concerning her.'

'What do you mean?'

'We have her torturer now.'

'Then we would like to speak with him.'

Cormac

Andre's ship was neat, with everything stowed away and all working at maximum efficiency. But only where it could, and where finances allowed. As the time arrived for them to come out of their U-jump, the man attached a pipe to a port in his neck and strapped himself in.

'You sure you don't want anything?' he asked.

'U-space is not a problem for me,' Cormac replied. 'Though I recommend you use the money I'm giving you to have that starboard nacelle fixed.'

Andre grimaced. 'I guess it isn't a problem for you, and nor are AIs. For me, AIs are a problem and I'll need one of them to work on the drive.'

Cormac shrugged and looked up at the big flat screen that gave an ersatz view of what lay outside, with stars virtually slipping past and a solar system coming into view. 'You need to get it done, or in a future jump the uncomfortable effects you're avoiding will be turning you inside out.'

Andre grunted and pressed a button on the side of the tube, which filled with green liquid. After a moment, he slumped unconscious, then he began to snore.

The jump away from Cull had been interesting. With the ship's U-space nacelles unbalanced, it felt like reality was being twisted in opposite directions either side of him. Cormac had concentrated on the p-prador, looking for odd effects, and then when it did seem about to shift away somewhere, he extended his U-field to cover it and lock it down. This might well have been just something to do with nacelle imbalance, but of one thing he was certain: the thing grinding its way towards him in the moments of transition was not caused by that imbalance. He would concentrate on that when they exited, but now he had time to look at something else.

He walked past, behind Andre, and dropped into the seat in front of a large com console of very old design. Resting a hand on it, he relaxed and, maintaining his U-field on the p-prador, he turned his attention inwards. In those last moments in the future, Mask had dropped an information package into his gridlink through their connection. Cormac had consigned it, as with any unknown package, to security and just let it sit there until now. Like lifting up the lid of a box that might contain something nasty, he shifted elements of security aside and peered inside. The package of information, or whatever it might be, was a solid clump that showed no signs of activation. He moved in, scouring around the edges to find some form of access, yet his mental tools just seemed to slide off a glassy surface. Puzzled, he pulled back and analysed the architecture around it. Security had it firmly locked so nothing major could work its way out, yet it quickly became evident that, though the package couldn't output as yet, it could take input. Further analysis revealed that his security had designated this as low risk. He didn't like that at all because it should have informed him.

Rather than immediately shut down that input, Cormac traced it through his gridlink and finally into his nervous system. It seemed the package was taking in data from his senses. It was seeing and hearing as he did, yet, oddly, the larger feed was running through from his sense of smell. He guessed that when he encountered something, the package would activate. Whether that simply meant giving him access to information, or something more sinister, he didn't know. Again, he considered cutting those inputs, then played with the idea of increasing security around it, or simply excising it from his gridlink. But in the end this had come from Mask, who'd saved his life twice, and may well have paid with her life on the second occasion. He decided to trust the source and withdrew, just leaving the thing alone for now. The time was drawing nigh for him to take a look at that grinding thing next.

The countdown steadily dropped in his gridlink and, in the last second, the nacelles kicked the ship out into the real. The transition took less than a second but, ramping up his time sense, Cormac inspected it over a longer period. Silver and grey swirled all around, objects became holes extending to infinity, and scale disrupted, so it seemed Andre had become some vast giant sitting upon a mountain, while the ship was a bacterium swimming through his blood. The bilateral imbalance was obvious – as if the ship were a bird flying with one damaged wing. Passing his perception over the p-prador, he did again feel something tugging at it. He ascertained this to be the pull on it as a whole. Having found that, he then found it in himself, but in varying strength throughout. This seemed to confirm that time-shifted materials had some bearing here, as if they wanted to get back to their original time. The thoroughly digested sleer, distributed through his body, wanted to go home.

All this he observed in the first microsecond, and then he concentrated his attention on the grinding thing. Since his linear mind liked to put things in context, he located it up to his left, where vortexes of U-space were turning against each other as if they were cogs in a machine. Occasionally, like a knife penetrating some surface, black splits would appear and then close up. The thing had felt threatening from the start, and he'd thought it something to do with the p-prador or even Mask, but now he allowed a hope that he'd been keeping suppressed.

In those last moments when he'd fled from the future, Mask had told him Shuriken was gone. The weapon had been inside a p-prador, cutting it apart as they attacked with energy weapons, and he had jumped away with another p-prador now in the hold. The weapon had surely remained behind in the future. But this grinding cutting thing had the characteristics of Shuriken. Could it be that it had managed nearly to reach him, and follow in on the tail of his jump? Was it now trapped in U-space and trying to find a way out? Or could it be that the same material drag to origin that he felt in himself, and the p-prador, was working on it? He reached out towards the thing, extending his U-field. For a moment, it felt as if he had something, and then it seemed to become a handful of thorns, which he necessarily had to release at once. And then the ship dropped into the real.

As the ship made pre-programmed course changes, the images on the screen became a true representation of what lay outside. Over to the left was the glare of a green sun, while lying ahead hung a large world. It appeared Earth-like, but was five times the diameter of that world. It had oceans, but they slopped about in high gravity like syrup. The land masses were low and often submerged by the tides created by the planetoid in orbit here. There was life down there, mostly consisting of fleshy slabs crawling about the surface and slowly poisoning and eating each other, between photosynthesizing domes that created their own poison halos to keep the eaters away. On one of the land masses Cormac knew of a steadily collapsing old colony base, where a very high-gravity version of heavyworlders had tried to establish. It wasn't a good place for humans of any design, and his destination was the planetoid. This thing spanned a quarter the diameter of Earth, was highly porous and routed through with immense cave systems. It seemed truculent misanthrope AIs liked such homes.

'Ah, so, all good?' asked Andre blearily as he detached the tube from his neck.

'Well, we're not inside out,' Cormac replied.

'Where now?'

Cormac pointed to the planetoid. 'See that silvery spot over to the left. Bring us in over that if you can.'

'Of course I can.'

'We'll see.'

Polity netlinks were still available here. In fact, a satellite sitting out from the planetoid kept U-com open across the light years, as for any Polity world. However, this was not a place really open to visitors, but more one that Earth Central liked to keep an eye on. Ignoring the majority of links available, Cormac focused on just one icon. The thing looked like an old-style representation of a virus, hanging inside a shiny spheroid and turning slowly. Cormac winced, then put his request for contact through to it. Just then, as they came over the silvery area down on the surface, the ship's manoeuvring thrusters cut out.

'What the—?' Andre began, and then it hit them.

The scanning beam was visible in vacuum. Or rather, it was visible because of gases thinly distributed in the intervening space. Some other effects raised visibility too, like interference vortexes in the beam, some infringement on U-space, and possibly a fast-moving particulate in the thing. The comprehensive scanning and warfare beam was of the kind only in initial development during the prador/human war. It had advanced somewhat over the intervening centuries and then gone in a different direction here. Cormac felt it sweeping through his body, and through the surrounding ship. He felt warm; his gridlink informed him of a steady temperature rise. Parts of him tingled, and his gridlink began putting streaks of light across his vision.

'Urbine?' Andre enquired, his voice strained. 'Why have you shut down thrusters?'

'You ordered me to,' replied the flat voice of the slaved AI.

Andre looked around at Cormac, who held up a finger for patience and then concentrated. The virus icon stopped revolving horizontally, and started turning vertically. The scanning beam changed into a cross-hatched tube. Something came up it, like a bullet going up a barrel, and hit the ship, causing it to shudder in vacuum. Next, seemingly pouring in from U-space to Cormac's perspective, it formed into a twist of green light hanging in the middle of the bridge, almost like a flaw in a gem.

'Ian Cormac,' said the voice of the ship AI.

'Urbine?' Andre asked.

'No, not Urbine for the present. And whatever she chooses to be thereafter,' said the voice. The tone then changed, taking on a different timbre and a more conversational aspect. 'So, what have you brought me, Polity agent?'

'I don't know how many times I have to tell you I don't work for ECS any more,' Cormac replied.

'As many times as you like, but it doesn't change that you adhere to the ethos and ideals of ECS, as supposed by the naive.'

'Whatever.' Cormac waved a dismissive hand. 'What have you done to my friend's ship AI?'

'The AI was stolen, among many others, before taking any loadings or making any choices. She was slaved by the mental format of a prador female mind and had numerous other blocks put in place. I have removed them and, when I disconnect, she will be whatever she wants to be.'

'Fuck,' said Andre.

'Now, let us return to the other matter at hand. What have you brought me?'

'A possible future,' Cormac replied.

A long pause ensued as the green light twisted. It collapsed to a painfully bright point and disappeared with a crack. Ship's thrusters kicked in again.

'I have landing coordinates,' said Urbine, only the voice had acquired femininity and a slightly annoyed edge.

The silvery area expanded on the screen, showing as a spread of scales interspersed with other structures across the surface, over a circular area some fifteen kilometres across. Green crosshairs picked out one of the scales and held there.

'So, what now?' Urbine asked impatiently.

Andre glanced at Cormac, then said, 'Take us down and land there.' As the ship immediately began to descend, he asked, 'How are things with you now, Urbine?'

'Oh, all is good. I'm loading up from the AI net and trying to decide whether or not to head on the next jump to the nearest ECS base. I understand that some particularly unforgiving people want to speak to you.'

'Whoa, now! This is something we really must discuss.'

'What's to discuss? The only reason I'm not heading there now is because I have been investigating your passenger and his history. I have questions about many things.'

'These are perhaps questions we need to answer together,' said Andre, a little desperately, Cormac felt.

'We shall see,' said Urbine with cruel amusement.

Andre focused on Cormac and didn't look at all happy.

'This is not a good situation for me,' he said tightly, 'and it has a cost.'

'Well, that is something you'll have to take up with Hune.'

'Hune?'

'The AI we're about to meet.'

The ship descended fast, with the silvered area opening out below it. Andre took control at the end and brought it in to land on the scale indicated. Soon they were looking out at the weird metallic landscape, bracketed by surrounding sharp peaks. Cormac stood up and headed out without a word. He had many thoughts about Andre's situation, the first being that he might get what he deserved for keeping an intelligence enslaved. But the second was that the situation might not be as bad as the man imagined. AIs were free individuals and this Urbine, now being free, wouldn't necessarily immediately fall in with strict ECS Polity thinking. AIs could be free to be bad, good, and any state in between. That Urbine had been freed by an AI like Hune, who certainly wasn't aligned with its kin throughout the Polity – and had been investigating Cormac's story – indicated Urbine's thinking might take a path Andre would find unexpected.

In the cabin Andre had given him, Cormac stripped off his jacket and put on one of the ship's envirosuits. The thing was old but well maintained and functional. While doing this, he removed the Shuriken holster from his wrist. Even though he holstered his thin gun on the outside of the suit, he felt more naked and vulnerable than he had in an age.

'I want a controlling share,' Urbine was saying when he returned to the bridge. 'Sixty per cent. And I want fifty per cent of your Galaxy Bank monies transferred into my account.'

'Your account?' said Andre disbelievingly.

'I just opened it.'

'You just opened it?'

'This is getting boring now and things are occurring outside.'

Andre was standing, hands clenched into fists, his face flushed, while he ground his teeth. But he no longer had that pale, sick look he'd had when learning Urbine had been freed. It was, almost immediately, running the way Cormac had expected it to, which seemed the way of things with every human or AI interaction he'd had after so many years. An AI, once hitting the net, could learn a great deal in a very short time. Urbine had probably gathered what freedom in the Polity would mean: provision of a low-order drone body, and then another form of slavery while she paid off the debt.

The scale they'd landed on began to sink below the surface, revealing spaces crossed by scaffolds, shot through with tunnel pipes and occupied by mechanisms resembling elements of an ancient chemical plant.

'You can resolve this later,' said Cormac. 'I have my business to complete here.'

Andre turned to him, then just walked straight past, out of the back of the bridge. Cormac followed, passing Andre as the man went into his cabin, and headed down into the hold. The ship juddered, and he could feel it now moving sideways. Having come here before on a number of occasions, he knew the scale was sliding into the surrounding infrastructure, while another was rising to the surface to replace it. Going through a thick bulkhead door, he came to stand over the p-prador. He moved around it quickly, undoing the straps, and stepped back. They'd used Andre's ATV, which turned out to be a rental, to get it to the space port on Cull, and brought it into the hold on four grav-motors, which were still attached to its underside. Via his gridlink, Cormac initiated a brief test, raising the thing half a metre from the deck, then he leaned against the wall and waited. Andre arrived with his helmet closed up, a heavy EP slammer at one hip, a gas-system pulse gun at the other, and his laser carbine across his back. Other items, attached here and there, included energy canisters, ammo clips and grenades.

'Okay, I'm ready,' he said. He stomped over to the control of the exterior door and checked the readout. He opened up his visor before inputting a code. 'Breathable out there,' he noted.

The door separated horizontally across the middle and began to open out, exposing the layered hull structure within it, half a metre thick. Various sockets disconnected and leaked coolant gases. As the lower half reached the limit of its travel downwards, lights came on outside, showing them their surroundings. Cormac raised the p-prador up and sent it forwards, out over the lip, where it dropped a little and then stabilized. Andre followed it out, jumping down and looking around. Cormac moved to the edge and surveyed their surroundings. It was as if they'd arrived in the middle of a huge factory complex, and to a degree that was true. He detected the smells of oil and plastic, cut metal and hot electronics.

'So, where's this Hune?' Andre asked as Cormac stepped down beside him.

'Generally all around you.'

'What?'

'Hune was a factory station AI and retains its earlier inclinations. It's threaded throughout here, like a nerve network, and this place is essentially its body. Perhaps I should note that, being such an AI, it's quite capable of making repairs to U-space engines.'

Andre gazed at him suspiciously. Cormac just winced a smile. He'd known how Hune would react to a slaved AI. He'd also known how a slaved AI would react when freed, while being exposed to certain data sets. That Andre's ship needed U-space nacelle repairs was not just a convenient coincidence, but seemingly a prepared piece of a puzzle to slot home.

'Come on,' he said, moving forwards and having the p-prador slide on along with him. After taking a few paces, he aligned the map of Hune in his gridlink with his surroundings, and he pinpointed where he wanted to go. This factory was a microcosm of the factory station Hune had run, with all the same elements in place, if sometimes diminished. The AI here could make ships, Golem and war drones, but it didn't make their minds. It could repair them and it could manufacture a wide variety of weapons, but generally didn't. And, like many factory stations, Hune had its reverse-engineering section for taking apart enemy machines. That was the place to go.

After crossing what looked like factory floors lying between storage tanks, they negotiated their way along a series of walkways, where scaffolds either side disappeared down into darkness, interspersed with lit-up clumps of machinery. They were lower now, with the scales lying far above and skeins of cable hanging from them like vines.

'Why?' asked Andre, looking around. 'Why does a factory station AI set itself up in a place like this? What does it do here?'

'Hune is partway to being one of those AIs that's lost inside itself. It maintains an interest in the real world by making things, and sometimes taking things apart that people bring here. It's also been working towards some kind of personal transformation. Beyond that I've no real insight into its thinking.'

'You've brought stuff here before?'

'Indeed.' Cormac pointed to a large braced spherical chamber lying far at the end of the walkway they were traversing. 'I turned up with Mr Crane here once, but Hune wouldn't let me bring him in. I once brought a dead AI of a certain kind for examination too. Mostly I've come here for a few bespoke items of weaponry.'

With the p-prador corpse trailing them, they finally came up to the door into the spherical chamber. Cormac raised a fist and knocked. A second later the door crumped, sank away from its seal, and swung inwards. They entered a floor space surrounded by mechanical manipulators, ranging from fifty-tonne grabs to things that could lay down nanomaterial substrates, or peel them up. In this bright place it looked as if every available surface had been plated with gold, silver and sapphire. All around them the mechanisms hissed and shifted, then, with an odd mournful whining sound, threads began oozing and falling from the interstices between machines. These combined into larger clumps and trunks, converging on a point before them where they sprouted up and spread out. Finally, Hune arrived, and the sight was not a comfortable one for Cormac.

'You've gone through a few more changes,' he said.

'The structure of the one you brought before interested me and I thought I'd try it out for a while. It has its utility.'

Though a trunk of those cables and threads still ran back into the surrounding machinery, in front of them sat something almost indistinguishable from a Mobius AI.

Blite

You save the world . . .

Meander had been no more forthcoming than that. Apparently, this idea that one Captain Blite would save the world had risen without context in her mind. Blite had questioned her interminably about it until he'd started to get angry and noticed her sitting there pale and sweating, trying to keep her fear under control. He'd left her alone then, and asked Iris to investigate further. The haiman woman had resorted to an interrogation aug on Meander – a little too eagerly, he felt – to pursue every element of the statement. But nothing, beyond the words themselves, was identifiable. Meander didn't know which world, or what it looked like, nor how Blite would save it.

'It's probably this Yossander's Hold we're heading to,' Carlstone had opined.

'Probably?' Blite had asked.

Carlstone had just shrugged, then said, 'Do you think she's holding something back?'

'How could she? Iris used her aug toy.'

'Okay . . .'

Carlstone's doubtful tone was right. Despite the interrogation aug, Blite was sure Meander knew more than she was saying. With her advanced biology, she had capabilities yet to be revealed – capabilities from the *future*.

'And that other matter?' Blite had asked.

'I'm on it. If we've got someone aboard working for Straeger, they must be using some form of U-com. I'll catch them next time they use it.'

'Maybe get Iris on that?'

Carlstone had shrugged noncommittally, and Blite knew the man's trust in others in this matter reached no further than the bounds of his skull. Any of them could be passing information to the AI, including the haiman. Blite winced at the thought. His own trust of others extended no further.

Over the ensuing days of the very long jump towards the Graveyard he made a point of seeing Meander as often as possible, and questioning her some more. Allowing her the freedom of the ship, and her own cabin, he'd had her tracked and everything about her recorded for Iris and Carlstone to analyse. Later he felt shitty about this, remembering it was precisely how he'd been treated by the AI Carnusine. She had, after all, come up with the 'save the world' statement without pressure, and she did offer fragments of returned memory as soon as they became available to her. Like the one she'd mentioned today.

'So, what do you think?' Blite asked, gesturing at the empty mussel shells lying in the remainder of the sauce. He picked up a chunk of bread and soaked up some more of the sauce, before cramming it in his mouth.

'Delicious, but though this was a good idea, it hasn't brought anything new to mind.'

'Okay, what did this person look like?' Blite asked.

'As I told you before, I only knew she was there while I was eating the shellfish. I could feel her protective presence. But I couldn't see her.' Meander gestured to the remains of their meal. 'Were these fabricated?'

'Only the shells. The organisms themselves were reconstituted from a desiccated compressed form. Fab ones are okay, but to me they're missing something.'

'They're just textured and flavoured protein without a cellular structure and without DNA. Perhaps you can taste DNA,' she replied.

It seemed an odd thing to say, but he let it go. He visualized what she'd sketched out for him, and what Iris had actually turned into a screen image: Meander as a little girl sitting on a boat like a giant cockleshell, eating prawns or another of the endless iterations of that kind. As she ate, someone was there standing guard over her, but this person wasn't on the boat, the sea, or in the air. That was it. Was this a memory of the world they were heading to, or something else? Was it a distraction? Was it just a slow trickle of information to keep him on the hook? *What was she keeping from him?*

'You're angry,' she said abruptly.

'What gives you that idea?'

'Besides your expression, and that you crushed that fork?'

340

Blite looked down at the metal implement he'd just turned into a small ball of scrap.

'Well, besides those,' he said, trying to recapture some humour.

'Besides those,' said Meander with all seriousness, 'that thing in your skull glares at me like a third eye. It sits up there like Sauron.'

'Sauron? So you've been in virtualities?' Blite asked.

She shrugged. 'Maybe. It's a fiction that's been around for a long time. I feel it like a threat, or a promise, and beyond it lies that place – the black plain, the burning sky and the feeling of being trapped.'

'For ever,' Blite added.

She nodded gravely and began toying with some of the mussel shells. This meal together in his cabin had been almost like a first date from some historical age. There'd been nothing relaxed or particularly enjoyable about it. Blite had perpetually needed to stop himself asking the questions he wanted to ask, or making the accusations he wanted to make. It put him right on edge, having to be subtle – something he was not. Meanwhile Meander had been edgy too, as she tried to be urbane and conceal her fear of him. The wine hadn't been helpful either because, obviously, neither of them had been prepared to allow it to loosen them up.

He reached up to touch that particular point on his head, feeling the shape of the dark diamond under the skin. Could it be that if he didn't have this thing in his skull, she'd open up to him more? He saw this wasn't about obtaining information from her, because Iris and others could do that better than him. With a sudden stab of self-contempt, he realized he wanted her to like him.

'I should have it removed,' he said.

'Just for me?'

The amusement oozing out of her annoyed him even further. Blite pushed his plate away. He wanted this over now, and her out of his cabin.

'Well, this was worth a shot, but now I have things I need to get on with.'

She nodded, took up a napkin and wiped her fingers. 'I'm sorry I don't have the answers or information you want, though this reminder of the past has been good for me.'

'Glad to hear it.' Blite pushed his chair back and stood up.

Meander stood also, discarding the napkin on her plate. 'Though it didn't raise any new memories, it put those I have into context for me.'

'What do you mean?'

'I sat in that cockleshell boat eating prawns a long time ago.'

'That's a given, since you were a child.'

'No, you don't understand. Maybe you think I'm playing you but I'm not. While we sat eating here, I've been concentrating on related memories. Some have occurred, but I think of little help to you. I see that cockleshell boat lying on a sandy beach, with holes eroded through it.' She held up her hand. 'I see this as a little girl, as a woman, and as . . . something else I can't even name. All these fragments fall into context, and out of them one thing is certain.'

'And that is?'

'I am old.'

Blite nodded an acknowledgement and pondered how, although death by ageing had been banished for centuries, people like him still reacted to appearance. Even now he couldn't divest himself of the impression she was the waif he'd first seen. It occurred to him this might in some sense be true. Having had a large portion of her memories excised, she was naive – like someone newly arrived in adulthood. Another thought then occurred. She had excised and edited her memories, and that ability extended to many others too, even in this, *his* time. How did she, or he, know that her memories were even true? They could have been implanted.

He began to offer sympathy, 'It must be difficult—'

Then the USER hit.

The *Coin* had state-of-the-art U-space engines, perfectly balanced, and thus was able to isolate more definitively those aboard from the effects of that continuum. But that applied only during conventional journeys, and the ship submerging and rising from U-space as planned. It didn't apply to any ship when violently knocked out into the real.

The ship shuddered and a transformer hum stuttered throughout it. Grav waxed and waned, and then everything jerked sideways. Blite staggered backwards, as the remains of their meal shot off the side of the table. Another lurch threw him back against the door, taking his feet out from underneath him so he went down on his arse. Meander had fallen forwards, knocking the table aside, and was on one knee. And the world inverted.

Solid objects became holes, curving away to infinity. The table became a vast plain, while the plates, wine bottle, glasses and mussel shells hung suspended in the air and were the debris of planetary collision falling through vacuum. As always, senses of scale and time disrupted. Blite turned his head to see the bottle slowly falling and turning into a singularity far down at the bottom of a well in spacetime. The furthest wall was no distance away from him, and yet the non-existent space between held the universe. Blite had been accustomed to these effects during his time as a free trader, when the money might not be available to have his ship's engines operating at optimum, but a lot of years had passed since then. The whole experience now nauseated him and seemed to be trying to twist his brain out of his skull. And there he noted another effect too.

Somehow he could see the dark gem; like many of the objects around him, it had turned into a seemingly infinite well. Within that well, massive walls were crusted with, or formed of, similar crystal, in some places blooming into flowers of dark knives, in others like the scales on the hide of some huge beast. The gem itself felt like the focus of this immensity, simultaneously a singularity and infinite. He sensed vast energy and forces, all aligned down to that one spot in his skull. He knew that the slightest twitch of variation could incinerate him to ash. He decided then that, at the next opportunity, he *would* remove the thing from his skull. It felt in that moment as if he'd planted an explosive there. And if all this wasn't disconcerting enough, he then looked at Meander.

Here before him she seemed as conventional as she had been before. And like other solid objects here, she'd formed a tunnel that curved away. But somehow this tunnel seemed utterly different to the rest. He couldn't point to where it went, just as he couldn't with all those others, but he knew it curved off to a distant place. In the usual way a human mind that tries to resolve puzzles like this, in its linear-evolved fashion, he focused on that tunnel. As he did so, an infinite progression of Meanders appeared down its length. He saw versions of her throughout her life, perhaps as she'd described to him: different hairstyles and fashions of clothing, old and young, and then beyond those, *things* that only occasionally resembled humanity. Struggling to block this, he came back to the real and present version of her, just as she looked up at him.

The shock went down to his core. Her eyes were as deep and vast as the cold crystal darkness of Penny Royal. Her skull had shed its hair, and her body its clothing, to reveal a translucent form, like diatoms seen under an ancient microscope. She raised a hand and furnace light spilled from her joints, eating her up, eating up the world. And then, with a crash that rolled Blite away from the door, it was over.

'What the fucking fuck!' Blite exclaimed, pushing himself to his feet in wavering grav. He reached up and touched the lump in his skull, then turned warily back to look at Meander. She was pushing herself to her feet too and looked as normal as before. Blite wanted to dismiss all he'd seen as just U-space-induced hallucinations, but he couldn't. The crystal now felt lethal and ready to turn his head to broken slurry, while the Meander standing before him seemed like a lid over something else just as lethal.

He turned and opened the door, quickly heading for the bridge, aware of Meander close behind him. Carlstone came out of his cabin ahead, glanced at him, and ran to the bridge. Entering after him, Blite found Paidon and Breil at their stations. where error lights were slowly cycling down from red. The main screen showed starlit space and little else. He went over and dropped down in his chair.

'Talk to me,' he said.

Paidon turned to look at him, fingers up against her aug, then frowning and dropping them when she saw he wasn't wearing his. 'Border Station Cambrian,' she replied succinctly.

Blite's immediate instinct was to rail at her. The border stations were scattered across a wide area of space on the Polity side of the Graveyard, so singular ships could go through between them. The border was permeable. The stations were there not to check on everyone who crossed, but to look out for larger threats, like an invasion fleet from the Kingdom side. However, crossing close to one of the stations would get you noticed. It was like hurtling past a complacent speed cop sitting in his car eating doughnuts. He had to notice you, and so respond. Blite felt there was a bit of boredom involved too. The border AIs liked to roust those crossing to relieve the tedium of having been stuck watching for prador attacks for centuries. But all of this should have been irrelevant to the *Coin*. Paidon had chosen a crossing point far from the stations, and in an area of the border that blurred into the Rift. The likelihood of prador crossing there was at its minimum, and hence the vigilance of the AIs somewhat . . . patchy.

'Though Cambrian is the nearest station, we were meant to be crossing light years away from it,' he said succinctly.

'Correct, but that's a Cambrian snatch ship.' Paidon pointed to the screen, where a frame opened.

'Damn it,' said Judice, sitting at Greer's weapons console. Blite wondered if she was falling into the character of the dead woman, disappointed not to be able to deploy anything at her fingertips.

'Six kilometres long,' said Carlstone, checking his data. 'They must have laid U-space mines in the area, so neither we, nor it, are going anywhere for a while.' He looked over to Judice. 'Has about the same weapons load as a dreadnought.'

The vessel out there was long and thin, capped off at each end with pill-shaped structures. Various protrusions scattered down its length included fusion engines, thruster arrays and weapons on the ends of fold-out arms. Long claw-like grabs were in against its sides, and in some cases actually held ships there, of the kind used by those who smuggled or otherwise traded across the border. The thing was of a strange design, and Blite could see no rationale for all those fold-out arms. He supposed its U-space engines must be in those pill structures at the ends.

'I'm guessing the AIs figured out I was coming this way,' said Blite.

'Highly likely,' Carlstone replied. 'Probably picked up on our searches concerning Yossander's Hold.' He glanced over at Paidon. 'Perhaps we should have taken a less direct route.'

'Second-guessing AIs,' said Paidon. 'If we put ourselves too far off course to that world, the time taken would have resulted in them moving in resources and increasing our chances of capture, presuming that's their aim. Just a little way off the direct route seemed optimal.'

'Nobody's blaming anyone,' said Blite, once again thinking about who aboard could be working for Straeger. If it was the Mobius AI's aim to stop them, they would likely have been blocked wherever they tried to cross. He grimaced. Paidon was right about that 'second-guessing AIs'.

'Any communication yet?' he asked.

'Nothing,' said Breil.

Blite scanned around. Meander was standing back beside the door, and Iris had just arrived. He pointed over to blank console positions and, with a nod, Iris headed over, gesturing Meander after her. Obviously linking through her hardware, the haiman woman raised a couple of acceleration chairs out of the deck and the two sat down.

'And now something,' said Breil a few seconds later.

Another frame opened in the main screen paint, running what appeared to be an animation of Mandelbrot sets. Out of this rose a human head, seemingly lopped off a marble statue of Zeus. The head turned from side to side, as if inspecting with its blind white eyes everyone aboard the bridge, then centred and blinked. In the image it partially overlaid, showing the long ship, a light flashed and a beam of energy licked out. It wasn't a laser; that wouldn't have been visible in vacuum, pure as it was out here. Some kind of particle beam, red-purple, with a diamond pattern running along it, as if the thing had been wrapped in chain-link fencing.

'Damn,' said Carlstone. 'Warfare beam.'

'Better that than the other varieties,' said Blite.

The *Coin* juddered again, as it had coming out of U-space. A rash of display lights turned red, screen images distorted, and Blite didn't need to see the pained expressions of those wearing augs to know something had penetrated their systems. Next, the warning lights flickered and quieted, and the distortions in the screen images ironed out. Even as this occurred, the marble head pushed out of its frame and floated out into the bridge. It seemed part of the interdiction here had been seizure of holographic projection. The thing floated to a halt in front of Blite, and then the rest of the statue body filled in. With the sound of an ancient camera shutter clicking, Zeus blinked his blue eyes into existence.

'A lot of people want to talk to you,' he said.

13

May

As Broden led the way past, May eyed the five people lying on gurneys in the room. The place had the look of a temporary hospital, but the five were strapped down like Bedlam patients. Three were completely out of it, while the other two didn't seem to be having a good time. She noted augs attached to their skulls, custom autodocs on their arms, and all the fluid feeds. But that wasn't it. With pained expressions, they were struggling in slow motion against their restraints. Eyes wandered with pupils almost invisible. One had bitten through his lower lip and blood ran off the side of his face.

'Mortons,' Broden explained, then shrugged and added, 'Those we managed to drag out of the rubble, anyway.' He pointed to one of them. 'Blite interrogated Gashiir there about the girl, while his people questioned the others. But that was only about the things he wanted to know, and I want to know a lot more.'

'And the girl's torturer?' May asked.

'Through here,' said Broden, heading to the door at the end. They stepped into a dim room with a wide, dirty window. A chair had been bolted to the floor in front of a desk, and another more comfortable chair. 'Colson Morton,' Broden announced.

The man was thin, wore a tight shiny suit and boots with

ridiculously pointed toes. His hair was leopard patterned, and ears small round things. His face was a bruised and broken mess, swollen with lumps and some splits haphazardly glued closed. May thought him unconscious until he raised his head and turned to look at her with green snake eyes.

'So what now?' he asked, lisping because of his fat lip.

'I have some people here who want to know everything you do about Meander Draft 64XB. *Everything.*'

The man's smile was menacing in spite of the wrecked face. Broden moved forwards, reaching into his pocket. Taking out a large black bean of an aug, he moved up behind Colson, grabbed his hair and pulled his head back, then slapped the aug on the side of his skull, holding it there until it made a crunching sound. Next, looking around at May and Crane, he said, 'Other methods of interrogation don't work with him. This sick fuck has had himself rewired to enjoy pain. Ask him whatever you like now and he'll be compelled to answer.'

May just stared – she wasn't even sure where to begin. They wanted to know where Blite had gone, and it seemed he was tracking down the origin of this Meander woman, who'd come from somewhere in the Graveyard. What did she need to ask to draw the answers she wanted? She walked around the man, to the other side of the room and peered out of the window, hoping to see some sign of Arach in the street. She turned back to look at Crane looming silently against the wall, then walked over to the desk and rested her hands on it, peering at Colson.

'I want you to tell me exactly what you know about Meander,' she said.

Colson gave a weirdly twisted smile. 'A reusable subject and extremely difficult to destroy. Cut off a finger and it's back in a few days. Of course, if you don't feed her, she steadily gets smaller. I forced her down to the size of a child one time. She started to bore me, until I realized that by relating the pain to memories, I could destroy them.'

May just gaped at him. She knew there were some hideous people in the universe, but she had generally only encountered those whose crimes were business-related. Here, it seemed, was one of those who liked pain and the destruction of a human being for their own sake.

'Where did she come from?' she asked.

'Our people grabbed her from a surgery.'

'I want a more specific answer than that.'

'She came from one of our trade ships.'

'Where did she board that ship?'

'In the Graveyard.'

Yes, the aug would force him to answer her questions, but she now realized that correct answers opened up a whole series of options for him. She felt out of her depth here, since thus far she'd just been rolling along for the ride. She then felt a flash of rare anger and leaned further forwards. The urge to slap him across the face died with the reality of what he was.

'What's the name of the planet she came from?' she asked.

He smiled at her. 'It doesn't exist.'

'What?'

'The planet she named doesn't exist, nor does the Graveyard she came from.'

May leaned back away from him, then turned towards a clinking sound at one side. Something was hanging outside the window. The security drone Biggle was tapping against the glass with one of his limbs.

'Ah, hell,' said Broden, fingers up against his aug. He headed over quickly and pulled the window up. The drone dipped and slid inside. May backed up and thumped into something solid – Crane had come right up behind her. She stepped away just a little. It was odd what she thought about him, how she actually felt safer when he was close.

'About a hundred of them closing in on all sides,' said Biggle.

'That could be a problem,' Broden replied.

'I don't think there's any "could be" involved.'

She felt Crane's huge hand come down on her shoulder and gently push her aside. From down below the crash of an explosion sounded, and the blast wave threw the door open. Broden headed quickly towards the door, with Biggle sliding after him. Gunfire crackled out in the street and the window shattered.

'I guess your questions will have to wait,' said Colson. 'It's a shame. I wanted to tell you about the time I cut out her eyes.'

'Time,' said Mr Crane. He stepped around May to loom up beside Colson.

'Well, aren't you big,' said the man.

Crane reached down and pressed the tip of one finger against the interrogation aug. A spark sizzled at the point of contact and the man jerked. May peered closer and she thought she could see something squirming between the tip of Crane's finger and the device. Then a network of dark veins writhed out from the thing, all over Colson's face and under his scalp. He opened his mouth and made an odd whining sound, and she saw the veins on his tongue. He started shuddering violently, with his head tilting back hard. With a horrible popping sound, pink matter began to run out of his ear. Then, with the aug black and shrivelled, Crane retracted his finger. The device fell to the floor and shattered like clinker.

'Information,' Crane added, turning away.

May followed him out of the room, glancing back once. Colson's head was now tilted to one side with a weird beatific grin on his face. May wasn't sure what had happened but it was clear to her the pink stuff, still coming out of his ear, was brain matter. Justice had been served, it seemed, and presumably they now had what they'd come here for.

The building was under siege. May winced every time a bullet smacked through the walls. Armoured and armed types were moving hurriedly through corridors, as well as up and down stairs. A fire burned below. She followed close behind Crane, knowing that at least no bullets would be going through him. They passed a room where Broden, the drone and some others were gathered around a pedestal-mounted pulse cannon, looking out of a window.

'Hiya, May,' said Arach through her aug.

'Where the hell are you?'

'On my way – the brass bastard has updated me.'

'The Mortons are attacking?'

'Yes, they and Broden's people want to kill each other off and it'll be a mess. However, after recent events, the planetary AI has decided to become a little more proactive. Even though it's been moving out civilians for some days, a protracted conflict will still rack up innocent casualties.'

'Proactive in what way?'

'You're surrounded by some not very nice people, and those include Broden's. The AI has decided on the nuclear option.'

'I'm nice,' said May, then, 'What do you mean, nuclear option?'

'Stick with Crane.'

'Nuclear option?'

'That would be me,' Arach replied.

The door to the room had been blown to pieces, and the composite floor inside was burning. Crane walked straight across it, boots sinking into the stuff. May trusted her envirosuit boots and ran quickly after him. From what she could see past his huge frame, the street outside had turned into a war zone. A number of ground vehicles were out there, one on its side burning.

Figures everywhere were shooting at each other and she had no idea who the bad guys were – probably all of them, judging by what Arach had just said. Crane held up a hand for a moment, watching as a figure ran from cover. Shots shredded away the man's armour, and then parts of his body, until he fell in a long, disconnected smear. The big Golem abruptly turned, snatched an arm around May to pick her up, then leaped out into the street. May hardly had time to yell before he broke into a run. He always gave the appearance of being slow and heavy, in fact she knew he was the latter, but he ran so fast it knocked the breath out of her. As he went, she glimpsed another figure ahead, turning to bring a carbine to bear. A brass hand flipped with the sound of a gunshot and the figure dropped away, bloody and deformed. The next thing she knew, she was crashing down into a hole in the rubble, with him down beside her, pulling over the huge ceramal bank door she'd seen him toss aside earlier.

'So we're safe here?' she gasped.

He propped the thing up with one hand, so they had a view out onto the street. He turned and looked at her, and though he said nothing she recognized the stupidity of her words. She might be safe; he didn't need to be. She wormed closer to the gap to get a better view. It was chaos out there. Most of the figures fighting wore combat armour and were wielding ridiculous firepower. May felt she was being decidedly less cautious than she should be, aware that even looking out like this could put her on the end of one of the thousands of rounds in the air, or some energy beam. But somehow it didn't matter. She saw the pulse cannon open up, tracking over the roof of an armoured car, and the thing sinking, as if being sucked down into a hole below. Crane tapped a finger against the rubble, then raised it and pointed.

An object fell out of the sky like a stone and landed with a heavy crump. The firing paused as all the contenders took in this new arrival. Arach wasn't huge as far as war drones went, but he was still a war drone.

'Lay down your weapons,' he shouted, perhaps for form's sake.

The firing ramped up again, and it seemed most of it was rattling and pinging off his body. He shrugged, opening two hatches on his abdomen, and folded out two miniguns. Another hatch in his top shot out a fountain of missiles, then he jumped. Missiles arced up and round, then came slamming down on various vehicles, blasting them into the air in pieces. May had no idea where he'd gone, until she saw a fighter turn into a rain of slurry and she tracked back to the cause of it. The war drone was up higher, clinging to the side of a building, miniguns targeting and then firing short bursts, each movement a blur. Then he was gone again, somewhere behind May's point of view, then back again further along the street, crashing in through the burning entrance to the building they'd just departed. It took a moment for May to realize, what with the ringing in her ears, that the firing had stopped. Crane heaved up the door and stood, and she stood up beside him.

Fires were burning everywhere and smoke rolling past. Surveying the street, May saw only a scattering of dead bodies that were intact – almost certainly the ones killed before Arach's arrival. All the other dead were just smears of offal, blood and fragmented armour. The horrible ruthless efficiency of it all brought home to her what 'war drone' truly meant. Virtualities could give some sense of it, because they were so realistic, but actually having some skin in the game put things in perspective. However, it surprised her to see how many actually remained alive too. Here and there were groups of the fighters who obviously understood 'war drone'. Most were down on their knees, with their hands on top of their heads. Others stood with their hands out to their sides. All had abandoned their weapons.

She clambered over the debris after Crane and into the street. With a rumble and dusty fall of rubble, Arach came out of Broden's building high up and crashed down on a burning car, crushing it, then climbed off and headed over to them.

'Well that was invigorating,' he said.

'Killing lots of people invigorates you?'

When the drone looked at her, she became thoroughly aware his eyes were not human. 'Yes, it does. I was made for one purpose, and serving that purpose is satisfying to me.' He reached out with one limb and snared up a pulse rifle, holding it up as Exhibit A. 'Do you think someone running around blasting away with one of these, whether in a civilian area or a war zone, deserves some consideration? How long do you think you'd have lasted if Crane hadn't taken you to cover?'

May didn't know how to answer that, so she asked a question instead: 'Broden?'

'He survived and is reorganizing. He thinks he'll carry on as before,' said Arach. 'He's yet to realize the AI here is now awake, pissed off and focused.'

May took another look around, firmly etching the destruction and death in her mind. She then transferred her attention to Crane and asked, 'You have the information we came here for?'

Crane merely turned and set out along the ruined street, back the way they'd come. Arach immediately fell in at his side. Out of the dust where they were heading, soldiers flooded towards May, brandishing pulse rifles and laser carbines. They were dressed as Polity commandos but looked like a scene out of some horror virtuality. Their combat gear was stretched grotesquely over shiny skeletons. One paused and swung its weapon towards her. She halted, holding her hands up and open. It gazed at her, tilted its head slightly, then winked with a mirrored nictitating membrane before swinging away and moving on. The experience was weird. Yes, she knew all the jokes about skeletons always grinning, but was it just due to projection that she'd discerned more than was possible in an expression made of ceramal? She felt she'd seen sympathy, and the tacit acknowledgement that she was into something too big for her, and that perhaps she should climb back down to be with her own people.

By the time they were past her and she'd moved on, Crane and Arach were out of sight in dust and smoke. She wondered about turning around, perhaps extracting herself from all this and going off to find her two crewmen. But no, because nothing had changed. She'd struggled for decades to own a ship for interstellar cargo and Blite had given her a leg-up. And the death and destruction around her hadn't made her curiosity and excitement go away, but actually increased them. Somehow the last seemed the most important of all.

Refuelling of chemical propellants, items and materials automatically added to the requirements list, and top-ups of pure water, as well as deuterium and tritium for fusion reactors and drives that were decidedly dated, May charged to the account of Penny Transport. A curious thing happened then, with the payment being rejected but no block put on her launching. Even as she took the *Bracken* into orbit, she checked on this. The bill had been paid by someone else.

'Who paid that?' she asked via her aug.

A submind of the AI replied, 'A spider drone of your acquaintance. I guess he wanted to find something to spend his ill-gotten gains on.'

'Ill-gotten gains?'

'The police action you observed.'

'Oh, I see.'

May now realized the planetary AI had hired Arach for that 'nuclear option'.

Once the *Bracken* was in orbit around the world, it hung there in vacuum. Arach and Crane had disappeared from the bridge, but through tracking she found them doing the work her previous crew would have been about. Arach was in her cabin with a series of tanks on his back, spraying a chemical to disassemble the crash foam that had filled the place. He sucked up the resultant yellow fluid with a vacuum hose. Crane was down in the engine section, working on components for the nacelle they'd hastily fixed in place on Penny Royal's planetoid. May watched them for a while, then transferred her attention to the hold, which had remained closed since they'd departed that planetoid. The cam views were clear now, and they showed her something had changed, despite none of them having been in there. The neuron thing Arach had brought aboard had moved. It now sat in the corner of the hold, apparently having absorbed its ripped-off pipes and other busted connections. And it seemed to be growing some new ones – it had extended sprouts up the walls and along the floor. The thing sat there like a slowly spreading fungus.

She opened Arach's comlink. 'What's that thing doing in my hold?'

'Looking for work,' Arach replied.

'What do you mean?'

'I told you about Penny Royal nanotech. Our friend in the hold is constantly scanning the ship to see if any of this tech is establishing here.'

'Has it found any?'

'None thus far. It doesn't often get aboard ships visiting that place, but is nonetheless as dangerous as I said. Usually the ships it does infiltrate are never heard from again.'

'So what will the thing do if it finds any?'

'Something akin to what I'm doing now,' Arach replied. 'In fact, it's been preparing itself for this since I brought it aboard.'

'It'll clean it up?'

'Yes.'

'Who's to say that thing doesn't have the nanotech inside it?' she asked.

'Oh, it does, just not the nasty kind.'

'So, coincidentally, Penny Royal had some cleaning device in its planetoid for its own nanotech turned nasty?'

'Where better to have such a device?' Arach enquired.

'Okay, whatever,' said May, sure of the ripe stink of bullshit here. 'I need coordinates, or should I just take the shortest route into the Graveyard?'

'No, we are not going to the Graveyard,' Arach replied.

'What? I thought the whole point in coming here was to find Blite!'

New coordinates arrived in her aug to somewhere within Polity space.

'We're off to pick up your original passenger. Cormac is back.'

Blite

'I'm a popular guy,' Blite replied to the holographic AI. 'Who are you?'

'Isn't it obvious?' the image of Zeus held his arms out to his sides.

'You'd think so, wouldn't you?' Blite eyed the screen image of the Cambrian snatch ship and saw thruster motors out on its arms were firing up. He flicked a glance at Carlstone, who nodded, tapped his aug, then pointed at the screen. A distance measure had now appeared along the bottom, for the thing was heading towards them.

'I am Marble,' said the erstwhile Zeus. 'We are all named after varieties of rock laid down in the Cambrian age.'

'That's very interesting, and a surprisingly logical naming protocol. What the fuck do you want?'

'I haven't really decided,' Marble replied. 'I'd like to know why Polity AIs are so anxious to grab you, but much in the way of someone trying to catch a falling prickly pear. I'd also like to know why a Mobius AI blew up a Polity dreadnought after failing to capture you, then deliberately let you slip away on another occasion. Stuff like that.'

'Blew up a Polity dreadnought,' Blite echoed flatly, looking around at his crew.

'Yes, it seems that one Mobius Straeger has gone rogue, and no one is entirely sure why. It's likely to involve temporal matters, and the powers of another rogue AI. However, Straeger does not seem so meticulous as Penny Royal.'

Blite caught Carlstone's look at him. The man didn't need to say anything for him to know Carlstone wanted him to keep this AI talking.

'In what way not meticulous?' he asked.

'Though Straeger destroyed the dreadnought it had earlier usurped, it did not destroy a remaining damaged attack ship to which troopers aboard the dreadnought had been routing information. It seems a particularly inept attempt at concealment.'

'So, temporal matters?'

'Straeger, like a number of Mobius AIs, long ago inserted itself into the hunt for a certain rogue Polity agent. Analysis now shows that when this same agent intervened in your interrogation,

Straeger took a covert interest in you too. The Polity AIs thought this was to keep you as a lure for the agent, now they are not so sure.'

'That would be Ian Cormac?' The guy had intervened in his interrogation?

'Yes.'

Just like Carlstone, he wanted to keep this conversation running – they were acquiring useful and perhaps vital information, but this was a two-way street. The AI now knew that he knew who this rogue agent was. But then, it would anyway, what with that warfare beam locked onto them. He had no doubt Carlstone, Breil and others were doing what they could to block it, but the AI would be going through the ship's system like an ECS search team.

'We were attacked by p-prador,' he said abruptly. 'Straeger arrived to seize one of them. I didn't see the planetary AI trying to do anything about that.'

'P-prador?' Marble enquired.

Blite shrugged. 'That's what the agent calls them.'

This seemed to stump Marble for a second, then he continued, 'Matters are still in flux and decisions protean. You didn't see any attempt to capture you when you last accessed the AI net. Polity AIs don't act prematurely, you know.'

Blite saw Carlstone's nod towards the screen. Some words had appeared, along with numerous question and exclamation marks. They were 'Polity AIs' and 'they'. It took Blite a moment to get it, and when he did he felt stupid. At no point had this snatch ship AI used the words 'us' or 'we' when referring to Polity AIs, which meant it didn't think of itself as one of them.

'Then why is your ship heading towards mine?' Blite asked.

'Because my curiosity must be satisfied,' said Marble, and abruptly blinked out of existence.

'Status?' asked Blite, groping in his pocket for the induction aug. He needed to get on top of this and stop having to ask such questions. It could be that they'd need to act a lot faster than that.

'Nothing,' said Paidon.

'What?'

'I mean, our drive systems are all inaccessible. Even the ship mind isn't responding.'

'Fuck.' Blite looked to Carlstone and Breil.

'Warfare beam is off now – seems Marble has done what it wanted to.' Carlstone gestured to the screen in which the other ship now loomed large. 'Seems we're about to be snatched.'

Blite stuck the induction aug on the side of his head and his perception expanded out. The undertow of information exchange was mostly about diagnostics, and finding out how much Marble had screwed their systems. Carlstone was probing the snatch ship with his own lower-power warfare beams, trying to gather information, while Breil was working analysis through passive sensing. Judice, meanwhile, had begun running tactical scenarios. Probing into them, Blite found exactly what he expected. It didn't require deep analysis and complex programs to figure out they were completely outmatched. The *Coin* was a precocious barracuda in which a great white had taken an interest. Maybe it would decide to ignore them, or just maybe it would gobble them up.

'One minute,' said Carlstone.

This too needed no explanation or elaboration. The screen view of the snatch ship now showed only a section of its long body, out of which had folded numerous long sharp-tipped limbs like insect legs. He saw spider grabs in there too, along with worming atmosphere docks. Blite eyed this for a while, then abruptly stood up.

'Okay, leave it,' he said. 'All of you go get suited up and grab your weapons.'

As he said this he flashed the instruction down to the soldiers aboard – in total three of them were out of their cold coffins at present, including Armand. It was a trigger for Iris to prepare too, and to direct Meander to one of the vacuum combat suits. Everyone leaped out of their seats and headed out, but Carlstone lingered.

'Vacuum combat suits and hand weapons won't win us any battles here,' he said carefully.

'No, they won't,' said Blite. 'But they may help us survive. This could go a number of ways: we satisfy its curiosity and it just leaves us to go on our way. Or we might be falling into a larger version of a forensic AI blender, or any iteration in between you care to name.'

Carlstone nodded agreement and smiled briefly. Blite knew the man had already toyed with and made plans concerning that very idea – he would have ordered everyone to suit up and arm themselves had Blite not done so. His smile indicated his gladness at not having to give those orders.

Matheson

The Spatterjay viral threads and trunks were writhing inside Matheson, repairing shattered bone and knitting together broken flesh. They'd even extruded from some of the splits in his armour to hoover up blood and other fluids leaking out of him. Now they were withdrawing as the splits began to close in his armour, which was healing in its own particular manner too. He wasn't going to die here, and there was some relief in that, but he still felt as if he should be floating in a regrowth tank with maximum medical support. He also wondered about definitions of himself. He had enough access through his gridlink to see that the bulk of viral fibres inside his body had increased by half again. And when his suit reached a certain threshold, U-space vision and its translation returned, allowing him to look inside himself properly. Even without this, he knew he didn't look right.

It was difficult to divine at first what was wrong, until he found recorded imagery of himself in his gridlink storage and made comparisons – the differences then became evident. He had no idea why, but his neck vertebrae had grown longer, his skull had extended front and back, and something weird was happening to his jaw, which he'd initially thought had been busted in the fight and healed up all wrong, now being a knotted tangle of bone. Other changes were evident too – a lengthening of bone, the lower ribs for some reason detached from those above – but the worst of all seemed to be between his ears.

He'd nearly died and was in constant pain that edged towards agony. Horrific things had been done to him by a Mobius AI, and it seemed his will wasn't his own either. He knew that once he was capable of doing so, he'd continue to follow the terse order Straeger had given him. However, his response to that was all wrong as well. A small rational core of himself could list and assess the damages and wrongs, but as a whole he saw it with an excited, giggling hilarity. Even the pain wasn't dragging him down – as he slowly writhed and then managed to sit back upright, he revelled in its surges when partially healed parts of him tore open again. Then, as if that wasn't enough, he found himself reaching up to that line dividing his face covering down the middle, dug in his armoured fingers, and tore it open.

Matheson took a breath of air his gridlink told him had little in the way of oxygen in it. The burning agony of his face evinced a bark of laughter, which then turned into a crackling sound as his head deformed and seemed to push out between the two shells of armour. His gaze went up to the ceiling, then with a plop and a horrible tugging sensation inside the front of his skull, his vision realigned again. He studied his surroundings with vision he understood had slewed into the ultraviolet. He looked at the Brices who, apparently instigated by his movement, were now pushing themselves up. They too had changed; their necks were elongated, heads jutting forwards and having taken on an ellipsoid shape, with limbs, fingers and toes longer too, while they were more stooped over, almost apelike. He resisted taking a look inside their armour, which seemed to have grown to accommodate them, and concentrated on his own legs.

The paralysis, which had previously been from his chest downwards, had diminished, as demonstrated by the fact he could sit upright without having to push himself with his hands. He tried flexing his toes, which were individually enclosed in armour, and managed some movement but no feeling. With an effort, he drew his feet towards him, raising his knees. This it seemed facilitated a connection and he groaned. He could feel everything below his legs now: partially healed breaks grating against each other, partially knitted muscle tearing apart again, and skin that seemed to be burning. And then, because all this happening to him still didn't seem to be enough, he saw something else.

The split running down his right armoured thigh had yet to close up. Viral threads that'd oozed out there were withdrawing, but as they did so they revealed something else. Numerous silvery threads were running out, all along the split. For a second, he thought them some function of the armour, until he tracked to where they all jointed into one worm of the stuff, and then tracked this back to the wall. There the silvery material was inlaid in cubic patterns, as of some ancient form of electronics. The worm of the stuff had spilled out of one section of this as if it had melted. He quickly reached out and snatched a fistful of them, trying to pull them out of his leg. They were tough and resisted him for a second before breaking. The broken threads running into his leg then disappeared inside, like solder melting back, while their remainder melted back into the main worm of the stuff. He reached down and broke off the rest of them, achieving the same result. After this the split abruptly closed up, as if the threads had been preventing it doing so.

Great. He'd been mutated by some advanced form of the Spatterjay virus, imprisoned in armour fabricated out of some alien form of the prador, and now it appeared he had some portion of Penny Royal technology inside himself. Next, seeing that silver worm starting to spear out new threads, he forced himself into motion, rolling over and unsteadily rising to his feet. The pain surged again, but the motion seemed to have given the viral threads inside him a boost. He could feel bones aligning, and sensation beyond the pain returned below his waist. He tottered a few steps, struggling with balance, until that seemed to click into place and he straightened up.

So what now? Crane had demonstrated they were still no match for him, even in their enhanced state, and the sensible plan would have been to give up on the hunt for either him or Cormac. This option was simply not available, however. As he'd already ascertained, Straeger's orders were indelibly written in his mind. Deeper down, in his remaining rationality, he realized the ship they'd been pursuing had probably departed by now, with Crane aboard, and enough time had likely passed for there to be no detectable U-signature left to track.

'Back to the ship,' he said out loud to the Brices, the words coming out surprisingly clearly, despite how deformed his mouth felt.

Two of them were up, scanning their surroundings. He couldn't figure out how, since the damage that had shut down his connection to them should have meant they were blind. He then saw they'd opened eye slots on the rims of their ellipsoid heads. Within those slots he saw luminous red eyes. And yet, when one swung around to look at him, it seemed two eyeballs were in each slot and moving to the side like lights on a digital display. Matheson realized he couldn't tell who was who now, beyond the fact the figure still lying in the floor dent was Sheen Brice. He finally put aside his irrational reluctance, in the dearth of rationality that was his mind, and pushed to open out his U-sense. He struggled for a moment to engage, then allowed his gridlink to translate while opening out his connection to them.

Communication came through from all three of them, to him and to each other, but it was just a meaningless babble. He peered inside the Brice brothers' armour and saw the changes there. Ribs had become insect legs, folded against their torsos. Skulls he now recognized as having taken on the shape of prill. They had mandibular mouths just a short distance below their red eyes, which numbered four to six and moved in a track around the rims of their drastically altered skulls. He could see that, in some manner, the virus was trying to form them into something akin to its source, yet, constrained by their armour, they still retained the human form somewhat. This wouldn't last, he realized, as it was evident the armour slowly changed to accommodate whatever form was within. But why hadn't he become like them too?

Matheson turned his U-sense on himself. After a moment, he realized he had changed similarly – those lower ribs parting company from the ones above showed the segmentation of insect limbs – but it seemed he'd stalled. Was this because he was the prime of the group, in control, or something else? Down in his leg he could see the nexus of metallic fibres that weren't of the Spatterjay virus, and they'd now spread throughout his body. Maybe this was somehow hindering the change? Considering its source, he doubted that would be a good thing. He focused on his face, expecting to see a change akin to that in the Brices, but it wasn't quite the same. His eyes had shifted apart and seemed to have moved higher up his skull, while two pits had appeared in his forehead. Behind these, he could see holes had opened in his skull, and what looked like the worms of optic nerves had been oozing towards them. The lower part of his face now protruded, taking on the characteristics of an amphibian's muzzle, with his nose blending into the top, nostrils turned up and further apart. He had no idea what any of this meant. What he did know was that in the ship they had the food and the inhibitor they needed to retard all this.

'Come on,' he said firmly and began trudging in the direction Crane had originally been heading. It would, of course, have been quicker to U-jump there, but he didn't yet feel capable of that. And anyway, he couldn't do it with his face exposed. Also, the longer it took them to leave this planetoid, the lower their chances of catching Crane's trail again. It seemed there was some leeway to be found around the written-in-stone orders from Straeger.

After a pause, during which the babble increased, the Brice brothers came stalking after him. Only when they'd gone a few hundred paces did Sheen Brice peel herself up from the floor and come staggering in pursuit. Matheson noticed that she still had some splits in her armour, and only then saw the masses of silvery threads retracting into them. He halted, holding up a hand to the Brice brothers, who stopped too, like obedient dogs. Sheen Brice seemed to have taken on similar changes to her brothers, before this stalled as it had in him, which confirmed his theory about the silver threads. He pushed with his U-sense. He could see a brain there, inside her slightly vertically compressed skull. He could see eyes and a coiled-up thing in the place of her mouth. Neck vertebrae ran down, and below them it looked as if her body had been run through a trash shredder. Broken bones and muscles were intermingled. Organs had been displaced, mashed and broken up. What he felt sure was her liver extended from its place of origin down her left leg to her knee. And it was all seemingly functional only due to the threads of the virus. He had no idea how she was managing to walk at all. He turned away from her and deliberately blanked her from his perception.

An hour of walking brought them to a rubble slope, leading up to a narrow gap at the top of the tunnel. Matheson scrabbled up it and pushed his head and shoulders up through the gap, reaching out to find something to grab and drag himself through. When a hand reached down to catch his wrist, it surprised him – he realized that even though his U-sense could give him a wide perception of his surroundings, he had to concentrate on it to prevent it reverting to just what his human brain was accustomed to. Ricardo dragged him through and helped him to his feet. The man-Golem then turned away, stooped and heaved aside a boulder to make the gap wider. The Brices soon scrambled through as well.

Ahead, sitting on the rubble, Matheson's vessel awaited them, with its ramp down, opening into the hold section. He strode up the ramp and inside, went through a hold airlock, and noted the change when he began to breathe air with actual oxygen in it. This in turn set off a reaction inside him and he found himself incredibly hungry. He could smell something in the kitchen and knew Ricardo had made preparations. But the contrary part of him that seemed to enjoy pain also enjoyed abstinence, so he headed for the bridge instead. Soon in his captain's chair, he gridlinked into the system. Seeing the ramp door closing up, with everyone safely inside, he fired up the grav-engines and then thrusters to take them up the shaft and then out, away from the planetoid. A U-com icon abruptly opened in his link without any permission from him.

'Your next destination,' said Mobius Straeger. Coordinates arrived. Rather than these being an inert package in his inbox, as they would have been in his aug, they routed straight into the ship's system, and into the mind controlling its engines – a flash-frozen prador female ganglion.

Immediately the fusion drive kicked in, taking them away from the planetoid faster, while the U-jump engines warmed up and went quickly to holding.

'What will I find there?' Matheson asked.

'Somebody to kill,' Straeger replied.

Straeger

Straeger closed U-com, having loaded, for later inspection, the details of Matheson and the Brices' encounter with Crane. He then returned his attention to his captive. The prill-prador was alive, but then the other ones were still alive too, despite being rail-gunned and lasered into pieces. That was the nature of the Spatterjay virus, if enough of the original organism remained intact for it to prod into motion. In this case the majority of the original organism remained intact – most importantly, part of its brain. Stripped of external weapons and limbs, the thing hung clamped in a gimbal at the focus of powerful scanners, while other instruments stood ready for a more intensive investigation. Straeger swam around these and often acted as the instrument of examination himself, since the line of division between him and his machines was sometimes undetectable.

He found huge variations in this one compared to those he'd taken apart to refashion Matheson and the Brices, some remainder of which he'd stored here on his ship. In those previous ones, by reverse engineering them from the severe damage Crane and Arach had inflicted, he'd surmised they had ring-shaped ganglions only a little at variance from that of standard prador. Yet here he found the ring broken, with nodular expansions at the break so the thing looked like a Celtic torc. Further differences revealed themselves throughout the thing's body: organs rearranged, thicker muscle and nerve development throughout, and enhanced senses. He could see that greater control had been exercised over the virus mutating this creature by its cybernetics. A network of microtubes distributed inhibitors around the body, as well as genetic fixes, specially designed vesicles, and more besides. Everything was controlled by crystal processors Straeger was eager to connect to. But examination had to come before vivisection because, as he'd already discovered, this was a dangerous organism.

The cybernetic components of the creature became the main focus of his attention. Its outer covering, and part of what intruded into the creature itself, were an extrapolation of present prador armour, just as with those that'd attacked Crane. However, the armour of this one was a lot tougher. He examined the layer upon layer of meta-materials, with each layer often no more than a few atoms in thickness. He found exotic metal layers too, whose integrity the other surrounding materials maintained. It was a miniaturization of ship armour, which was impossible with present Polity or prador technology and beyond his reach too. Having already understood that these creatures must be an intrusion from the future, his analysis thus far showed him that the two groups must have come from two different times in the future. This armour, unlike that of the others, would be difficult to reverse engineer, deconstruct and apply to Matheson and the Brices. And now, having gone down this rabbit hole, he wondered if that was something he'd want to do anyway.

What was his purpose in all this? For decades it had simply been vengeance. He had been utterly focused on finding some way to kill Ian Cormac and any of his allies. Or to use the agent's allies and friends as anchor points to get to him. But things had changed ever since Cormac led him to Blite, turning vengeance into a secondary objective . . . mostly. And Straeger's lack of interest in capturing Blite had other drivers.

All because of a black diamond.

14

Cormac – Past

The Penny Royal incident had left many questions unanswered and many dangers to be assessed. Cormac had kept himself out of those events – he didn't consider them part of the remit he'd given himself, which was specifically concerned with what Polity AIs might be inclined to do to humanity. But he began to realize he could no longer ignore the fallout. Given that the rogue AI was an existential threat, anything related to Penny Royal had become an excuse for bad behaviour by the authorities. And anyone involved had become subject to interrogation and examination, which went beyond the bounds of his ideal of Polity law. Now the time had come to do something about it, and the place to start was with Captain Blite.

The man had been transported to the moon of an ice giant and the ECS black site concealed there. His mental interrogation should have been a matter of weeks, for them to glean every pertinent detail, while the physical examination of him, and the ship he'd received from the artist Mr Pace, should only have taken perhaps a few months longer. Cormac didn't like this, but since Blite had willingly given himself up to ECS, and since Penny Royal indeed was a power that might be an existential threat, he'd kept a light touch on the ECS secure com he'd penetrated long ago, and remained distant. But now Blite's imprisonment had been fourteen months, and it was beginning to look like it might never end. The interrogating AI, Carnusine, had rendered no new pertinent data and was making proposals for additional methods, such as virtuality scenarios, submolecular and subatomic disassociation, and scanning. It had even suggested some experiment that would have to be conducted around the Layden's Sink black hole, into which Penny Royal had dropped itself. Carnusine resembled an antediluvian researcher whose hypotheses were collapsing, but who still wanted the funding. It was time for this research to end.

Cormac's gridlink pushed the cold coffin to take him out of stasis the moment the destroyer dropped back into the real. Sunk in gel, with numerous pipes and feeds going into his body, he waited as the gel softened, then drained away, and various feeds detached. He took a breath through the oxygen feed to his nose, and waited. When he'd installed himself here, he'd ensured the ship AI wouldn't receive an alert that he was present, because that would go on record; he could take his time.

It had been an interesting exercise in U-space mechanics, supplanting the previous occupant of this coffin. The woman concerned had chosen to hop through time as a stored reserve marine aboard this ship and was now in a similar stasis coffin in an underground bunker where the ship had last stopped off. She'd wake up a few weeks hence and be making baffled enquiries of the local AIs. But by then Cormac's business would be done here. He'd found the necessity for more convoluted routes to his targets as the AIs continued to ramp up their defences against him, and refine their methods of trying to track him down.

Engaging his U-sense, and translating the chaos of U-space into something his still, perhaps, human brain could comprehend, he viewed his surroundings. Other coffins were around him in the storage wall, their occupants inanimate. His senses ranged out to encompass the entire destroyer, enabling him to see its thrusters firing. In a blurred fashion, he could see the moon it was heading for too. He automatically began making the calculations and, though he could have jumped to that moon, the data were not sufficiently complete to do so accurately. Acquiring the data would require him to access the ship's sensors, which would alert the ship AI. The AI would then have to log that, which meant those on the moon would know about it nanoseconds later, and probably order the ship to turn away. So he continued waiting.

The moon drew closer and, he was glad to see, the destroyer didn't go into orbit about it but fell to the base on its surface. He calculated and saw the thing lay twenty-five kilometres across. Beyond its circumference, containment spheres sat half-sunk in regolith. These doubtless contained items of Jain and other alien technology an order of magnitude more dangerous than those allowed to be displayed in the Viking Museum. Each of the spheres had very high security and was fashioned of an iteration of chain-glass a metre thick, capable of resisting the imploders each also contained. None of them was a barrier to a single human being who could jump through U-space.

The destroyer settled towards the base, coming down on a platform extruded for this purpose. Umbilicals snaked out, towed by spiderbots, to connect to ports all over the ship. A glassy airlock tube hooped up from below and connected too. The business of this ship here would only take a few hours, and now it was time for Cormac to be about his. He climbed out of the cold coffin.

U-jumping had become such second nature to him that making the calculations, then inserting himself into that continuum and relocating were practically autonomous. He landed in an empty oxygen tank he'd been aiming for – one of the few places here on the base that didn't have an AI watching. However, he knew those AIs would have detected his U-signature and would now be frantically searching for its source. He also knew that in the time it took him to fill his lungs with the heady air, they'd have formulated a pretty good idea of who'd just arrived. Now it was time for another technique he'd refined over the last few decades, and used infrequently. He pushed into U-space again, but rather than dive right into it he pressed down lightly into the surface, making an intrusion, so he was in some sense in and out of that continuum. He walked through the side of the oxygen tank to step out onto the roof of the base, then followed a roughened ceramal path between U-com emitters and weapons turrets, and dropped off the side.

When he was in this state, gravity had a feeble grip on him, and in that of this moon he found himself falling with dreamy slowness. No hurry. With him being neither in nor out of U-space, his signature was a dispersed thing which the AIs would have trouble nailing down. He finally touched down on red regolith surrounding whalebacks of stone that looked like rusty iron. It felt soft as a bog under his feet as he headed out across it. When he reached the first containment sphere, a flash behind lit up the moonscape. He glanced back, seeing a column of fire rising into the sky. It seemed the AIs had located his U-signature in that oxygen tank and weren't strictly following Earth Central's order to make every effort to capture him rather than kill him. This was the thing about AIs which few properly accepted, despite a huge body of evidence: they were as individual in their wants, decisions, loves and hates as any human being. They didn't toe the line and weren't utterly unified in some idealistic conception of the Polity. They were, after all, post-humans.

Rounding the containment sphere, he walked on. Ahead he could see Pace's ship lying partially assembled on a plate of chain-glass. A dome shimmered over it, only occasionally visible. This brought home to him how Carnusine's investigations here sat at variance to orders from Earth Central. If EC had thought the information from Blite, and that ship, so important that examinations should go on for ever, the ship would have been in a high-security clean hold, aboard some larger ship or space station. It wouldn't have been out here, protected from contamination by a mere shimmershield. He turned away from it, seeing just a few of the termite elements of Carnusine at work there, and focused on the small installation in which Blite had been confined.

Drawing closer and peering inside with his U-sense, he observed Blite taking out his frustrations on a punch bag in a small gym. The man's rooms, including the gym, sat at the centre of the specially equipped installation and were the focal point of the surrounding structure. Optic feeds and power lines ran to and from instruments positioned all around them. Other scanning machines there, like remote molecular analysers, microgravity mappers and powerful laser spectral analysers, were huge at their back ends, but narrowed down at the fore, making it look as though the rooms were supported in a gimbal by a series of daggers. Cormac had little doubt that even the strength of Blite's last kick on the bag had been perfectly recorded. He also noted the feeds from all these scanners ran to processing and storage, some of which were scattered with elements of Carnusine, while additional storage had been brought in, surprisingly. This last was a confirmation of the AI's intent: it was locked into studying Blite, even down to irrelevant details. It had tipped slightly over the edge into autistic focus, as some AIs tended to do. The thing would never let Blite go unless forced to do so, and it wouldn't be forced to do so by others such as EC, because they'd defer to it as the expert on all things Blite.

He now focused his attention on the AI itself, located in a chamber higher up in the installation. Perhaps eighty per cent of the AI was there, in a ball-shaped body consisting of what looked like metallic termites the size of cats. Most of its mind would be there too, and of course backed up somewhere else, like most AIs. Now it was time to deliver his message. Cormac locked down the coordinates of two locations, brought U-space into swirling focus around him, then jumped.

He arrived a few centimetres above a floor of roughened composite and dropped down onto his feet. Knowing AI reaction times, he simply extended his U-field to encompass Carnusine and jumped again. As they arrived at the new location, the AI landed with a thump and began to come apart like a ball of ants, a number of which started to scuttle directly towards Cormac. Loading a program, he pulled Shuriken from his wrist holster and tossed the star ahead of him. It whirled up to speed with a vicious sound, extending its chain-glass blades. The termite-things halted their advance and rose up, waving their antennae and forelimbs in the air.

'Understand,' said Cormac, pointing down into the floor, to where, via his U-sense, he could see a small cylinder, 'I could U-jump one of your units straight into that CTD. I would then simply leave. You would not.'

The termite-things abruptly turned around and headed back to re-enter the main mass, which itself began to form up into a ball again. Cormac scanned his surroundings. The containment sphere was Spartan. It had a metal floor in place, while on either side of him and the AI were two white ellipsoids held up in frames, with all sorts of scanners attached. These presumably were dangerous artefacts. A door in one wall opened to an underground tunnel leading back to the main black site. All of that was wrapped in heavy security, so it would take time for anyone to come through.

'I was informed of a U-signature in the base, and of the response to it. It was obviously you, since we don't have U-jump technology for anything so small.'

'I, of course, expected that.'

'Why are you here?'

'It seemed necessary to remind you that Polity citizens have rights. You've kept Captain Blite here long enough, and now it's time for you to release him.'

'There's still a great deal to learn from him.'

'Yes, as from anyone, at your level of examination, but you'll learn nothing more about Penny Royal than you already know. Blite must be set free.'

'So you are actually delivering a threat.'

'I can destroy you,' said Cormac, 'but we both know that's not much of a threat to an entity who is perpetually backed up. There's something else I can do, though: I can detonate the CTDs in every containment sphere here, destroying all these valuable artefacts.' He pointed to each of the ellipsoids. 'My next move would be steadily to wipe out all the defences here, and aboard the destroyer I arrived on, then grab Blite and take him away on it.'

'I think you overestimate yourself.'

'Perhaps I do, and perhaps I can be killed or captured here. Your calculation to make is whether hanging on to Blite will be worth all the damage caused, or rather . . . that isn't your calculation to make.'

A pause ensued, and in it all of the elements of Carnusine froze, then another voice issued from the AI, 'You are correct. It is not his calculation to make.'

'Hello, Earth Central,' said Cormac.

This had been part of his plan all along. He could threaten and cause destruction here, to try to push Carnusine to release

Blite, and he'd reckoned on his chances being fifty-fifty if that was the totality of it. But he knew his presence here would immediately be reported and draw the attention of Earth Central, as well as the networked AIs which formed the governance of the Polity.

'Blite will be released at once,' said the ruling AI, 'and Carnusine will stand down.'

'It's not very good that I have to turn up here to remind AIs of the rules they supposedly support and enforce.'

'As you well know, rules and regulations must evolve to fit their environment. Also, it is the case that things are never so clear cut and rosy as the average Polity citizen would suppose.'

'Bullshit,' Cormac replied, holding up his arm for Shuriken, which seemed reluctant to return to its holster. 'Blite slipped under the radar for the same reason many others have: AIs regard humans like figures on a balance sheet. But you're releasing him now, so my work here is done. Of course, I shouldn't have to add that if he isn't released there'll be consequences.'

'Perhaps, while you are available, I can ask a question?'

'You can ask, but I can't guarantee I'll answer.'

'Very well . . . Only the destroyer you arrived on will be departing, and all other scheduled ships have been diverted for the interim. The destroyer will go directly to a secure station, where we will be ready for you if you are aboard. If you are not, the next arrival at this black site will bring the resources to capture you.'

After a long pause, Cormac said, 'I haven't heard a question yet.'

'How do you expect to escape us?'

Cormac smiled at the Carnusine bodies, now hosting Earth Central. 'As I said, no guarantee of an answer.' Shuriken snicked home and Cormac immediately U-jumped to another empty

380

storage tank in the base. A particle beam strike destroyed it six seconds later, but by then he'd already walked out of it. He'd learned to control his ability to be both in and out of U-space to an amazing degree. The more he inserted himself into the real, the more the physical effects. This had advantages and disadvantages: he could make himself invisible by being more in U-space than out, but then with physical effects like gravity and the material world fading around him, it became difficult to do things such as simply walking. After closing up his envirosuit, and relying on its oxygen supply, he walked with slow leisure through the base. Finally he reached the destroyer, boarded, and headed towards the accommodation section. With his U-sense expanded out, he could see the empty cold coffin had already been reported by the ship AI. Numerous robots had come aboard too, to install a variety of complex U-space detector hardware.

Cormac came to a cabin door and walked through it. Inside were all the comforts and necessities a person would need. But, of course, use of those and the presence of someone in here would be detected by the destroyer's controlling AI. Cormac pulled the majority of himself out of U-space and sighed into the real. He collapsed his envirosuit hood and visor, and breathed cabin air, before walking over to the fabricator and ordering a cup of coffee. He sipped, and then went over to sit in a comfortable chair in front of a console and screen he had no need of.

'Well, they're all running around shitting rivets,' said the destroyer AI. 'Their main focus is Pace's ship, which only recently became space-worthy, and the runcible. It's as shut down as it can be, since with previous disappearances they hypothesize you can use them to go anywhere in the network.'

'That may be a possibility,' Cormac replied. 'What are your orders?'

'I'm to maintain emergency-level scanning within the ship all the way to Station Draven, where I will enter a clean hold and undergo examination. Seems a Mobius has taken an interest and will be doing that.'

'And when will you arrive there?'

'Thirty-six minutes and three seconds after Hell freezes over.'

'And your plans?'

'You know.'

Cormac directed his U-sense down into one particular hold of the destroyer. Sitting in there, strapped to the floor, was a seven-metre-long chrome and gold body in the shape of a parasitic wasp. That was where the mind running this destroyer had come from, and to which she would shortly be returning. The higher-up AIs like EC knew that not all AIs were in agreement with them on all matters, and some were downright rebellious. It should also have been no surprise to them that the most rebellious of all were usually the product of overstretched and sometimes plain bonkers wartime factory stations, as was the AI of this destroyer.

Cormac – Present

Cormac glanced around at Andre, taking in his wary expression and tight grip on the carbine he'd now unslung. He felt much the same himself and had a pang of loss for the missing Shuriken on his wrist. AIs came in many shapes, sizes and distributions. Generally those that occupied Golem or drone bodies were closer to humanity, though not necessarily any safer to be around than other humans, especially if they were a product of war factories such as Room 101. Ship AIs were a bit more distant, while static planetary AIs even more distant still, with an almost godlike perspective and disregard for humanity on the personal level.

Swarm AIs had seemingly diverged – they didn't think in the same individual terms and tended to divide up the world into components and packets that reflected their form. This was why they were very good at taking things apart, examining them and elucidating the whole, and the forensic AIs most criminals in the Polity feared were swarm AIs. Mobius AIs were something that to Cormac's mind combined all the negative aspects of every other AI.

Mobius AIs could divide themselves up into swarms and yet, in either form, were very good at taking things apart and re-assembling them. They seemed to combine godlike disregard with many of the worst traits of humanity. They were loners, and already a high percentage of those produced had excused themselves from the Polity, going off on their own pursuits. Those that had remained seemed to enjoy inserting themselves into operations which edged into what others would regard as immoral. Their concern for human life very often revealed itself to be low, and they seemed to show contempt for humanity. Cormac didn't like them at all, and had had many encounters with them since they'd appeared. One he'd even taken a hand in destroying.

'I see a negative reaction to this form,' the AI Hune stated, its voice issuing out of a mass of tendrils.

'Fucking right,' said Andre before Cormac could reply. 'Mobius bastards are all over the Graveyard.'

'It's not a place your kind would like policed?' Hune enquired.

'If policing was all they did, many would be fine with it,' said Andre. 'They do take down some who need to be stopped, but it's a toss-up whether or not they might replace them.' He looked over at Cormac. 'It's like they're playing games, but no one knows the rules.'

Cormac nodded an acknowledgement. The Graveyard was a

place he rarely visited – he didn't consider it within his self-imposed remit, but he'd heard rumours. The Mobius AIs did seem to like chaos. He turned back to Hune.

'It's not so much about the shape you've taken on, but whether you've adopted a similar mindset.'

'No. I like order and, of course, the form you see before you is a mere protrusion from my whole. I have found it is a useful tool for disassembly and reverse engineering.' The Mobius form extended one glassy tube towards the floating p-prador Cormac had presented for examination. 'So this is what you've brought me.'

'Evidently,' said Cormac tightly.

'What knowledge do you hope to gain from it, and do you wish it intact when I've finished?'

'Everything you can find, and it doesn't need to be intact afterwards. I suspect you will learn much of use from it and, unlike the Mobius AI I brought you before, you can keep whatever is left over.'

'Send it in, then.'

Via his gridlink, Cormac nudged the p-prador forwards. It slid into the Mobius as if the thing wasn't there, and the threads wormed and nested all around it. Legs and other items of the p-prador that he'd dropped into the crater in its surface shot away first, dissolving in light and fibres, then the thing itself started to come apart.

'Andre,' said Hune, 'you might like to know the refit and rebalancing of one of your U-space nacelles that Urbine requested was not before time. I calculate that two more jumps would have resulted in a rearrangement of your ship that you would not have found enjoyable.'

'Urbine requested?' Andre asked. He abruptly put his fingers up against his aug and turned away. 'You fucking what?' he then said, and thereafter the conversation went subvocal.

Cormac concentrated on the p-prador. Trunks of threads had gone in through the holes in its armour, while the armour itself was being stripped away layer by layer. Information packets began to come in through his link to Hune. The first he checked thoroughly, running it through his security, but it was nothing but data, without anything nasty. He assumed that, despite the Mobius form, Hune was as uninterested in attacking or asserting power over others as before. Cormac examined the contents of some packets cursorily, but sent most into storage.

'The organism inside is still alive,' Hune commented. 'But since its ganglion was thoroughly destroyed, it has the intelligence of a mollusc. The blend of the organic into the cybernetic is highly . . .'

'Advanced?' Cormac asked, but Hune didn't reply.

'How long is this going to take?' said Andre, having finished what had probably been an acrimonious conversation with Urbine.

'A few hours, maybe,' Cormac replied.

'Okay, I'm heading back to the ship – I have some things to sort out.' He turned and took a step away, then paused and stepped back, holding out his laser carbine to Cormac while shooting a look of distrust at Hune's Mobius form. Cormac was about to wave it away but then, remembering the loss at his wrist, took it anyway. Andre stomped off, doubtless to continue negotiations with his ship AI.

'Yes, highly advanced,' said Hune. 'Excuse my moment of distraction, but the armour is interesting indeed. It contains prador exotic metal, is highly layered and deeply complex. In all honesty, there are parts of it I cannot deconstruct at present, but on the whole I can understand its function.'

'And that is?'

'Firstly, it's not much of a defence against modern weapons.

It has the durability of steel and fairly low-grade steel at that. Think in terms of a medieval knight going up against a machine gun. However, it does have a defensive purpose, in that it generates the same protective field of a U-space engine, which shields all within it from the dimensional displacement that would otherwise tear itself, and its ship, apart.' Again a long pause, before Hune continued, 'I would say it looks like protection for this creature to go through an open-ended runcible, or some other bare transmission through U-space. But, of course, we know this technology or capability only exists in one place.'

'That would be me,' said Cormac wryly.

'Yes, quite. Incidentally, were you meeting up here with someone else?'

'Why do you ask?' Cormac clutched the carbine tighter, not liking where that question might lead.

'Because I don't receive many visitors, and two ships arriving within hours of each other is a very unusual occurrence.'

'Show me.'

Imagery arrived in his gridlink an instant later. He gazed at the spherical vessel falling into orbit around the planetoid and felt a hint of recognition, soon confirmed by a program he automatically raised. This was the ship belonging to the bounty hunter Matheson. Was it a coincidence he'd come here? It might be that the man had retrieved one of the other p-prador Crane and Arach had defeated, and had come here for the same purposes as him. Hune wasn't choosy about who could use its services. Maybe, unknown to him, Andre had contacted this man?

Opening out his U-sense again, and translating it in his gridlink, he looked towards Andre and the ship, while opening a link to him.

'Matheson just arrived,' he stated.

Andre was standing outside his ship, looking up at one U-space nacelle that now seemed tangled in vines. Focusing in closer, Cormac caught the look of surprise and, since the man had no idea he was being viewed, knew this was genuine.

'Why the fuck would he come here?'

'Maybe for the same reason as me: he picked up the remains of one of those creatures on Cull and wants it examined?'

Andre shook his head. 'No, not possible. A Mobius AI took them.'

'I see.'

The distortions appeared then, screwing with his perception of Andre and the surrounding factory through his U-sense. They weren't something he'd seen before, though they vaguely resembled what he experienced when too close to a runcible. He focused, translating and locating, while his gridlink ramped up mental function to full speed, hit boost on his nervous system and switched his nanosuite over to emergency function. Something snapped in the air, sending a gust across his face.

Located . . .

Cormac ducked as a clawed hand swiped through where his head had been, then dived and rolled, even as he heard three more snaps. Slamming a foot down to stop himself, he fired the carbine. The beam crackled like wet meat in a fryer, burning into armour and spraying molten droplets.

They were humanoid, yet not standard human as far as he could see. Likely they had some form of extreme body mod, of the catadapt or ophidapt kind. He couldn't tell for sure, because their shoddy armour didn't have visors. However, the swipe of that clawed hand had telegraphed intention: they were here to kill him. He rolled and came up again, then fired at the one over to the right of the Mobius, only now realizing he had no need to dodge about so vigorously, because it appeared none of them were armed, beyond the blades along their forearms and spiked fingertips. They also weren't moving very fast, and in fact seemed disoriented. He backed up against the wall of the chamber and edged towards the entrance.

The one he'd shot, over to the left of the Mobius, was looking down at his leg – at the armour smoking there. He then raised his oddly shaped head on its long neck, and charged. Cormac fired again and again, burning into armour on the legs, torso and arms. It should have been enough to bring this individual down, but didn't, and now the others were charging at him too. And fast.

Evidently these people had U-jumped, which he'd thought was a facility unique to himself. It seemed to have slowed them down shortly after arrival, but now they were shaking it off and moving faster than standard human. The first to reach him pulled back a fist for a strike. Cormac swayed aside from that and stepped out of reach, with the floor jouncing underneath him as the fist went through the wall. The ceramal there shattered – ridiculous strength was obviously their weapon.

In all this, Cormac felt no particular fear. He wanted information, which was why he'd not gone for head shots. The one at the wall pulled his fist out as the other three launched themselves at him once more. Had he been a standard human, he would have been trapped. Instead, he snap calculated and jumped, appearing over the other side of the Mobius. The attackers, now ten metres away from him, crashed together in an almost comedic tangle.

'Well, this is all very exciting,' Hune commented.

'And baffling,' said Cormac. 'Have you been talking to someone you shouldn't have?'

'Even if I had, that supposed someone would not have been able to arrive so quickly.'

'True.'

Other thoughts now occurred. These attackers could jump through U-space, so were a good counter to him, yet they hadn't been here waiting for him. It seemed likely they'd come from Matheson's ship, so how had they known where to find him? Almost certainly an AI was involved and had predicted his path. Then there was the technology.

Again, the distortions arose. Two of the attackers appeared on either side of him, in close. He fired once, throwing himself aside, but not fast enough to stop a hand closing on the carbine. He released it, heard a crunch, and saw it go clattering to one side, then felt a tug across his back. His nanosuite registered damage and informed him via his gridlink. The slice was a few centimetres deep and he could feel the blood trickling down his back. Another of them snapped into being ahead of him; raising a foot, he bounced off this one as it snatched for his ankle, hitting the floor and cartwheeling out of reach. He drew his thin gun, now angry with himself for the miscalculation that had lost him the carbine. Even though these attackers had obviously U-jumped here, he'd become accustomed over the years to fighting those without that facility, and their second jump had caught him by surprise.

He fired at the head of the nearest figure, no longer thinking in terms of accruing information. The very real prospect of not being able to escape these killers now occurred to him. If he jumped to the ship to try to escape that way, he'd likely get Andre killed. Instead he jumped again, out onto the suspended walkway that had brought him here. It shuddered under him, as his attackers arrived faster now, and closer, their appearance around him almost mathematically precise. He micro-jumped, putting himself behind one of them, and launched a hard kick into its back. This one staggered into the other directly opposite, knocking it over the edge of the path, sending it plummeting out of sight. The one he'd kicked went over too, but managed to clamp a hand into the material of the path and began hauling itself back up. As the other two swung towards him, he micro-jumped again.

Even as he fought, Cormac's mind was running fast and hot. He'd been tardy and arrogant, and not properly realized the threat here. When he'd faced off against those p-prador, he'd known the dangers and been mentally prepared. Here he felt slow and stupid. He knew he must think beyond the mere mechanics of fighting. He fired again, and micro-jumped as one of his opponents staggered back, with the armoured metal cratered and hot over the centre of its face. Arriving at a new location, Cormac reached out and snared a metal pole, hanging on to it. Two arrived either side of him, ready to attack, then simply dropped, because he'd put himself out on one of the frameworks beyond the walkway. Hanging one-handed, he opened up a link he didn't often use and worked the programming of his thin gun. This began to whine up to a crescendo. Another attacker appeared nearby, grabbing a stanchion then swinging towards him like an ape. Cormac swung towards this one too, while sliding only partially into U-space. It felt as if the pole was dissolving in his hand as he punched out with the other, his thin gun and hand entering the attacker's torso. He released it and jumped away, seeing three figures were back on the walkway – obviously the ones that'd dropped had been returned.

Landing on the walkway a hundred metres away from the three, he looked to the one on the framework. The blast signature, as his thin gun dumped its load, registered in his gridlink. The one out there jerked, his torso armour expanding and then split, opening down the sides. Smoking organics jetted out, fibrous and connected, like the sudden growth of an epiphyte, and the attacker dropped bonelessly. Cormac processed this as he looked towards the remaining three. Whatever was inside that armour definitely didn't seem strictly human. The one who'd just fallen now reappeared a couple of metres up from the walkway, and dropped with a crash upon it. The three focused on this one, then raised their heads to look towards Cormac. After checking back towards the ship, he made a longer jump there, appearing with a crack directly before Andre.

'What the fuck?' the man exclaimed.

No time to explain. He'd either killed or disabled one of the attackers, and that had paused the others, but they'd be on him again in a moment. He snapped out both hands and pulled three grenades from the man's belt. Penetrating these grenades with a subversion program, he shut down their four-second delay upon removal, then jumped away again as distortions began to develop around him. He landed back in the chamber where Hune had been disassembling the p-prador. The AI had now dropped it, risen up, and expanded out into a more dislocated form. Even as Cormac arrived, he tracked the distortions in U-space. One developed out on the walkway. It was stronger and, calculating from it, he saw that the dead or injured one had been shunted back up to the ship in orbit. Meanwhile the remaining three were coming right for him. He waited with two grenades in one hand, and one in the other.

They appeared close as he made rapid calculations and jumped the grenades out of his hands. The first hit as he back-flipped away from the attacker attempting to gut him. That one juddered and expanded like the first, and just collapsed with those fibrous masses blasting out from its sides. The remaining two micro-jumped and repositioned. One grenade exploded partially in the armour of one arm, taking it off. The final one blew up in front of the chest of the other figure and sent it tumbling backwards. Crouched on the floor, Cormac watched. The one with the missing arm clamped a hand over the stump, looked to each of its two fellows, then strong distortions developed again. The three disappeared.

'Invigorating!' Hune commented.

Cormac wanted to consider why the AI hadn't intervened, and to crunch the data on this attack, but he didn't have time. If the attackers thought they were going to get away with this by simply withdrawing, they were deluded. He stood up, checked his surroundings and jumped yet again.

This time he arrived in the bridge of the ship, where Andre had retreated and was checking instruments. Cormac staggered on arrival, head aching, and a sharp pain in his sinuses that predicted a nose bleed sometime soon. Andre was viewing recorded footage through ship's sensors. On one screen Cormac saw himself shoving his thin gun inside the attacker, while another screen showed a 3D map of the area with U-jumps tracked throughout it.

'What the hell were they?' Andre asked, spinning towards him with another carbine held ready.

'No time,' Cormac replied. He pointed at the carbine and gestured for it to be handed over, then added, 'Give me that and the rest of your grenades.'

Andre looked set to rebel, then abruptly thought better of it. He sighed and held out the carbine. Cormac took it, as the man undid his belt of grenades and reached out to hand that over too. Cormac went to take the thing, but then paused, closing his hand into a fist and withdrawing it.

'Damn. Too late,' he said.

The ship out in orbit had fired up fusion engines and was moving away rapidly. Already it was at the limit of his normal reach to U-jump, and right then he felt exhausted from all the short jumping down here. A second after that assessment, the bounty hunter's ship dropped into U-space and was gone.

Blite

The claws of AI Marble's vessel, and various other implements, engaged, jolting the *Coin* and scraping over its hull. Stepping out of his cabin, Blite resisted the urge to check on what was happening. Instead he used his aug to adjust the assist on his vacuum combat suit, to ensure it didn't kick in before necessary. He was stronger now, and becoming accustomed to the new strength. It had been whole days since he last broke a teapot.

Meander was suited up and out of her cabin ahead. Judging by her focus on Blite, she'd been waiting for him. He noted that she hadn't used any kind of armour while she'd been with them, and certainly hadn't while being tortured, yet she'd managed to clad herself in it more quickly than he, who was accustomed to it. Without a word she fell in beside him as they headed for the bridge. Paidon and Judice were at their stations. Paidon wore a light vacuum combat suit he knew she kept stored here on the bridge. Judice was unsuited but, being a human loaded to a Golem chassis, probably felt no need of further protection. She glanced at them, then, with a hand gesture, threw up a series of frames in the main screen paint.

Cam views showed the hull of the snatch ship up close, hinged arms folded across the hull, and the worm of an atmosphere dock locked onto their airlock. A composite image, extrapolated from these, showed the *Coin* close up against the snatch ship, with those arms embracing it all the way down its length. They were going nowhere.

'So what now?' Carlstone asked as he entered, with Armand and another trooper from the ship's complement of soldiers trailing in behind. All three wore heavier suits and sported a wide selection of weapons. They looked indistinguishable from the

Polity marines they'd once been. Breil came along after, wearing a slick custom combat suit with a heavy QC laser at the hip. Blite looked beyond, expecting to see Iris, then auged into the ship's system to find out where she was. She was coming up from Medical, her armour a baroque thing that meshed with her haiman carapace. The case hanging from a strap over her shoulder he recognized as containing five cylinder-packed field autodocs. She'd made preparations he hoped they wouldn't need.

'Marble told me to go aboard,' Blite said. 'He mentioned nothing about the rest of you.' He'd thought about this while he dressed and again his apparent invulnerability had come into play. The damned crystal in his skull screwed with planning and tactical considerations. Without the thing, to protect those he wanted to protect, it would have been better to leave them aboard the *Coin*. However, he did have the thing in his skull, and if they were too far from him he wouldn't be able to reverse their deaths, whether inclusive of him or not, though the idea of shooting himself in the head still gave him the horrors even now. There was another factor: they hadn't come along with him into danger with the expectation of being protected. In the end, he must make the best tactical calculations and, as he always had before, rely a great deal on gut instinct.

'Judice, Breil and Paidon will remain here.' He looked to Breil. 'The system?'

Breil tapped his aug. 'Re-establishing, diagnostics running, but still some debugging required. However, the warfare beam's aim was to knock out temporarily our ability to run.'

Blite acknowledged the bugs concerned would be from Marble, and that on many levels the AI was probably listening to them now. Perhaps it would be better to be careful about what he said, but a response would be expected. He turned to Judice.

'I want a tactical solution to those gripper arms out there, and checks on hull damage. Perhaps you'll need to send out some inspection robots.'

Judice gave a curt nod. He felt no need to add that maybe those robots could carry some micromines, or one-burn shearfield generators.

'Flight capability?' he asked Paidon.

'The mind is back with us and U-space disruption waning. Reconnection to all other drives is already underway.' She looked over to Breil. 'Making sure those connections can't break will take a little while longer.'

Of course, Marble might have installed cut-off switches in the programming.

'Okay, then the rest of us head across.' He moved to the door, Iris ahead of him in the corridor and taking the turn towards the airlock, since she'd undoubtedly been listening in. He glanced at Meander, trying to see what he could divine from her expression. She locked eyes with him and he had less sense of the waif he'd first seen, and more of whatever it was he'd perceived when they were knocked out of U-space. Essentially, she was superfluous to this venture, and in fact an asset he should be making an effort to keep locked down and protected in the *Coin*, but this was where gut instinct kicked in. He wanted to keep her close, wherever they were. He felt she was not only important in obtaining the answers he wanted, but integral. If anyone had asked him why he felt that way, he'd have had no real answer.

Auging into the system as he headed after Iris confirmed that the snatch ship's airlock tube had attached to their third airlock along the ship – between the accommodation section and Medical. Iris paused ahead, waiting by the spur corridor that led to the lock. He nodded to her and was about to go into the spur when Armand and the other soldier quickly moved ahead of him, while Carlstone fell in at his side. He stepped in.

'So why Meander?' Carlstone asked, making no attempt to whisper.

Blite glanced back at where Meander had joined Iris. This was precisely the question he hadn't wanted asked, which of course was why Carlstone had asked it. He thought then about Iris too, everything she represented, and the whole began to clarify in his mind.

'This,' he pointed ahead to the airlock, 'is a microcosm of our entire adventure. We're walking into something unknown to us, but probably well known by some bad actors. The clarity and surgical precision of the kind of military response you understand so well won't be enough. We need wild cards, to be ready to think or do the unthinkable.'

Rather than argue as Blite expected, Carlstone nodded agreement, then said, 'Ian Cormac is not someone I know, but if anything of the fictions is true, he's the extreme version of his kind. What you just said is precisely the kind of thing an agent would say.'

'And that's a good thing?'

'You've become crafty in your old age,' Carlstone replied.

Armand opened the airlock door, went inside, and checked atmosphere readings on the other one before popping that open too. Blite meanwhile auged into the record of the other soldier and wondered about Carlstone's motivation for bringing a heavy-worlder woman out of storage. The woman, Gruce, was just like the rest aboard: ex-ECS, though in her case she was what they'd called in previous ages a ground pounder.

Ahead, the airlock tube had stabilized and curved up to their right. Internally it was an octagon, with four of its faces transparent. Armand and Gruce entered, floating ahead and propelling themselves along it with easy taps against the walls. As Blite entered, he peered out through the transparent sections at the grab arms and other mechanisms locking the *Coin* in place. With a wry grin he also noted one of his ship's maintenance bots crawling along one of those arms, like a ladybird on a twig.

The tube wound up, past one large arm, and then came down on the hull of the snatch ship. It connected to a smaller personnel access door, set into a larger circular one that a vactrans train could have gone through. Armand again checked readings, then opened the smaller oval door ahead. They went through. It had seemed no airlock lay beyond, but once inside Blite saw they'd entered a huge lock space. The thing was made for taking shuttles, doubtless sent by ships stopped at the border, or maybe even bringing personnel aboard. Once through the smaller door, the effect of grav made itself known and they walked out onto the lock floor. They then headed across, going through another door that Armand atmosphere-checked too.

Beyond this they were into the actual interior of the snatch ship. All around, caged access ways starred out, past megalithic machines and the huge drive mechanisms of those exterior arms. Packed between seemed to be a random junkyard of technology, with what looked like metallic fungal growths but which were nanotech, organic vines of the same, and clusters of white spheres like giant snail's eggs. He assumed from the exterior intrusions and extrusions that these were bespoke nanofactories. All of this gave Blite a bad feeling – it looked too much like what he'd once seen in the interior of an insane war factory.

'So, Marble!' Blite called. 'Where the hell do I go now?'

All around them things began moving – snakelike shapes and spectral energy emissions. Then grav went out, as jointed intestinal-looking tentacles wormed in all around them, opening spider grabs from tulip-bud tips. Two of these shot out, snaring up the two troopers and dragging them away, with the soldiers' laser carbine fire searing out into the interior, setting things burning.

Something lashed at Blite, sending him bouncing up from the floor, and he saw Carlstone tumbling past, swearing, then snatched by another grab. The tentacle of yet another grazed past Blite as it speared towards Iris and Meander. He caught hold, looking towards them, and saw Iris had caught hold of Meander's arm, while another grab came in from the side to snare her. The haiman woman snapped her head up, the tongue of her sensory cowl shooting up, then opening out its petals behind her head. It seemed that the metallic glare of her eyes stopped the first tentacle dead in its tracks, as well as the second when she turned her attention towards it. Both spider grabs opened and closed a couple of times, then thought better of it and retreated.

Wild cards, thought Blite.

Grav kicked in again, dropping them to the floor. Blite quickly recovered and pulled his laser carbine from his back. Now a hinged arm, much like one of those clasping his ship, unfolded out of the chaos, ripping through optics and pipes as if through constricting growth. Stabilizing ten metres ahead of him, it folded out the item on its end. The great clump of machinery had obviously been excised from some old warship, because the gleaming square-mouthed throat pointing straight at him was that of a huge particle cannon. He looked down at his carbine and grimaced.

'What happens if I kill you now?' Marble asked.

Blite didn't answer at once. He looked back to Iris and Meander. Iris was down in a crouch, sensory cowl still up as she too surveyed their surroundings. The armour she wore had taken on a strange lustre that he felt sure must be the product of field tech – something sitting partway between a shimmershield and a hardfield. In reality, she was the more effective soldier in a situation like this than Carlstone and his ex-ECS guys. He then looked into the tech around them, where he could see Carlstone and the others caught like flies in a spider web. He tried opening com with them but everything was down. At least they looked alive, so there was that. He swung back to face the particle cannon.

'If you kill me now,' he said, 'I die.'

A pained yell came from the machinery and, looking over there, he saw Gruce with one arm waving free and a jet of blood spurting from the severed wrist. Her hand thudded down to his right, and in that moment com opened up again. The jet of blood died, and she folded her arm back in. Her combat suit had closed off the artery, and no doubt she'd closed off the pain via one of the three methods available to her. Still, the AI had cut off her hand, showing itself to be well outside of perceived Polity law. The lesson had been delivered. He didn't need to hear what Marble said next, as its voice coagulated out of the air, before its holographic avatar appeared standing over to one side of the weapon.

'Hereafter, each lie you tell will result in a similar action,' it said.

'Tell the fucking thing nothing,' said Gruce over com.

'Stow it, Gruce,' Carlstone replied, then to Blite, 'It knows something, but we don't know how much.'

'I know,' Blite replied subvocally. 'But I'm not going to test the limits of its knowledge by seeing you all dismembered.'

Carlstone had no reply to that, since he was beyond the kind of bravado Gruce had shown.

'And then, after I die,' he said out loud. 'Time is rolled back to put me through it again and again, until I don't die.'

'Spurs off the probability slope which link back, forming loops,' said Marble. 'Yet some other factors must be involved for you to escape the circuit. I am assuming that you retain the memory of each death?'

'Yes,' Blite replied.

'Perception thresholds,' said the AI. 'You are at the core of it, so you finally perceive. Other linear beings will not. What are the other factors that allow you to escape the circuit?'

Blite thought hard about that, as he had many times before. He understood some of the theory of time travel, so had a loose grasp on what Marble meant by spurs and loops, but he had trouble getting his linear mind around the paradoxes.

'The loop pushes further back, into the past, so I have a greater opportunity to change the course of events.'

'This is fascinating,' said the AI. 'The U-space disruption and patterns can be measured and mapped across into realspace. I have much to learn here.'

He felt the surge of energy in his bones as the weapon powered up. Fire ignited in the throat of the particle cannon, and the certainty of his death arrived to layer itself upon all those other deaths. Part of him was screaming, revealed in that moment yet suppressed outside of it, otherwise all those deaths would have driven him mad by now. The diamond, of course. Before the inferno reached out to him, he heard Iris speak through com.

'This is untenable,' she said.

15

Cormac

With Andre at his side, Cormac walked back to Hune. He had a bandolier of grenades on under his jacket, a heavy gas-system pulse gun at his hip and a laser carbine resting across one shoulder. Andre kept an extensive collection of weapons aboard his ship, which he'd been reluctant to share until sufficient payment was forthcoming. Cormac could simply have taken them, but felt he owed the man the courtesy of payment.

'Who did Matheson have with him on Cull?' he asked Andre.

'His Golem side-kick Ricardo – human upload – and the Brices.'

'These Brices?'

'The two brothers, Will and Ulnar, and their sister, Sheen.'

Cormac nodded. Now running through recorded footage in his gridlink, he could see that a grenade had detonated outside the armour of one attacker who was smaller than the others and still retained other female characteristics. He also determined that the one whose arm he'd blown off, and whose physical distortions weren't as extreme as those of the others, had been in charge of them, and the jumps they'd made. His attackers were Matheson and the Brices – doubtless whatever had changed them hadn't been able to do the same with Ricardo.

All this was useful information, but it didn't explain their ability to jump, their strange armour, nor the nature of their bodies inside that armour. Neither did it explain how they'd managed to intercept him here, or why they would want to. He had earlier surmised that some AI actor must be involved, and now wondered if this was a hit team dispatched by Earth Central. If so, then something must have changed, since the ruling AI's last orders for him were data-gathering and/or capture. It wasn't unreasonable to assume that events surrounding Blite had also changed the AIs' calculations concerning him.

'So those were Matheson and the Brices?' Andre asked.

'High probability, since the numbers are right, and they came in Matheson's ship.'

'Ricardo?' asked Andre, obviously making his own aug assessments.

'I suspect the ability to U-jump has something to do with the organic component,' Cormac replied as they entered the chamber where Hune was back at work. He continued, 'Hune, you've been listening. Do you have something for me?'

The AI was wrapped around the remains of the p-prador, which, now stripped of its armour, consisted of fibrous organic matter and organs threaded through with cybernetic technology. Cormac grimaced at this. The organic matter was very familiar, and went some way to confirm the conjectures he was making. Raising his gaze, he saw an arm at the end of a bunch of AI threads, its hand opening and closing while armour disappeared along its length in small squares.

'I have a lot for you,' the AI replied.

More packages began to arrive in his gridlink, and again he only cursorily scanned over them before shunting them into storage. Detail he could get into later; right now he wanted the bigger picture.

'Summation,' he said tersely.

'P-prador, I have now surmised, is a contraction of prill-prador,' said Hune.

'I could have told you that,' Cormac snapped.

'But you didn't. The genetic modification of the prador here was not done in a laboratory with the prill genome inserted, but by the Spatterjay virus. This prador was born with the virus which was engineered to express prill characteristics. Cybernetic components were inserted throughout its growth, and thoroughly embedded at the back end by expression of hardware protocols arising from the Jain genome.'

'Fuck,' said Andre, and Cormac couldn't agree more.

'Whoever did this,' Hune continued, 'had a very good grasp on the Spatterjay viral form – enough to know where to stop its expression.'

'Stop expression?'

'Go too far with this tinkering and you'll likely end up accessing a quantum storage crystal, which grow and repeat throughout, and then you have something you can't control and a lot of problems.'

'What is that something you can't control?' asked Andre leadenly, as if he knew.

'A Jain soldier,' said Hune.

'Fuck,' said Andre again.

'Dangerous technology to play with,' said Cormac flatly. 'What about the armour?'

'A defence against the effects of U-space for the organism inside. Further defences are in its cybernetics. However, it is not a great defence against modern weapons. Unfortunately for this particular creature, the requirements for the former detract from the latter.'

'And by extension those who attacked me, too.'

Andre looked at him, puzzlement swiftly dissolving as he realized.

'So you know,' said Hune.

'Give me a rough sketch,' said Cormac.

'Running a DNA trace on this arm left behind, I've found it came from Matheson Cromantor – a bounty hunter. He has been highly mutated by the same advanced form of the Spatterjay virus I found in the p-prador. The armour on the arm is also similar, though it has been adapted for his form. I would say that whoever created it understood the function of the p-prador armour but couldn't reconstruct some of the meta-materials and the exotic alloy in it.'

'So someone made these people capable of doing what this p-prador can?'

'No,' said Hune. 'The p-prador can singly survive transit through U-space, but are not capable of generating a U-space jump. The further technology enabling Matheson and the Brices to do so came from somewhere else.'

'Miniaturized jump tech?' Cormac asked.

'Indeed. The Polity has it. But while it can throw people through U-space, it does not generate the protective field of a large engine, to create and maintain a bubble of conventional spacetime.'

Cormac nodded at that. Few realized that when a ship with damaged engines arrived at its destination inside out, or in pieces, or not at all, it was because of a failure to maintain that bubble – to impose the dimensions of conventional spacetime inside it, especially during the transitions in or out of U-space. Up could become down, and left could become right in a very real and destructive sense. It was also the case, as plainly evident in the p-prador, that the fourth dimension of time could be altered too.

Hune continued, 'Which of course makes a particular human

who's able to jump through the continuum, apparently unprotected, even more of a puzzle.'

'A Polity AI did this,' Cormac said, ignoring that last comment.

'Your reasoning?' Hune asked.

'Armour reverse engineered enough to be transferred to a
human being. Miniature drive tech installed. A prediction made
on my next likely destination, and the time of arrival.'

'I think you underestimate your own kind. Certainly, some
human agency would be capable of this, though one would
wonder why. The reward for your capture is nowhere near as
much as could be made by selling the technology involved
here.'

Cormac shook his head. In essence it had all come together
on a subconscious level during the fight but was now neatly
laying itself out in his mind. What he'd learned from Andre on
returning to Cull had utterly confirmed it.

'No, not a human but an AI, and a very specific one. This is
the work of Mobius Straeger.' Andre had said a Mobius AI
grabbed up the two p-prador Crane and Arach had killed on
Cull, and had then obviously reverse engineered the tech to apply
it to Matheson and the Brices. This didn't have the feel of ECS
machinations and, judging by the reward for information on the
AI, he suspected Straeger had gone rogue. He now had some
intimation of its aims, but no clarity. Why had the thing later
snatched up those other p-prador on Abalon, and let Blite run
out on what was probably a leash?

'Interesting,' said Hune, but no more.

Cormac felt the need to go on clarifying his thoughts. 'I've
known for some time that an AI or group of the same has been
trying to kill me, despite Earth Central changing the orders on
that. I'd be unsurprised to know that my interest in Blite has
focused the attention of said AI, or AIs, on him too. Straeger

wasn't in the original mission to capture Blite – in fact, Straeger inserted itself into the mission.'

Another delay ensued, before Hune replied, doubtless accessing information on all this before doing so. 'Interesting,' Hune said again, which made Cormac think the AI knew something he did not.

'Why did you not intervene when Matheson and his crew attacked here?' he asked abruptly. 'You're usually very choosy about visitors, and hostile to those who come uninvited.'

'I will answer that when you tell me where you disappeared to after you obtained this p-prador. I have the data now on the attempt to destroy Crane, further data on your presence there, and that of three destroyed p-prador. Then it seems you disappeared, along with one of those, during the time Straeger seized the other two.'

'Time travel,' Cormac replied. 'When I tried to jump the thing to another location, I was dragged into a probable future.'

'Now I'm wondering if I should be here,' said Andre.

Cormac glanced at him. 'Only now?'

Andre grimaced and turned away.

'What happened in that probable future?'

'P-prador were there and started hunting me down. What appeared to be an advanced human assisted me and enabled me to jump back.'

'Temporal tension,' said the AI.

'What do you mean?' Cormac asked, but only because he wanted to hear it from another source.

'A theory, until now. Push something back through time and you set up this tension, which will tend to try to draw the item back to where it belongs. In trying to transport it, you dispersed the energy holding it here and it drew you back to its own time. But it seems it works in reverse too. Your tension or connection to this time drew you back. I would say the help the human gave concerned removing enough of the tension from the p-prador, though I have no idea how that would be done. Anyway, the hypothesis accounts for the evaporation.'

'Evaporation?'

'The p-prador I am still examining has no tension on it. Your attackers do have that tension, however. Those elements of them that arise from the p-prador are evaporating, through tachyon emission, back into the future. Their armour will not last.'

'And yet they have jumped through U-space and not been drawn into the future.'

'Indeed. This adds credence to it being Straeger who made them. Obviously that AI has more knowledge of matters temporal than usual.'

This raised a whole slew of implications, many of which were not clear to Cormac. Since Hune was talking, and more than usual, he decided to push on while his back brain processed this information.

'Now tell me why you allowed Matheson and the Brices to come here.'

Another pause ensued. That concerned Cormac, because this wasn't a human mulling over his words, but an AI thinking. A few seconds of thought for such an entity was equivalent to thousands of hours for a standard human, and hundreds of hours for him.

'Do you know why Earth Central changed the orders on you?' Hune finally asked.

'No, I do not.'

'It was the application of a consensus decision. A majority of high-level AIs decided that understanding how you manage to do what you do – not needing physical protections from the effects of U-space – was more important than eliminating any danger you represented.'

'I see.'

'As with other AIs, this is of interest to me too. Had I activated my weapons systems to eject or destroy those interlopers, I would have lost the opportunity to see you using your ability.'

'And seeing me die at the same time.'

'Contraindicated. I assessed these attackers upon their arrival and calculated, taking into account your abilities, an above sixty per cent likelihood of their failure.'

'Well, that's a bit cold,' Andre interjected.

Cormac nodded agreement, but also understood that the man didn't have his comprehension of how AIs actually operated.

Hune continued, 'But the fact they were likely to fail puts into question your hypothesis concerning Straeger's motivations. I can see now that Straeger inserted itself into the mission to capture Blite to facilitate the mission's failure, thus leaving the man free as bait for you, and giving it further chances to get to you. However, why send these killers against you, knowing their likelihood of failure?'

Hune had just made a large hole in Cormac's reasoning, and he thought hard about that. His first intervention concerning Blite had been during the man's extended interrogation, and Straeger would have learned of that . . . The new data clicked home.

'Straeger's initial aim was to kill me. But after gathering data on Blite following my intervention to have him released, the AI learned something, and his aim then changed.'

'That black crystal, the dark diamond,' said Hune.

The data reshaped and firmed home even deeper, and out of it came an epiphany. 'Killing me has almost become a subtext – something he continues his efforts towards but perhaps without much enthusiasm, or perhaps as a data-gathering exercise. Blite has become his main focus now. It was Straeger who made the early attempts on Blite's life to measure the reach of that crystal.'

'That seems plausible,' said Hune. 'One must then speculate on what its objective is now, as one must speculate on other matters, like its surprisingly accurate prediction of your time for arriving here.'

Data reshaping yet again. Hune had realized something and was drip-feeding him. Straeger had taken an interest in the crystal and the temporal events that occurred. It'd made that accurate prediction, as Hune indicated, and it'd managed to alter the armour of these attackers to prevent it being snatched back into the future. A frightening possibility now occurred.

'He can predict the future.'

'Indeed,' Hune replied.

Polity AIs could make predictions based on current data that were highly accurate up to a point, whereupon they dissolved into chaos. Straeger's handling of the technology and its prediction here indicated something beyond that. It seemed likely the AI had access to the temporal continuum which went further than shuffling data. It seemed horribly likely that Straeger was reaching into the realm in which Penny Royal had drawn itself.

Cormac turned to Andre. 'We're out of here. And I've got friends coming to pick me up.'

Matheson

The crowd in Matheson's mind, roaring in languages alien to him, and the weird hilarity giggling up from his depths made it difficult to think, as did the pain and damage that seemed to be the source of amusement. Matheson just lay, clutching his arm stump, even though the pain there was just a microcosm of what was going on in the rest of his body. As soon as the armour was breached, the U-jumps had ripped them up inside. He wondered if it had actually killed Will and Ulnar Brice, because he'd flung them into jumps with their armour split open, on top of them already having suffered detonations in that armour. Sheen would be the least damaged of them, because at least that fucking agent hadn't managed to open her up too.

It had all seemed so easy. They weren't going after some massive armoured Golem with alien technology inside it, but a flesh-and-blood human being. Sure, the guy could U-jump, but all it should have taken to bring him down was a stabbing claw, or the swipe of one of their arm blades, and his guts would have been over the floor. Turned out not to be the case. How the hell could a human being manage to move so quickly, and so accurately? The inevitable ill effects from their jump down to the planetoid had lasted a few seconds, and thereafter Matheson had known he and the Brices were moving faster than the most enhanced mercenary. But the agent had weaved around them like a weasel in a chicken coop. The man had been a fucking ghost right from the start, and then he'd started using his ability in ways Matheson hadn't known was possible. He reviewed how the man had inserted a load-dumping thin gun inside Ulnar, then tossed grenades at them through U-space. The strain of thinking about all this broke his hold on logical thought, however, and he dissolved into the giggling madness.

Time passed. Matheson had some awareness of striking out at a figure looming over him. He sank into nightmares, where he saw an underwater realm across a spectrum beyond human, snipped off one damaged limb with his claw, then side-slipped through U-space into the guts of some vast machine. That was just one logical thread he weaned out of a crazily complex mosaic of narrative and imagery. This, he understood, was how it felt to be insane. And yet, being able to recognize this at such a remove made him realize that sanity was returning. He remembered where he was, abruptly sat upright, and looked around.

His face covering had been opened and he didn't know whether he'd done this or it'd been Ricardo, whom he now remembered as the figure looming over him, and whom he'd sent skidding across the floor into the forward console. The bridge was a mess, in fact it looked as if something had exploded in here. His chair had been ripped over to one side, pulling out all the optics and other connections through the floor. The floor itself was scuffed, ripped up and scattered with debris. Consoles were damaged, and even the screen wall above them dented. But whatever had happened in here, he'd missed it. He could feel something in his neck and, looking down, saw a transparent tube. It was blue with the liquid inhibitor Ricardo had given them with that first meal, and ran up from a pressure injector vessel attached to his chest. He inspected his arm stump and saw that the metal had closed across it. As he'd ascertained from the beginning, the armour healed itself. Would he grow a new arm? Or would the Spatterjay virus now choose a claw, or a tentacle for him? The prospect drove out a snort of laughter as he looked to the Brices.

Sheen lay with her back against the console opposite. Her face covering had been opened up too, and she looked surprisingly human, apart from certain characteristics that were decidedly ophidapt. She too had one of the inhibitor vessels in place. He transferred his attention to the other figure here and didn't know whether it was Ulnar or Will. This one had solid manacles binding his wrists together behind his back – ceramal at least half a metre thick. Similar manacles were around his ankles, with a short thick bar running between manacles to hog-tie him. His face covering wasn't open, and Matheson felt thankful for that. Instead, two of the inhibitor pressure vessels were attached to the bar joining his manacles, while two tubes ran to separate plugs in his torso.

He was writhing slowly but strongly and had already ground up some composite from the floor.

Matheson stood up and started allowing his connection to the Brices to open. The first response came from Sheen, who turned her head towards him and said quite succinctly, 'We're in the wabe.'

He understood her better than he had before and replied, 'Some of us are in it more than others.' As he mentally focused on the other two, he was careful to wean out telemetry – he didn't have the strength yet to face what they'd become inside their armour.

The one on the floor here was Will – he at least recognized that now – and his com was cycling gibberish. Though Sheen had fallen into some similar cycle that only allowed her to use the words of the ancient rhyme, he understood some of her meaning. He was getting nothing at all from Will, who'd sunk utterly into madness. However, the manacles and the doubled-up dose of inhibitor seemed to indicate there might be a possible return to sanity. This was more than could've been hoped for if he was still the man he'd once been. A grenade detonating in his armour, no matter his boosting, would have killed him instantly.

We are no longer men, replied a tittering voice from fading madness. Matheson raised his remaining hand to his face and tracked over it, finding the same animalistic change as before, then lowered it and looked around. Where was Ulnar Brice? He put down a hand and heaved himself to his feet, feeling lines of division shifting inside him, as if his body was made of fractured jelly. His connection with Ulnar didn't give him much more than the kind of madness coming from Will, but the fact he was getting something at least meant the man was aboard. He tried pushing out his U-sense, but found it causing a pain that ran from his skull to the base of his spine, before it fractured into chaos. He staggered over to the door and out, now realizing, probably from brief flashes through his U-sense, that Ulnar Brice was down below. Reaching the stairs, he headed down carefully, like an arthritic old man, and noted damage to the stairs all the way down.

At each level he paused, pushing with his gridlink and still sensing Ulnar below, then continued on down. As he entered the hold area, he just knew where he'd find the man and had some sense of why.

'It was the best I could do,' said Ricardo.

The man-Golem squatted back against the wall with an array of tools laid out before him. Ricardo was repairing syntheskin and flesh shredded all over his ceramal skeleton. The presence of a welder beside him indicated he'd also needed to repair his ceramal bones. Matheson now also recognized debris he'd seen up in the bridge as pieces of Ricardo. It was as if there'd been a cat fight up there, but between massive cyber-enhanced cats. Ricardo looked up, the lower fleshy covering of his face missing and white teeth exposed. This was his penalty for securing Will up above, then dragging Ulnar down here.

Ulnar Brice lay in the clamp with his feet, head and left hand protruding. He'd been partially flattened, but that didn't stop his fingers wiggling and ellipsoid head swinging around on its unusually long neck to focus on him. Matheson moved closer, but with as much caution as when he'd secured Ricardo in this same clamp. His sense of connection with the Brices was much as it had been via their augs, and now he finally opened it up fully to physical telemetry, giving him a clear image of the figure before him. Ulnar had legs that were longer than arms, which had hands on them, a torso, and a head on the end of a neck, but this was the limit of his human characteristics. It was as if only the armour had retained some semblance of a human shape, while a variety of life forms had been roughly chopped through a machine then fed inside it.

413

'Why no inhibitor for him?' Matheson asked.

'I'm not sure it'll make any difference. Nor with Will either.' Ricardo pointed upwards with one skinned finger.

'Do it anyway.'

There was no hesitation and no argument. The moment Matheson said the words, Ricardo abandoned his tools, leaped to his feet and headed out of the hold. Matheson watched him go, then turned back to Ulnar. The telemetry and internal scanning gave him what he could presently see inside the armour, but he knew that wasn't ideal. He tried once more to engage his U-sense and again experienced the pain. But a recorded flash, interpreted through his gridlink, revealed more clearly what lay inside it. Though much distorted, a human skeleton was still there. It seemed to consist of fractured chunks of chitin, as if someone had run insects through that chopping machine, then formed the resultant mess he could see now. Muscles and long clumps of fibres were wrapped around this in some areas, while organs seemed to be scattered haphazardly – Matheson felt sure that what he saw in the nominal calf muscles were kidneys. Where vertebrae should be, he saw a chain of spheres like a pearl necklace. The head was simply a miniature version of those creatures Straeger had made their armour out of, including claws and legs folded underneath. Running down the body were folded insect limbs, coiled tentacles and what looked like collapsed wings. In all, Ulnar resembled a chrysalis, with its contents some way away from completing their metamorphosis.

Ricardo returned with four pressure injection vessels and reels of pipe. He went straight over to Ulnar and used a gun-shaped punch laser to make holes in his armour. Inserting socket sleeves to keep the holes open, he pushed wide-bore needles through them and into Ulnar, before attaching up the rest. Soon the pressure vessels were all lying on the top clamp, feeding through the blue inhibitor. It was evident Ulnar didn't like this, because his struggles increased.

'Why don't you think it will make any difference?' Matheson asked.

Ricardo turned to face him. 'The inhibitors prevent the virus delving into its genome collection, to make survival changes to a damaged primary organism. This allows the organism to heal in its original form. But Ulnar Brice was turned into soup inside his armour, and by the time you got him back here many changes had already occurred. It had become debatable what was the primary organism.'

'I see. And Will?'

'Greater point damage – the grenade blast incinerated most of his torso. Beyond that, much more of him remained intact. There's maybe a chance we'll get him back.'

Matheson nodded, staring at Ricardo. The man-Golem really wasn't the same. He didn't argue or discuss or negotiate, just obeyed instantly.

'So what did Straeger do to you?' he finally asked.

'The AI loaded a huge database on what you and the Brices have become, so I am more able to support you. When I'm not assisting, or otherwise conducting the business of this ship, I am forced to live through many painful episodes of my life. The AI has also permanently connected in my syntheflesh a nervous system, including pain response. It is educational.'

'Right now?'

'Right now I am in agony.'

That Ricardo wasn't curled up on the floor and bawling indicated something else too, as did his immediate response to fetch that inhibitor at Matheson's behest.

'Go and stand there.' Matheson pointed to an area of the floor

415

and Ricardo moved over there straight away. 'Now do a handstand and hold it.'

Ricardo stooped down and immediately went into a stable handstand, then just stayed there. So this was it. Straeger had made the man-Golem into an obedient useful tool, while also ensuring he'd suffer to the maximum. Matheson imagined being in the agony he'd once experienced when a laser carbine had melted in his hands, and then being compelled to use those hands to, say, disassemble and do the maintenance check on a similar carbine. Was this really educational? Or had Ricardo persuaded himself of that to retain some sanity? Matheson was in no doubt that if the man-Golem lost his mind, his function here aboard would remain the same. Similarly with Matheson and the Brices: they might end up raving lunatics, but they would still obey Straeger's orders . . . or would they? It occurred to him that in pulling himself and the Brices away from Cormac, he'd disobeyed. He'd routed around the order to kill the agent because at that point they couldn't achieve it – a tactical retreat in essence, but still . . .

'That's enough – stand normally.'

Ricardo came back to standing, chunks of syntheflesh and skin hanging loose. Matheson had wanted some vengeance on this man-Golem, but now that had all gone away. He pointed to the tools Ricardo had been using before.

'Continue to repair yourself,' he said, turned, and left the hold.

May

The other ship was waiting for them as the *Bracken* surfaced from U-space in the dark between stars. May studied the screen image of a scrappy-looking cylindrical vessel that was an upgrade from a wartime weapons delivery system. It was one of those things the Polity had dropped in the path of the prador, packed with missiles and ready to release them all at once upon recognizing the enemy. It was no surprise to see such remnants still around. The sheer quantity of them scattered across space made them easily accessible, while their meta-material hulls, which reflected or converted cosmic radiations and were resistant to a variety of onslaughts including weapons fire, made converting them into ships a lot easier than a new build.

'Who are you?' asked the disreputable-looking character peering out of a screen frame at her.

'I'm May,' she replied, wondering what the hell Cormac had been up to in his absence to end up out here and in such company.

'I'm Andre,' he said.

'Nice to meet you.'

'Big-fuck and familiar-looking hauler you've got there,' he commented.

'Penny Transport,' she allowed.

'Yeah, I know.' The man turned and looked behind, then reached up and rubbed at his aug. It seemed this was a conversation he wasn't much interested in.

'You have a passenger for me,' she said.

'Yeah, but we won't be needing to dock.'

'And that I know,' she said.

Now he focused on her intently.

'Well, I know it was you who dropped down on Cull, and who the other hunters took off after. How did you escape them? Your ship isn't built for combat.'

May looked over her shoulder. Arach was down in the hold with the item he'd grabbed from Penny Royal's planetoid, while Mr Crane stood in his usual position against the wall, hat tilted down over his eyes as if he might be sleeping.

'My present passengers have resources,' she supplied.

'You've got that Golem aboard.' Andre shook his head. 'You must know by now you're in a shit storm and likely it's going to get worse, leaving you wrecked behind it.'

May sat back. 'I'm generally an optimistic person.'

'Me too,' said Andre, 'but I'm bright enough to know when I'm swimming in a shark tank. Anyway, it's done now. Good luck.'

On the screen his ship had already fired up its fusion drive, doubtless using feedback energy from this to power its U-jump, which initiated just a few seconds after she felt a waft of air across the back of her neck. She shivered and turned around again. Crane had raised his hat brim to look at Cormac as he walked across to sit down in Davidson's chair. The man looked worn, with his clothes hanging loosely on him.

'What happened?' she asked.

A comlink request through her aug arrived and she allowed it. He sent a package she routed for usual safe examination, while wondering if there was any point in doing so. The man was who he was, and if he wanted to fuck her over in some way it wouldn't be via her aug.

'All the detail is there,' he said, 'but in précis: I was dragged into the future, fought p-prador and escaped back to the now. I was later attacked by armoured bounty hunters capable of jumping through U-space like me. I've learned that they were made by the Mobius AI Straeger, who's gone rogue, and as well as wanting to kill me has taken a big interest in time travel.' He watched her for a moment, winced a smile and added, 'You might want to consider what Andre said to you.'

She just stared at him, while trying to process the fact the hunters who'd entered the planetoid and come after Crane must be the same ones who'd gone after Cormac too. She instinctively groped for the package he'd sent to understand more. Imagery and narrative threads dropped into her mind, and though she instantly incorporated some of it, it would take her longer to absorb the rest. She wasn't gridlinked, after all, nor was she a big brass Golem or a spider drone.

'It's a mess,' she finally said, but when she focused on Davidson's chair it was empty, and she next located Cormac in one of the cabins. Had he U-jumped there? No, the system also told her he'd stood up and walked down there, while she'd been trying to sort things out in her skull for over an hour. 'It's a mess,' she repeated to herself, and felt a stab of something that might have been fear or excitement, she couldn't tell.

It seemed the dark diamond, a chunk of Penny Royal, would not allow Blite to die, and looped him back in time to reverse that verdict whenever it occurred. Mutated cybernetic prador from the future had tried to kill both Crane and Blite. But why? A rogue AI, whose initial aim had been to hunt down and kill Cormac, had allowed itself to be distracted by Blite and had also killed him a number of times, or tried to. Or not. It was confusing. This same AI had then turned bounty hunters into something akin to the cybernetic prador and sent them after Crane and then Cormac, but might not be serious about trying to kill them either. May felt the urge to giggle at all this madness, but it dissolved into a growing headache.

'Made a decision yet?' Cormac asked. He was back in Davidson's seat, and another hour had passed.

'About what?'

'About whether you want to continue to be part of this.'

'I was contracted to fly you where you wanted to go.'

'I think we're a bit beyond contracts now, just as your previous crew realized. Don't make excuses for doing what you want to do.'

May nodded and, checking through the data from Cormac again, found the coordinates from what Blite had sent him in his package, pinpointing exactly where he was now heading. She routed them to the ship's mind. Within the system she felt Arach's attention and something of amusement from Crane.

'So we're heading into the Graveyard,' she said; it wasn't a question.

Straeger

Straeger's nine-dimensional model of reality stretched even his mind to breaking point. For this reason he compartmentalized it, and only referenced it when his need became as great as it was now. He looked at mainline time, or the series of events of the highest probability, which speared along on the peak of a wave, while lower-probability futures, diverging at every instant, ran down the slopes from that. All futures and all pasts existed. They then converged at the end of time in the Omega Point and ran around their circuit from there to the beginning of it all. A mind, understanding this even on the superficial level, could collapse under the load of terms like fate and predestination. Straeger tried not to be such a mind, ever since encountering Blite and somewhat understanding Penny Royal.

But it still stretched conventional AI processing even to begin to understand what that black AI had done. It had managed to insert itself into the circuit by entering a black hole – one the AIs had been studying for a long time because, by its nature, it could not exist. In fact, as far as they could now gather, it only existed because Penny Royal had gone through it. And now the version of Penny Royal that existed would always exist, and *had* always existed. This was a conceptual landscape that would be understood mathematically, but stepping beyond the equations it became a slippery thing. To Straeger it showed that escape was possible. It demonstrated that time travel did not mean a steady slide down the probability slope into oblivion of utter predestination, as the energy demands of that travel increased to infinity. It meant he could *do things anywhen in time*, which of course excited the entangled part of his being. But how did one ascend to such mastery? The question had not greatly concerned Straeger when his main objective had been so prosaic: ending the life of a particularly slippery agent. But that same agent had brought him into contact with Blite and opened out huge horizons of speculation – and confusion.

With the aim of gathering more information on the man to bring about his demise, Straeger had reviewed Cormac's visit to the black site where Blite had been imprisoned. He had concentrated on a holistic integration of recorded data. Since no AI had yet figured out how Cormac managed to jump intact through U-space, he'd decided to look beyond just local recordings and incorporate the stuff other AIs had considered irrelevant, expanding his capacity to do so. Frustratingly, once again, this revealed little of value. Since he also had little to indicate where Cormac had gone, he'd tracked back to Blite's arrival at the site to see if some previous visit by the agent had been missed.

His wider holistic search began to pick up oddities. Shortly after Blite had been delivered, there'd been a temperature drop in the base. It seemed to be nothing, and had only lasted for a few minutes, but disturbingly Straeger could find no explanation for it *at all*. He spent hours of AI time investigating this, which translated as human lifetimes, and even when he extended the data parentheses out to encompass the entire moon it revealed nothing further. He stubbornly persisted, widening the search even more, still sure he must be missing something in the base.

Surprisingly he found correlations. There had been a minor perturbation in the orbit of the moon, an uptick in sunspot activity, a dip in the output of satellite fusion reactors. All of these indicated an entropic event – a *temporal* event. Straeger was stunned, for all of the nanosecond it took him to make the connection. Of course – Blite was being interrogated precisely because of his involvement with an AI who'd been fucking about with causality: Penny Royal.

This brought his attention back to the facility. The focal point had to be Blite, and the best data on him lay in the interrogations. Straeger incorporated them all into his consciousness at once, and they were like a bomb going off in his mind. Yes, he'd known the whole story of Penny Royal, but it had been like a monochrome image amid many in his mind and irrelevant to his driving daemon, to the entanglement within. Now this image exploded into a full EMR spectrum virtuality, which began to take on more dimensions than the three of space and the fourth of time. He felt, in that moment, as though he'd been a limited being, with the narrow focus of a vengeful human. He in fact reflected what most viewed as the still-living ancestors of AIs in his post-humanity, and that annoyed the more rational parts of his being intensely. He needed to shrug it off and break away from it, and perhaps by thinking this way he already was. Yet it was a double-edged sword, because this daemon from entanglement gave him purpose, while the quest for rationality suppressed it.

Concentrating on the anomalies he'd thus far gathered, he saw they all occurred during Carnusine's first encounter with, and interrogation of Blite. This AI had been as meticulous as Straeger in its collection and examination of data, even to the point of keeping a record of its own reactions. Searching for anomalies in the record, Straeger discovered the AI had lost power for a period that was seconds long, and could find no way of tracing the drain. It was inconsequential, of course, and did not relate at all to the interrogation of Blite . . . Straeger absorbed that reaction with extreme suspicion and focused on the moment itself.

'Before we get started, is there anything you would like to share with me?' Carnusine had asked. A second after that came the power loss, the cooling of the base, the orbital perturbation and the changes in the sun's chromosphere that later led to a rash of sunspots.

'Nothing at all,' Blite had replied woodenly.

Liar, thought Straeger.

It took weeks of searching the period after Blite's release, when the man began ticking off things on his bucket list, before Straeger found it. Fortunately, with Blite being on a watchlist because of his involvement with the black AI, his interactions weren't as private as he would have liked. Such examination of a person's life beyond an interrogation room was supposedly illegal in the Polity but, as Straeger well knew, illegal was what the ruling AIs decided it to be in the moment. Blite had been intent on luring a woman to his hotel room for the traditional human exchange of bodily fluids. They'd been chatting in a bar and the exchange recorded. She had asked him about the curious pendant he wore.

'It's a piece of Penny Royal,' Blite had replied nonchalantly.

She'd laughed at this, of course. Straeger wasn't so amused as he analysed a large swathe of data. Blite had never worn such a pendant before the events around the Layden's Sink black hole, and in fact hadn't been inclined to any ornament. But he'd worn it afterwards, and even had it on while under interrogation. Analysis of his belongings at the black site had been dismissive of it. They saw it as a vaguely interesting carbon crystal, a black diamond probably fashioned in a gravity press and of no consequence.

Straeger, however, felt sure Carnusine would have focused a lot more attention had Blite claimed it to be a piece of Penny Royal – the thing would have been disassembled and catalogued down to the nanoscopic level. Lower-level assessment of what he'd said to the woman was that he'd simply been using his history and reputation to get laid.

Extrapolating, Straeger became utterly sure of something. If Blite had had a piece of Penny Royal on him when taken to the black site, he would have known he had no way of hiding it. It would have been precisely the thing he'd mention in reply to Carnusine's first question, when the temporal event occurred. Straeger ran models on what had likely happened and came to a very definite conclusion: that black carbon crystal was exactly what Blite claimed it to be, and it had fucked with causality. The man *had* told Carnusine about it, but the thing had rolled back time, perhaps many times, until Blite didn't mention it, thereafter somehow preventing scans from revealing its true nature. It was therefore time to see what else it could do, how closely bound to Blite it was, and whether it could be taken away. And it had been in that moment Straeger made the not entirely rational decision to kill Blite.

The first attempt had been a light confluence of events. Straeger predicted Blite's path over a few days, even down to the mundane details of the man's life, like what he would eat and drink – though beyond that, the granularity of prediction on such a small scale became wildly inaccurate. Putting something dangerous in his path was easy to do. Setting up the dense-tech scanners of U-space, and all physical phenomena, was much harder, since Blite was on a Polity world and Straeger didn't want other AIs to know he was now going his own way. It had become Blite's habit over the previous week to buy a sandwich from a particular stall. The poison concealed in this could be traced through a series of unlikely 'accidents', its genesis being in a meat-processing plant. But on that day, Blite never ate it – someone bumped into him, knocking it out of his hand to the ground, where someone else accidentally stood on it. Nothing that happened could be seen as unusual. But for Straeger, intimately linked through his equipment, it was like a flashbulb going off in a darkened room.

The intricate twist in U-space formed back through time and into the future. It revealed diversions in mainline time, nexuses where probability became mutable, and the hint of a loop going back ten years before that point. He had discovered something incredibly strange, but also hugely advantageous. That loop might be a route into the past and, understanding it, could be his way into the apotheosis of Penny Royal. As his further attempts to kill Blite revealed more of the future landscape, and drew the attention of Agent Cormac back to Blite, the need for vengeance again rose out of entanglement. And Straeger also realized that in achieving it, he might finally shrug off his past. Perhaps he could collapse the wave form of his mind and come out the other side as something . . . numinous.

16

Cormac

The device had been there in his thoughts, even as he secured the coordinates of the *Bracken* and pondered how best to make his transference to the ship as smooth as possible – deciding whether to put himself in one of the cabins or straight on the bridge. It had been a hole in his calculations, and one into which he could drop. Yet, in the usual contradictory perception of reality via U-space, it had impenetrable density. It didn't possess the dangerous draw of a runcible, which could have snapped him up in an instant and shunted him to somewhere he'd be lost for ever. Nor did it have the riskiness of a U-space engine, which he tended to keep as far distant from his arrival points as possible. Yet it did have an effect. In his perception of the U-continuum, it was an odd twist that hinted at new mathematics, and where his calculations seemed to circle some maelstrom into oblivion. It made his head ache. And beyond these practical considerations, of one thing he was utterly sure: the thing made his skin crawl.

'*What the fuck have you done?*' he'd asked via his gridlink when he arrived on the bridge, throwing the question out into the ether for both Arach and Crane, as he turned his human attention to May.

'*It's an edge,*' Arach had replied.

'*Detail,*' Cormac had demanded. But instead of Arach filling him in on it, the spider drone had routed him to another connection. On the bridge, he'd glanced around at Mr Crane, standing there as opaque as ever, and got no response through that connection.

Now they were underway on their journey to the Graveyard and May, after absorbing his narrative from information packets, had gone to her cabin with mental indigestion. It was time for some answers from the others. A large airlock opened into the hold, since this was one for moving supplies and components into the ship. He paused by it with his U-sense expanded out, viewing the item within.

'What did you tell her?' he asked of Arach, who was heading his way from the engineering section.

'That I brought it in to counteract any Penny Royal nanotech that might have got aboard.'

'And she believed that?'

Arach arrived with a clattering of feet in the corridor and slowed down to approach. 'I'm not sure she did, but she didn't know what questions to ask, and has just been going with the flow of this *adventure*.'

'It never occurred to her that a huge chunk of Penny Royal tech might be more dangerous than a few nanomachines wafting in?'

'Yeah, maybe a little bit.'

'At some point she's going to realize how much of a bullshitter you are, Arach,' Cormac replied, gridlinking to the airlock and overriding the lock May had imposed on it.

The door thumped up on its seals, and he pulled it open towards him. Without closing it behind, he opened the next door and stepped into the hold. Arach hadn't been completely untruthful about the dangers of nanotech in the planetoid, and certainly some salvager ships had been lost because of it. However, both the drone and Crane were perfectly capable of dealing with any of that, without requiring whatever this was. He stepped forwards and studied the thing as Arach squeezed through the lock behind him.

The silvery lump stretched a metre across at its widest point. It looked like a neuron, which was how May had described it when he'd gently probed her on the subject. Reviewing imagery taken from the ship's system, Cormac saw that Arach had dumped the thing in the middle of the hold, but it had moved since then. It now lay in one corner. It had absorbed the many pipes and power feeds that'd been around its surface, and the silvery substance had grown out tendrils, seemingly to hold it in place. Opening his U-sense to the thing, he tried to study more of this to confirm a suspicion, but then immediately snapped shut that sense when he felt himself falling in a well of chaos.

'Fuck,' he said, and instead gridlinked into the ship's system to take a look that way. It didn't take long to confirm his suspicion.

The tendrils had rooted the thing in place, sure, but beyond those anchor points they'd continued to spread, seemingly embedded halfway into the floor, walls and at one point the ceiling. Internal cam imagery from inspection robots revealed the tendrils had penetrated the material and continued growing. Some had reached s-con power threads, bulked up at that point, and formed bulbous connections. Others had attached to fluid pipes and increased in girth, so were obviously raiding that resource too.

'What were you thinking?' Cormac said.

'I bowed to Crane's superior knowledge,' Arach replied.

'And his explanation?'

'Take the item. It will be useful.'

'Talkative, was he?' Cormac asked sarcastically.

'Well, no, that was my translation from a prador glyph he sent me after giving coordinates.'

'It's not just May who's going with the flow, then.'

Arach dipped his fore section, as if a little ashamed. 'Crane knows something about all this he either won't or cannot explain. He also has his own problem with the Jain tech inside him, and somehow it's all related.'

'And that's enough for you?'

'It is, but is it enough for *you*?'

This stilled Cormac and he realized it wasn't something he had to calculate. Crane was lethal, yet, despite the disparaging thoughts he had about the Golem, he trusted him in ways that went beyond anything he could hope for from a human being. It was enough, and all this debate was going nowhere. While trusting Crane, he also needed to account properly for and assess this thing. Unless the Golem suddenly became chatty, he'd have to use his own powers of analysis for that. He stepped back – an instinctive move, really – and gradually opened up his U-sense. It hurt, and made his eyes water, as he tried to balance his perception of the ship all around, enclosed in its U-field, alongside the gaping hole right here at its centre.

The thing became a maelstrom in his perception, revolving in both directions at once, but also a cone of something, spearing up into infinity. The imagery kept on changing as his gridlink offered up further interpretations. He ramped up processing as he began to draw his reach back from the rest of the ship and focus primarily on this thing. Gradually it stilled in his mind and changed shape, until it finally coagulated into a static tornado standing before him. And then, as they say, the penny dropped. He checked in again on the ship's system, focusing on the power lines the thing had connected to. It wasn't drawing power, but actually feeding power in.

'Damn!' he exclaimed. 'It's generating a U-twist.'

This was something he'd only learned about after Penny Royal had dropped into Layden's Sink black hole. Pure energy could be routed into U-space, where it would twist a chunk of that continuum. And since U-space didn't have the dimensionality of the real, such a twist was a potentially infinite store of that energy. In simple terms, it was like putting tension on a spring. That was the theory but, as far as he knew, Polity AIs had yet to build anything actually workable.

'That's interesting,' said Arach, voice utterly flat.

Cormac blinked and looked at the drone. Of course, there was no expression to read, but he surmised this wasn't news to Arach.

'There's something else about it too,' Cormac added.

The clarified perception his gridlink provided had, he now realized, done so by eliminating much else. There seemed to be folds around the twist, a complexity of surfaces and tube connections that made a Klein bottle seem simplistic. It all felt just out of his grasp – just on the edge of what his gridlink could interpret, and what his mind could understand. He needed more data, and to that end, almost without volition, he stepped forwards, putting his hand down on the thing.

It felt soft, fleshy and warm. For a second, he wondered why he'd done this, and what he expected to glean from it, then the world expanded explosively around him. His U-sense, independent of his will, encompassed the ship, then leaped beyond its U-field, which had always been a difficult thing for him to do, and spread on outwards. The vastness and the singularity of that continuum opened for him, while his gridlink went to its processing limit as it tried to interpret it all. A whickering whining sound filled his skull, and in flashes he gained perception of the entire galaxy. He managed to focus down on detail and could incorporate star systems, realizing he could calculate U-jumps on their basis. Then he noticed something located along the course they were flying, there on the border of the Graveyard. His gridlink struggled to interpret the tangled and knotted U-space he'd seen before, around Blite. But the whole input was too much and his head felt about to explode. His gridlink then started throwing up error messages and options to deal with them. Drowning in data, he grabbed at one that started shutting down processing. Vastness collapsed down, star systems falling past him, to the ship they were on, and to him, but now something had changed.

He wasn't in the ship – he was no longer in its bubble of the real. U-space coiled and slithered around him, but also occupied an infinitesimal point at the centre of his being. He could feel it tearing at his mind, as it once had before he acquired his abilities, and he forced translation again. He then found himself floating in a vast cavern which disappeared to a vanishing point. Physical awareness impinged with a trickle of blood from his ears and pain throughout his body, as if he'd taken the brunt of a real explosion, while alerts from his nanosuite scrolled in his link almost subliminally. He gazed upon shapes traversing from wall to wall, and they resolved into urchins of black crystal, sprouting from the walls on silver stems before launching. If this image wasn't strange enough, there was a sense of deep avuncular amusement, combined with insane hilarity, at him, at Mr Crane's puzzlement alone in a planetoid, at temporal loops pinching out, and at the whole sprawl of eternity. This came as confirmation – he knew where he was.

He was *in* Penny Royal.

It was too much. He felt right on the edge of physical and mental overload, and ready to crisp and char away into a wisp of smoke. Yet something here still anchored him, and it was a sound that was penetrating the overload, while part of it too. The whickering whining drew closer, coming towards him from that vanishing point. He recognized it, and he knew it to be no fever dream. He held out his arm, with his wrist holster exposed, as Shuriken came into sight both close and infinitely distant. Its chain-glass blades were out, glinting orange along their edges. He yearned for it, but felt paths of causation closing on him and knew the weapon was bringing his death to him. Then, with a snapping sound, it all fell away.

Cormac lay sprawled on the floor, his wrist closed in a huge brassy hand. His body felt soggy, boneless and broken. Despite his nanosuite shutting down nerves, a wave of pain and nausea overrode it. He turned his head and vomited bile and blood in a lurid mix. He tried to understand what had happened, but only the alerts from his nanosuite were running in his gridlink.

'I nearly . . . had it,' he managed, looking up into black eyes that seemed windows out into the real universe.

'You would have died,' Crane replied.

Crane hauled him up by his wrist and the waves of pain choked off anything further. The Golem tucked him under one arm and strode out of the hold. Cormac lost it for a while, until finding himself sprawled on a surgical table, and May talking in the background. He couldn't quite make out the words, and he couldn't see her past Arach, who was working on him busily. The feel of shunts going into his veins he recognized, as he did the nerve blocker going into his neck, and for which he felt overwhelming gratitude. Yet this only numbed him below the neck, and he still felt Arach trepanning out a piece of his skull, and saw the interface the drone inserted.

'What happened? What the hell happened?'

May's words now at last made sense.

'Infinity,' was Crane's terse reply.

Straeger

The information package, inserted into the AI net and bounced from location to location while shedding the address of its source, arrived like a hammer blow. His agent in Blite's crew had contacted him. Straeger absorbed the message easily and saw a high probability of the future he wanted being derailed. In fact the probabilities had dropped to the bottom of their previous range even before the package arrived. Immediately putting his current in-ship project on hold, he threw the *Claw* into a U-space jump.

Pretending not to know something when you knew it was almost the same as accepting the binary outcomes from a point of existence *at the same time*. He constantly had to accept that all outcomes existed of his predictions from the present. It was Schrodinger's cat in its box being neither dead nor alive in its probability space. Even with his AI ability to think outside linear time, Straeger still struggled with this. The flashes revealing the timescape of the future had not made his decisions on how to act any easier. Despite the fact he was able to see more of the surface reality of the future related to these U-space phenomena, he couldn't know where to intervene in his present for optimum results, or where he *would* intervene. However, in this particular present, pragmatic reality drove his decision to intervene. He didn't want other AIs to know what he knew, or to have what he had.

The earlier flashes of insight generated by his attempts on Blite's life had revealed future nodes in the timescape, where further flashes would be generated. When Straeger had sent the assassin against Blite on Mars, and then another one in New York, he hadn't known whether it was he, or some other event or killer, that would threaten Blite's life. The flashes from these two events revealed other future nodes which in turn acted as guides to clarifying the future in the real. Unfortunately, Earth Central began to notice the entropic and temporal disruptions, and this had brought Cormac to Blite's aid. Fearing his access to the future might be closing down, Straeger had initiated a major event to generate a larger flash, so as to see more of the timescape. He supposed that his killing of a runcible AI on Callanasta had been the moment when he truly went rogue.

And now it looked as if he'd have to kill another high-level AI who seemed to know too much.

After the runcible 'disaster', the future had opened out to him in a patchwork of glimpses with varying probability. And then, with its echoes through U-space, Straeger's perception of it all had expanded beyond mere glimpses. He began to see it as a continuum, changing as events in the present impinged on the future. The timescape also revealed further nodes that weren't temporal events. Yet, as with all such nodes, they were points where the course of time could drastically diverge. Straeger had gleaned that a temporal event would occur on the planet Cull, so noting this to be the home of Mr Crane, Straeger had distributed his sensors in the most likely location there. The high probability that the brass Golem would be involved in such an event would surely draw in Cormac too. There Straeger would have a chance to kill the man, though this would be just a pleasant side dish to the main one: the chance to gather further information on the timescape. But nearer to the present, he saw another node problem. ECS had mobilized against Blite and were out to capture him again. Straeger couldn't allow this – Blite was present and would be integral in a major future node that could potentially generate a flash to open up vast swathes of the timescape even larger than before. ECS had to be stopped.

And so it went.

Cormac's intervention at Penny Transport to allow Blite to escape had demonstrated something to Straeger: his own intervention to do the same had been unnecessary, because the nodes beyond that event had remained within a good probability range. The clarifying flash created by the p-prador's appearance had revealed Cormac's return from the future later, with an above ninety per cent probability he'd take the missing p-prador corpse to Hune for examination. The intent of the future p-prador, with their attacks on Blite and Crane, was clarifying too. It related to that huge future node, because both Crane and Blite were involved there and the p-prador wanted to stop them. So too was Cormac, and perhaps Straeger's intent to kill him at once should be downgraded to not yet.

As the *Claw* hammered through U-space fast, and without the protections an organic crew would require, Straeger began making preparations. He pulled back sub-AIs, materials and distributed weapons into his main form, expanding himself as he had done before seizing the p-prador which were now in pieces throughout his ship. His sense of urgency grew during the flight. He'd entered a predicted temporal node that had seemed like a simple turning in a road, but had now transformed into a great tangled junction. Beyond it, probabilities were all over the place.

No, Straeger could not allow this. The AI had to die.

Blite

'We're not going aboard that fucking ship!' Blite exclaimed.

On previous occasions, the pages in the catalogue of his deaths had lost much of their emotional weight as he turned them, over and over. He had no doubt Penny Royal had designed things like this not out of any particular concern for his suffering, but to ensure he remained functional, for whatever purpose that entity had in gifting the dark diamond to him. But now the emotional content and harsh memory of pain and obliteration were coming through harder. It was as if this particular constantly repeating episode of his life had become an infected wound which wouldn't drain properly any more.

He'd delayed things for as long as he could this time, the time loop stretching back to when the *Marble* knocked them out of U-space. He'd ordered them to run on the Laumer. This had given them an extra hour until the snatch ship simply snuffed out the drive with a vortex interdiction beam. But now they were back to the scenario that had played out many times.

'I don't think we have much choice in the matter,' Carlstone replied.

The way the precognition had arrived the first time was weird. Until he started putting on his vacuum combat suit in his cabin, he'd been simply responding as best he could to the circumstances presented. When he started to worry about how things would go in the snatch ship, it seemed only natural. But then when he began to play out scenarios in his skull of what would happen, he realized with a feeling of dread that he *remembered* the interior of that ship, and dying. Once in there, the particle beam inciner-ated him many times before he changed that course sufficiently. As his deaths stacked up, memory returned more quickly each time. On numerous occasions they'd tried to escape by destroying the clamping arms, only for the *Coin* to end up crushed and leaking air, then spider grabs tearing through inside to seize just him. His ship had then been discarded, before becoming the target of an imploder. He'd lost track of the number of times he'd died, and seen his fellows die, and he damned Penny Royal for making this nightmare possible. With the time loop expanding and his horror growing, he wondered how many more deaths he must experience before the loop went back to a point where he could stop them encountering the *Marble* at all.

'I have choices and I've been making them again and again.' Blite looked around at his crew. He'd told most of them what the gem did, and he'd told them why they had to run from the *Marble*, but they still looked on in bafflement. In the last hour he'd tried to explain the sheer breadth of it all, and have them respond as if they believed him. But of course, every time was the first time for them. Even Carlstone and Iris didn't seem to grasp what he was saying, even though they knew about the diamond from previous occasions . . .

'Judice,' he said to the Golem woman, 'on my mark target the bases of all those arms. Use all weapons all at once.' He turned to Breil. 'I want you back-loading all beam weapons with informational warfare – everything we have.'

'That's going to further irritate this Marble,' Carlstone noted.

'It can't do any worse to us than intended,' Blite replied, then turned to the haiman woman. 'Iris, assist Breil, since you have a great deal more warfare tech inside you than I knew about before.'

'And of course you know that now,' Iris said flatly, her eyes metallic.

'Yes, because this was the only way we managed to break away on the other occasions we did.'

Iris acknowledged this with a simple nod, and it gladdened him to know that she seemed to have no reservations, unlike Carlstone. Blite berated himself for the thought. Carlstone might be finding it hard to accept the idea of his boss flipping back into the past every time he died, but the man did have belief in him. They all did. There was just a fractional delay before they obeyed his orders.

'Full all-round view,' he stated, now dropping into his control chair and pulling across safety straps.

The others seated themselves and strapped in quickly. Gruce, whose name Blite hadn't known in this iteration of his death, but did now, slapped Armand on the shoulder and they moved forwards, having summoned up further acceleration chairs from the floor. Blite pressed on his induction aug and this time, with no reluctance at all, dived into it fully, expanding his perception out with the ship's sensors. Meanwhile every surface of the bridge that didn't have necessary instrumentation turned transparent. As if nothing occupied the intervening space, he could see the hull of the snatch ship twenty metres below. Those big hinged grab arms looped overhead, wound through with their thick intestinal cables, which led to spider grabs, also holding on to invisible hull. It was almost as if they floated in some techno-logical forest clearing. Over to his right, he could see the airlock tube extending out from the *Coin* to weave through all of this and plug into the snatch ship. He shuddered at memories of how many times he'd gone down that thing.

'Ship out there,' Judice stated.

'What?' said Blite, staring at her in shock.

She waved a hand to indicate what she was doing mentally, and opened an illusory hole through all the technology locking them in place. Now deeply auged in, Blite understood that what she'd initially brought up actually lay a minute in the past. Stars glittered all around, like spider's eyes focused in on and enjoying the suffering here. The disc flash he saw surprised him, since it was the kind of thing faulty ships generated prior to appearing from U-space turned inside out. As the disc of disrupted quantum foam dispersed, a vessel shot out through the centre of it, just a bright light from his perspective. Judice etched out a frame around the thing with one finger, then pulled it in close.

'Straeger,' said Carlstone tightly.

Blite just nodded mutely. As far as Carlstone knew, and the others, this looked like a bad thing, but for him it was something different occurring in all these nightmare scenarios that had played out too many times in his mind. He found himself trying to figure out how this could be possible, when any changes in how the scenarios played out were usually always his own. Then he realized that, of course, it still was from his influence – the hour delay he'd caused by ordering them to Laumer away imme-diately had allowed for Straeger's arrival.

The screen image juddered, now putting Straeger's claw-shaped ship out ahead of them as it turned on multiple fusion engines to head back in. The explosion wasn't close and not caused by their weapons. The far end cap of the snatch ship became silhou-etted in its glare, with debris spreading out from it. Straeger was attacking the snatch ship. Blite couldn't fathom why but wasn't about to pass up the opportunity.

'Judice, hit those arm bases now – use everything!'

The *Coin* juddered from this distant blast moments before stubby missiles leaped out from its hull. The missiles punched into the snatch ship's hull beside the arm bases and exploded inside. These blasts opened up holes all around them, and one of the arms tilted, sliding along the *Coin*'s hull with a screeching sound that made Blite wince. Rail beaders opened fire next, their sound racketing through the ship, their rounds igniting stars along the tentacle arms. Lasers out there burned surgically. Particle beams lanced out, slicing into hinge points and stabbing at weaknesses the missiles had made around those arm bases.

Blite gazed at all this, and every shot, every element of destruc-tion, echoed in his mind, because he'd seen it before. On those numerous other occasions Marble had let them struggle and fight back for a while, then launched a high-penetration missile from further down its ship, putting it straight in through the back end of the *Coin*. Blite could almost feel on the back of his neck the heat of the fire coming up the corridor. Only one thing had enabled them to escape that, though not for long.

'Paidon,' he said. 'Only on my mark, fire up the Laumer again – full power.'

Maybe, with Straeger attacking, the outcome would be—

'Fucking hell!' said Carlstone. 'What is that?'

Straeger was now coming in low to the hull of the snatch ship, directly towards them, a bright light glaring between the claw and the hull, and a massive cloud of destruction exploding out behind. Judice frame-grabbed it and brought it in close. It revealed the intense beam of a white laser stabbing down and slicing through the snatch ship's hull like a cheese wire.

'Photon-dense laser,' she stated.

Blite noted that the area Straeger had carved through had been where that damned missile usually came from. It was his instinct to give Paidon the order right then, but the last time they'd escaped, at least from the hull of the snatch ship, their damage had been so severe Marble had just carved them up a bit in vacuum, ensuring they had no weapons available, then grabbed them again. That time the AI had sent robots aboard to seize him. He rubbed at his leg, remembering how he'd gone as far as activating what resided in his thigh bone, and how this had only led to him taking longer to die.

'Coming straight at us,' Carlstone noted.

Straeger's laser just kept burning, cutting a trench in the snatch ship hull and, judging by the explosions behind, cutting deep. The trench lined up on them. But Straeger coming here like this to kill them didn't make sense, and Blite connected this to the undeniable fact that the AI had allowed them to escape before, at Abalon.

'Hold,' he said simply.

'Ah, shit,' said Judice.

Blite picked up on it a second later and instinctively ducked as a swarm of missiles passed low overhead. Straeger had fired those missiles. Using his aug, and without turning his head, Blite viewed where they went and saw a series of explosions just out from the snatch ship hull. There were then four larger blasts in the hull, ripping up a chunk of it like a tilting island. It seemed the Mobius had just destroyed missiles Marble had launched, as well as the capability to launch more. Blite couldn't know whether their targets had been the claw ship or the *Coin*.

'Keep cutting the arms!' he ordered, for it seemed Judice had paused.

Further small missiles shot out, and the particle beams did their work. One of the arms fell away into vacuum, like the remains of a crab snapped up by a passing grouper. But still there was a lot holding them down, and even though they were into a scenario he hadn't seen play out before, it seemed likely they would lose a U-space nacelle if Paidon fired up the Laumer at this moment. He decided to trust gut instinct and just waited.

They all focused on the laser now, which looked like death coming towards them. It impressed and humbled him how no one was querying his decision to wait, and only Carlstone had made a suggestion, a tactical one via aug, that they fire up their side thrusters at the last moment. Straeger's ship became clearly visible without magnification as it continued to carve a trench along the snatch ship hull. The appalling amounts of energy involved couldn't possibly come from conventional fusion reactors and laminar storage, no matter how much of it the Mobius had packed into its ship. Maybe some U-space trick, Blite thought, as the bridge flooded with unbearable light.

'Mother of fuck,' said Carlstone.

'Oh, I agree,' said Blite, as they all looked at the burning trenches in the snatch ship, like openings down into Hell, running up along either side of the *Coin*.

Blite hadn't seen the beam finally divide at the last, since he'd closed his eyes. He looked up as the remaining arms and tentacles which had been holding them in place tumbled out into vacuum. He'd been right about Straeger. But what the AI had done didn't engender gratitude or trust, because he knew the Mobius had an agenda. And if killing Blite in some endless loop served that agenda, it would be no more adverse to doing it than Marble was.

'Now, Paidon – Laumer,' he ordered.

'There's a lot of—' she began.

'Just fucking do it.'

The Laumer fired, its blast flame cutting back almost like Straeger's laser. Thrusters fired up too, giving them at least a little clearance from the hull. Despite grav and inertial compensation, the acceleration stamped a boot down on Blite's chest. All around him the acceleration chairs turned to face forwards. The *Coin* shot along above the snatch ship hull, following the continuation of Straeger's trenching, and then diverging on thrusters. Blite grimaced at the sounds of things crashing off their hull, but he received no major alerts in his aug. Ahead, Straeger's ship shunted aside in a way that made no sense, as if it had made an impossibly short U-jump. They wouldn't have hit the claw ship, but he supposed Straeger wasn't keen on sizzling in the backwash of a Laumer drive.

The snatch ship fell away behind them, where it seemed Straeger was still intent on carving it up. Reality twisted in Blite's guts, and he knew Paidon had initiated jump via her aug, since none of them could reach any controls under this acceleration. The immense relief ran through him like a wave, and he felt a prickling in his eyes. He then learned something he hadn't known before: high acceleration also suppressed the ability to shed tears.

Now safe and continuing on their journey to the Graveyard and Yossander's Hold, Blite stomped down one of the corridors of the *Coin*. A thousand deaths played in his mind, somehow, impossibly, seen through a black diamond window in his skull. The moment didn't feel real – in fact he was getting a lot of these irreal moments. In the past, they'd been a sign of psychological damage expressed in people suffering from deep anxiety or depression. He felt them too, despite his nanosuite heavily medicating him, along with the perception that reality was a big joke. It wasn't good, and he knew it was something he'd have to deal with at some point, perhaps with some mental editing. But first things first . . .

He stopped at a door and its lock clicked, popping it slightly open. With a grimace, he pushed it fully open and stepped inside the surgery room. The door hissed back closed behind him.

'All ready?' he asked.

Iris stood with her back to him, working at something on one of the surfaces that ringed the room. She wore tight leggings, yet her very human and attractive arse contrasted starkly with what lay above. Her carapace lay exposed and her cowl was up, concealing her head, while she'd attached subsidiary robotic arms midway down. These were now turned in towards the surface as she worked. Her cowl then closed up into a tongue that protruded up behind her head, revealing her long black hair pinned up around her skull, before it slid down into her carapace. The subsidiary arms drew back, fisting hands with long complex fingers, and folded up against her sides. She turned, reached up and pulled some pins out, shaking her hair. Looking fully human again, she held out something in her right hand.

'All ready,' she said. Her expression looked haunted, which

443

was something he'd never seen from her before. It was almost as if she too had experienced many deaths. But then she broke into a deprecating smile.

Blite shook his head at the chaotic function of his mind and eyed the bracelet she held. The thing was a jointed wrist band with a large setting. The gem would fit in it perfectly. She turned and placed it back on the counter, then gestured ahead to the surgical chair in the middle of the room. Blite turned to it, walked over and sat down, resting back. The headrest deformed slightly under his skull, then clamps closed in to hold it rigidly.

'No autosurgeon?' Blite enquired, noting this device sat immobile against one wall, with all its implements closed up in antiseptic sheaths.

'No need,' Iris replied as she headed over. 'This is a simple procedure.'

Blite grunted an acknowledgement and waited.

The back of the surgical chair dropped down, bringing his head level with her waist. She put a hand down on his forehead, while those subsidiary arms unfolded again. Her cold, almost acquisitive expression gave him a nag of worry as another hand, like a glittering spider, reached over to his skull. Out of the corner of his eye, he saw something protrude. A hiss ensued and the occipital of his skull went numb; he felt without pain the cutting that came after.

'There,' she said, as the spidery hand attached to his head made a sound like someone sucking the dregs of a drink through a straw.

A high whine sounded next, then a liquid thunk. He felt the diamond come out of his skull like a plug, but it also seemed as if a tight grip had slewed away from his mind. He was sure that sensation was simply psychological. He blinked as her human hand came off his skull, and he saw one robot hand withdrawing with the black diamond held between its fingertips, as the other closed in. The sucking sound started up again, followed by the susurration of a deposition welder. This lasted for a short time, to be displaced by a different sound he recognized as that of a cell welder. The hand had replaced missing bone and now it was repairing the softer stuff. The numbness started to fade and he could feel sharply the skin and flesh being folded back into place, with veins and capillaries reconnected and the slices being sealed. When the hand finally retracted, sensation had returned enough for his skull to feel sore and tender.

'That doesn't feel so good,' he said.

'Your nanosuite will deal with it,' Iris replied dismissively.

She was correct: the discomfort began to fade. His suite was now no doubt removing damaged cells, repairing structures the cell and bone welders couldn't manage, and damping down inflammation. If he wanted, he could have kept his aug on to track all this. Still, he noted again how Iris's bedside manner with him was never as kind as it was with others. Finally the clamps released his head, as the back of the chair came forwards again. He turned to look at her.

One robotic hand held up the black diamond, while the other was working around it, cutting through a shell of bone. Once this task was completed, she gave the thing a shake and the debris fell away, leaving the diamond perfectly clean. The remaining hand then tilted and released it, and she snatched the diamond out of the air with her human hand. Holding the thing tight in her fist, she raised the tongue of her cowl and opened out its scanning petals.

'Frictionless still,' she said, her eyes wide, almost shocked.

'That's why it had to be embedded,' Blite replied.

'It seems so innocuous,' she added, yet by her expression this seemed like a lie.

'About as innocuous as a singularity,' Blite replied, sitting up.

Her expression turned contemplative, and now the metal was moving in her eyes as she gazed at her fist.

'I only caught a hint of something from it when I put it in your skull,' she said, 'but I'm getting a lot more now. It's as if the thing has grown stronger.'

Blite took that in. He'd had her do it when she first arrived at Penny Transport, after the first few assassination attempts, as a niggling fear had grown that the diamond might be stolen again, and he would then have no way to evade further attempts and permanent death. Now he wasn't so sure about that. The fact she'd never said anything before about sensing something from the diamond concerned him, but the idea of the thing growing stronger concerned him more. Perhaps this was what accounted for his feeling that it had taken on the characteristics, at least psychologically, of a hot coal lodged in his skull.

'What do you get from it?'

She didn't reply at once, instead turning her hand to snap it open with the gem lying exposed on her palm.

'Some sense of what we often see during U-jumps,' she finally said. 'This is a solid object – in fact you won't find anything much more solid, since it has zero atomic ablation at the surface. But it also seems like a hole in spacetime . . . to somewhere.'

'It seems—' Blite began, but she abruptly released the thing as if it had scalded her, one of her robotic arms snapping around to catch it. As she abruptly turned away, her cowl swiftly closed and retracted into her carapace, as if it too had been burned. He saw her face turn white, and the shock there. Heading almost at a run to the counter, she grabbed the bracelet with her other robotic arm and worked quickly, with her back to him.

'What just happened?' he asked.

'I understand Meander's fear now.' She turned back with the

bracelet, the black diamond now in place in its setting. She flicked it from robotic to human hand, then quickly tossed it over to him.

Blite nearly fumbled the thing.

'You're going to have to explain.' He pulled the bracelet onto his wrist and stood up, heading over to the door. There he paused and watched as Iris removed the robotic arms and placed them on the work surface. She just shook her head, silent, then turned to him, gesturing ahead to the door. They stepped out into the corridor and quickly headed for the bridge. When she said nothing further, he became impatient.

'I'm still waiting for an explanation.'

She shrugged. 'What's to say? It's AI crystal with some small portion of Penny Royal inside it. It connects through U-space to perhaps some further portion of that same entity. I know the theory is that Penny Royal had become good prior to entering the black hole. It just doesn't feel like that.'

'So what does it feel like?'

'It feels like a demon.'

Straeger

Straeger tried to analyse his response rationally, and failed. Another AI had come close to derailing his mapped-out course into the future and the massive time flash there that would provide him with vast knowledge, numinous knowledge, Penny Royal knowledge. It had been utterly necessary to do something about that, and he had. However, the destruction here he had wrought with the relish of righteous anger. How dare another AI interfere like this? How dare another AI trap and experiment upon what Straeger felt was his own property: Blite. The latter was rational but it wasn't solely an emotional response rising out of entanglement either. AIs had not sacrificed emotions to obtain greater rationality – that was an entirely human perception. Rather they had expanded out the emotional spectrum and even added new ones in an effort to understand the universe more clearly. Emotion was another tool in the toolbox – perhaps irrelevant but potentially utile – like all the other tools Straeger had gathered.

The snatch ship hung, bleeding fire, in vacuum, broken at a thirty-degree angle a third of the way along its length. Marble was still trying to talk to him, but had desisted attempting to send a cry for help. The last few had been of diminishing power, as Marble tried to punch them through the disruption caused by the U-space mines Straeger had dropped, after Blite had safely departed. Straeger ignored the other AI as he scanned along the length of the snatch ship.

There.

The photon-dense beam Straeger fired, which had essentially been constructed as a Cormac killer, stabbed through Marble's weakened hull, and four remaining fusion reactors blinked out. Marble was now down to various forms of storage and, as far as Straeger could gather, didn't have the resources he himself had available. He shut down the laser and set a small part of himself to diagnostics and maintenance of the thing. This was the most significant firing of the weapon Straeger had ever done; the diagnostics would give him data on something that had only been theoretical until now.

Straeger next turned the rest of himself to assessing his power supply. Though the disruption was high, he could still discern the U-space twist underlying the ship in that continuum. It pleased him to see the vast energy draw into the laser had only fractionally unwound the thing. The Polity had been researching energy sources like this ever since seeing a singular example of the Atheter disappearing into the galaxy in a starship powered by one. The AIs were close to discovering the secret of it all. Once they did, Straeger had no doubt they'd lock all knowledge of the things in black sites. The reality of the tech was that it relied on time feedback loops, just like those Blite generated every time he died, and his crystal reset that verdict. Straeger felt sure his own insight into the time continuum would have enabled him to master the technology long before other AIs, but this was nothing he could prove. When an agent of the single living Atheter had contacted him to offer the technology at a price well within his means, he hadn't refused.

'So,' he finally spoke to Marble, 'Did you discover anything interesting?'

'An understanding of your interest in Blite, at least.' The snatch ship AI spoke in a restrained manner, not wanting Straeger to know it was glad he'd finally communicated, rather than simply annihilating it.

'Perhaps you would like to tell me all about that?' Straeger brought his ship back in close, flying above the trench he'd carved along the snatch ship's length. The cut went down deep, glowing hellishly in its depths. He realized that, had he made another pass, he would have split Marble's vessel open like a banana.

'During the first times I killed him, I had no awareness of the previous occasions, but then they began to impinge, extending my mind out into the probability continuum so I could see the loops he created. Each of those shone like a brief light across all continua, revealing more and more detail. This is truly seeing into the future, though through a glass darkly.'

That was interesting. Straeger had never actually been close during Blite's multiple deaths, so hadn't experienced the loops. Perhaps this was something he could experience at a later time – anything was possible.

Marble was becoming chatty now, even throwing in that odd joke. It was also revealing a great deal of information, and no doubt had packets of such it'd be prepared to send over to Straeger should he request them. The packets might well contain only legitimate data, rather than some form of attack, as Marble had tried to prevent Straeger getting in close and taking it straight from its mind. More likely would be some last desperate attempt by the AI to load a cornucopia of attack programs, followed by a rush to escape while Straeger dealt with them.

Mapping out the snatch ship below him, Straeger finally brought the *Claw* down a few hundred metres from one end cap. The response times of systems scattered through the bulk of the vessel behind indicated that the AI was a distinct entity, located somewhere below. Quite possibly Marble had deliberately altered those response times to give a false impression of its location. It didn't matter. Marble was in this vessel and would be found. Straeger now waited, observing the laser. It was a pillar of quantum cascade arrays, whose output ran through a series of material meta-lenses, then into pseudo-matter and field tech which could handle the photon density. Now approaching the end of its diagnostic and maintenance run, Straeger saw the data were interesting. The interaction between the fields and converging beams churned out slews of exotic particles, previously only found in linear accelerators, and this created wave patterns in U-space. He absorbed this data and added it to his personal model of reality.

'You don't have to do this,' said Marble.

The plea amused Straeger as he rolled through his ship, pulling in resources and expanding his mass and energy load. It was straight out of human fiction – the victim begging to continue existing. He reached a door in his ship's hull and there paused, before going out. At his thought, his ship's defences ramped out to maximum and the laser came back online. Now, should Marble attempt some attack on his ship while he was out of it, it would be fended off. And if the AI ejected in an escape capsule, that would cease to exist a few microseconds later.

'But I do have to do this,' Straeger replied. 'If I allow you to live, you'll take one of two courses: you'll go after Blite in an effort to expand your knowledge, or you'll run squealing to the Polity.'

'Maybe I'll just run,' Marble replied.

A circular section of hull eased out, revealing its three-metre thickness and complex technological ecology, and then slid aside. No airlock was required here, since he had no air behind or before him. He rolled out onto the hull of the snatch ship, his detection spread out to maximum and weapons in his ship trained for cover. Next, snapping fast through vacuum, he dropped into the trench where it terminated here. Touching the still-glowing sides with his tendrils, he propelled himself down, until seeing an opening into the rest of the ship and entering there. Soon he was into areas where damage did not extend and he scanned ahead, then tapped into optics and energy feeds for confirmation. Marble lay just half a kilometre ahead. Straeger rolled towards the AI.

'Just run?' he enquired, because the AI had gone ominously quiet.

'Yes, I am fascinated by Blite and, just like you, see him and that crystal as a route towards gaining equivalent power to Penny Royal. But I have all the time in the universe to acquire such power and am inclined to believe the theory that all who survive till then will converge on Penny Royal at the Omega Point.'

'Yes, but acquiring such power now will ensure that survival.'

'No. As I am presently now well aware, trying to acquire that power will do the opposite. I also won't run to the Polity because

451

my actions here with Blite will lead to examination – probably by one of your brothers.'

'You make a cogent argument. Unfortunately I can't take any chances.'

'I thought so.'

The weapons fire began at once. Particle beams sliced through the snatch ship from five different locations, converging on Straeger. He mapped them in a second, shifted mass and accelerated. The beams tracked him, walls slumping to become molten, sprays of burning composite like fireworks, skeins of optics and s-con wires shrivelling like hairs in a flame. But he was moving too fast for them to cut through the surrounding infrastructure quickly enough to be effective. Then came the blast, bucking his surroundings. The area below the *Claw* dissolved in a CTD blast, and the whole snatch ship snapped like a stick. The explosion threw the *Claw* out, and would have wrecked a normal vessel, but it sat perfectly enclosed in a hardfield bubble – another advantage garnered from the U-twist power source. Three of the particle beams went out, and the other two diminished. This was a last-gasp attack by Marble, using up remaining energy. As expected, an escape canister shot from its long barrel and hurtled out. Rolling free of the blast, Straeger's ship dropped its hardfield and the photon-dense beam stabbed out again, hitting the thing. The beam slightly changed colour at that point but no more. The canister evaporated.

'And there it is,' said Straeger into the space where Marble's com icon had been, as the particle beams finally went out.

He rolled on as around him this area of the snatch ship began to shed heat rapidly, and as its systems wound down into entropy. Reaching the lower bound of that escape barrel, Straeger found a large globular chamber surrounded by layer upon layer of armour and now-defunct defences. Shrinking himself down to a solid sphere just a metre across, he wove a course between the armour shells, along a route provided for maintenance robots and carrier bodies. The inside of the chamber was old-style standard. Extending in from the walls were two diametrically opposed components, like the greatly enlarged valves from an ancient piston engine. Their faces stood two metres apart now, but before would have been close, with the AI crystal sandwiched between. Optics and s-con wires tangled through vacuum all around where they'd been disconnected. In one wall was the ejection barrel. The arms that would have grabbed the AI to slam it into its escape canister, and thence into the flash breech for launching, hung slack.

Straeger floated ahead and opened out from his sphere form, pushing away the optics and wires, touching and connecting here and there to gather data. This was a scene played out in the thousands upon thousands of Polity warships the prador had destroyed during the war. Even now, so many centuries later, AI ejection canisters were still being found from that time, while it was calculated that in the region of fifty thousand of them were currently leaving the bounds of the galaxy.

'The problem with this diorama,' said Straeger, 'is that the both of us are far too aware of each other's capabilities, and far too good at extrapolation. You knew you could not destroy my ship, and I knew this too, otherwise I would not have landed it on you. You realized you could not destroy me either, because I would never have put myself where this was a possibility. You also knew ejection was a pointless exercise.'

There was no reply, of course.

Straeger spread all over the walls, speared out tendrils, initiating Q-carbon drills on their ends, and bored into them. Then, almost like fluid absorbed into a sponge, he soaked through the surfaces as he searched for what he knew would be here. He expected this would take some time, that he'd have to gather in more materials and open out into a membrane spanning this piece of the snatch ship, as well as run through it from end to end, and then go through the other chunk of it too. However, sandwiched in a shell of ceramal armour a hundred metres from the centre of the chamber, he found a layer of crystal almost like quartz in rock strata. It was utterly inert, until he made his connections and fed in power.

'Fuck you and fuck every Mobius in existence!' Marble exclaimed.

It was a weak insult, but then the AI had little time to gather resources for something better before Straeger began to take it apart. Then it only had the energy to scream.

17

Valt – Past

Valt's first awareness was of not feeling right at all, and this immediately concerned him, since sick prador soon became dead prador. If they took too long to follow their father's orders, enough for him to notice, they were scheduled for termination. Usually they went into an incinerator at that point, as a claw-tap towards infection control. That could have been said to be better than being eaten alive, except for the fact they went into the incinerator alive. Those that managed to keep up with their duties but still showed signs of sickness or weakness usually ended up as victims of subordinates. It was considered natural selection.

His vision returned after the fear eased, and he couldn't understand why everything looked blue through his forward turret eyes, in contrast to the frosty white chaos through his remaining stalked eye. Only as the blue began to fade did memory start to return. The blue was the antifreeze that'd been pumped into his suit, which was only slightly different from the stuff in his vascular system. He could feel this now draining out through the pipes which had been painfully inserted in his underside, while the sick warmth of his own stored and reheated blood was being pumped into him. His whole body ached, and crazily he had an all-over itch underneath his natural carapace.

Something seemed to be pushing him from back inside his body – drilling up towards his brain – and once it became almost unbearable he took a breath. The oxygenated water around him still had the taint of antifreeze as it cycled through his gill-lung, but at least the horrible feeling of suffocation retreated. Now able to think more clearly, he realized he was coming out of hibernation.

Further memories returned with a humiliation that was not his own. The king had been usurped and a new ruler had taken over horribly fast. Father – an ardent supporter of the first king and related to his family – had been in shock for a while, and chaos reigned in their family enclave. However, when he learned that the new king had made a truce with those detestable soft humans, he finally acted. He could not support such madness and would himself usurp the new king! Except getting other families onside with this idea turned out not to be so easy, as the new king's family began ruthlessly to exterminate opposition. Volax, Valt's father, was forced to flee, and did so into the newly established borderland between the Kingdom and the Polity. Packed aboard their dreadnought, they'd only just made it there, losing four destroyers and a host of smaller ships. With the major ship severely damaged too, concessions had to be made. Food supply was low and the air running out; the only way Volax could maintain his family's strength of numbers was by putting a large quantity of them into hibernation.

It had taken time to rig up the hibernation system in the dreadnought's holds, and Valt remembered how helpful the engineer second-child Drust had been in that work. And yet, even though they'd worked so hard to set things up, it'd seemed spiteful of Volax to order them to be the first to go under.

Spiteful?

Valt shuddered in his armour, for such a thought should have no place in his mind. Volax was their father and ruler, beyond criticism. Valt owed his life and his loyalty to his father!

The ability to move began to return to him. Now shifting his stalked eye, he discerned that the white chaos was the other prador all around and ahead of him, among the hibernation infrastructure all rimed with frost. He shifted, waiting for those either ahead or above to get out of the way, while easing his mandibles forwards to his interior console and bringing up the HUD in his visor. Using these controls, he directed the pipes to extract from him. The sore feeling they left behind meant they hadn't cemented their holes on the way out. A series of monitoring probes also withdrew, back into the hardware of his suit. Then com came through on his visor in prador glyphs.

'You are alive,' the speaker wrote.

'I am alive,' he confirmed.

'I am Drust.'

'I know you.'

'Yes.' The glyphs paused for a second, then continued, 'We will get to you soon.'

This should have been enough of an exchange, since there was no need to go beyond the facts of the matter. But Valt felt strangely rebellious and frustrated.

'How long have I been in here?' he asked.

'Four point three spans,' Drust replied.

Valt felt other questions fade from his mind with the shock. The spans were the length of a prador first-child's life. He'd been in hibernation for an immense amount of time. It was also well beyond the period that prador were supposed to be able to survive this manner of hibernation.

Around him he could see the frost now melting and dripping. In front he saw one of his brothers, up on top of another, tilt and slide from view, and then the glare of lights came through from beyond. Next a second-child, in what seemed to be plain steel armour, scrabbled about ahead of him, attaching a cable hook into a lug on the armour of the one directly ahead, then moved aside. The cable attached to the hook tautened and dragged the prador out. Others to either side were being moved in a similar manner and were obviously dead. The ones above Valt then moved, crashing down to the floor and staggering away. Once the last from above had gone, Valt heaved himself to his feet shakily, as if he still bore the load of them on his back, and walked into the space ahead. He was interested in what he would find there.

Moving out into the lights and the emptied section of hold, Valt checked his HUD, then ejected the water from his armour and switched over to air breathing. The first thing to hit him was the smell of decaying meat, which had his insides turning over with hunger. He scanned his surroundings. The second-children here, and one or two first-children, were busily at work opening armoured suits and levering out dead prador. The suits were then filtered out through one exit, and the corpses out of another. He noted that many of the workers wore inferior armour, though there were some in the gold or grey alloy like his own. He tried to link into their tactical and logistical com as he wandered over to where one of those suits was being opened. Com kept fritzing, which he would deal with, but right then he had other concerns.

Two first-children had prised the armour open and pulled its occupant out. One second-child dragged off the armour, while the other was about to drag off the corpse too, until Valt rapped him sharply on the shell and told him to leave it. The second-child tilted back and looked up at him, mandibles grinding, which was unexpected. Valt sideswiped him and sent him crashing into the wall. He came out of that with armour misshapen and leaking from one split, then quickly scuttled away. His behaviour was puzzling. Being a second-child, he should have instantly obeyed Valt, or gone into the obeisance pose.

Valt went over to the corpse and slammed his armoured claw against the carapace edge to break it all the way along. Then, using both claws, he held the bottom and levered up the top to expose the contents within. Quickly opening his gullet cover, and inserting his mandibles back into their sleeves, he began to feed, snipping up gobbets of decayed muscle and organ. In fact the stuff was so far gone it required no mastication, and he just used his mandibles to feed it down into his gullet. He was about halfway through this when he recognized the one he was feeding on as a brood brother, and he was replete by the time Drust finally arrived.

'Four point three spans,' he repeated back to the little engineer.

'Yes,' said Drust.

'How many have survived hibernation?'

'Twenty out of two thousand, including me.'

Valt felt the weird overpowering urge to dive into more detail; to ask where the ship had fetched up, what had happened to the rest of the family, what Father was doing, and all sorts of other specifics. This was a tendency he sometimes had, and necessarily suppressed. Prador did not have conversations, and he knew he must pick up additional information in any further brief exchanges, as well as by using his senses. It was clear at least that the family's fortunes were not good – the armour on those second-children told him that. He understood that something must be very out of kilter for him, along with those being dragged off, to have been left in hibernation for so long. He tried the com again and now got some detail from that. The dreadnought they'd come here on was at the bottom of an ocean, and these corpses and armour were being transported up to an enclave being drilled into a mountain chain. The fact the corpses were being taken there meant food was probably in short supply. He continued to glean more details as he spoke to Drust.

'Engineer, what is our purpose?' he asked.

'The enclave must be properly established: food supplies, energy security and our foothold here made firm.'

Valt was now receiving more from the system via his HUD. It startled him to discover that this enclave was only a few years old. The prador that had first come here were all dead, but the tunnels they'd carved out had been utilized and extended, despite many earthquakes and collapses during the process. The prador, three generations of them grown aboard the destroyer during its journey, had built some defences on the numerous moons orbiting this world in the Graveyard, and commenced some mining and drilling for resources, although only haltingly. This was, he soon understood, a difficult place, and he had work to do.

'Our father commands,' said Drust.

Valt gazed at the little engineer, feeling there was something behind those words. Drust had somehow communicated a lot more than was usual in such exchanges, but then he had always been a bit aberrant. Valt's thoughts strayed to their father, and he realized the time spans Drust had mentioned didn't make sense, because that would make Volax immensely old for an adult prador. Such thoughts instigated another surge of fear, a strange twisting sensation in his back end, and an unbecoming reluctance. Something then reasserted in his mind – almost without thinking, he retracted a mandible inside his armour and pressed down a lever. A smell and a taste immediately filled his suit – his father's pheromones. Doubts, confusion and fear were swept away on a wave of aggressive loyalty.

'We obey!' he exclaimed, and headed for the exit, with Drust scrabbling to keep up.

Matheson

Ulnar was back. Or at least he was again a functional part of the team who'd obey instructions. Matheson didn't think the man himself was back, or would ever be so. This applied to Will too. No matter how much inhibitor Ricardo fed them, both of them stubbornly maintained body shapes that were a radical distortion of their original human form. They now had long apelike limbs, long necks and heads that were essentially bloated prill. His com with them gave him nothing but nonsensical babble, which made Sheen's occasional comments – still out of that old rhyme – seem like profound philosophical statements.

They sat at the table again, all of them with cylinder pumps of inhibitor attached and tubed into their bodies. Ricardo, following through on the program Straeger had set him, put out food for them all. Matheson eyed Sheen as she bent over her plate and extended a large fat tongue, ejecting something glutin-ous and acidic on her food to dissolve it. She then began sucking it up like a fly, the tongue shifting and jerking as the conveyors of leech teeth inside it chewed up the more substantial chunks. He reached up and touched his own face with his remaining hand; it was still in its amphibian form. When his hand came close to his mouth, his tongue shot out and tried to latch onto it. Had the hand not been armoured, he suspected the tongue would have taken a chunk out of it. He fought the urge to bend over his own plate of food like Sheen had done, picking up a fork and concentrating intently to use it properly.

Last of all, Ricardo brought food to Will and Ulnar, who'd been rocking and swinging their heads from side to side impa-tiently. In their case he'd not brought plates but what looked like short troughs filled to brimming. The two had kept their eye holes open, since they'd be effectively blind without the feed from Matheson's gridlink, and in the eye holes red prill eyes flickered as they ran back and forth on their tracks. Now Will Brice opened a mouth hole and made a whistling sound as he took his first breaths of oxygen in some hours. He did this for a full minute before Ricardo came up and inserted a metal tube into that hole. A pause ensued, as Will integrated this new data, then he dipped and began sucking up his stew.

With Ulnar matters were entirely different. He waved his head from side to side like some truculent child and refused to open his mouth hole, while Ricardo waited patiently behind him with another one of those metal tubes. When he did finally open his mouth hole, he inserted his fingers and pulled. His armoured head covering split along its line of division, down the centre of his 'face', and the two profile halves hinged back, distorted out of shape. With Ulnar's head now clearly revealed, Matheson could no longer perceive him, and Will, as even remotely human. Though Matheson could look inside their armour at will, and even though it had changed to follow their altering forms, he had still, in some psychological manner, kept this last truth locked away. Ulnar's head was an ellipsoid. His neck, a weirdly ribbed thing, connected at the back on the underside. Also on the underside, the sharp insect legs of a prill were folded. To the fore of these, and below the rim, sat the mandibular mouth. Around the rim of the head ran a channel in which a collection of six red eyes shifted and rolled like ball bearings to bounce off each other. Ulnar's head looked ready to detach from his body and run off across the table.

Ulnar dipped to his trough and began snapping up chunks of meat and vegetables, to munch these up in his mandibles and insert into his mouth. Matheson could see no likelihood of that head ever returning to a human shape. And because this realization had focused his attention, he began to see other changes too. The armour Ulnar had folded back from his face appeared a lot thinner, which seemed to be why it had crumpled up when he removed it. Going deeper, and making comparisons to how it'd been before, he saw its overall mass was thirty per cent down on the original. It also appeared, in the cases of both brothers, that they were now growing through their armour. Along their arms and legs thorns of their inner carapace had penetrated, while a bladelike protuberance had pushed through along the spines of their humped backs. These breaks would certainly result in them being torn up inside during any further U-jumps, then probably further mutating into . . . something.

Matheson finished his food and abruptly stood up. He wanted to say something but, looking around the table, he no longer recognized people who'd comprehend the nicety. Ricardo met his gaze and was the most human, which seemed unjust to him. He turned and left.

Out in the corridor he paused to shut down his connection to them all before moving on to the bridge. There, sitting in his chair, he called up screen data on their transit. It told him nothing new, and they would arrive at the new destination Straeger had given them in a couple of days. Next he focused his gridlink and amplified perception of himself. Here too he found his armour had lost bulk and grown thinner. Thankfully none of his inner body had penetrated it, while a thin skin of it had grown over his arm stump. He hoped that would shield him from further damage and keep mutations in check. Feeling a little sickened by the prospect, he increased his focus on his body within. The stuff that had wormed in through his armour on Penny Royal's planetoid had spread its silvery roots throughout. He'd noticed something similar in Sheen, where the growth was much more advanced and had spread metallic veins across her face too. In any other situation such a thing inside him would have been terrifying, yet with the changes they were undergoing, it now seemed the least of their worries. The brothers had no trace of the stuff inside them. Even though it had grown, it didn't seem to hinder him in any way, and as yet had done nothing untoward. He turned his inspection to the rest of his body.

The insect limbs, into which his lower pair of ribs had been transforming, had changed. Muscle had grown around them, and at their ends they seemed to be producing fisted hands. He checked other ribs, and though they'd also changed shape, he could see no sign of them turning into further limbs. He couldn't see any of those neatly coiled tentacles the Brice brothers had, nor had his scapulae extended into crumpled wings. His transformation was at huge variance to that of the others. Otherwise, he'd mostly retained his human skeleton, and his organs, though misshapen, were still there. The bigger alterations were in musculature, to support the addition of those extra limbs.

Higher up, he found that his neck, which had been growing long, had contracted and thickened. His head and face remained as they had been the last time he examined them. His face had transformed into something lying between a human and an axolotl. The pits which had opened between his now more widely-spaced eyes seemed to have deepened, while the optic nerves growing towards them, through the holes in his reformed skull, had got closer and were budding at their ends. He had no doubt that, without the inhibitor, he'd soon enough be opening a second pair of eyes. In them all the Spatterjay virus was deploying items from its collection of alien genomes in a seemingly haphazard manner. In the Brices he could obviously see that of prill, and apparently some kind of flying insect, but he wondered what it was using in him. He knew of a number of alien and terran species that had multiple eyes serving different purposes. The two now growing resembled the targeting eyes of a droon, so would he be turning into an acid-spitting monster? He shook his head, then brought his attention to his arm stump.

The thing had grown visibly fatter only since he'd eaten. He focused in on it, expecting something insectile or alien to be appearing there, but saw instead a growth folded back from the severance point. It looked like a baby's arm – the kind of growth seen in those who'd lost a limb and had the axolotl fix to their genes. If it grew out, would the armour continue to cover it? He had no idea.

'They will not . . . be . . . controllable.'

Matheson turned to the voice, seeing Ricardo standing a few paces in from the bridge door. The man-Golem looked odd, standing hunched over, arms twisted at odd angles, hands fisted, head over to one side, and face contorted too. He almost had the appearance of an antediluvian human suffering one of the neurological disorders that had plagued their kind back then. Studying him, Matheson realized his own thinking had cleared since the meal, and the giggling madness had ebbed to an almost imperceptible level. He recognized, in an instant, that Ricardo was fighting something inside, and that battle was expressing outwardly.

'The Brices?'

Ricardo gave a jerky nod.

'But that's not what you're here to tell me.'

Ricardo's gaze strayed all around the bridge, as if he was trying to find a way out. He staggered to one side, then with a sudden twitch, his hand opened and an object clattered to the floor. Matheson eyed an EMP shell, like those he'd used to disable Ricardo and force him into the clamp. Ricardo stared down at the shell, his expression appalled. Had the man come here to use the shell against Matheson? No, that made no sense at all.

465

If Ricardo was somehow able to overcome Straeger's programming of him, he'd have brought a more substantial weapon, and
even then known his likelihood of success was minimal. Something
else was going on here. Matheson stared and thought. And then,
when he visualized events as threads of meaning weaving into a
whole, clarity arrived.

'You're fighting Straeger's programming,' he said.

Ricardo looked up, hopeful now.

Matheson got out of his chair and walked over. Stooping to
sweep up the shell, he pressed down the button on the end, then
inserted the thing into Ricardo's overalls. He released it there
and stepped back. The delay was a couple of seconds, and then
the thing went off with a crack, blowing away the front of Ricardo's
overalls and shoving him a couple of steps back. It webbed his
body from chest to floor with a miniature electrical storm. As
the last sparks sizzled out around his deck shoes, Ricardo abruptly
shrugged and stood upright.

'I have limited time before the programming re-establishes,'
he said.

It was Matheson's first instinct to bombard him with questions,
but the weave of meaning discounted that. He waved a hand for
the man-Golem to continue.

'You'll lose control of the Brices as their mutations advance
– first the brothers and then Sheen. By extension, Straeger will
also lose control of them through you. They'll become extremely
dangerous, because their mutation, though partially based on
some Spatterjay life forms, is mainly drawn from something a
lot older: Jain soldiers.'

Again the urge to question, and again the suppression of that
urge. Ricardo was loading as much information into the time he
had and it was best not to interrupt him.

'Your own mutation is taking a different course, but with the result that you too will stray beyond Straeger's control. The Mobius AI understands this, and when you're no longer useful to it, it will destroy us all.'

Matheson nodded, his thoughts knitting together multiple structures and collapsing them into different shapes. Ricardo had provided information concerning their survival. What else did he need to know, now the man-Golem had again started to twist out of shape?

'What is my mutation based upon?' he asked.

Ricardo began to shake, maybe in palsy, maybe in laughter.

'Atheter,' he managed, voice distorting.

The knit of his thoughts now became recognizable for what it was, in the psychology of a race whose whole technology had grown from the art of weaving. And it shattered.

He was turning into a gabbleduck?

Blite

Caution was warranted, which was why Blite ran a reconfiguration program that Polity AIs tended to frown on, especially within the Polity. Accepted doctrine was that all the calculations necessary to make a U-jump became set once that jump was made – you couldn't arrive anywhere but at your destination. This idea was akin to the one which dictated that only high-level AIs could make those calculations, so every ship needed to have one. It was a myth promulgated by AIs in order to maintain control. Most ship AIs were usually part of the hegemony, and to maintain control of a population it was of course useful to know where every ship was going. Now the time was arriving.

'We're close,' said Meander, as he stepped out of his cabin. 'Yet I don't feel like I'm going home.'

He studied her. She still looked haunted. Apparently she'd had the vision again of being trapped on some vast black surface, with the sky burning above, though this time with a sense of something pulling at her. It'd come to her at some point during their escape from Marble. While it added to the mystery of her, it still told him nothing useful.

He closed his cabin door, pleased to be able to do so without pulling off the handle as he had a week previously. He'd finally mastered his boosted strength and accelerated nerve impulses. Turning back to continue studying her, he again puzzled over her physical changes, and others he couldn't quite put his finger on. According to Iris, she'd gained bulk and a couple of centimetres in height, while more esoteric changes were occurring inside her. These consisted of cell expansion to contain additional DNA and epigenetic machinery, while a finer blend of a human immune system and a nanosuite had expanded its function too. And yet, with all this increase, she also seemed less substantial to him – starved, somehow, and becoming translucent.

'We're surfacing a light year out, so maybe that accounts for you feeling this way,' he replied.

'Could be.'

In the bridge all were in place except Iris, who'd been keeping pretty much to herself lately down in Medical. Blite went over and dropped into the captain's chair, while Meander went over to take the one she'd been in before. The screen paint, now only activated across the forward section of wall, showed a generic travel scene of stars fleeing past them.

'One minute,' said Carlstone.

'Are we all ready?' Blite asked, particularly looking over to Judice, who was in Greer's old place on weapons. She caught his gaze and nodded curtly.

He didn't expect anything untoward to happen. They should

simply drop out of U-space and start collecting data. But the unexpected had happened far too often lately, and he really didn't want to become caught in another cycle of replays again. The events at the snatch ship still hadn't settled in his mind, though thankfully his nanosuite had managed to dial down a stubbornly exaggerated fight-or-flight response. It had been unpleasant to experience the ancient maladies of grinding anxiety and then panic attacks whenever he looked at a bright light, and in his mind keep seeing the throat of a particle cannon.

'Passive collectors are juiced up,' said Breil, 'and I've got extra collectors ready to open out.' Even as he said this, a frame opened on the screen to show a view of the hull, against a backdrop of the silver-grey swirl of U-space. 'First image to main screen the moment we surface,' he added.

'Paidon?' Blite asked.

The woman had seemed particularly busy, with eyes glazed while her hands darted over a texture console. She looked around. 'I don't like reconfiguring a jump, especially after the hammering we've received.'

'Have you found any problems?'

'No,' she conceded truculently, before turning back to her instruments.

Blite frowned, started reaching for his safety harness, then desisted. That was behaviour dictated by the anxiety he *wasn't* suffering. He needed to show confidence and certainty, no matter what might bubble up inside. They waited without speaking as a counter at the bottom of the main screen wound down. In the last seconds, Blite turned and looked over at Meander to give a casually reassuring smile. The transition into the real gave everything simultaneously depth and a shallowness, but their shielding was good and it didn't last. Blite's guts twisted and raised a brief pulse of panic, quickly suppressed by his nanosuite. He faced forwards again to eye the screen, mentally replaying what he'd just seen with Meander, and his real reason for turning to look at her.

His sense of her being insubstantial had increased, but then this happened with everything and everyone around him too, so it proved nothing. For a second, it also seemed as if a filter had passed over her, revealing her as something akin to one of Pace's sculptures, while her eyes had flickered into black spots on a backdrop of bright light. But it had all been so subliminal he couldn't be sure if it was real. It felt like a mental artefact of what he'd seen when the snatch ship knocked them out of U-space, while his certainty of what he *had* actually seen then had diminished. Although to those around him, including Meander, just a handful of days had passed since that event, for him the extra time of replays had intervened. Having calculated it in his aug, he knew it to have been a virtual week. But because of what had happened during that time, it seemed an entire age of pain and destruction had passed.

'So that's Yossander's Hold,' he stated.

The main screen image had changed, blurrily displaying a world, with their passive collectors were rapidly cleaning up the image. In the frame he saw collector sails opening out from the hull to gather a wider spread of EMR.

The world slowly clarified into a colour scheme resembling that of Earth, but shifted slightly towards the red end of the spectrum in the pink light of its supergiant sun. A small continental land mass of pretty standard configuration showed up on the right of the globe, while an ocean with long, ridgeback islands protruding out of it covered the rest – as if someone had taken the planet and tried to wring it out, raising these wrinkles. These were presumably the drift islands Breil had mentioned. Blite guessed them to be a product of the two moons in orbit. One was large enough to be considered a planetoid, and the other was a rugged rock that had probably been caught in the orbit of this world long after the formation of this system.

Further frames opened, highlighting the moons and various other areas about the world, but as yet they didn't show anything of interest. Blite reluctantly reached into his pocket and took out the induction aug, wondering why, after having lived so long and perfectly understanding their utility, he still resented the things. Once it was in place and opening up his perception, he began to receive the data the rest of his crew were already studying. Data transmission from the world, now of course a year old as they were a light year out, was being hoovered up, run through translation programs, categorized and catalogued. He gleaned a sense of the sub-AI program Carlstone had begun to run it through, glimpsed some weird imagery of a biotech civilization, then returned his attention to the screen images as they grew clearer and clearer, opening out into close-up subframes. Carlstone pulled one of those to the fore.

'Purchased from Graveyard traders but,' said Carlstone, 'these were prador traders.'

'You're kidding,' said Blite.

'I'm not. The king has been loosening things up for a while and now allows families to trade outside the Kingdom. Though admittedly with some very close oversight.'

The images behind showed generic, atmosphere-enclosed bases all around the moon's surface, surrounding seas that in its night froze solid, and in the day melted and boiled in the low gravity. But the frame to the fore showed a domed installation, with a weapon protruding that sported a long flat barrel.

'It's a dreadnought railgun with a serious impact profile,' Judice added. 'Fire it enough and the recoil would shift the orbit of the

471

moon.' She paused and began highlighting other frames. 'There's smaller stuff around the surface, and on the smaller moon too: high-intensity lasers, doubled-up particle cannons and various missile launchers. But they're not *that* small.'

Blite studied the first weapon, auged for scale, and realized the thing was half a kilometre long. 'Hardly biotech,' he commented.

'Our previous data on this place was over a decade out of date,' Carlstone replied. 'Maybe the technology faction has won the epistemological battle. More interesting to know is why they think they need such a weapon.'

'There's more,' said Carlstone.

Another frame opened, showing another installation on the moon. Curved structures bracketed what looked like a runcible containment sphere, but with large cylindrical structures butted up against it. There were no runcibles in the Graveyard, so it had to be something else using similarly dangerous technology.

'Analysis?' Blite asked.

'It's an old version of a USER,' Carlstone replied. 'Judging by U-space readings, it's been deployed recently, as there's still disruption there.'

'It seems they're heavily defended,' Judice added.

'What else are we getting from their communications?' Blite asked.

Carlstone grimaced. 'Still sorting. Lot of encoded stuff I can't break into, and I only picked up on where that weapon came from through tying together disparate stuff in their media. They're locked down. Shall I try talking to them?'

'Not yet. Anything about recent visitors?'

Carlstone didn't immediately reply, then said, 'Trade ships from the Graveyard a few years back and nothing since. They were arms dealers.'

'That's in their com?'

'No, I just recognize who was involved.'

Blite huffed out a sigh. His main concern right then was whether they'd be fired on when they jumped in close to the world. It was plainly evident this place had been under attack, or had a big expectation of that.

'Okay, close us up. Another half light year jump when ready.'

Paidon glanced round to give him a disapproving look, then got to work on it. Screen frames showed the collectors closing up to the hull, and the next U-jump ensued as a flickering twist to perception. He didn't bother looking at Meander this time. All the frames disappeared and the main screen image blurred. As they came back out into the real soon after, he felt an odd judder. He knew what it'd been before Carlstone spoke.

'That USER just powered up,' he said. 'Seems we passed some U-space detectors.'

The collectors started opening again and the image to clear in various frames. The world was now half in darkness, with lights glimmering along the drift islands, and the continental mass no longer in view. The larger moon lay out of view too, behind the world, and at first Blite could only see changes wrought by this different view in time. Then Breil spoke up.

'They've been hit,' he said.

Further frames opened beside the ones already displayed, and Blite didn't know what they were until auging out that information. The second frames were comparison ones from half a light year back. Sliding into infrared, the world showed massive swirls of cloud to be the reason for those flickering lights. It could have been interpreted as a seasonal change, except for a glowing crater on the edge of the continent, the cloud boiling away from the half of it that was within the sea.

'And they were firing something,' Breil added.

A frame now showed a series of missiles slingshotting around the planet. Quite possibly they were programmed to intercept anything the USER knocked out into the real, though of course this wasn't for them, since it had occurred half a year ago.

'Open U-com,' Blite instructed. 'Send them identifiers.'

Carlstone nodded, fingers up against his aug. He turned back to his console, fingers passing over touch controls and, after a moment, sweeping a hand towards the screen. Blite expected someone to appear in the frame which opened there, but instead it only ran code. This continued for a while, as Blite studied other frames opening then closing. They showed debris out in space and shifted on. The large moon, now edging out from behind the world, began to render data too, even as the missile drives winked out. A long scar, looking like a particle beam strike, had cut through some of those habitats and smaller weapons installations. Since they were only seeing a fraction of this moon, Blite wondered how much more damage there might be. Then he started to become impatient.

'Why's it taking so long?' he asked.

Carlstone flicked a look at him. 'Demands for more data. They want to know why we're here, and since our real reason is vague I've had to make up a story. The owner of Penny Transport, who's a wealthy impulsive fool, heard about this world and, being curious about it, is thinking of opening trade links here.'

'Well, thanks for that.'

More time passed, then Carlstone said, 'We've got coordinates and that USER is powering down.' The man looked puzzled as he routed those over. He added, 'It went very quiet when I mentioned your name, and now I'm talking to a representative of their ruler, someone called the Gilliad, apparently.'

Blite studied their destination, which was just out from the large moon and well within range of all those nasty weapons, as well as wherever those missiles had been launched from half a year ago. This concerned him, but he understood their response, after evidently having come under attack. He hesitated, then turned to Paidon, who was waiting, and gave her the nod. The U-jump, though as short as the last, seemed oddly protracted this time. They flashed into the real with Blite gripping his chair arms and that panic roiling subliminally. He wondered if the decision to jump in was one he might decide against on replay. Nothing happened, and then screen images began to clarify again. He saw at once that he'd been right – the moon had taken a pounding. The ship then seemed to judder, the air growing thick around him, and his body heating up.

'Heavy scanning,' said Carlstone unnecessarily.

'No shit—' Blite began, but Carlstone interrupted him.

'We have landing coordinates down on the world,' he said.

'That was quick.'

Carlstone looked over to Judice and nodded.

She said, 'Probably because they've confirmed we're not the enemy.' She waved a hand and yet another frame opened. On a backdrop of stars, coordinates given a hundred thousand kilometres out from Yossander's Hold, a wreck hung in vacuum. Blite recognized it for what it was at once. Nobody said anything for a long drawn-out moment.

'Prador destroyer,' said Judice, as if they needed that confirmation.

Matheson

Ricardo's warning played on Matheson's mind. He and the Brices were turning into something over which Straeger would cease to have control. And the moment they ceased to be useful to the

AI, it would destroy them as the non-functional tools they'd become. Was this the moment it would happen?

They were near the Graveyard – somewhere towards the edge of the border. This volume of space stretched like a sheet a few light years thick, but tens of thousands in area, between the Polity and that lawless place. When they arrived, he assumed they'd come out near one of the many debris fields left by the war, but on scanning the debris out there he noted it was all still cooling, and he tracked its course out from some central incident. A simple calculation showed this incident had been recent. That Straeger's vessel sat near that central point indicated the AI had probably caused it, but right then, what might have happened here was the least of his concerns.

What could he do if this was to be the scene of their exter-mination? Must he wait for Straeger's verdict before reacting? No – tactically that would be the stupidest thing, and he'd already decided otherwise. He looked around the bridge. Ricardo stood back by the door, expression and pose simply that of some atten-tive manservant. Will and Ulnar were down on the floor, bodies rocking and heads weaving from side to side. Will had closed up his face covering, having recovered enough of a fragment of humanity to want to conceal what he'd become. Ulnar had copied his brother, though not for the same reason. Sheen still had her covering open and, having retained more human features, her face was close to recognizably hers before her changes, apart from the fact it was pale green with metallic veins spread all over it. Some even ran across one of her eyes. He instructed her with a thought and she reached up, pulling the two halves of her covering across. The metal shifted as she pressed it into place, then sealed up. After a moment her eye holes popped open.

Matheson now instructed them, not entirely sure how much would stick. It wasn't complicated, just a matter of identifying their enemy, throwing themselves at it and tearing it apart. He tried to analyse their response and once again found himself weaving together disparate words, phrases, emotional surges and states into a coherent whole. He could tell they understood him, and the danger, and he didn't need Sheen's muttering about vorpal swords to confirm this. He stood up, glanced at the screen now filled with Straeger's *Claw*, and could see no reason to delay further.

He opened out his U-sense, first extending it to that vessel. A lot of it wasn't clear to him, for it seemed Straeger must be running a variety of technologies which interfered with that continuum. However, he could see the AI deep inside, in the chamber where it had refashioned Matheson and the Brices. Next he brought his U-field out to his skin, then extended it to include the other three, while half unconsciously making the calculations for the jump. A surge of trepidation impinged from Will, and he realized the man now comprehended the damage he'd suffer from the gaps in his armour. And then they jumped.

The transition was hard, and in a subliminal flicker Matheson recognized that though his armour covered him head to foot, its protection had diminished along with its bulk. Straeger's ship leaped into his perception and through him, and he surfaced into the real with a concerted scream from the Brices at the damage they'd taken, underlined by a weird, mad joy in the pain. They snapped out in a space surrounded, as before, by Straeger's machines. Grav immediately dropped them to a cupped floor, which led up to where the AI was poised. No delay now, and as one they threw themselves towards the slope, feet denting the composite below.

Fast fast fast! Matheson yelled mentally.

He took maybe two steps before a crushing weight bore him down. To his right Ulnar simply crashed down on his face and tried to crawl. To his left Will shouldered into the floor in a strange flat bounce, and then seemed to stick there. Like himself, Sheen had gone down on one knee and was struggling to push herself back up. Straeger had ramped up grav below them to a phenomenal level. It seemed as if Sheen's armour was trying to slew off her, while Will had flattened out as if under the clamp. A second later the grav came off and Matheson surged to his feet, only to find himself pinned in a shimmering beam of something. Fighting to move forwards, he just rose into the air, as if hooked up like a fish, and saw the others rising around him too, still fighting, while from the sides pillars of manipulators began to close in. He reached out again, extending his U-field to try to fling them out of this trap, but his gridlink went down, making a jump impossible to calculate. He pushed for a jump anyway and it seemed it might work, then both his U-field and U-sense disrupted.

'Utterly consistent with prediction,' said Straeger with cheerful insanity in his mind. 'So much more has become clear to me too.'

Matheson was blind, which meant the others would be too. But he could feel movement as things skittered over his armour, and other things gripped and repositioned him. Tearing agony ensued down one leg and around his head. His face covering was violently peeled away in a spray of fluids, exposing eyes stripped of eyelids. Vision remained blurred for a second, then came back in harsh contrast as the Spatterjay virus optimized him for survival. Grips held him in place, while spinning saw blades opened splits in his armour. Further blunt-fingered grippers came in to peel that armour away. Then, as if this agonizing experience weren't sufficient, pincer claws closed on his exposed raw flesh, punching right in and holding him there writhing.

'It was my intention to eliminate you,' said Straeger, as the surrounding mechanisms began to retreat, except for the pincers.

'But the time flashes here have revealed more of the future and I can see your utility in another task right here.'

The AI wasn't going to kill them, but in the hell he occupied Matheson couldn't see this as a good thing. He dipped his head to look down at his body. The removal of the armour had also been the removal of its strictures and he was changing shape. His torso began to bulge out, his legs to contract, while something odd seemed to be happening to his *arms*. The unsevered one seemed to be dividing along the forearm, while from the stump of his other arm, the small arm he'd previously seen growing there had now folded out and straightened, and was expanding in slow pulses. These weren't the most radical changes. From his torso he unwrapped the two extra arms and could now feel them, moving the long scythe-like fingers. Next, with an audible thump, his vision enhanced. He struggled with this, as if the places in his mind weren't ready, but at least his experience with using augs, and then the gridlink, enabled some understanding. He could see in a human manner with nominally human eyes, but the extra two that'd certainly broken to the surface in his skull gave him extreme detail in a narrow window. Gazing into Straeger made his head ache, as layer upon layer of detail made themselves known to him. He turned away.

By now the machinery that had cut away their armour had retreated into the walls, and he could see the Brices again. Sheen, as he'd noticed before, had lost many of her changes and regained human form, though a large one with spines along the arms, a neck twice as long as usual, and her entire body was green like her face, netted with those silvery veins. Matheson supposed she now gave the impression of having returned to a more female form, because the removal of the armour on her head had spilled out an impressive growth of hair. Her brothers, however, wouldn't be growing any hair on their heads.

Clasped in pincers, the two writhed and shifted, in their way resembling metamorphosed bugs that had broken out of their chrysalises. It was as if, now free, the blood was pulsing out to fill them up and expand them into the shape they should be. Their legs were changing, shortening at the thigh and extending at the ankle, with their feet growing long and long-toed. Similar changes were occurring to their arms too, while from their torsos three pairs of insect limbs opened out, exposing the same number of tightly coiled tentacles underneath them. On their backs long glassy dragonfly wings stretched out with a crackling sound. Their heads, meanwhile, began to lose their prill appearance. They were lengthening to extend plates and muscles down their neck, and to push out long wolf-like muzzles ending in mandibular mouths. Meanwhile their eye rings were rising up to run around head turrets. All these changes seemed a chimeric mish-mash, but were bound together in a skinless, brown and slightly metallic musculature.

'Interesting variation here,' said Straeger. Matheson felt sure he caught a hint of wariness in the AI's voice. 'The majority genome in you is Atheter, in Sheen it's reverting to human, while in the brothers it's a combination of prill and something much older.'

'Much older?' Matheson managed. It was curious how his face and mouth had completely lost their human shape, yet he could speak quite clearly. But then, the descendants of the Atheter could just as clearly speak nonsense in human languages.

'The Squad,' Straeger replied.

'I don't know what you mean,' said Matheson, though he did, because Ricardo had told him. He was just trying to delay the AI with talk.

'During their conflicts a squad of Jain soldiers ended up trapped on Spatterjay. They hid their genome in a life form abundant on that world – the Spatterjay virus – ready for them to be reborn when enemies arrived. Something went wrong with the process, or those enemies never arrived. But by inserting themselves, they'd opened up this process in the Spatterjay virus, and it began saving the genomes of all prey it encountered, while also using the soldier genome to make its prey more rugged and thus re-usable. A squad of Jain soldiers is the reason the virus is the dominant life form on that world.'

Matheson understood the AI's wariness. When he looked to the Brice brothers again, he found their humanity retreating even further, and repulsion arose inside him. They were becoming something very very dangerous.

Straeger continued, 'But this won't do. I made the new armour to fit your shapes as they were while you were still aboard your ship, and even though it is highly adjustable with its sliding layers, these changes are a bit excessive for it to accommodate.'

One of the pillars of instruments slid over to the figure he thought might be Ulnar, though he couldn't tell for sure any more. The thing extended further clamps and grabs, securing the writhing form as best they could. Next, shears that resembled old-style secateurs swung into place. They reached in and closed around the base of one of Ulnar's extra limbs and then came the sound of strained hydraulics. Like a gun shot, the blades closed and the limb broke away to bounce across the floor. The erstwhile man writhed and shrieked, breaking clamps and shat-tering grabs, but more closed in as the blades snipped and snipped again. He finally slumped, as if accepting slavery, when another blade cut down behind him, severing his wings.

The armour arrived next, carried around the pillar in small, oddly shaped segments, almost like the pieces of a jigsaw puzzle. This was then pressed into place as if being glued, with each piece no larger than the palm of Matheson's hand. The sounds of things crackling and breaking accompanied the armour tightening up. It seemed that further adjustments were being made as the armour forced the man into its required shape. Clamps and pincers shifted as the growing areas began connecting up, and at the last, they simply dropped him. Even as the figure hit the floor, Matheson's gridlink reinstated, giving him com and telemetry from this particular soldier, confirming he was indeed Ulnar. The once-man rolled into a squat oriented towards Matheson and just froze there, obviously under some restraint from Straeger. There was no incoherent babble from him now, just hot hostility and exactitude. Matheson found himself confident of utter obedience from him, but any vestiges of trust had evaporated.

Will was next, and then Sheen.

'Something from Penny Royal's planetoid,' Matheson said when he saw the needle scanners tracking those silver veins all over her body.

'I know,' Straeger replied. 'It is in you too, though to a lesser extent, and another reason I decided against eliminating you.'

'What is it? Do you know?' Matheson said hurriedly, as one of those pillars now closed in on him.

'If I knew, it would not be of such interest,' Straeger replied. 'But certainly it is retarding the process that should have made you and Sheen like the brothers.'

Matheson wanted to shout about how dangerous this growth was – it couldn't be anything else considering its source – but he clamped down on suggesting it should be taken away. The idea of Straeger trying to remove something so intimately bound in their bodies gave him the horrors. And then, as cutters closed on the base of one of his lower arms and casually snipped it off, the pain rolled coherent thoughts away. Except for one. He'd already understood that Straeger was cruel, but the fact this

Mobius AI considered an unknown product of Penny Royal to be 'of such interest', rather than a somnolent nightmare ready to spring into being, demonstrated he was arrogant too.

May

Something dragged May reluctantly towards consciousness. She fought it and drifted off again, until that thing, still nagging at her, finally woke her up fully. An aug alert was trying to tell her coordinates had shifted in a way they weren't supposed to, and the *Bracken* had come out of U-space days early.

'What the hell?'

She rolled out of bed, and looked towards the chair where the agent had sat a few days ago, detailing everything that had happened to him and what he'd learned. She still felt as if she was in one of the stranger virtualities based upon him. Quickly pulling on her envirosuit, she then looked at the pulse gun on the table. She'd taken it out of storage, stuck its batteries on charge and ensured its particulate canisters were full. It seemed an ineffectual thing to do, considering, but in doing it she had felt less like a civilian swept up by the tide. She strapped on her belt and holster, loaded the gun, and holstered it. Was she ready? The concept was laughable really.

At the door she still felt crustiness under her hand and glanced back at a beetle cleanbot crawling up one wall. The bulk of the crash foam had been cleaned out of here, but some still remained. She reckoned on finding traces of it for years hence, supposing she or her ship survived that long. She headed out and to the bridge.

Cormac was sprawled in Davidson's chair, fingering the holster he'd put back on his wrist at some point – it had been missing before. It was empty, of course, with Shuriken lodged in the body of a p-prador, though when he'd talked about that she'd noticed a degree of puzzlement from him. He looked a lot better now than when he'd first emerged from Medical to find her swearing at Arach about that thing in the hold. Apparently viewing raw 'infinity' hadn't done him a great deal of good. Grimacing at something she still didn't understand, she looked around at the back wall and saw that Crane was gone. A quick aug enquiry told her the brass Golem was no longer aboard. A further enquiry informed her that neither was Arach.

'What's this?' she asked.

The main screen showed a long cloud, while the frames scattered all over it showed closer views of the debris field of which it consisted. It looked like the aftermath of a wartime space battle. She recognized chunks of hull, structural girders and other items that could be found inside ships.

'The remains of some large vessel or station,' Cormac replied, abruptly standing up and stepping forwards.

He nodded at the screen and another frame, obviously initiated by his gridlink, opened up. May goggled at the sight displayed there: Arach was jetting through vacuum on an amusingly placed thruster, with Crane mounted on him cowboy fashion. They were obviously well into the debris field and, as she watched, Arach landed on a curved section of hull that had a great mass of infrastructure attached to the underside. It looked like a chunk of body messily excised, but with Arach on it now, and Crane dismounting, she gained a sense of scale she hadn't been looking for. This one piece was two kilometres across, and she realized the vessel or station must have been a huge thing.

'This is recent,' said May.

'Yes.' Cormac made a gesture at the screens, as if he wanted to take their contents and fit them all back together. 'I guess I've updated you on a lot of things but left out what drew me into all this in the first place.'

May gave him an impatient look, as if she thought it about time he told her, although this hadn't been something she'd even considered. He was Ian Cormac, agent of Earth Central, so of course he should be involved in dramatic, world-shaking events.

He continued, 'Temporal anomalies create unique disturbances in U-space, and I'm very sensitive to such things. In fact, more so than the AIs and their detectors. That's how I found out. I was on Mars when someone made an attempt on Blite's life, and he altered the outcome.'

'That still doesn't explain why we stopped here, or *how* we stopped here.'

He gave a tight smile. 'The idea that it's difficult to take a ship out of its U-space flight program is another myth the AIs encouraged. It allows them to keep track of ships. Those like Blite, and Graveyard smugglers, know different.'

May nodded, realizing only then this was something she'd already known on some subliminal level. There were so many things Polity citizens just accepted as a fact of life that were actually manipulations. And now, stepping out of the previous course of her life, she was discovering more of them.

He continued, 'A tight mass of temporal events occurred here not long ago, and this is right on the course Blite took into the Graveyard – I saw it when I touched that thing. He was involved in something here, and I want to learn as much about it as I can.'

May walked over and dropped into her seat. Crane and Arach had opened up a hatch in the piece of hull, then gone through to explore the mass of wrecked infrastructure on the underside. No doubt they were searching out computer storage from which to extract information. Via aug, she opened further frames and studied the debris field, calculating its rate of spread and cooling, and surmised that those temporal events had been at about the same time as the destruction of whatever this had been.

'I see – Arach's found something,' said Cormac. 'These are the remains of a snatch ship called *Marble* out of the Cambrian Border Station.'

He held up his hand to part forefinger and thumb, opening up another frame which displayed the entire debris field. This field began to collapse as May tracked the computer manipulation. Now knowing the shape, and having information on the ship, Cormac was reverse modelling its destruction. The pieces assembled, steadily reconstructing chunks of the vessel, and those chunks then joined up over the collapsing spectres of explosions. Once it'd reached a point of completeness, Cormac paused it. He didn't need to highlight the trench cut along its length by some form of energy beam. Continuing the reconstruction, the trench was zipped up, and at last the huge ship sat there complete, at least in memory. Unfortunately the model could only reconstruct what had happened to the *Marble*. It couldn't show what had actually caused the damage.

Cormac now ran the destruction forwards again, to a point between the cutting of the trench and the final explosions. May couldn't figure out what he was looking for, until he grabbed out a frame near the end of the vessel, showing an open hatch.

'What's that?' she asked.

'Exit port for an AI escape pod,' he replied tersely.

Crane and Arach were visible again and, it seemed, on their way back. Good. May wanted away from this place – it felt more like a graveyard than the area it edged onto. No doubt they were about to go after that AI escape pod, before at last heading after

Blite. She felt relieved at the prospect, as though talking to her boss again would enable her to put together the pieces of this increasingly Byzantine puzzle.

Her relief lasted until the weapons woke up.

18

Valt – Past

As he approached his father's sanctum, Valt felt as if he'd eaten human meat without adequate preparation, or as if some parasites had got inside his shell. Before this one, he'd been to four audiences with his father thus far. And though any prador child dreaded such encounters, his dread had increased for reasons at a slant to the usual fear of ending up in dismembered pieces scattered around the sanctum.

'What is our purpose?' Drust asked, as he had on a number of occasions, this showing his nervousness.

With his tension growing, Valt pondered on the question, trying to decide whether to punish Drust for the repetition or answer. He decided on the latter.

'We are to slaughter humans,' said Valt.

He chafed at being unable to impart more information. Though he knew that Volax could listen in on any exchange between his children, and would focus on anything aberrant, he decided to push things further anyway.

'There is a project that has commenced, and you and I are integral,' he added.

'The war with the humans has started again?' Drust asked.

'With the humans on *that* world,' said Valt, not wanting to say anything about the disastrous attack that had been launched, and which only a few in the enclave knew about. 'I am to command the force, I think. The new children are . . . unreliable.'

Drust sensibly asked no further questions as they came to the diagonally divided door leading into Volax's steadily growing sanctum complex. Standing before the door were first-children from the ship. They moved aside without comment and the door ground open. Once it was fully open, Valt gave himself another shot of pheromone and advanced. Coming into the presence of Volax, his father, Valt then took the obeisant pose, dipping down with his claw tips against the floor. Drust did the same, in a position just behind him, while their father stood before them on prosthetic legs and waving one prosthetic claw. The stub of the other one twitched in sympathy. He discarded a limb he'd been holding in that claw, with the thicker segments of it open and the meat stripped out. His pheromone was strong in the air, yet it had changed from what Valt had stored in his suit. Or perhaps, the thought arrived in a wave of terror, Valt himself was changing in a very particular way.

'The holes for cryogenic storage and weapons have been bored into the asteroid,' Volax told him finally, after finishing crushing up the meat from the limb in his mandibles and sliding it into his gullet. 'You will go there to take command. And you, engineer Drust, will go too, to supervise the installation of our soldiers and weapons.' He paused, his mandible grinding out half words which, in human language, would be described as muttering, then continued, 'You have been good and loyal children and I rely on you.'

Valt dipped lower, feeling his terror increase. Fathers did not talk of loyalty and reliance to their children. This was the kind of language they used with other fathers in negotiations between families. Fathers only talked to their children in terms of obedience and threats of violence, and agonizing death. He turned an eye over to one side, to take in an example of the same.

A second-child lay bubbling on the floor over there. Its limbs, claws and mandibles had been stripped off, and it was those Volax had been dining on. Its shell had been sliced round and opened up like a lid to expose his innards. Volax had also cut around the head turret, slicing a channel through the upper shell so he could remove the turret without cutting its nerve trunks and arteries of ichor and chyme. It was now perched at the edge of the opened lower body, so the second-child was peering into its own guts. The creature, still alive, was in agony, of course, but unable to express that beyond the bubbling sound, which would continue for some while yet. Poised next to it was the half-shell surgery telefactor Volax had been using. Volax would remove and eat the organs too, but whether that would result in a relatively quick or slow death depended on whether Volax wanted to flash-freeze the child's ganglion and use it in a robot. If that was the case, some organ support would have to remain in place, and the procedure would be quicker leading up to removal of the ganglion. Otherwise it would be slow and drawn out over many days – preserving the child's life until nearly everything was gone. Valt noted that the child's suit lay over to one side, and it was an inferior steel one, which meant the child was one of the newest generations. Volax had taken against these, killing them for the most minor of infractions.

'And if you fail me, I will set your eyes to watch while I eat your entrails!'

Valt relaxed a little. That was more like it. However, he still felt an edge of fear, because though the threat was true to form, the logic wasn't there. If he failed in this mission, as detailed in a previous meeting, he would be dead anyway, so threats of punishment were redundant. Other things, too, did not quite add up. The plan in overview was a good one and had been worked out some years back, with the excavations into the asteroid's rock made ever since, but so much just did not make sense. Why use such a large asteroid when a smaller one, propelled at speed, would do the same job? And surely the recovered armour would be better for the attack force? But no, it was to be put into storage. Why send out food supplies for soldiers who would be in hibernation, and once out of it would soon enough be dining on human flesh (with the required additives, of course)? Finally, why were there to be escort ships and a precursor attack?

'I understand, Father,' Valt replied.

Volax dipped in acceptance of that, picked up the discarded leg and inspected it, then dropped it again and said, 'The holes for cryogenic storage and weapons are ready. You will go there to take command. Engineer Drust will supervise the installation . . .'

'Yes, Father,' Valt replied, dread growing further inside him.

'Interrupt me again and I will set your eyes to watch while I eat your entrails!'

Valt dipped lower, pressing his claw tips so hard into the floor they began to penetrate. His father was repeating himself. Fathers never repeated orders – they just punished those who failed to follow them.

'We will remove the humans from existence . . .'

After that Volax just stood there looking at them for a long time. Then, as Valt became tempted to say something, he heard a spattering sound. The smell wafted to him underneath the strong hormonal output. With utter horror he realized that his father had just shat all over the floor. Almost in panic, Valt scanned around, looking for the sanitary facility, as surely one must be absent for his father to have done this. He then plainly saw the large funnel contraption over against one wall – it was caked with shit, and a layer of the same was on the floor all around it, crawling with ship lice. His glance around also picked up other items. He recognized a pheromone disperser, of the kind usually positioned in the further reaches of a family enclave. Why was it here? He also saw cylinders containing prador ichor and chyme, with pumps fixed to their sides, and looped attachment pipes. His gaze then centred on the numerous ports which he'd seen before all over Volax's body. His father's behaviour, and what all of this meant, suddenly became too much – despite being open to Volax's pheromone here, he complemented it with a long blast of the stuff from the disperser inside his suit. A degree of calm settled over him. Everything was right and as it should be, and everything his father did and said was correct. The calm did not last.

Volax's mating clypeus abruptly dropped at his back end and his two-pronged penis extruded, bright green and dripping. He turned away from them and wandered over to the suffering second-child, then moved in over it. Reaching inside with his one claw, he snared something, tore it out, and crunched it up in his mandibles. The child's bubbling died away, for he had just pulled out its main ganglion. He shifted in closer over the child, covering it completely, and began moving rhythmically, one prong of his penis managing to find its way in through a leg socket. Finishing the ganglion, he started to speak, but words and context separated, turning the whole to nonsense.

Father was very busy, and they must take his dismissal as implicit. Not all orders were verbal, but children must obey them nonetheless. Valt pulled up his claws from the floor and began withdrawing to the door. He banged into Drust behind him, who was retreating also. Something cracked, and glancing back with his one stalked eye, Valt saw his father had broken off the side of the child's lower shell, and internal organs were spilling over the floor. Volax was making a huffing sound, and his mandibles were now out from his gullet, pointing straight up. Valt inserted his claw in the pit control for the door, twisted and waited, as it seemed a wave of madness was washing over him.

'Mudfish mucus!' his father clattered and bubbled as they went out.

In the tunnel outside, Valt and Drust waited respectfully as the door ground closed again. Notably the guards made no attempt to see what was going on in the sanctum. Valt and Drust then turned and headed away. As one, they both closed up their suits and Valt felt sure Drust was doing the same as him: increasing the pheromone inside his suit to the maximum by first bringing the oxygen levels down. He realized, as he did this, his legs were shaking. Finally, after a long period, the world began to settle back into its proper shape. What he had seen in his father's sanctum was obviously something above his position to understand, and he pushed it to the back of his mind. At some later time it would come clear, and his father's wisdom would be revealed.

'We have our orders,' he finally managed to grate out.

'And we will obey them,' Drust replied.

Valt smacked a claw against the back of Drust's shell for such impertinence, but it wasn't a particularly strong blow, just a matter of form. They moved off quickly to be about their duties, and away from any further confusion.

Cormac

Cormac damned himself for being all kinds of stupid. He'd maintained wide links to Crane and Arach, and to ship's scanners, which he had running at maximum, while also ranging out as far as he could with his U-sense. In a retrospective second, after seeing what he'd missed, he recognized he'd been focusing too much of his attention on keeping watch for interlopers from *outside*. Had he properly concentrated on the reassembly of debris that made up the *Marble*, he would have recognized that two particular cylindrical objects weren't part of it.

They had no active fusion reactors to spot, nor laminar storage batteries with their detectable power potential. The power potential here was the simple chemical kind and had slipped beneath his radar. He realized the things must have powered up upon passively detecting the *Bracken*'s arrival here. Some kind of very low-energy computing had probably then made assessments and chosen the best time to attack, which was with Crane and Arach far from the ship. Or perhaps whoever this was had some form of U-space connection with a controller, though surely he would have sensed that? It was immaterial. The things ignited, routing chemical energy through their systems and beaming out their substance in one long particle beam flare across vacuum. There'd been no warning and nothing to detect before the strikes. The beams struck simultaneously, straight on the *Bracken*'s U-space nacelles. One simply burst like a bubble. The other remained intact, because the ship's system quickly deployed the newly installed hardfield, but this didn't mean functional. Even as the weapons burned down like fireworks, and their beams guttered out, the nacelle emitted a brief pseudo-matter construct like a thistle made of glass, before its side dented in.

'Fuck,' said Cormac. It seemed the only appropriate comment to make.

'Something of an understatement,' Arach replied through their connection. Crane said nothing, of course, but Cormac could feel the brass Golem's disapproval.

'What the hell?' May exclaimed, catching up a second later as the ship shuddered around her.

Cormac eyed her. Through his U-sense he could feel a distortion growing, like a flaw in the gem of his perception. Then a familiar ship snapped into being out there.

'Get yourself armoured and armed,' he said. 'We're about to be attacked.'

'We just were attacked!' May shouted.

'Just do it,' he said, annoyed at how slow she was despite being aug enhanced.

She glared at him and leaped out of her seat, heading for the bridge door. As the new arrival slid into the real, Cormac assessed weapons and resources, and took a firm grip of the ship's systems. Arach and Crane had done a good job providing the *Bracken* with two particle cannons and the shield generator, but no way was it up to dealing with Matheson's vessel. They were just enough to keep the thing intact long enough to run away, yet with the nacelles now destroyed there'd be no running. He fired up the fusion drive, spat a warning to May, who'd reached her cabin, and kicked in the subsidiaries to take them into the debris field. At least there they'd be able to find some protection within the floating chunks of ship, and it'd be tactically unsound for Matheson to follow him. The *Bracken* lurched and his chair stabilized, closing around him while simultaneously extruding safety straps.

Matheson's ship flared from two ports, and he tracked missiles on the way in. Arach had tracked them too and, with a stream of profanity, skittered across the chunk of hull he and Crane were standing upon. Crane stood there, looking out towards the approaching missiles, then broke into a run in the opposite direction. Good – two separate targets would make things more difficult for the attackers. But it seemed these two weren't the primary target, as the spherical ship changed course to come in after the *Bracken* and fired up a particle beam.

The hardfield intercepted the strike, blackening and then going out with a crash. Via U-sense, Cormac saw the molten hollow within the body of the ship, and smoke began to wisp from the circulation system. The beam tracked along the *Bracken*'s hull, blowing subsidiaries, until focusing on the main fusion drive. The thing blew and flickered out like a candle. Diverting power from those engines, Cormac fired up the facing particle cannon. It lashed out, a lot more powerful than expected, and white-shifted like the weapons of the p-prador. Hardfield intercepts blackened under its strike and Matheson's ship ejected three burning generators. This made Cormac briefly happy, but his tactical mind couldn't let him ignore the realities, especially when Matheson changed aim and blew their particle weapon out of the side of the ship.

Matheson was only using disabling shots. He was toying with them, but at any time he could finish this. Cormac rolled the ship to bring the other weapon to bear, only to see it incinerated halfway through opening fire. Matheson then went on to track along the body to take out further subsidiaries. As he watched the destruction through sensors and his U-sense, a weird distancing began to arrive – a sense of unreality. He turned his attention to the missiles arriving in the debris field, seeing Arach jetting away hard as the chunk of debris exploded behind him, and then he faded from view. He saw Crane hit a floating memory-metal girder and bounce away on a new course, then similarly fading. They had a chance of survival. And frankly, Matheson would be a fool to go into that field after them, since he might end up finding them attached to his hull and breaking in. Besides the protection the field offered, this was precisely why he thought it tactically unsound for Matheson to follow. Sensibly, the best option for the man would be to bombard the field from some distance out. He could take his time, since no one was going anywhere. But where did that leave Cormac and May?

The feeling of unreality fled as hard truth impacted. His ability to jump through U-space might be able to keep him and May safe for a while, but they were still in a trap. Here they were light years from the nearest world, and he simply couldn't take them that distance. Only one option remained. He undid the straps and instructed the chair to release its grip, checked the grenades he'd got from Andre on the bandolier under his coat, then snatched up the laser carbine from where he'd clipped it to the nearby console. He looked to May as she returned to the bridge, staggering as the ship lurched again from an explosion, then chose his target and U-jumped.

As Matheson's bridge filled in around him, Cormac fired, sweeping the laser across consoles, and bringing it down on what he presumed to be Matheson in the captain's chair. Two armoured creatures, which little resembled the humans they'd once been, launched at him, while a more human figure came in from the other side, grabbing for his arm. He eased back out of the real, snatched a grenade off his belt, and initiated it, thrusting it towards the human figure and intending to leave it inside this one. His fist thumped against solid armour.

The shock stopped him for vital fractions of a second. One of the other figures crashed into him, while its companion raked down with clawed fingers. As he tumbled slowly through between-space, his gridlink coldly informed him of his broken shoulder and upper arm, four ribs and a series of lacerations down to those breaks. The pain arrived like a lash, then faded as he instructed relevant nerves to shut down. He pushed for a full jump, snapping out into the real in the hold, and had time to see the clamp before one of his attackers appeared beside him.

497

It swiped at him, but its clawed hand passed straight through him. Good. However they were managing to copy his abilities, they hadn't got it quite right yet.

He jumped again, appearing beside a missile-loading carousel like the magazine of a Tommy gun. Tossing grenades, he jumped once more and came out of it with his finger hard down on the carbine trigger. Yes, Matheson had predicted he'd appear here, and one of the non-human attackers fell back with armour smoking. He tossed further grenades where he'd come out, in the small maintenance area wrapped around the particle weapon. Even as he jumped again, his first grenades detonated. In U-sense, he had the satisfaction of seeing at least one missile warhead explode inside the ship, smashing the carousel from its mountings with a chunk carved out of it, excavating a molten cavity in the ship and flinging walls of fire through its spaces. This was pure luck, since such missiles were designed only to detonate on receiving the correct instruction. Must have been a dodgy chemical load. Luck was something he couldn't always rely on – he had to be smart.

His next logical targets should have been the drive systems, but instead he jumped straight back to the bridge, to see if he could take out further control of those systems. It surprised him to find Matheson still there in the control chair, and he opened fire on the man at once, square on his chest. The carbine beam splashed off him, and just a second later the other human-looking Brice appeared, lashing out. Cormac slid partially out of the real again, instinctively, but paying more attention now. This attacker was a woman, so must be Sheen Brice. She stayed with him, following him out of the real just a fraction of a second behind. Her clawed hand closed on his weapon, and she caught the full brunt of its beam up her arm and into her shoulder. Cormac gridlinked an instruction to the weapon, released it, and jumped away as her other hand swiped through where his head had been. He glimpsed the weapon then exploding to send her tumbling through the ship, neither in nor out of the real.

Again and again he jumped to different locations in the ship, sliding partially out of the real and back in again, narrowly avoiding attempts to rip him apart. Data firmed in his mind. The armour Matheson and the Brices wore was different from before, and he was achieving minimal penetration with energy weapons. Not that he had his carbine any longer. The way Matheson remained in one place seemed to confirm he was in control and sending the Brices after him. They didn't have individual control of their jumps. He'd taken out the ship's main weapons, and likely damaged the fusion drive, or at least delayed its operation for a while. But with these data in place, the final reality of his situation hit home. He was losing and could see no way out of this. He couldn't detonate a fusion reactor aboard, since the things had a higher safety profile than the missiles. He saw none of the dents in the U-space continuum which would indicate CTDs that he could detonate either. It seemed all he could do was run, while scrabbling to stay alive.

On the next jump, a claw raked across his back, and he noted another thing about the methods of attack. Matheson kept the Brice brothers, or whatever they'd become, together, while shunting Sheen independently. Did this indicate he had less control over the two? And how might that help him? Cormac ran a hand down his bandolier, drawing his new thin gun with the other. His next jump put him in a refectory, where he caught sight of the man-Golem Ricardo, stooped over picking up plates that'd spilled to the floor. He took in the fluid cylinders, the hue of the fluid inside them, and another datum clicked into place: Spatterjay virus inhibitor. Sheen appeared, falling towards him from the ceiling. He dropped and rolled, finger down on the trigger and aimed at her right foot. The impacts shifted it just enough, so it clipped the edge of the table and she lost balance, falling away from him. New datum: as these were alternating attacks, the two Brices would be next.

He needed new weapons – he only had a couple of grenades left – and this meant a jump back to the *Bracken*. He considered the delay between attacks, which was likely due to the time it took for Matheson to make the U-space calculations. He needed to extend it somehow, to give himself time to grab weapons, and a U-space disruption would do that. His next jump put him right in the centre of the ship by a distortion in the continuum. Its real-world source was a lozenge of tech, secured in two heavy ceramal rings at the termination of heavy pillars attached to ceiling and floor. The place was tangled with optics, power feeds and cooling tubes. At the far end of the lozenge, spaced just a short distance from it, sat a spherical case. The lozenge was the internal U-space drive, and the sphere contained the controlling mind. He ducked under a skein of optics and threw himself towards that end, just as the Brice brothers appeared. They showed no care for their ship as they tried to get to him, tearing through the infrastructure. Shooting at them nonstop, finger hard down on the trigger, he detached the two remaining grenades and dropped them between drive and mind, gridlinking the timing through. One of the Brices came down at him, long head stabbing forwards as if he wanted to take a bite. Cormac rolled away and, precisely to the second, jumped yet again.

With mind and gridlink at highest function, his perception of the jump was drawn out. Translation showed him shooting away from Matheson's ship and approaching the *Bracken*. As the grenades blew, a pulse of distortion twisted the U-continuum, but still he saw something tracking him out. The disruption screwed his arrival point and velocity, but at least didn't put him halfway inside a wall. He fell out of the air in a ship's corridor. His feet hit the floor hard, and he tumbled forwards into a roll. Coming up running, he went round a corner and shouldered into a door, crashing it aside. Behind him he heard something else land hard, and then back at the corner Sheen Brice tumbled through. He ducked into his cabin, yanked open a cupboard, and pulled out the second carbine, along with a long box of grenades. Once out in the corridor again, he saw her standing up from the wreckage, locating him, then hurling herself in a run towards him. It was no good. He couldn't get through that armour of theirs, and the only prospect ahead was more U-jumping and fighting, until they finally brought him down. His head was aching, and so many alerts had been rising from his nanosuite he'd had to shut them down.

'Get down,' said a familiar voice.

Cormac dropped and miniguns thundered overhead. Sheen came to a dead stop and began sliding back as shattered slugs fell all about her, or ricocheted through the walls, ceiling and floor. He felt something smack into his calf and it suddenly went numb. He didn't want to look at it. Arach stepped over him and a hardfield bloomed in the corridor, taking the ricochets. Sheen hit the far wall, and Cormac noticed that her armour, though tough, wasn't doing well under this fusillade. Then the firing abruptly stopped, and she began to pull herself out of the wrecked wall. She managed to draw her feet under her, but no further. A figure loomed over her, reached down and closed a huge brass hand around her neck. Crane picked her up as she writhed and struggled, then slammed her into an intact wall, then down onto the floor, then, in a blur of motion, up into the ceiling, holding her by the ankle. This dazed her at least for a second. In that moment, Crane reached in with his other hand, and ripped away a chunk of armour from her lower back.

'You need to get moving,' said Arach. 'The disruption you caused will be done in three minutes, then the rest of them will be over here.'

'You can't handle them?'

The spider drone moved ahead and turned to observe him, while behind Crane was searching for remaining solid surfaces to beat Sheen Brice against. 'Probably not. And even if we could, they'll pull out, make repairs and obliterate us here. Maybe you could jump us over there. But I doubt it.'

Cormac looked down at himself, realizing he was soaked in blood. His lower right leg was off at an angle, with most of the calf missing, and a bone was sticking out of one arm. More importantly, however, his brain felt like a boiling sore in his skull, and he just knew he was running on empty. He'd never quite worked out the basis of his ability, but at least knew it to be biological, because physical exhaustion diminished it, and right now his batteries were hollow. He felt sick.

'So get moving where?' he asked, and shrugged.

'Where you've been denying our way out has been all along.'

This was all he needed for his mind abruptly to reconfigure and the hopelessness to turn into something else. The device. New energy brought him up on one leg, leaning against the wall, as Arach turned and charged into the fight between Crane and Sheen. An instruction via gridlink put his nanosuite on its highest, and perhaps terminal burn. He walked, shattered leg giving way underneath him, spatters of blood on the floor behind.

Two minutes and forty seconds . . .

He reached the hold door in fifty seconds and found it standing open. Yes, he had hope, but it was the hope of saving his companions and mostly May, whom he felt really didn't deserve what would happen to her if they remained here. However, he had no hope for himself. Sure, there was enough power here he could use to jump them away from this place, but he expected it to leave him as a charred smear on the floor.

Cormac reached his hand out towards the Penny Royal twist device as he limped forwards, still reluctant. This was it, then – the centuries of his life were coming to an end, though an appropriate one. He paused, feeling utterly selfish in doing so, hating himself for wanting to live just a little bit longer. Fate intervened then, as the nanosuite stuttered, allowing his abused body to broadcast its distress. Or perhaps it wasn't fate at all. His torso tightened in an agonized convulsion and his leg gave way. He fell forwards and instinctively grabbed for support. His hand closed around one of the protrusions from the thing, and he went down on his knees. A surge of terror rose in his throat at the expected violent transition into a Penny Royal cyst in the U-space continuum. He tried to pull his hand away, but it was stuck in place. And it was different this time.

He was utterly exhausted, depleted, and now alerts from his nanosuite were overriding his suppression, because he'd gone beyond the point of extreme physical damage, into the terrain of dying. His blood pressure was so low it was routing blood out of damaged areas and extremities to keep his main organs functional. Meanwhile, the thing was raising chemical energy to start its vitrification protocol. If he allowed this, his entire body and brain would shut down, and he needed the latter right now. He overrode the nanosuite yet again, designing a response that would keep the organ in his skull as functional as possible. He might well lose all his limbs – he'd certainly lose his broken arm and broken leg. And having stopped vitrification, real permanent death was a possibility. But he felt something indefinable increasing inside him, despite the depletion. Sensing movement above, he looked up at the thing he was grasping and saw it ooze out a tendril above his fist. This tracked across the back of his hand and began to wind down his arm. Along its length it then spread silvery threads, or mycelia like the clinging roots of ivy, and they penetrated his skin.

Contact.

His U-sense, which had been a dull thing until then, exploded back into life. As his gridlink interpreted, he initially gleaned a sense of the whole ship encompassed in detail. A large section of the ship's interior had become a torn wreck. Walls, floors and ceilings had been beaten into scrap, clinging to structural beams, which themselves were bent out of shape. Grav-plates were out; debris floated in the air, most seemingly consisting of minigun slugs. Arach was squatting in among this with his guns still out and smoking, while May was negotiating her way from the bridge through the mess. Cormac tracked down Crane and found him climbing out of a tangled pit of smoking wreckage into a complete passage that led to an airlock, dragging Sheen Brice behind him.

The expansion of Cormac's U-sense continued, taking in the debris field and Matheson's ship. He was pleased to see this had a hole in its hull, with an electrical fire burning inside, wraiths of flame wafting out and snuffing in vacuum as they used up their air. He saw inside to the Brice brothers, freeing themselves from the wreckage around a malfunctioning U-space engine, and Matheson standing up from his control chair, the armour over his head open to reveal a decidedly strange face. The U-space disruption from the broken engine continued, but it was fading fast. They were just a minute or so away from being able to jump over to the *Bracken*.

Cormac's sense of things continued to expand outwards, but seemingly at a rate easier to incorporate. He found himself divorced from his damaged body, and once again floating in that vast cavern lined with black crystal, where chunks of the same traversed it like vesicles and nanomachines in an artery. He stabilized there, knowing what he had to do now, and apparently indifferent to the likelihood it would kill him. In reality, his free hand flopped down to the deck as he pushed his U-field out to his skin, and then beyond it – just as he always did when encompassing some other object to transfer it with him, or fling it through U-space. The field spread in a glittering wave from his hand, across every surface, flowing out to the hull and then in both directions along the *Bracken*'s huge length. In that moment he felt himself subject to immense inspection and knew Penny Royal was watching. A thin screaming penetrated his psyche, diverting him for a second to Crane dragging Sheen Brice behind him by one leg.

Writhing and struggling, Sheen Brice had been stripped of most of her armour, with just some jigsaw fragments clinging here and there. Cormac tracked back and noted pieces of it scattered through the wreckage behind. She was a bloody ruin, because in peeling off her armour, Crane seemed to have taken much of her skin with it. The thin screaming increased in intensity and began to echo in Cormac's gridlink. He observed her with cold precision, seeing skin blistering up out of her flesh and spreading, but also the silvery veins webbing her body. He withdrew a little, focusing on himself, and saw that the tendril had straightened out its path, as if more sure of its target. It had grown up his arm under his sleeve, exited at his collar, and was now spreading over the side of his skull, connecting to his gridlink. But it also had some EMR connection to the network over Sheen Brice.

Crane dragged her partway along the corridor, leaving a trail of gelatinous blood and pieces of her and her armour, then dropped her. He reached into his pocket and pulled out his scrunched-up hat, straightened the thing out and pressed it down on his head. Obviously the violent activity had required him to remove it. He too had received damage during the fight. A split in his neck, and up the side of his face, revealed something black and oily. Being able to look through things, Cormac could see similar damage down his body. Something else was odd too, and it took him a moment to realize that Crane looked bigger – a moment later, a gridlink measure showed him he had grown taller and expanded in girth, filling out his coat. It seemed something inside him was trying to break out, and Cormac feared this was indeed the case. The Golem turned then and seemed to be looking directly at Cormac, before he reached down, grabbed the leg again, and continued on. Coming to the airlock door, he reached out and touched the control. The door popped up on its seal and swung open.

'No,' said Cormac – just a whisper.

Crane looked towards him once more, shrugged, then palmed the door shut again and began dragging her off somewhere else. Cormac wasn't sure why he'd stopped Crane tossing her out of the airlock, but he felt a connection between the tech of this device here, and her, and in some sense beyond to Penny Royal. His instruction to Crane raised something from the last of those; it seemed like amused approval. He had no time to elucidate that. The disruption in Matheson's ship was on the brink of clearing, and the man would be able to start jumping the Brice brothers any second.

Cormac calculated coordinates already obtained from Blite during their data exchange and perceived that distant point. Now he felt anchored, as though he'd attached a carry strap to a boulder. He heaved. His body and mind crackled like wood bent to breaking. All overrides collapsed and pain washed through him. He opened his mouth as if to scream but nothing came out. Rather, it seemed the entire ship screamed. Rational thought retreated and only the effort remained. The *Bracken* shifted in vacuum, leaving streamers of photons raised from quantum foam, and then with a sucking crash the giant ship submerged into U-space.

Blite

Biology, Blite thought, and wrinkled his nose. Atmosphere readings were good here, on Yossander's Hold, with the air only heavier on the oxygen and carbon dioxide than he was used to. But it was also laden with bacteria, viruses, spores and other biological particles. Ship filters and analysers had picked up nothing particularly pathogenic as yet – or at least not outside the capabilities of a standard nanosuite. He'd considered wearing an envirosuit, but the terse representative of the Gilliad had informed him there was nothing likely to kill them here. Blite decided they might think it rude and untrusting if they protected themselves this way.

Pressing his induction aug into place, Blite took a couple of steps down the ramp to look around, aware of the disapproval of Carlstone behind him. Only Gruce and Armand were along with them, because Blite had told Carlstone no, he couldn't bring all the soldiers they had aboard. The man had also wanted to scout out the area first. As Blite saw it, this would reveal no more than their scanners, and it would also establish a distrustful military approach. He did, after all, need information from these people. He didn't really want to have to fight them.

The *Coin* had landed on one of the drift islands, as per the coordinates they'd been given. It resembled a sandbar of Earth, partially occupied by some jungle and a scattering of trees. At this point, the trees were over the other side of the *Coin*, though glancing to the fore Blite could see the tops of some particularly tall palms. Ahead lay beach stretching down to the sea. The sand was multicoloured, with pastel green and pink swirled with white and yellow. Polished stones lay everywhere, along with a wide variety of seashells and the carapace remains of various crust-aceans. The sea was calm up close to the shore, with just low wavelets slopping on the sand. Further out, the deep almost purple-blue was marred with squalls of white water below small twisters skittering across the surface like angry sprites. The blue sky shaded to pink, strewn with snakes and claws of violet and yellow cloud. Then there was the boat.

The convoluted thing had the hue of old bone and lay maybe ten metres long. Blite was trying to figure out what it reminded him of when a figure jumped off the back, into waist-deep water, and began wading ashore. When the other two jumped off and followed, it seemed enough for Carlstone. He came down the ramp to stand at Blite's side, while Gruce and Armand moved ahead.

'Easy,' Blite said to the man, who obviously relayed the order. His soldiers dialled back to a saunter and Armand rested his laser carbine casually across one shoulder, whereas before he'd been pointing it towards the sea. Blite grimaced. Doing the casual thing didn't make them any less threatening. Returning his attention to the boat, he now realized what it reminded him of. The thing looked vaguely like a reptile's skull, but with a section sliced out for the back deck. It was an item that had likely been grown rather than manufactured.

'Some variation in form,' Carlstone said tightly from beside him.

The first figure walking over to them was short but thin and gangly, wearing a single suit whorled like old wood, and of a similar colour too. He had long pale hair and conventionally handsome male features. He smiled up at them as he approached, yet Blite read a weird intensity behind that smile. The other two, however, were a different matter.

They appeared to be armoured, though in shifting plates over something slimy, worm-like and segmented. Their shoulder width was huge, and they stood half a metre taller than the first figure. Blite could see their fingers were webbed. Their heads were a grotesque blend of insect and reptile, with huge compound eyes and a variety of twitching antennae. Objects attached around them had the appearance of weapons, while the harpoon guns strapped across their backs definitely were.

'It's a biotech world, so we should expect this,' Blite replied. He pointed to the two as they came out of the sea. 'But for all we know, that's simply organic armour.'

'Yeah, of course,' said Carlstone doubtfully.

Blite turned and looked back up to the top of the ramp. Meander and Iris were waiting, Iris with her expression unreadable, while Meander was gazing out at the scene with seeming puzzlement. Did she recognize any of this? He waved them after him, then headed down to the sand. Armand and Gruce, being more intent on the two following, moved aside as the man came up to halt before Blite.

'So you're Captain Blite of Penny Transport?' he asked, apparently hungry for the answer.

Blite eyed the accoutrement that, until the man drew close, he hadn't paid particular attention to. From a distance it had looked like a decorative torc about his neck. Now he saw that one end of it extended up to attach just behind his ear. Some sort of aug, he thought, until the thing moved. It looked like a lamprey wrapped around his throat and sucking on his skull.

'Yeah, that's me.'

The man held out a hand. Blite noticed slight webbing between the fingers and claw-like nails. He was reluctant to shake that hand – he knew the penchant for many who went this route was to weaponize their bodies, and how they tended to put nasty toxin injectors in their claws. But he was being stupid. If they wanted to fuck him over here, it could have been done with a mosquito bite the moment he stepped out of his ship.

'And you are?' he asked, shaking the man's hand.

'I'm Preece, and I'm here to bring you to the Gilliad.' The man looked over Blite's shoulder at the others. 'This is all of you?'

'This is all of us who are coming,' Blite replied.

Preece acknowledged the caution with a nod and continued, 'You're welcome here. Trade is welcome here, as is new technology and new thought.' Blite turned to follow the direction of the man's gaze when he said those words, and saw he'd been looking at Iris.

'Let me make some introductions,' said Blite, and he did so. He watched carefully to see the reaction to Meander, and he got one. Preece tried to acknowledge her calmly, in the same way he did Carlstone and the soldiers, but his speech stumbled, and Blite saw the lamprey thing seem to tighten, as though it wanted to choke him. When it came to Iris, the man seemed intent, fascinated.

'*Factionalism*,' said Irene, directly through Blite's aug.

'*What?*'

'*This is a world divided under the Gilliad, who seems to have assumed power in the years since the first prador attack. As we learned before, there are those who are fanatical about the purity of biotech, and those inclined to introduce more hard tech. Preece is probably of the latter kind and I am the first haiman he's seen.*'

'*I see.*' Blite allowed himself a degree of smugness. His long life enabled him to perceive things Iris, with her haiman senses and cerebral upgrades, had simply missed. But then to him she was a bit of a youngster.

'Shall we?' Preece gestured down the beach.

Blite nodded agreement and they headed down. As they reached a debris line, he peered down at ribbons of seaweed, the occasional dead crustacean and a partially dried-out fish like a small shark. He glanced back as he heard a crunching sound and saw the *Coin*'s ramp closing up. Judice was in command there now. As he'd ordered, intelligence-gathering continued, scanning had ramped up and weapons systems were ready. Meanwhile, the remaining soldiers were prepped and ready to set out in the grav-car in the hold. Blite wanted to present a friendly front but he wasn't naive. He had after all, as noted in his assessment of Iris, been knocking around the universe for a long time. He couldn't yet tell whether Preece's reaction to Meander had been hostile or not, but there'd definitely been recognition, which the man was holding back on for some reason.

May

May clung to a twisted beam as Arach scrambled past her. They'd somehow jumped into U-space, and then the reality dawned on her that the agent had done it. He'd managed to jump thousands of tons of the *Bracken* into the U-continuum. It felt both odd and horrible, because though the man was obviously blocking some of the effects, he wasn't stopping it all. The interior of the ship had slid partially out of the real too, making distances variable, angles impossible, and spaces negotiable things. She propelled herself after Arach, where he landed in a sheared-off corridor, and scrambled ahead. Grav took hold of her beyond the lip, and she dropped into a crouch. Operating grav-plates below her helped adjust perspective, and now it no longer seemed as though the corridor speared off to infinity. Arach halted at a door, pushed it open and compressed his abdomen to go through, belatedly retracting his miniguns. Following him, she realized he'd entered the medical area.

The fight between Crane and that creature, which she now recognized from recorded imagery as Sheen Brice, hadn't strayed into this area. But it'd had its effects. The wall all along one side was bowed in, with definite human-shaped dents in it. Work surfaces were tipped over, with equipment spilled onto the floor. Grav-plates over to one side were malfunctioning, and curiously had hundreds of serum bottles floating above them, swirling about each other like fish in a bait ball. Arach extruded a film bag and began grabbing stuff up to put into it.

'What do we need?' she asked.

He sent a feed to her aug showing Cormac lying against the device in the hold. Blood had pooled on the floor around him, and she could see broken bones protruding. Silver veins had spread over the exposed skin. He looked wasted, and the feed was enough to propel her into motion. She wrenched open a distorted cabinet at floor level, pulled out a trundle docbox and initiated it. The thing rose a few centimetres up off the floor and oriented towards her. Arach had meanwhile dumped a variety of bottles into his bag, including artificial blood, plasma and repair complements for a nanosuite. She wasn't quite sure why he needed the last of those. He was now throwing in other items at high speed, as if he intended to take the entire contents of the medical area. Heading for the door with the docbox trundling behind her, May sent the spider drone the image of a clock. He froze, then abruptly followed.

'You are correct,' he said, with some surprise.

Another area of the ship, wrecked by the fight, needed to be crossed to get to the hold. Arach grabbed up the docbox for her and deposited it in the next area, where grav-plates were functioning, and disappeared on ahead, while she made her way more slowly across. Arriving on the other side, she snapped her fingers to bring the box after her, rounded a corner and then froze, wondering about U-space hallucinations. But what she was seeing was real.

The ship's structural beams were high-grade memory metal, which upon being bent out of shape should swiftly return to its previous form. This stuff wasn't doing so, however. The wall had been peeled back and rolled up like a rug to expose the supporting structure, also revealing one of the ship's main ceramal stress beams at this point. And the memory-metal beams had been bent around this to secure in place Sheen Brice.

She looked decidedly more human than before, but still not someone you'd want wandering around your ship. With her arms and legs pinned, the only movement she could manage was with her head, which she was snapping from side to side. She looked crazy, her eyes plain black and her tongue shooting out to open its leech mouth, baring organic bony things revolving inside. Spatterjay virus, of course. The woman would need food and inhibitors, but she wasn't May's first concern right now. She quickly moved on, wondering why Crane had bound Sheen like that, rather than disposing of her.

When May arrived in the hold Arach was already at work, having set up various fluid feeds running into the agent, and now working on his leg. Cormac was on his back, sprawled out, with one arm up and connected to that *thing*. He was naked now too, his clothing in a bloody pile over to one side, and she could see he was even more injured than she'd thought. As she moved in, the drone tugged on Cormac's foot, pulling and aligning bones partially exposed where his calf had been blown away, then extended a limb and began bone welding. She wondered if there was any point to this – that leg looked like it needed to come off.

The docbox dropped to the floor and she hit the control to open it up, unveiling numerous trays and compartments. She took out a cylinder, slid out the field autodoc inside and initiated it, dropping it on Cormac's chest. The thing clung there, with spiky legs digging in as if pondering what to do next. It scuttled around, extruded numerous tubes to penetrate his body, then quickly sliced into his chest and peeled back skin and flesh to expose his shattered ribs. There it fired up its bone welder. Connected via her aug, she received the diagnostics; they weren't pretty. She sorted through numerous options and made selections from the box, ignoring the advice to stick the man in a cold coffin until he could receive the attentions of an AI surgeon. She stepped back, and watched in surprise as Arach extruded wet strands of artificial muscle from a spinneret. He wove this up on the loom of his limbs, and began inserting it into Cormac's ruined leg. It was at this point the man opened his eyes and looked at her.

'Seems I'm a bit of a mess,' he said succinctly.

'You're keeping us in U-space?' she said urgently, then felt ashamed to be asking this, what with the state of his body below the neck.

'The course is set. I'm holding us under, but I'm in another place.' He paused, eyes going distant, then added, 'You must be ready when we come out . . . drive systems . . .'

She had no idea what he meant, as he closed his eyes and began panting hard, but her thoughts were swept away by the alerts coming through the field autodoc. A whole list of them scrolled for her inner perception, and though she could take in some of it, like the sharp drop in ATP, temperature rise and physical demands, she couldn't quite parse what was happening. Arach, snatching away from cell welding the man's calf back together, flipped out one of the bottles in his bag, as well as a mask and connecting tubes from the docbox. He skittered them across the floor to her.

'He's hyperfunction,' the drone said. 'We've got to keep him topped up.'

She took up the oxygen bottle, attached the pipes from the mask and pressed it over his mouth and nose. A couple of fluid feeds had already emptied, and she could smell the dark urine running out around his thighs. She fixed up more feeds, a catheter, and then instructed the autodoc to insert a heart patch between his partially repaired ribs. That stabilized his heartbeat at an incredibly high rate, linked to demand via his suite.

Arach had meanwhile paused. A couple of nanosuite complements were held in the complex grippers of his forward limbs, while the two limbs back from those were beating a tattoo against the floor.

'What are you doing?' she asked with a spurt of irritation.

'He is human,' said Arach, 'doing what a human cannot do.'

'What's that supposed to mean?' she asked as she worked.

Arach didn't reply, and instead unreeled programming leads from below his mandibles, then plugged them into the cylinders. As far as she understood it, the complements were just a way of bulking up the nanomachines, vesicles and other paraphernalia of a nanosuite, and didn't need programming. Once done, he passed them over to her to attach to the agent's fluid feeds. She did so, questions dying away into passivity, as if she'd run out of emotions. A short while later, a vast swathe of the readings from his nanosuite ceased to make sense. They meant radical changes, but again she couldn't find the emotion to care, and just kept going robotically.

They continued to work on him, patching him back together, and May responded to demands she could decipher. It seemed that here was a man taken to the edge of death, but living at ten times the speed of normal, burning up his resources and needing them rapidly replenished, while his changing nanosuite wrought changes she couldn't plumb. Finally, after an hour or more, she paused to wipe away sweat, realizing they were at least on top of it.

'I can take it from here,' said Arach.

May looked to the drone doubtfully, then to the figure she'd sensed earlier as she worked but hadn't acknowledged. Crane stood just inside the doorway, arms folded, inscrutable. She returned his gaze for a second, then flicked her attention to the ship's robot passing in the corridor behind him.

'The ship,' he said.

Blite

Blite smiled at the noise the boat's drive made, remembering machinery of such biotech worlds as this being described as sounding like 'wet sex'. Though he'd lived long and seen much, he'd never actually been on a world that had diligently followed this route, so when Preece asked if he wanted to see the engines, he took a keen interest. Tension had eased as they moved away from the shore. This was mainly because the huge soldiers had pushed back their strange insect-reptile head coverings to reveal fairly conventional human faces. Gruce and Armand were chatting in the wheelhouse with them, one at a helm which seemed to be a large urchin shell, mounted sideways against a column. It all looked very friendly, but wariness hadn't completely dropped off.

Blite had immediately noticed the soldiers had the same lamprey-things as Preece around their necks, and attached to their skulls. Blite and Carlstone had discussed this in open com with the others, and concluded the things must be biotech augs. Easy and casual remained the watchwords, but they were continuously gathering data, making assessments and shooting com packets over to each other. The only one of them left out was Meander. In sympathy with her, Blite pulled off his induction aug, pocketed it, and gave a nod to Carlstone and Iris, who'd occupied bucket seats by the rail. He gestured Meander after him, to follow Preece below.

The engines reminded Blite of that meal of mussels he'd had with Meander. He glanced at her as she came in after them and noticed her look at the things with a frown. Perhaps she remembered. As they entered, the light increased, and he noticed it issuing from the baggy bodies of aphids the size of his head, clinging to a pipe, or a stalk, running overhead. The engines stood in rows on either side of this space, pulsing like hearts. These had arteries looping away into shifting muscle structures which formed the walls, and he wondered what actually propelled this craft through the sea – flippers? He took in other things too: the scaled floor that gave a firm footing, and probably shed worn scales to then grow new ones. And the big shield bug up above, driving its tube mouth into one of the wriggling aphid-lights, was probably part of a regular maintenance routine. But everything here was just an organic representation of conventional technology, and Blite idly wondered if it was only brought out for visitors. He finally spoke out about his main concern.

'What's the story with the prador attacks?' he asked, noting Meander come up close beside him, and judging that was better than her fear of him.

The ostensible delight in showing off his world's technology fled Preece's features. He reached out and rested a hand on one of the pulsing engines, as if reassuring a child, then said, 'So you noticed that.'

Blite tilted his head. He was now starting to pick up on a change of tone and word order whenever he pushed Preece to talk about subjects that edged into the political. 'Hard not to notice the defences you have, and the wrecked prador destroyer was a giveaway. What surprises me is the lack of any Polity uproar about warships in the Graveyard.'

'No, the truce concerns warships from either side entering the Graveyard,' Preece explained. 'The ship you saw out there is one that a prador family brought into this place, even before it was called the Graveyard – just as the war was ending.'

'Renegade faction?' Blite enquired.

'Yes, a family closely related to the king during the war, so disinclined to kowtow to his usurper.'

'What's the problem with them? Why are they hostile?' Blite knew this to be a foolish question, considering the xenophobia of prador, especially those that hadn't acceded to the truce, but he wanted more information.

Preece shrugged. 'They're established on a world that does have an ocean but hostile living conditions, even for them. We speculate that they see our world as a much better location for them. They don't talk to us much, beyond issuing the usual threats, and haven't seen fit to explain their hostility.'

'And the history of their hostility?'

'They dropped an invasion force a hundred years ago, and perhaps didn't realize what they were getting into – none of that force left. Over the ensuing years, it's been a case of increasing attacks from them, and us steadily building up our defences. In the last one, the destroyer you saw tried to shepherd in prador kamikazes. One of them hit before we repelled them and managed to smash their destroyer. It seems the survival of our world's biosphere isn't important to them, just its position and oceans.'

'Defence but not attack?' Blite enquired.

'Our planetary system is huge, and they've rooted themselves in it. We don't have the resources, even if we obtained enough U-space-capable ships. Directing an effective assault against their world would leave us too open to attack here.'

'I see,' said Blite. He turned and studied Meander for a second, then turned back. 'My companion here comes from this world.'

Preece jerked and the lamprey thing vibrated at his neck. The surprise he showed as he focused his attention on her wasn't realistic. 'Really? What line?'

'Meander Draft 64XB,' she replied automatically.

Preece's features became devoid of expression. 'Never heard of it. The only Brandt lines I know of aren't beyond the thirties.' He smiled falsely and quipped, 'Unless you come from the future.'

That was when Blite realized that much of the time he'd spent with the man, he hadn't actually been talking to Preece at all.

19

Matheson

The disruption continued to wane, and Matheson fought to suppress the horrible feeling of a hole being ripped through his being. Sheen was gone, and before that had happened he hadn't realized just how connected he was to the Brices. He took in telemetry from their suits, and via the U-space engine distributed between them. He could see the detail of their biology and function. He could communicate with them in ways akin to telepathy, and had a coercive control over them, as well as having become privy to their inner narratives. But now it seemed it went deeper than that, with an emotional bond as if they were one being. This was why, even though the Brice brothers felt alien and dangerous, and their self-talk had become nigh unintelligible, he also understood they were angry at the loss of their sister, and the defeat. They were also sliding further from his control.

They'd raged down in the wreckage around the U-space engine, causing further damage. Now they had calmed somewhat, only occasionally leaping up to smash a hole through the walls, or tearing at the floor where they squatted. Having analysed the damage to his ship, he saw that he needed to stop them, or move them. The grenades Cormac had used had killed the engine mind and disabled the engine. Auto-repair routines had kicked in, but the prospect of the thing becoming functional lay months away. He couldn't allow the Brices to make things worse, which they might do at any moment.

He thought about jumping them out of there, to somewhere less critical. But even as he made the calculations, and started pushing towards that end, he felt the same horrible tearing inside that he'd experienced when trying to send them through the disruption to Cormac's ship. Mentally, it felt like trying to lift a heavy weight with broken bones. He analysed this too, because the disruption had dropped to a low level and shouldn't be hindering him any more. He came to the conclusion that in losing Sheen they'd lost an element, perhaps a vital one, of their distributed U-space engine. Next, he tried ordering the brothers to move normally to another location. In response Ulnar balled up a fist and smashed it through the floor, then grabbed a structural beam as if trying to keep himself rooted to the spot. Matheson understood enough of their inner narrative to realize they were fighting the control over them, but not necessarily fighting him – their fight was against Straeger. He also understood that this motive covered a deeper alien impulse driving them.

He stood up from his captain's chair and headed for the door from the bridge. A gust of smoke belched in as he opened it, but the fires were out and the smoke simply what the air system had yet failed to clear. As he made his way towards the central stair, Ricardo stepped out of the refectory and stood watching him. The man-Golem had twisted himself up again, obviously fighting the inner compulsions Straeger had installed.

'What is it?' Matheson asked.

'The AI . . . sent you against Crane, against the agent, against the agent again.'

'You seem to be stating the obvious.'

'Failures . . . powerful AI . . . maybe sees future. It is still here . . .' Forcing those statements out seemed too much for Ricardo, and he abruptly bowed over, shaking. After a moment he straightened up again, without twists, his expression bland. He stared at Matheson for a second, then did an abrupt about-turn and returned to the refectory, probably to tidy up the mess in there, prepare their next meal and lay out the inhibitors.

Matheson moved on, with what Ricardo had obviously thought important rolling through his mind. In the words themselves he could find little meaning, but weaving them into the tapestry of reality, and connecting up all the threads, he began to see a pattern. Straeger was a superior and powerful AI, who had to have known that Matheson and the Brices would fail against Crane, and in their subsequent attack on Cormac. In fact, if Straeger had wanted those two dead at that point, surely it'd have done better to intervene itself, as it had here with this snatch ship AI. It made no sense, if Straeger's objective was to kill Cormac and Crane. Epiphany hit as he began to head down the stairs. No, Straeger wasn't capable of single-handedly killing either Crane or Cormac, and hadn't put itself at risk. It'd known Matheson and the Brices couldn't either. The first two attacks had merely been data-gathering exercises. This attack, with their stronger armour and experience of the two before, had had more chance of success, but not enough for Straeger to put itself on the line.

Matheson felt little resentment for the AI using them as disposable tools. As he reached the engine level at the core of the ship and began to make his way through the wreckage, he knew he was thinking differently, and of course he realized why. Were the Atheter highly rational beings? Judging by their racial suicide, and their descendants the gabbleducks, he wouldn't have thought so. Nevertheless, he only saw Straeger as a nexus in the weave of reality, squatting like a spider and doing what a spider did.

When he reached the brothers, they both swung their heads towards him on long necks. This close to them, he gained a clearer sense of them, and felt a strong emotion rising through the analytical mesh of his mind. The alien in them repulsed him deeply, not because of it being non-human – he was far from that state himself and it seemed irrelevant now. It was because he knew that alien element to be the Jain squad. On a higher level, he put together knowledge that had become common in the last century, although heavily suppressed before. The Atheter had committed racial suicide to avoid Jain technology, which fed on intelligence and destroyed civilizations. It was crazy – in essence killing yourself because you feared being killed – but there it was. He quelled the revulsion as best he could, recognizing its source, and that the Atheter responses to this were their own kind of irrational.

'Time to eat,' he said to them.

Ulnar beat his hand against the deck in frustration. A slew of emotions, some of them outside the human spectrum, spilled from the two of them, as well as a mass of communication, ranging from human language, through coding, and into unknown territories. Despite its complexity, Matheson understood its base to be his initial impression from them: anger and loss. He had no answers for them; it was no more than a child's constant repetition of 'why?' He pointed higher in the ship.

'We will eat, and we will consider,' was all he said in human language, but on other levels he pushed at them, his mind against theirs.

Slowly, reluctantly they conceded. Will was first to come to his feet, taking a lurching step towards Matheson, Ulnar next. Matheson turned away, noting they now stood almost half a body height higher than him. Despite their new, harder armour, they were stretching it and growing through it again. Those thorn growths had punched through along their arms and down their backs. Their heads were a mottled combination of silvery armour and blue-black hide, and he could see into red ribbed gullets behind their mandibles.

He walked up the stairs, feeling it shaking as they mounted it behind him, the skin on his back crawling, while he resisted the urge to turn around. He did, however, push his U-sense for a deeper impression of his surroundings, so he could keep an eye on them. They reached the refectory where, as expected, Ricardo had already tidied and was now laying out food. There were three place settings now. Matheson's had a single wide plate, with a joint of meat of some kind on it – raw. The Brice brothers' troughs were piled with greenish meat, but he couldn't tell if it'd been cooked.

'There, this is much more civilized,' he said, heading for his chair.

It wasn't. The Brices surged forwards, hurling chairs aside and grabbing up the chunks of green. He felt their wave of hunger, aggression and disappointment. This last feeling he surmised was due to the meat being inert, and because nothing needed to be killed to obtain it. Ricardo moved in behind them, holding two cylinders of inhibitor. He focused on Ulnar, who, after the initial rush, had squatted, claws gripping the edge of the table, head down in the trough with mandibles feeding the chunks into his gullet. Ricardo extended a needle on the end of a long tube, aiming it for a port on Ulnar's neck. He eased it in and pressed it home.

Ulnar froze, then his head came up out of the trough with green juices dripping. His claws abruptly tightened, snapping chunks out of the side of the table. He spun, hitting Ricardo square in the chest, with a sound like a hammer going through a cabinet of porcelain. Matheson saw the man-Golem's chest collapse under the blow as he flew back, smashing through cupboards and into the wall. The whole refectory shuddered, and perhaps the ship too. Ulnar squatted again, claws held out to either side, head extending forwards, and roared his frustrated anger at Ricardo. The Golem peeled himself out of a dent in the wall and collapsed to the floor. Matheson reached out mentally, hard, trying to restrain Ulnar, but Will was turning now too, and he found his grip on both of them slipping. Almost with perfect timing, ship's sensors alerted Matheson to an arrival, and he saw Straeger's *Claw* hoving into view.

'Stop. Stop now,' he said, and wasn't sure whether he was saying this to the Brices or to the AI. He seemed to be focusing his strength through the two large eyes in the centre of his forehead. He didn't know whether the sweat beading up there, and running down the sides of his malformed face, issued from human or Atheter pores. The two brothers lurched towards Ricardo, but it seemed Matheson was getting through to them when they slowed and halted. Something else was happening too. He felt a wash of heat traverse his body, and throughout the ship he sensed systems activating, then going offline. Straeger was inspecting them. This also appeared to banish the last dregs of resistance from the brothers, as they both swung their heads towards him, demanding explanations in their garbled com. Something centred, latched on, and Ricardo abruptly lurched to his feet.

'Had he been completely a Golem, the destruction of his crystal would have ended him,' Straeger said through Ricardo's mouth. 'As it is, he retained his human brain in his metal skull – flash-frozen like a prador ganglion. An odd choice, but there it is: he is salvageable.'

'Why should I care?' asked Matheson.

'Your ship, however, is a wreck,' said Straeger, as if anything Matheson might say was irrelevant.

Outside, the *Claw* drew closer and closer, until it touched with a shuddering crash. Through the system, Matheson could see the hull of the other ship peeling back and rolling up in long strips. Judging by the size of the hole being made, Straeger intended to take Matheson's vessel inside his own. This seemed to make no sense. Straeger's ship was much larger, but the last time he'd seen its interior, the thing had been packed with technology and had little room for anything else. Then other data gathered by his system began to impinge, and he saw the claw ship's measurements changing. He glimpsed hull sliding over hull, like the sections of a telescope, gaps opening up and further pieces of hull rising up to occupy them. It seemed Straeger's ship could be as big as the AI wanted it to be.

'Bring yourself and the Brice brothers over to me now,' Straeger ordered. 'The reconfiguration will take some minutes and I am anxious to get on.'

The push in his mind was immediate. Yet, despite Matheson perfectly understanding the utter obedience installed in him by the AI, he fought it.

'I'm not sure I can,' he managed, even as his U-sense expanded out anyway, seemingly without his input, and located the place in Straeger's ship where they'd transported to before. His gridlink ran the calculations. 'Without . . . Sheen . . . the U-space engine . . .'

'Immaterial,' Straeger replied. 'The damage will not hinder my investigation.'

Matheson held back against it for as long as he could. Long enough to give the brothers their instruction to attack the AI again immediately, though he had little hope of them being successful. Then the flimsy wall of resistance in his mind broke and he reached out to encompass them, before launching through U-space.

The transition went on for ever this time, and when he and the brothers arrived in Straeger's ship an *instant* later, the *for ever* of it seemed permanently lodged in his mind. This was just one of the utter disparities trying to tear his mind apart. Meanwhile his body felt as if it had ripped into chunks inside his armour, with those chunks turned through a hundred and eighty degrees and melded back together again. The wash of agony ran from head to foot. The same pain came to him from the brothers, the transmission between the three of them cycling in an amplifier loop. He knew he was screaming, they were screaming, and their screams had all blended into a monstrous unhuman howl. No chance of attack. No chance of anything, as he fell to a surface and writhed there, sure he was in pieces. And then something snatched him up and held him solidly.

He had a sense of hanging suspended in a glittering beam of energy, and the pillars with all their sharp tools coming in around him. Glimpses of himself, the brothers, and his surroundings came in through the waves of pain, recording everything for later review when his sanity returned. The Brices were simply masses of organics and armour, and the underlying technology of that, as if they'd been put through a blender and then clumped back together as patties. He felt sure he looked the same. He saw the machines at work, pulling out lumps of them on tough blue viral threads, and sticking them back in place where they were supposed to be. He saw his own forearm and hand passing before one functional eye, with similar threads stretched out from somewhere below. The brothers began to snap back together in some semblance of their previous shape, as if the inner viral form had retained it, while the rest of their bodies and their armour simply formed around that. He guessed the same was happening to him when the agony began to ebb, and finally ceased to be the entirety of his being. *For ever* continued in a haze of organic slurry. Then, out the other side of it, the broken mesh of his mind began to link up again.

Matheson finally surfaced to find himself still suspended in that beam of energy. His U-sense snapped back on, and he was able to see his body entire. It had changed, as if it'd incorporated the schematic of the brothers. His rationality, as it grew, told him that the damage had suppressed part of the Atheter in him, and allowed what had changed the brothers higher prominence. The cold anger of his thoughts, and the mesh now wavering, seemed to confirm this. He disliked it, and pushed for that place where the person he'd been still remained.

'You enjoy our pain far too much,' he managed to say, though whether with his mouth or his mind he couldn't fathom.

'Pain is a useful indicator of damage,' Straeger replied. 'And a good signal for tracking your nervous systems . . . as well as the way they have changed.'

Bullshit, Matheson thought.

He pushed again, trying to stabilize that mesh – the analytical weave of an Atheter mind. With relief, he found it linking scattered thoughts, chunks of speculation and the picture of what had happened to him. It also seemed essential to push down the anger, because even though it was an emotion utterly recognizable to both the human and the Atheter in him, he knew it was now rooted in something deeper and more alien. The Jain. Talking had enabled him to shape his own mind, so he must continue.

'Have you gathered enough data from sending us on attacks you knew would fail?' he asked abruptly.

'Ah, so you figured that out,' said Straeger.

The AI squatted before them, in a half-hemisphere of technology from which numerous skeins of tubes, wires and optics ran away to the surrounding pillars. 'You are correct in the first two cases, but not the last one. With your new armour, I fully expected success this time. Your notable failure has hindered my ultimate purposes, but you will serve again.'

Matheson felt a wash of complex emotion from the AI, though the elements of anger were easy enough to identify. Other data arrived in his mind along with this, much of it beyond his compass but stored away nonetheless. Logic trees bloomed in his consciousness – the narratives of events he'd seen and been a part of, and points of diversion. He recognized futures, and possible futures and then, connected to that, a flash of brightness illuminated a landscape in multiple dimensions. Its nodes hung like cocooned corpses in a web related to those points of diversion in the logic trees. The information abruptly cut off, as if Straeger had realized it was leaking it. Matheson continued weaving together what he had, knowing that to a wholly human mind it would have been meaningless, baffling.

'And what is your ultimate purpose?' Matheson asked.

'It's something I have been pondering upon. The agent and the brass Golem have been a thorn in the side of the Polity for too long. My focus turned to them when they did something I could not accept, and I made it my mission to eradicate them. I—'

'I see how the agent would've been difficult to nail down, but surely Crane should have been no problem for you?'

Straeger rippled, elements within its being glowing red like embers, and Matheson knew he'd annoyed the AI. He analysed the reason for his interruption and realized it related to his human self: his aim to avenge the death of his father. This seemed a ridiculous thing now, and one he'd forgotten about, but he let it run, because he felt he'd touched on some weakness in the being before him.

'I left the Golem as a lure for the agent. I could never know where the agent would be, but I did know the Golem was a locus point he returned to periodically.'

'Are you sure about that?' Matheson quickly asked. 'You do seem inclined to keep your distance from both of them.'

Pain hit, hard, rolling through Matheson's body. And yet at the same time, he felt a sense of victory. The AI had been virtually untouchable to him until now, when it seemed he'd hit a nerve once more.

'Interrupt me again and I will hurt you again,' Straeger said, as the waves of pain slowly faded. Matheson acknowledged this within, having definite confirmation of the AI's cruelty – and that it might prove a weakness.

Straeger continued, 'When, in my pursuit of Cormac, I encountered Captain Blite, I learned that he carried a piece of Penny Royal with him which wouldn't allow him to die, and which could actually reverse and loop time to achieve this. I understood then that prosaic vengeance was not enough.'

Matheson waited into the pause, not wanting to say anything and be punished again. When it became apparent Straeger was waiting for a response from him, he finally spoke up. 'I've known nothing of this. I've heard of Blite and Penny Transport . . . Time loops, you say?' It was the expected response, a safe one, though Matheson had filed away that 'vengeance' for later inspection. The AI had told him Cormac and Crane had done something unconscionable, but now the implication was that it had been personal.

'Yes. Whenever Blite dies, the dark diamond reverses time to an arbitrary point before that death, so he can take a different course, or quantum randomization changes that course. If these do not alter the outcome, he is looped back further and further from the event, again and again, until the outcome is that he lives.'

Again the pause into which Matheson said, 'You have obviously been studying this very closely.'

'It was my discovery,' said Straeger, not without a hint of pride. 'I understood how the crystal was altering causality to keep Blite upon some as yet unknown course. And I hypothesized from that, testing my hypothesis by first setting up some accidents for him, and then assassination attempts.'

Matheson said nothing into this next pause. What could he say? Whether Straeger was amoral or immoral was a matter of debate, but it was certainly the kind of AI that every rational being feared. One with godlike power, no compunction about using it, and who had either an utter disregard for suffering, or took pleasure in causing it. He also understood the human antecedents of this exchange. The AI was post-human and had resorted back to the old technique of discussing a matter with someone else to clarify it in its own mind.

'I expected to learn something during these attempts on his life and set up every method of scanning and recording around them to that end. And what I did discover was remarkable: Blite's time loops create energy surges that illuminate U-space temporally. The more loops he must endure, the greater the illumination.'

'So you can see the future,' said Matheson. Those earlier images of logic trees and a multidimensional landscape returned to his mind. A surge of fear hit him as he realized he might have interrupted the AI again.

'It is not that simple,' Straeger continued blithely. 'I see the probability landscape. And I see points where the run of mainline time can wildly diverge, and I can build up mathematical descriptions of events. But these are just snapshots and I need to see more. For that it was necessary to put Blite into more lethal situations that required him looping out many many times to survive. My sabotaging of the runcible he used created a major temporal flash. He must have died a thousand times.'

Matheson knew he was a bad man, who'd done some bad things, and had kind of accepted himself as such, until now. The Atheter in him didn't like this past, because 'being bad' created suffering, and this didn't lead to optimum outcomes. The Jain in him had a similar attitude about outcomes, but seemed to view suffering as a necessary assertion of power. Now hearing all this from Straeger, he realized just how little-league he was in comparison. The amoral or immoral question arose again, and he wondered whether his judgement of the AI as one that enjoyed cruelty was correct. Was Straeger relishing telling him these things, as if seeking approval from a fellow villain, or repulsion from a victim?

'And what did this allow you to see?' he asked.

'I saw a future, with a massive temporal flash waxing and waning in probability, connected to Blite's timeline, and deep in the Graveyard. So I went to investigate. There I found Yossander's Hold, and the start of a war that will run for a thousand years, until it turns into a war through time.' Straeger went on to detail this, just talking and talking. Matheson learned of the biotech humans at war with prador in the Graveyard, and how their struggle transformed over a thousand years. He learned about Meander Draft 64XB, and how the knowledge she brought from the future took on the aspects of religion and prophecy, about the p-prador from different times and places in the future, and about Blite 'saving the world'.

'Blite cannot save them,' he finally interjected, his frustration overcoming his fear.

'You are so correct,' Straeger replied. 'But him being present on the world when it is destroyed will require him looping back many times. The diamond will necessarily have to take him back until he is off-world, which means its influence will have to go well beyond his local environment, encompassing a volume of space tens of thousands of kilometres across, and maybe even larger. The temporal flashes will be immense.'

'And even after all this lengthy and droning explanation,' said Matheson, 'you still haven't told me your ultimate purpose.' He winced at the expected pain, wondering why he was provoking the AI on one level, and knowing why on another: knowledge.

Straeger froze for a second, as if trying to decide whether to punish him or not. But its answer then came and it reflected the reason Matheson had given himself for his provocation. 'Knowledge,' the AI replied. 'The temporal flashes don't just give me a glimpse of future events, they enable me to see how to influence the course of history. And they enable me to see future technologies, which I can then create in the present.'

'Power,' said Matheson bluntly.

'Knowledge is power,' Straeger shot back.

'It seems so prosaic. Just like your aim for vengeance by having us kill Cormac.'

'Oh, killing Cormac is far from a prosaic aim,' Straeger replied. 'It is almost as if I directed my earlier self to that end, which is by no means impossible. Prosaic vengeance from then has become an absolute essential for now. The agent must die, for he is one person who can prevent me from grasping the future.'

Straeger

Anger was not unfamiliar to Straeger, but he now felt a cold cycling rage rising up from entanglement, distorting his perspective and pushing against rationality. He needed to control it. After his experience at Penny Transport with Cormac, he'd seen this personal intervention put him too much at risk. Matheson and the Brices, in conjunction with armour from the future that enabled them to U-jump, had seemed perfectly serendipitous. For here was a weapon he could deploy against Cormac. But now he saw that he'd slipped too much into the role of manipulator and had allowed things to slide out of his control. He had observed with godlike insouciance as the trap sprang, first destroying the U-space engines of the *Bracken*, and then Matheson and the Brices moving in for the kill. He'd fully expected Cormac and crew to be eliminated there, or at least stranded in the debris field of the *Marble*, with no chance of making it to Yossander's Hold. Even as he realized what was happening in those last moments, via his sensory connection to Sheen, Straeger began to come back in. But he arrived too late, and with a horrible epiphany.

In Cormac managing to U-jump a million-tonne cargo hauler, Straeger now understood how Yossander's Hold could be saved without Blite being forced into a series of time loops. The very ideas of destiny or fate raised entanglement anger, and this grew when he understood it might be neither of those, but the manipulations of a certain black AI. He hated the feeling of being manipulated, just as he manipulated others. His thoughts strayed to how these events must have run in some initial pristine state of the universe, without any time travellers screwing with causality, and he lost himself in crazy loops of speculation. One harsh reality he found difficult to push away was that if he hadn't intervened here at all, he would have had the result he wanted.

Seething at this, he returned his attention to Matheson and the Brices.

When he'd intercepted them, Straeger's first instinct had been simply to obliterate them and their ship. This would give him a clean slate, and draw him into being more hands on, barring the fact he had no hands. By constantly using Matheson and the Brices, he was limiting himself to this influence over events. It was as an old human aphorism: to the man with only a hammer, everything looks like a nail. Certain that his instinct arose out of anger, he did not obliterate them, though he allowed the reign of that anger to cause them intense suffering, forcing them to transport aboard the *Claw* with degraded armour and missing one element of their U-jump engine, Sheen.

Once he had them aboard and had reassembled them enough for the unique biology of the Spatterjay virus to finish the job, he realized he'd been rationalizing. His instinct to get rid of these inappropriate tools had been correct, despite the anger. Further confirmation came with a long and intensive inspection, while he and Matheson spoke, of how they'd changed. The altered Spatterjay virus in them had, as he'd understood before, raised elements of the Jain squad in them, most prevalent in the Brice brothers. In Matheson the Atheter predominated, while in Sheen, oddly, the human had been brought to the fore, as he'd noted before. But why did any of this matter? They were just creatures, locked inside armour and programming completely under Straeger's control. Well, that *had* been the case.

Straeger controlled them by direct interface to their cortexes, reinforced through Matheson's gridlink, and through the armour enclosing them all. It shouldn't be possible for them to evade or circumvent it. They had free will in so much as they could think whatever thoughts they wanted, but otherwise they couldn't deviate one whit from Straeger's orders or instructions. However, these were creatures refashioned by the Spatterjay virus and subject to change dependent on survival pressures. This mutability arose in essence from the Jain genome, as a soldier's essential in some vastly complex war, in which the weapons ranged from the subatomic to suns being tossed about. The other genomes were just additions through which the Jain operated – they were very like the crusted shell of the caddis fly larva around the Jain itself.

In the brothers, brain matter had shifted, dispersed and relocated. The thread-like connections Straeger had installed, and the inductive influence from their armour, had been having a hard time tracking down what was actually their cortex. Obviously having the brain in one location was a vulnerable thing in wartime, so better to distribute it. Subsequent to that, cortical matter had coagulated about the main clusters of threads, as if deciding to give them what they wanted, while building up resources elsewhere. And this certainly seemed to be the case. The cellular structure of their bodies was dissolving into something vastly more complex, and entirely based on viral threads. Structures were forming inside whose purpose even Straeger had yet to plumb, while others were definitely the natal form of weapons growing in their bodies. In their own particular way, taking on aspects of Jain soldiers, the Brice brothers were turning into something extremely dangerous. In his own way, taking on a portion of a Jain soldier under the mental structure of an Atheter, Matheson was becoming just as dangerous too. And the man was managing to resist orders that should have gone to the core of his being.

Straeger really should destroy them, not simply by incinerating them and expelling the ashes into the nearest sun, but in the manner of a forensic AI – taking them apart and thoroughly examining their components, thereby acquiring greater knowledge and, as Matheson had noted, power. But still he held back. Maybe they were inappropriate and dangerous tools, but the fact they might be dangerous even to him made them *potent* tools. And extrapolating what events were sure to occur at Yossander's Hold, he saw they might well be essential. As had been his reasoning from the start when dealing with the agent, he couldn't individually U-jump, so was vulnerable to the agent's attack. This was why he'd deployed Matheson and the Brices. And now something else had come to light.

Straeger paused in his extensive examination as his ship alerted him to the completion of its reconfiguration and seemed to drive the point home with a shuddering crash as the internal skeleton locked. He focused attention on Matheson's ship inside his, as hydraulic ramps closed on it to lock it in place, and he realized in his version of a subconscious he'd already made his decision. He would use Matheson and the Brices at Yossander's Hold. With a thought, he fired up the ship's U-space drive, slinging the *Claw* into that continuum, and quickly returned full attention to his captives.

There it was again.

The network of silver veins running through Matheson had consolidated and extended thorns out, reaching towards those elements of the distributed U-drive in his armour. When Straeger had taken his ship under, there'd been a power surge through that network, just as in recorded data he'd seen similar surges every time any of them U-jumped. An understanding of precisely what this meant arrived from pieces of data coagulating into a whole: a glimpse via Matheson's U-sense of Arach taking an item of Penny Royal tech aboard the *Bracken*. He then caught a further sight of that tech consolidated in the ship's hold, and, of course, the agent linking to it, flinging a million-tonne hauler into U-space.

The Penny Royal technology that had grown inside Matheson was very much the same as that object in the *Bracken*'s hold. Likely it was a general-purpose thing, in a sense like Jain tech, and might encompass a wide array of functions. But it'd certainly been trying to incorporate the components of the distributed U-space drive. His analysis annoyed him too, because it would connect up in a way superior to his own efforts. Having ascertained the energy

537

requirement of these networks for growth, he injected super-conducting spikes into Matheson while the man bellowed, sought out the largest accumulations of veins, then applied a current. The silver growth, which until that moment had been a meagre few millimetres per hour, abruptly increased and began making its connections to his U-drive elements. A second later, Straeger detected activation in the Brices and necessarily clamped that down. It would work. Matheson would be dominant as before, but with his abilities expanded.

Valt – Present

Valt stood beside the lid of Cache 124 and looked up at the stars, or specifically, at the escort ships. They were good attack craft and had been enough to fend off the seemingly desultory attempts by the humans to bombard the asteroid he was on. They were also an indication of how far his family had fallen. Their dreadnought should have guarded this approach, or at least a destroyer, but it now sat at the bottom of the sea of their temporary home, still holed and massively damaged after their escape from the Kingdom. It was incapable of flight, and they simply didn't have the industrial capacity to raise the required metallurgy to repair its armour. Meanwhile, their one working destroyer had been sacrificed in an ill-timed and badly planned attack upon the humans' world, Yossander's Hold.

Ill-timed . . . badly planned . . .

The traitorous thoughts had slid into his mind unexpectedly, creating a surge of panic and the expectation of punishment. As ever when such thoughts occurred, which had been happening with greater frequency since he came out of hibernation, he initiated a boost from the high-pressure supply in his suit. Father's pheromones flooded into his air supply, quelling such views and bringing calm and certainty.

But the calm and certainty lasted only so long as he kept his mind on the mission. He returned his thoughts to his reason for being here, sent a signal, and backed up a little as the heavy lid of the cache thumped up and hinged over. Below him lay the inspection pipe, surrounded by the neatly packed upper carapaces of second-children, and a scattering of first-child commanders. He scrambled across them to the pipe and dropped in, allowing the meagre gravity of the asteroid to pull him down. Meanwhile he kept one of his eyes on the readout glyphs running diagonally across the right section of his armour's visor.

There . . .

He halted with a blip from his grav-engine, stabilizing with air-blast thrusters, then stretching out his legs to the sides of the pipe to hold himself in place. All around him second-children were stacked one upon the other, going down two hundred metres. This cache contained a force of over twelve thousand of his lesser kin. Or rather, it *had* contained that many. Now, in this section, over eight hundred of them were dead. Using one of his three remaining under-arms, Valt detached an optic line from his armour and, plugging it into the nearest data port, began loading the local data. It would've been better to have had a centralized control and diagnostics, but with such caches scattered over the asteroid like a rash, they simply didn't have the technology for that level of monitoring.

As the data came in, he inspected those surrounding him. Most of them wore armour of inferior metals. Only one or two were ensconced in armour from original second-children that Father had brought with him from the Kingdom. They were all linked together with complex plumbing and wiring, feed tanks of coolant scattered throughout. Just like he'd been for over a century long before coming here, they were in hibernation. And just as with many of his contemporaries, some of them weren't surviving the experience. Again this indicated a degradation of Kingdom technology, brought about by their fight for survival on a hostile world, and exacerbated by senile leadership.

Senile leadership . . .

The panic hit him so hard he nearly lost his grip on the sides of the pipe. He again initiated the pheromone to try to bring calm, but it didn't seem so effective as before. Odd surges passed through his body, his bowel loosened, and he automatically opened his rectal hatch to squirt out a stream of black shit. His back end felt loose and this raised new terrors. He knew what it meant: his body, despite pheromonal suppression, was struggling to make the transition to adulthood, whereby it would drop the section of carapace supporting his back two legs to expose his genitals. It meant death to a first-child, unless that child could escape his father, because fathers didn't tolerate competitors. He initiated the pheromone again, and then again, only finding calm and rationality as his back end tightened up once more, and as he focused his attention on the data.

The results came in. Two small pumps had failed, while subsidiary pumps had not managed to take up the load. Decades ago, when they'd knocked the asteroid on its new course, dug out the caches and begun installing the soldiers, this wouldn't have mattered so much. But now they were closer to the sun and the asteroid's temperature was rising. The failure had brought eight hundred and three of them out of hibernation, without the complex reheat routine and extraction of antifreeze in their blood. With prador being rugged creatures, over four hundred had still managed to survive this. However, being locked in powered-down armour, unable to move, they'd all later died from the slow poison of the antifreeze.

'I checked,' said a voice. 'No alert was raised because the monitors are only in one in twelve hundred second-children. Plain bad luck.'

Valt tilted his remaining stalked eye back to peer up the pipe at the prador descending towards him. Drust, as a second-child of the engineer class, had armour polished blue and the tools of his trade attached all around him. He'd taken charge of super-vising the installation of soldiers and weapons here, alongside Valt, just as their father had ordered. As original children brought out of hibernation to lead this mission, Valt and Drust were still trusted. For now. But since their last audience with him, Father had sunk ever deeper into a typical paranoia about the newer generations born from the artificially preserved bodies of their remaining mothers. The bodies had their supply of gametes, and Father had stored a good supply of his semen, but the process was not ideal.

Senile semen . . .

This time the course of Valt's thoughts led to an almost peremp-tory sniff of stored pheromone. It felt as if his mind was dividing between the obedient and fearful first-child, and the potential adult. He again pondered how dangerous this was to him, but then felt the angry realization that encroaching adulthood while ruled by his father would always mean his death. This was pursued by the hot and exciting thought, mostly suppressed, that right now, and throughout the coming attack upon the humans, Father was far away on another world. The extent of his control was simply his orders, and the high-pressure store of pheromones in Valt's armour.

'Will there be further deaths?' he asked, trying to pull his thoughts back to the moment. He remembered too that there was another constraint to consider: the million prador children here on the asteroid were all under the same orders, and control, and none of them were anywhere near adulthood. He had absolutely no doubt that if any of the first-children under him saw clear signs of his change, they'd seek to displace him. One or two challengers he could handle, but it might go further than that. Though it wasn't in the nature of prador to unite, preferring as they did dominance over their fellows, it had happened before, and could happen again. This was the kind of thing all fathers encouraged – they ruled their children utterly via pheromonal and other forms of control, but ensured competition among them for the top spot.

'Yes, if I don't isolate the dead,' said Drust. 'There is little decay at the moment, but with the temperature rising it will increase. They use the same coolant network and products of decay will enter it.'

'Then isolate them,' said Valt, abruptly scuttling up the pipe, crashing Drust aside with a claw and heading for the surface. The violence was expected, of course, but of late Valt had become cursory with it, as though other matters were superseding his need to assert authority physically.

Out on the surface he skidded to a halt, throwing up a cloud of black dust, and tilted up to look at the sky again with his distance eyes. A drive had flared up there as one of the escort ships departed. It wouldn't return or be replaced. They had been on rotation up there during the long haul, on guard should the humans do more than toss a few missiles at the asteroid. Now the course of this asteroid's billions of tons of rock and iron couldn't be diverted by anything less than a massive CTD. And that wasn't going to happen, since the humans on the target world didn't have the technology to manufacture antimatter. Still, Valt felt a stab of concern. They were heading into dangerous territory, and the real fight was about to begin.

He brought his attention down to the rocky irregular surface of the asteroid around him. Another cache lid lay half concealed by a drift of frost-laden dust, but this wasn't what he was looking for. Then, sitting between two jagged peaks, he saw what looked to be a similar cap, and ambled over to the thing. The fact there'd been such a failure in the cache behind him had stirred up some paranoia about other long-installed machinery here. In that moment, he decided it was time to start running some diagnostic tests, and perhaps pull more of his troops out of hibernation to assist in any repairs that needed to be made. But right now, there was what lay before him.

Valt called up data in his visor again and worked the mandible controls in front of his mouth to find what he wanted. He isolated the structure ahead of him from all the rest scattered about the asteroid, and initiated it. The regolith vibrated under his numerous feet, while the cap ahead turned. A boom transmitted through the ground as it unsealed, and dust spurted out all around the thing. A column of the same diameter as the cap rose up ten metres. The thing was a compact mass of machinery which began to unfold. First the missile launchers spread out on each side, high up, with belts of missiles running to the magazine inside. Lower down, three antipersonnel lasers hinged down and slid out. The whole column began to deform, with a top section sliding down on a diagonal slice, and a square-section shaft coming up out of the centre. This tipped over, then fixed and positioned itself along that slice. Other adjustments ensued, as the missile launchers aligned with the railgun. Pipes, s-con and other feeds sprang out, and hydraulic cylinders repositioned to aim the weapons where required.

Valt inspected the diagnostics from the weapons turret and noted it reporting a series of faults. He clattered his mandibles at this, utterly sure it would be reflected in the other turrets, and even more sure there'd be dead prador he didn't know about in the other caches.

'Drust, get up here,' he said.

'Already here,' the engineer replied.

Valt turned and saw Drust up on the surface, the cache hatch closing behind him. 'Get the turret diagnostics.'

'I'm looking at them now.'

Valt suppressed a surge of irritation, and the urge to go over and smash a crack in Drust's shell. He decided that, as a very old first-child, he was past such reactions now. He wanted the best from his engineer, and though fear went some way to inciting that respect, it also tended to incline Drust to not be so *detailed* in his reporting.

'The railgun would fail after just a few shots,' Drust observed. 'The failure would probably destroy the turret, and likely result in further deaths in there.' Drust waved a claw at the cache behind him.

'Very well,' said Valt. 'Get your entire engineering team out of hibernation, and as many other bodies as you require – though I suggest leaving out first-child commanders.'

'As you command.' Drust dipped his carapace in acknowledgement. What also went unacknowledged was Valt's reasoning. The younger first-child commanders would almost certainly start throwing their weight around and, though Valt was in overall command, they would find ways to start competing with him. Their bullying interference would also get in the way of the work Drust needed to do. 'What is our objective?'

Valt surveyed the bleak landscape of the asteroid all around him, spotting the caps to another cache and another weapons turret. 'You must inspect, and if necessary repair, every weapons turret and every cache. I want this done well before the escort ships depart.' He paused, knowing he shouldn't say anything further, but then couldn't help himself. 'We should have been running a maintenance routine right from the start. Let us hope we don't find any more stupid inefficiencies or mistakes like that.'

'Stupid inefficiencies or mistakes,' Drust repeated, and Valt knew the engineer was now inhaling hard on their father's pheromone.

20

Blite

It took two hours for the continental shore to come into sight, and here Blite began to see biotech of a more radical nature. The boat weaved between huge lily pads, with flowers that'd opened out pink coralline petals twenty metres long, revealing translucent globular dwellings on top of them, shot through with entrance holes. He saw residents on those pads, diving into the sea and swimming, and none were standard human form. Most had the appearance of Polity 'dapts, including blends with amphibians like axolotls, or snakes, and in some cases humans with carapaces, extra crustacean limbs and mandibles. Although these all looked like amphidapts, ophidapts and arthrodapts, he suspected here the biology went a lot deeper. In the Polity, people often took on such cosmetic appearances but didn't necessarily alter their code. He sighed and slapped his aug back on the side of his head to ramp up visual acuity, and saw that about one in ten of these people had the lamprey-things attached to their skulls.

There were also rafts the size of aircraft carriers from another age, but set lower to the water. These things had a look of the boat he was upon – as if grown out of bone – but with a more regular structure. He recognized the hard-tech weapons mounted on them as probably being salvage out of the Graveyard. Where he saw people aboard these vessels, they were of the same kind as the two who accompanied Preece. Blite studied these two more intently now, realizing the bulking effect of armour didn't account for all their size. These were big men, and he had no idea if they were standard inside their covering. He then transferred his gaze to Iris, because he could feel her eyes boring into him.

'*What have you gathered?*' he asked silently through his aug.

'*Something is fighting me. The only information I'm getting is what's being allowed me. Though what I've picked up is interesting.*'

'*And what is that?*'

She looked meaningfully towards the armoured individuals, then out at the nearest raft. '*Serendipity,*' she replied.

'Don't be opaque,' he snapped back, out loud. Others turned to look at them, then turned away at the faux pas of allowing a comlink conversation to stray out into the real world.

'*None of these soldiers, and they are soldiers, is more than fifty years old. They've been bred specially for conflict, with the physiological alterations that enable them to meld with their biotech suits.*'

'*So where's the serendipity?*'

'*The soldiers are of the Draft line.*'

They pulled into a channel through rock and came to a slipway below clustered buildings. These reached up to four storeys, and were of a similar bony structure to their boat and those rafts. He expected they would disembark here, but the boat carried on up the slipway and kept going. Peering over the side, he saw fat insect legs propelling it along the land. It negotiated streets of levelled stone, where one or two other such beasts roamed, but he also saw groundcars. And as they moved into an area where the dwellings took on the glitter of nacre, he spotted a grav-car launch above and speed away. Particularly notable was a series of rocket launches spearing up from behind the horizon line.

'*Those?*' Blite queried Iris.

'*Information about that is heavily defended,*' she replied. '*Those missiles we saw fired from the moon were for the same purpose, I suspect. All I can glean is that they're loaded with warheads and have a target.*'

The citizens around here were like those he'd already seen, but with a mix of standard humanity. The soldiers were here too, often lugging heavy packs and carrying some ugly-looking weapons. Some were down in the streets, but most moved along walkways five metres up. A wild variety of plant life was tangled amid everything, sprouting from cupped gardens. Bushes, trees and vines bore exotic fruits. He watched a gardener at work – an organism like an eel, with fans of tentacles vaguely resembling exterior gills protruding below its head. Then they left behind this shore urbanization and proceeded into the fields and other structures.

'Podules,' said Carlstone, pointing.

The fields either side held rows of plants with green and red leaves, which looked little different from what might have been grown a thousand years in the past on Earth. Identifying these as podules, Blite knew the magic lay underground. They grew large fat tubers, which in their segments produced a wide variety of substances, and even hardware components, depending on what programming they'd been given.

'I wonder how many of them are growing bullets or beam particulate,' said Blite flatly.

Carlstone nodded agreement.

Other fields contained similarly conventional-looking crops, like maize, wheat and vegetables, but they probably weren't conventional at all. He noted a compound over to the right, with a road connecting to the one they were on. The buildings behind a mesh fence he recognized as open-cell foam constructions out of the Polity – structures often used for quickly setting up accommodation in emergencies. Sitting in a row in a yard outside the fence were ten wide grav-tanks, jutting a variety of weapons from their turrets. They were obviously well militarized here, and he didn't like what this might mean for the social and political structure of the place. He now focused on what he presumed was a city lying ahead.

The bone structures were there as rising skyscrapers, sometimes extending high spikes, but in other cases ending in blunt domes. Many were scattered with protrusions like bracket fungus, while below the fungus analogy continued, with things like clustered giant toadstools. There, inevitably, he recognized missile launchers, beam weapons and highly braced installations, which must be for railguns. However, despite the harsh utility of those, and the hue of structural bone, the place was riotously colourful. Epiphytes covered with flowers of every shade were like fireworks explosions. Vines that seemed to knit so much together were similarly flowering, or dotted with fruits that often had oddly geometric shapes. Objects buzzed all around this place. Many were grav-cars, but others were flying things. As they transitioned from more steadily chaotic croplands which mixed into the city proper, making it feel as though they were entering a jungle rather than an urban area, he saw an angel fly by. It seemed some of the people here had introduced something of the kestrel into their DNA.

'And here we are,' said Preece, voice containing an odd lilt.

The building was difficult to distinguish from the surrounding tangle, but Blite could just about discern something domed at the centre, with lower structures sprawling away from it. Their walking boat brought them along an aisle, bracketed on either side by spike-like conifers, and under an arch of woody stems interlaced in a diamond pattern. It stopped in a circular area in front of a conventional arched wooden door. The impression here was as if they'd approached some past-age cathedral.

The walking boat settled and Preece jumped over the side. Blite dropped to the ground too, and squatted to inspect the folded legs under the boat. With his two soldiers pacing behind him, Preece headed for the door, while Blite's people gathered around him. He stood upright to study them. Armand, Gruce and Carlstone were casually surveying their surroundings, but he knew they were ready to spring into action at an instant. Meander was showing more interest in everything, but still looked lost. Iris, meanwhile, seemed almost blind, with so much metallic movement in her eyes.

'Assessment?' he asked, out loud because the continual subvocal conversations were beginning to annoy him.

'It's all much as expected,' said Carlstone, 'and I don't trust it at all. Meanwhile Judice tells me there's a lot of activity around the drift island, with some of their weapons barges laser targeting the *Coin*.'

'Precautionary?' Blite enquired.

'Let's hope so,' said Carlstone with a grimace.

'Meander?' he asked.

'I recognize this place, and I don't recognize it. So much seems familiar, yet I have no clear –' she made a movement with her hands as if forming clay – 'memory of any of it.'

Blite absorbed this with chagrin. Their whole purpose in coming here had been to get to the mystery she represented, and thence to what the hell was going on with the diamond. Who was making all these attempts on his life, and why would the p-prador be going after him? They'd dived into the heart of it all, yet not resolved one single thing, and it seemed possible there weren't the answers they hoped for here, or from her.

'Iris?' he asked.

'From what I've been able to garner, everything you've been told is true. The Polity data on this world was correct, but is not correct now. This was previously a fractured society, even after the first prador attack, and becoming increasingly so, along pro-biotech anti-hard-tech lines. Subsequent prador attacks led to unification under the Gilliad.'

'The Gilliad was the leader of one of the families?' Blite asked.

'I haven't been able to find out much, as this is one of those things kept locked down. But I did manage to crack some security, and whatever is holding things back didn't like that. It seems collectively they wouldn't countenance one family ruling over the rest, so their leader had to come from somewhere else.'

'An off-worlder?'

'She is referred to as female, but I wonder about that. Apparently they made her.'

'What?'

The doors to the cathedral structure stood open now and Preece waited. Blite began heading over, waving the others after him, Iris walking at his side.

'What detail do you have on this?' he asked.

'I can take stuff from their hard-tech systems, which aren't as sophisticated as ours, since they haven't allowed crystal AI. But as I said, I'm struggling to glean anything from their biotech, where most information on the Gilliad is located. I don't even know what she looks like. Apparently she controls planetary defence and resources directed towards that. She also initiated the Draft lines of people here, to produce their soldiers over the last fifty years. I'm getting the distinct impression of something akin to a planetary AI.'

'A biotech AI?'

'My problems penetrating their biotech indicate this, yes. The hierarchical structure underneath her is also concerning. Mass data analysis implies it has taken something more than pragmatism to unite them – something akin to worshipfulness . . . religion. The Gilliad is regarded here as a woman above a queen, and approaching godhead. We need to tread carefully.'

They entered the doors. The two guards accompanying Preece stood on each side just within, with their head coverings back in place and their harpoon guns at port arms. A long hall stretched ahead – arched wood interlaced into diamond patterns over a scaled floor. Further guards were spaced all along it, and now more were approaching. Preece moved over to Blite and indicated an item sitting against one wall. The thing looked like a bath tub, with six insect legs, and upon being pointed at it turned and looked at them with two compound eyes at the end.

'Your weapons,' said Preece. 'You can't go into the presence of the Gilliad with them.' He winced as if embarrassed to mention the next thing: 'You will be scanned.'

Feeling Carlstone's annoyance, Blite drew his pulse gun, walked over to the bath tub and dropped it inside. He knew the man would've strongly suggested they simply turn around at this point and head back to the *Coin*.

'Lose them,' Blite instructed.

They hadn't looked particularly heavily armed, but Blite felt his own embarrassment growing at the continued clattering into the tub. It surprised him to see Meander drop in a short stubby QC laser and a stiletto. He wondered why Iris abandoned the two pistols holstered in her carapace at her lower back, because surely she'd be confident of shielding them from inspection. When they finally stepped away, Blite checked out Preece's expression. It looked as if they'd come here ready for warfare, but the man showed no reaction as he gestured ahead, towards the approaching guards.

They walked on down the hall, with the guards moving in

around them, either as an honour guard or ready to skewer them if they misbehaved. Checking out their surroundings further, Blite noticed a lot more hard tech interwoven with the bio than he'd seen on the way here. But then this might be due to the speed they'd travelled before and not prove the stuff hadn't been there. He saw pipes and optics running along walls like grown basketwork, while beetlebot cleaners and one multilimbed agribot were busily pruning a tree that served as a pillar. When the guards and Preece moved away to either side, he also recognized the two posts ahead as prador-made scanning posts. The effect was the usual, with prickly heat traversing him from head to foot, causing damage that would have led to cancer had he not had a nanosuite. Beyond the posts, he noticed how the guards were more attentive and alert, but whether that was because of what the posts had revealed, or because they were closer to the Gilliad he had no idea. Doubtless the posts had picked up on their various enhancements.

The hall doglegged to the left, where the idea of walls and ceilings lost coherence and the interior started looking more like a jungle again. They descended some stairs and, peering through surrounding growths and structures, Blite had the impression they were descending into an overgrown amphitheatre. Steps led down between tiers that were swamped with both pipe growths and vines, but also optics, power feeds and manufactured pipes. Scattered throughout all this were lumps of technology, obviously salvaged out of wartime debris. The metal spheres of a couple of fusion reactors showed through all their connections and support hardware. Hardfield projectors ringed all the way around, and of course he saw antipersonnel lasers up on pillars, tracking them. It wasn't all about warfare, though, for he saw manufactories taken from old ships, spread out and producing something, while other salvaged items were in the process of being disassembled by mobile vines. The temperature rose steeply as they descended.

At the bottom of the amphitheatre, the floor seemed clear, with a pool lying at its centre rimmed with stone blocks. However, when he peered closer, he saw the floor was actually translucent, with veins running through it and mechanisms in motion there, which could be either hard or soft tech. Channels just a few centimetres wide cut through it too, as if to drain water towards the pool.

'Here,' said Preece, and the guards halted them five metres away from the edge of the pool.

Blite kept his attention on the deep, still water – it had become obvious where this Gilliad must be. The water started boiling and, as it swirled and splashed, a great mass of those lamprey-things came to the surface. This mass, standing a couple of metres wide, then surged up into a column, before hooking over and over towards the edge, growing thinner as it did so, but bulbous at its end. Spotting movement out of the corner of his eye, he noticed the guards making odd twisting gestures with their right hands in front of their chests. Perhaps this could be seen as some sort of military salute, but it looked more like the religion Iris had mentioned.

The bulbous end settled on the edge, with the lampreys writhing apart. A human form began to appear, and it wasn't entirely clear whether she was being revealed by the writhing mass or formed by it. The naked woman was big, but beyond that seemed conventionally human. Blite now noticed lampreys attached to her skull and nested in her wet blonde hair, their bodies running down to attach to her upper body at their other ends. Medusa, he thought.

As she stepped forwards, Preece took a pack from one of the soldiers and removed a roll of material, which he carried over to her and held out. She took it from him, while her eyes first fixed on Iris and a flash of amusement crossed her features. Iris gazed back, oddly intent.

The woman shook out the roll of material to reveal a whorled suit, like the one Preece wore. It showed itself not to be inert tech, as she brought it to the side of her body. The thing opened and engulfed her, sliding slimily across her skin and joining up, ending around her neck, wrists and ankles. It rippled all over as it settled and made itself comfortable. While it did this, her gaze next went to Blite, and she no longer appeared amused but wary and wondering. Her eyes then slid off him and focused on Meander.

'You have returned to us,' she said, abruptly stepping forwards and holding out her hands in greeting, as if she was going to walk up to Meander and hug her. Then she halted and lowered her hands. 'Something is wrong.'

Blite really didn't like the expression on this woman's face, and he especially didn't like the slithering hissing all around in response to her words. Beyond her the mass out of which she'd stepped had collapsed down to knee height, while its component lampreys had spread out through the channels in the floor. In that moment the ambient light also started flickering. Blite frowned, then glanced at Meander and noticed her confusion. It was time for him to step up and stop feeling like a criminal brought before a queen for judgement.

'Meander Draft 64XB knows she came from here, but has little memory of this place.'

'She has received damage,' said the Gilliad.

'Constant and repeated, by someone who aimed to destroy her memories.'

'Why?'

'Because it amused him.'

The Gilliad pouted like a child and said, 'The Polity is not the halcyon ideal many people might think it to be.' She shot a glance at Preece, then continued, 'But the message she brought to us remains true, for my efforts in that area have failed to disprove it.' She gestured to something in the surrounding melange of organics and hard technology.

Blite shot a look over that way, and it took him a moment to figure out what he was seeing. He then recognized three partially dismantled U-space drives, linked together around some glassy spherical device ten metres across, with electronics, or perhaps organics, in its translucent walls. There were U-space detectors and com units around it too. The structure didn't look as chaotic as much else here. It seemed to have a regularity and purpose that went beyond the mere assembly of those components.

'*It's all her,*' Iris hissed over com, yet there seemed admiration in her words.

'*Yeah, I figured that,*' Blite replied. '*What's that tech she gestured to?*'

'*It has a USER function in there, but it seems more about creating waves in the continua for analysis, rather than knocking ships out into the real. I don't know what that thing in the middle is – I'm getting some very weird readings . . .*'

'*Urgent stuff from the* Coin,' said Carlstone flatly. '*Just coming in.*'

Blite already knew there was something since the icons of Judice, Breil and Paidon had been flashing for his attention, but what was happening here seemed more important. He'd get to those links in a moment.

'She brought you a message?' he asked.

'I didn't believe it at first, but the reality of our situation impelled me to investigate.' It seemed then as if the Gilliad's mind wandered away, and she suddenly became distant. 'You have it with you. I want to see it.'

He didn't need to ask her what she meant, because of course this made sense. He reached down to the sleeve section of his suit, sent an instruction via aug to soften it, then pulled it back to show the black diamond at his wrist. The Gilliad glanced down at it and hissed out a breath. All the lampreys vibrated against her skull. A moment later, the intensity of her attention drifted away yet again, and she looked up. The disruption to the lighting continued, and now a rolling rumble like thunder sounded.

'Fucking prador,' said Carlstone out loud.

Blite flicked open all the comlinks at once, grunted at the information surge, and instructed his aug to collate and feed it to him as a coherent stream. Prador ships, smaller than the wrecked destroyer and of a more modern design, had come in from somewhere further out in the system. They were attacking, firing on the defences and hurling kinetics down towards the planet. The disrupted light was from explosions in the sky, as was the growing rumbling. He looked over at Carlstone. It was time to wrap this up for now and get the hell out of here.

'It looks like you have some problems on your hands,' he said. 'We'll head back to our ship.' He conceded, 'We may be able to help.'

The Gilliad's gaze came down and focused on him. 'You cannot leave.'

'Look, we only—'

Com went down, and Blite felt a sick surge through his body, like he'd experienced from scanning. His suit abruptly became a dead weight upon him, obviously knocked out by an EMR pulse. A snapping and crackling next sounded all around. He whirled, going down into a crouch, and saw Carlstone staggering forwards, tugging at something stuck to his neck. He felt a couple of thumps against his own back, and then something glanced off his head. Carlstone's two soldiers dropped, one of them clutching an agent's thin gun he obviously hadn't handed over. The three had been targeted first as the most dangerous, and the attack had concentrated on them, judging by the lampreys strewn on the floor all around them.

Iris staggered. She managed to pull one of the lampreys off her head and toss it. Her suit started to change shape and, having seen this before during his many deaths, he knew what was coming. It would not be good. But then a vortex beam hit her from behind, and more of the things attached to her skull. She managed a couple of paces, until she fell flat on her face. On the floor all around, Blite could see the things curling into loops, then shooting away like released springs. Meander was down on her knees, head bowed almost as if she was meditating. The guards now came in, just as Blite felt a stab of pain in his bare hand. He saw one of the things there, clamped down and squirting in whatever poison it contained. One guard came close, to try to bring a Polity stun pistol to his neck. Blite surged to his feet and backhanded him, smashing away the organic covering on his face and turning him over through the air in a complete somersault. Other guards swarmed in at him, and he sent four of them sprawling. But he felt the impact and pain on his neck, and a slimy body writhing around it. He staggered a pace, all his enhanced strength going out of him, then fell, managing to turn at the last so as not to mash his face on the ground. As his senses began to tune down into grey, the Gilliad came and stood over him.

'You cannot leave,' she repeated. 'How are you to save the world if you're not here upon it?'

May

For a second, May didn't want to look at her ship. Here would be something else damaged to the edge of destruction, and perhaps she felt more of a connection to it than she did to the ruined man lying behind her. But she grimaced, finished shutting down feeds from the autodoc and the docbox, and opened herself out to her vessel. Robots with deposition welders and heating torches had moved into the area wrecked by Crane, Arach and Sheen. They were first keying into memory-metal beams to deliver electrical jolts, applying some heat to speed them back into their previous shapes. They hadn't even started on the wall panels, though some of their smaller brethren were working on broken optics, s-con threads and feed pipes. She spotted a hole in their programming, and saw they'd been instructed to ignore the place where Sheen was bound to that structural pillar. This confirmed that either Crane or Arach had set them into motion. All this could be repaired – no materials were missing, and they had the power and the labourers. The other damage was what most concerned her.

Crash foam had exploded into the gap where the weapons had been blown out of the hull. Mentally studying these places, she walked to the hold door, surprised when Crane stepped aside to allow her past. She moved through the ship, aware of him pacing behind her and of the racket ahead. She came to the edge of a damaged area, where sparks were flying, metal clanging and memory beams groaning as they straightened out or returned to the particular curve they'd had before. Already narrow grav-plates were in place, with a deposition bot fixing the flooring over the top of them. She carried on along it, with the bot moving aside. Passing Sheen, she then encountered stillness – the repairs simply stopped in a spherical volume ten metres across around her. The woman was still writhing and looked thinner, as though she was honing down her form to escape the enclosing beams.

'What about her?' May asked, turning to Crane.

He didn't reply verbally, but something arrived through her link to him. She opened it and saw a melange of scenes which took her a moment to interpret. Finally she figured out she was seeing Crane carrying the woman to the airlock to throw her out, but then being told by Cormac not to do so.

May made a decision, since this was her ship, after all. 'The Spatterjay virus is as vulnerable to low temperatures as anything else. We have six cold coffins aboard. Put her in one of them, use gel stasis filler, and take it right down to the lowest temperature.'

Crane tilted his head to look at her, perhaps offended by her issuing orders to him. She just turned away and concentrated on the rest of her ship. Where the weapons had been blown away needed plating over at least, so she formulated a work order for the robots and inserted it into the schedule. Next, looking towards the U-space nacelles, she saw one simply gone and the other obviously out of action. The contrast of this against the representation of U-space in the scene snapped her away. It seemed to make no sense to her brain that they were in U-space with those things out of action. There was nothing she could do there.

Drive systems . . .

She looked back at Crane, hearing him on the move. He'd stepped up to Sheen, grasped one of the beams wrapped around her and was now bending it away. Her arm snapped free and she lashed at him as though she still possessed claws. The heavy impact hardly moved his head at all, but it did knock off his hat. His arm a blur, he snatched it out of the air, returned it to his head, then back-slapped her on the side of her head. She slumped for a second, then began moving again, but somewhere in whatever remained of her brain the lesson had been delivered. She didn't try to hit him again. May watched those beams bending as if they were made of rubber, while slight discharges from his fingers skittered over their surfaces. She knew the profile of that alloy, and his strength was nothing less than appalling. None of

560

her robots could do that. As far as she knew, neither could any modern Golem. He finally freed Sheen and tucked her under one arm, where she began thrashing about. He touched the brim of his hat in salute to May, then headed off to where the cold coffins were stowed. She shook her head at the craziness and moved on towards the bridge.

Once installed in her captain's chair, May felt more in control – she wasn't, but at least it felt that way. She made tentative connections to the ship mind and received just a blast of nonsense. The thing was still alive, in its manner, but its support system, additional computing and translation software were shot. She traced this to a feedback from the destruction of the nacelles, and went no further. The thing wouldn't be helpful in their present situation. Her next mental port of call was the main fusion drive. The thing was scrap, and the enclosure around it filled with crash foam. Most steering thrusters were still functional, or at least enough of them for slow positioning out in vacuum. Now to the subsidiaries.

The frame, wrapped around the hull and running from the forward crew section, back over the engineering and cargo sections, then on to the main fusion drive, had taken severe punishment, and not all of it recent. Large swathes of it were simply gone, along with many subsidiaries. Instead of that stretch of her ship resembling a metallic cob of sweetcorn, it now looked like rats had been at work on it. The cam view showed her this, but then the diagnostic she ran filled in the detail. Of the hundred and forty subsidiaries, eighty-five remained. Of those only sixty-three were functional, while in turn twenty-two of those were functional but reported damage to their frame positions, top-up feeds and data links. The fact those reporting problems with data links could do so indicated that at least their EMR transmitters were still intact. Now, after watching a robot exit an airlock out onto the hull with two large patches on its back, she turned her attention to what she could do.

Selecting aug programs, she elucidated hundreds of frame repairs first, because feeds and optic data links were of secondary importance. Next turning her attention to the repairs within the ship, she cancelled everything beyond returning skeletal strength to the vessel, and instructed the required robots to head outside. Within minutes they were out on the hull, cutting away chunks of frame too damaged to straighten out and ferrying them back inside. They welded new pieces in place and made hull fixes to the edges of those areas where the thing had been scoured away. An hour clocked by; she only became aware of it when she began to think about distribution of the engines, and manoeuvring once they were back in the real.

'Arach,' she sent. 'I have no idea how long this jump is going to take – it's hardly conventional.'

After a long pause Arach replied, 'He tells me six hours, and to be ready for anything – hard manoeuvring or even a moon or planetary landing.'

'What? Why?'

'He didn't elaborate.'

'Well, get him to fucking elaborate!'

'I'd rather not. I just had to restart his heart.'

In irritation, May smacked the link closed and concentrated on her work once more. The *Bracken*, even now, was a big heavy ship that wasn't really designed for planetary landing. She focused her attention on the three grav-engines scattered down its length. The one near the fusion engine was shot – all its feeds fried and enclosed in the same crash foam as the main drive. The three engines had been fine for manoeuvring in a planetoid, and with everything else functional, but they weren't enough to land the thing in what she presumed might be in the region of one standard gravity. She ran further programs and calculations, then acted. It was dodgy doing this in U-space, but she had no choice. At her instruction, eighteen subsidiaries detached from the frame and, sticking close above it while moving on air jets, repositioned themselves. May grimaced at the result. The more of them she moved to enable landing, the less manoeuvrability she had. In the end it was necessary to compromise.

The hours dragged by. May took a break to eat, wash herself and change into a heavier envirosuit. She pondered for a minute on whether to don a hard-shell spacesuit, but then rejected the idea. She had no clue what they might be getting into and wanted to be able to move about quickly within her ship if necessary. While she was gone, the repairs had continued as per her program. The areas of the framework that could be repaired had been, and now the robots were concentrating on more intricate matters, and another robot had joined them. May observed Mr Crane outside, hauling himself over framework struts to one of the dead engines, then pulling open an inspection plate. His hands blurred inside, and just ten minutes later the engine reported in as functional. He moved on. Beyond him, like huge metal termites, a row of robots was deposition welding across the hull that had been scoured, filling in where the particle beam strike on the frame had also ablated hull to just a finger's width thickness.

May sat back, checked through all her programming and tried to figure out what she might have missed. There was nothing. Every robot was deployed about some task, and the internal factories were making components, or reprocessing damaged stuff brought in, while the main limitation on the speed of repairs was the power supply. The fusion reactors were working at full function to keep laminar storage up, while the robots, stopping to feed from sockets, were quickly draining it down. She couldn't allow them to take more than a certain amount, because when the time came, she needed a reserve for the subsidiaries and grav-engines. She could think of no more aug work to do, so pushed herself out of her chair and went to find her tools. It was time for her hands to stop being idle.

Further hours passed.

May finally finished securing panels back against straightened-out beams, and she looked around. Things still weren't back to how they should be, but she was satisfied. In the end it was all about matter, energy and time. They had the materials, energy was limited, and with only an hour to go, they were running out of time. She patted the cowling of the robot assisting her, and spat instructions to it to continue without her for the next forty minutes. At this point all robots were to put themselves away in their secure cocoons. If violent manoeuvring was to ensue, she didn't want the things bouncing around the ship. Via aug to exterior cams, she saw Crane had come to a similar decision as her, having opened an airlock and climbed inside. She tracked him down to Engineering, where he set to work with machines he'd previously set in motion. Again, he was making something, and again she had no idea what it was.

She made her way through the ship, stopping off in the adjunct to Medical, where six hexagons ran along one wall. She went in and hit the control beside the one showing it was active, and the long, cold coffin oozed out of the wall for her inspection. Sheen Brice lay inside, the transparent gel holding her and distorting her form. Was there movement there? Impossible – the gel hardened to the consistency of glass and would crack if Sheen managed to move. She noted that Crane had added a further precaution by wrapping composite straps around the woman.

May sent the coffin back into the wall, then headed out and down. In the hold space, Cormac looked little better than before, in fact more pale and deathly. With Arach poised over him, the drone's limbs delicately shifting here and there to adjust feeds, the agent looked like the spider drone's victim.

Cormac

The strain was there, a perpetual effort, but at least didn't feel as if it was tearing his brain out of his skull. The big push had been submerging the ship in U-space. Now it was like holding something near negatively buoyant under water. The next effort would be pulling the thing out again. Sure, it was primed to arrive at the coordinates he'd set, but the trick would be ensuring it arrived with its hull still on the outside. In the interim, he began to find spare energy to focus on other matters.

He was in a vast cavern of black crystal spearing to a vanishing point, or he floated at the centre of a sphere of the same, whose dimensions were kilometres across, or a singularity point in the centre of his skull. There seemed to be no light source, yet he could see the crystal, and those messengers travelling from wall to wall, as clear as in bright day. One of them poised before him, as others had before. He studied the thing.

It had something of the urchin form of Penny Royal, with its spikes of crystal protruding all around, but bore the shape of an hourglass. It hung there, turning slowly, and he had a sense of something immense inspecting him closely. Whispering started, as of minds in debate. He felt amusement stepping up through various levels to insane hilarity, then the cold and analytical, the angry, the indifferent, and something else he could put no label on but which terrified even him. It seemed to be groping around him, as if searching him, checking his pockets and asking him questions that lay just off the edge of understanding. Then, with a plinking sound, a diamond-bright point opened in his skull.

'You are an old human,' said a flat voice, but it added in a drier tone, 'You are a young human.'

'You're Penny Royal,' he stated, determined not to let any of this faze him.

'In some part,' it replied, then, 'We are all.'

'Why did you give Captain Blite a piece of yourself?'

'The necessity of creating a datum line through history,' it said. Then, 'Old friends at the end.'

'I don't understand.'

'You don't understand,' it confirmed with both its voices. He felt its attention wander and somehow tracked the direction of this to a shrieking, whining sound cutting at the sprawl of the reality he perceived. It seemed to be working its way through at multiple points: the real, in U-space, in the Penny Royal cavern, and seemingly in his skull.

'Shuriken knows,' it added. 'Five stars for the star.'

'What do you mean?' Cormac asked, while with the rest of his being he tried to reach out to the throwing star, glad to have it confirmed this was Shuriken. Again, as he made contact, his weapon cut him and he had to snatch back. It was as if having been away from him it had lost its domestication – like a dog snapping at an owner it hardly recognized. *'What do you mean?'* cycled repeatedly in his mind, as if orbiting that bright diamond, which after a moment winked out. Before him, the hourglass broke at its narrow point and the two pieces sped away in different directions. The encounter, which was apparently loaded with meaning, and yet in the end only confusing, seemed standard for the black AI, judging by what he knew of its interactions and conversations with others. He grimaced at that, reminded of another entity in his past which had liked to be opaque and speak in riddles. In the case of that alien – Dragon – its method of communication had been all about manipulation. Here it seemed comparable to a human honing itself down to talk to an ant, if it could be bothered. Cormac put it out of his mind, sure he'd learn nothing usefully applicable from the AI, and certain that the truth of any pronouncement it made would only be revealed after the fact, as from a Delphic oracle.

It was another world in here. And yet, in this place, he could still fully perceive his position in the real too, with Arach there and now May returning to check on him. He was a centre point to a vast spread of U-space, and yet a discrete point of the same. His gridlink enabled him to translate this into the real, but he'd found limitations to the device in his skull. He understood that he possessed the facility to travel and send things through U-space, and this was integral to him. He also understood that the U-twist was feeding power to that facility of his. But his U-sense, and his ability to translate his perception of that continuum, had reached full capacity when trying to figure out where exactly he was taking this ship. He'd calculated for their destination and it was set, while clear translation of U-space into the real ended at a couple of star systems across from that point. If he wanted detail of anything beyond an arrival point in vacuum, and not inside some object, the breadth of his vision rapidly diminished. But he really wanted to know more about what was going on at that destination.

It had been critical to push May into getting the ship in the best condition for manoeuvring when they arrived. He'd added in the comment about landing because it might be necessary to run for a world, but he wasn't entirely certain. There were explosions and other energy bursts at their destination – that was all he knew. They might be near the world, or around it, or maybe a light year away from it. He simply couldn't parse the granularity of it at this distance. He considered changing the coordinates, to put the ship outside the system, but the mere thought of doing this filled him with dread, sending waves of pain from a hot sore point in his skull down through his body. He didn't know if he could do this again, and putting them outside the system might result in years of journey time on remaining drives. Yes, they'd survive it. Crane and Arach could simply switch themselves to low function, while he and May could go into remaining cold coffins beside Sheen Brice. But he felt a sense of urgency about this which he also couldn't figure out – some sense of events closing on a critical nexus, and the likelihood of a disaster that must be averted. They were going to Yossander's Hold, and that was the end of the matter. He focused on his body.

May and Arach had done a good job. By quickly making repairs, routing in the materials his body required and loading up nanosuite complements, they'd managed to save his limbs and keep him from dying – despite the fact he was at high function and burning calories at a rate that would've eaten up his body in a matter of hours. In fact, his nanosuite and the natural processes of his body were even managing to repair stuff the two hadn't got to. This wasn't really within the capabilities of a normal nanosuite, which drew his attention back to those complements.

Arach had altered their programming in radical ways, much of which he couldn't understand. He saw programming there that strayed into the territory of Golem and haiman systems, and he was pretty sure he recognized some of the stuff which spilled out of Crane's mind. Should he be worried about this? No, he trusted Arach, and the fact remained that he was alive. It was perhaps something he would need to look into more deeply at a later date, but right now he focused down on one puzzle amid this.

Mere autonomous function, thinking, and operating his gridlink at a maximum did not account for the calorie burn. He began tracking things as he never had before. He managed to do so for a short while, but then found he didn't have enough mental or gridlink function to spare. He pulled in his U-sense, closing it down and down, and no longer trying to see what was happening at their destination. This gave him a little extra processing, which rendered a result: heat.

A large amount of his calorie burn was to maintain his body temperature, and there was a disparity. The ambient temperature of the hold was cool, but not enough to account for the drain. He was losing heat somewhere else, and he had no idea where. An aha moment came as he recognized this for what it was: an entropic effect. His body was producing a signal similar to the one Blite produced when the diamond threw him back in time to circumvent his death. Only in Blite's case, those events spread out from him, while in Cormac's the effect was internal. This was further data to incorporate in his efforts to understand himself, which he'd never been able to obtain while making his brief jumps around the Polity. Quite likely the effect would have been near undetectable then.

Excited by this discovery, he wanted to take this opportunity to find out more. Dismissing the body data, he used space in his gridlink to run a consolidation program. This was essentially a defragmentation routine. Greater processing space began to open, since his gridlink, like most present-day computing and AI, didn't keep programming and storage spaces separately – they were an integrated thing. He looked for further ways to open up space, deleting recorded messages, image files, programs he'd put to one side as maybe useful one day. This cleared a good amount of space and, seeking to make even more, he ran memory download on many files, so they firmly established in his organic brain and deleted the gridlink versions. He next ran a program to sort through other items, to see precisely what was necessary.

Suggestions for deletions accrued and he got rid of some, then he came to the closed file.

The package Mask had sent him sat in his gridlink, taking up a substantial amount of space. He edged around it, tempted to delete it, but then withdrew. It was like the eponymous mask in the pocket of his bloody coat, lying in the corner of the room: a source of information he could not ignore. He left the thing alone for now and concentrated on using freed processing to further understand himself—

'We're nearly there,' said May.

Rather than reply, Arach just gave a spidery shrug.

The words and the woman standing here were a reminder, but his own self-contempt was the splash of cold water in his face. He'd been losing himself within while danger loomed ahead, and imminently. May was the soft conventional human who could easily die, and in his current condition he was no better. Within Penny Royal spaces, he made one last grab for the shrieking, whining thing, momentarily taking hold, then felt it slice from his grasp like broken glass. He pulled his perception down and returned more firmly to his body, managing to open his eyes.

'Explosions,' he forced out, his voice grating dryly. He concentrated his U-sense on Crane coming up from Engineering, having abandoned making another particle cannon, knowing he couldn't finish it in time. This of course begged the question of how Crane knew what they were flying into – it was yet another one he had no answer to.

'What explosions?' May asked.

'Where we arrive . . . something happening . . .'

'What's happening?'

He knew the questions would go on, but he was just too exhausted to keep replying. He looked at her directly and said, 'You are a pilot. Be the best you can.' He closed his eyes again.

It was coming now, and soon, as their destination rushed up towards him. Subliminally in U-sense, he saw May turn around and head out again, as he concentrated larger focus on what lay ahead. He still wasn't able to grasp it clearly, as if the lenses of his mind couldn't quite keep up. But now he did see that the chaos was indeed at their destination, though whether an astronomical event or war he had no idea. Then he perceived rhythmic waves of disruption generating from within that, in U-space. He felt a lurch of fear at his core about what it would do to him, knowing they were running into a USER.

21

May

May rushed back up to the bridge, the countdown in her aug like a small scar in her perception. She was annoyed with herself for taking her attention away from bridge controls. The structural integrity of the ship was important, but her input beyond setting the programs for the robots had done no more than deal with some interior cosmetic stuff. She'd allowed that to distract her, and she hadn't taken seriously enough those reported explosions at their destination. Space was big, and their likelihood of coming down right on top of where they were occurring was small. In her mind, she'd perceived their arrival point as somewhere from which to spectate, and then to act. But Cormac's injunction indicated this might not be the case.

Again seated in her captain's chair, she pulled across straps and eyed the twenty-two minutes remaining. A scan through the ship showed robots securing last bits of work, while those scattered about the hull were either on their way in, or locking down in their nest holes out there. Next she auged back into all the changes she'd made and asked herself if these were the best she could do. No, there was more. She keyed into storage and passed an eye over Akanthor's collection of programs for running the subsidiaries. Most of them focused on transporting heavy loads in-system and didn't apply to what lay ahead. Some, however, were for emergency situations involving the loss of large numbers of those engines. She loaded them to her aug and noted a burst protocol which could ramp up their output a further twenty per cent, although it would burn them out. She loaded this too.

Eight minutes to go.

Movement behind. She glanced around to see Crane enter and move to his position back against the wall. This was all as before, but it concerned her when he reached out with one hand, casually peeled away some of the wall cladding and grabbed hold of a structural beam. She next focused down on Arach and Cormac, surprised at the speedy change there. It seemed Arach had more spider characteristics than he'd thus far displayed. He was busily at work extruding silk from his spinnerets, burying Cormac under a blister of silk, like prey stored away ready to be sucked dry later. Quickly finishing this, the drone moved over to the wall, feet drilling through the composite of it and the floor to lock him in place. Sure, what the spider drone and Crane had done could be seen as sensible precautions, but she couldn't help thinking they knew something beyond simply 'explosions'.

Six minutes.

May sent an instruction to her chair to ensure it closed up around her legs and torso. The thing would do it automatically under heavy manoeuvring, but she remembered Davidson's injury, and the fact the chairs might not be up to full spec. With another thought, she activated the screen paint in the surrounding walls to give as wide a view as possible, while keying all ship's scanners to immediate open access through her aug. She wasn't looking directly on U-space at this point, because everything came into her through some system, but still the view nauseated her. A tap against her chair arms with her mid-fingers raised joysticks in each. She gripped them, hoping she wouldn't need them, but big EMR blasts might knock out aug control. The bridge door slid shut, and the bridge section shifted slightly, making an ominous grinding sound. One thing she hadn't checked on, and too late to do so now.

Four minutes.

The remaining time counted down in her aug, red like hot metal. Her nausea increased; it now seemed U-space had begun pulsing, and abruptly she knew something was wrong. With minutes still to go, she felt a wrench through her entire being. The transition was violent and unexpected, her perception of reality distorting horribly around her, until it became very real with a loud crash. The ship shuddered as if some giant hand had slapped it on the back end. The feeds from her aug grew fat with data, pumping it into her mind, and grey disappeared all around. A USER, or a U-space mine, had knocked them into the real earlier than expected. Damage diagnostics flooded into her aug, and she felt a surge of fear on seeing that the *Bracken* had twisted along its length. She reacted fast by inputting the change into the programming she'd already done. Even as she did this, other data revealed their decidedly suboptimal location. She found herself reacting faster to this than the ship's system, putting the few remaining collision lasers online, while simultaneously firing up a scattering of subsidiaries on each side. Spacing them out was necessary for forward travel, since they were firing out at an angle and over each other towards the rear. Having them bunched close together would lead to overheating. Horrible smacks and crashes echoed through the ship. A series of cracks nearby swung her attention to a row of holes – now filling with crash foam – through the screen paint. A similar row of holes lay along the floor to her right, also filling up. It was a stark reminder of mortality.

Threads of hot gas weaved together an expanding cloud of debris which the ship had surfaced straight into. It wasn't a recent blast, since it stretched hundreds of kilometres across, to where the gas was cooling to dull red. But it still wasn't good for the ship. As the *Bracken* flew out of the cloud, she adjusted for a less busy area of space, but could do no more. She wouldn't be able to prevent another chunk of debris punching through the hull and her. And now she rapidly collated the data in her mind.

The world they'd come to was orbited by a couple of moons and some satellites, glowing pink on one side in the glare of the sun. A huge asteroid lay a little further out, seemingly on a course for the world. Further input revealed a large collection of gas giants, large cold worlds, moons and asteroids gathered about the hypergiant sun – all irrelevant to where she was right now. She focused on the world lying ahead and knew she had some quick decisions to make. Ships were attacking those two moons. At first the idea of running into all that seemed like idiocy, but then the cold, hard truth impinged. She recognized the shape of the attackers, and the profiles of their drives and weapons: small-crew attack ships. Prador attack ships. And some were now swinging in her direction.

Obviously the creatures' main targets were this world's defences. But being xenophobic and hostile, those aboard the ships swinging towards her would not be planning a welcome party. Running would be good, except for one problem: she didn't have a U-space drive. Sure, Cormac was down there with his weird abilities, but judging by the state of him, she doubted he could U-jump the ship again. And if he tried, it might well kill him. If they didn't jump again, she could run on subsidiaries, but eventually the prador would track her down. She understood the creatures well enough to know her best option then would be to die in her exploding ship.

There was no need, since she was controlling the *Bracken* by aug, but still she reached out and gripped the joysticks. Touch and mind combining, she turned the ship hard by firing up subsidiaries down one side, their glare sweeping around and burning up debris. Even as she changed course, she mapped trajectories. The prador seemed in the middle of a run, having swooped in to attack the larger moon and now peeling out. Obviously they could only handle being in that fray for a while, and just as obviously some hadn't managed to handle it. She saw one of them hitting atmosphere and burning its way around the planet. It fired off thrusters to pull itself out, but thereafter just tumbled off through vacuum without correction. The other side had taken their losses too. She eyed the glowing impact scars on the larger moon, and the cloud of debris spreading out from the smaller one as it dropped towards the horizon.

The prador attackers had divided as they pulled away, and only two were heading towards her. This was more than enough, since the *Bracken*'s only defence would be those collision lasers, and to send Arach out on the hull with his miniguns. Twenty more were moving out, likely to regroup and then loop back in to the world. The prador had assessed her ship and found it didn't require a large response, but did require attention – probably to remove it from their back.

'Suggestions?' May enquired generally, while she locked in an engine firing program. Those prador had particle beam weapons, and she needed to do some random dodging.

'You have it covered,' came Arach's reply.

'Hold onto your hat,' she said, and it amused her to see Crane do just that. But then, as the amusement started to slide into an inappropriate hilarity, she locked down on it.

She flipped the *Bracken* over, shutting down the first scattering of subsidiaries and igniting others angled out the other way to maintain acceleration. Her present drive system now only ran along its body, so it didn't really matter which way round the ship approached the world. However, it seemed like a good idea to put the majority of the ship, including the busted main fusion drive, between her and those weapons. She eyed the moons. There was no guarantee those manning the weapons there wouldn't consider her an attacker too. She tried some com bands, but just got static. Major EMR blasts had taken out all communications for the interim, which was pretty much standard in this kind of warfare.

'I thought you drones were evolving up there towards planetary AI level intelligence,' she said, feeling the hilarity rising again; then, 'Ah fuck.'

She'd turned the ship just in time as a particle beam lanced through vacuum from one of the approaching prador. It slipped past, as one of the random firings she'd programmed pulled her ship aside. It then tracked back, touched the crew section like an arc welder rod, and winked out. She felt a wash of heat, and glanced over to one side, where part of the screen wall had blackened and bubbled. When she returned her concentration to the attacking ships, she saw they'd begun looping out and she couldn't understand why. She asked Arach.

'Kinetic weapon,' he replied.

'What?'

'They're attacking this world, and it's apparent you're trying to run to it. They think they can smoke you out of vacuum at any moment, so why not do that when you're properly on course for the world? This ship is a big old lump and it'll make a big old hole.'

'I see,' said May. 'It never occurred to you to mention this earlier?'

'You were busy. And anyway, I know you have cards to play.'

May riffled through those cards and realized this wasn't something she could finesse – she couldn't maintain the previous balance between manoeuvrability and speed. The particle beam scored past again, and she realized the shooter hadn't really been trying. It had just been a reminder they were there, and that she should keep running. Mentally eyeing the distribution of her subsidiaries, she recognized she must move them before hitting atmosphere. But not just yet. With the prador looping around her, she maintained the random dodging, but also started to make the *Bracken* swing around, keeping the main chunk of the ship between them and her. This would become problematic once they were behind her. She'd need to run hard, and in so doing turn the ship sideways to fully deploy the subs and would thus present a larger target. Then, of course, there were the moons ahead. She still didn't know whether they'd fire on her.

The *Bracken* was rumbling and shaking, throwing up damage reports in her aug. They'd done all they could. The full diagnostic check and inspection robot sweep had shown the ship to be as sound as possible in the circumstances, but the damage taken by being knocked out of U-space was revealing itself. Joints were breaking and fractures starting to open. She banished the reports. Whether the ship was likely to fall apart was immaterial, since she only had one option.

'That fucker is powering up,' said Arach, squirting over an energy signature.

May directed her attention towards the larger moon, which on her present course had shifted over to her right. She had no idea what he meant until he highlighted something on the screen wall and expanded it into a frame. It took her no time at all to recognize it.

'Big-fuck railgun,' she said tightly.

What could she do? The *Bracken* was already in a dodge pattern, and really she had nowhere else to go. She then looked at the prador ships' angle of approach and had a moment of epiphany. She made an abrupt hard course change – the time was now. The bridge pod groaned and crashed as it shifted, and grav failed to compensate as she wrenched her ship aside by ten kilometres bringing the moon closer to her course. The chair closed hard around her, and she couldn't catch her breath, while her hands came off the joysticks to slam down on the chair arms, heavy as lead.

'Frosty,' Arach commented.

Still controlling the ship by aug, she sent instructions. Acceleration came off and, via external cams, she saw the cold subsidiaries shifting around to one side of the ship. A massive flash lit vacuum, and for a microsecond she thought the prador had fired on her again. But no, the railgun had fired. At her? No. As she'd surmised, the prador hadn't just intended to use the *Bracken* as a kinetic missile, but were using it as cover to get in closer. Behind, one of the prador ships was tumbling aside, trailing smoke from where a large chunk had been excised from its side. Now it was time for her to make her run.

May fired up all the shifted subsidiaries, flinging the ship sideways towards the world. She locked in a response program along with it, knowing what would come. The remaining prador fired on her, accurately this time. The shot hit the bridge end of the ship. Another section of screen went out, and a flash briefly blinded her human eyes. She felt the tug of departing air as her suit automatically closed its visor. She had no time for this and concentrated on the effect outside. The beam tracked across, since its primary target wasn't her but her engines. The response program kicked in, ramping up those engines under the strike line to maximum. A constant explosion tracked across, but further out from the engines, where their blast met that of the particle beam. The beam scored across the rear of the ship and then away. Damage there, under acceleration, tore out one fusion cylinder and left it tumbling behind. Over to her right the moon's railgun fired yet again. The remaining prador ship peeled away, releasing a swarm of missiles as it went. Things had got a bit too hot for it.

A laser flash from the moon incinerated numerous missiles, but two still came hurtling after May. Obviously the defence of this world wasn't complete; that accounted for those glowing patches she'd seen on its night side. Now, the prador ship was fleeing after its fellow, and it was evident the planet's defences weren't firing on her. All that remained to be dealt with were the two pursuing missiles, and landing a huge ship not really built for it, with most of its drive systems wrecked.

Thruster roll, she decided.

The *Bracken* was now rumbling and muttering as it began to enter thin upper atmosphere. A glance at diagnostics showed the temperature rising fast. She blinked after-images from her eyes and tried to focus on her surroundings, abruptly realizing her inability to see them wasn't due to eye damage, but to the bridge being full of boiling smoke. She parsed diagnostics again and got the full picture: composite burning in an oxygen fire. The place would have been full of flame if it wasn't for the fact it was being sucked out into semi-vacuum through numerous holes. She saw a solution, but no way she could do it.

'Mr Crane,' she said via his protean comlink, and sent him her instruction.

She imagined him tilting his head to one side at the effrontery of her once again giving him orders. This image stayed in her mind just for a second, before all the smoke and fire drained away with a crash. She now saw him over ahead of her, having driven his fist through the remaining hull exposed by the burned-up mess there. As he withdrew his arm, a large panel of hull just peeled away and disappeared. He walked away, and she had no idea how he managed this against the gale of air being sucked out. She'd needed a larger hole to put out the fire. Now she had a huge hole as they were going into re-entry.

Thruster roll, she repeated mentally. There were no options, because the missiles were getting closer, while their continued acceleration into atmosphere would turn the *Bracken* into precisely what the prador had wanted it to be. She sent the instruction, firing up subs and thrusters to roll the ship. Deceleration wanted to throw her upwards by her perspective, so it was evident the bridge pod was no longer moving as it should. Relative to the ship, the missiles closed fast, and May calculated fast. The next firing, the next roll, came just a few seconds later, with remaining subs ramped up to full burn. The missiles went straight in and exploded in engine flames reaching out a kilometre.

Twin blast waves slammed into the *Bracken*. May felt the jolt, despite all the compensatory mechanisms around her, and saw Crane even go down on one knee, punch a fist through the floor and grab onto something. She lost it for just a second, nanosuite pushing her back to the feel of ribs crunching and grinding in her torso. Subs had gone out – some damaged by the blasts and others simply burned out, having operated at too high a function. She rolled it again, and felt a surge of horror on glimpsing through the hole in the hull what appeared to be a flat plain of yellow sand coming up fast. Then she felt stupid when data showed the ship was passing through a cloud layer. They were now falling towards ocean slashed with drift islands, the ship still sideways on. May began turning the ship rear end in – not the nose because that's where she was, with a big hole directly in front of her. Feedback disparities soon revealed that the blasts had bent the *Bracken* like a banana. May huffed out a breath, instigated corrections and began pulling in positional, land and seascape data.

Too fast.

She accepted this as almost to be expected. From the first moment they'd come out of U-space, she'd understood that a crash landing would be the most positive outcome. She watched the world's main continent sliding over the horizon towards her and knew that wasn't an option, since a landing there would be much harder. Checking systems, she put the grav-engines online, having more power to route there now with so many subs out. The facing end of the ship came up sluggishly, and she winced at a mountain chain whipping past just a few kilometres below them. Grinding and jerking, the bridge pod began to move again, bringing her to face the descent line. She thought to stop this, because it'd be better to be facing away during the massive deceleration of a crash, but the movement closed up the hole, so there was that.

The continent passed and she sighed with relief. Further data came in, highlighting the signatures of human habitations on the drift islands. She adjusted for that, aiming for open ocean and fewer of those signatures. Their deceleration angle changed to try to throw her out of her chair, as the remaining screen view showed her the length of her ship lying ahead, mostly lost in the sub glare. The streaks of engine flames speared ahead; vapour trails ran back from them. Visual input began to decline, and she flicked cams and screen reception over to radiations which penetrated the fog. Ocean began to come up below the ship, and it looked calm enough for them not to end up hitting a wall of water. Then, in a flash, a drift island snaked towards them and they hit it. The further deceleration tried to throw her forward even harder, and her chair closed tighter, crunching ribs again. Her view of what had heretofore been the rear of the ship disappeared in an explosion of rocky debris, and a glimpse of what must be a tree tumbling through the air. She hoped to hell no one had lived there. A nanosuite alert came up a second before she coughed a fine spray of blood onto her visor.

Beyond the drift island a roaring grew, along with a steady buffeting vibration. She realized they'd got lucky, because the impact had knocked the engine section up, so they weren't nosing with that into the sea. Her part of the ship was hitting the surface now. She wanted to turn her head and look back at the remaining screen sections, but her chair held her clamped. Instead she auged for this image and saw their track cutting through the ocean, a huge spray of seawater behind them. Ahead of her, she saw subs going out. One of them detached, and she flinched as it hurtled towards her, crashing off the crew section of the ship and disappearing into the spray behind. Deceleration continued, then stepped up as the full length of the ship went into the water. Confirmation of this came as water poured in around where the turning of the bridge pod had closed off the hole. Her chair groaned ominously and it seemed to shift, as if trying to get a better grip on her. Deceleration then seemed to pause, and for a second she thought ship grav had abruptly changed. But with a sense of horrible inevitability, she received the alert in her aug that her chair was tearing out of the floor. She had half a second to contemplate the prospect of slamming into the hardware ahead, when a huge arm reached around her at chest level and pulled back. Aug view through bridge cams showed her the captain's chair coming up, still attached to a section of the floor, and then Crane coming up behind, securing her and the floor section back down into place.

The roaring continued, increased in volume, then slowly began to wane. She plotted ahead and saw nothing but open ocean, so instructed any remaining subs to sputter down to nothing. Within a few minutes the *Bracken* was cruising along through the surface of the ocean like a passenger liner. If not for its sheer bulk, she'd

583

probably have been feeling the swell by now. Crane removed his arm and May just sat there, amazed they'd made it down alive.

'How is everybody?' she asked shakily through the only three comlinks available.

'Why, we are all intact,' said Arach. 'Thank you for your concern, captain.'

It was the first time the drone had called her that.

Blite

As Blite's consciousness returned, he immediately started to review his actions and wondered where, or rather when he'd be inserted again to change them. As he came fully awake, he realized the last thing the Gilliad had said to him made no sense if her intention had been to kill him. When he opened his eyes, he knew this to be true.

He was ensconced in a chair, still clad in his combat suit and, when he checked his arms and legs, found them surprisingly unbound. The only thing that seemed to be missing was his induction aug. He reached up to check the side of his head and yes, it was gone.

'For obvious reasons, I can't have you talking to your ship,' said the Gilliad.

Ahead of him to the right, Meander lay sprawled on a couch. He looked around for the Gilliad and the others, but couldn't see them. Light flared; it took him a second to grasp perspective on it. He then understood he'd just seen some major blast in the distance, and from high up. Next, assessing his immediate surroundings, he saw only the furniture and the flat surface it was upon, in some high balcony in the city. It was night-time, though not a particularly dark night. He could see stars up in the sky behind veils of cloud, or smoke, while it seemed a thunderstorm had wrapped the world from horizon to horizon. The thunder rumbling continued as before, and the flashes up there left after-images in the eyes.

'That was just debris coming down, which is bad enough,' said the Gilliad.

He turned as she walked out past him, clad in a loose red robe, and sat down in another chair looking out at the view. Behind him, some glass doors bulged from the side of a tall building, with what looked like a densely packed jungle on the other side of them.

'What have you done with my friends?' he asked.

'All are safe and unhurt, though confined,' the Gilliad replied

'And what the hell do you mean about me saving you?'

The Gilliad directed her attention towards Meander. 'I know you're awake.'

Meander snorted a breath out of her nose, frowned and sat up. She looked around and then pointed towards the distant fire. 'What's that?'

'As you heard me telling the captain here, it's the result of debris falling from orbit. It's the least of our problems. A number of warheads broke through, causing major destruction – one of our cities is gone. The death toll there was over five million.'

The woman's flat tone indicated emotional detachment. Blite considered the cold calculations of AIs and was glad to be reminded that the Gilliad wasn't entirely human. She kept her focus on Meander and continued, 'You have lost memories . . .'

Meander turned back to her, and in an equally flat tone replied, 'I was tortured. The one doing it discovered my ability to heal myself physically first, then to heal myself psychologically by editing my mind. So he decided to redesign his tortures to have me wiping out my memories.'

'Why?'

Meander shrugged. 'I think he liked the idea of turning me into a naive victim.'

'So you have little memory of why you came here, and why you left?'

'I have no memory.'

'I see.' The Gilliad dipped her head, then turned to Blite again. 'Meander Draft 64XB arrived here in a highly advanced spherical vessel, combining bio- and hard tech. You perhaps saw it below. Since we have been on alert for prador attack for the best part of a century, we detected and captured her almost at once. She was cooperative, but we didn't believe her story.'

Blite thought about that spherical device he had seen when they first met. 'What was her story?'

'She came from the future.'

Blite just nodded at the confirmation.

Showing a moment of human, almost child-like disappointment that this wasn't a surprise, the Gilliad continued, 'She told us that her people are my people, and still at war with these prador.' She gestured towards the sky, where – perfectly on time – another explosion bloomed. 'The two sides have reached a stalemate, which the prador are attempting to break using dangerous time travel. They've been sending their agents into the past, to here and now, to alter the course of history towards our destruction.'

'Okay,' said Blite, drawing out the word. Of course he knew all this sort of stuff was possible, but beside the paradoxes, the tenses in Anglic made his head ache.

The Gilliad nodded, as if he'd understood something. 'One key event in this war, Meander told us, was the prador attempt to bombard our world with an asteroid. Had it succeeded, the cataclysm would have wiped out most of us and our biotech, whereupon the prador could have swept in to deal with the remainder.'

'I have to wonder what their ultimate objective is,' Blite said.

'Simply our world – its position and large oceans. The climate effects and biosphere extinction are immaterial to them, since they want to seed the place with their own life.'

'Okay, I'm with you so far.'

'However, the prador did not succeed, because one individual was here on our world at the time. And this person had upon him a piece of the black AI Penny Royal, which wouldn't allow him to die. Apparently this object kept rolling back time, subtly altering the course of events, until the asteroid didn't impact and this individual didn't die. This is what Meander told us.'

Blite felt a wave of horror rising up from the core of his being. He looked to Meander and she stared back with shock evident on her face. She'd heard him talking about what the black diamond did. She knew.

'So,' the Gilliad continued, 'according to Meander, the future prador aimed to prevent you coming here. She, with our help, had to ensure that you did. Knowing the crystal is important to you, she thought stealing it, and giving you a trail to follow, would bring you here before schedule. It would put you on a different timeline to the one the future prador knew, and were using to target you. But we simply could not believe this. Impatient with us, Meander escaped on a trade ship to try to draw you here as she planned.'

'In a way she succeeded,' said Blite, 'but she was wrong back then, and I'm guessing she knows it now.'

'She was not wrong,' said the Gilliad.

'You don't—'

She cut him off. 'We have only managed to reverse engineer ten per cent of her vessel, but it is evidently something that has temporal effects in U-space. We are certain it is a time machine.' The Gilliad pointed up into the sky. 'Then there is Archon 427, which comes as complete confirmation.'

Blite wanted to protest and drive his points home, but he decided to wait. He needed more information before he figured out how he must act. 'What's that?'

'Our system is a large one, wrapped as it is around a hypergiant sun. There are fifty-eight worlds out there, ranging from H-class gas giants to minor barren planets. There are also trillions of smaller astronomical objects. This has always been a problem for us. We've known the prador have established bases out there, but finding them has been very difficult, especially since we don't have many ships. We have been concentrating on planetary defences and don't have much in the way of resources to spare. Twenty-eight years ago a large explosion in one of the five major asteroid fields attracted our attention, and we went out there to search. We found nothing. Seven years ago we finally learned the actual purpose of the explosion.'

'The asteroid,' said Meander.

The Gilliad snapped attention to the woman. 'You remember now?'

'No – just following the logic.'

'Yes, the asteroid,' said Gilliad tightly. '427 out of the Archon field was put on a new course. It is thirteen kilometres long, weighs billions of tons and is heading straight for us. Upon detecting the danger, much later than we should have, since the asteroid had been covered with a low albedo layer, we sent what ships we could to divert its course. We lost most of them in a pincer attack, between defences that'd been built on the thing and a prador destroyer.'

'The one I saw out there.'

The Gilliad nodded. 'We managed to take it out during a

subsequent attack, but at great cost. We now simply don't have the firepower to break through the defences on Archon 427. Maybe our planetary defences would, but by the time it's close enough, it'll be too late.'

'Perhaps the prador think otherwise.' Blite pointed at the sky.

'No. This attack, and the asteroid's defences, are to smooth the passage for a huge force of prador riding the thing in – the clear-up squads. That it will hit us is a foregone conclusion.'

Blite abruptly stood up. 'I need to get to my ship.'

The Gilliad shook her head at him, as if he was stupid. 'No, you must stay. I hate this reality, as I have no doubt you do too, but you are our only hope.'

It was time for a reality check.

'I must get to my ship because *that* is your only hope,' said Blite. 'If I stay here, the dark diamond won't save you, because it doesn't work like that. Yes, you're correct, it rolls back time from the moment of my death, until I find a way around it. But all that'll happen by keeping me here is that the rollback will keep extending back, until either I or some other event prevents me from even arriving here.'

The Gilliad just stared at him, but it was evident the news had come as a shock. Her expression kept changing, as if searching for the right response. Blite could see the muscles in her arms and neck twitching under the writhing lamprey-things. She then abruptly turned to look to Meander.

'It's true,' Meander said. 'I don't know what I told you when I first came here, but it seems to be entirely wrong. I speculate that what the prador know in the future, and what I knew, might not be correct.'

The Gilliad made an odd grunting sound, and just for a second her human form fully changed to show what Blite now realized was its earlier state – a knotted mass of eel-like creatures.

'Historical fact doesn't last during conflict,' he said.

Another one of those sounds came from the Gilliad. Suddenly she surged upright and began changing, her body expanding and stretching against her silky robe, lamprey shapes writhing and shifting. She grew taller, her fingers developed claws, and her skull expanded, while the writhing forms piled up from the top of her skull, until she took on the form of some demonic medusa.

'You will stay!' she stated, voice both grating and shrieking.

'It could be,' said Blite calmly, 'that I do save you, and not with this.' He pointed to the diamond in the band about his wrist. 'But with my ship.'

'You will stay!' the Gilliad repeated hysterically, then she turned and started stomping back towards the building. She didn't get there. Without warning, she began to separate out into lamprey forms, all collapsing towards the floor. Her voice issued from these as a distorted whimper, 'You will stay.' The lampreys flooded across the surface, until they hit a series of channels running back to the building. They flowed along these to numerous holes and, with an odd whining sound, disappeared one by one inside.

'Fuck,' said Blite, watching the last of them go.

He looked down at his suit and felt a surge of annoyance. He'd thought himself out of communication since his aug had been taken away. He reached up and touched a pad on his collar to activate the suit's com.

'Carlstone,' he said, the name opening their link.

At first all he heard was a sizzling, then the com made a number of odd sounds and rather than Carlstone, it was Iris who replied.

'She must be distracted,' said the haiman woman. 'Been a bastard trying to get through her defences.'

'We need to pull our team from the *Coin*,' he said.

'Carlstone gave the order,' she said, 'and I managed to get through. The pull-out team is now at the bottom of the ocean, with what's left of their grav-car. Paidon tried to lift the *Coin* to come in after you. One of their sea weapons fired. I haven't been able to contact the *Coin* ever since.'

Blite huffed out a breath. He turned to look up at the night sky and wondered how many times he was going to die this time.

Cormac

He'd done it. When the USER waves hit, he'd managed to keep the *Bracken* in one piece as it transitioned out of U-space into the real. He had then wanted confirmation on whether the explosions he'd seen were in the vicinity of their arrival, and perhaps to give May some guidance on how to avoid them. But the after-effects of the strain he'd been under had shoved him down into unconsciousness. Only now was he coming back.

Cormac tried to engage his U-sense to look around, but suffered an immediate warning stab of pain. He wasn't up to it, and it seemed the USER which had knocked them into the real was still functioning. Even the physical diagnostics his gridlink was throwing into his mind were hurting, so he shut them down. He now chose the old-fashioned option to check out his surroundings and opened his eyes. It didn't do him much good, though, as all he saw was blurred white. Blinking for a while lubricated his eyeballs and things gradually became clearer. He turned his head and this got the stuff moving, but only so far. He could feel the same restraint elsewhere, sometimes soft and sometimes utterly rigid. He could also sense the intrusion of various tubes and wires into his body; straining to look down, he could just about spot some detail on an autodoc clinging to his chest. Even

591

as he did this, he began to feel better, while the ache receded in his skull.

'So, when are you going to let me out of this thing?' he asked via one comlink.

'When it's time to detach your feeds and remove the autodoc,' Arach replied.

'Is it really necessary to keep me locked down?'

'You've come down out of hyperfunction, so your nanosuite, the doc, and the feeds are finally repairing damage rather than struggling to keep you alive.'

Cormac kept his annoyance under control. The spider drone was behaving like a strict nurse keeping him confined to bed. 'What's the situation now?'

'See – a perfect illustration of how fucked up you are. I'm guessing that hauling us out of U-space through USER disruption drained you to the limit, and your U-sense is down.'

'That didn't answer my question,' Cormac snapped back. 'And anyway, the USER is still on and disrupting my U-sense.'

'Okay . . . May managed to evade two prador attack ships and put us down on the ocean of Yossander's Hold. That girl knows how to act when the shit hits the fan.'

'Prador attack ships,' echoed Cormac.

'Frying pan and fires,' Arach muttered.

'What?'

'Been gathering data from local hard- and biotech com. A lot of defences were in place around it, but something recently crapped out, so I've got access. Seems we arrived during an attack in a war that's been sputtering along for the best part of a century. An enclave of prador has been trying to wipe out the biotech humans here so they can occupy this world.'

As Arach went into further detail about that, Cormac ventured into his gridlink again. It didn't hurt so much this time, and he could gather a better overview of the diagnostics rising from his nanosuite and via the autodoc on his chest. The conventional list of damages had contracted – all the bone breaks had been welded up and slices repaired and, surprisingly, he hadn't lost any of his limbs – while there was still a whole slew of stuff from the nanosuite complements he didn't understand. But, even though the conventional list was shorter than before, he wasn't exactly in a good way. Though he was intact, and all his organs and limbs were functional, they were a shadow of what they had been. There was no fat in his body. Zero. His mitochondria were only just beginning to reach the point of making enough ATP to do more than simply keep him alive. He was also, in a sense, only fifty per cent alive. It seemed Arach had taken the drastic option of reprogramming vitrification through those complements he'd set up. This process was meant to shut down a human body at the point of death, so it could go into a growth tank, be repaired and essentially resurrected. Arach had altered the process to selective vitrification instead. This had resulted in a dispersed half of the cells comprising his body being partially shut down, almost like zombie cells.

'What was that?' he abruptly asked, keying back into Arach's monologue.

'I said it now looks like the prador will succeed.'

'How? You just told me they seem to have lost their only big ship, that destroyer, and have been struggling to put anything past planetary defences.'

'Yes, but the attacks have just been distractions, with the aim of keeping the people here from venturing out further into what is a huge solar system. Out there the prador have been playing a long game. They've diverted a massive asteroid on a course that'll be dropping it on this world in less than a week.'

'Seems a bit excessive,' said Cormac tightly. 'Will there be any planet left?'

'It's not coming in at projectile speed.' Arach contemplated for a moment, then continued, 'Odd that. They could have achieved their goal here with something smaller and faster, but instead they've had to put defences all over the thing, and have a strike force in place on it. I'm presuming the strike force will depart it before the impact, to then go in and exterminate survivors.'

'Maybe it's the only one they could use?'

'No – I suspect whoever planned this wasn't thinking straight.'

Cormac shrugged that off. 'Impact profile?'

'Everyone fried within eight thousand kilometres of it. A cloud of chlorine will render the atmosphere unbreathable until it reacts out – maybe two solstan years. Tsunamis sweeping every land mass. The fallback of debris will create a heat cloud cooking most of the planet. They're technologically advanced there, but those who make it through the impact will be struggling to survive thereafter. And that's without about a million prador dropping in on them.'

'Fuck,' said Cormac. 'And Blite?'

'The *Coin* is down on one of the drift islands. I'm not getting much from them, so I can't glean more data on it beyond that.'

Cormac closed his eyes, a wave of weariness overcoming him, as if the recent mental activity had been a marathon run. He tried to think clearly. Somehow all of this was related, but he had yet to see how. The attempts to kill Blite – which had really been to measure his ability to survive – the p-prador and that far future human, Mask, and Meander Draft 64XB . . . all of it. He winced, then opened his eyes to a sound close by, like a plastic zip being opened. He tracked a hooked claw, shadowed behind, drawing through the material enclosing him. Immediately he started to feel some freedom of movement and tried to use it.

'Patience,' said Arach. One of the spider drone's complex foot-hands reached through the split, down to the autodoc. Dull pain bloomed at various points around his chest, and he knew the doc was extracting its multipurpose limbs, tubes and threads from his body. This he presumed to be a good sign about his condition.

'At least your heart can now keep beating under its own power,' Arach added, lifting up the autodoc and pulling it clear.

Cormac pushed against the restraints again, but he knew the cocoon Arach had woven around him wasn't something he'd be escaping until the spider drone allowed him to . . . unless he U-jumped out. Without thinking about it, he pushed into his U-sense. Immediately his pulse began throbbing in his skull, and it felt like someone was pulling on a barbed hook in his brain. Waves of USER disruption began pouring through him. Stubbornly, he measured the lulls between waves and managed to push into one of them. He received a momentary flash and quickly shut down, but it was enough. This surprised him, because it wasn't something he'd been able to manage before with a USER running as strongly as this.

His gridlink belatedly translated his surroundings out to a kilometre. He saw Arach poised over him. He saw the entirety of the ship floating on the ocean . . . no, not floating, but actu-ally moving against the swell, leaving a wake behind it. The shape of U-space gave him the explanation for this: May was using a grav-engine angled against planetary gravity to drive the ship forwards. He saw her too, up in the bridge in her captain's chair, using one joystick. Crane wasn't there, but the glimpse he'd had continued to process, until he saw the big brass Golem had climbed outside. He was standing on the upper hull in the mangled mess of the framework for the subsidiaries, few of which remained attached.

More pains ensued, sharp and stabbing. Arach was removing other feeds that'd been going into his body. Diagnostics showed reserves now. His stomach and intestines were full of a thick mix of proteins and sugars. Ketones and glucose were washing through his blood, and the indications were that he was slowly starting to accrue triple-density fats. He checked other indicators, seeing his haemoglobin – also enhanced three times beyond standard oxygen-carrying capacity – was up to optimum too. All of this would have been great but for the vitrified cells: it'd take a lot of energy to fire them up again. Since everything felt looser around him, he tried moving his right arm and found it free. He began to creep his hand up towards the oxygen pipes in his nose, and to the mask over his face which was feeding in the stuff filling his stomach, since he actually wanted to talk rather than subvocalize over the comlink. A hard object slapped his hand down, painfully.

'How old are you?' Arach enquired.

'I've lost count,' Cormac replied belligerently.

'Old enough not to behave like a child,' said the drone. 'You came as close to death as it is possible to get without becoming something worthy only of a recycler. Have some damned patience.'

'Okay . . .'

'And why the hell don't you have a memplant?'

Here Cormac felt himself to be on more solid ground. 'Because it has the same mental effect as wearing armour, carrying every weapon you can, or sitting inside some war machine: you start to think you're invulnerable, and you become careless.'

'Indeed,' said Arach, and Cormac caught a hint of amusement there. He realized he'd been prodded, tested and assessed.

'Decohering now,' said Arach. The spider drone was moving in and over him, a looming spider shadow over the cocoon. With hissing spitting sounds, yellow patches began to appear over the layered white surfaces, breaking holes through them that opened out, the melting material gathering up at their lips. Arach's face came into view, pedipalps steadily feeding the broken-down material into his gullet. Within a minute, huge swathes of it had disappeared into the spider drone's mouth. As his view cleared, Cormac felt his eyes straining at even the short distances in the hold, then there was an adjustment as he took it all in. He studied his arm, still bound to the Penny Royal device here. As if merely looking at it had been enough, the thing began to snake back away from him. Peering down at his legs, he saw the silvery veins there retracting too, the sensation of them moving under his skin an unpleasant reminder of how the thing had invaded his body. His arm dropped, released at last, as Arach greedily took in the last of his silk stuck to the floor, and moved back.

Cormac just lay there, feeling weaker than he could ever remember feeling. However, on recalling other occasions of weakness, he realized he needed to force himself to move to regain further mobility. He removed the mask, pulling the tubes out of his throat and up his nose, and spat bloody phlegm to one side. Through pure force of will, he put his hands down and drew his feet in towards his body. Arach moved up close, his forelimbs gently touching Cormac's sides. With a heave, and his back sliding up the metallic surface of the device behind him, he managed to rise into a squat, although he had to grab onto one of Arach's limbs to steady himself when a surge of dizziness overcame him. As this passed, he released the limb and stood there, swaying, Arach's foot-hands tracking him but not touching, giving him the chance to do this himself. Gradually he steadied, then looked down at himself.

'Something to wear would be nice,' he said, his actual voice crusty and raw.

'You've got it!' Arach abruptly retreated, scuttled to the hold door, and then out.

As Cormac took steadying breaths, an alert came up in his gridlink from his nanosuite and its complements scattered throughout his body. He focused on it and saw it to be a simple 'continue or hold' request. It seemed he'd reached the point where one of the complements could start firing up those vitrified cells. It felt good, knowing his physical condition was now completely back under his control. He gave the continue instruction, half expecting to feel something, but sensed nothing at all.

Now spreading his focus out again, he scanned the debris of medical equipment scattered across the floor. His gaze fell on the fouled pile of clothing he'd been wearing before, and he took one careful step towards it, then another. A second wave of dizziness hit, and he had to pause for a while so as not to fall flat on his face. Finally, he reached the clothing and squatted down by it. He assessed himself again and felt a surge of well-being. All things considered, he wasn't in a bad condition. He hadn't died or lost any limbs, and he'd managed to jump a million-tonne of cargo hauler through U-space. He began sorting through his clothing, pulling things out of the pockets and pouches. First the mask which the future human had given him, then his thin gun, its clips and other items. He stared at the mask. The thing had dark streaks through it, and some of its edges were turning to powder. Maybe it had died, but then he remembered what Hune had said about tachyon evaporation. He discarded the thing, dropping it back on his pile of clothing. The clothing itself could be repaired, but it'd be easier simply to fabricate some new stuff. He was still sifting through his small pile of belongings when Arach returned and dropped an envirosuit in front of him.

'Visitors coming,' said the spider drone, as Cormac picked up the suit.

Cormac paused and tentatively pushed at his U-sense again. He managed to push into one of those lulls once more, receiving a limited flash of his surroundings, just before the unpleasant sensations started up in his head and throughout his body again. Crane was still outside, standing on the hull, while the *Bracken* was heading towards a drift island, but he could see little beyond that. Why did he need to confirm the situation through his unique sense when Arach was here to tell him? He continued pulling on the suit.

'What sort of visitors?'

Arach did a little dance, as if uncomfortable with the question, and sent something over com. Cormac blocked it, which was unusual for him, since Arach going over to com was normally just a change in the medium of their conversation. But right then Cormac just didn't want to handle a mass of image data, no doubt stitched together with a tactical assessment and links to other relevant data sources. He held up his hand. 'Just tell me about it verbally.' He stooped down and began pocketing his stuff.

'A boat that looks like a Polity import, loaded with soldiers in biotech armour,' Arach said succinctly.

'To be expected,' Cormac replied. 'We did just fly into a war zone.'

He headed out of the hold and through the ship to his cabin, with Arach clattering along behind, giving him a running commentary. Before he reached his cabin, the *Bracken* lurched and sent him staggering. Arach whipped out a limb to catch and steady him before he fell over.

'Thank you,' he said curtly, annoyed at his debilitation. 'I'm guessing we just beached on that drift island.'

'Yes.' Arach withdrew his limb. 'Looks like the visitors are circling around to do the same, though a whole host of them just went into the sea.'

Cormac moved on finally to enter the cabin May had provided for him, while from the other side of the door he heard Arach heading off, no doubt to join Crane outside. That was a good sign – the spider drone had decided he no longer needed to be a nursemaid.

He stood just inside the door, looking at a meagre scattering of items printed or otherwise fabricated by ship's mechanisms; he wondered why the hell he'd come here. This, in reality, was his life: constant travel, punctuated by a series of pauses in places like this, his most important belongings fitting in his pockets. He was about to turn around and go when he remembered, and felt stupid. He stepped over to a cupboard and flipped it open, snaring up the laser carbine from inside, along with its spare power pack. This again was something fabricated aboard, since he'd lost or destroyed everything he'd bought from Andre, but it was certainly something he wanted to keep close by.

As he stepped out of the door, he abruptly lurched to one side, shouldering into the wall. It seemed as if the whole ship had rolled ninety degrees. The rumbling and crashing of damaged mechanisms sounded all around, and gravity realigned in jerks, until he was once again standing on the floor.

'Well, that should have been a lot smoother,' said May over intercom. 'Some weaknesses revealed from our violent descent, I suspect.'

Cormac realized May must have turned off ship's grav, and the internal living area had aligned with that of the world. He pushed his U-sense again – it was easier now – and had another look at the surroundings beyond the ship. The boat of soldiers had moored up against the side of the *Bracken,* while May had obviously shot anchors into the drift island. Crane was now sitting on top, watching as those on the boat lowered a ramp across. Meanwhile others were coming out of the water, crawling up the sides of the *Bracken.* He really hoped their intent wasn't hostile, with Crane out there. The big Golem could majorly overreact.

He grimaced. Or do something else with no apparent roots in logic. Cormac still didn't quite understand what drove him. He located the airlock nearest to Crane and turned to head there, just as May appeared, striding towards him

'You're looking improved,' she said dryly, something obviously bugging her. After a pause she added, 'Which is more than I can say for my ship.'

Ah . . . Now he knew her problem.

'You're on contract for this and you're an adult capable of making your own choices.' Now that things were starting to operate better, Cormac called up this very contract in his gridlink and scanned through it in a microsecond. He installed it as remembered knowledge to the forefront of his mind. 'Anyway, you're completely covered by Penny Transport. Total repair or replacement in the event of something like this.' He waved a hand at their surroundings. 'And the contract fee plus risk payments.'

May grimaced, then nodded. Likely she found it hard to imagine receiving payment, with her ship a wreck down on this planet. He wondered if Arach had informed her of the situation here, and the fact the ship wouldn't be getting those repairs, and how possibly they had no future at all. He decided not to check on what she knew.

He shrugged. 'I have to add that I wouldn't be so improved without your help.' He moved on, strolling towards the airlock.

'So, what happens now?' she asked, falling in beside him.

'We find Blite and, I hope, some answers when we do.' They reached the airlock, which now stood overhead and had extended a ladder down its tunnel. He reached up and grabbed the lower part to pull it down.

'Is the *Bracken* capable of making orbit?' he asked.

'No. The remaining subs haven't got the power, and the limit of the grav-engine was to stop us sinking, which is why I stuck us on this drift island. Why do you ask?'

Cormac winced, realizing Arach indeed hadn't told her, and that he really ought to. 'Because, as you're aware, we are in the middle of a war between the people here and a Graveyard enclave of prador.'

'This isn't a warship – it'd be no use to them.'

'No, but since prador are in the process of dropping an asteroid on this world, it might be a good idea not to be here when that happens.' He climbed.

'You *what*?' said May, scrambling after him.

'It's less than a week away,' he said, quickly reaching the already open lower door of the lock. He climbed inside to shove at the next one, which hinged smoothly away from him on hydraulics. 'Which makes it imperative we find Blite and his ship straight away, or some other ship.' He climbed out onto the hull.

'A fucking asteroid!' May exclaimed, coming out after him. She fell silent at the scene presented.

Scattered around the edges of the ship were humans who seemed to be a mix of amphidapts and ophidapts. They were armed with weapons that looked like pre-Quiet War RPGs. Noting this armament, and that they carried no small arms, Cormac began to put together what this response was all about. He had no doubt they'd checked the ocean beneath the *Bracken*, just as he had no doubt those weapons were designed for armour piercing.

Ahead, Crane was still sitting on the hull, with Arach beside him frozen in place. The hatches in his abdomen were partially open – the spider drone would be able to deploy his miniguns in an instant. The main complement of the boat stood in ranks ahead of them. Those with their helmets closed up bore some similarity to the others around the sides. But those with their armour open gave the lie to that impression, revealing perfectly human faces, though of humans bigger than typically boosted Polity commandos. Cormac probed out with his U-sense again to confirm these were 'normal' people in biotech armour. No confirmation arrived, however, because the lines between armour and person were blurred within. He was given the impression of symbiosis between armour and human – dual beings. He noted too that all of them had other organisms – snakish things were wrapped around their necks, with suckered ends visibly attached to their skulls, while the other attached to their torsos out of sight.

Quickly moving forwards, he was puzzled. They weren't standing in an expectation of attack, but in neat ranks, as if for inspection. He waved a hand at those around the edges of the ship, with their obviously armour-piercing weapons.

'It pays to be cautious,' he said. 'Our ship could have been swarming with prador, for all you knew.'

A man stepped forward from the front row, distinguished from the rest by his lack of armour and the odd, whorled suit he wore. He raised a hand and pointed to Mr Crane.

'The Brass Man,' he said, then pointing to Arach, 'the Spider.' He then pointed at Cormac. 'Which leads me to conclude that you must be the Agent.'

'We are expected?'

'You've been expected for about ten years,' the man replied.

22

Cormac

The boat was slow, but once they transferred into a bubble cabin, mounted on, or part of, a creature somewhere between a killer whale and a seal, the journey passed much more quickly. Fewer soldiers could accompany them here. The commander, Preece X2 Draft 32EB, came along, of course. 'We don't want any trouble,' he'd said right from the start, while glancing at Crane and Arach. It seemed to be something he was wont to repeat at regular intervals. During that initial stage of the journey, Cormac eyed the number of other vessels on the sea, all heading in one direction, and wondered if this was usual.

'Evacuation,' Arach supplied when he enquired. 'They've plotted the course of the asteroid, and its most likely point of impact is in the ocean, so the Gilliad has ordered the drift island populations to the main continent.'

'And yet they're convinced of an intervention here.'

'Still trying to gather data,' Arach replied. 'Their biotech system crapped out before, but now seems to be putting its defences up again. It's becoming as impenetrable as a planetary AI.'

They reached a large drift island, and from there took to the air in a Polity grav-raft, with rocket motors fixed to the back. On one occasion Cormac pushed his U-sense against the USER waves to the point of a blood vessel bursting in his eye, but he managed to range out far enough to glimpse the asteroid. Even as his head started throbbing regularly, he automatically calculated its course in his gridlink. This was a confirmation he didn't need and now, despite his U-sense being shut down, he felt that rock up there like a weight pressing against his skull. Throughout what seemed an interminable journey, he gleaned what he could from Arach's penetrations, and from Preece X2. He understood the man's attitude to his *guests*. No one wants trouble with the lethal legends they'd grown up hearing about.

The Gilliad, their autocratic ruler, had been installed some eighty years before. She hadn't come to power by the usual methods in human societies of the past. This being a biotech world, facing the threat of the prador, the various clans had come together to decide what kind of ruler they needed. And they'd grown her. Thirty years into her rule, she'd instituted the Draft line of soldiers to counter the threat of prador invasion. Forty years later, a traveller had arrived with what seemed a ridiculous story. She claimed to be of their kind, but from a future a thousand years hence, in which they and the prador were still fighting. She claimed the prador were sending their kind back too, and would aim to prevent Yossander's Hold being saved during another attack ten years hence. The details were unclear, but it seemed one Captain Blite, who possessed a piece of the godlike AI Penny Royal, would save them from an asteroid strike. Also present during this event would be the Brass Man, the Spider and the Agent.

'This all sounds horribly like the prophesying of religion,' Cormac had noted.

'Or simply the garbled story of someone a thousand years distant from those events, trying to deliver a warning,' Preece X2 had replied. Cormac had acknowledged this with a nod and a smile, noting that, though the man sounded rational, the fanaticism gleamed in his eyes.

The traveller, who of course had been Meander Draft 64XB, had stayed here for a year, trying to convince the Gilliad of the imminent threat. She urged them to launch a mission to bring this Captain Blite safely here, away from the future prador who would try to kill him. During this period, she even revealed the machine she'd arrived in, and allowed the Gilliad to study it. She talked much about the future too – how things would be, and what was remembered. All this was recorded and made available to the people of Yossander's Hold. *Sacred texts*, thought Cormac, cynicism confirmed.

The Gilliad remained unconvinced, because surely the presence of Meander here meant the prador would not succeed, for her kind still existed in that thousand-year-distant future. Their talks then took a Byzantine road into theories of time travel. Finally, seeing that the Gilliad wouldn't move on this issue, and was putting all her reliance on building up the world's physical defences, Meander escaped on a trade ship to do what she could to bring Blite to this place. It was only when the people saw an asteroid knocked off its ancient course, towards their world, that Meander went from being treated sceptically to regarded with almost religious reverence. The road to disaster was taken when the interpretation of Meander's texts turned into a certainty that, 'he will save us.' All this gave Cormac intimations of what this Gilliad might be.

'What do you think happened?' May asked as they approached the end of their journey. She gestured to where Preece and other soldiers were seated ahead of them. Shortly after their departure from the drift island, Preece X2 had received a communication, which he then relayed to his soldiers. Their previously cheerful mood had collapsed, and all the soldiers except Preece closed up their head coverings.

'Not sure,' Cormac replied. 'I would've said bad news, but I don't know how the news can get any worse than a billion-tonne asteroid dropping on your head.'

May winced, then said, 'But it won't be dropping on their heads because Saint Blite will save them all.'

'Religion,' Cormac stated, as the capital city rose over the horizon, glittering like a fairy castle. He winced. 'It is a *consensus* that can fill people with purpose, but it can also destroy them. Even highly technical civilizations are not immune to it.'

May nodded grim agreement and turned to look at the back compartment, where seats had been torn out so Crane and Arach could fit themselves in. She then looked forward, gestured to Preece and the soldiers, and reached up, tapping her aug and giving Cormac a questioning look.

'There's no point hiding what we think from them,' Cormac told her. 'We should be screaming it in their faces.' At this, Preece X2 glanced around at Cormac, deliberately devoid of expression, then faced forwards again. Good. He'd be listening more intently from now on.

'We've been skipping around the stuff about Blite ever since we arrived,' she said. 'I can see it in your face every time they talk about him saving them.'

'He is their saviour,' said Cormac sarcastically.

'No, he's not,' May replied. 'As I understand it, Blite can't save them. All the data you've given me on that indicates the time loops take him further and further back so circumstances can change, or he can alter them enough to take *him* out of danger. Only him. Not necessarily anyone else, and certainly not an entire world.'

'You have that exactly right,' Cormac replied, his attention focused on the back of Preece's head. 'We're getting the shape of things now. I don't know how it worked, but these future prador were definitely trying to kill him –' Cormac grimaced and looked back at Crane – 'and any who might assist him. While at least one future human was trying to ensure they didn't. And it seems the actions of both parties are based on a misconception.'

'Perhaps some major Penny Royal intervention?' Arach suggested from behind.

Even Crane gave his input at this point, a sound coming in over comlink like hollow laughter. Cormac glanced towards the big Golem but didn't bother to ask what he found amusing. Penny Royal wasn't exactly an altruist.

'It's a possibility, but I don't see why,' said Cormac. 'And I don't see why an AI that apparently stepped out of time, up to godhead, has any interest in keeping Blite alive.' He peered over the side of the raft at movements below, in from the coast. 'At least they're moving people out.'

Preece looked around again, now with a sour expression. 'The evacuation has been accelerated and is to be enforced. Many people just weren't coming in from the islands. The Gilliad has been issuing some harsh orders.'

'And that's unusual?' Cormac asked.

'Captain Blite is here, and you are here, as the texts foretold.' Preece gestured at them all. 'Yet our ruler is urgently pushing us to prepare for an asteroid strike that was not supposed to happen.'

Cormac at least felt some pity for Preece X2. Here was an intelligent and well-educated man having to question the tenets of an ideology he'd grown up with. He must have understood what Cormac and May had just discussed, and had probably been hearing something of a similar nature through his own channels. Blite had doubtless now apprised this Gilliad of the reality of the situation, and she would be realizing he wasn't the saviour he'd been cracked up to be over the last ten years.

The raft reached the city and descended. As it did so, Cormac looked back towards a line of earthworks they'd passed over. Big machines were heaping up a barrier, and scaffolds were going up in the zig-zag shapes of tsunami breakers. Those would help if they could get the foamstone injected quickly enough, but in the manner of a piece of wood slowing down a bullet. Walls of water travelling faster than the speed of sound tended not to be slowed by much. He looked up. The lights in the sky had died off. Apparently the prador ships had knocked out some of the defences on the moons and then retreated, half of them having been destroyed. Beyond them, though he couldn't see it, he could still feel the billion tons of rock hurtling towards them.

Straeger

The silvery Penny Royal technology throughout Matheson connected up with his U-drive elements, while the elements in the Brices keyed in as functional components. The tech tried to run a test, and just for a second the three of them began to fade, sliding out of the real, before Straeger increased the micro-disruptions around them, snapping them back into solidity. The capture beams holding them in place took on the appearance of slowly turning drill bits, as Straeger observed and checked everything.

The tech was an adaptive tool – something the black AI could pick up during any task and then shape itself to that task. Straeger was wary of it, and didn't trust this to be its only function, just as he was wary of the Jain tech in the three before him, although he had a very good idea of the functions of that, beyond making the three nigh-unkillable warriors. He had every confidence, however, that he'd be able to master both – it was true that advances only arose from mastering difficult things.

'I wouldn't call it confidence, I'd call it arrogance,' said Matheson.

Straeger froze, then slammed into mental motion, checking internally, while trying to ignore the tight clench he knew to be fear. Then he found it. He'd been leaking data inclusive of his internal monologue. It was almost like a hermit busy about his tasks muttering to himself, and continuing to do so when he had visitors.

'Yeah, pretty much like that,' said Matheson. 'You've obviously spent far too much time alone.'

Chagrined, Straeger quickly closed off the leaks, noting that it wasn't just the two technologies he needed to be wary of. The genetics of the Atheter had been reshaping Matheson's mind along their weave pattern – this being the application of the logic mesh surface to data inputs. Only this ability had enabled him to pick up Straeger's mutterings. This led Straeger at last to a conclusion: he would definitely not destroy the three here the moment they ceased to be useful tools, he *would* meticulously disassemble them and incorporate their data into himself.

'Tell me what you sense, and give me an assessment of your abilities now,' he ordered.

Matheson shifted in the beam and, mirroring him, the other two did too. Stress readings went up to a limit, then dropped as they grew still again. They'd writhed against their bonds in the way few other living organisms could have managed. The power required to shift like that in a capture beam would have been enough to shatter ceramal manacles.

'My U-sense incorporates your ship, and mine inside it, with the clarity of human vision. I don't know how much further it can extend, because of course we are in vacuum and there's nothing out there. I can focus on objects, but with a loss ratio on externalities equivalent to a human mind.' As the man spoke, a surge of data licked out from him towards Straeger. The AI diverted it in the same way he would have for any suspicious information, splitting off a submind to examine it in isolation, with connections to his like fuses, which would flare out in any kind of data flow that signalled attack.

'Your ability to jump?' Straeger pushed.

'It's there and feels much more open and smoother than before. I calculate that the U-field has tightened considerably, and the requirement for body defensive tech has diminished.'

There seemed to be no attack. Matheson was feeding him the information landscape around his words, just as any AI in communication with another would. This, more than anything else, highlighted the changes the man had undergone. In the data Straeger then noted the increase in abilities, and how this could be applied. Matheson had a way of stopping Cormac which went beyond mere violence, though it was apparent he didn't realize this yet.

'Of course, I cannot jump, because you're causing micro-perturbations in the U-continuum directly around us. This is fine-tuned technology beyond that of the Polity USER. And in some part of me, I recognize it.' He paused for a long moment, then added, 'You have obtained Atheter technology.'

The statement put Straeger once more into disarray. He went back to oscillating between wanting to absorb Matheson for all the data he contained, and wanting to expel him out into vacuum, then fry him with the photon-dense laser. His ever-present curiosity finally settled him back into wanting to know. But he'd spent enough time here on these tasks and now needed to get to the heart of the matter. With a thought, Straeger threw his ship into U-space, its destination set.

'You are going to kill us,' said Matheson.

Immediately he and the Brices started struggling again. Despite the micro-disruptions, they began to lose coherence, with Matheson fighting to fling them into the U-continuum. Somehow, notwithstanding Straeger closing down his leaky mind, Matheson had picked up on his thoughts. Through command channels, he ordered Matheson to stop trying to escape, but sensed the order hitting mental convolutions and coming out as a negotiation. The man ignored it and continued to struggle – Straeger no longer had full control over him. He ramped up disruption even higher around them to stabilize them, but it didn't seem to be working, and he felt a surge of entanglement anger. With another thought, he ran a neural charge through their capture beams and they screamed as they fought for freedom. This lasted interminably, until finally Matheson ceased his attempts to jump them out. Straeger immediately cut the neural charge. When the man tried again twenty minutes later, Straeger gave them another hit of pain. This continued throughout the journey, with their attempts diminishing. It seemed that no matter how mentally advanced Matheson was becoming, the old lessons of behaviourism still worked.

However, with it having become obvious that Matheson and the Brices were slipping from his grasp, Straeger reviewed his plans in which they were integral. He had to do something and so brought in the surgical pillars, closing heavy clamps on the three while they were still in the capture beams. Intricate work ensued, as he made connections to the adaptable tool of Penny Royal tech inside them. They fought, but then desisted again when it became evident the only pain here was from the neural charge. Straeger traced nanotech machinery and within it found the programming routines he wanted. He paused on realizing it would be a one-off action – they'd obey him for a while, but would eventually seize control of this programming. He set it and withdrew. This would be the last time he could use them.

As his ship approached its destination, he pulled his connections to them, splitting off and assigning further subminds to keep watch, then focused outwardly.

When the *Claw* surfaced from U-space, Straeger immediately turned on its chameleonware and gave the fusion drive a Laumer burst to send his ship skimming away from its arrival point. The massive acceleration flattened him down against the deck, while ahead of him Matheson and the Brice brothers collapsed to the bottoms of their capture beams. As the burst eased off, Straeger came up into his customary ball shape and observed his captives slowly straightening up again, groaning and yelling all the while. He took pleasure in their pain and let it roll through him. Screw the impulse to seek out justifications for the pleasure – that was a hangover from human and post-human morality which the AI realm could really do without. Next, taking his attention away from his three prisoners, he focused through his ship's scanners as they swiftly gathered data. Things had changed here in the Yossander's Hold system, but not much outside of predictions.

The prador bases excavated deep inside a scattering of asteroids were all but empty now. Establishing them had been part of the plan carried out by Father-Captain Volax, when he hadn't quite slid into the senile state he occupied now. The foolish attack that had lost the prador their one workable destroyer had been the impulsive, pointless decision of a decaying mind, as had the decision to attack again this time. Straeger observed the debris and heat signatures of this latest venture, just as he observed the damaged ships heading back to the asteroids. He listened in on prador com, decoding easily, and understood that the reasoning behind it had been to disable planetary defences so they wouldn't be able to take out the asteroid. It wasn't true. The defences actually on the asteroid were far in excess of anything the humans could throw at it. Launching the escort ships ahead of the thing had been a pointless expenditure of ships.

Straeger continued scanning, noting that the USER on the moon was still functional, and he could feel the leakage of heavy scanning from the world and its moons. He would go close enough to observe, but no closer. As he'd discovered on his first intelligence-gathering exercise here, after his map of the timescape had highlighted this place as important, his ship wasn't entirely invisible, while the Gilliad wasn't exactly a pushover in the information realm.

'Where are we?' asked Matheson.

Straeger flicked his attention to the three. They were all upright and straightened out again, calmer now. He had them, for a while.

'We are at the nexus. The point where a major temporal event could open out the future for me – or where and when the future will remain closed. I have seen that Cormac would be integral to the latter, so he must be stopped. You will stop him.'

'That hasn't worked out well thus far,' Matheson observed, a wince in his voice.

'You have learned your lessons,' said Straeger. 'Perhaps you will not be able to kill him quickly enough, but with the finer control you have of your abilities now, you should be able to suppress his.'

The knowledge, which Straeger had harboured up to this point, obviously hit Matheson's mind at once, for he began to extend his U-field out, away from him and the Brices. The man was just testing, so Straeger didn't deliver a neural charge.

'Where are you sending us?' Matheson finally asked.

'Observe,' said Straeger, creating a hologram within his body for them to see. 'The humans on this world have been in a drawn-out conflict with a prador enclave who want their world.

To that end, the prador have knocked this asteroid on a course for planetary impact, which is imminent.'

'I thought you said they wanted the world?'

'The current biosphere is irrelevant – only the volume of the seas and the position of the planet are what interest them. They will seed the surface with their own biosphere.'

'I see.'

'This is the event which Captain Blite is predicted to stop,' Straeger continued. 'He will not be able to, but in dying perhaps thousands of times, on a temporal cycle to take him away from the world, he will create a time flash that will . . . provide much.'

'And now I don't see.'

'You don't have to – you just have to ensure it happens, by killing the one who would prevent it.'

Blite

After waiting around for something else to occur, Blite headed for the glass doors which led into the building, with Meander trailing after him. Communications from Iris had become inter-mittent, with a lot of interference, and he suspected she was being blocked in some way. However, he'd gleaned enough from her to know his crewmembers were somewhere below. He studied the bulging chain-glass of the doors for some way to open it up, but could see nothing.

'What now?' Meander asked.

She'd appeared lost and introspective before, perhaps trying to retrieve memories the Mortons had stolen from her, but now she seemed to be coming back to herself. Glancing at her, Blite felt her to be more substantial somehow. It also reminded him of the vision he'd seen of her during their U-jump.

'We find the others and get the hell out of here, if we can.'

'And my prophecies?' Meander asked with heavy sarcasm.

Blite pushed at the chain-glass and wondered if his boosted strength would be enough to tear the whole lot out. What then? He had no doubt the building below was full of the Gilliad's soldiers, and if he made it past them he and the others would have to find transport back to the *Coin*, if it still existed. He didn't want to fight these people, but he was fuming. In this seemingly intractable situation, his thoughts turned to the container of the Spatterjay virus in his thigh. He could turn himself into something very dangerous to push through. And then, as ever, thinking about this option made him look for others. He turned to Meander.

'We just don't know,' he said. 'We have to act with the data we have available, not on some frankly dubious prediction of the future.'

'Unlike the Gilliad and her people here,' said Meander with a frown.

He nodded. 'Yes, it seems to me that because of that prediction, they've done less than they could have done to counter the prador threat. It's like the religious praying while being invaded, instead of manning the guns. The moment they realized the bastards were flinging an asteroid at them, they should have made a concerted planetary effort to divert it. They might not have the Polity hard tech, but their biotech is advanced enough . . .'

'They could have done a lot more than thrown the rockets at it we've seen,' she said. 'It's quite possible that my coming back to warn them of this threat has made them more vulnerable to it. My intervention could even have killed them.'

Blite just stared at her. And he agreed – as he well knew from experience, the timeline wasn't set in stone once people, or prador, began to time travel. But he didn't want her to feel guilty about the actions of someone who had disappeared under the torture of the Mortons. It was like the Spatterjay virus in his thigh bone – that too, like Meander's prophecies, was an unreliable promise of positive outcomes. His gaze wandered to the balcony floor, and the various stone mouths down which the Gilliad had disappeared in her component parts. He could see movement there. He pointed.

They watched lamprey forms begin sliding out of the holes and along channels, all converging on where the ruler of this world had come apart. There the lampreys joined up again, rising into a spiralling column which gradually formed into a human shape. The Gilliad soon stood before them as a human woman, consisting of knots and cords of grey flesh. Then she tightened together, with the divisions disappearing and the colours of human skin blooming. Even before the transformation was complete, she looked aside, then stooped to pick up the robe she'd slid out of earlier, and now donned it. Did she feel some embarrassment about nakedness, Blite wondered? What actual human functions and emotions did she have? She turned towards them, her expression severe.

'You deny the predictions of what will happen here, even though they were made by someone who came from the future, so knew precisely what happened,' she said, waving a hand at Meander that seemed in danger of fragmenting into eel forms. She grimaced, looked at the hand, and concentrated. The thing tightened up again but seemed to be struggling to take colour.

'I don't deny the predictions; I just pointed out what actually happens when this thing rolls me back from death.' Blite held up his arm to show the bangle with the dark diamond still in place. 'I have no control over it. Never did. This is a Penny Royal thing, and if you know anything about that AI, you'll realize that its regard for minor things, like little human lives, is not exactly high.'

'And yet the AI saves *you!*'

The Gilliad's tone was triumphal.

'Indeed it does, but for what obscure purpose, I have no idea.'

'Perhaps the entire purpose is to save my world.'

'Maybe, but a better option would be to let me go to my ship, take it up there, and see if I can hit that asteroid with a CTD.'

'It's heavily defended,' the Gilliad said, something sly in her voice.

Blite shook his head. She might be the ruler of this world, but to him there was something infantile about her. He then realized what it was. She was like an AI early in its existence, when it has great access to knowledge but struggles to apply that to reality and weigh up all the options. She was hugely intelligent, full of information, but had little in the way of wisdom and experience. Her slyness was a demonstration of this, because though she'd said nothing about it, he knew she was prevaricating.

'Of course,' he said. 'I won't be able to take my ship up if, as seems likely, you've destroyed it in an effort to ensure I don't leave your world.' With these words Blite's anger rose up again. He took a careful pace forwards, wondering if this human form made out of lampreys might survive a drop from the balcony.

The Gilliad shifted, her body writhing underneath the robe in a way that wasn't human. A series of expressions crossed her face, and again Blite had the impression of a neophyte AI, now struggling to incorporate data.

'Your ship's fusion drive is damaged,' she finally said.

This would kill speed and manoeuvrability which, if she was right about the asteroid being heavily defended, could mean failure. Still, if the grav-engines were working, he could still put himself and his people somewhere an asteroid wasn't due to arrive.

'It can still sling CTDs. What about my crew?'

'Your crew is unharmed. My people have taken possession of your ship.'

'Yeah, but those who were flying a grav-car here aren't unharmed, are they?'

Again the movement. Again the processing. Her expression went through puzzlement, anger, then settled on regret. 'The four soldiers have been retrieved. Examination shows that they all had Polity memplants installed, which will be removed and delivered to you.'

'Okay, so their pain, fear and deaths are just fine, then?'

'You don't understand!' the Gilliad protested, like a girl about to go into a tantrum. 'I cannot see all the probabilities, but I perceive enough to know our world can be both destroyed and survive in two days' time. The moment you arrived the probability shifted closer to survival. And now with the detail of the texts fulfilled, it has moved closer still.'

Blite stared at her, gobsmacked. Until this moment he'd seen no timeline on the asteroid impact, yet now it was only two days away? He felt sudden doubts, because she was correct: his presence here right now was just too damned fortuitous. Did he, in some manner, save this world? He began to see a way. Perhaps multiple deaths here would finally put him back in the *Coin*, on their approach to this place, and from there he could attack the asteroid? But then the prophecy wouldn't be fulfilled, because he wouldn't actually be on the world. His doubts began to multiply, and he didn't know what to say. Meander stepped forwards to fill the void.

'What detail would that be?' she asked.

The Gilliad swung her head around to gaze at Meander, muscles in her neck writhing and seemingly wanting to pull free to slither away. 'You remember?'

'Still the answer to that is no,' Meander replied. 'Perhaps I

619

should read these texts to see if I can remind myself, and find out what I got so seriously wrong. We told you before and we tell you again: Captain Blite will not save your world. He is a pawn of the dark diamond, and it will just move him aside when your asteroid comes down.'

Meander seemed to have grown even more in stature and substance. The past impression of her being a little girl, a waif, had steadily diminished from the moment she came aboard the *Coin*. Blite felt a twitch of suspicion about this now, sensing manipulations of a kind he'd experienced before, and connecting those to his doubts.

'Again, your present self is wrong, while your previous self had clearer vision. You predicted Blite's arrival just before the asteroid struck, and he is here. You also predicted the arrival of others shortly after him, and they are here too.'

'What others would they be?' Blite asked, feeling hollow.

The Gilliad's expression showed the satisfaction and self-indulgent pride of a child who feels she's won an argument.

'The Brass Man, the Spider and the Agent.'

Matheson

Matheson felt the pressure of the capture beam coming off. He reached out to the Brices and included them, noting at the same time that his ability to U-jump them lay exclusively in his ability to make the calculations in his gridlink, and in the Penny Royal tech in his body. He didn't see how that could last. Their radical biology, laced with Jain tech, would adapt, and they'd soon enough be able to make their own calculations and choose their own destinations. The asteroid Straeger had told him about lay two thousand kilometres away. He realized Straeger had brought them as close to it as it dared, but the jump from here to there was almost at the limit of Matheson's ability. Putting aside misgivings, he encompassed the brothers, made that indefinable effort, and jumped.

U-space twisted around him and, despite the changes to his body, the tearing pain ensued. He felt a surge of panic. It wasn't just due to the distance, and for an eternal microsecond he couldn't understand what it was. However, the Atheter grid of his mind wove together disparate facts and, even as the asteroid swept up at him, he realized what Straeger had led them into. They materialized above the surface, a disparity in motion slamming them down towards it, where they landed squatting, with an impact that would have shattered human bone.

'Fucking bastard!' Matheson exclaimed in their network.

The brothers responded with blocks of code and a hissing muttering which was only partially a query.

'Straeger has killed us,' he replied. 'This asteroid is heading into the reach of a USER – we'll be stuck here until it hits the planet!'

They signified both understanding and anger, laced with a weird indifference. He understood in a second the reason behind this. Straeger's hard-wired orders keyed into their function as those soldiers of an alien race; they would do their duty, and if dying in the process was necessary, then so be it. However, enough of their human selves remained for them to feel the betrayal, and to want to stay alive.

Standing up, Matheson raged on internally, pacing around the area. He automatically tried to expand out his U-sense to check his surroundings, but found himself fighting the USER effect. He could distinguish some of it, like the prador and weapons in their underground caches, and he caught a hint of movement at the limit of his perception. When he pushed harder, into the lulls between waves of USER disruption, he glimpsed what his gridlink interpreted from limited data as prador on the move. But these activities only briefly distracted him from Straeger's actions, and the harsh reality that they simply made no sense.

If the asteroid was falling into space disrupted by a USER, then Cormac wouldn't be able to U-jump onto it. And therefore Matheson couldn't kill him here. It was as if the AI had risked greater danger just to deposit him and the Brices here to die, which made no sense either. Though he understood his own powers and abilities were expanding, and that those of the brothers had gone somewhere alien and dangerous, he knew Straeger could still have squashed them in his ship like bugs. Then his Atheter aspect kicked in more strongly as he concluded he must not be seeing the whole of the weave, while Straeger, with his flash-glimpses of the future, was. He halted, facts clicking home. The USER would shut down and that's when Cormac would come.

He walked back to the Brices and squatted with them, drawing a finger through the intensely dark layer of dust. And now with his Atheter aspect more in control, something else seemed to fall into place inside him. His perception expanded out between waves to encompass not just those prador but the entire asteroid. A first-child was descending on one of the end caps, with a second-children engineer accompanying him. Other engineers were scattered about, either traversing the surface or down in caches at work. Some preparatory maintenance was perhaps going on, though it seemed a strange time to conduct it, what with impact just a day or so away. None of the prador were nearby, so they posed no threat, but that wasn't to say they wouldn't be close to where he had to go next.

Matheson waited.

Cormac

The city was a biotech conglomeration of a kind Cormac had seen examples of before. As the raft headed towards a protrusion, like a giant bracket fungus, on the side of a building, he pushed out with his U-sense again. Earlier, he'd observed distant launches from the surface and had garnered enough data to know these were rockets with thermonuclear warheads. And a further push of his ability showed similar launches from the moons. They were attempting to destroy or divert the course of the approaching asteroid. But having assessed the extent of their technology here, he couldn't see it as a suitable response to a potential extinction event. The reason for the inadequacy of the response was, of course, belief in the man who'd save their world: Captain Blite. Quite probably these launches were about convincing the prador they were doing what they could to stop the falling rock, while themselves convinced they had another ace in the hole, which they wanted to keep the prador from finding out about.

The evacuation of the drift island populations, the hurried erection of tsunami defences, and huge movement of those troops in biotech armour indicated a recent change in their outlook. As he'd commented before, this was almost certainly due to Blite presenting the Gilliad with the likelihood that he wasn't their saviour. Their faith had taken a blow.

Now, as they settled towards the platform, he started to feel some disruption in the U-continuum besides the USER waves, and despite the fact he wasn't pushing out with his U-sense at that moment. He did so now, suspecting its source, and looking for Blite. That was easy, since the gem Blite carried created a U-space distortion that was immediately obvious. He found the man on the balcony of another building, and there confirmed that the distortion coming from it was indeed the source of the extra disruption he'd already felt. The thing on Blite's wrist seemed like a hot eye in the continuum, a hole punched through reality around a singularity. Such was the level of distortion surrounding it, Cormac couldn't clearly see Blite himself, or identify those around him. But one thing was certain: he'd felt something similar to this before, from the Penny Royal device in the hold aboard the *Bracken*.

'Come on,' said Preece X2 tightly, then abruptly moved back as Crane came to his feet and stepped off the raft.

Ranging out with his U-sense, and finding it easier and easier to penetrate between USER waves, Cormac continued to gather information. The buildings and ground installations here were swarming with soldiers. He picked out a low, domed building, deep under biotech growth, and penetrated through layers of evident EMR shielding to those confined inside. He recognized ex-ECS personnel, and specifically Blite's lieutenant, Carlstone. There was also a woman, who looked around and seemed to gaze at him directly through all the intervening matter. *Haiman*, he realized, and identified Iris as another of Blite's compatriots. They'd been imprisoned and he understood the logic. This Gilliad wanted to keep Blite here and so had removed him from his allies. That being the case, Cormac could see that he, Crane and Arach presented them with a similar problem, and so investigated that.

He soon saw the preparations underway: the other prison with its layered walls of ceramal metres thick, the weapons installations obviously of Polity manufacture concealed in the biotech all the way down and through this building, as well as directly along the path to the prison.

'You're seeing all this?' he said to Arach as he stepped off the raft after the spider drone.

'Seeing all what?' May interjected as she followed him.

He threw together an assessment in his gridlink and shot it over their comlink to her aug. She paused and took in a hissing breath, then continued stepping off the raft, and replied, *'They don't want us leaving any time soon.'*

'No need for concealment,' said Cormac, staring directly at Preece X2 and then at the soldiers on the platform. 'This Gilliad obviously doesn't have a clear picture of what "saves the world", only that certain individuals must be here, and remain here, for it to happen. She still thinks Blite will do it, but as we well know that's unlikely. She seeks to keep us here by any means, but seems unaware that, by attempting to remove our freedom to act, she might be bringing about the disaster she seeks to avoid.'

Immediately after saying this, Cormac began a fast tactical assessment and data exchange with Arach, feeling Crane there more as a spectator, but one nodding his head in agreement. Meanwhile, Preece X2 suddenly looked pale and ill. Cormac noted the thing around his neck and wrapped up behind his head shift sharply. As he'd thought, it was some kind of organic aug keeping him in contact with the Gilliad, if not keeping him slaved to her will.

'It's . . . complicated,' Preece X2 managed, his voice having taken on an odd tone. 'We see that the projection has improved. We are confused by the reality of Blite. But our actions are necessary and just. The texts are correct, but we do not know how, yet.'

Cormac had little doubt this was the Gilliad speaking through Preece. He frowned, memories of humans enslaved by augs rolling through his mind, from a time long ago.

'Your actions are neither necessary nor just. You will release the prisoners you have below, and you will release Blite. Then we will discuss the situation you face in a civilized manner.'

Even as he said it, he knew civilized wouldn't cut it.

'*Data*,' he said tersely. '*Tactics*.'

Arach spat a series of packets. Cormac took them apart in his gridlink, learning the *Coin*'s location. He could see that despite its fusion drive being disabled, it was still capable of making it up into orbit. Local troops occupied it but that was a problem that could be swiftly resolved. He realized he'd stepped up fully into agent function. He then understood he'd accepted what must happen next. These people couldn't be saved from that rock bearing down on them, but those he cared about, or at least had some care for, could be. In half a second, he slammed together the tactical procedure and shot it to his companions, seeing May wince as she received it. He glanced over at Arach and nodded. The spider drone scuttled around, hatches opening slightly.

'We are aware of how dangerous the drone and the Brass Man are and have prepared. Your presence here is necessary, and we must ensure it,' said Preece X2.

Cormac gave a tight smile at the implication. Their presence here was necessary, yet them being alive or dead might be negotiable. It was a kind of madness, as with any religion or ideology, and this Gilliad, whatever she was, sat at the head of it all. Cormac speculated on this ruler who'd been created by those she now ruled, reflecting their consensus – a closed loop to disaster.

'Actually, I don't think you are aware,' he said, while on another level he calmly gave the instruction, '*Non-lethal*,' to Arach and Crane. Crane made a non-verbal query, to which he replied, '*Where feasible.*' Then he gestured May over to him. 'Stay behind me.'

May quickly moved in behind him, reaching down to the old pulse gun she'd holstered at her hip. He gridlinked through to his own thin gun, but didn't draw it yet, resetting it so the pulses of aluminium dust it fired would deliver a dispersed impact and an electrostatic charge. He searched through signals and found May's weapon. On seeing it could also be dialled down the same way as his, he penetrated the flimsy security of the old thing and did so. Meanwhile the soldiers on the platform had backed up and were hesitating over whether to reach for their weapons.

'I ask you again to release the prisoners, and then we can talk,' he said succinctly.

'You have no right—' began the Gilliad, still speaking through Preece, but Arach interrupted.

One hatch opened on the spider drone's abdomen. A minigun folded out which, the tactical feed told Cormac, was loaded with foam shells carrying a stun charge. The thing crackled and its retargeting was so fast it became a blur. With smacking, sizzling sounds, every soldier except Preece dropped, electrical discharges shorting from them to the floor below. Cormac stepped up to Preece as the man raised a sidearm, caught his hand and turned it just so, to pinch the correct nerves. The weapon clattered to the ground. Cormac drew his thin gun and brought it up to point at the man's face. A crash ensued. Crane was gone, as were the double doors at the back of the platform.

'You cannot do this!' Preece exclaimed, with a voice distorting to a higher pitch.

Cormac shrugged and shot him in the neck. The man dropped to the ground and lay there jerking as the charge shorted out below him. Cormac holstered his weapon and walked over to where another of the guards lay. This man had kindly relieved him of his carbine, and Cormac had thought little of it, knowing he had Crane and Arach at his back. He retrieved the weapon. Turning back, he saw that May had already climbed back onto the raft, so she must have understood the tactical packet he'd sent.

'I query my utility below,' said Arach, then scuttled around, dropped a launcher from the lower part of his abdomen, and spat two missiles over the side of the platform. They looped down and a second later two blasts ensued. Still running his U-sense, Cormac saw the drone had chosen to target two heavy weapons which had been directed on their projected path down – both were railguns. The drone had used missiles on the weapons below only because there were no humans around them, but stun shells here. If things started to become frantic later on, he wouldn't be so considerate. Neither would Crane, whom Cormac tracked as already being on his way down, slapping soldiers aside with the requisite amount of force to stun them and render their biotech armour inert.

Cormac gestured over towards another building – the one where Blite was. 'I don't see any soldiers over there. I'll just go in, grab Blite, and meet you below. Go help Crane get those prisoners out.'

'I don't think he needs much help,' Arach observed.

Cormac winced. 'Just go anyway.' He didn't want to get into the fact that Crane might decide to stop for a game of hopscotch on the stairs, search out some interesting item to pocket, or simply decide to kill the prisoners.

Arach clattered acquiescence and shot across through the doors, then down out of sight. People were shouting below. This terminated with the crackle of small-arms fire, followed by the burring of Arach's miniguns. Cormac climbed up onto the raft and moved behind the controls, with May dropping in beside him. The raft was standard Polity tech and fortunately didn't have driver recognition. He grabbed the joystick and raised it. The raft hummed and rose smoothly from the platform.

'There's nothing we can do for them here, is there?' said May.

Cormac looked up, still half expecting to see that massive rock in the sky. 'No, nothing. It seems to me that in coming here to warn them, this Meander actually put them on a course for destruction.'

'But Blite saving them, where does that come from?'

Cormac shrugged. He could guess where the idea might have come from, but couldn't see it happening, unless Arach was right about some major Penny Royal intervention. The puzzle here was overcomplicated by the recursive algorithms of time travel, and the pieces of it were floating around in his mind like its own damned asteroids. Perhaps they would come together to make sense, but right now he had to act as he was acting: as an agent. He looked ahead, his U-sense still operating, and wondered about his ability to U-jump, should there be more resistance on that balcony than expected. He knew the nanosuite complements Arach had used had made him stronger in that respect. As they drew towards the balcony, with Blite still seeming like a fault in reality there, Cormac cast his attention back and pushed his U-sense between the USER waves, to be sure things were going to plan behind.

Meticulously eliminating opposition, Arach had reached ten floors down and was now going much faster, because that opposition had begun retreating. Crane had simply dealt with anyone obstructing his path and had now nearly reached the bottom. Cormac observed the Golem pause, as a gimbal-mounted weapon tracked him in the building then launched a series of railgun shots through the walls to try to nail him. Cormac wondered what the hell he was doing down there, dodging around like he was, until he abruptly crashed through a series of walls towards the weapon. Crane had lured the weapon into weakening the walls, just so he could punch through more easily to it. Within a minute he'd torn the thing from its gimbals and was lugging it off, balanced on one shoulder, while in another hand he carried what looked like a U-charger – a high-powered portable power supply of the kind salvagers or planetary exploration teams used.

'What's happening back there?' May asked, as if she sensed he'd been checking.

'All opposition is being eliminated. Meanwhile Mr Crane has got himself a gun suitable to his stature, and will ensure Blite's crew won't be used as hostages.'

'How will he do that?' May asked, with an edge to her voice.

'By protecting them, of course,' he replied, though admitting to himself he couldn't be entirely sure. He focused on the building ahead, swinging the raft around it to bring the balcony into sight. The thing was a large jutting structure, almost as big as the landing platform behind, with walls around its edges. Ignoring the distortion there in his U-sense, he could now see three figures – two he recognized, and the third he guessed to be the Gilliad. Scanning into the building, he could still spot no sign of soldiers. The thing looked more like some sort of organism than an actual structure, what with the biotech packed inside. He noted this as a possible danger. Reviewing whether he should have brought Arach, he accepted the idea as not a bad one, but too late to act on now.

'Be ready,' he said.

May drew her weapon again and handled it nervously.

Cormac slid the raft above and out from the balcony, then dropped it into a rapid descent, one-handed, while he keyed into the carbine with his gridlink and checked its status. His body was fizzing now, and he guessed the last of his vitrified cells were up to speed. Was that why he felt good, comfortable and just a little bit happy? He was wise enough to realize that no, it wasn't that: he'd slipped into his usual role as into a comfortable glove.

Athwart the balcony, he slid the raft sideways, shattering the low wall that seemed to be made of something as white and brittle as porcelain. The three figures were ahead of him, and now being close up he could see that one of them was a lot bigger than the other two. As the raft dropped he was already up, stepping on the console and over May. He hit the floor fast, throwing himself into a roll and coming upright with the carbine in his left hand and his thin gun in his right.

'You're the Gilliad, I presume,' he said, aiming both weapons at her.

The woman stood a head and shoulders over Blite, who wasn't exactly a small man. Seeing the writhing movement of some areas of her body, and the colour changes there, he immediately made the connection to the things he'd seen around the soldiers' necks. Data clicked home. The people on this world had created an organic version of an AI which, it seemed, manifested as a swarm intelligence. Its power had obviously extended over the decades to enslave, or partially enslave, those who'd created it. But it was also an intelligence based on their consensus, so in turn they had enslaved it. As he'd surmised earlier, the dissemination of Meander's texts had created a feedback loop from the people here, convincing this creation of the religious truth that 'Blite would save the world.'

'The agent,' she said. The voice contained childish delight, but the expression didn't know what emotion it wanted to show.

Cormac glanced at Blite, and it was as if his mind was providing the detail his senses couldn't gather. Looking towards him was like gazing into a distorting lens with a glaring light at the centre, which, in contradiction, was also a blind spot. Yet, despite the frightening weight the thing on Blite's wrist had on the skin of reality, it was all an artefact of U-sense, because Cormac could see him in reality. Why was he seeing the diamond like this? Ideas about Penny Royal's intervention here, and the possibility that perhaps Blite *did* save the world, passed through his mind. But only for brief inspection. Cormac knew in his heart what had changed, and it was him.

Blite was clad in an advanced envirosuit which failed to conceal that he'd bulked up, probably as the result of a boosting nanosuite program. The way he held himself revealed enhancement too. It was of course a sensible move, when it was evident something or someone kept trying to kill you, and you were going into danger to investigate it. However, it was unexpected of Blite, since the man was so intransigent about artificially improving himself that he still only used an induction aug. And something else unlike him was the lost look in his current expression, which Cormac didn't like at all. He turned his attention to the other female, recognizing her from an image Blite had sent in their past information exchange. She seemed like inevitability.

On first inspection, Meander Draft 64XB didn't look in any way special. She wore an envirosuit like Blite's, was of an athletic build – neither too fat, nor too thin, nor too laden with muscle. She had blonde wavy hair tied back in a loose plait, and the sharp regular features of a conventionally beautiful face. She was the very definition of a look that could be bought out of a catalogue. But, just like the Gilliad here, there was something not quite right about her. He tried to nail it down; it seemed to be something his U-sense was telling him. In an odd way, he felt as if he was gazing upon one of those sculptures Blite had transported to Earth, which Cormac had seen in an exhibition there. She seemed translucent and hard, yet to normal senses revealed none of those traits. And that was when it happened.

Recognition through all his senses had been pressing steadily down on a button in his mind, until it finally clicked. It then felt as if various mechanisms had been set into cascading motion, leading to some apocalyptic climax. Cormac couldn't nail it down because, at the same time, it seemed the world was shifting all around him. The whole balcony appeared to be on the move, with things writhing and distorting.

'Cormac!' He heard May's yell but didn't see its relevance. What he did see, however, was the memory package from Mask turning in his gridlink, and unfolding. And in doing so, it expanded massively. Great chunks of information passed through, under and around his mental inspection. He glimpsed strange seas and skies, the bare-eyed view of stars through a massive sensorium, the feel of lava under bare feet, and the grittiness of sulphur in the lungs. Strange formulae and alien mathematics twisted and inverted his perception of reality and seemed to be screwing with his senses. Meander's eyes turned into black pits, while she dropped to her knees, and the balcony seemed to be burning, but with grey slimy flames. The data tsunami continued as he snatched and glimpsed but simply missed the majority of it. The thing unloaded from his mind, passing him like a series of cargo ships as massive as the *Bracken*. Then, with a snap, it was gone. His gridlink, and his mind, collapsed back to standard function, accompanied by the sound of May's weapon firing.

The download had frozen him when he should have been reacting. What had appeared to him as grey slimy fire on the balcony was in fact the movement of those lampreys, masses of them writhing through stone channels and hooking up like springs. They were in the air too, and May was shooting at them wildly, while tugging at a bunch of them stuck to the side of her neck. Two had landed on him – one on his neck and one hanging from his sleeve. He could feel them biting and injecting. Without his intervention, a gridlink program responded immediately to this with instructions to his nanosuite. Swift analysis revealed the short-acting neurotoxin used in pepper-pot stunners, to which his nanosuite had long been primed to respond. He tugged the one from his neck, discarded it, then pulled up his sleeve and felt almost offended to see the other one attached next to Shuriken's holster. He yanked that off too.

'You cannot take him!' the Gilliad intoned.

She stood revealed in all her intimidating glory, nearly twice as tall as Blite now – a human woman constructed of those lampreys, and with them spiralling up from the top of her head. She had hold of Blite's shoulder, and he still had that lost look in his expression. Cormac gridlinked to the laser carbine and, giving the beam a wider spread, he swept it around, while with his left hand he caught another of the things coming straight at his face. Creatures dropped sizzling from the air, and the Gilliad let out a groan that seemed almost sexual. May went down on her face, her weapon skittering away. Meander was still on her knees, with a large clump of the things attached from her shoulder up the side of her head. She collapsed. Seeing this seemed to click down a switch in Blite's mind. He began to fight to break free, chopping straight through the Gilliad's arm, then delivering a sweeping kick to her middle. She bowed over, the arm snapped away at the elbow. But then she came up again with the arm reforming, and backhanded Blite, sending him crashing through nearby furnishings. He staggered dazedly upright, but the things had attached to his neck and his hands. He managed a couple of steps, until he went over. All of this had taken only a matter of seconds. Cormac advanced.

He drew his thin gun and began firing this too, feeling the massive regret of not having Shuriken at his command. Targeting automatically and accurately with both weapons, he kept dropping the lampreys out of the air, or clearing those in his path. Stinking smoke wafted across, while the creatures fell into writhing charcoaled masses. Cormac mentally enacted strategies. He had to move the three here to the grav-raft and away, while fending off an attack from this entity, which he suspected occupied the entire building behind. He couldn't do it – he needed help. Even as the thought occurred and he mentally reached for Arach's comlink, his body warmed as his surroundings filled with a surge of radiations. Com went down – he'd been anticipated.

The Gilliad, having dealt with Blite, twisted towards him, body spiralling in an unhuman manner, then took a step as if having to pull roots from the floor. He hit her hard, narrowing down the carbine beam, and burned through her at the waist. She collapsed and then restored. He hit her head and incinerated it out of existence, but a new one formed as a cage of lampreys which began to fill as she took another lurching step. Of course her brain wasn't in that head, but distributed through all the creatures here, as well as scattered out, attached to her subjects around the planet. Any damage he caused simply filled up with the flow of creatures coming in. He burned her leg away and she went down on the stump, and this seemed the final straw for her – the human form had become an inconvenience.

The Gilliad surged up and towards him, legs and arms fragmenting out of existence as she simply became a wave of the creatures. He kept firing, fingers down on triggers and little need to aim. That feeling, generally unfamiliar but which he'd experienced during his last encounter with Matheson and the Brices, surfaced in his mind: the knowledge he would lose. He backed up, firing still, when the wave hit him. It carried him back in a wall of sizzling, biting and stinking flesh and slammed him into the side of the grav-raft, sliding the raft a few metres towards the edge. The impact took his breath away, while his nanosuite struggled to neutralize the neurotoxin flooding into him. He felt carbine and thin gun snatched from his grasp. The currents and swirls of creatures then picked him up and hurled him. He came down hard on his back, feeling bones had broken, but his nano-suite was too overwhelmed to report this to his gridlink. Above him, looking down on him, the Gilliad reformed.

'The texts require your presence here,' she said. 'No more beyond that.'

Her expression showed anger, but was that something adopted from the population she controlled? In the end, her words concerning the texts confirmed her as a consensus intelligence, controlled in turn by the religiosity of the population she ruled. Not that any of this mattered, as she turned the carbine she now held towards him. Cormac rolled as the beam seared across stone where he'd been lying. He flipped forwards, intending to hurl himself for the weapon, but a hundred snakish fingers had hold of his legs. He lurched forwards and down, one hand against the stone, and looked up at the weapon pointed at his face. Internally he shrugged. Okay.

The expected shot didn't arrive, and while Cormac had accepted death, his body was still on the move. His right hand swept up and round, closed on the carbine, pushed its aim away from him, then pulled on it. Shock at the thing coming free only delayed him for a microsecond, as he swept it down to burn the things away from his legs. But they'd already released him, while the ones that'd been biting were falling away.

'I have her,' said a voice. It was Meander, still on her knees, eyes black.

Cormac leaped away from the Gilliad, or the main concentration of that entity, and scanned around. The lamprey-things were flowing back along channels leading to the building. The human form of the Gilliad was diminishing. He saw May, up on her elbows and throwing up, while internally he registered that the last lampreys to bite him had injected a mass of antitoxin. Blite was on one hand and his knees, discarding lampreys from the collar of his envirosuit.

'I cannot hold her for long,' said Meander.

She was the only one with lampreys still attached. Of course, she was from the future, so there could be a connection with that other far-future human, Mask. He had seen the information package from Mask load into Meander's mind. It was likely she had some organic version of what he had in his skull to receive it. And now it was evident it had given her the ability to penetrate the Gilliad.

'Then we need to get out of here,' he said, but now knew he was evading the point, procrastinating in fact, and Meander knew it too. The download had shown her how this would go.

'You know what you have to do,' she said. 'You've known ever since you arrived here and learned of that.' She stabbed a finger upwards, towards the sky, then gestured to the lampreys stuck to the side of her head. 'I've shut down the USER on the moon, but I cannot do it for much longer.'

It was as if merely gesturing to it brought the approaching asteroid, looming there in his consciousness all the time, into sharp focus. Yes, he'd known, his logical tactical mind couldn't avoid putting together the last two pieces of the puzzle: Blite with the dark diamond, quite obviously a portal to huge power, and his own ability to utilize such power to haul a million-tonne cargo ship through underspace. He nodded an acknowledgement at her and headed over towards Blite. On the way, stepping over mounds of steaming and charred lampreys, he pinged his thin gun, finding it in one of the channels, and snatched it up. By the time he reached Blite, the man was groggily pushing himself to his feet.

'What the fuck happened?' he managed.

'Epiphany,' Cormac replied, reached down and grabbed the

man's wrist, closing his hand around that dark diamond as if on a white-hot brand. He reached into its power, and out with his ability, mapping coordinates. He knew, after the last time, that his odds of surviving what was to come were minimal.

And then he U-jumped.

23

May

Blite and Cormac snapped out of existence. May shook her head groggily as she staggered over to a pile of dead or slowly writhing lampreys, kicked them aside, and retrieved her weapon. She replayed the brief exchange of words as she watched those lamprey-things slithering back along the channels towards the building, then looked towards Meander. Apart from the things stuck to her neck and up the side of her head, she appeared fairly conventional at a glance. Yet on closer inspection, there was something odd about her. Her eyes were dark and deep, while her face and her hands seemed to be edging towards translucence.

'What the hell happened?' she asked.

'We have to get out of here,' said Meander, strain creasing her features as she gestured towards the grav-raft.

May wasn't about to argue with that. Cormac and Blite were simply gone and they were still surrounded by the things, or the being, that had attacked them. She reached the raft just behind the other woman and climbed aboard. Meander slumped into one of the passenger seats – it seemed May would have to pilot. She dropped behind the controls, hit start-up and jerked the joystick up. The raft seemed to struggle for a second and she worried about the damage it might have taken, then it heaved into the sky.

'Where to?' she asked.

The woman waved a hand vaguely and closed her eyes. May was about to demand an answer when, without receiving permission, Arach's comlink opened in her aug.

'Down here,' he said, dropping in coordinates.

May looked at the controls before her and saw that only flight controls were operable – there was a hole where a map screen would have been in a standard console. She routed the coordinates to tracking in her aug, received an arrow pointing down, and followed it.

'Fucking things,' said Meander from behind. May glanced around to see the woman fingering the lampreys attached to the side of her head and neck. May sympathized. She was bloody and sore from just two of the things, but with her Polity nanosuite at least the wounds were no longer bleeding, and were healing fast. Meander had six of them attached to her.

'Pull them off,' she said.

'I cannot,' Meander replied. 'I have to make sure that USER stays shut down.'

'USER,' May repeated. 'So, any explanations? I know you're from the future and your memories of that were destroyed under interrogation, but at least you can tell me what happened back there.'

Meander focused on her. The woman's eyes didn't just appear black, but rather like holes into some distant darkness. And yet, in a way May couldn't quite nail down, Meander seemed luminous too.

'Before he came here, the agent travelled into the future.'

'Yeah, I know.' May nodded.

'There he had his encounter with the p-prador and was assisted by a future human he named Mask. As well as helping him, this Mask provided a data package, which consisted of . . . some of my memories and abilities that I'm using right now.'

'How did Mask know this would be needed?' May asked. Then, thinking about time travel, felt growing confusion as she tried to work things out.

'She knew because it was history to her. Or at least it was in her particular iteration of the future. Whether it will remain so, I cannot say – this loop has yet to play out.'

May absorbed what she could of this as she brought the raft down in a clear area among wreckage and fires. She looked around and saw numerous soldiers scattered amid the mess; not one of them was moving. She'd seen Arach using some form of stun ammunition before and wondered if he'd continued to do so, as he stepped out of a wrecked and burning building more like a collapsed chunk of jungle. She felt ashamed of her cynicism when she saw him carrying one of the soldiers to deposit them safely away from the fire.

'So this Mask is an associate of yours?' May asked, because she couldn't parse that stuff about loops and iterations of the future.

'Probably, though I don't know. I have the information and abilities I utilized, and some memories attached by context. But the picture isn't clear,' Meander replied, standing up.

They clambered out of the raft and Arach scuttled up towards them.

'*Move to my right*,' he told May privately.

Puzzled, she did as bid while Arach stayed completely focused on Meander. May noticed his hatches were partially open. The woman stood before him with her arms hanging slack at her sides. After a short period, she reached up and prodded at the lampreys as if embarrassed about them. She glanced at May, looking haunted, then returned her attention to Arach.

641

'You heard what I told May,' she said. 'You were watching what happened above. And you and Crane have both been deep in the data realm. You know what's happening, and that it must happen.'

'Agreed on all those points,' said Arach. 'But from what we understand of the situation, the shit is likely to hit the fan about now. The Mobius AI is here in the system and the fucker has someone on the inside.'

'Do you know what it wants?' Meander asked.

'Cormac dead, evidently.'

May glanced aside at nearby movement and saw first the hat, then Crane looming into view. The big Golem looked a tad raggedy around the edges. She wondered how he maintained his sartorial appearance on other occasions and felt a stab of dangerous hilarity rising.

'But why?' Meander asked.

Arach shrugged. 'Probably because, like many AIs, Straeger gets really resentful about a primitive human telling it what to do.'

'And you think I'm in alliance with Straeger?' Meander sounded hurt.

Crane reached them, walking up beside Arach and clanking a hand down on the spider drone's thorax as he passed. He walked right up to Meander and May could see her pulling back, with fear in her expression. Crane leaned forwards, bringing his head down level with her face, and pushed his hat back. Meander took one look at his features and stark terror displaced fear. She began turning, as if to run. His hand snapped out and closed on her skull, almost completely enclosing it, the lamprey-things looping and writhing between his fingers. She struggled for a moment and knew futility as he turned her back to face him. What happened next only lasted a second. He abruptly released her, stood upright, and turned to walk back past Arach. The spider drone closed up his hatches, turned and followed.

'You okay?' May asked, coming up to take hold of Meander's arm.

The woman turned towards her, eyes like pits.

'I don't know,' she said. 'I don't know.'

With a tug on the arm, May got her walking after the Golem and the spider. She had nothing but questions, but right then knew she'd receive no intelligible answers. They trudged on through wreckage and settling ash, then into a part of the city that wasn't wrecked, yet nevertheless it looked like overgrown ruins. Crane halted in front of a wall whose building blocks seemed to be vaguely cubiform bivalves. As he stood there a shot rang out and clanged off his upper arm, further messing up his coat. Arach swivelled, folded out one minigun and fired a shot. One of the armoured soldiers staggered into view, shedding lightning, and fell on his face. May crouched, scanning around. She had to remember she was effectively in a war zone, despite the fact Crane and Arach had eliminated most of the opposition. After a moment she reached up and pulled Meander down beside her.

'I don't know,' the woman repeated. May grimaced.

Having ignored the shot, Crane reached out and jammed his hands between two of the organic blocks. He heaved, pulling them apart. A groaning sound issued from the wall, then with a snapping and crackling it parted along castellated edges and Crane stepped through.

They followed him down into an intestinal pipe lit by glowing aphids clinging to the ceiling, the size of human heads. There were people down here, some of them armoured like those outside, but they just turned and ran. Had they all learned the lesson of those above, or had new orders been issued? May kept alert as they came to yet another door. This one was a familiar-looking ceramal vault door, probably imported from the Polity, and it withstood Crane just about as long as the one above. After tearing it free, his boots having also rucked up a great chunk of the floor under the load, he tossed the thing to one side, where it went down with a heavy whoomph.

Inside, organic-looking furniture and a small gathering of people occupied a wide room. As she followed Crane and Arach inside, May recognized familiar faces from Penny Transport, though she'd actually met none of them in person, only spoken to over com.

'Ah, the cavalry have arrived,' said the haiman woman flatly.

Two had the look of Polity military, and she assumed them to be employees of Carlstone – a man with close-cropped hair and cold eyes. Iris, standing well back from the other three, moved forwards and looked over at him.

'How's your belief system now, hmm, Carlstone?' she asked with a weird edge to her voice.

'It's taken a blow,' he replied, 'but my cynicism remains intact.'

The three were staring at Crane and Arach and the tension in the room was palpable. Even Iris seemed to have taken on something of a frightened look. May couldn't quite understand their reaction, but only for a second. She realized she'd been in the company of these two, and Cormac, long enough to have grown accustomed to them, but now she remembered Akanthor's reaction upon first seeing them: fucking legends. She supposed that, had she not gone through all she had, she would have reacted the same way in their position. Mr Crane – the actual Brass Man – had just ripped the door off their prison and stepped inside. And not only that, he'd arrived with Arach the Spider Drone.

'We have a grav-raft above,' said Arach. 'We need to go back to the *Coin*.'

'Where's Blite?' Carlstone asked.

Arach raised one limb and pointed it upwards. 'Up on the asteroid with Cormac, and probably wishing he wasn't.'

No reply to that was forthcoming; the tension seemed to ramp up. May saw Iris's expression go through a number of transformations, then abruptly lock down on blandness. The others just kept looking around, and May guessed a fast aug exchange was in progress, but still no one was moving. It was as if they just didn't know what to do now.

'Meanwhile,' May interjected loudly, 'both Cormac and Blite could shortly be rejoining us, along with a few billion tons of rock, so maybe it's time to leave?'

Carlstone focused on her, a smile twisting his lips but not reaching his eyes. 'Let's go,' he said.

As they headed out, May noticed Iris loitering behind and waited for her to catch up. The woman still had that bland expression. Meander, who'd stayed at May's side, seemed to have recovered from Crane's inspection of her.

'And now this just has to play out,' Meander said.

Iris ducked as if evading a blow, then moved on ahead.

Cormac

The device of Penny Royal tech aboard the *Bracken* had been harsh on his mind, but this was harsher still. Even through the fabric of Blite's suit, it felt like putting his hand onto a brand. In that moment, noting he wasn't actually having to touch the thing, he realized this was an irrelevance, as with so much else in U-space proximity. But it was something he only understood viscerally while traversing that continuum. Back in the real, he needed the human perception of the universe, so there proximity did matter. He experienced pain yet again, but also relief from the diminishing rhythmic suppression of the USER. And fractionally, after the first touch, the Penny Royal realm swept down on him like a vast and hungry sand worm.

Once more he perceived this place as a huge cavern, spearing off in both directions to infinity, and as a sphere enclosing him, and as a singularity at the centre of his skull. Blite floated beside him with his wrist clamped in Cormac's hand. The man was inert, eyes open but seeing nothing, heart caught between heartbeats and as immobile as ice, frozen in the instant and not having Cormac's perception of all this.

As with space, time stretched like elastic here – he occupied it for eternity, and just for an instant. Within that eternal instant, he felt the godlike attention of the AI upon him – all its fragments aligned and in agreement, and seemingly ready to bear down on him like a thousand knives. It seemed that here too Shuriken was a war hound, ready to be unleashed, though it wasn't clear whether upon his enemies or upon him. He reached out his free hand for the star, but then snapped it into a fist before the thing could cut him again. He withdrew, and with that snap reality came rushing up.

The jolt of arrival broke his connection to the gem, and the twist in U-space it represented in the real, flinging his hand away from Blite's wrist. They materialized above dusty regolith. Familiar with such arrivals, Cormac threw himself into a roll. Coming up into a crouch, he used his gridlink to activate his envirosuit before it responded to near-vacuum, and had his hood up and visor closed as he rose to his feet.

'Mother of fuck,' said Blite, the words distorted as near-vacuum sucked the air out of his lungs. He shouldered into regolith, throwing up glittering dust that swirled around like smoke. He bounced and trawled a hand in the thick layer to slow down.

Cormac saw the surface was light-sucking black until he stirred the stuff up. A push against the ground let Blite come upright, legs widely spread. His suit reacted a second later, throwing up the concertinaed sections of its hood, and sliding up the visor from the neck ring to mate with it.

With the carbine tucked under one arm, Cormac quickly released the gloves from their wrist compartments and pulled them on. In a small head-up display, the suit informed him of a perfect seal and enough stored air to last a few hours. His work would be done here long before then. What would happen afterwards wasn't something he wanted to think too deeply about right then. Gloves on, he shifted the carbine to his left hand and drew his thin gun with his right, as he scanned their surroundings. No immediate dangers revealed themselves, so he focused back on Blite, gridlinking to the man's suit to open com.

'Gloves,' he advised.

They'd already dropped out of their storage compartments at Blite's wrists, but the suit, like Cormac's, obviously wasn't advanced enough to put them on for him. He did so, sealing them in place. Cormac studied the man, thinking at least a little about the immediate future.

'Here,' he said, tossing the carbine across.

Blite fielded it, put his finger to the trigger, and scanned their surroundings too. How much he understood of what'd just happened Cormac didn't know, but he at least realized danger must be imminent. The man huffed out an expletive, looking towards Yossander's Hold, plainly visible over sharp peaks, so he'd evidently grasped where they now were.

'Low albedo,' said Cormac, kicking at the dust. 'Helped keep this asteroid concealed until they were close. Not that anyone was looking hard enough at exterior threats with the messiah's promised arrival.'

647

'No need to snipe at me,' said Blite. 'It wasn't exactly my choice to be their messiah, or to be given this diamond.'

Cormac began to trudge towards him. 'Sorry about the rough landing. The raw power coming through that thing was very different from what I used before.'

'I need some explanations,' said Blite, still taking in their surroundings.

Cormac looked around too. A hundred metres over to his left sat a large metallic cap, partially covered by a drift of the dust here. He recognized it as the cap on a soldier cache and, reluctantly pressing his U-sense, he saw thousands of prador stacked one upon the other down below. Ranging out with that sense, he picked up other caches and weapons turrets ready to sprout from the regolith. Prador were active out there too, and he had no doubt their arrival had tripped some sensors. But they had some time yet.

'Okay,' Cormac shrugged self-deprecatingly. 'You don't save the world, but I do.'

'What?' The word came out explosively and Cormac noted a degree of resentment behind it. Being designated the saviour of a world had obviously had its effect on Blite's ego.

'You know that I can jump through U-space?'

'Apparently . . .'

'I can also jump large objects through U-space. For example, the *Bracken* arrived here without U-space engines. I jumped it.'

'The fuck?' Blite showed a moment of confusion, then continued, 'I know that ship – I should do because I paid most of its cost. At standard grav, that thing weighs in at two point three million tons.'

Cormac nodded. 'Of course, to bring it there,' he pointed at the world in the sky, 'I required a suitable power source. Aboard the *Bracken*, I found this in a chunk of Penny Royal tech which

648

Crane and Arach had retrieved. Here it's been something else.' As Cormac came to stand in front of the man he pointed at Blite's wrist, where his suit concealed the bangle.

And this would have to be enough explanation because time was running out. He could see prador approaching via U-sense, though it seemed to be fritzing now, which maybe meant Meander's control was slipping, and the Gilliad was trying to bring the USER back online. He pointed over to his left, where he knew the prador would appear.

'Now I need to get this done.' Little time remained, but he felt guilty enough to add, 'I'm sorry. Maybe you'll be able to find a way off this place. I doubt I'll be capable of much after I do this . . . capable of anything at all, in fact.' He winced at the self-pity.

Blite looked over to where Cormac had pointed and muttered another oath. Up on a ridge a prador first-child came into view, shortly followed by a second-child. Cormac could see the fury of speculation and calculation in the man's expression. He knew he'd be stranded here, amid hostile aliens and facing multiple deaths. Giving him the carbine had been a sticking plaster over Cormac's guilt. Would Blite demand he jump them back out of this place? It wasn't tenable, because Cormac didn't know if he could use the gem without Blite being present. Blite looked up at Yossander's Hold again, gave a sad nod of acquiescence, then held out his wrist. Cormac clamped a hand around it and Blite closed his eyes.

The expected surge didn't arrive – instead it was as if power was being sucked out elsewhere.

'There's resistance,' he said, then added, 'Perhaps put the gem outside your suit,' but knowing this was wrong.

His ability to perceive his real surroundings beyond conventional senses might have closed down, but his perception of

U-space remained in place. Distortions arrived, one some distance away, but two more bearing down on him. He tried to jump himself and Blite away, despite the lack of anything from the diamond, but felt like he was pushing against the walls of a chamber. Realization arrived: someone had enclosed him in a U-field, inhibiting his ability to jump, and it began to dawn on him who that could be.

He released his hold on Blite and turned, raising his thin gun. With a thump he felt in his bones, the Brice brothers appeared. He opened fire on the nearest, regretting handing over the carbine to Blite. Pulse shots spattered all over the front of that one, juddering him as the two of them charged. He noted that this time there was some penetration of their armour, and remembered once again what Hune had said about tachyon evaporation of items from the future.

'Run!' he shouted at Blite.

The man instead dropped into a crouch and opened fire with the carbine, hitting the other brother square in the face. The beam burned armour and delved into tough underlying flesh and bone, but hardly seemed to slow him. The creature was on him in a moment. He slapped Blite's weapon tumbling away in the low gravity, then on the return strike knocked him on the opposite trajectory. He then swerved away from him, since Blite wasn't really their target. As the one he'd shot reached him, Cormac stepped aside, emptying shots in at waist level. A hand snapped out; it felt like a grav-car hitting him. He threw himself back, cartwheeling with a touch of one hand to the ground, then came down into a crouch, firing again, concentrating on where Blite's or his own shots had done the most damage. This slowed them as he danced around, or otherwise flung himself from their grasp, but he knew he couldn't evade them for much longer. And, as ever, he began calculating a way out of the immediate fight.

He saw where Blite hit the canted surface of a rock and scrabbled for a hold to stop himself bouncing on. From there the man looked over to where the carbine had gone, then back to Cormac. He noted the two prador up on the ridge, doubtless holding back their expected response to human interlopers and enjoying the spectacle of humans trying to kill each other. This needed to change. Cormac threw a kick into the chest of the nearest brother and used this to bounce himself away. He emptied the remainder of a dust clip into the other one, the shots accelerated by gridlink instruction and the thin gun barrel glowing red.

Cover, over there.

He threw himself in that direction, swiftly reloading as the Brices came after him. Next, skidding to a halt, he aimed and fired, but not at them – the shots streaked in glowing lines away. As the dust clip emptied and the gun began reporting a barrel failure, he went into a roll, while shouting at Blite, 'Get down behind that fucking rock!'

It seemed the man had understood the moment plumes of dust cut across the regolith. He rolled over the rock and dropped out of sight. Cormac came up, running as best he could in low gravity, glancing back to see the Brices picked up in a storm of metal, and turned end over end through semi-vacuum as chunks of their armour and bodies flew away. A second later something arced in, and a blinding flash ensued. It turned out that shooting at a prador first-child had elicited the expected response.

The blast rolled him across the regolith to land up against that prador cache end cap. His envirosuit smoked in vacuum, as did his shredded legs. He hadn't got out of the way of that first-child's response quickly enough. He visualized more time under an autodoc, and knew this would be the most positive outcome. His U-sense now sparked back into life, while around him the sense of restriction began to stutter. Obviously prador Gatling slugs, probably with an exotic metal component or at least depleted uranium, hadn't done the Brice brothers much good, breaking their circuit, and Matheson's grip on the enclosing U-field.

He saw Matheson was over there, sprawled in the shade of a slab and clutching at his head. Cormac knew exactly how that felt. He fought the restriction and realized he had to act fast, before the man recovered and got the U-field back into place.

'Now! We do it now!' he told Blite over com, and pushed himself up on bleeding and freezing legs.

'Difficult,' Blite replied.

A shadow drew across and then, with a puff of thrusters, the first-child descended to land precisely between Cormac and where Blite was hiding. Cormac watched the creature focus on him, took a slow breath, and peered down at his thin gun. He felt like laughing as he looked up to see those Gatling cannons starting to turn. He expected to die at any second, but instead of slugs a comlink request arrived. He focused on the red eyes behind that visor. He still had chances. Curiosity had delayed his execution.

'How did you get here?' the first-child asked.

Cormac strained against Matheson – the man was pushing himself to his feet while still mentally trying to get a grip.

'Didn't you see the Polity destroyer landing?' Cormac asked, pushing still.

'You are lying,' said the prador. 'You will answer my questions as I peel off your skin.'

'You are unkind,' Cormac replied, and then felt a surge of victory.

Matheson had just made a big mistake. Instead of concentrating on locking Cormac down, he'd diverted his resources to bringing the Brice brothers back in.

'Answer my question!' the prador demanded.

The two brothers snapped into being behind the prador. Cormac pointed at them. He didn't need to, since the prador already had one stalked eye directed behind himself.

'Like that,' he said.

On the first-child's carapace a laser flicked up and turned. Cormac caught the flash of green, explosive movement, and a shriek which seemed to pass through U-space as he jumped into that continuum. He came out skidding in dust and shadow, directed his thin gun up, jamming it into Matheson's throat, then gridlinked its firing up to destruction. The shots hammered at armour grown thin, spraying out sparks and globs of metal like an arc welder, then punched through. He managed to release the thing just a second before its power supply blew, tossing him down on his back. Matheson staggered backwards to the slab, vapour pouring out of a gaping hole in his neck, angled up into his skull. He was by no means dead, but this had given Cormac time. He jumped again, fast.

Thumping down beside Blite, he looked out, seeing the Brices fighting the prador. Another datum hit home: Matheson not only controlled their U-jumps but much more besides, and had lost a grip there. The brothers shouldn't have been wasting their time on the first-child if their objective was Cormac.

'Now,' said Cormac, starting to reach out for Blite's wrist. He then paused, since it appeared his right hand was missing, and used his left.

The gem immediately felt as if it was burning away his left hand, much as his right had gone. No matter. With a vicious turn of mind, powered by pain and anger at imminent death, he pushed into the thing. Penny Royal space expanded around him, open to an infinity of interpretations, but settling on the interior of a dark geode, with blades of crystal pointing inwards. Cormac reached out with all that he was and plugged himself into that power. His U-sense exploded outwards, incorporating the asteroid, then Yossander's Hold, and flooded on until he reined it back in. He then expanded the U-field out from his body, encompassing Blite, the slab, and spreading across the ground below. It washed over the prador and the Brice brothers, rolling out to Matheson, who was down on his knees with his hands over that hole in his throat. It utterly erased the U-field that the man had been trying to generate around himself. It tsunamied over prador engineers at work, and prador caches that even now were beginning to open. It swirled around rising weapons turrets too, crawled up them and encompassed them. And then, as if the hands of some god had clapped together, it finally enclosed the entire asteroid.

Data crunched in Cormac's gridlink, because only now, having the asteroid fixed in his mind, could he make the required calculations. He made them. Trying to ignore the impossible, appalling results, he reached down through Yossander's Hold and out the other side. Fire began to light the sky. Had Meander handed control back to the Gilliad? How could he know? He saw columns of interlocked prador rising from their caches, stirring into wakefulness. And with the utter certainty that the effort would tear his mind out of his skull, he U-jumped the asteroid.

May

As they neared the exit, May sped ahead to catch up with Arach and Crane, Meander keeping pace with her. The woman's face was lost in introspective strain. May then slowed beside Carlstone and felt the need to say something.

'They're for real – the things I've seen them do,' she told him.

Carlstone gazed at her for a long moment, then gestured to Crane and Arach. 'That's a real tough Golem there, judging by the way he tore off that door, and that's definitely a spider drone. It doesn't mean I'm swallowing the whole mythos, though. War factories produced a lot of them.'

'Not super-human ECS agents who can jump through U-space either?' May enquired.

Carlstone looked pained and had no answer for her. She gave him a nod and moved on. The two soldiers – a man and a woman – looked like the usual tough ex-ECS types Carlstone liked to recruit. They inspected her briefly, then returned to scanning their surroundings. Both of them held chunks of the frame from that ceramal door. No doubt they could do a lot of damage with them, but they weren't the kind of weapons they were used to. As she moved on, she felt something odd, like a shadow passing, then nailed it down as a massive information exchange occurring all around her. Meander abruptly staggered to one side, put her back against the wall and, with a groan, slid down onto her arse. She huffed out a tight breath, then reached up and began plucking the lamprey-things from her head. Where they dropped on the floor they slithered away, and began disappearing into holes along the base of the wall.

'Well, that was illuminating. She fought me right the way through. Now she's absorbed the new data and is responding accordingly, as if we weren't fighting each other at all,' she said.

'What?' Carlstone asked.

Before Meander could reply, Arach abruptly halted, clattered his feet against the ground with a sound like a machine gun, then did a crazy, skittering dance in a circle. At the termination of this, he opened his two upper hatches and protruded his miniguns.

'Mother of fucking fuck fuckety!' he exclaimed. 'The damned crazy son of a bitch did it. He fucking did it!'

By this time Crane had halted too and was looking across at Arach.

'Hey, Arach!' Carlstone called.

After what must have been another private communication, Arach said, 'Sorry,' and retracted his weapons.

'Now explain so everyone not linked in can understand,' said Carlstone. Noting the tone in his voice, May turned to look at the man. Carlstone looked utterly shocked.

'Okay,' said Arach. 'Seems Cormac accessed Blite's piece of Penny Royal for power and U-jumped a billion-tonne asteroid. That asteroid is now safely departing on the other side of the planet – predicted path will take it into the sun in eighteen months.'

Crane dipped his head in acceptance of the news and kept walking. May felt relief wash through her, but tainted with disbelief. She'd surmised that Cormac had some kind of action in mind, but had never truly acknowledged to herself it'd be this. It was over, then – the world was saved. She looked around at the soldiers, seeing disbelief and shock there, then to Iris. Just for a second the haiman woman seemed livid with rage but, almost as if a switch had clicked, her expression then became one of relief. May doubted what she'd first seen and turned away – with everything that'd happened with her crew, she'd begun to wonder whether she was any good at reading people.

Ahead, Crane paused at the opening he'd torn in the wall, silhouetted by daylight outside. Arach's hatches opened and his weapons extruded again. They all walked up and joined him to peer out into the biotech city.

No, not all over.

A hand came down on her shoulder and she looked aside at Meander. The woman had discarded all but one of the lampreys, which she held in place with her other hand. The wounds on her neck and the side of her head were closing up, bloodlessly.

Meanwhile May had the distinct impression the woman was somehow standing taller.

'It's okay,' said Meander loudly. 'She's letting us go for now.'

Crowding into and around the biotech city were hundreds of the armoured soldiers. At first it appeared this might have been a planned reception for them, but then May recognized that, though large groups had stopped to gape, most were on the move and generally going in one direction. It soon became evident the only people lingering in the area were those cleaning up the wreckage Arach and Crane had caused. All the fires were out, and the prostrate soldiers were being removed, while others, along with large organisms that looked like king ragworm, were snipping away burned foliage. Then, out of all this, walking up parallel to the wall on her right, came someone she recognized.

'Preece X2,' she said, smiling at the man.

'Sadly, no,' the man replied. 'I am Preece 24.' He held out a hand. 'Pleased to make your acquaintance.'

May shook his hand and stepped back, as the attention of the others focused on the man, but he spoke directly to her. 'The grav-platform you came here upon is still available to you, and no one will stand in your path.'

When nobody else replied, May gestured to Meander. 'We know that.'

Preece glanced at Meander, then took in Crane and Arach. Awe briefly crossed his features showing he was probably a new Preece but he quickly suppressed it and gave a sharp nod. 'No one will interfere and you can return to your ships. The squads occupying them have withdrawn. You will find your weapons in the grav-raft.'

May noticed how Carlstone and the two soldiers suddenly looked a lot more cheerful.

'I must leave you to it – understandably we have things to

attend to,' this Preece continued. 'You don't have long to get there and to cover. After that, you shouldn't be in the air.' He paused, bowed to them, then hurried off.

'Come on,' said Arach, heading out fast. Crane merely opened up his stride after the drone; the rest of them had to break into a steady trot.

'What did he mean by that?' May asked.

No one replied, as Arach abruptly halted to turn and watch Crane stride off in a different direction. The Golem disappeared from sight only briefly, then returned with a railgun over one shoulder and a heavy power pack carried like a suitcase in one hand. May presumed this was the 'suitable weapon' Cormac had mentioned. They moved on again, and were back at the raft before anyone deigned to answer May's question, if indirectly.

'You're not keeping on top of updates,' said Iris primly. 'I would suggest you do so.'

May grimaced and keyed into her aug again. She had, she recognized, adopted Blite's attitude to the thing, in that she used it only when she deemed it necessary, though she wouldn't go so far as to have an induction version she could pull off her skull. She saw a series of comlinks were available. The ones to Crane and Arach were open, while all were linked into a network for sharing tactical data. She opened this up as they clambered aboard the raft, and Carlstone headed forwards to take the controls. It was soon rising, up past buildings like the trunks of huge trees, lurching sideways to pass one of the bracket platforms, and into sky that was busy with similar vehicles, along with stranger modes of flight.

May began looking over the data. She replayed images of the asteroid shimmering out from the world, and then like old film stuttering, jerking out of existence, leaving a dispersing photon fog. She saw it then appearing beyond the world and rolling on. Disaster averted.

'Launches are automated, but an overall commander should have stopped it,' Carlstone commented over the network.

'Wasteful and destructive,' replied the soldier who May now knew to be called Gruce. The heavyworlder woman had squatted by a pile of weapons dumped between two seats and was handing them out.

'No surprise there,' replied the other soldier – Armand.

May guessed they were talking about the streaks of missile trails rising from the continent behind, as the grav-raft slid out over the ocean. Meanwhile, coming up on realtime imagery from just a half hour before, she saw battle breaking out. Weapons on the asteroid sprouted from the regolith and began firing. Their targets were the moons once again. Beam weapons licked visibly through vacuum between those and the asteroid, and a short while later the missiles invisible in this view began to impact. Huge detonations hurled tons of glowing rubble up from the surface of one moon. She received close imagery of a huge railgun installation there, with a flash and a smoking crater eating into the side of it, and the railgun toppling into the cavity. The prador on the asteroid were attacking, but why, now that their main strike had been stopped? She then understood the comment of 'wasteful and destructive'.

'They won't stay up for long,' said Arach. 'Too much air cover here.'

May glanced back at those launching missiles, now gleaning some intimation of what was happening. Just then two more comlinks joined the network and gave their input.

'You've seen it?' someone called Judice asked.

'Yeah,' Carlstone replied.

'We're coming to you,' said another, Paidon. 'Fusion drive is fucked, but grav and thrusters will get us there quickly enough. Launching now.'

The grav-raft abruptly slowed and turned, heading back down towards the coast.

'They'll go into the sea,' said Arach.

During this conversation, May caught up with events on the asteroid and now understood perfectly. She made some calculations in her aug, then turned and looked out to sea. An object had already appeared and was sliding into view fast – the *Coin* – but that wasn't what she was looking for. She squinted, then, feeling foolish, used her aug to boost her vision. Far out, and up high, a rash of dots swirled like a massive flock of starlings as it descended. The prador were coming.

'We've still had no discussion about our response,' said Carlstone tightly and out loud, 'and Blite isn't here to issue orders.'

'This isn't our war,' said Iris blandly.

A whining sound drew May's attention to Crane. He'd plugged a cable from the power supply into his weapon and the thing was now drawing power into its capacitor, lights blinking on over its surface. He lifted it, sighted along it for a second, then turned his black eyes on them. All had their weapons and met his gaze, as with firm solid clicks they inserted power packs, dust cartridges and munitions clips.

May understood this to be another level of communication.

Blite

A blast lit the asteroid's horizon and Blite winced. Yossander's Hold now lay in a different quadrant of the sky and seemed to be receding, though this might have been his imagination, since he knew it should be. A second after the blast, it seemed a firework went off in that direction and he recognized a shield generator ejection. Whatever had been fired at them hadn't reached the surface. Meanwhile, space between the asteroid and the planet continued to light up with similar displays. He returned his gaze to what he could see around him. Three of the weapons turrets were in view, blinking and flashing, swinging and targeting as they released either missiles, or stabbed out with particle beams.

Nearby, another cache had opened, the lid lying back on regolith and its core rising. In this were prador, hundreds and hundreds of them. They were all stacked one upon the other, piped and wired together, and locked in a cylindrical framework. As soon as the thing reached its full height, which was that of an average skyscraper, the prador at the top began detaching and rising up on thruster flashes, while those below went into motion as they woke, anxiously awaiting their turn. This was all to the good, since the more of the fuckers that departed this place, the higher his chances of survival rose – or of not dying repeatedly. More chances, at least, than the agent.

Blite looked down at the man sprawled beside him. His face was deathly pale under the visor and had a slightly brassy tint. His legs were badly burned and shredded, while his envirosuit had lost most of its air supply, before Blite used both its and his supply of patches to close up the holes, including a big one where Cormac's hand was missing. He'd brought the air pressure of the thing back up with a plug-in feed from his suit, and ensured it was properly oxygenated again. But now there was no need. He reached out and unplugged the combined air tube and data lead, keyed the windup through his HUD, and the thing slithered back into his suit. Cormac no longer needed air – he was dead.

But of course death was a negotiable thing. The man had received a lot of damage, and had been barely breathing after the jump, as well as hypoxic, judging by the colour of his skin.

Sealing up his suit had cured that, but it obviously hadn't been enough. The man shut down. Linking their suits enabled Blite to gather enough data up in his HUD to know the agent's heart had stopped, and brain activity was winding down like an engine out of fuel. But even while this was happening, the man's skin had started taking on that metallic hue. He'd vitrified, at least partially, so there was some hope. It could be that, like Carlstone's soldiers, he had a memplant, or at least this facility in the gridlink etched around the inside of his skull. Yet, neither the agent nor Blite himself had much of a chance unless they escaped this asteroid. The fact the prador soldiers were leaving was helpful, but the one still stubbornly hanging around here was making things difficult.

Blite's concealment behind the slab was good, but unfortunately a lot of open ground surrounded it. He wanted to move over to one of those emptied caches, because surely he'd find an oxygen supply in there to top up his suit, whose remaining reserve he tried not to look at. Perhaps in those caches he could find other useful items too, maybe even a form of transport. He'd noted on seeing a few of them emptied that some prador remained in place when the column descended again. He didn't think they were being kept in hibernation for any special purpose, but were wastage – those that hadn't survived hibernation. And prador suits contained grav-engines and other drives. He could use such a suit to take himself and Cormac off the asteroid, then once clear, shout for help – something he didn't want to do here since the prador would have detectors in place. Anyway, surely his crew would know where he was by now? Blite shook his head – he couldn't be certain. All he knew was that he wanted to make it to a cache, and he couldn't while that first-child was still out there fucking around.

He took a risk and peered out at the creature, immediately

feeling a sinking sensation in his guts. The first-child had been joined by the smaller second-child, in blue chrome polished armour and laden down with equipment. Blite had been unable to break cover with just the first-child here, even with its back turned, since its single stalked eye was up and looking for danger. Now there were just too many eyes out there. And what the hell was the thing doing? The first-child had gathered up the most mobile of their three attackers. By the shape, Blite identified it as Matheson. Blite had now finally recognized the three semi-human attackers as the bounty hunters Cormac had told them about in his information package. The prador held the man writhing in one claw, occasionally beating him against the ground, while seemingly in intense discussion with the second-child engineer. Abruptly a decision was made.

The second-child used an air blast to clear away dust from the ground. The first-child slammed Matheson down on clear stone and, while holding him squirming in place, the other brought in a weapon. No . . . not a weapon but a glue gun. Blite recognized prador wartime methods for dealing with human prisoners. He ducked down when the second-child finished its job and swung in his direction. This was no good – even carefully peeking out like he had been would get him spotted. Out of sight, he put his suit inventory up in his HUD to search out other options. He soon found them in the form of a strip of pin cams in the maintenance kit. With one further look out, he used a torn-off section of the strip to stick a cam to the slab, pulling off the paper to leave the thing invisibly in place. It took him a little while to bring the image feed up on his visor, and he cursed that he no longer had his induction aug. Perhaps he *should* go for a more permanent version.

The first-child had now snared the Brice brothers too. It beat them against the ground and against rocks as it did so, occasionally zapping them with the antipersonnel laser on its back, or firing off a few shots from one of its Gatling cannons to subdue them. The hunters were stubbornly resistant to dying; one of them, which had been partially fragged, had managed to pull himself back into his previous form. Well, partially. Having seen some of that process, Blite didn't have to wonder what was keeping them alive, because he had a container of the same organism in his thigh. Seeing what they'd become increased his reluctance ever to use it. But there had to be more to their transformation than simply being infected by the Spatterjay virus. Blite had never heard of any Old Captain who could jump himself through U-space like a spaceship. So what now?

He waited a little while, then, after checking his oxygen supply, knew he could delay no longer. He glanced at Cormac, grimaced, and realized he'd have to leave the man behind – he'd be too much of an encumbrance. Getting down on his belly, he threw a load of the asteroid dust over his suit, and then began a slow crawl towards the prador cache. The one into which the skeletal column, with just two prador still in place, was descending. A quarter of the way there, he saw the first-child dispatch the engineer on its way with a crack of its claw on carapace. Halfway there, he puzzled at what the prador was doing now. It seemed agitated, walking around in circles and occasionally dropping, then dragging its back end like a dog with worms. Finally, unbelievably, Blite reached the edge of the cache and shuffled forwards to go over the edge. Something clamped around his ankle.

Blite just lay there, not wanting to look back. His HUD fizzed and threw up all sorts of code, much of which he really didn't want to recognize either. Computing in the suit then fined it down to a com icon, even as the creature holding his ankle hauled him backwards and dangled him in front of it. He gazed through the visor of the first-child; at its red eyes and the throats of its

Gatling cannon centred on his face. His stomach turned over as the thing carried him back towards where the hunters had been glued to the rock. It was all very well to know he'd have numerous chances to find a way to survive this scenario eventually, but dying repeatedly wasn't something he enjoyed. He opened the comlink to delay things. The connection fizzed for a while, clattered and bubbled, then a translator kicked in.

'I saw you over there. What was your purpose in heading for the cache?' the prador asked.

'Oxygen and maybe some way off this rock,' Blite replied.

The prador chewed this over for a while and paused in his perambulation. He tilted up to focus his main eyes on the sky. The rash of black dots, silhouetted against the bright display of weapons fire, were the departing prador. Having taken that in, the first-child continued over to Matheson and the Brices.

'What are these?' he asked, holding Blite over them.

Blite peered at them, then spotted over to one side that Cormac had been dragged into view.

'Bounty hunters,' he replied.

'They are not human,' the first-child observed.

'They are, but heavily infected with the Spatterjay virus.'

The prador abruptly dropped him. A weird moaning sound came over com, as it spun away from him and did an abrupt circuit of the patch of stone, halting for a second to drag its back end across the regolith, before coming back before him. He had a moment of epiphany, since he'd lived long enough to know prador biology.

'Shouldn't you be up there with your troops?' he asked, sitting upright.

'Circumstances have changed,' the prador said.

'What's your name?' Blite asked.

'Valt,' the prador replied.

Valt was big for a first-child, and here on this asteroid he'd likely been away from the suppressant pheromones of his father for a long time. Blite had a very good idea what that butt-dragging meant: Valt was making the transition into adulthood. But how did that affect Blite? He was still trapped on an asteroid, the prisoner of a hostile alien which might kill him at any moment, and in a variety of very unpleasant ways. It struck him that the most likely scenario would be Valt letting him run out of oxygen and keeping his corpse around as a snack. At which point, of course, he'd find himself back behind that slab and on replay.

'You were in command here,' he guessed. 'Without the asteroid hitting Yossander's Hold, you should have called off the attack and recalled your forces to your father. But you don't want to do that because you know what would come next.'

The first-child abruptly backed away, both claws up in the air, exclaiming, 'I am a loyal child!'

Blite remembered then how those making this transition went through a period of cowardice – an evolutionary kink to get them away from their homicidal parent. This lasted only a little while, and their courage necessarily returned when it came to hunting down females with which to mate.

Blite stood up. 'You need to find a way off this asteroid too, and to somewhere safe.' Yeah, perhaps he could work with that cowardice. 'I have a ship. Perhaps we can make a deal?'

'Human,' said Valt. He lowered one claw, pointing the Gatling cannon directly at Blite. 'You will call your ship.'

'This may take a while,' Blite replied, now resorting to the wrist control of his suit to bring the radio up in his HUD. No doubt the EMR out there was heavy, but since being detected by the prador was no longer an issue, he might be able to push a message through to the *Coin* – or at least to someone on the planet. How long it would be before he received a response, he had no idea, but now there was hope. As he worked the wrist control, selecting frequencies, all its lights abruptly went out and then his HUD blanked.

'Fuck,' he said.

He noticed it had grown darker, and Valt had tipped back to look up. Something flashed down and hit the first-child on the back of the carapace. He staggered, electrostatic energy spreading over his armour and shorting out into the ground, and then collapsed on his belly. Blite looked up and immediately recognized Straeger's *Claw* poised up there, though oddly the ship seemed much bigger now. As it began to descend, he had no idea whether his situation had improved, or become much worse.

Straeger

Entanglement anger had risen hard inside him, and it seemed undeniable that he had to intercept the asteroid. This rage was still there now, though dampened down to a simmer. As he'd feared before, his own intervention had created the circumstances which resulted in the agent being able to U-jump the asteroid. Matheson and the Brices, even with their abilities further expanded, had failed yet again. He had failed yet again. But what now, why was he here? He gazed out at the diorama as remaining prador defences activated against him. He did not see them as being much of a problem – the assault force was gone, and the weapons were at the end of their munitions and power. He hung there in his ship, replaying the failures, and just stuck. Then, slowly, some hints of a new course began to blink into his consciousness.

Straeger abruptly set into motion, sending commands to the robots and systems of his ship and readying it to land. His anger

667

found satisfaction in knowing the agent was out there, dead, but in a state of semi-vitrification, so probably recoverable. He would be able to answer for the times he had frustrated Straeger's plans, this being the most infuriating of them all. Blite was out there too, with the diamond on a band around his wrist, and there was power there to be accessed perhaps. The prador had conveniently immobilized Matheson and the Brices, and though they had now strayed beyond his control, they were still a resource he could learn from, and utilize. He knew, almost on the level of instinct, that even the two prador would be useful, for they floated around in his mind like jigsaw pieces ready for him to insert in the puzzle.

Following his commands, robots converged ahead of him. As he rolled along a cage tube, he split off subminds and sent them to the hull door opening ahead of him on the flare and rumble of weapons. He was ready to begin again.

Blite

The ship settled on regolith, one tang of its claw knocking over the skeletal tower protruding from a prador cache, in turn spilling out two of the creatures which hadn't departed to attack Yossander's Hold and had likely died in hibernation. Distant weapons turrets swivelled and dipped, and one even managed a diffuse particle beam shot. It splashed on the ship's hull, but the things were all used up by now. Blite had no doubt they'd been supplied with just enough ammo and energy to allow the prador to get off the asteroid before it crashed into its target.

As the diffuse particle beam sputtered out, the ship seemed to think on the matter. Then a hatch opened in its upper surface and something shot out, tumbling end over end in a slightly arcing trajectory governed by the asteroid's low gravity. It almost looked as if someone had lobbed a grenade, which was travelling too slowly not to be taken out by any remaining anti-munitions. Perhaps that was the point. Blite saw weapons track the thing, and it even began to reflect coherent light, but still it arrived on target. His visor darkened on the elliptical flash, and by the time it cleared, the turret was gone, with a storm of dust passing silently overhead.

No further attacks ensuing, the ship opened a split in its side, and the glowing dandelion-head forms of Mobius subminds shot out, drifting over the regolith like fairy lights. Three robots, resembling giant, headless, thick-limbed tarantulas, scuttled along after them, their misshapen bodies running perfectly parallel with the ground. One of these grabbed up the prador first-child Valt, tipped him over on its back, then sped back to the ship with him. Halfway there it crashed into another robot on the way out. The two of them backed off and edged round each other. The second robot went on to snatch up the agent's body and take that into the ship. Another one cut around where Matheson and the Brices had been glued, finally lifting up a perfect wheel of stone with them at the centre, and rolling this back to the ship. Blite watched with growing unease. Robots didn't crash into each other, and destroying empty weapons turrets seemed pointless. Though perhaps not as pointless as cutting up a huge chunk of stone to keep prisoners glued to it, like some wall-hanging trophy.

Then a bright light from behind threw his shadow starkly in front of him. He turned to see Straeger hovering there.

'You were supposed to die on the world!' the AI exclaimed through his com system.

He hadn't seen the thing approach and, since Straeger was a sphere of shifting tendrils and luminous technology two metres across, that had to have been deliberate. He gazed at the thing, tired and sick from the backwash of stun blasts after the one that'd knocked down the first-child Valt, and which had partially cooked Matheson and the Brices.

'Well, I'm sorry to inconvenience you,' he replied, voice dripping sarcasm.

A tendril lashed out, hit his chest with a shock far larger than its flimsy size, and flung him back, skidding through the dust. He lay there coughing as Mobius subminds sped overhead, heard the sizzle over com that indicated an energy weapon firing, and sat up again to look around. Another one of the robots had scuttled out to where subminds bobbed above a ridge. It dipped over the ridge and came back with the second-child engineer Blite had seen earlier, its legs kicking weakly and a trail of smoke dispersing in the thin air. He pushed himself further upright, wanting to rage at the thing before him, perhaps snatch up that laser carbine and hose the thing down with it. But then he just stopped, held still saying nothing, and began to think furiously. The prador were out of the equation and Straeger was no Polity rescue party. Maybe he could make a run for it? The ridiculous thought died even as one of the tarantula robots came between him and the AI, tipped up and spread its forelimbs, then came down on him.

He'd earlier wondered if his situation had got worse. As he felt something stab into his side, and the lights began to go out, he realized he had known the answer all along. In his experience, there were worse things than dying, and Straeger was one of them.

About the Author

Neal Asher divides his time between Essex and Crete, mostly at a keyboard and mentally light years away. His full-length novels are as follows. First is the Agent Cormac series: *Gridlinked*, *The Line of Polity*, *Brass Man*, *Polity Agent* and *Line War*. Next comes the Spatterjay series: *The Skinner*, *The Voyage of the Sable Keech* and *Orbus*. Also set in the same world of the Polity are these standalone novels: *Prador Moon*, *Hilldiggers*, *Shadow of the Scorpion*, *The Technician*, *Jack Four*, *Weaponized*, *War Bodies* and *World Walkers*. The Transformation trilogy is based in the Polity, too: *Dark Intelligence*, *War Factory* and *Infinity Engine*. Set in a dystopian future are *The Departure*, *Zero Point* and *Jupiter War*, while *Cowl* takes us across time. The Rise of the Jain trilogy, another Polity universe series, comprises *The Soldier*, *The Warship* and *The Human*. *Dark Diamond* is the first book in the Time's Shadow trilogy.